THE COMPLETE COFFEE AND GHOSTS

COFFEE AND GHOSTS SEASONS 1-3

CHARITY TAHMASEB

COPYRIGHT

CONTENTS

AUTHOR'S NOTE

COFFEE & GHOSTS is a cozy paranormal mystery/romance serial told in episodes and seasons, much like a television series. Think *Doctor Who* or *Sherlock*.

I've recently consolidated the episodes into three season bundles. This makes the episodes easier to find and—I hope—more enjoyable to read.

This compilation contains all three seasons, every last story, in one handy place. Pour yourself some Kona blend and get ready to binge-read.

∾

If coffee hasn't yet topped your list as the most versatile substance on Earth, consider
"The Ghost in the Coffee Machine" by Charity Tahmaseb.
~ **Lori Parker, Word of the Nerd**

COFFEE AND GHOSTS, THE SEASON LISTS

Season 1:

Episode 1: *Ghost in the Coffee Machine*

Episode 2: *Giving Up the Ghosts*

Episode 3: *The Ghost Whisperer*

Episode 4: *Gone Ghost*

Episode 5: *Must Love Ghosts*

Season 2:

Episode 1: *Ghosts of Christmas Past*

Episode 2: *The Ghost That Got Away*

Episode 3: *The Wedding Ghost*

Season 3:

Episode 1: *Ghosts and Consequences*

Episode 2: *A Few Good Ghosts*

Episode 3: *Nothing but the Ghosts*

MUST LOVE GHOSTS

COFFEE AND GHOSTS SEASON 1

GHOST IN THE COFFEE MACHINE

COFFEE AND GHOSTS: EPISODE 1

WHEN IT COMES TO GHOSTS, my grandmother has one solution: brew a pot of coffee. Like today, in Sadie Lancaster's kitchen.

Sadie clutches her hands beneath her chin and stares at our percolator, her eyes huge. The thing gurgles and hisses as if it resents being pressed into service. My own reflection in its side is distorted. When I was younger, I thought this was how ghosts see our world.

In places with bad infestations, they swirl around the percolator. I can reach out, touch hot moist air with one hand and the icy patch of dry with the other. One time, a ghost slipped inside. It rattled around until the percolator sprang from the table and hit the floor, splashing scalding water everywhere.

I still wear the scars of that across my shins.

But Sadie's ghosts are barely ghosts at all. I'd call them sprites. They might annoy you on the way to the bathroom at three a.m., but little more. They also, as my grandmother points out, help pay the bills. So I remain silent while she pours the coffee: three cups black, three cups with sugar, three cups with cream, and three cups extra light and extra sweet. Twelve cups. Always. If anyone complains, my grandmother snorts and says, "As if no one has a preference once they've died."

Don't get her started on instant coffee, either. Since I was five, my job involves carrying the cups throughout the house, up and down stairs, into bedrooms, dining alcoves, walk-in closets. We never skip the bathroom, no matter what.

"The last place you'd want a ghost," my grandmother says to Sadie. "Lecherous little beasts."

I walk past the two women, my steps slow and steady. I still burn myself, make no mistake. My hands wear the scars of multiple scaldings. We keep a burn kit in the truck. But as I place the last cup on the edge of the sink, I smile. At least I won't need that today. I rush back to the kitchen for the Tupperware.

Some ghost catchers use glass jars, but ghosts confined to small spaces can manifest images—grotesque or obscene or both. Ghosts, generally speaking, are pissed off and rude, which is why you don't want one in your toilet. We buy the containers with the opaque sides, since what you can't see won't offend you. I use several at Sadie's that afternoon, although truthfully, I only snag three little sprites in the den.

"She's imagining things," I whisper to my grandmother.

"Yes." Her hand steadies my shoulder. "But how many repeat customers do we get?"

She has a point. We're good. When we're really in the zone—the right type of coffee beans, perfect brewing temperature, clean catches—a house might stay ghost-free for decades. If we're not careful, there won't be any ghosts left to catch.

With the sprites in the back of our pickup, we rumble down the county road that leads out of town and into endless fields of corn and soybean. Ten miles out, there's a windbreak with a little creek. This is where we'll set the sprites free. They'll be, if not happy, content at least, and in no hurry to find other humans to haunt. I'm setting the sprites free —legs braced, container at arm's length—when my grandmother speaks.

"When I'm gone, Katy-girl, I'll come back and show you how to rid them once and for all."

I sigh. I've heard this before. "But then I'd be getting rid of you."

"You wouldn't like me as a ghost. Besides, they don't belong on this plane. This has been my life's work." She touches three fingers to her heart. "I don't see why it shouldn't be my afterlife's work as well."

She always says this. I always tell her she'll live a good long time. Then we drive home, empty containers rattling against the flatbed, percolator perched between us, belted in, our third—and quite possibly most important—passenger.

~

THAT WAS THREE MONTHS AGO. If my grandmother raged against the dying of the light, it didn't show in her expression the following morning when I found her. She left me her house, the family business, and of course, the dented, silver percolator. I have yet to see a hint of my grandmother's ghost. I'm not sure I want to.

The house is quiet without her in it. Even the ghosts have stayed away. I shake the canister of roasted beans, give it a sniff, certain I'll need to dump it and buy fresh within a matter of days.

Sadie Lancaster calls as the first cascade of beans hits the garbage sack. I decide on those fresh beans now, and instead of running next door, I jump into my truck and head for the Coffee Depot.

Ten minutes later, I pull up in front of Sadie's house, but I don't find her cowering on the porch (her usual position pre-eradication). Percolator under one arm, I ring the bell.

"Oh, Katy," she says, urging me inside. She beams like she has a secret. "There's someone I want you to meet."

This is it. My grandmother has chosen Sadie's house as the spot for her grand reappearance and that's why Sadie isn't scared. My steps quicken, heart fluttering something crazy. Do I want to see my grandmother like this? I've never been afraid of ghosts, but this is different.

The aroma hits me first—rich, aromatic, turmeric, saffron, and a hint of rose petal. Sun glints off the sides of a samovar squatting in the center of the kitchen table, in the very place I always set the percolator. I clutch the thing to my chest as if that can protect us from its flashy usurper on the table. The samovar is gold-plated brass—I squint at it—in the Persian style instead of Russian.

"Katy," Sadie says, throwing her arms wide, "I want you to meet Malcolm Armand. He catches ghosts with tea the way you do with coffee." Her fingers twitch as if she's urging us closer together. I stand my ground. "You two have so much in common," she adds.

Malcolm runs a hand over smooth, dark hair. His white dress shirt gleams in the sunlight streaming through the kitchen windows. I'm in torn jeans and a T-shirt. Why anyone would attempt ghost catching in something so fancy is beyond me. Even so? I can't help but feel grubby in comparison.

"It's nice to meet you," he says, extending that same hand, one without a single blemish or scar.

I fight the urge to whip my own hands behind my back, out of sight. I gulp a breath and shake his hand, breaking contact the second it's polite (okay, maybe a couple of seconds before it's polite). I try not to stare too hard at Malcolm, so I let my gaze travel the kitchen, the dining alcove. No ghosts here. I'd be surprised to find even the weakest sprite. And certainly, my grandmother isn't in residence.

That leaves me alone with Malcolm—and the tea-scented suspicion about where all my business is going.

When I walk into Springside Long-term Care, the first thing I see is Malcolm standing in the center of the common area, enchanting all the residents, the gold-plated samovar glowing on a side table next to him. I freeze, so every time the automatic doors try to close, they bounce back open again. This draws attention. I sigh, give up my plan to sneak out, and step forward to meet the facility manager.

"Oh, Katy," she says, a flush rising up her neck, "I meant to call, so you wouldn't make the trip out here." She waves a hand at Malcolm. "He offered a "try before you buy" and well ... the residents just love him."

Or at least most of the female ones do. They gather around Malcolm and his shiny, shiny samovar, their *oohs* and *ahhs* mixing with the scented steam.

I don't point out that Springside is—and always has been—a gratis account. Older people, my grandmother always said, are haunted by many things. It's only right that we chase some of their ghosts away.

I'm backing toward the door, willing myself not to inhale a hint of rose petal and saffron, when a bony hand grips my wrist. The percolator crashes to the floor, adding one more dent to its history.

"Katy-girl, are you going to let him get away with that?" Mr. Carlotta nearly growls the words. He may hold the world's record for longest unrequited crush, in his case, on my grandmother. Even now, sorrow lines his eyes. His fingers tremble against my wrist.

"What can I do?" I wave my free hand toward Malcolm. "He's so flashy."

"More like a flash in the pan. Mark my words."

A part of me grabs onto what Mr. Carlotta says. Be patient. Business will pick up the second it's clear you can't catch ghosts with tea. Because honestly, who ever heard of that? My practical side—the side that pays the property taxes and utility bills—wonders if the local coffee shop is hiring.

I trace the scars on the backs of my hands while waiting for the Coffee Depot's assistant manager. My qualifications are thin. I know ghost hunting and how to brew a damn good cup of coffee. But customer service? Well, when you ghost hunt, people don't mind if you shove them out of the way, not if you trap the otherworldly thing shaking their house to the foundation.

At the Coffee Depot? They probably frown on customer shoving. Still, the converted train station is quaint and life as a barista can't be that bad, can it?

The assistant manager plops down across from me. He wipes fake sweat from his brow and gives me a grin.

"So," he says. "Tell me a bit about yourself."

"I make the best damn coffee you've ever tasted." I declare this because I've read online that you should be confident in your interview.

He chuckles but doesn't sound amused. "I'm sure you do. But tell me," and now, the amusement is back, "what about frothing milk?"

I like cappuccino, even if frothing milk is something I've never done. Likewise, I'm sure there are many fine answers to his question. I do not choose any of them.

Instead, I say, "Why would you want to do that?" It's like I'm possessed by the spirit of my grandmother, since in that moment, I sound just like her.

"Right," he says. He clears his throat, then gives me a long look. "I'll take that challenge. Go make me the best damn cup of coffee I've ever tasted."

So I do. I stand, and with his nod, round the counter so I'm on the other side. My fingers barely brush the silver, industrial sized coffee machine when it starts to tremble. The thing wheezes. The tile beneath my feet shudders, sending a shockwave that resonates from toes to jaw. Next to me, the barista's teeth clack together, and she pitches toward the cash register, clinging to it. Then, the machine erupts, spewing water and coffee grounds with so much force, they coat the ceiling, the walls, and all of the tables.

I offer to clean up. I offer to rid their machine of its ghost—for free. Everyone is damp, but since the water was only lukewarm, no one was scalded. This is why the assistant manager pushes me out of the store instead of calling the police.

As the door closes, his voice echoes behind me. "Yes, do you have the number for Malcolm Armand ...?"

Something won't let me leave the sidewalk in front of the shop. My feet remain rooted there, next to the planters with the sugar maples. I stand there so long it's a wonder I don't sprout leaves. But since I do stand there so long, I'm treated to the view of Malcolm Armand double parking and springing from his two-seater. In the passenger seat, belted in like a trophy girlfriend, sits the samovar.

"That's not very practical," I say.

He halts in his trek up the walk, samovar held away from me. "What?"

"Where do you put the ghosts? I mean, once you capture them." I point at the convertible. "There's no room."

He eyes me, my coffee-soaked shirt, stained slacks, and all. He sniffs, nose wrinkling, and tromps into the shop without another look in my direction. I turn, uproot my feet, and inch toward the front window.

Inside is the mess I made, but I ignore that. What I want to see is how Malcolm works, what he does, how he entices the ghosts. I stare so long, the sun dries the back of my shirt. I study the inside of the shop, the placement of the samovar, and track Malcolm's every move until the assistant manager jerks a cord and Venetian blinds block my view.

Whatever grips me about the shop—the ghost or Malcolm—loosens its hold. Dismissed, I trudge home, leaving a set of coffee-colored footprints in my wake.

"K-k-aty? Are you there?"

The call comes at nine in the morning, on a day so sunny and bright, only the most dedicated pessimist could remain that way. Since I have all my overdue bills spread out on the dining room table, I'm well on my way to joining their ranks.

"Sadie?" It sounds like her, but I've never heard her voice so shaky.

"Please hurry."

"What's going on? Where are you?"

"My porch. They won't let me inside."

"Who won't?"

"The ghosts."

"Why don't you call Malcolm?" The question comes out sharp, laced with acid and jealousy.

"He's t-trapped inside."

"Trapped?"

"Dead?" Sadie's voice hitches.

"Ghosts don't …" *Kill.* No, normally ghosts don't. But they can. "I'll be right over."

The second I pull the half and half from the fridge and give it a good whiff, I realize *right over* isn't happening. I toss the reeking carton into the garbage and head to the canister with the beans. A few lone ones rattle in the bottom. I haven't been back to the Coffee Depot since my disastrous interview, but it looks like I'll be stopping there today.

With the percolator strapped in its seat, a four-pound bag of sugar snug against it, and several containers of half and half on the truck's floor, I run two red lights on my way to the Coffee Depot. By the time the little bell above the door stops jingling, the assistant manager is rounding the counter. He stalks forward, arms loaded down with bags of coffee beans. He skids to a halt and shoves the beans at me.

"But—" I begin.

He holds up a cell phone. On the screen, a message reads:

Malcolm: Give her anything she wants.

Still uncertain, I blink at the words. In my arms, I hold everything I want, or at least need. For now. I head for the door.

"Call or text if you need a resupply," the assistant manager shouts after me. "I'll have someone run it over."

The door whooshes closed before I can say thanks.

I TEST OUT THE FRONT DOOR, the garage, even the window to the bath-room. Every surface I touch ices my fingertips. Sadie Lancaster's house is in full-on ghost infestation. Usually something like this takes years to build up, or a sudden invasion of strong ghosts—a group of them. True, I haven't cleared the sprites in a month or so, but that can't be the cause of this.

My gaze travels the structure, from chimney to foundation. All the windows are black, the cheery blue paint molting into a dead gray. I need to get inside. I need to do that now. So I do the most logical thing. I march up the porch steps, press my palm against the doorbell, and let it ring for an entire minute. Then I cross my arms over my chest and tap my foot.

"Nobody's getting any coffee if someone doesn't open up this door." I sound bossy, just like my grandmother. I kind of like it.

A moment later, the door creaks on its hinges. I scoop up the perco-lator and my bag of supplies and race for the kitchen.

"Malcolm?" I call out. "Are you okay?"

Is he even here? Maybe he went out the back once the ghosts released their hold on the doors. I plug in the percolator and take a few deep breaths so I don't rush the preparations. Ghosts this strong will need the best coffee I can brew.

I survey the beans the assistant manager shoved at me. One hundred percent Kona? Really? Shame to waste that on ghosts. But the air prickles the skin on my arms. It must be fifty degrees in here and getting colder. One hundred percent Kona might not do the trick if I don't hurry.

"Katy?" A voice rasps.

For a second, I mistake it for a ghost.

"Katy?"

No. Too deep, too human for that.

"Malcolm?"

"In the dining room."

I set the percolator to brew and run. On the threshold, I trip over something bulky and sail through the air. I land hard, but manage to tuck and roll. When I stop, the blown out end of a gold-plated samovar fills my view, the brass twisted into vicious curlicues.

A groan comes from the threshold. Malcolm props himself up on one elbow, his cell phone clutched in one hand, his shirt, torn and tea-stained.

"What happened?" I say.

"It just ... blew. I was adding in a sprite when—"

"Wait. You've been storing all the ghosts." I heft the samovar, careful of the edges. "In here?"

He nods.

"You don't release them?"

"Never have." He shakes his head, eyes downcast. "Honestly? I don't know how."

This sad, honest confession tugs at me. We don't have time, however, to go over the finer points of ghost hunting.

"Can you stand?" I ask. "Walk?"

"I think so."

"Then you can help."

In the kitchen, I pour the twelve cups. Malcolm adds the half and half and sugar. His hands are steady, and he stirs each cup without spilling a single drop. My grandmother would approve.

From there, we divide and conquer, carrying the cups to various spots in the house.

"Be sure to put one in the master bath," I call from the living room. "There's bound to be one in there."

"It won't let me in," he says a moment later.

Oh, really? Nasty little bugger. Ghosts and their toilet humor.

At the door to the bathroom, I ease the cup of coffee from Malcolm's hands then kick on the door. It flies open with all the strength of the supernatural behind it.

Malcolm places a hand on my arm. "I don't think—"

"It'll be okay." I hear it for the lie it is, and so must Malcolm, but he lets me go.

I close the door and place the coffee on the vanity. That icy patch of air flutters past, swirls into the steam, and revels in it. Oh, it is having the best time—at everyone's expense, too. Before I can trap it beneath some Tupperware, that same feeling from the coffee shop washes over me. This is the ghost in the coffee machine. This is ... my grandmother.

The realization makes me drop the container. Malcolm pounds on the door, but I ignore him.

"Grandma?"

Now, the ghost swoops around me, a frigid caress against my cheek.

"What are you doing? I thought—"

Something that sounds like *hush* fills the air. Whatever her mission, it's not for me to question.

"I love you," I say. "And I miss you."

I pick up the container and my grandmother flows inside, compliantly. I secure the lid and hug the Tupperware to my chest. During her life, my grandmother was right about most everything. But here's where she was wrong:

I do like her as a ghost.

WE DRIVE OUT TO THE NATURE PRESERVE, a good thirty miles from town.

In a deserted campsite, I demonstrate how to open containers and set ghosts free. I even let Malcolm release a few. (Only the sprites, but you have to start somewhere.)

"Will they come back?" he asks.

"The strong ones can, but most choose to stay here, or find an old barn to haunt. Something's got to scare all those Scouts on camping trips, right?"

Malcolm studies the backs of his hands. The beautiful olive skin is pink from scalding.

"You should put something on that," I say. "Before it scars."

"A little scarring never hurt anyone. I'm sorry for a lot of things." He raises his hands. "But not for this."

I nod and he gives me a piercing look that I swear could scar—if I let it.

"You know something," he says, "I think this will work."

"What will?"

"You and me. I'm all sizzle, and you're the steak."

"I'm a vegetarian."

He throws his head back and laughs. And while I have no clue what he means, I can't help but like the sound of his laughter.

I LET MY FINGERS TRACE the gold lettering on the window—for the tenth time in as many minutes. I can't help it, can hardly believe the words are real.

K&M Ghost Eradication Specialists

In the store window, the gold-plated brass samovar sits, backside hidden in midnight velvet. Somehow, Malcolm talked the bank manager into a small business loan. Somehow, we're on retainer with the only law office and investment firm in town. Somehow, my worry about bills and property taxes has evaporated.

Malcolm still wears the scars from what we call the day of the ghosts. He boasts a few fresh ones as well. So do I. We take a new, electric samovar with us when we go out on a call. Because even I must admit: some ghosts prefer tea. Sometimes I feel that particular presence and an icy caress along my cheek. Sometimes I say things that make Malcolm throw his head back and laugh.

What I don't tell Malcolm: I do it on purpose.

What I don't tell my grandmother: I know what her afterlife's mission really is.

And I love her for it.

GIVING UP THE GHOSTS

COFFEE AND GHOSTS, EPISODE 2

CONTRARY TO POPULAR BELIEF, it's hard to find a ghost in a cemetery. But a mausoleum? Like the sterile one Malcolm and I are now walking through? That's going to be even harder. We trek along the endless halls. Wall after wall. Drawer after drawer. The interior is all windows, steel, and marble. Sunlight pours through the glass and makes me wince. Even so, Lasting Rest Mausoleum is—quite possibly—the coldest place on earth, or at least in this county.

"I don't sense a thing," I say to Malcolm. Actually, I whisper it, which is ridiculous, since we are the only two people on the third floor.

"Let's keep going," he says, voice equally hushed. "Maybe there's something. Plus, I promised."

We seldom turn down a ghost eradication job, it's true. Often it's no more than a mischievous little sprite. They love to play jokes. If anything might haunt a cemetery, it would be a sprite. Whatever else you think you sense, see, or experience is a product of your imagination, fears, and repressed feelings. You don't need an exorcist. You need a psychiatrist.

I know how to deal with ghosts. But this place? The space feels hollow in the wrong sort of way. At least in a cemetery, grass cushions your feet. The grave markers hint at stories, lives, and loves. Birds chirp. Dragonflies buzz.

"They should pipe in some music." I glance toward the ceiling as if in search of hidden speakers. Nothing disturbs the smooth marble surfaces.

"I read an article once, about the cleanup at Chernobyl," he says. "They had to pipe in music for the workers since there were no other sounds."

I wonder if he realizes he's compared the Lasting Rest Mausoleum with the world's largest nuclear disaster.

He coughs, glances around—maybe so I won't see the blush in his cheeks. "But it's a clean, well-lighted place."

Yes. He realizes. "I don't think this is what Hemingway had in mind," I say.

Malcolm chuckles. I love his laugh, but it's the wrong sort of sound for this place. "Let's replay the video," he says. "We're getting close to the spot."

I think it's an excuse to hear something other than our footfalls and breathing. He pulls out his phone and brings up the recording. In it, our client, Doug, is touring the mausoleum much as we are, only with a video camera in his hand. Occasionally he speaks directly into the lens, but mostly it's a rocky, virtual trip through these halls. I sway, motion sickness overtaking me.

"You okay?" Malcolm steps closer, places a hand at the small of my back. A hint of saffron from the tea he carries reaches me.

He is very much warm and alive in a place that is not. He smells of nutmeg and Ivory soap. I like being close to him, but I don't want to give him the wrong idea. I don't want to give *myself* the wrong idea.

I keep my distance.

On the screen, Doug's trek continues.

"Doug didn't even notice the ghost while he was filming," Malcolm says. "It was only after he reviewed the video that he noticed something odd."

This does not lend credence to Doug's claim, but I remain silently skeptical.

"There!" Malcolm says. The cold marble walls bounce the word back at us and seem to gobble it up all at once. The space is greedy for all things alive.

What looks like a white bed sheet flutters on the screen. It's a child's idea of a ghost. I've said as much to Malcolm, but feel compelled to mention it again.

"Ghosts don't look like that. It's probably something he edited into the video."

"I don't think so. He's not that tech savvy."

"You don't have to be that tech savvy these days. You could hire someone to do it."

Malcolm turns to me now, arms crossed over his chest, phone still clutched in his hand. "Why would someone do that? He's paying us money, good money that we need, to investigate—"

"And eradicate."

"And eradicate, if necessary. Why go to all that trouble and expense?"

Oh, there are so many reasons. When I worked with my grandmother, we encountered them all. Some people crave the attention, or are so lonely, they desperately need it. Having a ghost select them—or their house—to haunt? Well, that must mean they're something special. Or so the reasoning goes.

But Malcolm is new to the business. He is what my grandmother would have called feral—not in a bad way. Ghost hunting is both an inborn trait and a skill that is passed down through generations. Long ago, his ancestors no doubt made a living doing what we're doing now. But when I met him, he didn't even know how to perform a proper catch and release.

We match our steps to those on the video to where that white fluttering vanished into the wall. A fan is stationed at this corner. In fact, several fans are positioned throughout the building. Clean. Well-lighted. Not ventilated. But then, the dead don't need to breathe, do they?

"The fan would account for the fluttering," I say. "Some fishing line, a bed sheet or an old bridal veil? Instant ghost."

"And they rigged it up how, exactly?" His gaze searches the walls and ceiling.

Oh, yes, he has a point. No place for a pulley and ropes. No place for a co-conspirator to hide. It's a mystery, but I doubt it's an otherworldly one.

"Malcolm, I just don't think—"

"I'll be honest, Katy." His words are rushed, anxious. "I've already spent the deposit."

I know ghost hunting, but Malcolm knows business. His words send a chill through me that rivals the temperature in this place.

"Rent, on the office space," he says. "Bargain eradications aren't going to keep us in business. Some people are starting to embrace their sprites and live with them." He shrugs. "It's sort of a thing now."

My grandmother and I always made ends meet—more or less. It took Malcolm to untangle the mess of property taxes on the house I inherited from her. I don't have any savings and only just started a retirement account—and only because Malcolm insisted. When it comes to money, I trust him.

I ease the pack from my shoulders. "I guess it wouldn't hurt to set up the coffee, at least. If there's a ghost, it will come out for that."

The long marble bench makes an excellent station. Malcolm unloads the cups and thermoses. I pour. Twelve cups, like always: three black, three with sugar, three with cream, and three extra light and sweet. Everyone has a favorite, even ghosts.

"We could get out the tea, too," I say to him.

The smile melts some of the worry from his face. "Let's see how picky they are."

Usually, I brew the coffee on the premises, but we decided for this first run to use the field kit. If it works well enough in abandoned barns and warehouses, then it should work here. Steam rises from the cups, warming the air, infusing it with a tangible thickness.

"Ow." Malcolm sticks a finger into his mouth, although that's no way to treat a burn. "Careful, it's still scalding hot."

"Good. Have you ever seen what a ghost does with a lukewarm cup of coffee?" I ask.

He shakes his head.

"It's messy." I have a dozen coffee-stained shirts to prove it.

He holds his hands over the rising steam. "It feels better in here."

It does. Even so, the air is devoid of everything but the coffee's aroma. No glimmer. No swirling in the steam above a cup. I have the Tupperware ready for the catch, but at the moment, there's nothing to catch.

I'm about to suggest tea, since perhaps this is a particular sort of ghost, a choosy sort who is only lured by the exotic. Malcolm's tea recipe, an old Persian one, is all kinds of exotic. Before I can say a word, a screech echoes down the long hallway, the sort of sound that raises the hairs on the back of your neck.

Something swoops. Something flutters. Bed sheets. Bridal veils. It might be either or both of those things. The force of the swoop upends the coffee cups—all of them. The liquid splatters everywhere. On the tombs, the silk flowers that adorn them, the floor.

Me.

Black coffee strikes my thighs, the scald instant. I yelp, then pluck at my jeans, the material too hot, too tight, too slippery for me to grip. I can't move fast enough, pluck hard enough. My skin flashes with pain. At last, I unbutton the fly and yank.

By the time the material is past my knees, it no longer has the power to burn. I slump on the damp, coffee-covered floor and push my palms against my eyes. *I will not cry. I will not cry.*

"Katy!" Malcolm slides to the floor next to me. "Jesus, let me look."

He eases me back. His intake of breath is not reassuring.

"How bad?" I ask, palms locked on my eyes.

"Hospital bad, as in I'm dialing 911 bad."

I peer through my fingers at him. "We don't have money for an ambulance." We are two townships from home. An ambulance will cost what? More than I think we should spend, perhaps more than we have to spend.

"We'll make the money, somehow."

"My truck. It'll be just as fast, and there's a burn kit in the glove compartment."

"The EMTs—"

"Can't do anything more than I can on my own." Honestly, he can't lecture me about finances then expect me to be fiscally irresponsible.

"Compromise." He holds up a finger. "You're not walking anywhere." He tugs off his fine white dress shirt, which is now speckled with coffee and less than fine. He helps me stand, helps me ease the jeans off my legs, then creates a makeshift skirt from that shirt.

Then, in knight-in-shining-armor mode, he sweeps me into his arms and carries me down the hall.

"I can walk," I protest.

"But you're not going to." He heads down the stairs.

"There's an elevator," I point out.

"And with our luck, we'd end up trapped. No thanks."

He has a point. Whatever that thing was, it has a vendetta. Messing with the electrical system is something a strong ghost might do, on occasion, although I'm still uncertain that's what we encountered.

"Maybe we should've served it tea," I say.

He grunts a laugh and crushes me closer to his chest. Nutmeg. Ivory soap. If there's an upside to being a damsel in distress, it might be this.

Malcolm secures me in the truck, seatbelt and all, as if he's afraid I'll bolt back inside to fight more ghosts. His instincts are spot-on, for I point and say, "Our stuff. We just can't leave it."

Those are precision-made German thermoses and matching cups, not to mention everything else in our field kit.

"But I'm not sure you should go in alone," I add.

His gaze darts from the mausoleum to me. Fine grooves form around his mouth and eyes. "You're right," he says. "But someone has to. Stay."

Like I'm going anywhere half-dressed. I give him a mock salute. Malcolm rushes off, and I stare after him, tracking his progress inside through the window as he dashes up the stairs. Then, he vanishes.

I wait. And I wait. My thighs sting with enough force it steals my breath. I should pull out the burn kit, start in on first aid, but my eyes are locked on the mausoleum. My shoulders tense, and I inch ever closer to the windshield. That's when I see it. That's *why* I see it. Something white. Something that flutters. Bed sheets. Bridal veils. Whatever it is, it circles the mausoleum in what can only be described as a victory lap. The thing is ... gloating.

Malcolm bursts through the glass doors of the mausoleum, field kit clutched to his chest. I nearly tumble from the truck with my efforts to point toward the sky. But the thing is gone, and when Malcolm turns to look, all that greets him is blue sky.

He throws the field kit at my feet and clambers into the driver's side. "Katy?"

"I saw it," I say.

"It?"

"The thing. The thing from Doug's video."

"Do you know what it is?"

The truck rumbles to life and he throws it into gear. The way is smooth, but the suspension bad, so we bounce down to the main road.

In all my years of ghost hunting, in all the stories my grandmother told me, I've never seen or heard anything like this.

"I have no idea."

My ARM ACHES from the tetanus shot. This small annoyance bothers me more than the swath of bandages across each thigh, and the fact I can't tug any of my jeans up and over the bandages. I'm reduced to wearing a short, flirty skater skirt. This skirt, which is really too short for most activities, might be the only thing I can wear for the next week.

This does not bode well for ghost hunting.

I sit on the couch in our office, tray propped up and over my thighs—a bridge over my bandages. In a wise move, Malcolm brings in a cold lunch—sandwiches and icy lemonade from the deli next door. I am not in the mood for coffee.

"You okay?" he says. Actually, he has said this about once every fifteen minutes. Until now, I haven't felt like answering.

"I've never blistered like this before," I tell him.

"The doctor said it wouldn't scar—"

"That's not what bugs me."

Oh, I have scars, many of which are on view, thanks to the skater skirt. I look at them more as badges of honor, a legacy of working with my grandmother. "I was totally unprepared for what happened."

"We both were."

"But I shouldn't have been."

This still eats at me, hours later, has led to endless Internet searches, and has left me so frustrated, I'm afraid most of my words will emerge with more than a growl—I will bite, too.

"It's different for me," I add. The words hang in the air, and I realize just how arrogant they sound, and how it's too late to take them back.

He studies his sandwich, a Black Forest ham with baby Swiss, on rye, his favorite. Instead of eating, he sets it on his paper plate.

"You know what I think?" he says.

"What?"

"You're right, sort of. It *is* different for you, but not because you think you went in unprepared. No one is more prepared than you are."

"Then what was it?"

"I think it was ... a trap, an ambush. Whatever that thing was, it targeted you."

"You think that?"

Malcolm tips his head; it's a slow, thoughtful sort of movement. He rubs his jaw. "I don't have proof, but I sense it. There was nothing when I ran back inside. I couldn't even smell the spilt coffee."

"You were in a hurry—"

"And I had to pick up all the cups and the thermoses. You know the smell of cold coffee."

Do I ever. An involuntary shudder runs through me and has Malcolm securing a fleece throw and wrapping it around my shoulders. I don't refuse.

"The place should've reeked." He sits on the coffee table so his gaze strikes me dead on. "I'm telling you, there was nothing, no odor, and it's not like that place smells of anything except stale air."

"The fans?" I suggest. "They were going full blast."

Instead of responding, he pulls the field kit out from under the table. Inside, the contents rattle. He lifts a silver thermos from the pack, the one we use for the extra sweet, extra light concoction. The sides should be damp and sticky. No matter how carefully we pour, this is our messiest thermos. The silver gleams. Malcolm unscrews the cap. He waves it under his nose, then mine.

Nothing.

"That's weird," I say, "but it doesn't prove this thing is after me."

He directs a pointed look at my thighs. Okay, maybe it does.

"Vendetta," he says.

"What?"

"The word is stuck in my mind. Vendetta. Only I can't figure out why.

Who, or what, would have a vendetta against you? You've never done more than catch and release, have you?"

I shake my head. No, that was always our strict policy. Ghosts can be nasty, it's true, especially those who resent their afterlife. For the stronger, meaner ones, the solution is nothing more than driving them farther out, and around in circles, until they lose all sense of direction. Sure, once released, they might make their way back. More likely, they'll find a new spot to haunt.

"What about your grandmother?"

"Not that I know of, and I learned everything from her."

He props his elbows on his knees and plants his chin on his fists. His dark eyes are fringed with black lashes. This close, the effect is breathtaking. No wonder the women who work the deli counter toss in dessert for free.

"Maybe we need to expand our search," he says. "Maybe this thing isn't a ghost. I told you about the old Victorian I lived in back in college."

It's where he picked up his ghost catching ability—or maybe it picked him.

"People thought it was funny I could catch ghosts and put them in my samovar, but I always thought it was kind of sad."

By *people*, he means his fraternity brothers, and he had amassed quite a collection by the time I met him. I had to teach him how to release ghosts, although he still doesn't have the knack. Half the time, they double back and smack him in the head.

"But there was other stuff going on. Not ghosts, but …" He pauses, presses a finger against his lip. "Definitely supernatural. I never knew what they were, only that I couldn't catch them."

I don't like the idea of things that can't be caught. I think of that white fluttering—of bed sheets and bridal veils. Merely a ruse, then? Something to grab our attention—or the attention of a potential client? If so, it worked.

"Maybe you should talk to Doug," I say. "Give him an update."

Malcolm groans. "If I do that, he's going to blather it all over the internet."

"One, there's already so much ghost crap all over the internet, what's a little more? Two?" I catch Malcolm's eye. "Maybe that's not such a bad thing."

~

I DON'T KNOW what it is about the internet and ghosts, but it has a way of bringing out the frauds. Or maybe that's the internet in general. Long ago, I stopped trying to explain properties of light to potential clients. It simply doesn't matter. If someone wants to see a ghost in a spot in a photograph, they will see one.

I've never once captured an actual ghost on film, although I've taken hundreds of lousy pictures trying to do so. Even when they swirl in the steam of a hot cup of coffee, ghosts simply don't show up on film or the digital version of it.

Less than twenty-four hours after Malcolm updates Doug, the phone calls and emails flood in. I am still couch-bound and still in my skater skirt. I scroll through the photos attached to those emails, and scan the paranormal chat boards, looking for a connection.

When my cell phone rings, I answer automatically. "K&M Ghost Eradication Specialists."

"You're on the wrong track." The voice warbles, like it's streaming through an electronic filter. I place the call on speaker and wave Malcolm over.

"What did you say?" I ask the caller, then press a finger against my lips.

Malcolm nods, once, and crouches next to the coffee table, ear aimed at my phone.

"You're on the wrong track, and your client's an idiot."

"How so?"

"Do you really believe he can see ghosts? Capture them on film?"

"Well, whatever he saw, I did too."

The caller snorts. The resulting burst of static has me clamping my hands over my ears.

"But you're not dim enough to call it a ghost."

"You don't like Doug," I say.

The silence stretches for so long I think the call has dropped.

"This has nothing to do with Doug. You should know that … Malcolm. Yes, I know you're listening in."

Malcolm slams a hand on the coffee table. I jump back, my heart thudding.

"Who is this?" he says. "I demand to know who this is."

He's always so cool, so calm, so Malcolm. But this? This is a side I've never seen of him. My ears strain for the caller's response, but it's Malcolm who holds all my attention.

"Can't you figure it out? Oh, Malcolm, really? I never thought *you* were that dim." A static-laden sigh travels through the speakers. "And your business partner is so pretty. Be a shame if those burns ended up on her face, wouldn't it?"

"Who is this?" Malcolm's voice cracks.

Mine doesn't. "Don't be stupid," I say to the caller. "An empty threat is just that, empty and stupid."

"Who says it's empty?"

"I do. The victim has to care, and I don't. Burn my face. I don't care. I don't care at all. But I do care about my friends—"

"Are you sure you know who your friends are?"

The speakers let out one last burst of static before going silent. My gaze meets Malcolm's.

"What the hell was that?" I say.

"Katy." He shakes his head. "Katy, I—"

"Please tell me this is not where you make some horrible confession that changes everything."

I consider my demand—and the call. I've only known Malcolm for four months, and for one of those he was my rival in the ghost hunting business. How well can I claim to know him? Would I swear he is good and honorable and all those things a person should be, especially your business partner? Would I? What's the alternative?

"Oh," I say, the realization sinking in, my lungs pulling a full breath at last. "Of course. Seeds of doubt. Who hates you—or me—enough to do that?"

"Then—" he begins.

"I think we're being played. What do you think?"

He props his elbows on the coffee table and rests his head in his hands.

I ignore this. "This is personal, not paranormal." Bed sheets and bridal veils. The thought strikes me hard. "You didn't break an engagement or something before you moved here, did you?"

I'm praying he'll say no, or shake his head, or something. He remains statue-like still, as if in mourning.

"Malcolm." I leaned forward, smooth his hair, and then place a gentle hand on his shoulder. "What's going on?"

"Once upon a time, I had a brother," he says. "Nigel."

Once upon a time? Despite the fairy tale start, something tells me this is going to be a dark story. "*Had* a brother." I say the words slowly.

"Technically, I still do. Around the time I discovered I could catch ghosts, my brother did too. Only instead of putting them into something, he swallowed them."

"Swallowed them? Is that even possible?"

Malcolm gives me one anguished nod.

"He's filled with ghosts?"

Malcolm nods again.

"And resents you because?"

His eyes meet mine. They are dark and damp and filled with so much sorrow, my heart constricts.

"Because of you."

I SINK into the couch cushion as if Malcolm's confession has knocked the wind from me. Perhaps it has, figuratively, at least. An eater of ghosts. I've never encountered such a thing; my grandmother never mentioned it.

"How do I figure into all of this?" I ask.

"You ... saved me. I was using the samovar as a holding place, so I wouldn't swallow the ghosts, wouldn't be tempted to." He heaves a sigh. "Now that I know there's an option, that I don't have to carry them with me or inside me, I can live a normal life. You know why I was fired from the brokerage, don't you?"

"I thought it was the recession."

He shakes his head. "That's the excuse. A layoff. After I graduated, my brother followed me there. My first job after college. I thought I was all set. Then Nigel shows up one day. He ..."

Malcolm breaks off and searches the ceiling as if the words he needs are there. "He would stand in the public lobby, like some sort of crazed prophet, talking about ghosts—and of course, me. He harassed people, the women brokers in particular. It was..." He shudders. "Awful."

"Why didn't you tell me?"

"I thought it was all over. I took one suitcase and left everything else behind, except the samovar, and drove until I was nearly out of gas. I stopped here. I liked the town. I heard about you and your grandmother. I thought maybe you had the same problem I did." Here, he shrugs. "It made sense to stay."

I guess it would. "I kind of hated you when you first showed up."

Malcolm tips his head back and laughs—the first light sound I've heard from him since yesterday. "I know," he says once he's caught his breath.

"Do you want to swallow ghosts now? Is it like being an alcoholic?"

He shakes his head, his smile still there, although his eyes grow somber. "No, fortunately. I don't think I could function when we go out on calls if I did."

I wonder how true this is, but don't contradict him. "What happens to the ghosts once your brother swallows them? Do you know?"

"He says they give him strength, but I don't know if they're there inside, if they disappear or dissolve." He shrugs, palms skyward. "Maybe they become part of him."

At his words, one horrible thought strikes me. "My grandmother!"

"What?"

"She's ..." I choke back the words.

I've never told Malcolm my secret, that my grandmother's ghost haunts me. Or rather, she has a series of haunts, and when our bank balance dips to a certain level, she kicks up a ruckus—and we get a call and some much-needed cash.

"My grandmother is a ghost," I admit, at last. There. Now we've both confessed. I want to sink into the cushions, but the expression on Malcolm's face won't let me.

"How can you know? You've said yourself that most ghosts lose their human personality."

"Most do, or they cling to one aspect of it. In life, the thing my grandmother wanted most was to take care of me. So in her afterlife?"

"She's still taking care of you—or us." This time, his laugh is soft. "Last month's ghost in the bank vault?"

I nod.

"I suppose she's the one who shows up in the law offices as well."

"That too."

"What about Sadie?"

Sadie Lancaster is my next-door neighbor, one who believes herself continually plagued by ghosts. "No, Sadie just has a low tolerance for sprites. But that isn't my point."

Malcolm raises an eyebrow.

"What if your brother finds my grandmother and swallows her?"

WE'VE RETURNED to Lasting Rest Mausoleum. Autumn chills the air. Although I've pulled on a pair of over-the-knee stockings, the strip of flesh between the wool and the bandages breaks out in goose bumps. But my feet are toasty in leather hiking boots, the rest of me in a leather jacket.

I've spent the entire drive here ignoring glances from Malcolm, but now in the parking lot, I spit out an annoyed, "What?"

"You look—" he begins.

"Like you've walked out of his dreams, my dear."

It's the voice from the phone, but where it comes from, and how it seems to echo both in my head and all around us, I can't tell. It is yet another thing that defies logic and physics, like the floating bed sheet of the ghost from earlier.

"Is this what you meant by harassment?" I whisper. "He made it ... personal?"

Malcolm's face contorts. He gives me one quick nod.

"I'm sorry." I mean it, too. I suspect this first volley is merely a hint of what his brother can deliver.

The world around us has gone quiet. A breeze flutters my skirt, but I don't hear the wind. No birds sing. It is nearly as quiet as I'm sure the inside of the mausoleum is. But this is where we need to be, if only because there are no ghosts here. My grandmother isn't here. At least, I don't sense her. Would she face off against this ghost eater if she thought he might hurt me?

I know the answer and decide not to think about it, not now.

"Why are we here again?" Malcolm asks.

"Because this is where it started, because when you have so many different people inside you, you probably need a quiet place. Isn't that right, Nigel?"

Silence answers me. Malcolm eyes me. I want to protest that no, I have not suddenly lost my mind. Instead, I say:

"Let's set up the camp stove."

We are outside, in the parking lot. If someone protests, we can point out that there isn't a sign that states: No brewing coffee. Or tea, for that matter. Malcolm sets up the stove on the tailgate of my truck. I unpack the percolator and the Kona blend. A job like this, with an untold number of ghosts? Well, we need the good stuff.

But his hands move slowly. His gaze darts to the bandages on my thighs. At last, he drops any pretext of starting the stove.

"I can't do this," he says. "I can't see you hurt again."

"I won't be hurt."

He turns and cocks his head at me.

"How about, I probably won't be hurt. I'll jump out of the way. We know what to expect."

"That's just it, Katy. You don't know him. I do. And he'll go to any lengths—"

"Ah, poor baby brother." The strange voice is back. "Always trying to play knight in shining armor. It's too bad your damsel in distress doesn't want to be rescued."

It's clearly the wrong thing to say, since the metallic words send Malcolm into a frenzy of activity, and soon the camp stove is pumping propane and heat into the air. I set the percolator on it, and the aroma of coffee joins the heat. Then I pull three more percolators from the front seat of the truck.

Malcolm scowls at the sight. "Katy, what the—?"

"How many years has your brother been swallowing ghosts?"

His mouth draws into a thin, hard line. "I'm not certain. At least three, maybe more."

I expect that strange, metallic voice to cackle, but all is still. "That's a lot of ghosts, and they're going to want some coffee."

Malcolm blinks. "Or possibly some tea."

"Or possibly some tea," I echo. I want to hug him, but I'm not certain I should. That might only give Nigel more ammunition, and Malcolm is already skittish.

Wouldn't I be? I scan the parking lot. If we can hear him, his brother must be close. "All those ghosts," I say. "Do you think that helps him throw his voice?"

"Yes, actually, it does."

I jump and whirl around, but no one is behind me. Malcolm stands next to the tailgate, clutching a samovar, one he'll use to brew tea.

"Oh, you're clever," I say. "Isn't he clever, Malcolm?"

Malcolm stares as if I've lost my mind. Perhaps I have. "But there's a difference between clever and smart, and you're not being very smart."

A howl of protest goes up, but it's all air and golden leaves and little more.

"Because it isn't very smart to swallow ghosts." When there's no response, I continue. "How do you keep them all in check? Each one wants something, right? How do you manage? How do you keep them from leaving?" I return to the tailgate and the camp stove.

There, Malcolm sets out the cups. I pour. He adds sugar. I add cream. We work like my grandmother and I used to, our movements like a perfectly choreographed dance routine. I smile at him. Worry crinkles the lines around his eyes, but he gives me a small smile in return.

Scented steam fills the air. The parking lot is thick with the aroma, and combined with the cool autumn day, this could almost be paradise, or at least, a version of it. Barring Lasting Rest Mausoleum looming over everything, of course.

A cry rends the quiet, followed by a choking sound.

"They want out, don't they?" I say. I get no response.

"Katy, look!" Malcolm points, then reaches for one of our Tupperware containers.

Above one of the cups of coffee, something swirls. It's a puny thing, hardly more than a sprite, but its presence tinges the air, makes it glimmer in a way steam alone can't. Malcolm traps it easily in the container. The thing doesn't even put up a fight, but merely sinks to the bottom as if it needs a good rest.

He peers at the container and then at me. "It's exhausted."

I nod.

"Ghosts get tired?"

I shrug. "Maybe from being inside someone else, with so many others?"

Maybe. And maybe it simply doesn't matter, not when a second, third, and fourth swirl above two cups of coffee and one of tea. We trap them, one by one, and place the containers in the back of my truck.

The stillness catches us off guard. We've been so busy catching ghosts that only now do I notice that the air is stale. The steam sinks into the cups as if it has acquired weight. The world is silent and devoid of everything—smells, sounds. I inch closer to Malcolm, but even his Ivory soap and nutmeg scent eludes me.

"It's like the calm before the storm," I say.

He nods toward my truck, not so much at it as the space beneath it. He taps his fingers against his thigh, a countdown.

Three ... two ... one.

We both dive beneath the tailgate. The asphalt tears at my stockings, scrapes my bare skin. Malcolm tugs me close while around the truck, coffee and tea rain down. It's a storm and it's unrelenting. The laugh that follows rings hollow and makes my heart squeeze tight.

"Bravo, bravo. But did you really think *coffee* would work?" That metallic voice is triumphant.

Malcolm eyes me. I'm afraid my expression must convey it all: yes, I really did think coffee would work.

"The ghosts are exhausted," I whisper. "They really want to leave. They need a reason to break free."

That's when I feel the familiar and icy caress against my cheek. She must swoop in and nudge Malcolm as well, for his eyes go wide.

"Katy, that's not—"

"It is," I say. "That's my grandmother."

She continues to swoop and nudge, as if she could push me from beneath the truck. I flip over and low crawl my way from its shelter. I roll and miss most of the larger coffee puddles. They've lost all their scent, and the air above them is cold and stale, but as my grandmother whirls around the truck, a glimmer returns to the day.

Somewhere in the far-off tree line, a howl reverberates.

"More coffee," I say. "And tea."

Malcolm fires up the camp stove. I measure out the grounds. In the back of the truck, my grandmother swoops around the Tupperware containers, the ones with occupants. The ghosts rattle, then sink, rattle, sink. She darts back and forth before streaming across the parking lot. I catch the barest glimmer of her near the tree line.

I grip Malcolm's wrist. "She's using herself as bait."

His face is stricken. He shakes me off, then, before I can say or do anything, he bolts across the parking lot, toward the tree line, his brother, and the ghost of my grandmother.

FROM THE MOMENT Malcolm vanishes into the trees, my world goes quiet. Make the coffee, I order myself. Make the coffee, pour the cups, add the cream and sugar. Move your hands and everything will be okay. Move your hands.

My legs twitch. It's all I can do not to tear across the parking lot after them. But if the coffee isn't brewed, if the containers aren't out and ready to capture ghosts, then whatever happens to my grandmother and Malcolm will be for nothing.

I count the cups. I pull out extra containers and count those too. What I don't count on is seeing the fluttering bed sheet, that pretend ghost, in my peripheral vision. I cast my gaze toward the tree line, then back toward the fluttering. My heart sinks.

"Bed sheets and bridal veils," I say out loud.

That strange, metallic voice laughs.

"Vendetta?" I venture.

This time, there is no response.

"There are two of you," I say. Has it been this ... thing all along? I think I know the answer and dread washes over me.

"Ah, close enough, my dear. You are far cleverer than ... who is he, again? Your business partner?"

I clutch one of the percolators to me. It's not much of a weapon, but the metal heats my frigid fingers, and the handle is sure and steady in my grip.

"You are not Nigel," I say.

"Again, brava."

"Who are you, then?"

That laugh fills the air. With it comes the absence of everything—the aroma of coffee, the saffron from the tea. It's as if this thing—whatever it is—sucks up everything with a hint of life.

"It gives me substance," he says, as if reading my thoughts. "Not much, but I do appreciate your effort. You do make a damn fine cup of coffee." A sigh kicks up some dried leaves. "I miss drinking coffee, almost as much as I miss walking. It's strange, really, how much I miss the simple act of moving myself from one place to another. Of course, there are other ... *pleasures* I miss as well."

I scan the parking lot, but every time I catch sight of that fluttering bed sheet, it somehow whisks away.

"People imagine that to be ethereal is to be divine. It isn't, of course. In fact, you might say it's rather hellish, especially when all you want to do is stroke the cheek of a pretty girl."

That bed sheet appears before my eyes. It flaps as if draped from a clothesline. An edge touches my cheek. Before I can leap back, it entwines itself around my neck. Pressure against my windpipe makes me drop the percolator. Coffee splashes my shins, but I barely feel the heat. All my attention is on getting air into my lungs. I clutch at my neck, but all I do is rake fingernails across my skin.

Then, in a flash, the bed sheet flies away, once again teasing my peripheral vision.

"See? It's just not the same. Now, if I had a body ..."

I cough, unable—at first—to respond with words. I hold a protective hand over my neck; the other clutches the side of the truck. "Nigel," I say at last. "You want Nigel. You lured him here."

"With some help. You. His brother. That imbecile Doug. You see, my dear, for a ghost eater, I'm the ultimate prize. Of course, I'll have to do a little housekeeping once I'm inside. Kick everyone else out, for starters—"

"How does a ghost get so powerful?" I turn in a slow circle. His voice comes from everywhere. There must be some sort of trick.

The stale silence of the parking lot greets my question. "How does a ghost become so self-aware?"

Most, I believe, run on instinct, my grandmother a possible exception. But this thing?

"I am older than your grandmother. I am older than her grandmother. I am older than you can possibly begin to imagine." The voice fills the parking lot, seems to fill me. "I was here when mankind first crawled from the slime, and I'll be here when you bomb yourselves back into it."

"Then why would you want to be a puny human being?"

"I believe I already gave you my reasons. Indeed, I may have just added you to my list of those reasons."

"Seriously?" My neck aches, but my words come out strong. "Is that supposed to scare me?" I pick up a percolator, although this is only a ruse.

"It should."

I walk around the truck and open the driver's side door. I lean in, as if reaching for one of the bags of sugar. The bed sheet strikes the windshield. I pull my legs inside the cab and slam the door before it can follow me in. I start the engine. I'm about to peel out of the parking lot, in search of Malcolm, when in the rearview mirror I see that bed sheet flutter and dive.

The tailpipe.

I shift into first anyway. I press the accelerator. The engine sputters and dies. I reach for the key, determined to try again.

"I wouldn't, my dear. Carbon monoxide poisoning is a nasty way to go."

I concede that this obnoxious entity is correct. So I blast the horn instead.

Now, in the side mirror, I see two figures. Both run. Both glimmer. My grandmother must be keeping pace with them, blurring their images. No matter what Nigel has done, I need to warn him. He can't swallow this creature. This ... thing will kill him, erase any trace of the brother Malcolm knows and—I suspect—still loves.

But I can't leave the cab without the stupid thing choking me again.

"No, I'm afraid you can't."

"Stop that," I order.

"I'm not reading your mind, not really. It's just that all your thoughts play so clearly across your face. It's like watching a stage actress."

"Watch this." I hold up my middle finger.

The entity merely laughs that grating, metallic cackle. The sound freezes both Malcolm and Nigel in place. Then they both race forward again. This time, though, it's as if Nigel is bolstered by supernatural strength. He's thinner than Malcolm, but his legs stretch farther with each step, and he outpaces his brother easily.

He is nearly to the tailgate when I fling open the cab door.

"Nigel, no!" I shout. My throat aches and my words emerge with a croak. "It's a trap."

I'm right. It is. But not in the way I think. That bed sheet bursts from beneath the hood of my truck and drops down on top of me. Someone screams, but I don't think it's me. My mouth is too full of what feels like mist. I cough and choke. I push, but there's nothing to push against.

Nigel crashes into me. For a moment, we're both trapped beneath a fluttering white bed sheet that is there, and at the same time, not there. But he's done this before and knows what to do. He opens his mouth as if for a big yawn, and then I am free.

Nigel falls to the ground. His legs and arms twitch. I am only two feet away, but the chill that rolls off him is a force pushing me back. I can't get close. I can't help him. Malcolm catches me from behind, wraps his arms around my waist.

"The ultimate prize." Malcolm's voice is ragged in my ear. "That's what he kept saying. The ultimate prize for a ghost eater."

"A trap. That thing will ... use your brother, maybe already has been using him. I'm sorry."

Malcolm's arms tighten around my waist. He buries his head against my neck. "I'm sorry, too, Katy, for bringing this to you."

I don't want to watch, but know I should. If I must fight this sort of being, then I need to know all its tricks. Nigel rolls on the asphalt, through puddles of coffee and damp leaves. He clamps his hands over his mouth.

"He's not giving up the ghosts," I say.

"Is that good?"

"I don't know, but it isn't part of that thing's plan."

When I notice the darting glimmer, I can't say. Perhaps at first, I only think it a trick of the September afternoon light. But this light has purpose. It moves and swoops—just like my grandmother.

"Oh, my God, she wants in," I say a second before Nigel uncovers his mouth.

My grandmother dives inside.

This time, the scream is mine.

∽

NIGEL STOPS TWITCHING. He rolls onto his back, closes his eyes, his face almost serene. An infant asleep. Or a man near death. In my mind, I hear an echo of a voice, a command from long ago.

Katy-Girl, the coffee, now!

"Coffee!" This comes out as more air than word, but understanding lights Malcolm's eyes.

We race for the camp stove. Except for the pot I removed earlier, the rest remains, brewing and steaming and filling the air with an aroma to rival the best coffee shop. Malcolm pours cups of tea from the samovar. When that heady mixture of saffron and spice strikes the air, I think I hear a cheer, the sound both joyful and otherworldly.

"Katy, look!" Malcolm points and we round the truck together. "Do you see them?"

"I do!"

One by one, glimmers emerge from Nigel's mouth. Tiny ones, no more than sprites. They streak toward the brewing coffee. They dip and dive in the steam before compliantly sinking into one of the Tupperware containers by the truck's left rear wheel.

"They're happy to be free," I say.

And they are. Happy. Grateful. A few swoop by me, giving me a ghostly kiss on their way to a container. Granted, one smacks Malcolm on the back of the head, but it's more of a ghostly version of a buddy shove than any sort of retribution.

Sprites are one thing. Nigel has just swallowed something very nasty. We will have to face that.

During my years of ghost catching, I've only witnessed a full-on ghost infestation three times, two in homes, once in an old barn. Never have I seen one inside a person, but that can only explain Nigel's current state. He appears glazed over, as if a thin sheet of ice covers him. His lips turn blue; his eyelashes are frosted.

"More heat," I call to Malcolm. "More steam." I refill the percolator. Malcolm turns the knob of the camp stove to high.

"Let's bring the cups to him," I say a moment later. "Tempt them out."

When the coffee is ready, I pour. Malcolm adds the cream and sugar, the spoon clinking against the sides of the cups.

"Three black," he says, "three with cream."

"Three with sugar," I say, picking up the chant. "And three extra light and extra sweet."

"Because even ghosts have a preference."

Twelve cups. Always. The way my grandmother taught me. We rush the cups of scalding coffee across the parking lot. Hot liquid sloshes over the sides. My hands throb with the scalding, their skin bright pink. I keep up the run until a circle of coffee surrounds Nigel, the ceramic mugs gleaming in the sunshine, bright blues to rival the sky, the green deeper than the chemically enhanced lawn of the mausoleum behind us.

With all twelve cups in place, it's like Nigel is some strange offering to the god of caffeine. Steam rises into the autumn air, the vapor clouding my view of him. He is hazy, as if we've tucked him in for the night in a blanket of fog.

His entire body trembles. He cries out, once. Then, the world glimmers.

From his mouth, ghosts stream. The more powerful ones jostle the mugs, send coffee splashing across the asphalt, my hiking boots, Malcolm's loafers. They whirl, kick up leaves and pebbles with the force of their escape. We grab containers and catch the slower ones. Some bypass the coffee, intent on freedom—and that is anywhere but our Tupperware.

I don't sense my grandmother. I detect no hint of that ... thing, the one who flutters bed sheets and makes me think of bridal veils. Nigel bolts upright. He coughs. He strikes himself in the solar plexus as if giving himself the Heimlich maneuver.

What emerges from his mouth is an inky swirl of dark purple, tinged with green, like storm clouds during a tornado warning. It does not glimmer. It oozes. I take a few steps back and bump against Malcolm. He grips my shoulders, and it's his heat that keeps me steady.

The thing floats inches from my face. The air around it is stale, devoid of scent. Its presence fills my head. Cold metal. Gray sleet. And thoughts I force myself not to think. Bed sheets. Bridal veils.

"Know this, Katy," the thing says in its strange, metallic voice, words clicking against my eardrums. "You can't run."

Malcolm pushes himself in front of me, but the thing drifts skyward as if filled with just enough helium to give it lift. The breeze takes it and carries the inky mass away until the blot against the sky at last vanishes.

Malcolm swears softly in my ear, giving voice to my thoughts. Then I whirl.

"My grandmother!"

We rush to Nigel's side. He is still, his face pale, eyes shut. Malcolm sinks to one side, I land on the other. I close my own eyes to hold back the tears. True, I've lost my grandmother to death. That she follows me now during her afterlife has been more of a comfort than I'm willing to admit. Now I fear the goodbye is for real.

"Katy." Malcolm's voice is soft. "Look."

So I do. There, emerging from Nigel's mouth, is a soft, shimmering glimmer, robust and able to withstand the breeze. Thirsty, perhaps, for a cup of coffee—two sugars, extra cream.

"It's the yellow cup," I tell her.

Before she swoops in for her reward, my grandmother's ghost swirls against my cheeks and dries my tears.

Malcolm holds his brother's hand. "He's breathing, his pulse is fast, but I think that's to be expected."

"Should we—?" Before I can suggest calling 911, Nigel bolts upright.

He coughs, a shudder convulsing his body. His eyes clear. "Malcolm?"

Malcolm nods.

"I ... I ..." Nigel surveys the parking lot, the coffee cups. His gaze follows the tree line. I see the instant the memories come flooding back. The chagrin on his face is painful to witness.

"Oh, God," he murmurs and buries his face in his hands. "I am so ashamed."

Malcolm hugs his brother, but Nigel won't stop his litany of regret and shame.

"I don't know what I've done, and yet, I remember it all. I can't explain it."

"You weren't in control," Malcolm says. "It was the ghosts."

"Oh, but I swallowed them."

Malcolm casts me a desperate look. I inch closer. My red and white striped stockings are ruined, so what's a little more asphalt? I kneel and peer up at Nigel. Then I offer him my hand.

"Hi, I'm Katy. You saved my life."

Now I have the attention of both brothers. And yes, the resemblance is there, although where Malcolm's hair is a gleaming ebony, Nigel has a shock of pure white. Their eyes are dark, but Nigel's have the look of a man who has seen far too many things.

"I ... saved your life?" he says, each word its own question.

"That thing." I touch my neck. It's tender, and I suspect a bruise is already forming. "It tried to kill me. It would have, or taken me over, or something. You crashed into me on purpose, didn't you?"

Nigel is silent.

"You had second thoughts about it, didn't you?"

"I don't know." The words are rough and honest.

"I think you did, and you didn't have to save my life, but you did anyway." I'm still extending my hand. I nod to it.

He takes my hand, his skin nearly as warm as his brother's. A second later, he exclaims, "You're freezing." He turns to his brother. "Malcolm, she's freezing."

"I think there's some tea left," Malcolm says.

We huddle around the tailgate and sip the last of Malcolm's tea, my grandmother turning lazy circles in the steam from the samovar.

WE RETURN one last time to Lasting Rest Mausoleum. After Nigel gave up all the ghosts, a few mischievous sprites found their way inside. Apparently, they've been nipping at visitors and knocking over the fans. Personally, I think they liven up the place. But a client is a client, as Malcolm points out, especially with our cash flow the way it is.

On our final circuit through the building, we find a discarded bed sheet, some fishing line, and what looks like a pulley from a child's toy. The innocuous items feel menacing, but the air in the space smells merely recycled, not devoid of everything, not like before.

Still, when Malcolm gathers the things, worry carves a frown in his brow.

"Why bed sheets and bridal veils?" I ask both brothers later in the week. We've settled now into a new routine, one that includes Nigel. He lives with Malcolm, and knows his way around a computer. He plans to build us a ghost hunting database.

To my surprise, it's Nigel who speaks up first.

"Sex and love," he says. "That's what most of them want, some form of it. Attention, love, acknowledgement, to be desired." He shakes his head. "Even now, I can hear their chatter. It fills you up, but it leaves you empty."

And then he is silent. We've grown used to this, having him quiet, his gaze somewhere in the middle distance. I don't ask him what he sees. I know he will tell us when he's ready.

In the meantime, Malcolm and I have an incident at the local law firm.

"Your grandmother can't keep doing this," he says. "Someone will figure it out."

"You didn't." I have graduated back into jeans, my thighs healed, or mostly so. I've added a plaid blazer, but still feel underdressed for the gauntlet of lawyers we will need to pass.

"How about this," he counters. "She needs to be careful." He stops our trek down the sidewalk. "You need to be careful, Katy. That thing—"

"Is gone."

He stands firm in the center of the sidewalk so a mother with a stroller must scoot past us.

"I can't get that word out of my head," he says once she passes. "Vendetta. It wasn't about Nigel, and I don't think it was about me. That leaves you."

"That thing is gone," I say again.

"For now."

"Yes, exactly. And in the meantime, we have a job to do."

"But—"

I press my finger against his lips, a quick touch, there and gone. This close, he is all Ivory soap and nutmeg. "Let's go catch a ghost."

To my surprise, Malcolm doesn't protest. He merely takes my hand and starts walking.

To my surprise, I don't mind. Not at all.

THE GHOST WHISPERER

COFFEE AND GHOSTS: EPISODE 3

S FAR AS GHOST ERADICATIONS GO, clearing sprites from Sadie Lancaster's house almost never varies. I suspect they are the same two sprites, although with sprites, it's hard to tell. I suspect they hold a certain amount of affection for Sadie since they always return. They don't mind my efforts to catch them. At least, they don't mind the coffee I use to do so. All in all, clearing Sadie's house of sprites guarantees a certain amount of cash flow each month.

K&M Ghost Eradication Specialists appreciates and counts on that certain amount of cash flow.

"You know, Katy," Sadie says to me, hands fluttering. "I've been talking to someone who says I should embrace my sprites."

"You could," I say, mentally weighing cash flow against honesty. In my hands, I cradle a cup of coffee, one I plan to place in the master bath. Ghosts of all varieties love toilet humor. You really don't want one in your bathroom. The mug stings my fingertips and steam rises from the coffee's surface. In that steam, something glimmers. I may have my first catch already.

"She says they won't hurt me," Sadie adds.

"They won't," I say. "But they will play pranks."

Sadie gives her head an emphatic shake. "They're only trying to communicate. You should know that, Katy."

Well, no, they're not. And no, I don't know any such thing. True, ghosts have desires, but not in the way most people think they do. None of them want to sit down for a chat. They don't want to unburden themselves, no matter what you see on television. Like most things supernatural, information on ghosts is very misleading.

"Anyway," Sadie is saying. "Mistress Armand—"

"Wait. Mistress *Armand*?" My partner—the M in K&M—is Malcolm Armand.

"Well, yes. I just assumed she's a sister, or an aunt. Same beautiful black hair and all." Sadie waves a hand, dismissing my question.

Aunt. Sister. Imposter? My hands tremble at the thought. Coffee sloshes over the rim. My skin smarts. I swallow back the pain. When I reach the bathroom, I'll run some cold water over the burn. Now? Now I want to know more about this Mistress Armand.

Sadie clutches her hands beneath her chin. "She did a reading, right here in the living room." Her eyes glow. "She knows everything, about Harold, how even though he cheated, he still loved me ..."

What else would you say to a widow, especially one both grieving and wronged? I sigh, my breath chasing steam from the top of the cup. The sprite is there, waiting to be caught. This one is a tease.

"Cold reading," I murmur to myself.

"Pardon, dear?"

"I said, the coffee is getting cold. I need to take it to the bathroom."

What I need to do is think, and possibly call Malcolm, and catch a ghost. I can do all three in the bathroom.

I set the cup on the vanity, then return with a Tupperware container. I hold it open next to the rising steam. The coffee is cooling, and the sprite has had its fill.

"In you go."

I don't even need to scoop up the tiny thing. It floats compliantly into the container, settles at the bottom, and makes no protest when I snap on the lid. I hold the container at eye level and stare through the opaque plastic.

"We've met before."

In response, the sprite thumps the Tupperware's side.

Sprite secured, I text Malcolm. Nothing. I call Malcolm. Still nothing. As a last resort, I try the main number of the Springside Long-term Care Facility.

"Oh, hello, Katy," the manager says, her voice clear and light and full of humor. "Yes, Malcolm is here."

The fact I'm speaking with the manager—and she sounds so happy—can mean only one thing: Malcolm is holding court. The Springside staff and residents love him. Or rather, most of the *female* staff and residents love him. For a man so obsessed with our cash flow, he certainly doesn't mind spending hours at one of our few gratis accounts.

In the background, a cry goes up, a gasp as if a magician has pulled a bouquet of flowers from a hat and presented them to someone in the audience. Since Malcolm knows a handful of magic tricks, this is entirely possible.

The manager laughs. "Oh, his visits brighten everyone's day ... yours do too, Katy, I didn't mean—"

Whenever I visit, I only manage to mess up everyone's bridge game. So no, I doubt I'm a day-brightener.

"It's kind of important," I say. "Could you put him on the line?"

The manager sets the phone down. Sounds filter through the receiver, chatter and laughter. Someone squeals. When Malcolm picks up the phone, his voice is tinged with warmth.

"Malcolm Armand."

"It's Katy."

There's a pause in which I hear him mentally berating me. Yes, I know. I'm interrupting the Malcolm Armand variety hour and all his fun.

"Do you have a sister?" I ask.

This is a fair question—and not out of the blue as you might suspect. Up until a few weeks ago, I never knew Malcolm had a brother, one who swallows ghosts. It's entirely possible his family tree includes a medium.

"No."

"An aunt, then? Or a female cousin?"

"Maybe a second cousin. Or is that first cousin, once removed? I can never remember."

"How about a mistress? Do you have one of those?"

"Katy, what the hell is this about?"

"Someone is in town. She claims to be—" I pause and glance at Sadie, eyebrow raised in question.

"A medium between this world and the next," Sadie rattles off. She sounds like she's parroting an infomercial.

"A medium. She's been advising Sadie." Possibly for a great deal of cash, but I'll investigate that later. "And she calls herself Mistress Armand."

"Seriously, Katy," Malcolm says. "Assuming I had a mistress, which I don't, would she really go around calling herself Mistress Armand?"

"No .... I was just trying to get your attention."

The line goes silent, and then his laugh fills my ear. It's a rich sort of laughter that—if you could brew it and pour it into a cup—would taste like a sweet, dark roast.

"You've got it," he says, humor returning to his voice. "You always do."

My throat tightens. I'm not entirely certain what he means by this. However, I am certain I won't ask. Or at least, I can't ask. My throat won't let me. Through the receiver I hear the volume of the chatter in the facility drop, a collective hush that sounds like the rushing of air. Malcolm sucks in his breath.

"Uh, Katy, do you know what Mistress Armand looks like?"

I repeat the question. It's barely out of my mouth when Sadie hands me a trifold brochure.

"Long, dark hair," I say.

"Check."

"Could be anywhere between twenty-nine and forty-nine."

"Check."

"Long, flowing robe-like thing?" I add.

"I think they're called kaftans."

Yes. Leave it to Malcolm to know the correct term.

"Whatever," I say. "She's wearing a pink and yellow one in her photo. It's fancy."

"Blue and green. But yes, and it looks expensive, like it's made out of silk."

"It is made out of silk."

I jerk around because the lilting female voice seems to come from both the phone and the air around me.

"Speaker," Malcolm murmurs.

I mute my own phone and then press it close to my ear, unwilling to miss a single word of this exchange.

"I hear we share an interest in the supernatural and a surname," that same lilting voice says. "I am Mistress Armand."

"Malcolm Armand."

He sounds impressed, or like he's trying to impress. From the brochure, her image stares up at me. I assumed Photoshop. Perhaps I assumed wrong. My throat clogs again, the taste of it thick and salty. *Don't be stupid. Malcolm is your business partner. He's free to impress anyone he likes.*

If only I weren't so impressed.

"We need to embrace our otherworldly friends," Mistress Armand is saying. Her voice wavers in and out, like she's turning as she talks.

"Physically speaking," he says, "that's not possible."

Her laugh tinkles as if he's uttered the funniest thing ever.

"But you do catch them, don't you?" she says. "They must have some substance."

Well, yes, but not enough for a hug.

"And then you just set them free?" she asks.

"Of course." Malcolm's voice is sturdy and sure. "We are strictly a catch and release operation."

"But, in some ways, isn't that just as cruel?"

Cruel? My ears strain to hear what Malcolm says, what she will say.

"I don't see how," he says. "We set them free."

"Unmoored, unprotected, lost, in all that air? It's like releasing a laboratory animal or a house pet into the wild. Without their familiar surroundings, they're unable to survive."

Worry pings inside me. I'd never thought of what we do as deliberately cruel. It's a service, really, for both humans and ghosts. Most ghosts are more than willing to be caught. Many, like Sadie's sprites, find their way back to haunt yet again. My grandmother—who taught me everything I know about ghosts and ghost hunting—always said we were doing everyone involved a favor.

"I don't think that's true," Malcolm says, but the conviction in his voice bears cracks. At least, I can hear them even if no one else can.

"Here." Something rattles, something that sounds like paper, quite possibly a replica of the brochure Sadie handed me earlier. "I'm holding a séance tonight. Bring your little partner."

Little partner?

"Cups of coffee and Tupperware?" She snorts a laugh, one that does not tinkle, thank goodness. "Come tonight and watch how a real ghost whisperer does it."

MALCOLM IS NOT at our office by the time I arrive there, but his brother Nigel is. Nigel, who is also an Armand. Nigel, who knows a thing or two about ghosts, even if those things came from swallowing them. He's recently recovered from his addiction to that. Although sometimes his eyes glimmer, like he's contemplating a tasty sprite. He is also our resident computer expert. I hand him Mistress Armand's brochure.

"Whoa." Nigel runs a hand through his pure white hair. "She's … intense."

"A relation?"

"Not that I know of, but—" He shrugs. "The Armand family tree is kind of scattered."

He studies the brochure for a moment, then glances up, dazzling me with a rare smile. "She has a domain name. Where there's a domain, there's a trail. Let's follow it."

His hands fly over the keyboard while I pull up a chair to watch.

"Here we go," he says. "Looks like she maintains a static webpage. Not much here."

I lean forward for a glimpse of Mistress Armand's website.

Let Mistress Armand whisper the ghosts from your life. Guaranteed. Effective. Heal yourself and watch the ghosts flee.

I roll my eyes.

"Not impressed?" Nigel asks.

"Not really. She knew all about Sadie's marriage, and how Harold cheated on her, and probably how he died, too."

"How did he die?"

"In bed, with another woman."

Nigel cringes. "Really? Poor Sadie."

"Do you think she researches a town," I say, "then uses that as a starting point for cold readings?"

Really, it wouldn't be that hard to scan the newspapers for tidbits and then ask a few questions around town. Harold Lancaster's obituary was coy, but if you knew what to look for, you could read between the lines.

And although I haven't met her, Mistress Armand strikes me as the sort of person who knows how to read between the lines.

"Probably," Nigel says. "You can find out almost anything on the Internet these days."

"But why use your last name?"

"To get our attention?" A new voice joins the conversation.

Malcolm stands in the doorway to the conference room, which also doubles as Nigel's work area.

"What's your take on all this?" Nigel asks.

Malcolm gives a half laugh and shakes his head.

"Is she ...?" Nigel points to Mistress Armand's portrait. "In person?"

"Oh, yeah, and then some."

"What?" I demand. "She's what?" I glance from one brother to the other, but neither one will meet my gaze.

Nigel clears his throat. "Anyway, here's the thing about having a domain name. Even though her registration is private, we can take a trip in the Internet Wayback Machine to see if she's always been Mistress Armand."

He clacks the keyboard some more. Then, in triumph, he pushes back from his desk, fists raised in the air. "Lady and gentleman, meet Mistress Ramone."

Malcolm leans over one shoulder. I take the other. The website is unchanged except for the last name in the center of the screen.

Nigel peers up at his brother. "We should get on the ghost forums, see if anyone is chatting about her."

I almost never bother with the ghost forums since anything there is either completely wrong, or so filled with hyperbole it might as well be. But in this case, maybe it's just what we need.

Nigel pulls his chair closer to the desk and leans forward like he's about to run a race. "I'm on it."

WHAT DOES one wear to a séance? Certainly not a skater skirt paired with over-the-knee, plaid socks. Unless you're me. Because that's exactly what I'm wearing. The only other dressy item in my closet is the suit I wore to my grandmother's funeral. I can't bring myself to pull it on; I doubt I ever will. I can't bring myself to donate it, either, so there it hangs, haunting my closet.

Outside the Springside Community Center, a crowd is gathering. Residents from the long-term care facility make their unsteady way down the steps of the shuttle bus while others wait for the wheelchair ramp. I wave at Mr. Carlotta, who has just landed on the sidewalk.

"Katy-Girl, do you believe this bunk?" He takes my hand, like he always does. We proceed inside as if I'm his date for the evening, one of the attendants pushing his wheelchair.

"Bunk, I tell you," he says again. "You don't believe it, do you?"

"Of course not."

"Then what are you going to do about it?"

People swarm the lobby. A sticky, sweet smell rises in the air. Some enterprising soul from the school board has set up a cotton candy machine. Someone else—just as clever—is selling bottled water. Sweat trickles down my spine, and despite the two-dollar markup, I buy a bottle.

"I don't know what we're going to do," I say to Mr. Carlotta. "I'm meeting Malcolm here and—"

He snorts, a response that encompasses his entire opinion of Malcolm. Then a cloud passes over Mr. Carlotta's eyes. I see it, feel it, and kneel next to his chair.

"God, Katy-Girl, but I miss her." He clutches my hand harder, as if that could bring my grandmother back.

"I miss her too."

He was so in love with her. That he mourns—still—makes me just a little bit angry with her. She never encouraged him; it was true.

"It wouldn't be right," is what she always told me. "And it's not something I can do."

Before she died, I agreed. Mr. Carlotta's gnarled fingers pass across the top of my head, tangling in a few wayward strands of hair. Now I wonder if it really would have hurt that much. I disengage, slowly, standing first, then giving his hand a squeeze.

"I've been meaning to ask," I say. "How's Jack?"

At the sound of his grandson's name, Mr. Carlotta's spine straightens. The clouds clear from his eyes.

"Just passed the bar exam and got a job offer from one of those fancy law firms in downtown Minneapolis."

"Very impressive," I say.

"He's a good catch for a girl, steady job and all. Hard to make ends meet as a ghost hunter."

I swallow back the sigh. "Last I heard, Jack was engaged."

"Flighty thing. I knew it wouldn't work out."

I went to school with Jack Carlotta. We were in the same graduating class, and he once set my hair on fire with the Bunsen burner in science class, although not on purpose. I adore Mr. Carlotta too much to tell him that it's actually his grandson who's the flighty one.

"I need to find Malcolm," I say instead.

Predictably, I'm treated to another snort. "You tell him, for me, that I've got my eye on him. He mistreats you, Katy-Girl? Well, I'll have something to say about it."

"We're business partners."

"Yes. Of course." He gives me a sly look. "How silly of me."

Only after I turn toward the gymnasium do I roll my eyes.

At the far end of the gym, a platform sits beneath the basketball hoop. Except for an overstuffed chair in midnight blue, the platform is empty. From where I stand, the material looks like velvet and it matches the ruffle that surrounds the platform itself. The fabric—on the chair, around the platform—is so conveniently draped, it makes me wish I were five so I could lift it up, crawl beneath, and discover all the secrets that are no doubt hidden there.

But I'm not five, so instead I walk up the center aisle, gaze searching for Malcolm. I catch sight of his ebony hair first. He's in the front row, chatting with a reporter from the weekly newspaper. I don't want to sit in the front row. Indeed, nothing about the front row entices me, as a person or as a ghost eradication specialist. The back is the better option, the place where you might see the sleight of hand of the technical crew.

In the back, you can slip out and no one notices. In the back, you can see who is truly engaged from their posture. But Malcolm is in the front, so I continue my trek and take the chair two seats away from his.

When the reporter leaves, Malcolm eyes the space I've left between us, then skewers me with a look.

"What?" He raises an eyebrow. "Do I smell?"

Normally, yes, like Ivory soap and nutmeg. It's one of the best things about working closely with him. But when he scoots over, I end up with a nose full of musk. I scrunch up my face.

"Yeah, you do smell. Are you wearing cologne?"

He pushes a strand of hair from his forehead. "A little."

A lot. His white dress shirt bristles with starch. His loafers gleam. So does his hair. Extra product, I think.

"Are you going on a date later?" I ask at last.

He casts a glance at my stockings. "Are you?"

I look away.

Several banks of lights shut off, leaving the rows of chairs in the dark. A collective intake of breath echoes through the gymnasium. A hazy glow illuminates the chair in the center of the platform, the midnight blue like the night sky, sparkling with hundreds of tiny stars. It's low budget stagecraft, to be sure, but it's effective. I can feel people in the rows behind us leaning forward. The soft plinking of some new age tune fills the air. I turn toward Malcolm. He gives me a shrug.

Mistress Armand ascends the platform from the back, using stairs none of us can see. Her caftan flutters and glimmers a ghostly white. The image reminds me of a child's idea of a ghost. It also reminds me of something I saw very recently, something I can't explain, and something that tried to kill me. I lurch backward. My chair tips. The legs wobble, then Malcolm's arm steadies me. As an encore, the chair legs thud against the wood floor. The jolt travels from the base of my spine to my jaw.

"You okay?" he whispers.

I place a hand against my neck. That thing—the entity that attacked me—is not here. Nothing is choking me. I can still breathe. I nod.

Perhaps it's the light, but Mistress Armand is somehow lovelier than her own retouched image. Another murmur cascades through the crowd. Certainly Malcolm sits up straighter, as if she's captured his full attention. His arm slips from the back of my chair.

I pretend not to notice.

"Welcome!" Mistress Armand calls out. "Welcome friends of all kinds, human and otherworldly. We are here today to dispel myths about our friends on the other side. We are here today to communicate with them, to learn from their knowledge. We are here to heal past hurts."

I can't tell if she means all of us or is speaking in the royal third person. I'm not sure it matters, since most everyone is here to speak to ghosts.

If only the ghosts could talk back.

I listen, trying not to judge or roll my eyes. I fail on both accounts. I squirm in my seat, the metal folding chair making my hips ache. A chill rolls through me despite the body heat warming the air. Up on stage, Mistress Armand wants us to confront our ghosts, which is something I do every day.

"They are merely a manifestation of our inner turmoil," she says. "Rid yourself of that, and you rid yourself of ghosts completely. You will heal your body, soul, and spirit."

I raise my hand.

For a second, Mistress Armand's face contorts. "Let's save questions for the end, shall we?"

"But I have one now," I counter, and before she can cut me off, continue with, "Didn't you say earlier, in fact, earlier today, that ghosts are real and that our policy of catch and release was cruel? How can they be both things? Real and merely a manifestation of our inner turmoil?"

"You simply don't understand, my child. They are both. Don't you see? Catch and release is like denial. You're not facing your problems, simply pushing them aside. They return, stronger than ever."

"But—"

"Who would like to be healed of their ghosts?" Mistress Armand's caftan flutters with her movements. It billows as if to embrace us all.

Around me, hands shoot into the air until I'm surrounded by a forest of arms.

"You there, in the gray sweater and blue skirt. Yes, you."

I crane my neck to see who she's selected. To my horror, Sadie Lancaster makes her way down the aisle, hands clutched under her chin in excitement and pride at being picked.

"Ah, there you go, my dear." Mistress Armand extends a hand and helps Sadie climb the stairs to the platform. "You are plagued by ghosts, then?"

Sadie nods. "Normally I call Katy or Malcolm, but the ghosts always come back."

"Perhaps theirs is not the most effective business model."

Muted laughter ripples through the audience. I'm leaning forward, ready to raise my hand or possibly storm the stage, when Malcolm grips my wrist.

"Not worth it, Katy," he says under his breath.

"But—"

"Not. Worth. It."

I sit back, defeated—for now. Mistress Armand leads Sadie to the chair and rests fingers with long red nails against Sadie's temples.

"Ah, yes. I see your ghosts, my dear. The philandering husband. Am I right?"

"We have to stop this," I say to Malcolm.

"It's common knowledge. Everyone in town knows." He's still gripping my wrist as if he's worried I'll charge up on stage. He should worry, because I'm *this close* to doing so.

On stage, Sadie gulps a plaintive, "Yes."

"I count one, two … oh, my, *five* affairs."

I spear Malcolm with a look. So Mistress Armand wants to talk cruel? *This* is cruel. Sadie's lower lip quivers. She shuts her eyes only to have Mistress Armand snap her fingers in front of her face.

"No, my dear, you must face your inner demons, stare at them straight on. For this business, we keep our eyes open. *Always.*"

Mistress Armand goes on, although the details hardly matter. Malcolm is right. Everyone in town already knows. Everyone in town, except perhaps my grandmother, was party to the deception. When Mistress Armand is done, Sadie is in tatters, her mascara carving two dark rivers down her cheeks. Bits of tissue dot her skirt.

Mistress Armand clutches hands to her chest and turns her gaze toward the ceiling. "Wasn't that cathartic?"

"Actually it was horrid," I say, not caring who hears me.

Mistress Armand's jaw twitches.

"Now, my dear," Mistress Armand continues, "you will see the benefits and a distinct lack of ghosts. Mark my words on that."

Sadie makes her shaky way down the stairs. The assistant manager from the Coffee Depot helps her down the final steps and she gives him a wan smile. When she passes my chair, however, Sadie refuses to even glance at me.

"Who's next?" Mistress Armand calls out. "Who else wants the benefit of ridding their lives of ghosts?"

This time around, the forest of arms is not quite as thick. Still, plenty volunteer. To my surprise, Malcolm releases my wrist.

Then he raises his hand.

"How about a gentleman this time. You there, sir, are you haunted?" She points a red-lacquered nail at Malcolm.

"Constantly," he says.

She gestures toward the stairs. "Then Mistress Armand awaits you."

Oh, I bet she does. I cross my arms over my chest, then cross one leg over the other. Without Malcolm at my side—on my side—things feel wrong in a way I can't pinpoint. Mistress Armand doesn't lead him to the chair. Instead, she has him stand center stage, then circles him as if he's something she might like to buy.

"Oh, dear," she says. "Such a sad tale, such a heavy heart. Do you want to tell Mistress Armand all about the girl you left behind?"

"Yes." And Malcolm breathes this word more than says it. It's as if someone has hit him in the stomach. "The girl I left behind."

The *what*? I come undone, or at least, unfolded. My mouth? Hanging open. Yes, Malcolm's past is murky. I've only just learned of—and met— his brother. Still. Have I been too focused on my own mourning and the business of ghost catching to notice he was suffering from a broken heart?

I don't think so. But ever since Mistress Armand first uttered her breezy proclamations—just this afternoon, no less—I've started to doubt a great many things.

"Oh, you poor boy," she murmurs, her voice like velvet. She cups his face, fingers caressing his jaw. Malcolm stares at her, mouth agape, expression rapt.

I push from my chair and head, not toward the stage, but down the aisle. I can't take anymore. In fact, I may have taken too much already. I doubt I can scrub the image of her hand caressing Malcolm from my mind. At least, not any time soon.

I push through the gymnasium doors. Before they shut completely, Mistress Armand's lilting voice follows me.

"There are always unbelievers."

POLICE CHIEF RAMSEY is standing in the lobby outside the gymnasium, arms folded over his chest, his serious-police-business scowl firmly in place. For a moment, my mood lifts. Yes! Mistress Armand is a fraud and Chief Ramsey is here to arrest her—or at least to shut down the séance.

The hope must show on my face, since an almost-grin appears on his.

"Sorry, Katy, you'll have to deal with the competition on your own. I'm just here for traffic control when the séance lets out."

Mistress Armand was right about one thing: there are always unbelievers. Chief Ramsey? He's one of the biggest in town. When my grandmother was alive, every few months, she'd offer to help clear some of the unsolved cases clogging the files of the Springside Township Police Department. Half the vandalism in town is really the result of energetic sprites.

Chief always refused. Some people can't detect ghost activity. They chalk up odd occurrences to Mercury in retrograde or bad luck or superstition.

I glance back at the closed gymnasium doors. "Does she have—?"

"A permit? Why, yes, she does. You'll also notice she isn't charging anyone anything."

"Yet," I add. "She isn't charging them yet. The first hit is always free."

"Isn't that how you operate? Funny how the ghosts"—he draws little air quotes around the word *ghosts*—"always come back."

Yes. Like mice. Or insects. I don't say this. Instead, I say, "K&M Ghost Eradication Specialists is registered with City Hall. We're a limited liability company, and our business license is up to date."

Most of that is thanks to Malcolm. At the thought of him, my gaze once again goes to the closed gymnasium doors.

"Lose something?" Chief asks.

I choose to ignore this. "Let me know when you want me to capture the ghost in your garden shed."

Without waiting for a reply, I walk from the lobby area and head into the night.

The air cools my heated cheeks. Part of me insists I charge back into the gymnasium and put a stop to the séance. Part of me wants to argue with Chief Ramsey, but I can't force someone to believe in ghosts. I can't force anyone to believe anything at all.

I take a final look at the community center doors and wonder if that applies to me.

There are always unbelievers.

Maybe I'm one of them.

On the sidewalk, I find Mr. Carlotta. He glowers at the entrance of the community center. For a moment, I fear that glower is for me.

"Bunk!" he shouts. "Pure bunk! If only your grandmother were here, Katy-Girl."

Yes. If only.

"She'd know what to do. Oh, she'd take that charlatan down a notch." He wags a finger at me. "That young man of yours—"

"He's not my young man, Mr. Carlotta. He's my business partner."

"He's a disgrace, picking her over you."

"I don't think he's picked anyone." Although why, at the moment, I'm defending Malcolm, I can't say. Maybe I simply can't believe it. So instead, I say, "Can I wheel you home?"

"I know you *can*, Katy-Girl."

I sigh. "May I wheel you home, Mr. Carlotta?"

"No, but you may wheel me back to the care facility."

I sigh again.

The facility is lightly staffed. The few employees on shift seem resentful and disgruntled, as if we've kept them from all the fun at the séance. From what I saw, it was less of a séance and more of an exercise in public humiliation. They should probably thank us.

"Bunk!" Mr. Carlotta tells them, not that it helps. But he's right. It was that, too.

The wheels on Mr. Carlotta's chair whisper against the carpet. His room is near the end of the wing, and I wave at the residents still here and still awake. When we reach his room, a glimmer and flash of cold greet us.

"Oh, Mr. Carlotta, why didn't you tell Malcolm your ghost was back?"

He makes a noise, something that sounds like *harrumph*.

"He can catch ghosts just as well as I can."

"No, Katy-Girl, that's where you're wrong. Besides, I don't want just anyone catching this particular ghost."

It's a strong one, that's for certain, its vibe more sad than malevolent. For something ethereal, it weights the air as if it carries many burdens. It feels, if not ancient, then very old.

"Had it since Guadalcanal," Mr. Carlotta told me once.

I don't know if that's true, or if one ghost has been swapped for another. In the past few years, I've sensed it's the same one. Why it chooses to haunt Mr. Carlotta, I can't say, although I'm certain Mistress Armand would be willing to take a guess.

But that's all it would be. My theory? Ghosts latch onto emotions, either an overabundance of them or a complete lack, depending. It's why you so often find sprites annoying a humorless person. They think it's funny.

Sometimes it is.

But in Mr. Carlotta's case, I suspect this spirit merely wants to commiserate. Maybe it was a soldier, like he was during World War Two.

Maybe it suffered a great loss and feels that same loss in him. But it makes the air hard to breathe in here, dims the overhead lights. A well of sadness forms in my chest.

"Let me see if they have any coffee in the staff break room."

Mr. Carlotta waves away my suggestion. "You won't catch this one with that swill."

He's right about that.

"Go home, Katy-Girl. I've lived with this ghost for many a year. One more night won't matter."

"I'll be here first thing in the morning," I tell him. "With the Kona blend."

"Extra cream and sugar?"

"Of course." I lean down and let him kiss my cheek.

"Close the door and shut the light off on the way out?" His voice is quiet, just shy of plaintive. I don't want to leave him here, alone, in the dark. But I do.

On my way toward the lobby, a quavery voice calls out.

"Katy, dear, is that you?"

I pause in front of another resident's door. "Shouldn't you be asleep, Mrs. Greeley?"

"I wanted to tell you how much I've been enjoying your grandmother's visits."

I push open the door. The room is shrouded, the space lit by single nightlight. Not that Mrs. Greeley needs it. She's blind. I'm conscious—maybe self-conscious—about how I step, as if Mrs. Greeley can detect worry and stress in my footfalls. When I reach her bed, I take her hand.

She folds my hand between hers. "Are you all right, my dear?"

Nope, I'm not fooling her. "Tired," I say. "I went to the séance, then pushed Mr. Carlotta all the way here."

"Old fool. He should've called for the shuttle."

"I wanted to walk," I say.

Her skin feels papery thin against my own. She is so frail, her fingers like twigs. And yet, despite her blindness, I suspect she perceives more than the rest of us combined.

"I haven't seen your grandmother for a few days," she says.

"It's a busy time of year. Close to Halloween. Sprites like to make mischief then."

Mrs. Greeley chuckles. "Indeed they do. If you see her before I do, tell her I'd love to continue our chat."

"I will," I promise.

The night manager meets me in the hall, a few doors away from Mrs. Greeley's room.

"Oh, Katy, I'm so sorry." He's the sort of man who wears his anxiety all over his face, and now lines crease his forehead. "We've had her in for testing. Her memory is fine. Why she insists that she can talk to your grandmother, no one can figure out."

"It's okay."

"But it's not. You already do so much for the residents here. That you're reminded of …."

He can't bring himself to say *your grandmother's death*, so he lets the sentence trail.

"Every single time," he adds, with more conviction.

"It's really okay," I insist. "In some ways, it's like my grandmother lives on through Mrs. Greeley."

The night manager looks unconvinced. He crinkles his forehead, multiplying the lines there, then gives me a shrug. "How was the séance?" he asks.

"A waste of time."

With that, I leave, before I can confess more, before I can tell the night manager that Mrs. Greeley does talk to my grandmother. For my grandmother still makes rounds here at the care facility—as a ghost. Perhaps Mrs. Greeley has always been sensitive. Perhaps it's her blindness. Whatever the cause, she can communicate with my grandmother's ghost. The only other person who can is me. Not that we've actually chatted. Sometimes words or images float into my head, unbidden. Most of the time, I don't know what they mean. It's like putting together a puzzle, and so far most of the pieces are missing.

Outside, the wind ruffles my skater skirt, the night air colder, the sky black with a few pinpricks of stars. Goose bumps pucker on my bare skin above the stockings. I consider asking the night manager for a ride in the shuttle. But my feet have their own ideas. I'm two blocks away before I truly regret my decision to walk.

I ignore the car at first. Because it's cherry red and a convertible, this is hard. The driver revs the engine. He doesn't tap the horn because it's late, this town tucks in early, and he's far too polite for such things. Then he says my name.

"Katy, come on, I'll give you a ride home."

I stop my trek, turn to face the car, my arms clutched close for warmth. It really is too cold for the top down, but then, that lets Malcolm wear the scarf. It's dark gray wool, and he has it flung jauntily around his neck.

"You were brilliant tonight, by the way," he says.

"Brilliant?"

Did I miss something about the séance? I remember storming out, a lot like a jealous girlfriend might. I remember being rude and disgusted. Brilliant? I doubt that.

"She made a couple cracks about you," he adds.

Oh, how lovely. Of course she did.

"It was perfect. It's almost like you're here." He taps his temple. "Right inside my head. We couldn't have planned it any better if we tried."

I clutch my arms tighter. "I have no idea what you're talking about."

"The whole jealous routine. She totally bought it."

I still have no idea what he's talking about. Instead of responding, I shiver, icy air sneaking up my skirt, the cold making me feel both sleepy and wide-awake at the same time.

Malcolm frowns. "You weren't really ... jealous, were you?"

I'm not the sort of girl who might flip her hair and pretend the image of red lacquered nails running along the jaw of her partner-not-boyfriend doesn't bother her. So I tell Malcolm the truth.

"I was ... am." I shrug as if there's nothing more to say after confessing that.

"But why?"

"Because you're my partner, and—"

"I'm still your partner."

"Then—?"

"If you tried to fool her, pretended to be interested, tried to get close to her," he says, "do you think she would've believed you?"

"Probably not."

"Add your reputation to that, not to mention your grandmother's. Mistress Armand seems to know a lot about everyone in this town."

Yes. She does. Disturbingly so.

"But me?" Malcolm touches his chest. "When I'm, you know—"

"Soft-headed and easily swayed by a pretty face?"

My words ring cold in the night air. Perhaps I've shattered our partnership, which after declaring it so important is a rather stupid thing to do. Then Malcolm throws his head back and laughs.

"Get in the car, partner?"

"It's freezing out and you have the top down."

"And the heat cranked. Trust me, there's no better way to ride."

I don't bother with the handle. Instead, I plant my hand on the side of the car and vault over. I'm halfway into the front seat when I remember the skater skirt. The material flares, and I flash him a generous portion of my thighs and a glimpse of my underwear—pink with black polka dots. A fierce blush chases the chill from my face. Before I can read his expression, Malcolm glances away.

Then he puts the car into gear and we fly down the road. Whenever we go out on a call, we take my truck. The old, battered thing grumbles, but it runs. Plus, once we catch the ghosts, we can store them in the back until the release. There's no room in the convertible for ghosts. There's barely room for two. Despite the gearshift that separates us, I feel close to him, but not trapped or confined. No. Close. I feel close to Malcolm.

And yet? Not.

I exhale, sending my frustration streaming into the air that buzzes past us.

"Cold?" Malcolm asks.

"Tired. I pushed Mr. Carlotta all the way to the care facility."

"Oh, damn, that reminds me. I think his ghost is back."

"It is. But I didn't have any decent coffee with me. I'll stop in tomorrow."

"It's just as well." And here, I think the wind also steals Malcolm's sigh. "He doesn't much like it when I catch his ghost. Actually, he doesn't much like me."

I want to contradict this, but can't. Why this bothers Malcolm, especially when most everyone else in town adores him, I don't know.

The convertible rolls to a stop in front of my house. Next door, light blazes from all the windows. A muted glow comes from the bedroom. I suspect this night will be long for Sadie.

"I feel like I should sneak over and scoop up her sprites," I say. They're back already; I can tell. That accounts for the lights, and the enormous electric bill she'll need to pay at the end of the month.

"If you did, it would only prove Mistress Armand's point. I don't think we want to do that."

I turn toward him. "What happened at the séance?"

Malcolm sinks into the car seat. "What didn't? I know there aren't many secrets in a town this small. Still." He swipes a hand over his face. "I'm not sure we needed so much bloodletting. I don't know what else to call it. She left everyone bruised and bloodied up on that platform."

"Even you?"

He shifts in his seat and raises an eyebrow as if to ask, *Whatever do you mean?*

"You know," I say. "The girl you left behind."

"Oh. That." His laugh is soft. "I'll give Mistress Armand that. She's good at a cold read. We can't underestimate her. I must have twitched my jaw. She picked up on something, but she got it all wrong. There is no girl I left behind."

"Oh." Questions burn in the back of my mind. If there's no girl, then what is there? What is it I'm missing about him? After all, he's my business partner, and maybe my friend. Yes, he's my friend. So what does Mistress Armand see that I can't?

"Anyway," Malcolm continues, "she convinced everyone to embrace their ghosts and promised they would vanish. Business could be … thin for a while."

Like it wasn't already. My gaze is drawn back to Sadie's windows, which continue to pour light into the dark.

"Do you think it's on purpose?" I ask him.

"Well, yes, she's being very intentional with all this, most likely to fill her bank account, even if she hasn't charged anyone yet."

"No, not that. I mean, why. She claims to be getting rid of ghosts. So they must vanish, at least temporarily. If that's the case, where do they all go?"

We stare at each other, and I detect the moment horror fills Malcolm's eyes.

"Oh, no. No," he murmurs. He shifts into gear and makes a tight U-turn, nearly hitting a car parked opposite my house. It's a good thing I never undid my seatbelt. I'm tossed from one side to the other as we race down the road toward the center of town. Before I can ask, Malcolm speaks.

"Nigel," he says.

With that one word, I understand his fear.

MALCOLM RENTS an apartment at the center of town. The old, restored building has lots of brick and wood. We jog through the lobby. Malcolm punches the button for the elevator, but he's so jittery, I think he might rush up the stairs. The doors open with a soft ding before he's able to.

The fourth floor hallway is quiet. Either the walls are thick or his neighbors are polite. No drone of a television set. No loud music. At the end of the corridor, he pulls out his keys to unlock the door, and we step inside.

And I realize this is the first time I've seen where Malcolm lives.

He holds up a hand, stopping me from venturing farther than the living room. "Let me check," he says, voice low.

I nod.

While he's gone, I scan the space. A flat screen TV takes up most of one wall. A blanket and pillow sit neatly at one end of a worn futon. Is this where Malcolm's been sleeping? It strikes me as both uncomfortable and a little sad.

On the coffee table rests a laptop computer that I know belongs to Malcolm. On all sides, I'm surrounded by stacks of books, magazines, and newspapers. One pile teeters, then cascades over my feet the moment Malcolm emerges from the apartment's lone hall.

"Sorry, sorry," he says, scooping papers into his arms and a soiled coffee cup from the table. "The place is a mess." He dumps the papers into a bin and the cup into the sink. "Hey, do you want something to drink?"

"I'm okay," I say, even though my throat is dry.

Malcolm returns with two bottles of water despite my protest.

"It's a long walk from the community center to the care facility," is all he says.

I nod toward the hall. "Is Nigel—?"

"Sound asleep. If there are any ghosts inside him, I can't tell, but I doubt it. Insomnia is one of the signs, or at least it was before." Here he shrugs. "Still."

"Are you worried?"

"I'm worried how addictive it is, this ghost eating thing."

I wonder if some of that worry extends to Malcolm himself. He's new to ghost catching. It would be easy to slip, I think, to try something, to end up liking that something.

"Other than the name, I'm not certain there's a connection between Mistress Armand and either of you," I venture. "And I don't think Nigel—"

"It just ... it just hit me all at once. Things got bad between us before I left Minneapolis. Addicts lie, all the time. Nigel has only been clean for a few weeks. And I thought—"

"Me, too."

My legs ache. Malcolm was right. It *was* a long walk from the community center to the care facility. I cast a quick glance around. I don't want to sit on his bed. I decide on the coffee table.

"Before I left for the séance, I scanned the ghost forums." Malcolm kneels next to the coffee table and flips open his laptop.

"See?" He points to a message thread. "Someone called Mistress Ramone was in Waunakee, Wisconsin a few months back. And six months ago, a Mistress Williams was in Kendallville, Indiana. Oddly enough, there's a Williams in Kendallville who's a ghost hunter, and a Ramone who was a retired school teacher in Waunakee."

"So she borrows names? To get people to trust her?" I ask.

"Apparently."

"To do what? Séances?"

"People, it seems, were reluctant to talk about it. Lots of 'don't trust her' or 'stay away' messages, but nothing concrete, and nothing, really, to prove that either one is Mistress Armand."

"So what's her angle? What does she really want? I mean, other than to humiliate an entire town. Is that why people won't talk about it? I don't see the purpose in that."

"I don't either, except that some people are intentionally cruel."

Malcolm stands and shakes out his trousers. Despite the evening, he still looks clean and pressed and ready for a date. I'm fairly certain I look rumpled, disheveled, and ready for a shower.

"Come on," he says. "Let me drive you home."

"You don't have to walk me to the door."

I've said this before. Actually, I've said it a hundred times, at least, since Malcolm and I started working together. Even though my street is quiet and half my neighbors leave their doors unlocked (the others keep a key beneath one of those fake rocks), if the sun is flirting with the horizon, Malcolm makes the trip up the front porch steps and makes sure I reach my door.

He says nothing in response. I never push the issue and in return, he isn't pushy. He's just there, solid and sure. This one small thing defines who he is.

"In the morning," I begin. My hand lands on the doorknob. A second later, I jerk it away. What happens first, I can't say. Do I yelp? Or do I clutch my hand to my chest, the sharp sting of freezer burn making its way through my skin?

"Katy! What is it?"

I'm doubled over, but straighten just enough to test the door again. Frozen solid. My house? Malcolm probes the door, but yanks his hand back.

"Damn." His gaze meets mine. "It can't be."

But it is. My house is in a full-on ghost infestation.

He scans the porch, the roof, the yard. "Back door, maybe?" He takes my hand. His fingers are so warm, I don't want to let go. We race around the house, clatter up the back porch steps, and confront a door hoary with frost. Instead of letting go, Malcolm grips my fingers tighter.

"Now what?" I say.

"What did you do last time?" He nods toward Sadie's house.

Oh, yes! Of course. The full-on ghost infestation at Sadie's might count as our very first job together—even if we didn't realize it at the time. I clear my throat.

"All of you are aware that coffee doesn't brew itself, right?"

At first, nothing but icy silence greets my proclamation. Then, slowly, the back door creaks open. We're allowed only as far as the kitchen. When we try to push through to other areas of the house, a force pushes us backward, toward the percolator. Something much stronger than a sprite rattles the bin where I keep the Kona blend.

"Looks like we have our marching orders," Malcolm says.

Over the past few months, we've brewed so many pots of coffee together it's like a dance routine. He knows what pitcher to use for the half and half, which spoon for the sugar. It is, perhaps, not strictly necessary to use the same items in the same manner, but routine soothes both humans and ghosts. The air vibrates around us, a whole pack of ghosts anticipating the first hints of rich brew from the percolator.

I pour the coffee into the twelve cups lined up on the kitchen table. Malcolm adds the half and half and sugar. It's always the same: three black, three with half and half, three with sugar, and three extra light and extra sweet.

Aromatic steam fills the kitchen. It wavers, not just with air currents, but with the ghosts that fill the space, soaking in the warmth and flavor. The temperature in the house also rises, the thermostat nearly back to normal. I sag against the sink.

"What's going on?" I ask.

As if in answer, cold swirls around my ankles. Ghosts urge me forward. I glance at Malcolm, and he takes my hand again. Together we creep into the living room, the dining area, explore the entire house.

It's filled with ghosts, from attic to basement. I lose count sometime after ninety. Some I recognize, or at least they feel familiar when they brush against my skin. Others are strange, wild things, the sort that haunt deep woods or old, abandoned houses. The only ghost I don't sense is my grandmother's.

"Why are they here?" I ask Malcolm.

It isn't logical, not on the surface, anyway. I've been catching and releasing ghosts since I was five years old. I'm not scared of them, although I've encountered my share of stubborn ones. Still, ours is a relationship where I—more often than not—spoil their fun.

Malcolm holds out a hand, turning it in the air. The ghosts are so thick, I can see them swoop between his fingers. "I think they're scared," he says.

"Of what?"

"Mistress Armand?"

"Is she really a danger?" I ask.

Sure, she's a fraud and is planning to bilk people out of money—at least, I'm pretty sure she is. But dangerous? I don't see it.

"What if it's a distraction?" He points between the two of us. "For us." Now he waves that same hand in the air. "And for them. We're all in one spot. Who would want us all in one spot?"

"If I have all the ghosts, then it looks like Mistress Armand's methods work, right?" I say.

"What if it's more than that? What if she's the distraction?"

"You mean that thing ...?" I begin, but my words dry up. Dread fills my stomach; it feels as cold as the ghosts around me.

"Yeah, that thing that attacked you at the mausoleum."

"That was weeks ago."

"That's just it," he says. "I don't think it was the sort of thing that cares about time."

He's right. The thing—for I have no other name for it—is not a ghost. I don't know what it is other than some sort of entity. But maybe a few of my current houseguests might.

"Okay, you guys." I cup my hands around my mouth, letting my voice carry throughout the space. "Who wants more coffee?"

The air shimmers with excitement. A few sprites whirl around my head. Malcolm raises an eyebrow, a quizzical look on his face. It's really kind of adorable when he does that. But when I hold out my hand, he doesn't hesitate.

"You may have to make a bean run to the Coffee Depot when it opens," I tell him on the way back to the kitchen.

"What did you have in mind?"

"We're going to get these guys drunk."

"It's like pulling an all-nighter in college," Malcolm says. His eyes are both bright and half-lidded.

Because yes, we have indulged in several cups ourselves. There's no sense in letting the very fine and very expensive Kona blend go to waste, even if ghosts have been dancing in it all night. And dance they have. Several float in the air, languid and spent. Sprites still zip around, tripping me up whenever I try to go somewhere that isn't the kitchen. But then, sprites are like puppies—almost always active and nearly always causing trouble.

"You had a reason for doing this, right?" he adds.

"They might be able to tell us something," I say.

"I thought you said ghost whispering was a fraud."

"Oh, it is. I'm not talking about personal demons or healing, or messages from beyond the grave. I'm talking about what they see and hear. Each one might have a little piece of ... something that won't make sense. But together? We might figure out what's going on."

"And you know this how?"

"Lately my grandmother's been talking to Mrs. Greeley," I say, and then add with some reluctance, "and lately, I think I can hear her too."

"And you're telling me this now?" His eyes are wide, their expression tinged with fatigue and anger.

"I just found out about Mrs. Greeley." I shrug. "And it's not like I've been having actual conversations. I never thought you could talk to ghosts. I still think that. But I get words, usually ones that don't make sense. What if everyone here—" I wave a hand. "Has a word for us?"

A tired smile replaces some of the anger. "Especially if we ply them with a fresh batch of coffee?"

"Especially then."

"What if you lie down on the floor and I place the cups of coffee around you?" he suggests.

I eye him, uncertain if he's joking or not. "No. That's just creepy."

He laughs, the sound tired, but still, a laugh. "Kidding."

"But lying down sounds nice," I say.

He stifles a yawn. "It does."

We shouldn't, I know. Despite the coffee, I feel the night press against my eyelids. And lying down with Malcolm, even if it is on the living room floor, even if a good two feet of space separates us, is also a bad idea. But we do, gazes fixed on the ceiling. The ghosts there are so thick, their outlines swirl before our eyes, and the ceiling shimmers as if covered with tinsel. Although our fingertips don't touch, he's close enough that the warmth of his skin reaches mine.

"You," he says in no more than a whisper.

"Me?"

"The ghosts. They're talking about you. That's what I hear, or it's the word in my head. Katy. Katy. Katy." He falls silent. "They like you."

"I don't know why. I'm always spoiling their fun."

"I don't think they mind that."

I don't respond. Above us the ghosts continue their dance. A sprite nudges my foot.

"Do you hear anything?" Malcolm asks.

"I don't know. It's too silly to be anything real."

"What is it?" he says.

"Boo."

"What?"

"Just that. Boo. You know, when you want to scare someone. You pop out and say, 'Boo!' It's a little kid thing."

"A child's idea of a ghost."

With his words, we both turn our heads to face each other.

"No." And I hate the way the word emerges from my mouth, pathetic and small.

"He's not here, Katy." Malcolm pushes up on his elbows. "He ... it ... whatever it is. We're safe, you're safe, in this house."

"And you know this how?"

He glances around, waves his fingers through a ghost. "Probably because they're here. They're scared, too, remember?"

"I'm not sure this makes us safe," I say.

"Then what does it make us?"

"Trapped."

The walls around us shudder as if that single word has triggered such a trap. I scamper to my feet, Malcolm reaching a hand to help me up. We stand there, clutching hands, the walls trembling around us.

"Whatever it is," Malcolm says, "it's outside the house. We're safe."

I'm not so sure.

The greatest trembling comes from the front. That's where the threat is. That's where we must go, if only to see what we're up against.

"Come on." I nod toward what used to be the formal dining room of the house. The windows look out onto the front lawn.

We leave the dining room light off. Malcolm splits two of the venetian blinds with his fingers. He swears and lets the blinds fall back into place. Then he doesn't move.

So I repeat the exercise. There on the sidewalk is not the creature that haunts my dreams, not the thing that tried to kill me mere weeks before, but Malcolm's brother.

Nigel looks nearly ghostly himself, that shock of white hair, his thin, drawn face. He hasn't fully recovered, at least not physically, from ghost eating. He stares up at the house as if it's a banquet.

No wonder the ghosts are shaking my walls.

"It's okay," I call out to them. "He won't swallow you."

The trembling continues. Malcolm heaves a sigh. No one in this house, human or otherwise, believes me.

"I won't let him," I add, slipping through the pocket door that leads to the front entrance. I touch the handle, flinch and jerk my hand back so hard, I smack Malcolm in the chest.

"Sorry." I clutch my freezer-burnt hand with the other. "Come on, guys. Let us out."

Nothing. The doorknob is pale with frost. I know if we brew another pot of coffee, I'll be sick.

"He won't come in, but you need to let us out," I say, using my most reasonable voice. "You want to go back to haunting someone other than me, right? I'll just catch you all right now and drive you out to the nature preserve."

The doorknob thaws, warm brass breaking through the frost. I don't even have to turn it. A bevy of ghosts obligingly push open the door for us. We spill onto the front porch. The door slams behind us.

It will take another round of bribery to get them to open it again.

"Nigel?" Malcolm grabs the porch railing, the knuckles of his hands turning white. "What's going on?"

"Katy's grandmother," he begins.

I cut him off. "My grandmother!" I start for the steps, but Malcolm stops me with a gentle hand on my shoulder.

"She … your grandmother sent me," Nigel says. He stares up at the house, his eyes wide with both horror and hunger. "Mistress Armand. She's chased all the ghosts away from the care facility. She's there now … feasting."

"Feasting?" I can barely force the word through all the bile in my throat.

"Not like you think," Nigel adds. "She consumes shame, humiliation. In some ways, she's like me. I'm—" His gaze goes once again to the house. "Addicted to ghosts. She's addicted to shame—as long as it's someone else's. That's why she gets everyone to confess their deepest regrets, their most shameful experiences."

The notion hits me hard. "And she's at the care facility because people with long lives often have a long list of regrets."

"It's the ultimate in schadenfreude," Malcolm observes.

Joy in the misfortune of others. Joy and money. And how terrible is it to steal everything from someone?

"We should go," I say, casting Malcolm a wary glance. "They'll need our help."

Malcolm rests his head on my shoulder. "I can't leave him here," he says in a voice meant only for my ears. "I can't. You know that. And you can't go alone."

"I can go alone," I insist.

"No, you can't!"

The voice isn't Malcolm's. Nor is it Nigel who speaks these words. From next door, Sadie charges down her porch steps, her pink fleece robe flapping in her wake. Matching pink slippers encase her feet, and their soles slap the concrete with each fierce stride. She holds a broom like a sword. She is so ferocious that I take a step back, into Malcolm's embrace.

"I will guard the ghosts!" she declares. "I won't let this young man hurt himself further, and I won't let them"—she brandishes the broom at my house—"get into any trouble, either."

"Sadie, are you sure?" I say. This? From the woman terrified of sprites?

"You know who left me, right?" she says. "Harold. The whole town knows that, thanks to Mistress Armand. You know who didn't leave me?"

I can only shake my head.

"My sprites. Even though they were scared—yes, I could tell—they stayed with me all night. After reliving the humiliation of Harold at the séance, after everything I've tried to do to get rid of them, they stayed. Well? I'm here to return the favor." She shakes the broom at Nigel. "Don't get any ideas, young man."

Nigel steps off the sidewalk and lands in the gutter.

Sadie turns to us, broom at the ready. "Well? Don't just stand there. Go!"

"We can take my car," Malcolm says. "It will be fastest." He pats his pockets. "Damn, my keys are—"

My front door flies open. A second later, a key fob sails through the air and lands at Malcolm's feet.

"Well?" Sadie prompts again.

Malcolm grabs the keys while I launch myself into the convertible's passenger seat. We leave behind a motley crew in the exhaust. A reformed ghost eater, a woman petrified of ghosts, and a house filled with every spirit in town, except for one.

THE SUN RISES with a burst of orange and pink that makes the sandstone buildings along Main Street glow. Malcolm's red convertible streaks along the road, its reflection in the storefront windows like something from a movie.

"Do you think it's that ... thing?" I ask Malcolm over the roar of air. "He ... it was looking for a body." Not to mention, the thing had captured Nigel's for a short time.

Malcolm shakes his head. "No. She touched me, remember? On stage?"

Oh. *Yes.* I remember.

"I don't know who she really is, but she had too much substance and warmth to be anything but human."

I'm not certain that's proof. Then again, I can't shake away the image of her red nails clutching Malcolm's jaw, so my view is definitely skewed.

Malcolm parks in the roundabout driveway. From the moment he shuts off the engine, I can hear the cries. Sobs, heartfelt and deep—the sort that shake your entire body. I cast a glance at Malcolm. His worried frown must mirror my own. The crying continues, each wail squeezing my heart so hard it hurts.

My legs wobble when I hop out. Unsteady, I clutch the side of the car, not quite ready to burst through the double doors and into the care facility itself. Sweat bathes my forehead. A wave of dizziness pushes me back against the car door.

"Katy?" Malcolm is at my side. He appears to sway before my eyes.

"The all-nighter? I feel ..."

"Weak," he finishes. "Me too."

The cries continue unabated.

"I felt fine when we left," I say. "Tired, but fine."

He nods and rubs his temples.

Near the entrance, someone has left a walker. I stumble across the outdoor carpeting and make a grab for it. I miss. I tumble onto the ground and trigger the automatic doors. They whoosh open. From inside, the sound of crying increases, louder, more heart wrenching.

I pull myself up and onto the walker, triggering the doors each time they try to close. By the time Malcolm reaches me, his skin has gone a horrid shade of gray.

"You look awful," he says.

"That makes two of us."

We hobble toward the facility entrance, the doors wide open now.

With each step, the cries grow until I'm certain the sound is thickening the air around us.

"I have the strangest urge to tell you about the time I lost my shorts during a soccer game," he says, his breath labored.

"During the game? You mean on the field, in front of everyone?"

"Yes, it was ... humiliating, to say the least, and I wasn't wearing any—"

I place a finger over his lips. "Not now."

"But—"

"Someday, when this is all over, if you still want to tell me, you can. But not now. She only wants to feed on your shame."

Understanding dawns in his weary eyes. "Of course. That explains why I want to also tell you about all my bad dates."

"I can't believe you ever had a bad date," I say. He's too smooth and charming.

"I'm refraining." Somehow, he manages a wink. "Later, and you can tell me about yours."

"There isn't anything to tell."

I start up our trek again. We're almost to the lobby and the carpeted floor there. I'm not certain how much longer I can walk, and falling there, rather than the hard tile of the entrance, feels like the better option.

"So all your dates have been amazingly good?" he asks.

"There haven't been any dates," I say, palms sweating against the walker's handgrips. "Good or bad."

Malcolm halts, so I plunk the walker forward a foot or two without him. I'm on the carpet now, and the surface steadies my footsteps. When Malcolm doesn't catch up, I crane my neck to peer at him.

"You've never been on a date?" His gaze surveys me, from wobbly feet to the top of my head, his look incredulous.

"No." Only now that I've confessed do I realize how odd it is for a woman my age to have never dated. How ... humiliating.

Something crackles in the air, raises the hairs on my arms and the back of my neck, like a surge of electricity. A second later, a force knocks me across the room, into the reception desk and onto the floor. I fight to regain my breath, my bearings. My vision tunnels to a single point before expanding.

"Thank you, ghost hunter," a voice says, melodious and feminine, and just this side of seductive. "That was a most delicious bite of shame you served up. I do hope there's more where that came from."

Mistress Armand is still lithe and tall, her glossy black hair streaming down her back, her white caftan fluttering around her. And yet, something about her is massive. I'd call it her aura, but I don't believe in such things; my grandmother never did, anyway. Something surrounds Mistress Armand like a force field. It glows and crackles and gives off the occasional spark.

Any words I might say would be lost in the electricity that fills the air. Silence may be golden; in this case, I suspect it may be the only thing that saves us. *Don't speak. Don't utter a word. Don't feed her.* I frown, hoping to convey this idea to Malcolm with thought power alone. All I get for my efforts is Mistress Armand whirling to follow my gaze.

"Oh, and there he is, the man with so many secrets, and some of them are oh, so shameful, you bad boy. Do tell, Malcolm. I'm certain Katy will want to hear all of them. You know I do."

He is a man frozen, is what he is, whether from shame or for other reasons, I don't know. Then I see his fingers twitch. They twitch again, toward the hall that leads to the wing with the resident rooms, the wing from which all the crying still echoes. In that slight twitch, I discern a single message:

Go!

I crawl, knees scraping against the rough carpet. Before I vanish down the hallway, I hear Malcolm's voice, so strong and steady, I wonder how he manages it.

"I'll tell you my secrets, Mistress Armand, but you have to tell me some of yours."

THE SOBS and wails from the residents' rooms weaken me further. I continue forward on hands and knees. Every time I try to push to stand, another cry assaults my ears. At last I reach Mrs. Greeley's door and slump against it.

"Mrs. Greeley? Are you in there? Are you okay?"

"Katy, dear, is that you?" Her voice is anxious, but free of tears.

"It's me."

"I'm trapped. That witch jammed something in the door handle."

"Give me a moment," I say. Oh, the handle is up so, so high. Can I stand up to reach it? How can I not try? I let my head thump against Mrs. Greeley's door, the sound that of defeat.

"Close your eyes, dear," Mrs. Greeley says.

"What?"

"Close your eyes. They're blinding you to the falseness of her voice. With them closed, you will hear her for what she is."

Certainly I've blinked since entering the facility, but I haven't left my eyes closed, not for more than a moment, if that. I don't want to fight … blind. But that's exactly what Mrs. Greeley is doing, and so far she's the only one not caught in this web of sorrow and shame. I think about the séance and how Mistress Armand insisted Sadie keep her eyes open. To confront her personal demons? Or to let Mistress Armand feast on some shame?

I shut my eyes. At first, nothing changes. The crying rings louder in my ears. But strength returns to my limbs. I reach up and open Mrs. Greeley's door. It creaks, and Mrs. Greeley claps her hands together.

"Well done!" The tap of a cane accompanies her voice. "Now, we must get down the hall and tell the others to shut their eyes."

A shriek echoes through the hallway, wretched and otherworldly. In it, I detect the barest hint of Mistress Armand. There is no seduction left, but an occasional musical tone breaks through, tempts me to open my eyes.

"Don't," Mrs. Greeley says. "Yes, I feel the urge too," she adds, "but I simply can't comply. I'm certain Mistress Armand didn't count on me."

Indeed she didn't. I push to stand, then hold my hands out in front of me, fingertips straining against the air. I will crash into something on my trek down the hall, without a doubt.

"Stop!" The command is robust, so much so that I do falter in my steps. That low, musical tone is stronger. My eyelids flutter before I squeeze my eyes shut again.

"Go," Mrs. Greeley urges.

Yes, but where? I don't dare open my eyes. Before I can move in any direction, something crashes into the backs of my legs.

"Oh! Katy-Girl, is that you?"

"Mr. Carlotta?"

"Keep going," he says. "You're covered. Annabelle and I will guard your back."

"Old fool," Mrs. Greeley mutters, but her voice is nothing but tender.

I still don't know which way to walk, not with my eyes closed. Then something cold and familiar brushes my cheek. The words *Katy-Girl* float into my mind. My grandmother. She's here, and she's showing me which way to go.

Gingerly, I take a step, then another. My grandmother nudges my face, first the right cheek, then the left, helping me navigate around obstacles. Every few feet, I call out.

"Shut your eyes. Don't open them."

Bit by bit the sobs subside. Bit by bit, the care facility quiets. Despite the fact that Mistress Armand's words now cajole and mock, they hold no power. Not over me, and not over anyone in the facility who has their eyes closed.

Even so, or perhaps because of this, she comes for me. Where Malcolm is, I don't know, and I don't open my eyes to find out. Mrs. Greeley cries out. Mr. Carlotta calls, "Hang on! She's broken through."

I hold still. I've reached the lounge area. From the television comes the muted hum of a morning news program. The crying has all but ceased. Perhaps it's my imagination, but I think I detect snoring. My grandmother swirls around me like this alone will protect me. I feel her against my eyes, as if she's trying to remind me not to open them. Then the other presence enters the room.

"You think you know him," Mistress Armand croaks. Without everyone's shame, she is a weak thing. "That will be your undoing."

It's nearly enough to tempt me, nearly enough that I open my eyes. But I don't. I clench my fists against the urge. My grandmother whips around me like a cyclone. I think we might stand like this forever—

Mistress Armand too weak to attack with anything but taunts, me not daring to open my eyes.

Then a thump echoes in the lounge area and her presence vanishes.

"You can open your eyes, Katy." Malcolm's voice is calm and welcoming, and with my eyes closed, its rhythm is startling. I think I could listen to him like this for a long while. But instead, I open my eyes. When I do, his are the first thing I see. He glances downward.

There, on the floor, his foot secures a Tupperware bowl. Inside the bowl, the misty and shrunken image of Mistress Armand floats.

"Nice work," I say.

"You too."

We don't lift the container. Instead, the night manager brings us a thin cookie sheet from the facility's kitchen. We slide it beneath the bowl, and now our trap is mobile.

Malcolm drives. I clutch the two pieces—bowl and cookie sheet—until my hands ache. We drive past our usual release point, the windbreak with a little creek. We drive past the nature preserve and state park where we release the meaner ghosts.

We drive for another full hour after that. The wind chases my hair around my head, into my eyes and mouth. I still clutch the bowl and cookie sheet. Malcolm leaves the freeway, navigates back roads until he finds a deserted gravel road that's barely more than a path. Next to a plowed-under cornfield, he stops the convertible.

He holds up a hand. "Hang on," he says and rounds the car to open my door.

I step out, Malcolm's hands joining mine. Together, we stumble through the ruts and rows of the cornfield. We stand in the center of what must be the most desolate spot on earth—or would be if Malcolm weren't next to me. Then we set the container on the ground. We don't bother to remove the cookie sheet. The wind or an animal will knock it off soon enough. In the meantime, Mistress Armand can stew in her own mist.

We return to the convertible without looking back. Halfway across the field, Malcolm takes my hand.

"THINGS ARE CHANGING," I say to Malcolm right before we enter Springside Township. It's the first words we've spoken since leaving the cornfield. "I used to know what to do, how to capture ghosts. But ghost eating? Mistress Armand? None of this makes sense. I can't believe my grandmother wouldn't tell me about such things."

Malcolm is silent, jaw tense. In front of us, the stop light for Main and Fifth turns red.

"What do you think she was?" I ask. "You said before you thought she was human."

"I did," he says. "I think at one time, she must have been. I think the addiction ate away at her. I mean, look at Nigel compared to me. He's only two years older."

But looks at least twenty.

"I wonder if my grandmother ever knew of such things?" I think she must have. Maybe she died too soon to tell me.

"About what Mistress Armand said—" Malcolm begins.

I cut him off. "I doubt you have any shameful secrets. And if you do? So what? That's in the past."

I want to reach over, pat his knee or something. I don't. Instead, I clutch my hands together and hope I've said the right thing.

He sighs. The light turns green. With a single nod, he puts the car in gear.

Malcolm slows the convertible when we reach my street. We crawl up the road, well under the speed limit. In fact, I could walk home faster. All appears quiet. Still, my heart thumps with worry.

Inside my house, warm air greets us. The frost has melted from all the brass doorknobs. I do a quick circuit, but not even a sprite is in residence. The only proof I have of last night's ghost infestation is the mess —cold cups of coffee scattered all over the place, brown stains on the carpet, a splatter pattern on one wall that would be creepy if it were blood rather than Kona blend.

Malcolm casts a wary look around. "Where's Nigel?" He bolts and is out on the street before I can suggest an answer.

We find Nigel next door, in Sadie's kitchen, drinking coffee. Sadie chats happily over the drone of a talk show host. Nigel stares into the middle distance. Whether he hears Sadie or not doesn't seem to matter.

Odd contentment lights his face, and the man who stared mere hours before with horror and hunger is banished. Malcolm places a hand on his brother's shoulder and squeezes.

To my surprise, Sadie's sprites are basking in the steam of an extra-large cup. But other than that, her house is also ghost-free.

I point to the sprites. "Do you want me to take them with me?" I ask her. For certainly they are up to no good, no matter how complacent they appear to be.

Sadie considers, hand on her chin. "Maybe tonight, if they start acting up. But for now?" She throws them a stern look. "They can stay."

Malcolm's pocket buzzes. Or rather, his cell phone does. He pulls it out, raises an eyebrow, then meets my gaze.

"Looks like we're back in business," he says. "Want to go catch a ghost?"

"My grandmother?" I whisper on the way out.

"Possibly."

"Law firm again?"

"Bank. The manager is locked in the vault. "

"That's probably my grandmother."

"The tellers want us to bring extra coffee." He checks his phone again. "And one wants tea."

"We're going to have to charge extra if we're supplying drinks for ghosts *and* humans," I say.

Back in Malcolm's convertible, I realize I'm still in last night's clothes, the skater skirt limp, my stockings sagging well below my knees. I haven't brushed my teeth. My hair? After that ride in the country? I'm afraid to look. But when he puts the car in gear and gives me a grin, none of that matters.

"Ready, partner?" he asks.

"I am," I say into the wind. "I am."

GONE GHOST

COFFEE AND GHOSTS: EPISODE 4

I STAND OUTSIDE THE DOOR to the Springside Long-term Care Facility, my hands clutching an insulated carafe of the best Kona blend. I have a ghost to catch, one who is picky and prickly. Even with the most expensive beans, I might not be able to tempt it from its haunting.

The melancholy ghosts are the hardest to catch.

My business partner, Malcolm Armand, stands next to me. In the canvas bag we use as a field kit, he carries a collection of thermoses. They jangle as he halts, a hand on my shoulder to keep me in place. His brow wears a worried frown, and his lips are pursed.

"Malcolm?" I say. "What—?"

"Where is everyone?"

Through the glass double doors, I can see the woman who works the reception desk, but no one else. Above us, the sun is doing its best to pretend that summer hasn't faded. It's one in the afternoon, activity time. Most residents should be doing something. But the building feels quiet, as if everyone is tucked in for the night.

Malcolm's cell phone buzzes. He pulls it out and holds it so we both can read the text message from the facility manager.

Please stay where you are. I'll be out in a moment.

Malcolm and I lock gazes.

"Did we do something wrong?" I ask.

As if in answer, a breeze catches strands of my hair and chases them into my mouth. Since I'm holding the carafe, I blow and spit, and it's entirely unladylike. I ponder our last visit here: we rid the place of a rather obnoxious (if preternaturally beautiful) being, a woman who claimed to be a ghost whisperer, but instead feasted on everyone's shame. And when you've lived a very long life, you have plenty of shame in reserve.

The double doors whoosh open. The facility manager strides out, her heels clicking on the sidewalk, pant legs fluttering in the breeze and from her gait.

"I'm sorry you had to come all the way out here." She holds out her arms as if to herd us back toward my truck. "There's been a change in plans."

"Do you want us to come at a different time?" I ask.

I've been coming here for years, first with my grandmother, then on my own. Now, Malcolm and I visit. Springside Long-term Care is one of our gratis accounts. We don't charge for catching ghosts. My grandmother always said the people here already had enough ghosts to contend with—why not make things a little easier on them.

"Actually, we're changing our routine, and we won't be..." The manager trails off, bites her lip. "Needing your services from now on."

"But we're not charging you anything." It's a stupid protest. We all know this.

Malcolm's grip on my shoulder tightens. With the slightest bit of pressure, he eases me back, steps between me and the manager, and turns on the charm.

"Vanessa, what is this about? Have there been any complaints? I've been promising a taste test between Katy's coffee and my tea." He gives the canvas bag a shake, jostles the thermoses, and the aluminum sings out. "Today's the day. I'd hate to disappoint the residents."

By *residents*, he means the female residents, or at least most of them. While the Malcolm Armand variety hour goes on in the common area,

I'm always down the hallway, in residents' rooms, catching picky and prickly ghosts.

Vanessa wavers, swaying back and forth in the breeze and under Malcolm's gaze. Then she shakes herself and shakes a good dose of resolve into her features.

"This is hard for us," she says, "but we took a vote on it. And by we, I mean all the residents and the staff. We no longer want you visiting Springside Long-term Care. I'm sorry."

She turns and bolts toward the glass double doors, high heels striking the concrete like icepicks. With each step, I feel a sharp stab in my stomach. I loosen my grip on the carafe and press a hand against my belly, my pulse beating frantic beneath it.

I survey the building, the drawn curtains, and the now-empty reception desk. "They took a ... vote? What does that mean?"

He shakes his head. "I don't know."

"But I promised Mr. Carlotta that I'd take care of his ghost. No one else can catch it."

"I know."

Not even Malcolm. And for a while, I doubted my own ability to do so. Mr. Carlotta's ghost is very old and very sad. It weights the air, makes it hard to breathe in Mr. Carlotta's room. He claims the ghost has been with him since Guadalcanal, but I don't know how true that is. What I do know is that something about this is wrong.

I step forward, determined to find out what—exactly—that something is.

"Katy, no." Malcolm jogs to catch up. "If they don't want us here, and we barge in, that's trespassing."

"What are they going to do? Call the police?"

He points. "Maybe."

Through the glass double doors, I see Vanessa, cell phone pressed against her ear. But it doesn't matter. When I reach the entrance, nothing happens. The sensor that opens the doors automatically is switched off. I stand there, peering into the space, my fingers leaving smudges on the glass.

Malcolm takes that hand, the one glued to the glass, and folds it in both of his. He tugs me away. The movement is gentle, like a mother reluctantly pulling her child from a swing, a father urging his son away from a toy that's far too expensive. I think he might wrap his arm around my shoulder on the way back to the truck, but all he does is clutch my hand.

I can't explain how much this hurts. I can't explain why it plants an ache in my heart. It's just business, isn't it? But when Malcolm holds out his palm for the keys to my truck, I know he understands. I pass him the keys, not because I can't drive. I certainly can. But I want to take a long, hard look at the care facility. I want to study each resident's room. And when the curtains flutter in Mr. Carlotta's window, I want to make sure it's something I've really seen.

It's the late afternoons, when the buildings across from our office fracture the setting sun, that are the hardest to endure. That tender light signals another day without a client, another day without income, and one day closer to giving up this space if we can't make the rent.

I love our office, all of it. I love the gold lettering on the front window, proclaiming us *K&M Ghost Eradication Specialists*. I love that we have Malcolm's old samovar in the window, along with a vintage percolator that belonged to my grandmother, one I've recently retired from service. I love how unlocking the door every morning makes all of this feel real.

But when lunch rolls around without a call or email, when I peer through the large bay window and see the bank closing down for the day, it feels as though the ventilation system isn't pumping in enough air. It's been two weeks since Vanessa at Springside Long-term Care told us not to return. I've gone out on a few jobs, nuisance calls involving sprites that I handled on my own. But after that? Silence.

I've been here before.

"Maybe it's the change in the weather," Malcolm says.

We haven't been talking about the lack of work, but clearly it's on both of our minds.

"In college," he continues, "nothing supernatural happened until at least October."

"You were probably too busy to notice," I say.

Ghosts love autumn, and Halloween in particular, especially the sprites. They love to play pranks, and Halloween is perfect for that.

"Then maybe that's it," he counters. "People are too busy going back to school and with sports and all of it to care about a few ghosts."

"Maybe." I rub my neck. Across the street, the bank manager pulls the shades on the entry doors. I'm too far away to hear the click of the lock, but that doesn't stop me from imagining that I do.

"Staring out the window isn't going to get us any clients," Malcolm adds.

"It was just like this, you know."

"What was?"

"When you came to town and stole all my clients."

He bursts out laughing. "Oh, come on. I didn't steal all your clients."

I pivot from my contemplation of Main Street and confront him instead, hands on hips. "Didn't you? What would you call it, then?"

"Free enterprise?" He crosses the distance between us. "Besides, we both know how it turned out."

For a month, Malcolm was my rival, and he did steal all my clients, no matter what he says. For a month, I loathed the sight of him. And now?

He puts his hands on my shoulders. "Didn't it turn out?" His voice is lower, a near whisper, as if he doesn't want anyone to overhear what he might say next.

My heart thuds hard against my ribcage. I don't want to feel this way about my business partner. I'm not even certain what *this way* means, except that at times like this, his nearness clouds my head. He smells of Ivory soap and nutmeg and that does nothing to clear my thoughts.

"Katy," he says, "I've been thinking—"

The door to our office swings open, the chime promising a customer. Malcolm drops his hands as if my shoulders burn him. In the entrance, Officer Deborah Millard stands. She's been a police officer for as long as I can remember. Her partner is new, practically a boy. He gnaws on his bottom lip while the creases around Officer Millard's eyes deepen.

"Katrina Lindstrom?" she says, although why, I don't know. We've known each other forever.

"Yes?" I answer, although again, it seems silly, both my answer and the sound of my full name.

"I have a warrant for your arrest."

Or not so silly.

She pulls out a pair of handcuffs. "You have the right to remain silent..."

"No, really." Malcolm inserts himself between Deborah and me. "This is ridiculous. What are the charges? You just can't come in here and—"

"Sir, step to the side and let me do my job." Deborah's words lack any inflection. "There are penalties if you don't."

I shake my head at Malcolm. "You can't get arrested too." I let Deborah take my hands and secure them behind my back. The metal is cold against my wrists, and I'm shackled. There's no way I'm jerking free of this. At least she doesn't pat me down. Then again, it's not like I can conceal and carry a carafe of coffee.

"... Anything you say can be used against you in a court of law..."

"What are the charges?" He is fierce, but hovering, one eye on Deborah and one on the boy, who has pulled out his own set of cuffs. "At least tell us that."

"Grand larceny," Deborah says. "Seven counts."

I know I must be gaping. My jaw feels loose; air rushes into my mouth. I can't imagine it. What is it they think I've stolen?

"Katy?" Malcolm's eyes are wide and uncertain.

Well, yes, I've had money troubles. But I've never stolen anything, not even clients.

"You have the right to an attorney," Deborah is saying.

A lawyer! My gaze meets Malcolm's and his eyes brighten.

"I'll run down to the law offices," he says. "Don't say anything until I get there with a lawyer, okay?"

I nod. But really, what is there to say? I don't know what Deborah is talking about. Then again, maybe that makes this even more dangerous.

When I'm cuffed and Deborah has finished speaking, she leads me from the office. A town the size of Springside doesn't have much of a rush hour. But today, I'm on display for the one it does have. Malcolm locks the door and charges down the sidewalk.

"I'll be there as soon as I can," he calls over his shoulder.

Then he sprints, loafers clacking the concrete, his destination the law firm at the corner of Main and Fifth, where we're on retainer. Ghosts with a grudge like to pester attorneys, divorce lawyers in particular.

I glance around as if the people gathered can rescue me from this fate. Someone will step forward and confess or provide evidence of my innocence. But the only thing that happens is that people glance away. No one meets my eyes. Except for my neighbor, Sadie Lancaster, who drops her shopping bag on the ground, her mouth round with shock.

My cheeks flame and I duck my head. But a whisper, my name on the breeze, has me jerking it back up again. In the doorway of the deli, Malcolm's brother is hiding. Nigel steps toward me, but I shake my head. He can't help me, not now. Then my attention goes to Sadie. He follows my gaze and nods to show he understands. When Deborah places a hand on my head and eases me into a patrol car, Nigel slips from the shadows.

As we drive away, I crane my neck to peer from the back window, the hard, unforgiving seat digging into my hips. There, on the sidewalk, Nigel has his hands on Sadie's shoulders. The gesture is so like Malcolm only a few minutes earlier, my heart lurches. Then she's in his arms and he's holding her close. He picks up her shopping bag and seems to be talking to both the items inside and to her, comforting words, judging by the expression on Sadie's face.

And then we turn a corner and there's nothing left to see.

"Oh, goodness, Katy, I'm so sorry. Can we do this again?"

The metal bench I'm sitting on is secured to the wall. My spine is flush against that same wall. I stare at the blue dot next to the camera's lens. I don't smile.

"Of course," I say.

"Sometimes this thing goes haywire. You haven't moved, so I don't know why each picture is so blurry." Penny Wilson blows air through her bangs. She is the booking officer, the police chief's administrative assistant, and quite unaware of the two sprites darting around the camera.

They dip and dive. While you can't capture ghosts on film, they can certainly do plenty to mess up your glamour shot. Or, in my case, a mug shot.

"Cut it out," I whisper.

"What, dear?" Penny raises her head so her eyes peek above the camera.

"I said, maybe the power cut out?"

"Maybe that's it!" She ducks beneath the desk.

"You and you." I mouth the words and point at each of them. "Let her do this." Not that they'll listen to me. I don't recognize these two sprites in particular. But then, sprites have such a slight presence that that doesn't mean much. It's a sure thing, however, that I've caught them before—sometime in the past—and have spoiled their fun.

I don't suppose I can really offer my services now. Not that Penny would accept. She has an unusually high tolerance for sprites. The fact she hasn't noticed these two is proof of that. Also, Police Chief Ramsey has never been a fan of ghost eradication.

"It's not science!" he always told my grandmother.

He's right. It's not. Really, that's the point.

Besides, the charred swill wafting from the break area wouldn't tempt these two in the least. I'm surprised it hasn't repelled them, not to mention all the humans in this place. The scent alone makes the back of my throat ache. Then again, maybe that's something else, something like waiting for my mug shot to be taken.

Penny pops back up, her curls swinging in triumph. She slaps a hand on the camera, catching the sprites off guard. "There!" she cries out. "Perfect."

Oh, but there's still the fingerprinting to endure. This, too, is digital.

"Springside PD has gone high tech," I say.

And because this is Penny, and she's known me all my life, she brightens at my conversation starter, despite the circumstances. "We have! They even sent me to training."

Unfortunately, this training didn't include how to take a print when two sprites are covering your subject's skin. I blow at them—discreetly. Or rather I try, but I don't think there's a discreet way to blow.

"Although sometimes," Penny concedes, "the old-fashioned way is better."

By the time she's through, my hands are covered in black ink. There's a smear across Penny's cheek and several in her hair. The sprites zip around us, far too pleased with themselves.

"Wait," I whisper on the way to the holding cell. "Just you two wait."

Then Penny locks me in, and it's official. I'm a criminal.

A figure is huddled on the plank bed connected to the wall. I grip one of the metal bars, smearing it with black residue, and sigh.

"Katy?"

A voice creaks behind me. I whirl, heart thumping. A woman emerges from that huddled mass, her hair a blonde tangle that still catches the light despite its current state. Her blue eyes water, but I remember what they look like when they shine. Last time I saw Belinda Barnes, she was in rehab. The center called me since dealing with an alcohol addiction and a particularly nasty ghost is more than anyone can handle.

"Oh, Belinda." It's all I can think to say. The alcohol is stealing everything from her—her beauty, which is phenomenal, her brain, which is equally so, and her life. She could be anything, go anywhere. But she drinks and the ghosts find her. So she drinks some more. It's been that way since high school.

This must show on my face, for she gives me a rueful smile. "I know. I know. I already got the lecture from your grandmother."

I suck in a breath. True, my grandmother's ghost haunts me. Malcolm recognizes her presence, and Mrs. Greeley at the long-term care facility senses her as well. But this? This is new. I move to the bench and sit next to Belinda. This is not a conversation that needs to be overheard.

"Sorry." Belinda tucks the flaps of her overcoat beneath her thighs and then plucks at her shirt. "I refused the shower. I like to make them suffer."

An earthy smell rolls off of her, one laced with dead leaves and whisky. In some ways, it's a relief from the charred coffee stench in the booking area.

"You can talk to my grandmother?"

"She caught me drinking." She raises her palms skyward as if to say *obviously*. "She read me the riot act. At least that's the feeling I got. I know she cares. She's not like some of the ... others." She pulls her coat closer.

"Have they been bothering you?"

She shakes her head. "Clearly, I'm dry at the moment, right?"

"If they do, come find me. I mean that. No charge."

"Katy, you don't—"

"I do, and I don't mind. It would make me feel better. Okay?"

She nods, and it almost looks sincere. Nasty ghosts have a tendency to attract even nastier ones. Sprites are annoying and sometimes take their pranks too far. But the nasty ones linger. They clutch and cling, and those who carry that burden really are haunted.

"So, you know, I hate to ask," Belinda says. "But what on earth are you doing here?"

"Grand larceny, seven counts, only I can't tell you what I've stolen."

She snorts. "Idiots. They spend all their time rounding up drunks and arresting the wrong people."

"Are there right people to arrest?"

"Of course. Whoever's been stealing everybody's stuff. You haven't heard about the break-ins?"

Not at all. This worries me, as does the fact I haven't heard from my grandmother for a few days. Usually she's a ghostly presence, an icy kiss against my cheek when I go out on a call. But we haven't been out on any calls. Sometimes, when things get slow, she'll kick up a ruckus somewhere so we'll get a little business.

That hasn't happened either. This worries me even more. I shift on the hard bench, pulling my knees to my chest, wrapping my arms around my shins.

"Oh, no," Belinda says.

I turn my head so my cheek rests against my knees.

"You don't suppose that they"—she points through the bars, toward the front of the station—"think you're the one stealing, do you?"

"Grand larceny," I say. "Seven counts."

For a moment, we stare at each other. Belinda's eyes are clear now, like the September sky. Then she huddles into her overcoat, drawing the collar up around her jaw as if she's chilled. I turn to face the bars and the long night ahead of me.

"Katrina Lindstrom, you have a visitor."

Really, I don't think my full name is necessary. The holding cell is hardly teeming with violent offenders. Belinda stirs and shifts. I hope whoever called my name hasn't woken her. Sleep without alcohol or ghosts would do her good.

"Katy?"

This voice is different—low, masculine, familiar. But not Malcolm. I can't place it, not until its owner comes into view. Jack Carlotta bursts through the door. By the time he reaches the cell, I'm gripping the bars with both hands and peering out at him.

"Jack? How—?"

"My grandfather called me. He said you were in jail and that I needed to rescue you. His words, not mine. So I called down, and yes, you are in jail. So here I am." He holds out his arms. "Here to rescue you."

"But ... how did he know?"

Jack shakes his head, gives a little shrug. He's all suited up, very much the lawyer. Crisp pleats in each leg of his trousers, a tie with a red stripe. This is good. I need a lawyer, especially since Malcolm hasn't returned with one.

"You drove all the way down here?" I ask. "From Minneapolis?"

"It's not that far, and I've been meaning to visit anyway. Look, I've already made some preliminary calls—"

"On your drive down?"

"I multi-task. Anyway, they can't hold you. The evidence is way too thin. If it went to a hearing, the judge would throw it out."

"Then why arrest me in the first place?"

"Well, there was some pressure to do something about this rash of robberies, or so I'm told. There's the fact Chief Ramsey and your grandmother often had ... words."

"Neither of which have anything to do with me."

"The pattern of thefts does. Three to five days after you stopped in on a call, something goes missing."

All those nuisance calls. The thought of them makes me vaguely uncomfortable, like I should've noticed something about them. "And they told you all this?"

"They have to." He gives me that winning grin I remember from high school. "I'm your lawyer."

"Can you get me out of here, too?"

"Working on it."

"More multi-tasking?"

"Of course. I'm a pro at it."

The door bursts open again. This time, Malcolm rushes in. He lurches forward as if there's nothing more he wants to do than plant his hands on his thighs and suck in lungfuls of air. The sight of Jack in front of the jail cell halts him, but only for a moment. He starts at a run again and grips one of the bars next to my hand.

"Katy, I'm sorry. They closed the law offices for the day, and I wasted an hour calling around, trying to get someone at home. In the morning—"

"Katy has a lawyer," Jack says.

When Malcolm simply stares, Jack adds, "Me. Jack Carlotta."

He takes Malcolm's hand and it's all handshaking and elbow gripping. I think they must be passing secret messages to each other, since Malcolm's eyes narrow and Jack's lips curl into a grimace. Malcolm looks rumpled next to Jack, as if he's been tearing up and down Main Street, which, I concede, he probably has been.

I cough, hoping to get their attention. I am the one in jail, after all. "Jack," I say, "this is my business partner, Malcolm Armand. Malcolm, this is Jack Carlotta, Mr. Carlotta's grandson. We went to high school together."

"I even asked Katy to prom, but she turned me down." Jack winks.

I'm not sure if this is aimed at Malcolm or me. But, yes, it's true. In the week Jack was in off-again status with his on-again/off-again girlfriend, he did ask me. And I did turn him down. He ended up at prom with his girlfriend, as I'd known he would. I don't mention this detail.

Instead, I say, "Jack just passed the bar exam. Mr. Carlotta called him. He'll be my lawyer."

Malcolm's eyes light with the same question turning in my mind. "How did he...?" He trails off, casting a look at Jack.

I give my head the slightest of shakes and mouth, "I don't know." Later. We'll sort all this out later.

"Listen," Jack says, "no friend of mine is spending the night in jail. I'm getting you out. In the morning, I'll get all the charges dropped. This won't even go to a hearing. It's ridiculous. Give me ten minutes and you'll be on your way home."

He strides from the holding area very much like he entered it—a full swagger, suit coat swinging. Malcolm tracks him as he leaves, his eyes still narrowed, an odd expression on his face, one I can't read.

"Go with him," I say.

"I don't want to leave you alone." His gaze flickers to the lump that is Belinda.

"I'm fine. Nothing can hurt me in here, and the only two ghosts are the sprites in the booking area. Besides," I add, and lower my voice, "Jack can get ... distracted. He'll end up having drinks with Chief Ramsey and forget all about me."

"Are you sure?"

"Positive."

When Malcolm leaves, I sag against the bars. I don't know what to make of Jack's sudden appearance. I'm not ungrateful. I can get more done if I'm not in jail. Still, I must find a way to speak to Mr. Carlotta. I take a deep breath, and then slowly, I turn toward Belinda.

"Hey." I keep my voice low, in case she really is asleep.

"Katy, don't..."

"Okay, I won't, but I was just thinking—"

"You just promised you wouldn't. You said it yourself. He's easily distracted. I take more concentration these days. A lot more. And promise me this as well. You won't say anything once you're out, either."

"What makes you think I'm not spending the night?"

"The two guys out there who're about ready to fight over you."

"Don't be stupid," I say. "No one's fighting over me."

The lump that is Belinda stirs. "Don't think so?"

"No, I don't. I'm not that kind of girl."

"Well, take it from someone who used to be that kind of girl. Watch yourself, Katy. And choose carefully."

I don't know what to say to that, and she burrows further into her overcoat, cutting off our conversation. When the officer comes to release me from the cell, Belinda doesn't move, almost seems content in her pile of ragged clothes.

So I step from the cell and let the officer lock the door on the woman who went to prom with Jack Carlotta.

I AM RIGHT ABOUT one thing. By the time I meet both Malcolm and Jack in the main office area, Jack is slapping Chief Ramsey on the back. I sense more than hear the suggestion of Finnegan's Pub.

"Katy, come with us," Jack says. Deftly, he goes from slapping to urging, his fingers finding the small of my back and pushing me forward.

"Isn't that a conflict of interest?" I whisper. Isn't it? My lawyer with the police chief? It must be.

"I was thinking more of mending a few fences." Jack's mouth is close to my ear, his lips brushing the sensitive skin. It's almost like a kiss or a caress, these words in my ear. "Like the ones your grandmother burned down."

"I think you're mixing metaphors," I say, and I am trapped between his lips and his fingers.

"I was always lousy at English." Jack steps back, pulls his hand away as if he senses my discomfort. "It's why I'm a lawyer."

"I can't go." I scour my mind, searching for an excuse, any excuse. I never drink. Ghosts are not kind to drunken ghost hunters.

"We need to get back to the office," Malcolm says. And now his hand is at the small of my back, but this I don't mind nearly as much. "Ghosts don't wait, after all," he adds.

Of course, in our case they do, given our lack of clients. I decide not to contradict him.

"Next time." Jack leans closer, and it's almost like the three of us are conspiring, our heads are so close together. "Really, it would be good for your business to have the police chief in your corner."

Jack leaves me with that bit of advice and a kiss on my cheek.

OUR WALK back to the office is silent. Main Street has rolled up for the night, with only the pub casting a beacon into the dark. Even the deli next to our office is closed, and I despair that I must cook dinner for myself.

The samovar that sits in our front window throws a golden glow onto the sidewalk. This feels like home, but Malcolm is quiet, oddly so. I want to say something to him but don't know where to start. When I cast him a sidelong glance, he turns toward the door, wrinkles his nose. I step back, pluck my shirt, and bring the fabric close to my face. I sniff. The holding cell comes flooding back—all stale, burnt coffee, that earthy aroma, and a hint of whisky.

"I stink, don't I?" I say.

"Maybe a little."

"Maybe a lot?"

His laugh is soft. He nods toward the door. "Let's go inside."

Once we're inside, it strikes me. I can't smell him. Normally, he smells so warm, but when I inhale, all I get is stale air. The smallest bit of dreads worms its way into my stomach. This is so like before, when we confronted that entity, the thing that seemed to suck up all the life—and scents—around itself. I shake my head and try to shake away that idea. I can't smell Malcolm simply because I reek. Nothing more.

"So," he says to me now. "You and Jack Carlotta."

"Me and Jack Carlotta what?"

"You went to high school together?"

"Same graduating class."

"Who did you end up at prom with, if not him?"

"No one," I say. "You ... I mean, I told you that I've never dated anyone."

Before we managed to put an end to Mistress Armand, she had

coaxed that bit of shame from me. Even now, it stings. Even now, I know how odd it sounds, how odd I sound, how odd I am.

"No one wants to date the local ghost catcher, okay?" I shrug. "Maybe it's different in the city, at college, but here? They just don't."

"It's just that he—" Malcolm begins, his voice thick with something I can't name.

So instead, I don't. I refuse to name it, and I don't let him finish either. "Why are we even talking about this?"

Malcolm rubs his jaw. "I realized tonight that I don't know a whole lot about you or your life in Springside."

"I don't know a lot about you, either."

He takes up a perch on the desk, making certain to adjust the leg of his trousers first. "Maybe we should do something about that sometime."

His meaning is lost on me. I'm not certain what he wants. We're already business partners. I'd like to think we're friends. I'm not sure what comes after that.

"Maybe we could play truth or dare," I say.

He throws his head back and laughs. The sound of it is so rich, so real, and that earlier dread loosens its grip. Tension melts from my shoulders.

"What do you think?" he says, once his laughter has subsided. "Should we call it a day?"

"I need a bath," I say.

"You kind of do." He softens this with a grin. "I can give you a ride home."

"I'm fine," I say. "Really. But you can walk me to my truck."

He does, and even helps me inside it. Malcolm's brand of chivalry is solid and sturdy. It never feels like a trap.

I'm a block away, ready to make the turn off of Main, when I check the rearview mirror. In it, I see Malcolm, standing on the sidewalk, hands in his pockets, gaze on my truck.

Then I turn the wheel, the signal clicking, and he vanishes from my sight.

❧

THE RINGTONE on my cell phone jolts me awake at three in the morning. This isn't too unusual. Even the gentlest sprite can morph into something fearsome after midnight—at least in the imagination. Some people simply can't—or won't—wait until morning. Of course, when we inform them that all eradications between the hours of midnight and six a.m. are at double our normal rate, most find a way to embrace the supernatural—at least until the sun comes up.

But the number on the screen is for Springside Long-term Care. My heart thuds, the beat strange and worried, as if no matter how fast it goes, it can't push enough blood through my veins.

I answer, more dread filling my stomach.

"Katy-Girl," the caller says, voice low and hushed. "Is that you?"

Only one person, other than my grandmother, has ever called me that. "Mr. Carlotta?"

"Sorry to call you so late. I've been waiting for the night manager to take his long weekend. The substitute they get always falls asleep. I had to wait until no one was around."

"Why not shut the door and call from your room?" Every resident has a phone, after all. This seems like the most logical solution.

"They monitor outgoing calls," he says.

This I doubt, but I suppose it's possible. "Won't they know you called out tonight?"

"Just that someone did from the front desk. They won't know it's me."

Honestly? I think Mr. Carlotta is just having a bit of fun, maybe at my expense. Of course, if not for the fact that Springside Long-term Care is no longer a client, I might say this was a joke.

"Katy-Girl," he's saying now, "I'm sorry for what everyone did to you. There was nothing Annabelle and I could say to change their minds. It was our two votes against everyone else."

"But what did I do?" There's something awful about knowing that a large number of people simply don't want you around, that you're that repulsive or unpleasant or whatever it is Mr. Carlotta is about to tell me.

"It's not what you did, it's what you heard, when Mistress Armand was here."

"What I heard?"

The echoes of that day rattle around in my head—confessions and shame, sorrow and regrets. The things that tear at your heart decades later, big and small, the things you can't shrug off, pretend never happened, the things you keep locked away.

"You're like a granddaughter to us, Katy-Girl. For some of the residents here, the ones without actual grandchildren, you are the closest thing to it."

"Then—"

"No one wants their granddaughter learning those sorts of secrets, the indiscretions, the infidelity..." Mr. Carlotta breaks off, his voice rough as if it's coated with its own layer of shame.

Springside Township is small enough that no one can grow up here and remain ... ignorant to all the goings-on. Still, gossip is different than confession, and truth trumps rumor.

"So they didn't want us to come back?"

"They were too ashamed. Don't hate them, Katy-Girl."

"I don't. And maybe you could tell them I can't even sort out what I heard. It's all a jumble, and I don't know who did what to whom."

Mr. Carlotta snorts. "You're better off not knowing. Trust me."

In this case, he's right. I would very much like to remain the ignorant granddaughter. I would also like our account back as well, even if it's a gratis one. If I am the surrogate granddaughter, then these people are my grandparents.

"But here's the thing," he says. "We have worse trouble now."

"Is it the ghosts?"

"Someone new came around, claiming they could exorcise the ghosts from haunted objects."

"That's convenient," I say. I scoot up in bed and plump the pillow. I have the feeling I won't be falling back asleep after this conversation.

Mr. Carlotta snorts again. "It did work."

My heart sinks. This is just how it was when Malcolm first came to town and stole all my clients with his flashy golden samovar and tea. (Ghosts prefer coffee. At least, most ghosts do. A few odd ones go for the tea.) Someone new. Someone doing something different. It's the shiny factor.

"But there's a problem," he adds.

"And that is?"

"Not all of our items came back."

For a moment, I can't speak. I feel as if the breath has been knocked from me. Grand larceny. Seven counts. I kick off the covers, my feet bicycling furiously.

I think I've been framed.

I don't voice my suspicion to Mr. Carlotta—not yet, anyway. I want to hear the whole story, or at least, his version of it.

"There were three of them," he says. "But I think only one of them, the woman, could sense ghosts. The other two looked like hired muscle."

"But she didn't try to catch them?"

"No."

Sensing ghosts—where they are, their size, what they're up to—is an inborn trait. Actually catching them takes skill, finesse, hours of practice, and in my case, plenty of scalding with cups of coffee.

"Could you tell if all the items they took were haunted?"

"I'm sure they weren't. They took Annabelle's jewelry box. According to her, it's never been haunted."

Annabelle Greeley is another resident at the care facility. Whether it's because she's blind or extraordinarily sensitive, she has a feel for ghosts—my grandmother's in particular. She'd know if she owned a haunted jewelry box.

"Here's the thing, Katy-Girl. They brought that back."

"As a ruse?" I suggest. The jewelry box is something her grandchildren bought her, probably at a dollar store. I doubt you could pawn it or fence it or do whatever it is thieves do. Its only value is sentimental.

"My thoughts exactly!" His voice is charged with excitement.

"And I was in Mrs. Greeley's room not too long ago," I add. "But I wasn't there for the jewelry box." My grandmother likes to visit Mrs. Greeley and often swirls inside a cobalt blue vase on the nightstand—or the Kona blend I might happen to have in a thermos.

"And you were in my room," Mr. Carlotta says.

"Are you missing something?"

"My Purple Heart."

"They took that?" It's good I live alone. My outrage would wake the entire house.

"And my ghost as well."

Oh, well, this is different. I hadn't pegged his ghost as one that would haunt an item. Its connection to Mr. Carlotta feels far more personal than that.

"Have you told Jack this?" I ask.

"Yes, but don't you dare say anything to him. He's convinced I just misplaced it and forgot."

Mr. Carlotta still advises the Springside High School chess team. Of all the residents, I'd say his memory is the sharpest.

"But you called him ... Why did you call him? How did you know I was in jail?"

"Your grandmother, of course. She told Annabelle, Annabelle told me."

And then Mr. Carlotta embarked on his secret, after-hours mission. I sigh. "But Jack got me out of jail. He can make Chief Ramsey take this seriously."

"He'll just say I shouldn't bother you."

His voice tears at me, so glum, so forlorn. Mr. Carlotta is eighty-nine years old. I did the math once, figured out that he must have lied about his age to enlist during World War Two. Maybe this, too, is one of the reasons he doesn't want to involve Jack. I think about the collective shame of everyone at the care facility, the urge to salvage a last bit of pride. I think I understand.

"I want it back," Mr. Carlotta says, the declaration sudden, his voice firm. "Can you help me?"

"Your Purple Heart?" I ask.

"No. My ghost."

OUR TINY CONFERENCE room brims with caffeine. In addition to the coffee I've brewed in the percolator, Malcolm's tea scents the air with its exotic blend of saffron and spices.

"It's different today," I say to him, blinking my eyes against the steam.

He holds his index finger and thumb together. "Just a pinch of cardamom."

Nigel sits at the end of the conference table, which is really nothing more than someone's discarded dining room set. On either side of his laptop sits a cup—one of tea and one of coffee. He takes a sip from each, alternating precisely, never playing favorites.

"I've traced the patterns of the thefts," Nigel says after a sip of tea. "About three days after Katy went on a call, alone, without you"—he points to Malcolm—"something went missing."

"Which is why they didn't arrest me, I'm guessing." Malcolm leans over Nigel's shoulder, gaze on the laptop's screen.

"So it looks like I was staking out places to rob," I say, "after living all my life in Springside?" I roll my eyes.

I haven't been in everybody's house, it's true. Some people like their ghosts, especially the sprites, who are usually harmless. Some people refuse to believe, like Chief Ramsey. Still, this is a rather clumsy attempt, I think, to make me look guilty.

"Bad blood, Katy. Blame your grandmother."

The voice startles me. I shoot to my feet, my chair careening backward into the wall. In the conference room doorway, Jack stands, all dark suit and red lawyer tie. He has his hands in his pockets and he leans against the frame. It's a devastating pose, one he perfected against the lockers at Springside High School.

I grope for my chair and plant myself in it. "Who said anything about blood?"

"It's an expression," Malcolm says, his voice grumpy.

Well, yes, I know that. I cast him a quick glance and fight the urge to roll my eyes again.

"And I don't think that assessment is fair to Katy or her grandmother," he adds. This last is directed at Jack.

"You're new here, aren't you?" Jack says. He is frozen now, an ice sculpture of a man.

"I live here now." In the echo of Malcolm's reply, I catch: *and you don't.*

My gaze flickers between the two men, then lands on Nigel. He gives me a shrug, but I notice his lips twitch, as if he's trying not to laugh.

"Anyway," Jack says, turning his attention to me, a smile melting some of the ice. "The charges are dropped, but you shouldn't leave town."

"Funny," Malcolm says. "That doesn't sound like the charges have been dropped at all."

"Please, it's not like I ever leave town except to release ghosts," I say. "The last time I went anywhere was the school trip to the state capital."

This confession brings silence. I wonder if something of Mistress Armand lingers in the air of Springside, for certainly I've managed to blurt out several things that can kill a conversation. Again, that sense that I'm odd weighs on me. I don't feel deprived for not traveling. Sometimes I think the world comes to me, or at least, history does. I've trapped enough old ghosts that sometimes I feel old myself.

"When this is all over," Jack says, lawyer-striding into the room, "I'm making sure you leave this town—at least for a weekend."

"Is that a promise or a threat?" With Jack, it could go either way.

He laughs. "Katy, you know me better than that."

He's right. I do. And my question stands, at least in my own mind.

"What's missing?" I ask in an attempt to change the subject.

Jack pulls a cell phone from his suit coat pocket. "A couple of flat-screen televisions, some high-end video equipment, a brand new MacBook."

"And what would I do with those things?"

"Pawn them, I guess."

"Where? In Springside? Don't you think someone might catch on?"

"Up in the Twin Cities—"

"But I never leave town," I interrupt. "Remember? Has Chief Ramsey really thought this through, or am I just convenient?"

Jack folds his arms over his chest. "I think you're stubborn. His theory is you could also use the equipment in your business."

"To do what? Make ghost pornos?"

Once again I have silenced the room. After a moment, Nigel snorts. Malcolm glances away; I think he might be laughing. An angry pink blazes across Jack's cheekbones.

"You know it doesn't work that way," I say, more contrite now. "You can't film ghosts. Not really. I don't need all the stuff he says I do."

"Unless your business is failing." Jack pauses. "Is your business failing, Katy?"

His words sucker punch the air from my lungs. I open my mouth to contradict him, but I can't draw a full breath. Words lodge in my throat. I can't look at anyone, not Nigel, and especially not Malcolm. I don't understand, either, why Jack is acting this way. So I do what any wounded thing does when desperate. I attack.

"So I stole all these things *and* your grandfather's Purple Heart? How much sense does that make?"

Jack heaves a sigh. "He probably just misplaced it." His voice is patronizing. Does he speak to Mr. Carlotta this way? Has he always spoken this way? My mind searches the past, trying to dredge up old images of Jack. I don't remember him being quite so abrasive. I don't like it. I'm starting to not like him.

I turn to not Jack or Malcolm, but Nigel, who still has his hands poised over the laptop's keyboard. "Let's say someone came to town and did steal all those things. What would be the next steps?"

"Pawn them." Nigel's fingers fly over the keys. "Probably up in Minneapolis or one of the suburbs."

"Even the medal?"

His fingers stutter, then start up again. He squints at the screen. "Oh, well, this is interesting. Apparently there's a market for medals, Purple Hearts in particular. Collectors' items. Does Mr. Carlotta's medal still have the original box?"

"It does." This is Jack, his voice devoid of arrogance now. "And the citation."

"Could be worth something to the right collector," Nigel says. "And ... there's a Military Relic Show going on this weekend at the State Fairgrounds."

"That can't be a coincidence," I say.

Nigel shakes his head. "Doesn't look that way."

"When this weekend?" I ask.

"Tomorrow, eight to six and Sunday, nine to three."

"I think—"

I never get to say what I think. In that moment, both Malcolm and Jack burst out with something, something I can't understand. They talk over each other, talk about me, but neither considers that maybe they should talk *to* me. I'm about to climb up onto the table, maybe stomp my feet, just to silence them, when Nigel catches my eye.

"Oh, Katy!" Nigel stands, a feat considering Malcolm has an iron grip on the back of his chair. "I almost forgot. Sadie's sprites are getting out of hand. I don't suppose you could—" He nods toward the door. His lips twitch again.

I take the offer for what it is: a chance to escape. "Of course. I have supplies at my house."

Sadie Lancaster is my next-door neighbor. She believes herself plagued by ghosts, although in reality, it's only two mischievous sprites. I've caught them dozens of times. They always return. They have nothing but affection for her, but sprites being sprites, they're also annoying.

We escape, leaving Malcolm and Jack glaring at each other. I wonder if they'll still be like that when we return.

SINCE I DON'T NEED my truck, we decide to walk.

"I thought Sadie was going to embrace her sprites," I say.

"She was. She's trying. Thing is, they're troublemakers."

"Sprites usually are."

"And ... I'm coming over for dinner tonight."

Oh. Interesting. Something's been brewing there, between them. My mind goes to last night, how Nigel gathered Sadie's groceries, the comforting hands on her shoulders. Still, the two of them make such an unusual couple that I've dismissed the idea. Clearly, I shouldn't have.

"The steam from the food," Nigel continues. "You know how they like the steam. Well, if food goes in my mouth, and there's a sprite in the steam..." He trails off because I can fill in the rest.

Nigel used to swallow ghosts, was addicted to them, the way you might be to alcohol or heroin. He's only been ghost-free for a little more than a month, and I'm not sure that's long enough for any addict. Accidently swallowing a sprite along with the green beans? That could cause a relapse.

We turn off of Main Street. The wind whips up funnels of leaves. We're closer to winter than summer now. Soon it will be Halloween. Business should be good—there's something about the winter holidays that brings out the ghosts. Of course if everyone thinks I'm a thief, we won't get any business at all.

"Thank you," I say.

"Thank *you*," he echoes. "As excuses go, this one is real."

"I just don't—" I shake my head and try to shake off the image of the strange showdown in our conference room. "I have no idea what's going on."

"Don't you?" Nigel laughs, then pauses at the gate in front of Sadie's Victorian. "The thing about Malcolm is he's never had to work to get a girlfriend. You've seen how women fall all over him."

Yes. I have. It's disgusting.

"I don't know this Jack guy." Nigel plants his hand on the gate and drums his fingers against the slats as if he's thinking. "But I'm guessing it's the same for him, especially now that he's a fancy lawyer with a fancy car."

"He has a fancy car?" I ask. "I didn't notice."

Nigel throws his head back and laughs. In that instance, he is very much like Malcolm, especially along the jawline and with the humor lighting his eyes. But although he's only a few years older, that gap could easily be two decades. His hair is pure white where Malcolm's is inky black. The lines around his mouth and eyes speak of things he probably doesn't want to think about, never mind discuss.

"That's your charm, Katy," he says. "You didn't notice the fancy car."

"I was supposed to?"

"It was right out front."

"It was?"

"Yes, and you were supposed to be suitably impressed as well." He laughs again, softer this time, and more to himself. He unlatches the gate and holds it open for me. "And now? Well, now they're both gunning for the same girl, and the best part? Neither one may win."

"Do you mean me?" I step through the gate and start up the sidewalk.

Nigel doesn't answer. Instead, he hums to himself. I decide to put Malcolm and Jack, fancy cars, and all the rest from my mind.

I have some ghosts to catch.

I DO a quick check of Sadie's to confirm that yes, the sprites are in residence and they're in a particularly naughty mood. Grit beneath the soles of my sneakers tells me they've knocked over the planter with the fern—again. Certainly they would upset dinner plans.

"I think I told you," I say to the air. "That if you aren't good, you're out of here."

Something whirls by my face. Something else ruffles my hair.

"Kona blend."

I also say this to the air. Nigel is—wisely—waiting outside. Sadie is upstairs, I think. She will be where the sprites are not. I'm alone with the sprites, and speaking as if they can understand me. This last, I'm not sure of. I used to think I knew everything there was to know about ghosts. Lately? I'm not so sure I know anything at all.

In five minutes' time, I return with my supplies—the percolator, cups, sugar, and half and half. And of course, the Kona blend, not that these two deserve it. Still, it makes them easy to catch. I won't even need to pour twelve full cups, like I would during a normal eradication job.

The third cup does the trick, one with extra sugar and cream. They swirl in the steam, and the air sparkles with their presence. I trap them both in a Tupperware container. They thump the sides, more put out that I've spoiled their fun than in anger.

"You two," I say, "are causing problems."

Thump.

I snap the lid on tight before calling up the staircase.

"I've got them. You can come down now." I peek out the front door and wave Nigel inside.

I'm concentrating so hard on the sprites in the Tupperware that I don't notice Sadie at first. Then, all at once, she blooms before me. Her hair, which normally is a mix of salt and pepper, now glows with hot pink highlights. I step back, not certain about this new transformation. A moment later, I'm plucking a strand of my own hair and considering highlights for myself. Green? Or maybe a neon blue.

She shakes her head, the short curls bouncing. "Too much?" she asks.

"No, it's great. I was just thinking." I tug at my hair again. "Maybe blue?"

"The girl at the salon said even women my age are doing it now, so I figured why not? It's not like Harold's around to criticize."

And a certain ghostly-haired Nigel will understand. I remember, years ago, my grandmother and Mrs. Greeley talking. They kept calling Sadie a young bride. Looking at her now, I see that was true. She isn't even close to fifty, but she's always seemed old to me. I think that comes from having been married to Harold and then having him die in another woman's bed.

Nigel raps on the doorframe. "All clear?"

I hold up the Tupperware. The sprites whirl about. Often, when trapped, ghosts will manifest grotesque—or obscene—images. These two are all sugar and light, just like their preferred coffee.

"Would you like to stay for lunch?" Sadie directs this at both of us, but I suspect she only wants Nigel to stay.

"I'd better get back." I tap the container with my charges. "And do something about this."

Nigel opens his mouth. I think he might refuse, so I rush a few more words.

"Nigel, you should stay."

"But—"

"Stay, unless you really want to run interference between Malcolm and Jack all afternoon."

"You shouldn't have to alone."

I tap the container's lid. "Who says I'm going back to the office?"

His grin is filled with relief and gratitude. Sadie is already chattering by the time I'm at the front door. So I slip from the house, leaving them to their lunch. The ghost eater and the woman terrified of ghosts. It occurs to me, now, that this coupling is not as odd as it first seems.

I'M ONLY a block away from Sadie's when a cherry red convertible pulls up alongside me. Have I noticed his fancy car before? Honestly, it's hard not to notice Malcolm's car. But I'm not sure I've given it the proper consideration.

"Hey," he says, killing the engine. The street is quiet except for a crow and the light thump of two naughty sprites. "Catch of the day?" he adds.

I examine the Tupperware. "You could say that."

"I'm sorry," he says, "about earlier. I was a ... jerk to your friend."

"You mean Jack?"

Malcolm makes a sour-apple sort of face. Yes. That's exactly who he means.

"We went to school together," I say. "I've known him since kindergarten. But I'm not sure I'd call him my friend."

"He thinks you're friends."

"Jack thinks a lot of things that aren't always true."

Malcolm nods toward the Tupperware in my hands. "You want to get rid of them?"

"Yes, otherwise they'll ruin the romance."

His gaze goes from me to Sadie's Victorian. His eyes cloud. His mouth goes slack. "No. You're kidding me. Nigel and Sadie?"

I nod and then shrug. "Nigel and Sadie."

"It's kind of a ... not May-December, but I don't know. July-October sort of thing."

I choose this moment to launch myself into the front seat of his convertible. It's much too cold to have the top down, but Malcolm drives it this way every chance he gets.

"Older woman, younger man?" I say. "It's very twenty-first century."

"How far out do you want to drive?" he asks. "Should we lose these two permanently?"

At the suggestion, the sprites sink to the bottom of the container, as if weighed down by sorrow. I study them, considering their persistent haunting. They are so playful, like puppies or children. Oh. *Children.* Ghosts search out emotion, either fueled by their own or that of a living person. In this case, I think these two are filling an emotional hole.

I shake my head. "No, let's take them to the usual spot. They won't make it back before dinner, but they won't be missed for long either."

Malcolm has just put the car in gear when I cover his hand with mine. His skin is so warm in the autumn air. For a moment, we sit like that. I've held his hand before. He's taken mine while we're out on a call.

Something about this time is different.

"I want to find Mr. Carlotta's Purple Heart," I say. "If we leave early tomorrow morning, do you think we could be the first in the doors at the Military Relic Show?"

"Katy, you're not supposed to leave town."

"I don't care. Besides, if I find his Purple Heart, won't that clear me?"

"Maybe. Maybe not. Besides, you don't even know it will be there. Those exhibition halls at the State Fairgrounds are huge. Even if it's there, you might not find it. You could leave town, get in trouble, and it would all be for nothing."

"Where would you sell a stolen Purple Heart?" I counter. "Where would you sell a haunted one?"

Malcolm turns in his seat to face me full on. "Mr. Carlotta's ghost?"

"It's attached itself to the medal. Whoever has it will want to unload it, and fast. I think the show is the best option. It won't matter how huge the hall is. I know that ghost. I'll find it."

Malcolm drums his fingers on the steering wheel. He gazes through the windshield, then turns back to me. "How fast can you pack a bag?"

"What?"

Instead of answering, Malcolm puts the car in reverse and backs up until we're even with my house.

"How fast can you pack a bag?" he asks again.

"Five, ten minutes? Why?"

"Let's go now. I'll show you around the Cities, the U of M campus. We can park at my old frat house and jump on the Green Line."

"Green Line?"

"Light rail. We can ... go out to dinner?"

Out. To. Dinner. Is Malcolm asking me out? Should I say yes? Should I really date my business partner? But is one dinner really dating?

"There's this Persian place. It's where I get all the spices for my tea. I'd love to take you there." The words stream from him as if he's convinced the more of them he uses, the better the chances are that I might say yes.

His chances were already pretty good. "Is it fancy? Because all I really have to wear is my skater skirt."

His eyes light up in a way I can't decipher. He nods. "Pack the skater skirt."

So, I'm not supposed to leave town. I shouldn't go on a date—or an overnight—with my business partner.

I hand Malcolm the Tupperware container.

"Five minutes," I say. "Ten at the most." I leap from the car.

I make it back in seven.

I TRY NOT TO GAWK. But when Malcolm drives us through downtown Minneapolis, convertible top open to the autumn air, I crane my neck as far back as it will go and stare at the blue, glimmering buildings on either side of us.

He parks the car at his old frat house and we wander the campus until we reach the Mississippi River. Students stream here and there, some with backpacks, others with soccer balls tucked beneath an arm. I inhale as if that alone will let me breathe in the entirety of this place. When I exhale, it comes out as a sigh—a sad one.

"Didn't you go to college?" Malcolm asks, his fingers brushing my wrist.

"No. I ... we didn't have the money for that, and I didn't have the grades for scholarships. Besides, I was doing most of the chasing and catching by then." I turn from the view of the Mississippi and the paddleboat that's chugging its way up the river. "I couldn't leave her."

Her. My grandmother. I wonder where she's gone. I haven't sensed her for days, and that secondhand report from Mr. Carlotta wasn't reassuring, either. Every time I feel her presence, part of me is convinced it will be the last.

"You could still go," Malcolm says.

I nod, unconvinced. I like my work. I like catching ghosts. But as I take in the golden leaves, the green grass, the campus with all its buildings and that undeniable buzz in the air, a yearning tugs at me. There is so much more in this world than Springside Township—and I've been working very hard trying to tell myself there isn't.

My contemplation turns toward Malcolm. He had all this—the campus, the glimmering downtown. Does he miss it?

"Hungry?" he says.

"Maybe."

"Come on. You're going to love the restaurant. Actually, you're going to love the frat house."

"There's no way I'm going to love your frat house."

Granted, I've never been inside a fraternity house, but I've done my share of ghost eradications in the boys' locker room at the high school. I can't imagine it's all that much different.

"Want to bet?" Malcolm grins at me. Those fingertips at my wrist slip until our palms meet and our fingers lace together.

On our way back, I catch glimpses of dorm rooms. I find one I like and pretend it's mine. I pretend Malcolm and I are students here and we're on a study date. For the ten-minute walk, I don't think of ghosts, or Purple Hearts, or my grandmother. For those ten minutes, I simply dream.

THE SECOND WE step into the old Victorian that houses his fraternity, I know Malcolm is right. The rush is immediate, icy against my cheeks. Something tugs my hair.

"It's haunted!" I say.

"It is." Malcolm glances around as if tasting the air. "A few new ones since I was last here."

"Are they always this rowdy?"

"Only when there's a pretty girl around."

Since no one else is around, my cheeks blaze at this, more heat for the ghosts to absorb. But it makes me wonder where all the humans are.

"Is it always this quiet?" I ask. It is a frat house, after all. Granted, my only experience with them is what I've seen in the movies. Still. I was expecting more than ghosts.

"Everyone is either at class or getting supplies for tonight."

"Tonight?"

"It's Friday."

"So?"

Malcolm gives one of the ghosts a sidelong glance. "I know. She doesn't get it. Someone is out getting a keg as we speak."

"For a party?"

"Yes."

"What kind?"

"Friday. It's a Friday party."

As if to send the point home, two of the sprites go whipping around my head. I laugh and reach out a hand as if to capture them. "They're almost tame," I say. They're almost like pets.

He holds out his hand as if he, too, might like to hold or pet one. "I used to catch the nasty ones," he says, "and keep them in my samovar."

"At least now you can catch and release."

"At least now I can," he echoes, his voice oddly nostalgic.

Again, I wonder if he misses his college days, his life here. I think he must. It's in the set of his shoulders. They're not slumped in defeat, nothing like that, but determined, as if now that he's chosen a path, he won't alter his course.

But then he turns a grin on me. "Let's change and go out. Trust me, you don't want to be here when they tap the keg."

"Do ghost drink beer? Do they get drunk?"

I always thought they loved the coffee for both its heat and the flavor. But beer? Could you catch a ghost with that?

"They like the foam," he says. "And yes, they do get drunk."

The rowdiest ghost, the one that has been tugging strands of my hair, whips about in a frenzy of ghostly anticipation.

"Plus," Malcolm says. He has both our bags and is urging me up the stairs. "I don't want to introduce you to any of my fraternity brothers."

I climb the first steps. "Aren't they nice?"

"They're fine."

"Then—"

"I don't want the competition." With that, he dashes up the remaining stairs.

When I'm locked alone in the bathroom (yes, it really is just like the boys' locker room), I try to sort out what he means by that. I try to sort out how I feel about that—and him. Before I can, there's a thump against the door, jarring me from these thoughts.

"If you peek," I say to the apparition on the other side, "I will return with a Tupperware container that has your name on it. Don't think I can't catch you."

The door rattles a second time, but nothing more.

Before I can step into the hallway, my cell phone buzzes. The display reads Springside Long-term Care. My insides ice, and I'm so cold, I think there must be a ghost in here with me.

"Hello?" I keep my voice low, quiet. I glance around as if someone is listening in.

"Katy-Girl! Where are you?" Mr. Carlotta's voice is equally low and muffled, as if he's speaking from beneath a blanket or inside a closet.

"I'm getting your Purple Heart back," I say. "And your ghost." I hope both these statements are true.

"Jack was just here. He's looking for you. Chief Ramsey is looking for you. He wants you to check in."

"That's going to be hard to do."

"Come home now. I don't need my Purple Heart. I don't even need my ghost. I don't want you in trouble. Jack says it could mean jail."

"I was already there," I say. "Besides, Chief Ramsey let me go. He said I shouldn't leave town, not that I couldn't. I'm not under arrest. If they come around, tell them I'm doing a big release out at the state park."

"I have to warn you. Jack has your phone number."

"And he got that how, exactly?"

"Not me, Katy-Girl. I pretended I couldn't remember."

Of course he did.

"Works every time," Mr. Carlotta adds. "He asked the manager, and she gave it to him." His voice is now thick with disgust, at himself, it sounds like, as if he could have somehow prevented it.

"It's okay," I say. "I'm at the state park, remember? I'm probably out of cell phone range as well."

"Ah, that's my girl. Be careful and come home soon, ghost or no. An old man and an old ghost aren't worth it."

Before I can contradict him, he hangs up. Immediately, the screen flashes with another number, one I don't recognize. My guess? Jack is calling. My response?

I refuse the call and then turn off my phone.

FOR THE ENTIRE RIDE, I clutch my ticket for the light rail. It's an idiotic thing to do. It won't get lost in my bag. But it feels like a talisman, and I feel like a gaping tourist again.

"It's okay to have fun," Malcolm says, as if he's reading my thoughts.

We're sitting side by side. Even with the blast of air that comes with the doors opening and closing, I catch his scent—nutmeg and Ivory soap. His hair gleams. I can't decide if he adds product or if it's naturally shiny. Once upon a time, I might have reached out to test a strand in my fingers to see. That was before. Before what? This, I don't know. All I know is I can't bring myself to tease him about it the way I might have. I'm not sure I like this either.

It's only a few stops and a few blocks to The Taste of Persia. Inside, the entire space smells like the tea Malcolm brews—warm and rich, the scent has a life of its own, almost like its own ghostly presence. I cast my gaze about, breathing in the air, tasting it.

The space is split in two. On one side is a market filled with exotic fruits, spices, and mountains of rice straining their burlap sacks. On the other is a cozy restaurant with deep red carpets lining the walls and floors, and tiny tables lit with candles.

"Malcolm!" A man emerges from behind the deli counter and embraces Malcolm. "It's been too long!"

"I've moved out of the Cities," Malcolm says.

"Then you must need a resupply." His gaze darts to me. A graying eyebrow arches.

"Hamid." Malcolm's hand hovers over the small of my back. "This is my business partner, Katy Lindstrom. Katy, this is Hamid Kassem."

Hamid shakes my hand, inclining slightly, almost in a regal bow.

"And I do need that resupply," Malcolm adds. "Can I pick it up tomorrow? Tonight—" He nods at me and then the tiny tables to our right. "We're hungry."

"Of course!" He grips Malcolm by the shoulder, a gesture that's both familiar and affectionate. "Mariam will seat you."

I have never eaten in such a place. Springside has a pancake house and the Jade Dragon, and of course, all the fast food you could ever want.

There's the country club, but I've never been there, either. Here, it's like I've stepped into the Arabian Nights. Fortunately, I don't need to be Scheherazade, because I'm speechless for a good ten minutes into our meal.

"Do you like it?" Malcolm says at last.

"I love it," I say. "I don't even have words for how much."

"I'm glad."

He offers up a bit of his kebab, but I shake my head. I'm not so over-come that I forget I'm (mostly) a vegetarian. Besides, my baked eggplant is incredible. The tea, served in dainty glasses, is far more elegant than wine or champagne.

"Let's split a dish of ice cream," he says as the waitress clears our plates. "It's amazing."

The waitress returns with a scoop of rosewater pistachio in a silver bowl and two spoons.

"Try it," Malcolm urges.

So I do. With my first bite, I nearly drop my spoon. "It's soft!"

He laughs.

"It's like eating lotion," I say, "only lotion that's sweet and tastes good."

"It's the rosewater. They use that to make a lot of beauty products, so you're right. It's like eating lotion."

We scrape the bowl clean.

Outside, the street glows with yellow lamplight. My mouth is still cold from the ice cream, and I can feel the bite of October in the air. A shiver runs through me. Malcolm steps closer, eases an arm around my waist. The heat of his body sinks into mine. For a moment, we just stand there, although there isn't much to see. The station for the Green Line. Cars zipping past. A few stars strong enough to penetrate the city lights.

"Do you like music?" he says.

"Sure. Everyone likes music."

"Not everyone. But there's this great little club. I don't know who's playing, and sometimes there's dancing, but I think you might like it."

"In the same way I liked your fraternity house?"

"Maybe."

"Then how can I say no?"

What happens then—exactly—is hard to say. Malcolm turns one way. I turn the other. We're face to face, my hand planted on his chest. I tip my head back. He leans down. And then my business partner, Malcolm Armand, kisses me.

It's a soft, intimate thing because his lips are laced with rosewater. I clutch at his coat, wondering if this is a bad idea, while knowing at the same time that it is. I also know I won't stop this kiss. Not yet. I want more of his warm, soapy smell. I want to taste the nutmeg that's so elusive. I don't want this to end because I'm afraid of what might happen when it does.

Of course it ends. All kisses do. But he smiles at me, eyes bright in the dark.

"Has anyone mentioned you know how to kiss?" he says.

"Not recently."

"I thought you said you've never been on a date."

"That doesn't mean I've never kissed before."

With that, I break away and make a dash for the light rail station. I'm halfway there when he catches me by the waist and swings me around. We run the rest of the way hand in hand.

IF THE INSIDE of the restaurant was heavy with spice, the air inside the club is weighted down with beer. I could get drunk just from inhaling. The sprites that swirl around my head already are. They make clumsy passes at my cheeks, as if trying for a ghostly kiss. I wonder, just briefly, if we should switch from coffee to beer. It might make them easier to catch.

Bass thrums in my ears, vibrates through the soles of my Mary Janes. Malcolm's hand is snug in the small of my back, and we inch our way toward the bar.

"Something to drink?" His mouth brushes my ear, the only way I'll hear him with the unrelenting thump, thump, thump from the stage.

"Just water."

He goes fancy, getting me something bottled along with a beer for himself. It's too loud to talk, the music too jarring to dance to, although some couples are attempting it. We settle against the bar, me in the crook of Malcolm's arm, and it feels as though I've always meant to be here. With the thought, my heart races, its beat counterpoint to the one on stage.

I'm halfway through the water when something feels off kilter, beyond my erratic pulse, our earlier kiss, and the way his fingertips are playing with the fabric of my sleeve. The air is different, not lighter, but not as beer-drenched as before. I touch my cheek, then look for the tell-tale glimmer the sprites leave behind whenever they dance through someone's drink.

Nothing. In fact, I don't sense them at all.

"The sprites," I say, not that Malcolm can hear me.

Something flutters in my peripheral vision, something that makes me think of bed sheets and bridal veils, something that grips my throat so tight I can't swallow.

No. Not here. That ... thing can't be here. But bit by bit, the club drains of sound, of scent, of life itself. No wonder the sprites have fled. If I had any common sense, I would too. A screech tears through the speakers. People cry out, slam hands over ears. Several knock over chairs on their way out of the club. The lights flicker.

Malcolm and I exchange a single glance. Our hands lock together. We turn to leave, but the main door slams shut. The club goes dark except for a single spotlight that shines on the center of the dance floor. A low, metallic laugh fills the space.

"Ah, ghost hunter, you look lovely this evening. May I have this dance?" The voice clicks and grates, but it's stronger than I remember.

The last time I met this ... thing, whatever it is, I was outside. Perhaps the enclosed space makes it sound stronger than before. Perhaps this is my wishful thinking. I take a step toward the dance floor and the spotlight, but Malcolm's grip on my hand keeps me in place.

"It can't hurt me." I tug on my hand. "It's not strong enough."

"Is that what you think, ghost hunter?"

"It's what I know. You play tricks, just like any other ghost, but you're not any different."

The speakers erupt with a burst of static and smoke. Overhead, lights spark and pop. Behind us, bottle after bottle explodes, spraying shards of glass and streams of alcohol along the surface of the bar. We duck, but liquid soaks my jacket. The back of my neck breaks out in pinpricks. I swipe my free hand across the skin. It comes away red.

"Parlor tricks." Admittedly, I say this once I've caught my breath and wiped the blood from my fingers. Still, random and petty destruction is standard for an angry ghost.

Malcolm's grip on my other hand tightens. "Wrong thing to say," he mutters.

But the entity is silent. A bit of hope sparks that it has worn itself out. The air is still too stale, too lifeless. That fluttering again. This time, I swear I see an actual bridal veil.

"Why don't you step into the light, Katy dear," the entity says, its voice metallic-y sweet. "She looks so pretty tonight. Don't you agree, Necromancer?"

Necromancer? Next to me, Malcolm is statue-like. Despite the dim light, I can tell his skin has an ashen cast to it.

"Don't do this." Malcolm's voice cracks. In it I hear doubt and fear, and something that goes beyond both, something desperate.

"Do what?" The thing is gleeful in response. "You mean to say you haven't told her what you really are? And here I thought things were getting so cozy between you two. My mistake."

"Necromancer?" I try out the word. "What ... I don't understand."

"I'll explain," Malcolm says, "but not here."

I'm not certain I want an explanation at all, but he's right about one thing: here is a poor choice. I ease my hand from Malcolm's grip. He's in shock, I think. His normally warm skin feels chilled. I press my fingers against my throat and then my forehead. My skin is burning. Maybe I'm abnormally hot. Or the club is. It's hard to distinguish where the air stops and my skin starts.

"No, my dear, it's not hot in here, it's simply you."

This is one obnoxious entity. I step onto the dance floor. The soles of my Mary Janes are soft, so I don't make a sound on my way to the spotlight. I enter it. This, of course, is exactly what this entity wants me to do. With this thing, there is no around or away or under. I must barrel through, do what it wants me to do—for now—and look for a way out on the other side.

A dark, inky mass descends from the club's ceiling. How easily it hid itself in all the exposed pipes and vents. It's larger now, larger than when we encountered it outside the mausoleum, but then, my grandmother had just defeated it then.

The entity expands and contracts, contracts and expands, and each time an outline shimmers before collapsing. The thought strikes me that it's trying to take on the form of a man.

"I'm afraid we won't be able to dance tonight, my dear," the thing says. "I'm currently in no shape for it." It cackles, the laughter booming through the space. "But I can do this."

Before I can even think to move, one inky tendril surges forward and touches my cheek. I cry out, jump back, and Malcolm sprints forward, intent not on me, but that thing.

His hands reach for it, but despite its sluggish appearance, the entity shoots up toward the lights.

"Oh, no, you don't, Necromancer. I won't be captured so easily. Besides, I've marked my choice. See for yourself."

Malcolm turns slowly, almost reluctantly. "No, no. You can't do this to her. She has no idea—"

"All the more fun for me, then. Thank you, Necromancer. You've played your part brilliantly in all this. And, Katy?"

I crane my neck. One vent appears darker than the rest, more sinister. Once again, something flutters. Bed sheets. Bridal veils. The taste of metal against my tongue.

"I'll be seeing you soon."

With the entity's final words, the speakers burst back to life, music blaring. Colored lights flash. The disco ball above our heads throws out a million fake stars. The club doors open and people rush the stage, footsteps and bass thumping the floor. I can feel the crunch of broken glass in my jaw. Only now do fumes from the alcohol fill the air, mixed with the odor of a hundred bodies.

I don't search for Malcolm. I don't know what I'd say to him. I don't know what to think about him. Or this. Or anything. I push against people forcing their way onto the dance floor, grabbing elbows and shoulders to leverage myself out of this space. If I can leave this space, I can figure things out. If I can leave this space, it will all start to make sense.

When the cold air of outside strikes my face, I'm no closer to understanding anything but this: I must get away.

I run. Footfalls sound behind me. I think I hear my name. I don't look back. I don't slacken my pace. There's a train at the light rail station. I don't care what line or where it's going. I slip through the doors just as they're closing.

I'm without a ticket, without my partner, without a plan. I press a hand against the glass of the door and peer out in time to see Malcolm stumble to a halt, brace his hands against his knees. He looks up, mouths my name.

And then he's gone.

~

EVENTUALLY, I stagger to a seat. I dig through my bag and pull out my ticket. I clutch my talisman, although I doubt it's much of one. My ride time has expired. I scan the aisle, hoping there's no conductor on this train. A few people occupy seats in front of mine. A group of college-age kids lounge behind me, in the very back of the train.

I don't relax so much as pull in a full breath—at last. I'm on the Green Line, headed toward St. Paul. St. Paul. Where the State Fairgrounds are. I pull out my phone.

A flurry of missed calls and text messages assault me the moment I switch on the power. That number I assume is Jack's. Malcolm's number and a series of text messages, all frantic and popping up much faster than I can read them.

Katy, please...

I can explain...

It's not what you think...

That last text is a lie. I have no idea what to think, not about tonight or about him. I ignore all this and open up the map. The State Fairgrounds are on Snelling Avenue, about two miles from the Snelling

Avenue station, which is two stations up ahead. Plan in mind, I tuck the phone back into my bag. That slight movement kicks up scents from the club, the aroma heavy with beer. I reek. This might explain why no one has sat near me.

Then I catch my reflection in the window. There's something on my cheek, right where the entity touched me. I press my fingertips against the spot, and they come away chilled. I rub, but the spot remains. I can't tell what it is, but I can tell this:

Other people notice it.

At the Snelling Avenue station, I step off the train. I study the traffic, the pedestrians, but I see no sign of Malcolm. Will he follow on the next train? Double back to get his car and follow that way? My destination is a fairly obvious one. I check my phone. After that initial flurry, his messages have stopped. My first—irrational—thought is: I hope he's okay.

I give myself a shake and brace for the long trek to the fairgrounds.

I'm halfway there when the idea of a taxi makes more and more sense. Of course, now that I'm halfway there, a taxi is no longer an option. I tuck my hands under my arms to ward off the chill as best I can. My over-the-knee stockings keep slipping, reminding my legs that it is very much October and I very much live in Minnesota. My Mary Janes are more sensible than sexy, but they're not made for hiking.

I am alone, after dark, in a strange city.

I am certifiably an idiot.

Someone approaches me, an older man, stocky, but I tense. That could be muscle, not fat. He might not be fast, but he could be strong. Something predatory flickers in his eyes, but the moment his gaze lands on my cheek, it vanishes. Despite the traffic, the man steps into the gutter when he passes me. Horns blare. Even so, he gives me a wide berth.

I stop and stare after him, fingertips on the spot on my cheek. I need a mirror, I think. I need to get to the State Fairgrounds. I need ... a bodyguard?

Two sprites swirl around me. When, exactly, I picked them up, I can't say. Have they been following me since the station? The club?

"Hello, you two," I whisper into the night.

Yes, they plan to travel with me. In fact, they insist I start my trek again with a bit of nudging against my shoulder blades. So I do. With the sprites urging me on, I make it to the fairgrounds in time to slip through the gates before closing.

I'M HOLDING what might be the worst cup of coffee ever brewed. But since it's the warmest thing I've encountered in the last ten hours, I'm grateful. The sprites dip and dive in the steam rising from the coffee's surface. They shudder, and the steam breaks apart. The heat of it doesn't reach my face, but then, neither does the aroma. This makes it easier to drink.

"If you're ever in Springside," I tell the sprites, "I'll brew you some Kona blend."

They whirl around my head before shooting off into the crowd that's gathering by the exhibition hall doors. They will cause trouble today, I'm certain. But with them gone, I'm free to sip the coffee, warm my bones, and scan the area for Malcolm.

And if I see him?

I take another sip of coffee and burn my tongue.

Even though I spent the night hidden in the skeletal shadows of amusement park rides, I am not the first in line for the Military Relic Show. People glance my way before averting their gaze. I don't know if it's because I look like I've spent the night outside or if the spot on my cheek remains. I still haven't had a chance to inspect it or my face. My first stop once inside the doors will be the restroom.

When at last I confront my image in the mirror, I'm not sure what to make of it. Something blue and iridescent swirls beneath the surface of my skin. Its pattern is like that of a hurricane seen from above. The clouds of blue shift and grow thicker before thinning out. It's a slow movement. I must concentrate in order to track it. If there's a message in the pattern, I can't decipher it, although I spend several minutes with my nose grazing the mirror trying to do so.

When someone enters the restroom, I jerk back, heart thudding. Since I can't make the thing on my cheek go away, I must make do, and I must find Mr. Carlotta's Purple Heart. With caution, I ease open the door to the lobby area and scan the crowd for that gleaming ebony hair. Malcolm is tall. He should be easy to spot.

I don't see him and swallow back equal doses of relief and disappointment.

The woman who sells me a ticket for the show darts looks at my cheek. The line is growing behind me, and she counts out change one bill at a time, her gaze always lighting on my cheek. The question fills the space between us.

"It's a tattoo," I say when the silence—and the line—goes on for too long.

"Oh ... wow." She gives it an appraising once-over. "Wicked."

Yes, I think, it really is.

I walk into the exhibition hall, the enormity of it striking me all at once. Malcolm was right. It will be nearly impossible to find Mr. Carlotta's Purple Heart, but not because hundreds of vendors crowd the room. Finding a single ghost, even in a space this large, wouldn't be too difficult, especially one with such a distinctive personality.

No, it's the number of ghosts attached to all the items in this particular space. Old items with old ghosts. The air is thick with that telltale glimmer. Some people might mistake the closeness in the room for poor ventilation. I know better. Other than the time the ghosts of Springside gathered in my house, I've never felt so many spirits in one place.

Some are sullen, heavy things. Others careen frantically around their displays. Some are attached to the person working the booth. Some scare away potential customers, their presence making the air so unpleasant that people skirt the displays filled with medals and other memorabilia.

Except for me. I snag a few business cards. Maybe instead of waiting for the haunted to come to us, we should go to them. We. I freeze, the cards chafing my palm. Me and Malcolm. Is there a *we* anymore? Are we still partners? I glance over my shoulder but still see no sign of him.

I travel the aisles, all manner of apparitions surging forward as if to greet me. There is only one ghost I want. Even if I find it, I'm not sure what the next step is. I catch and release. I've never captured and returned before.

Then something familiar swirls around my face. This is a ghost I know. This ghost is not so old—at least in ghost terms—and not melancholy.

"How...?" I begin, but clamp my mouth shut. I'm already the girl with the freaky tattoo. I don't need to add *girl who talks to herself* to the list.

My grandmother swirls and nudges, swirls and nudges, leading me to Mr. Carlotta's medal. We arrive at a vendor who specializes in World War Two memorabilia, a woman who calls herself G.I. Joan. I'm pretty sure this is not her real name.

Her face lights up when I approach her booth. More than one ghost haunts her or her items—it's hard to tell with so many of them whirling in this space. But it's Mr. Carlotta's ghost that's scaring away customers. It thickens the air around the booth. Each breath is a chore. It's as if the glow from the overhead lights must fight to illuminate the items on the tables.

"How's business today?" I ask.

Joan gives me a wan smile. "You're my first. Is there something I can help you find?"

"My grandfather collects World War Two stuff," I say, "and his birthday is coming up. Do you have anything from World War Two?"

I've parked myself in front of a Pearl Harbor commemorative plate, so clearly she does. It's such a stupid thing to ask, but considering I'm in last night's skater skirt and have a swirling tattoo on my cheek, I figure I look less than erudite. Also? My credit card has a limit, one I'm dangerously close to. I can't act like I want the one item I so desperately need.

Joan pulls out several things to entice me: canteens and lighters, an equipment belt, a hat.

"What about medals?" I ask. "He likes medals."

Joan holds several in her cupped palms. None of them the Purple Heart. I want to confess that I can see all the ghosts. I want to tell her that if she sells me the Purple Heart, business will pick up. The other ghosts here are mild or apathetic—or both.

My grandmother whips around, nudging me toward the Purple Heart as if I can't see it. At last, I give in.

"What about this?" I point to Mr. Carlotta's Purple Heart. "That looks awesome."

"It's really more for the serious collector. I was hoping—"

And I don't have time. "How much?"

She rattles off a price, and my mind blanks. I keep my mouth shut, so neither *yes* nor *no* will pop out. I try to visualize my balance. Can I afford this? If G.I. Joan runs my card through her reader, will it come back declined?

Before I can respond, she says, "Well, I guess I can knock fifty off of that."

I shut my eyes, resigned to the whole exercise all over again. My mind is foggy from lack of sleep, and I've grown lazy with Malcolm as my partner. I never calculate anything in my head anymore, not with him around.

"Okay." Joan sighs as if she's about to make a great concession. "How about seventy-five off the asking price? I can't go any lower than that."

That should work. Or at least, it's worth the risk. From my bag, I pull my credit card and hand it over to her. My throat tightens, and my lungs feel as if they're taking in molasses. This last, though, is the fault of Mr. Carlotta's ghost. It has oozed its way over to me. It fills the space around my head and shoulders. Miffed, my grandmother's ghost bats against it. This thing? It doesn't care.

"Just sign here," Joan says.

I startle at her voice, not sure what she wants. Pen. Receipt. I release a sigh of my own and sign my name.

"Be careful with this," she says to me while wrapping my purchase. "It's not just a collector's item, but a significant part of someone's life. See that?" She points to a pin attached to the award. "That's an oak leaf cluster. That means he was wounded more than once."

I sway a bit, but manage a nod. "I didn't know."

"Most people don't, unless they know something about the military."

That isn't what I meant, but I don't correct her. I thank G.I. Joan, and I'm only a few feet from her booth when three customers converge, exclaiming over her display. The Purple Heart, in its case, feels heavy in my palms.

"You stay with me," I say to the air in front of me. "Both of you. We're going home."

Outside, I jostle the phone from my bag. I scroll until I find what must be Jack's number.

"It's Katy," I say when he answers.

"Good God, where the hell have you been? I've been running interference with Chief Ramsey, but he knows you haven't been home all night. He knows Malcolm hasn't been home either, and he's thinking of—"

"I have your grandfather's Purple Heart," I say.

This can't be the first time someone has silenced Jack Carlotta, but from the tense, edgy quiet that fills the line, my guess is that it doesn't happen very often.

"What?" he says at last.

"I have your grandfather's Purple Heart. I'll be standing outside the gates to the State Fairgrounds if you want to pick me up."

With that, I hang up. I'm pretty sure Jack will make the trip.

Sixty minutes later, a black BMW pulls through the gates. I am suitably impressed—that he broke the speed limit to get here. I don't say a word when I ease into the passenger seat. I only hold up a finger before he can put the car in gear, checking for my charges. Mr. Carlotta's ghost settles sullenly in the backseat. My grandmother caresses my cheek and then knocks Jack's sunglasses askew.

"Okay," I say. "Let's go home."

We sit in the Springside Long-term Care Facility parking lot. Both ghosts made the trip, and Mr. Carlotta's has inched its way from the backseat until it infiltrated the box that holds the Purple Heart. As heavy and melancholy as that feels, something clicks into place. For whatever reason, this ghost has claimed this item, and the medal wouldn't be complete without it.

"You want to come inside?" I ask.

"I was thinking about it, but you know what?" Jack shakes his head. "I don't want to steal your thunder."

I can't help it. I laugh.

He raises a hand from the steering wheel as if he's trying to silence my laughter. His grin says he isn't. "I'm serious. Besides, when I was there yesterday, I noticed my grandfather's chess set was missing a few pieces. I was going to pick up a new one, come back this afternoon and play a game with him."

This is a new side to Jack Carlotta. I kind of like it.

"Thank you for picking me up," I say.

"Thank you for finding his medal."

I lean in to kiss his cheek, just a friendly, thank-you sort of kiss. My lips have barely grazed his skin when he jerks back.

"Do I smell?" I did spend the night outside, hunkered down in State Fairgrounds debris.

Jack gives himself a shake. "Jesus, no. It's ... it's..." He reaches a hand forward, but doesn't touch my cheek.

Oh. It's that.

"I want to kiss you," he says. "I've wanted to kiss you from the second I got back into town. But I physically can't, and I can't explain why not, either."

"It's okay. It's been a long, strange sort of day—and night."

"Katy, are you okay?"

I nod. "I am." For now. "Things have been ... different since my grandmother died. Odd things have been happening. Every time I turn around, some new sort of ghost pops up, or someone comes to town. This never happened when she was alive."

"Maybe it's not your grandmother. Maybe it's this Armand guy."

I don't know what to think about that, because yes, it could be Malcolm.

"Be careful," Jack says when I reach for the door handle.

"I will."

"Promise?" He gives me that grin I remember from high school.

"Promise."

I watch him drive off, my fingertips exploring the mark on my cheek. The skin feels exposed, and the urge to pull out some lip balm and smear it across my face nearly overwhelms me. I know it won't help. So I turn and head for the facility's front doors.

I'm halfway up the walk when the manager strides through the double doors, her heels making that staccato click on the concrete. I deflate, my grip on the medal's box loosening. Mr. Carlotta's ghost senses our defeat and seems to gain five pounds. How a ghost can be so heavy, I will never know.

"Katy, Katy," she's saying, her words strung together so I barely recognize my name.

I raise the box. "I just want—"

"Please, let me go first. On behalf of everyone, staff and residents, of Springside Long-term Care, I would like to apologize."

"Apolo—?"

"Everyone was so ashamed. That whole thing with Mistress Armand, but then we heard you'd been arrested, and they insisted I call Chief Ramsey. He was here all morning, taking statements. You just missed him."

I send up a prayer of thanks.

"We gave him a description of the thieves," she continues, "and explicitly stated it wasn't you who stole from us. Katy, we're so sorry. I understand if you don't want to come back, but will you consider it?"

Stunned, I'm not sure what to say, but the burden in my hands has its own ideas. I lift the box so the manager can see it. "I have Mr. Carlotta's Purple Heart."

She clamps a hand over her mouth. Her eyes grow moist. "How...?"

"It's a very long story. Can I take it to him?"

She nods. "He might be asleep, but yes. Please. Take it to him."

Inside, residents wave to me. They are silently respectful, though, as if they know what I carry with me. When I reach Mr. Carlotta's room, I see the manager was right. He's asleep. Too many late nights of secret telephone calls. I leave the Purple Heart on the nightstand where he's sure to see it when he wakes.

In the corridor, my grandmother's ghost whirls around my head, caresses the cheek without the mark, then she shoots down the hall toward Mrs. Greeley's room.

Unburdened by ghosts, I leave the care facility.

OUTSIDE, the October air clears my head. I will walk home. I will collect all my thoughts along the way. Once there, I will take a hot shower. Then I'll be ready to face this thing on my cheek, and Malcolm, and all the questions I have about last night.

The red convertible at the end of the walk stops this line of thought. Malcolm leans against the door, his normally silky hair rumpled, dress shirt torn and stained. The knees of his trousers are embedded with grime. If he crawled through a sewer he wouldn't look any worse.

"Were you in a fight?" I ask.

"It only feels like it."

"I don't understand." I mean this in every way possible. I don't understand what he said. I don't understand what happened last night. I don't understand him.

"After I couldn't find you," he says, "I decided I'd try to find that ... thing."

"I'm guessing that didn't work."

Malcolm shakes his head, his mouth tight. His gaze locks on my cheek, and I can see the calculation in his eyes, the assessment. He takes a step forward and then another. I hold still, breath shallow in my throat. The skin on my legs puckers with goose bumps, but the cold is something I barely feel anymore.

He stops in front of me, the toes of our shoes almost brushing. He reaches a hand toward my face. My throat tightens, then my stomach. My heart pounds so hard, I'm surprised Malcolm can't hear it. His fingertips graze my cheek, a touch so light I'm not sure it's a touch at all.

Then, suddenly, Malcolm crumples to the sidewalk as if his knees have gone liquid. He clutches one hand with the other. He doesn't cry out, but the pain that etches his expression makes me wish he would. I collapse next to him, go to place a hand on his shoulder, then pull back at the last second. Will that hurt him too? I don't know, and I find I'm shaking my head like an idiot. In fact, I'm shaking all over.

"What is it?" I ask him. "Are you hurt?"

"I know better than to do something like that," Malcolm says, his words low and taut.

"What does it mean?"

"It means that thing has marked you."

Marked me. That sounds ... disturbing. "And what does that mean, exactly?"

"The thing, that entity, can find you again."

Even more disturbing. "Why would it want to find me?"

Malcolm shakes his head. Whether he knows—and won't tell me—or simply doesn't know, isn't clear.

"Why did it call you a necromancer?" I ask.

Malcolm eases from his knees to sitting. My legs are wobbly, and standing isn't something I plan to attempt just yet.

"Because I am one." He sighs. "I haven't told you the whole truth."

I cock my head to the side and give him a hard stare, because that? That is the only thing I do know at this point.

He raises a hand. "Yeah, I know. Pretty obvious, right? I'm a necromancer. I talk to the dead, or as the case may be, with ghosts."

"But ghosts don't really talk."

"Don't they? They communicate with you all the time. Besides, if you invited one inside, you'd hear plenty."

"You mean swallow ghosts, like Nigel used to? Is he a necromancer?"

"Nigel's what happens when a necromancer gets ... careless—or addicted. A true relationship between a necromancer and a ghost is symbiotic. Each partner helps the other."

Something Mistress Armand said to Malcolm echoes in my head. I've always thought he left more than simply his job when he came to Springside.

"The girl you left behind," I say. "That's what Mistress Armand meant. That's your ghost."

"That *was* my ghost," he says, "before Nigel swallowed her."

"Did she escape when we set them free?"

The crinkles around his eyes deepen, his mouth a grim line. "I don't know. Maybe. I didn't sense her, but it was kind of chaotic."

"What was it ... I mean. How...?" My words are nonsensical. How do I ask this question? Were they in a relationship? Can you date a ghost?

"How does it work?" he supplies. "What did we do?"

"Yeah. That."

"She helped me play the market. It's why I was so good. She listened in on phone calls, picked up gossip and pieces of information floating around on the floor, and brought it all back to me. Then I'd make a killing."

"That sounds like cheating."

"Or leveling the playing field. A lot of successful brokers are necromancers."

That sounds insane. I don't say this out loud, but I'm certain it shows in my expression. "What did you do in return?"

"Spent a lot of time in art museums."

"As a ghost, she could go any time she liked."

"According to her, it's not the same, not as enjoyable, not as ... sensual."

Okay, I've heard enough. Malcolm has—or had—an invisible girlfriend. My legs find their strength and I push to stand.

"Where are you going?"

"Home," I say.

"Do you want a ride?"

"No."

"Katy, I know it's strange, but give it some thought—"

"My grandmother never said anything about necromancers, ever."

"Then maybe your grandmother didn't tell you everything. They exist. I'm one. And I'm pretty sure you're one too."

"I'm a ghost hunter." I turn from him and start down the walk.

"Katy—"

"I'll see you Monday. At work."

This time, he lets me walk away without another word.

THE WALK HOME is long and cold. I pick up two sprites along the way—two that I recognize. They dart and spin about, feeling oh so full of themselves. When I pass Sadie's house, they peel off and zip to the roof and down her chimney.

My own house is dark. Only recently it started feeling like home again, but now, when I unlock the door, emptiness greets me. I think of all the things Malcolm said and all the things that my grandmother never did. I don't feel like Katy Lindstrom, ghost hunter. I'm certainly not Katy Lindstrom, necromancer.

For now, I'll go through the motions. I'll take a shower, brew a pot of Kona blend. I'll drink it slowly and study the walls. I'll pretend I know all the answers. I'll pretend last night never happened.

That will work. For now.

As long as I don't look in the mirror.

MUST LOVE GHOSTS

COFFEE AND GHOSTS: EPISODE 5

A MERE FOUR DAYS AGO, I was behind bars. So meeting Police Chief Ramsey on the front steps of the Springside Township Police Department?

Somewhat awkward.

Chief Ramsey's bulk casts a shadow across the steps. He studies the space behind me, around me, in between us. He coughs, once.

"You're not under arrest," he says. "You know that, right?"

I cock my head and stare. His gaze darts to my face and lingers there —or, more accurately, on my left cheek—before he can compose himself.

I resist the urge to touch my face.

"And you're free to leave town as well." He shrugs, as if the last forty-eight hours were a simple misunderstanding. "Seems there was a theft ring operating here. Pretty clever of them to follow you around. The Minneapolis Police have picked up their trail. We might even get some of the stuff back."

The traffic on Main Street consists of a single VW Bug, sky blue with a convertible top. From the Pancake House comes the scent of bacon wrapped in maple. I want to cross the road, leave Police Chief Ramsey behind, and order a stack of buttermilk pancakes. The fresh-squeezed orange juice is to die for. No coffee, though. They make the worst in town.

Instead, I work a few more degrees of frost into my stare. My grandmother would do this when whatever came from someone's mouth didn't match her expectations. During her lifetime, Chief Ramsey got the ice glare more than once.

"And I really appreciate you finding Mr. Carlotta's Purple Heart." His tone implies that these might be the hardest words he's ever uttered. "That was the one thing that insurance couldn't replace."

It's not much of an apology, but it's close enough.

"So ... you're free to go." He doesn't shoo with his hands, but his fingers twitch as if he wants to.

I would love nothing better than to comply, but I'm here at the police station for a reason. Before either of us can do or say anything further, a van rumbles up Main Street. The vehicle is strange, both in the sense that I've never seen it before—in a town the size of Springside, I've seen most everybody's car—and in the sense that it's ... strange. Bright yellow paint. Black lettering. Antennae sprouting like an untamed garden on the roof.

The van creeps past us, going well below the speed limit. The lettering on the side reads:

Ghost B Gone
Gregory B. Gone, proprietor

Chief Ramsey snorts and shakes his head. He doesn't believe in ghosts, although he should. He has two sprites in the booking area and a more substantial one that haunts his garden shed. We both track the van until it turns off of Main Street.

"What do you know, Katy?" he says. "Looks like you have a little competition there. Gotta love free enterprise."

He steps inside without bothering to hold the door for me. I let it shut, my gaze still on the intersection where the van disappeared. Choices, choices. Do I hop into my truck and follow it? Do I go to the office and confront my business partner, who's been lying to me, and maybe kissed me not so long ago? (Okay, he did kiss me, and I kissed back.) I peer up at the police station's façade. I have business here, too.

I step inside, since of all the things I must do, this is the most clear-cut.

Penny is working in the reception area, her hair frizzed as if she's clutched chunks of it several times in the past hour.

"Not again," she moans. "Third time this morning." Her fingers move across the computer's keyboard in the Ctrl-Alt-Del dance. She flops back in her chair, then jerks forward when her gaze lands on me.

"Katy? You don't … I mean…" She trails off, her stare more blatant than Chief Ramsey's.

She focuses on the spot on my cheek, her eyes glazing over. I've studied the iridescent blue that mars my skin in the mirror, and I swear it rotates oh so slowly. Penny's current state of hypnosis might be proof of that.

"Penny."

No response.

"Penny."

Still nothing. I slap my hand on the counter. She blinks.

"How can I help you, Katy? Did you leave something here from when … I mean, last Thursday?"

Yes, when I was incarcerated. "No, I'm good, but I need to know something else."

Penny leans forward.

"What do I need to do to get Belinda Barnes out of jail?" I Googled last night, but I'm still not certain what I might need to do in Springside —or rather, what I might need to do because of Police Chief Ramsey. "Do I pay her bail? How does it work?"

Penny's mouth hangs open. Her computer whirs. It's then I notice the source of her technical difficulties. The two sprites that haunt this place are at work—or, more accurately, play. Sprites love to annoy, startle, pull pranks. You find them in twos and threes because they also love an audience.

"Belinda?" I prompt. "Is she still here?"

Penny clamps her mouth shut and nods.

"Then what do I do? Penny, help me. Do I sign her out? Give you money? Talk to Chief Ramsey?" This last is something I'd rather not do, but I'll try anything.

She shoves from her desk. "Let me go talk to Chief."

Her chair spins as she passes by, then keeps spinning long after she's left the room.

"Nice trick," I say to the sprites. "Don't get out of hand, or I'll come back with Kona blend and some Tupperware."

The chair continues to spin. I continue to wait. All the while, I keep my palms glued to the countertop. I will not touch my cheek.

For a full five minutes, my resolve actually holds.

TEN MINUTES LATER, Penny ushers me into Chief Ramsey's office. He's a big man, and he has a big chair and desk to match. But the space we're forced to share is tiny. Morning sunlight filters through a window that's more of a vent. Dust motes dance in the sunbeam, but it's devoid of sprites. This is just as well. I'm not certain we could cram another being in here, ethereal or otherwise.

"Belinda Barnes is free to go," Chief tells me.

"Does she know that?" From what I gathered during my stay on Thursday, I'm not so sure.

He raises his hand and then tips it this way and that. Maybe yes? Maybe no? Then he uses that hand to rub the back of his neck.

"I'll be honest, I bring her in sometimes when I think she can use a shower and a decent meal, somewhere dry to sleep."

"So she really isn't under arrest."

"Drunk and disorderly. That's the charge, if anyone cares to check." Chief shakes his head. "Shame, bright girl like that, drinking her life away."

"But she *is* free to go," I say. "Right? She can come with me."

"To do what?"

"I have a job for her and a place for her to stay."

"A job." Chief shifts into full-on skeptic mode. Two words never held so much doubt.

Because what can the crazy girl offer the drunk one? I go with the truth, or at least, the piece of it Chief Ramsey might believe.

"It's been lonely since my grandmother died. My house has lots of bedrooms. I thought Belinda could stay in one." I give what I hope looks like an innocent little shrug. "Room and board in exchange for a few chores. That takes care of food and showers and a dry place to sleep."

Chief strokes his chin as if my request takes great consideration.

"And the only thing I have to drink in the house is coffee."

This gets a laugh, although he steels himself almost immediately. With a sigh, Chief Ramsey heaves himself to his feet.

"Go wait in the reception area. We'll start the paperwork and bring her out to you."

I don't release my own sigh until I've passed the front desk and landed in one of the hard, molded plastic chairs. Penny leaves her desk, and the sprites sag. Other than myself, Belinda is the only other person currently in the station who is aware of them, and I'm stealing their audience.

"Be glad I'm not driving you out to the nature preserve," I tell them.

"Oh, I don't know. That sounds nice."

Belinda's voice startles me. She's standing in the doorway to the booking and holding cell area, Chief Ramsey glowering behind her.

"I was just talking—" I begin.

"To yourself?" She nods toward the sprites. "Careful, or Chief Ramsey will start locking you up on a regular basis, too."

"Now, Belinda, I promised your father—"

"Oh, don't worry about Daddy. He's not around to haunt you. Trust me. I'd know." With that, she breezes out of the police station.

"Reckless girl," Chief mutters.

I dash out the door without a goodbye—or a thank you. No matter. Chief wouldn't hear me. No time, either. Belinda is halfway down the block before I catch up to her. At first, she won't adjust her stride. I'm not short, but Belinda is six feet tall, and most of that is leg.

"Thanks, Katy," she says, boot heels clacking on the sidewalk. "But I don't need your pity."

"Would you just stop, or at least slow down? You have no idea what you're talking about." I'm close to begging, but I'm not sure that will work with Belinda. Again, I try the truth. "I need your help."

She halts so suddenly that I shoot past her. I whirl around, afraid this is a ruse. But she's standing there, arms crossed over her chest.

"My help," she says, her tone nearly as skeptical as Chief's was. "What on earth could I ... what the hell is on your cheek?"

I deflate. I tried makeup this morning, but clearly it isn't working. "I wish I knew what it was. It ... happened on Friday night."

Belinda steps closer. "This doesn't look like the result of too much tequila and a trip to the tattoo parlor."

"It isn't."

She leans in. Since Thursday—when we shared the holding cell together—she's had a shower. Someone must have taken the overcoat she wears to the drycleaner. The khaki material hangs in smooth lines, the stains gone, or at least faded so you might not notice.

"Don't touch it," I say.

"Not going to. It's sending out a serious keep-back message."

"The last person who did got hurt," I add.

"Who was the last person to touch you, Katy?" Her provocative lilt implies volumes more than her mere words.

My heart beats volumes more than I think it should.

"That would be Malcolm." My throat is tight. I try to swallow, but it doesn't do any good. Malcolm, my business partner, the man I kissed not too long ago. Malcolm, who calls himself a necromancer. Malcolm, who is expecting me in the office about ten minutes ago.

"It's too bad no one was taking bets on that," Belinda says. "I would've made a killing."

"I don't want to talk about Malcolm," I say, hoping to steer the conversation in another direction. Except Malcolm's involved in all of it, and in ways I'm not sure I understand. "I want to hire you," I blurt out, certain this will do the trick.

"What?"

"I want to hire you."

"To do what? I have no skills beyond scooping ice cream."

"All I can do is make coffee."

Belinda snorts a laugh. "You can do a lot more. You didn't see Chief Ramsey go after Mr. Carlotta's Purple Heart, did you?"

"You heard about that?" I only arrived back on Saturday afternoon. But Springside Township is small, and word gets around.

"Penny." Belinda holds up her hand as if it's a talking puppet. "And the sprites. You'd be surprised how much I hear."

"Actually, I wouldn't. Not anymore. It's one of the reasons I need your help." I nod toward the Pancake House. "I barely ate yesterday, and I'm starving. Can we talk over breakfast?"

Maybe it's the maple syrup drenching the air, but she wavers. Hardly anyone turns down breakfast at Springside Pancake House. Belinda doesn't nod. She doesn't say a word. Instead, she strikes out across Main Street, cutting in front of the No Jaywalking sign.

I run to catch up.

ONCE UPON A TIME, I thought I knew everything there was to know about ghost hunting. You don't need high-tech gadgets or sensors or a (usually faked) connection to the other side. You don't need to wait for dark. What you need is a really good cup of coffee.

It might sound immodest, but I make a great cup of coffee. This, however, is the only thing I can do. As recession-proof skills go, it's a mediocre one. When she died, my grandmother left behind the family business. She left me her house. What I'm finding out now is that she left a lot of unanswered questions as well.

I think Belinda can answer some of those.

I wait until we've plowed through a first round of silver-dollar-size buttermilk pancakes. They cook them all day long and will bring you as many as you can eat.

"This beats the burnt toast Penny made me this morning." Belinda raises her glass of orange juice to mine. "Thank you," she adds. "That should've been my answer before. Thank you."

"I do need your help, but I don't know if you want to talk about it." When she doesn't respond, I say, "Ghosts. I know they've always harassed you."

Belinda sets down her glass. She's always been so golden—well-to-do, adoring parents, hair both naturally wavy and blonde. Add in academic success in high school, all the extracurriculars, and all the awards—prom queen, homecoming queen, most likely to succeed. It could make you crazy with jealousy, if you let it. Or if you could see what I do—and did see all through our school years.

Something about her attracts the nastiest ghosts around. Sprites are playful. The ghost that haunts Mr. Carlotta's Purple Heart is melancholy to the point of thickening the air. The ghosts that find Belinda are cruel, twisted things that resent not so much their afterlife but the life they missed out on. So they like to make hers as miserable as possible.

They can be difficult to catch, too. I've scalded myself more than once going after them. In high school, before big tests, I'd pack a thermos of coffee. During the four years at Springside High, I managed to splatter Kona blend over the tile of every single girls' bathroom in the building. The last of Belinda's ghosts I captured, in the rehab center, I drove out a good sixty miles before setting it free.

"You might not want to answer this," I say now, picking my way through the right words. "But can you hear them ... talk?"

Before my grandmother died, I would've said, with full conviction, that ghosts don't talk. They don't send messages from beyond the grave. They're not looking to unburden themselves so they can cross over into the light. Now? At least the talking part?

"I ask because I'm starting to think there's a lot I don't know." I cut a pancake into quarters, dip it in syrup, but don't bring it to my mouth. "And I'm starting to think I can hear ... suggestions?" It's more of a question than a statement.

Belinda nods. "It's like that. But when one of them latches on, it's like having your worst enemy in your head, criticizing everything you do. Only without words. Feelings, maybe? The meaning is there, even if the actual words aren't." She shakes her head as if to clear it of ghosts and words. "It's hard to explain."

"I think I know what you mean."

"And if you drink? You can blot them out for a while." She presses her fingertips against her temples. "At least until the alcohol wears off."

"Then it's worse."

She nods, once.

"Only now," I say, "I'm starting to hear them. I don't understand why."

"Oh, well, that's simple. Because your grandmother never wanted you to hear them."

Never ... what? I gape, and I must look hungry, because the waitress plops down another plate of pancakes in front of me. By rote, I spread butter, all the while searching for words.

"How do you know?" I ask finally.

Belinda shrugs. "She told me once, when she was trying to teach me, I don't know, self-defense. The whole coffee trick you do. Even when she made the coffee, I still couldn't trap them. She told me that a lot of it was up here." Belinda taps her head. "If she told you that you couldn't hear the ghosts, then you simply wouldn't. It would make you a better ghost hunter in the long run. More focused. Less distracted by their chatter." She pushes her hair away from her face. "God, they love to chatter."

I consider this. My grandmother taught me everything I know about ghost hunting. But lately, I believe she didn't teach me everything she knew. Each day, the gap grows a little wider. Each day, I worry I may miss something crucial, something I should know.

"I'd like to hire you," I say.

"Katy, I can't take your money—"

"Place to stay? Room and board? I live in a really big house with a lot of bedrooms. No ghosts. I almost wish there were. It would liven up the place."

Belinda laughs, and I decide not to mention the time when nearly all of Springside's ghosts invaded the old Victorian. It was harmless. Mostly.

"I'm lonely," I admit.

Belinda gives me a wan smile. "Me too."

"So? What do you have to lose? If we end up hating each other, you can move out. Deal?" I extend my hand across the table.

My fingertips are sticky with syrup. So are hers.

"On one condition," she says, scooting from the booth. "We stop at the drugstore first."

As a safety measure, I brew a pot of my very best coffee, a blend I make from a select group of beans. The aroma fills the kitchen, the steam of it warming every part of my face with one exception—the spot on my cheek.

Belinda waves a makeup brush in front of her eyes. "If I stare at it too long, it's like I forget where I am." She takes a breath and anchors me to a chair, her palm on my head so she can tip my face upward.

"I don't think you should touch it," I say.

"Why do you think we went to the drugstore?" She points the makeup brush at some cream foundation and a makeup sponge. "Tools of my trade. I don't actually need to touch your skin."

"Just be careful."

Belinda brushes and dabs, bottom lip caught between her teeth. The spot on my left cheek feels unreal and waxy. I hope it's not spreading. I don't want a blue face. I don't want to be unreal and waxy. At last she sits back as if the whole process has exhausted her.

"It's better. Here." She opens a compact and turns the mirror toward me. "Take a look."

Better. Not gone.

"I can still see it swirl," I say.

"Yeah. That's freaky."

"It's like a tropical storm has invaded my face."

"How did you get it, anyway? Thursday you were looking fine and had two hot guys fighting over you."

"First, no one is fighting over me."

Belinda snorts.

"Second, it's a long story. It wasn't a ghost, but it's a ghost-like ... thing. An entity, maybe? I think I walked into a trap." Or was led there. That the entity was lurking at the very club Malcolm and I ended up at seems less coincidental than I'd like to admit.

"I'm sorry," she says.

"It's not your fault."

"No." She shakes her head, and then her whole body shakes, like she's fighting a chill. "It's just when one of those ... things finds you, they have a hard time letting go. So, I understand, and I'm sorry it happened to you."

"That's why I'm brewing up some coffee." I try for bright and cheery. I pour the fresh brew into a thermal carafe. "This will keep it hot all day long. If you get an uninvited visitor, just uncap it and then run next door and call from Sadie's. She has sprites, but they won't bother you."

Belinda wafts some of the aroma toward her face. Her eyes close, and she sighs. "If I don't end up drinking it all first."

I divide the remaining coffee between a second carafe and a half a dozen thermoses. "That's what this is for. Plus, I need some for work."

She raises an eyebrow. How she makes that single gesture imply volumes, I'll never know.

"Malcolm is my business partner," I say. "Nothing more."

"Yeah, well, if he were my business partner, I'd work overtime."

I decide that doesn't need a response. I tighten the lid on my thermos and leave the house.

For a long time, I merely stand in front of our office, my eyes tracing the gold leaf lettering on the front window.

K&M Ghost Eradication Specialists

I was so thrilled when Malcolm unveiled that finishing touch. When my grandmother was alive, we always worked out of the house. But then, I'd been working since I was five. Something about that gold leaf makes all of this feel real.

Inside, everything is how I left it on Thursday, like nothing has changed. We have a reception desk but not enough money to pay a receptionist. We work mostly in the conference room. That's where Malcolm's brother, Nigel, keeps his computer. He's building us a ghost database, making a website, and can probably do other computer-related things I haven't even thought of yet.

The conference room is where I find both brothers. Something sparks in Malcolm's gaze when I enter the room. Relief? Hope? Or something I can't read?

"Is it…" Malcolm squints. "Is it fading?"

"Makeup. It was too distracting. It kept hypnotizing people."

He swears.

Nigel glances up from the computer screen. "Oh, Jesus, Katy, I'm sorry. Something like that shouldn't happen to you."

The spot on my cheek is not Nigel's fault. It might, however, be his brother's fault. But Nigel knows ghosts; he used to be addicted to swallowing them. And for a few minutes, he even had the entity in question inside him. He might be able to help, or at least have some information I can work with.

"Then did it mark you in a way, when it was inside you?" I ask.

"I didn't think so, not at first. But there are memories that are just out of my reach, and every once in a while, an inappropriate impulse." Nigel pulls his fingers through the shock of white hair on his head. "That's why I had you clear Sadie's house before dinner. It kept suggesting that a sprite side dish would be totally harmless."

So we're both marked. Through all this, Malcolm sits to one side, arms braced on his thighs, hands clasped. His gaze never leaves the floor. I won't condemn him, not yet. Besides, we may have other problems.

"Have either of you heard of Ghost B Gone or Gregory B. Gone?"

"Oh, sure," Nigel says. "He has a web show. I watch it all the time."

Really? A web show? "What does he do?"

"Ghost evictions, as he calls them. Streams them live over the net."

I pull a thermos of coffee from my bag. "So I don't need to bribe you with this to do a little research for us?"

Nigel grins. "You can always bribe me with coffee. What do you want to know?"

"What he's up to. He pulled into town this morning. I saw his van on Main Street."

"Seriously?" Nigel rubs his hands together and pulls his chair closer to his computer.

Within moments, we land on Ghost B Gone's YouTube page. He scrolls through videos and comments, and both seem to go on forever. One video starts to play, and the tinny, squeaking music makes me wince.

"Theme song," Nigel says.

"And you watch this?" Malcolm asks, stealing my question.

"Well, yeah. It's unintentionally hilarious. He doesn't actually catch anything. He just thinks he does because the sprites making mischief get bored."

"You can't see the sprites, can you?" I ask. Ghosts don't show up in photographs, digital or otherwise—or so I've always believed.

"No, you can't, but if you know the telltale signs, it's pretty obvious." Nigel leans forward now. "Oh, look at this."

On the screen is an announcement for the next episode.

Springside Township's Haunted Shame.
One family's dream became their nightmare.
On Halloween, Gregory and the Ghost B Gone team will rid this dream home
of its uninvited and malicious visitors. Live streaming! 8 p.m. CST/9 p.m. EST

The image of a house replaces the fading words. The Victorian is new construction. I recognize the forest green paint and white trim.

Malcolm turns toward me and gives his head a shake. "This isn't one of our clients."

"That's because it isn't really haunted," I say. "Well, it is, but that's not why it's empty. The builders went bankrupt, the buyers backed out of the deal, and now I think the bank owns it. It just sits there. Kids sneak inside, and it's attracted a trio of sprites who like to scare them. Halloween is their busy season."

"So no one's dream has been denied?" Nigel says.

I roll my eyes. "Hardly."

Malcolm looks at me. Despite everything that's happened, something zings inside me. A connection, the thought we both have at the same time. Like he's still my partner.

"Want to investigate?" he says.

"You read my mind."

"Katy, we should talk."

Well, yes, we should, but it would only be one of those messy, emotional talks no one likes to have. I'm overflowing with feelings and hollow at the same time. But I can walk and think and investigate. I don't want to spoil any of that. Because that? That feels right.

Having Malcolm at my side still feels right. He's all Ivory soap and nutmeg, with a hint of the saffron that he uses in his tea. It should be a crime for a man to smell this good.

"We should take my truck," I say, "in case we need supplies."

I keep an emergency stash in my truck—coffee, sugar, percolator, a little camp stove for brewing. The only thing I don't have is half and half. Some ghosts insist on it; trust me, you don't want to see what they do when they're presented with the powdered stuff. Catching a ghost that tough requires a more deliberate approach.

"Can we talk about what happened?" Malcolm follows me to the alley behind our building, where I park my truck.

The thing is old and unsightly, and the mayor has asked that I not park it on Main Street. Malcolm's cherry red convertible? That gets its own designated parking spot between our storefront and the deli.

I climb into the driver's side, put the key into the ignition, but don't turn it. I wait until Malcolm's seatbelt clicks.

"Are we still partners?" I stare straight ahead, as if I'm speaking to the windshield.

"Of course we are."

I shift slightly in my seat. He does the same.

"Then can you tell me the truth, from the start? Because I don't think I can be your partner if I don't know that."

So maybe I do want the messy, emotional chat. I'm certain I won't like what I hear. I also know I can't physically turn the key and drive to investigate Ghost B Gone with all these doubts in my head.

"I owe you that." His voice is quiet, contemplative. "I owe you a lot of things. And it's not so much that I lied. Well, not exactly. I just didn't tell you the whole truth."

"And what is the whole truth?"

"First? You saved me. I really did lose my job. Part of it was Nigel, but no one minded that, not when I was the top broker quarter after quarter. They threw bonuses at me, trips to Cancun. As long as Selena—"

"Wait. Is Selena your ghost?"

He nods.

Of course. Malcolm's ghostly girlfriend would have a glamorous name. I shake my head and try to shake off the irrational jealousy.

"As long as she was around," he continues, "things were fine. But when Nigel swallowed her, there went my streak." He shrugs, palms skyward. "I was still a good broker, but I wasn't spectacular—and people noticed. And they noticed enough that when things got tight and Nigel got out of hand, they fired me."

I'm torn between telling him I'm sorry and berating him for cheating at investing in the first place. But then, is it insider trading if your source isn't alive?

"I didn't come to Springside with a plan, but I did come here on purpose."

This gets my attention. I scoot against the slippery vinyl seat as if moving a few inches closer guarantees I won't miss a word.

"Your grandmother has—had—a reputation beyond Springside. I knew she didn't practice necromancy, but she was powerful. She could've been one of the best." He sighs. "I was hoping for some advice."

"But you found me instead."

The grin he gives me is a slow, seductive thing. "I'm not disappointed by that."

For three full seconds, my head buzzes. I blow out a breath and steel myself.

"I was at a crossroads. Catching ghosts with you was more fun than working at the brokerage, even if it didn't pay nearly as well. And you..." He breaks off, rubs the palm of one hand with the thumb of the other. "I'd never met a necromancer as strong as you are."

"I'm not a necromancer," I say.

"But you could be. Don't you see it, Katy? Part of the reason Spring-side is so haunted is you. Ghosts like you. You have an affinity for them. My grandfather would've called you a natural—"

"Or maybe a supernatural?"

Malcolm pauses, then throws his head back and laughs. Part of me melts, just a little. Part of me is thrilled I can still make him laugh like that.

"Yes," he says, still chuckling. "That. I've never seen anything like you, and I can't understand why you've never even heard of necromancy before now."

Well, I've heard of it, but that's not what Malcolm means. But ever since he zoomed into town in his cherry red convertible, I've discovered there are many things about ghosts and ghost hunting I never knew.

"I don't understand why your grandmother never told you, at least."

The sad thing is, I don't either.

"Wait." He sits up straight and strains against the seatbelt. "What about your parents?"

"They died not long after I was born. I don't remember them."

"How did they die?"

I bite my lip. "Car accident."

"Huh. That's a leading cause of death for necromancers."

"It is?" I shake my head because this? This is starting to get weird.

"When there's an imbalance, or when things go wrong—like with Nigel's addiction—accidents happen. If we hadn't intervened, at some point the ghosts would have decided to free themselves. Or sometimes, if a necromancer takes on a ghost that's too strong ..." He trails off. "Car accidents are good for that."

"So the ... host." Is that what you call it? I'm not sure, but since Malcolm doesn't contradict me, I continue. "Has to die in those cases?"

"I'm afraid so." His expression turns tender. He reaches out to touch my cheek—the right one. "One more reason I'm grateful to you."

I shiver, although the air inside the cab is warm. Our conversation has fogged the glass. If anyone walks by, they'll think we're doing something other than talking in here. For a moment, I ponder the possibility of my parents being necromancers. I don't remember them at all. Photographs of them evoke no memories, not even manufactured ones. My few questions always made my grandmother so sad that I eventually stopped asking.

"What about Friday, at the club?" I say now. This notion has been eating at me for the past two days. Did we walk into a trap or did Malcolm lead me there?

"I didn't know that thing, that entity, whatever it is, would be there. It was a coincidence."

"It's an awfully big coincidence."

"Maybe, but you know, ghosts gossip just as much as people do. Plus, I took you to a haunted dance club, a spot where a lot of necromancers hang out. If anything, it happened because I'm really predictable."

"You are?" If anything, Malcolm leaves me off balance.

"Sure. A trip to my alma mater? I was showing you around. Frat house, favorite restaurant, favorite club. That's Psych 101."

"Then why did that thing thank you for playing a part?"

"Because the part I was playing was simply a guy trying to impress a girl."

This should not please me as much as it does. Malcolm has lied. For all I know, Malcolm may still be lying. I will be cautious. I will clamp my lips together so no hint of a smile shows.

"If I'd been thinking—really thinking—I would've seen the theft of Mr. Carlotta's Purple Heart for what it was: bait for a trap." He sighs again, adding to the fog on the windshield. "Do you really care about anyone's flat screen TV?"

"I don't even own a TV."

"There you go. But you care about Mr. Carlotta. So this entity manipulates a couple of weak-minded individuals to steal a few things, including the Purple Heart, and I unwittingly do the rest. And I'm sorry, Katy, really, really sorry." He rubs his jaw as if it aches. "And I'm scared of what this means." He points to the spot on my left cheek.

"You said it meant that thing can find me."

"It does."

"Does it..." I begin, then pause. I'm so tired of calling it *thing* or *entity*. "Does it even have a name?"

"I'm sure it does. I was trying to find out more yesterday. Called in a few favors, talked to a few old friends, that sort of thing. Made me wish my grandfather were still alive. He would know what to do."

"So you don't know its name."

"You don't *want* to know its name. To speak the name out loud is to invoke the entity."

"You mean, poof? There it is in front of you?"

"That's exactly what I mean, and only a well-prepared necromancer would ever do that."

"So even if someone knows what it's called, they won't tell you."

"Exactly."

"Could you write it down?" I venture.

Malcolm laughs, not a full-throated one, but the sound of it fills the cab with warmth.

"You never give up, do you?" he says.

I shake my head.

"Katy, I don't want you trying anything. I'm worried what this might mean for you. Remember at the mausoleum, when I kept getting that vendetta vibe?"

I nod.

"I think it means you."

"But ... I haven't done anything to this entity."

"What about your grandmother?"

A week ago, I would've declared *of course not*. Now? Now I have to consider that I may have never fully known the woman who raised me and taught me all about ghosts.

"This thing is ancient," Malcolm says. "Time means little to it. So, if it feels like it, it might take its revenge on you. Or wait and take it on your granddaughter. But I think it finds you ... intriguing."

"So you're thinking sooner rather than later, but sooner for it could be when I'm sixty. Or it could be tomorrow."

He raises a hand and lets it drop onto his lap, defeated.

"Well, then," I say, and turn the key in the ignition. "We'd better get going and investigate Ghost B Gone while we still have time."

THE DOORS to the green and white Victorian are flung wide open. A tech crew is tramping up and down the porch stairs, lugging in all sorts of electronic equipment. Two people are wrestling a generator toward the side of the house. Out front, a card table holds sodas and sandwiches. Static buzzes in the air, and the tiny hairs on the back of my neck prick up, but it's not from fear or even the sensation of someone watching us.

No, just the cool kiss of a sprite before it veers off through the open doorway.

"See?" Malcolm whispers. "You brought them another ghost. They should put you on the payroll."

"Hardly. This?" I gesture toward all the activity. "Is like setting a cake in front of toddlers and asking them not to touch it. I'm sure the sprites are overjoyed. All this attention? On Halloween? The most they usually get is a few screeching kids."

Together, we take a few steps up the walk. When no one stops us, we take a few more. At last we cross the threshold without anyone noticing. Inside, we pick our way through cables and electrical cords. The buzz of static is more insistent here. Someone is feeding lines from the generator through an open window, and the breeze that sneaks in makes the space feel more abandoned, despite the crowd.

"Welcome!" someone booms out. "Welcome, friends!"

A man approaches, hand extended. His face, behind round lens glasses, beams. At sixty, he'll make a jolly mall Santa Claus. Now, at about thirty, he's wiry and bearded and quite possibly the true source of all this buzzing static.

He pumps Malcolm's hand and then mine. "Good to meet you! Good to meet you! I'm Gregory B. Gone, and this is my show."

"I'm Katy Lindstrom—"

"The ghost catcher! Of course." He turns toward Malcolm. "And you must be Malcolm Armand. So good to have the local talent on hand."

Local talent?

"Really lends an air of authenticity to the show. My viewers love that. Did you hear? I just broke one million."

I glance at Malcolm. Because really? I have no idea how to respond to such a statement.

"Any luck with sponsors yet?" Malcolm asks.

Gregory lights up. Yes, leave it to Malcolm to know what to say.

"Not yet, but I have a line on a couple. But then, you know how tough that is."

Gregory tugs Malcolm away in a move so slick I barely notice. That's fine with me. I head off on my own to peer beneath tables, thump on walls, and trace cables. I can't quite tell if this is nothing more than elaborate stagecraft or if Gregory B. Gone truly believes in all of this.

At my side, the thermoses of coffee I made this morning slosh in the canvas bag we use as a field kit. I push open a swinging door and land in the kitchen. The space is empty. No chairs. No table. I ease onto the island, a bare and icy marble slab, the rack above it like a black skeleton. It's just a little bit creepy sitting beneath it, like the metal arms will reach out and grab me.

I decide I need company, so I open a thermos, pour a small cup, and then hold it out like an offering.

"Yeah, I know it came from a thermos," I say to the air, "but I just brewed it this morning and it's some of my best."

The metal cup warms my fingers. The aroma flows throughout the kitchen as if this space has been longing for the scent of food. I study the steam rising from the coffee's surface. Within a minute, a glimmer appears. That didn't take long.

"Thirsty?" I ask.

The steam wavers, and the sprite basks in the heat and flavor, clearly enjoying itself.

"I'm not sure I know you."

Some ghosts feel familiar. My neighbor Sadie's sprites are like playful children or puppies. Mr. Carlotta's ghost is heavy and sad, and of all the ghosts I've encountered in Springside, it must be the oldest. My grandmother, whom I now realize I haven't sensed in the past two days, is vibrant, feisty, and very much like she was in her life.

This one, here in the steam? I think it's new. Or maybe we simply haven't crossed paths before.

I've just topped off the cup when the swinging door flies open. Gregory B. Gone fills the space with his booming words.

"So here's where you're hiding."

"I'm not hiding." I hold the cup so the steam—along with the ghost—is in his line of sight.

He eyes the coffee. "Doing a little reconnaissance? I think it's going to take more than that to draw these entities from their hiding places, and I'm not sure you should attempt it on your own. They have an evil reputation. But then, living here, you would know that."

I open my mouth to contradict him, but Malcolm stands at the threshold, a finger pressed to his lips. So I bite down on my words.

"Would you like some coffee?" I say instead. "For you and your crew?

It's perfect drinking temperature, so I won't be able to use it to catch anything. Hate to see it go to waste."

I'm certain my offer doesn't carry past the kitchen door, but it's like I've broadcast it through the entire space. The kitchen fills with people. Someone brings in the sandwiches. Someone else passes around Styrofoam cups. I pour out every last drop that I have in the thermoses. People tap cups, make toasts, and drink.

The sprite leaves in a huff, smacking Malcolm on the back of the head on its way out.

"Like it's my fault," he whispers when he reaches my side.

"Let me introduce you to a few of our regulars," Gregory says. "Nick, our tech support. Rajeev keeps us electrified. And of course, we couldn't make contact at all without our medium, Terese."

The two men nod, more interested in coffee than ghosts. Terese, ethereal, with flowing white hair and dusky skin, kisses first Malcolm and then me on both cheeks.

"And while you won't see much of his face, we have Tim, who runs the cameras," Gregory says.

I whirl around and confront the lens of a video camera, its eye trained on me.

"Are you filming this now?" I ask.

Gregory bursts out laughing. "Of course we are. And we'll be streaming live tonight for Halloween, when we'll finally rid this place of its ghosts. We'd love to have your help."

"Halloween is our busy night," I say.

"Trust me, all the action will be here. So, what do you say?" Gregory urges both Malcolm and me closer, placing a hand on each of our shoulders. "Can I count on K&M Ghost Eradication Specialists?"

I'm paralyzed by the lens trained on my face, but Malcolm's voice comes sure and smooth.

"Of course. We'll be here tonight."

Gregory does something—I can't say what, exactly—but Tim relaxes his hand and the camera sags in his grip.

"Perfect," Gregory says. "Splice together a promo. Be sure to include Katy saying 'Are you filming this now?' It's adorable. And plenty of Malcolm for the female demographic. In fact, fire up some of our sock puppets and have them start talking about the haunted hottie. That'll up the views."

He squeezes our shoulders before letting go and then claps his hands together. "Tonight's the night, people. Tonight's the night Ghost B Gone makes a true name for itself. No more scraps. No more begging. Everyone will come to us from now on."

He shoos them from the kitchen and, as quickly as they arrived, they vanish, leaving behind stains on the marble countertop, a scattering of Styrofoam cups, and the scent of stale coffee and sweat.

"Is he going to put me on the internet?" I ask, although I'm pretty sure I know the answer.

Malcolm frowns. "I think he already has."

"I don't like this," I say. "I don't like that I can't figure out whether it's stagecraft or if he believes in what he's doing."

"Or if it's a little bit of both."

"And what did you two talk about that I wasn't privileged enough to hear?"

Malcolm snorts. "He talked. Tim trailed us with his camera. I'm beginning to think I'm along just as eye candy."

"The haunted hottie?"

His lip curls as if I've handed him a cold cup of coffee. He looks as appalled as I feel.

"Well, you do dress nicely," I say. Malcolm does, in crisp oxford shirts and pressed trousers, all leftovers from his days as a broker for an investment firm in Minneapolis. "And you are handsome. You're probably photogenic, too."

"What did you call me?"

A flush invades my cheeks. Or more accurately, my right one. The spot on my left is stubborn and cold and waxy. Something about that pings in the back of my mind, but with Malcolm staring at me, one eyebrow slightly raised, I can't grasp what that might be.

"Photogenic," I say.

"No. The other."

"Handsome." My voice is maybe more breathy than it should be.

"Do you think that?"

"Maybe," I say, giving my shoulders a shrug. "Or maybe it's just a simple fact."

His lip doesn't curl at this, at least. For a long moment, he simply scrutinizes me. Then he laughs.

"So, partner," Malcolm says, the humor still in his voice. "What do you think we should do tonight?"

I survey the kitchen. True, the electricity is out, and I doubt Gregory B. Gone will spare any from his generator. Still, there's plenty of room for the camp stove. Through the window, I notice cloud cover has rolled in. The dark, menacing sky might just cancel Halloween.

"We could set up in here," I say. "Halloween is one of the few nights Sadie's sprites don't bother her. We might even find them here."

"So you don't think there's anything here but sprites?"

"I just saw the one. You?"

Malcolm shakes his head. "This place doesn't even feel haunted, just empty."

"Like it should have a family in it, some life," I add.

He opens his mouth to speak, but no words come out. He takes a slow turn around the kitchen. "Does this place feel *too* empty to you?"

"Too empty, like what?"

"The mausoleum?"

Before I can inhale a deep breath, gauge whether the air here feels like that of the mausoleum with all its stale, lifeless stillness, thunder rumbles the house with so much force, the windows rattle. The rack above our heads creaks and sways. A fine sprinkling of plaster from the ceiling coats the marble slab. Malcolm grabs my hand and jerks us both away.

"Why don't we go get ready for tonight?" he says.

"Are you sure?" I say. "This place could fall down around everybody's ears."

"If we're here, with supplies, we can stop things. If the sprites get out of hand, we'll just fire up the camp stove."

I nod. That makes the most sense. Once the ghostly word gets out that something is happening here, it will draw the sprites. So many in one spot can be a problem. They aren't the awful, evil things of movies and books, but so many together results in chaos.

"All right," I say. "Let's go get ready."

We race through the rain to my truck. By the time I fling myself into the cab, my hair is slicked to my scalp. Drops slither down my spine. Malcolm's shirt is so soaked, it's gone from light blue to dark.

"You might want to change before tonight," I say.

He squeezes water from a sleeve. "I think you might be right."

I drop him at his apartment, and we agree to meet back at the Victorian half an hour before Ghost B Gone starts streaming their show. But as I turn the truck around and drive back the way I came—a way that takes me by the house again—I wonder if I'm missing something about tonight.

I let the engine idle, truck blocking the road, but this is a residential street that never sees much traffic. I blink, certain what I see is my imagination—or possibly part of Gregory's stagecraft. The clouds hang lower over the place, the rain pelts harder, the air is darker, somehow.

Terese emerges from the house, hair whipping in the wind, and the strands look alive, like snakes or tentacles. I think that this, too, must be part of Gregory's stagecraft. Her gaze lingers on me before she offers a smile.

I blink again. In that moment, I lose sight of her. She is no longer on the front porch, hair taking on a life of its own. She is not in the yard. I did not see her step back inside. She is not here.

She is nowhere.

I LEAVE Belinda with a second pot of coffee and some sandwiches from the deli.

"I'm a terrible hostess," I tell her. "Leaving you like this."

"Are you kidding?" She already has the sandwiches cut into quarters, a cup of coffee poured, and my laptop fired up on the kitchen table. "This." She points a sandwich quarter at the screen. "Is going to be awesome."

On the screen is Ghost B Gone's YouTube channel. And on their channel, right now? The promo for tonight's show. Belinda has paused the video so I'm frozen in time, my mouth open to say: *Are you filming this now?*

I sigh. She laughs, then sobers.

"Be careful, tonight, Katy," she says. "I'm not sure I'd trust this Gregory guy."

"He's a lot of hot air and words."

"Yeah, and if he manages to say the wrong ones? Who knows what he'll conjure up?"

"It's just sprites," I say. "Malcolm and I checked out the place this morning. Low level, mischievous sort of haunting."

Belinda is silent.

"You don't think there could be anything more, do you?" I ask.

She shakes her head. "It's just that your grandmother always told me not to go around looking for ghosts, or even asking if any were around. It draws them out."

This is true. When we called out the meaner ones, we always did so with a cup of coffee and some Tupperware at the ready.

"They crave attention," I say.

"Then again, this guy is so obnoxious, he's lucky it's Halloween. Otherwise, he might not even get any sprite action."

"I was thinking of sneaking through the house and catching them all beforehand."

"Oh, wouldn't that ruin his day."

She clicks play on the video. I leave before I can hear myself utter those inane words one more time.

THE VICTORIAN IS ablaze with light when I pull up in my truck. Other vehicles crowd both sides of the street, so I have to park two blocks down and dodge raindrops on my way to the house. Someone on the porch is handing out candy to children and flyers to the adults. Someone calls my name, but when I turn around, I can't see who it might be.

I stand in the rain for a heartbeat, considering whether I really did hear my name or not. Too many children squeal and cry out, too many adults scold. I can barely hear my thoughts. Pink cotton candy dresses and sparkly tiaras compete with black capes and white fluttering sheets. My heart stops at this last.

A child's idea of a ghost.

Oh, there are so many tonight. All children, I tell myself. Just costumes, from the store. No bed sheets. No bridal veils.

No entity. Not here in Springside, and not here in this modern replica of a Victorian mansion. The rain splatters harder and chases me inside.

Gregory's tech crew crowds the front part of the house. I push past the flow of people and duck into the kitchen. There, I find Malcolm. I exhale. I didn't realize I'd swallowed a good dose of anxiety along with dinner.

"Hey," he says. "You okay?"

I nod. "It's just crazy out there."

"Yeah, I'm not sure the sprites wanted that much attention. I can't seem to tempt any of them out."

His samovar is throwing aromatic steam into the air. I catch the hint of saffron and other exotic spices. That alone should be enough to lure a sprite. It certainly works on me.

"Is there enough that I can have a cup?" I ask.

"For you? Anything."

He pours. I sip. The warmth spreads through me, melting away the last bit of my unease. Then I start in on my own brew.

"I'm beginning to think that if there's going to be a show at all," he says, "it'll be up to us to bring the sprites. I mean, really. Do you sense anything? You're better at that than I am."

Maybe, but not by much. After I measure the coffee and set the percolator to brew, I take a slow walk around the kitchen.

"I called out that sprite earlier today, but I'm not really getting anything. You'd think with all of that—" I wave toward the front of the house. "They'd be ecstatic. Kids, grownups, everyone shrieking at their antics."

The kitchen door flies open, and Gregory sticks his head in.

"Hey, you two, the show's out here," he says. "Don't want to start without you."

"We're just getting some supplies ready," Malcolm says.

"What did I tell you? Coffee won't catch this thing."

"It's for the crew," I pipe up. "In case it's a late night."

"How sweet." He trains a dazzling grin on me. "Come on. The viewers will be disappointed if you're not there when we start streaming. The haunted hottie already has a fan club."

Malcolm waits until Gregory vanishes. Then he lets out a groan. I can't help it. I giggle.

"Come on, partner." I hold out my hand. "We wouldn't want to disappoint your fan club."

He contemplates my hand, but the expression on his face is odd, like he's uncertain, but not about me. More like, he's uncertain about himself. But he takes my hand, his skin warm like always, and we push through the kitchen door and into the main part of the house.

IN A MATTER OF HOURS, the Ghost B Gone crew has transformed the living room from airy and modern to cramped and closed. The space feels as though it has aged. Heavy drapes hide the big bay windows. The fireplace mantelpiece is loaded with ornately framed photographs of unsmiling ancestors. The red in the rolled-out Persian carpet looks like blood. The muted lighting gives the space a dank feel.

It looks like a child's idea of a haunted house.

"Do you think he supplies his own ghosts, too?" I whisper to Malcolm.

He nods toward Terese, whom Gregory is leading center stage—for lack of a better term.

"Ladies and gentlemen!" he booms. "Welcome! Tonight Ghost B Gone will confront its toughest foe yet, but confront it we will. And we will drive this malicious spirit from this space and reclaim it for the family dream home it should be."

Terese stands beneath the lights. They cast a blue tint on her hair. The strands flow and undulate, and I glance around for a wind machine or even a fan, but I don't see any. Stagecraft, I think. He's nothing but stagecraft. Still, that doesn't explain why the floorboards rumble beneath our feet.

"Ah," Gregory says, his stage whisper echoing through the space. "As everyone knows, Mistress Terese does not speak until she's made contact. She saves her strength in order to communicate with those beyond our realm."

Terese shoots her arms into the air, a look of ecstasy on her face.

"Touchdown?" Malcolm whispers in my ear.

I stifle a laugh and nudge him. He squeezes my hand.

The chandelier above Terese's head rattles, the crystals clinking against each other. Plaster clouds the air and coats Terese's skin and hair, the red robe she's wearing fading beneath the dust.

"Terese," Gregory says, voice low and urgent. "Have you made contact?"

She looks as if she's about to speak, and her expression is that of an actress uttering well-rehearsed lines. So this is a play, I think, with some well-managed stagecraft, and we've all been fooled.

But Terese's words never come. Instead, her eyes grow wide with shock. She stares straight at the camera. Then she collapses to the floor, robes billowing around her.

"Terese!" Gregory throws himself at her. He kneels at her side, patting her hand, checking her pulse. "Get our EMT," he calls out.

Behind us, the crew chatters. A woman pushes through the crowd and shoves Gregory out of her way.

"She's unconscious," the woman says.

Gregory gives her a *no kidding* sort of look, then schools his face for the camera. "Ladies and gentlemen, it appears this entity is stronger than we first imagined. In fact—"

A howl echoes through the house. It's exactly the sort of sound you expect to hear on Halloween, low and almost mechanical. I've heard this sort of noise a hundred times while walking through the costume aisle at the store. And yet, something about it makes me grip Malcolm's hand even tighter.

"Perhaps our ghostly friend would like to make contact," Gregory says.

Behind him, the EMT continues to care for Terese, although I suspect the only thing to do is get her out of this place and take her to the emergency room. No one suggests this. I'm about to when something flutters in my peripheral vision. I whirl, but whatever it was has vanished.

"Malcolm," I say, keeping my voice even and quiet. "I think we should leave."

I turn to do just that, Malcolm's grip still firm, and watch as the front door slams shut. The fluttering comes again. Bed sheets on a clothesline. A bridal veil. The metallic undertones in that howl.

The lack of sprites. The empty feel of the kitchen. I shake my head, but denial isn't going to keep this entity away. My fingertips itch as if they long to touch that spot on my cheek. It's colder now, waxier, as if it really isn't a part of me.

"That's because it isn't, my dear. It's a part of me."

The voice trumps all other sounds in this space. The crew's chatter dies. Gregory stands, slack-mouthed, eyes darting, searching for the source.

"Have ... have we made contact with the other side?" he manages at last.

"That would be a first," one of the crew mutters.

Something inky peels itself from Terese's inert form. A blob at first, the thing solidifies into shape, more or less. It still lacks substance. It is still ethereal. But it looks like a man now, tall, with angular features. If you saw this silhouette and nothing more, you might think him handsome.

"Ah, yes, my dear. I thought you might like this incarnation. Tall. Dark. Handsome. Of course, I don't have my own fan club, but then I'm not as needy as some of the people in your life."

Gregory storms toward the entity. "Who are you? What do you want? Who are you talking to?"

He is either stupid or naive or completely clueless about this thing. Can't he feel its menace? How stale the air is? The taste of cold metal against his tongue? I break free from Malcolm and lurch forward. My fingers skim Gregory's back just as he reaches the entity.

"Don't touch it!" I cry out.

Too late. Gregory is there, ready to shove a hand through the thing's murky chest. His fist goes straight through. Gregory pulls back, studies his hand in awe.

"What the—" he begins.

Something flutters. Gregory soars through the air and crashes against the fireplace. The photographs teeter and rain down on him. Glass shatters, shards scattering across the hardwood floor and embedding themselves into the carpet. Drops of blood speckle the tile surrounding the fireplace.

Someone screams. Someone else barks orders. In between, voices rise again, the undertone frantic, panic filling the air.

"Silence!" The entity's voice shakes the entire house.

The shouts and urgent voices die, the only sound the hitched breathing of someone who might be crying.

"Much better," it says. "Now, could someone come sweep up this buffoon?" Again, a fluttering, a flick of a bed sheet. Rajeev from the tech crew rushes out and heaves Gregory to his feet.

The entity turns toward me. Or should I say, it oozes. It is not corporeal. This, I can tell. What it truly is?

I have no idea.

"Now, Katy, my dear. Didn't I warn you? You can't run. Not then, and certainly not now."

He is right about that. I will have to puzzle this out, figure a way to fight this thing. I can do this, I think, even if the enormity of the task overwhelms me. Despair—that this thing is too big to fight—fills me. I pull in a breath and widen my stance.

Malcolm slips in behind me, one hand at my waist, the other on my shoulder. He is warm and solid. Even in the stale air that surrounds us, I catch a hint of nutmeg and Ivory soap. I exhale.

I won't have to do this alone.

"Katy's not prepared," Malcolm says. "She doesn't even know what you are." He gives my shoulder a squeeze and then steps around and in front of me. "On the other hand," he continues, "we've been doing this dance for some months now."

The entity shifts, loses its new form for a moment, then solidifies its shape. "Necromancer, are you still here? How amusing."

"She isn't willing," Malcolm says, his voice preternaturally calm. "You can't take her if she isn't willing."

"I can be most persuasive when I wish to be. Once she understands what will happen to Springside Township should she refuse me, I believe she'll see things my way. I almost persuaded her grandmother, after all, and Katy isn't half the ghost hunter she was."

Something that starts as a cry clogs my throat. I move my mouth, but can't make actual words emerge. The thoughts that cloud my head I can't process. Malcolm? My grandmother? This entity? Why am I the only person here—other than Gregory B. Gone—who doesn't understand what's going on?

The entity oozes toward Malcolm. When they're a mere foot apart, it takes on more of his features. "I will give you this, Necromancer. There was a window of time when you were my equal. You and me?" The entity sighs, a strange sound of longing and regret. "It would've been good."

"It still can be," Malcolm says.

"Oh, but now your desire isn't pure enough. Your attention has been ... fractured. And who can blame you? I find myself unusually distracted by her as well. But you couldn't hold me. I'd burn through you in a matter of months. Look what I did to your brother in a meager five minutes. Love makes you weak, Necromancer. Remember that."

I take tiny, staccato breaths, as if some invisible hand is squeezing the air from my lungs.

"This isn't fair," Malcolm says. "It isn't fair to Katy."

"Fair? *Fair*?" The entity's scorn fills the room. Another dusting of plaster drifts from the ceiling. "Was what her grandmother did to me fair?"

Malcolm casts a glance my way and lunges. Before he can reach me, something white and fluttering snaps between us. Less bed sheet and more bridal veil, it cuts Malcolm from me. When I reach for him, my fingers become ensnared in what looks like an intricate pattern of lace and feels like a spider web. I jerk my hands back and cradle them against my chest.

"Are you enjoying the weather, my dear?" The entity shifts again, its attention on me now.

As if on cue, lightning flashes, illuminating the heavy drapes. The thunder in response shakes the house, knocking the last framed pictures from the mantelpiece.

The entity swipes the air. There, in the middle of the room, is a portal to the outside. It's like a viewfinder, and the scene shifts from one part of town to the next. The little creek where we release ghosts overflows its banks. In the Springside Long-term Care Facility, the staff races to place bowls and buckets beneath relentless leaks in the ceiling. Shingles fly from the roof of Sadie's house. She stands in the yard, drenched and miserable, her attention skyward as if she's praying to a cruel god.

"This is only the start," the entity says. "Thanks to your grandparents, I've spent a very long time ... restrained. I'm in the mood for a little havoc —physical, emotional, spiritual."

"The entire town," I say. "You would do that to the entire town simply because you want revenge?" I say these words to buy time. I say these words in hopes this thing will reveal ... something. I never knew my grandfather. He died long before I was born, or so my grandmother always said, but she kept his photograph on her bedside table.

It sits there now. I ponder what that might mean, beyond her love for him.

"My dear," the thing says now. "Revenge, by itself, is a rather petty emotion. I long for some companionship. I've decided yours will be most suitable."

"Katy!" Malcolm's voice is tight with fear. "It can't take you if you're not willing. That's the rule, the pact this thing has made with humanity."

Something flickers in Malcolm's direction, another fluttering bed sheet that sends him soaring into Tim the camera guy. Even as they crash to the floor, Tim keeps the camera elevated, lens trained on the entity and me.

"I must be willing," I echo. "In that case, I need a guarantee that everyone will be safe, that you won't hurt anyone, that..." I trail off, because this is the sort of bargain that cuts more than one way.

"But of course, my dear. I think you'll find me utterly obliging."

I hold up a hand. "I'm not through yet. There can't be any loopholes. When I say I want the town safe, you can't shrink it down and put it in a snow globe. Things like that don't count."

The house quakes. For a moment, I can't tell why or the source. Then the entity itself shivers. It's ... laughing. At me.

"Oh, my dear, you are a delight. I am so going to enjoy our time together. I may consider extending your existence, you delight me so. Would you like that?"

"If I go with you," I say, picking my way through words, through the right phrasing, like picking my way through a barbed wire fence. "I need to know that no one here will be harmed, that my words won't be twisted, that what I say won't be used against me or the people of Springside. No tricks."

"But I'm all about trickery," it says.

"Yeah. I figured that much."

"Ah, you drive a hard bargain. Your grandmother was especially good at bargaining. It must be a family trait."

The entity contracts and grows silent. Is it thinking? Devising some new way to trick me? I need to agree to its terms, eventually. But I won't do so foolishly. I won't throw myself at it in hopes of saving everyone else, not with this cold doubt in the pit of my stomach.

Before the entity speaks again, before I can do something foolish, a force shoves me to one side. Malcolm stands between the entity and me, his breath labored and harsh.

"I will be your willing sacrifice," he declares.

The house rumbles, the floorboards buckling beneath my feet. The entity expands and contracts again as if exhaling an angry breath.

"No interference, Necromancer."

"You can't refuse." Malcolm doesn't waver. "If a willing sacrifice steps forward, you must take it. That's part of the pact." He spreads his arms wide and tips his head back. "I am that willing sacrifice."

The thing expands again, larger this time, as if it means to encompass the entire room. I lurch forward, my arms outstretched to capture Malcolm around the waist, to pull him away from this thing.

One moment, he is there, solid and warm. The next, my arms meet air. I pitch forward, land on the floor. On hands and knees, I stare up at the entity. Its form roils with rage.

"Love makes you weak, Necromancer," it murmurs.

"Malcolm?" I glance around, but he is truly gone, all of him, his warmth, that nutmeg smell, his wonderful laugh.

The entity reforms, again into the shape of a man, more like Malcolm than ever before.

"Well, my dear, it seems we've returned to the status quo."

"Status quo?"

"Where I am.... sated by a willing sacrifice. Do you know who my last willing sacrifice was?"

That cold dread invades my stomach. I don't want to ask. I'm certain I don't want to know. Either way, I can't speak. I shake my head.

"Your grandfather. And do you know why I remained dormant for so long?"

Again, I go with a headshake.

"Your grandmother's tremendous love for him. She never wavered. Unusual. Humans are normally so fickle."

That bed sheet flutters in dismissal, as if this thing could flick away every last one of us.

"Her love alone kept the pact secure for decades, but when she died, so did its hold on me. Null and void, as they say."

And that was when things started to change. I shut my eyes.

"Yes, indeed they did," the entity says. "And now? Do you know what your love for Malcolm is like, Katy?"

I don't know because I haven't even given the feeling that name, not yet.

"It's quite beautiful, like a tender spring sapling. Oh, but so young! So weak! One gust of wind."

The entity expands again, a whoosh of stale, icy air flowing over me. Then the thing oozes forward, touches the spot on my cheek that I know —even now—remains.

"I won't say goodbye, my dear, because I'll be seeing you again very soon. Until then, I'll be anticipating our next meeting."

The entity solidifies into that silhouette of a handsome man. It brings what looks like fingertips to its lips and blows a kiss. The resulting sting flashes across my cheek.

Then, much like Malcolm did, the thing vanishes. I am on the floor, still on my hands and knees, uncertain I have the power to stand.

~

FOR SEVERAL SECONDS, no one moves. I'm not sure any of us dare to breathe more than quick, quiet breaths. I want to paw the floor where Malcolm stood, but I know it's no use. He's gone. I let that thing take him. I was too slow. And now? What do I do now? How do I explain this to Nigel? That cold dread in the pit of my stomach moves to my heart.

The chime of the doorbell makes us all jump. Rajeev stumbles to the front entrance and flings open the door.

"Trick or treat!"

The air that rushes inside is free of rain but drenched in the aroma of late autumn. Wood smoke and dying leaves. Someone, somewhere, is playing "Monster Mash" loud enough for all of us to hear the words. Children screech. Parents laugh.

It's the status quo.

From behind me, Gregory B. Gone springs up. "Tell me we got that on video!"

He rushes toward Tim, who takes a few faltering steps backward. A trail of blood follows the lines of Gregory's face. The right lens of his glasses is shattered in a star pattern. He grips the cameraman's shirt, a man desperate.

"Tell me, please tell me we got that on video." Gregory glances around, frantic. "Tell me we streamed it. Tell me—"

Rajeev fires up a laptop. "No streaming, at least," he says. "It looks like the feed cut out right when that … thing appeared."

"Damn." Gregory whirls again on Tim. "Well?"

"I was filming the whole time, but I don't know what I have."

The three of them huddle over the camera. A few members of the crew stand and stare. Some simply wander outside with bags of candy. No one bothers to check on Terese, not even the EMT. I crawl toward her. She is still a plaster-covered lump on the floor, and worry eats at me.

How big of a toll did that thing take on her? Her chest rises and falls, so there is that, at least.

"Terese?" I say, keeping my words soft. "Are you okay?"

She stirs, pushes against the floor, but her arms quake. I catch her hands. Slowly, together, we inch her to sitting. Terese stares at me, her eyes enormous. Her hair is pure white. Not artifice, as I thought before, but fact.

"It wanted you," she says. "I couldn't stop it."

"How did it ... I mean, do you remember what happened?"

She surveys the living area, eyes blinking, gaze confused. It's clear this is the first time she's truly seen it. "A few nights ago, I was conducting a séance."

Oh, those are always a bad idea.

"I often do one before a show," Terese continues. "I made contact with the other side, but this time..."

"It was the entity?"

"Yes. The rest is murky." She reaches out as if to touch my left cheek but is smart enough to pull her hand back before it grazes the iridescent blue spot. "But it wasn't after me. It wanted you."

"I should've known," I said. "You kissed both my cheeks. Were you trying to warn me or did it just slip up?"

She shakes her head, eyes brimming with moisture. Maybe that was an unfair question. I struggle to my feet and offer Terese my hand.

"What do you mean, it's not on video?" Gregory bellows. "We have the show of the century—no, the show of the millennium—and it's not on video? On audio? Did we get anything at all?"

Tim is jabbing a keyboard, mouthing soundless words, and shaking his head. Gregory paces and storms, hands alternately clutching his hair and hapless members of the tech crew. Between the blood on his face and the manic jerking of his limbs, he is fearsome. He whirls. I suspect his next target is me. Before I can dodge his questions or escape the house, a sharp whistle cuts through all the noise.

"This is the Springside Township Police Department! You are all in violation of the law. You have fifteen minutes to vacate the premises."

Police Chief Ramsey is standing in the doorway, bullhorn in one hand and nightstick in the other. While I can believe he'll gladly use the one, I can't imagine him resorting to the other. Officer Millard is standing behind him holding a Taser, so perhaps what I believe doesn't match this new reality.

Gregory charges forward. "I have permission to be here, from the owners. I am ridding this space of malignant spirits so the family may—"

"The Springside Bank owns this house," Chief says. "You're trespassing, and I'm not joking. Fifteen minutes and then I start arresting people."

Around me, the stagecraft disintegrates. Velvet curtains cascade to the floor. Two of the crew roll up the carpet. Near the fireplace, Rajeev clutches a broom, his gaze locked on blood-speckled glass.

From the kitchen, I collect our field kit. I dump the coffee and tea down the sink. It's cold and stale, and the aroma clogs my throat, triggers my gag reflex. For a moment, I clutch the marble countertop. Sweat sprouts along my forehead. I shut my eyes. I yearn for Malcolm's reassuring hand on my shoulder. If I try hard enough, I'll feel it. If I try hard enough, he'll return.

Nothing but the sound of Chief Ramsey's voice—amplified by the bullhorn—greets my efforts.

I pack the percolator into our field kit. There's no room for Malcolm's samovar, so I clutch it to my chest like a life preserver.

Chief grunts at me on my way out. "Funny," he says. "I'm not surprised to see you here."

Without a word, I continue down the steps.

"Where's your partner in crime?" he calls after me.

On the sidewalk, I turn and stare up at him and the house behind him. The green and white Victorian appears benign, like it always has.

"I wish I knew," I say to Chief.

I walk through the clear night to my truck with the knowledge that I am completely alone.

I LET my truck idle in front of my house and contemplate the light that spills from the kitchen windows. When I finally step onto the walk, a hint of spice and molasses fills the night. I stand there, clutching Malcolm's samovar to my chest, the metal a dull cold beneath my fingertips and against my heart, trying to fathom what is going on in my home.

There's one way to find out. I round the house and enter from the back. The moment I open the door, the kitchen wraps me in warmth and spice—nutmeg and clove, and the tang of ginger. Sadie is standing at the oven. She's wearing a pair of mitts I'm certain I don't own. Nigel is slipping cookies from a sheet to a cooling rack. Belinda is pouring a mug of something that she hands to me.

"Don't talk. Don't think. Just sit down and breathe for a bit." She steers me to a kitchen chair and with the slightest pressure on my shoulders, has me sitting.

With caution, I bring the mug to my lips. I brace for coffee or tea, not certain I could stand to drink either. Instead, sweet apple cider fills my mouth. I sigh. The apples are tart, the cinnamon smooth and comforting.

"Sadie's idea," Nigel says.

Sadie waves an oven mitt as if she could wave away his praise. "After the night you had, I didn't think you'd want another cup of coffee."

She's right about that. I survey the three of them, perplexed. "But the streaming cut out," I say.

Belinda wakes up the laptop. Frozen on Ghost B Gone's YouTube channel is the image of Police Chief Ramsey leading Gregory away in handcuffs.

"We don't know what happened, exactly," Belinda says, "but someone started filming again."

She rewinds the video. And yes, there I am, on my hands and knees, my expression shattered. Terese crumpled on the floor. Gregory shouting, arms waving, blood dripping. It's a jerky, chaotic montage of images and sound. Whoever this enterprising videographer is, they track me with their camera as I leave the house.

So there I am, staring up at Chief Ramsey, telling the entire world I don't know where Malcolm is.

I glance at Nigel and something inside me fractures. He already knows, and yet, that doesn't make it any easier. The fact that he—along with Belinda and Sadie—is trying to take care of me makes it hurt that much more. True, I am no longer completely alone. The thought fills a void while easing weight onto my shoulders. I shrug, not used to this new feeling.

"I'm sorry," I say at last.

"What for?" Nigel holds my gaze, his eyes dark and bright.

"For Malcolm. He's ... I don't know. Gone. That thing—"

"Malcolm knew the risks going in." Nigel rubs his hands across his eyes. They're dry and red. They hold sorrow I don't think he dares to speak. "And part of me is petty enough to think he got what he deserved."

I gape, but Sadie smacks Nigel with one of the oven mitts.

"He's your brother," she says, voice indignant. Then she softens. "It's okay to be sad. It's okay to mourn, even if the other person wasn't perfect."

Nigel takes her hand and presses it against his cheek. "Neither one of us is perfect. But yes, my brother—and my rival. It's the way it works in our family. We were both trying to capture this thing. May the best man win and all that."

"Why the hell would either of you want to do that?" Belinda's question echoes my own. She stands, takes my mug, and ladles in more cider.

"Power. Wealth. Lifelong security." Nigel gives Sadie's hand a squeeze and lets go. "A powerful enough necromancer could ... harness that entity. It's an exchange, but one with rules. At the end of the agreed upon time, there's a parting. It's risky, no doubt. But we both thought it would be worth the risk."

"What do you give it in exchange?" I ask.

"That's part of the deal you hammer out once you capture it." Nigel shrugs. "Honestly? It's not like some sort of demonic possession. And it's not like these things are sex-crazed."

Belinda snorts. Sadie's cheeks flush a deep pink, although that might be from the oven's heat.

"Often, all they want is to feel again." Here, even Nigel goes a bit red around the ears. "So, yeah. Sex, maybe. But just moving around, walking, eating. When I had all the ghosts inside me, one of the things they all loved was when I went running." He turns to me now. "It's why they love your coffee, Katy. The steam gives them a bit of substance, and the aroma and flavor make them feel ... almost human."

"So, both of you," I say. "From the start. You came here looking for that thing?"

"And we both knew the rules." Nigel leans forward and grips my hand. "Remember that, Katy. Malcolm knew, absolutely, what he was doing. We both knew that if we couldn't capture it, our fate wouldn't be pretty."

"So a willing sacrifice isn't the same as capturing this thing?" I say.

"No, not at all."

"Then what happens to a willing sacrifice?" I'm fairly certain I don't want to hear the answer, but I ask anyway.

He shakes his head. "No one has ever come back, so no one really knows."

"Then why did Malcolm—" I begin.

"Honestly, Katy? Don't you know?"

My gaze falls to the mug of cider. The surface is absolutely smooth until a single drop falls from my cheek and sends ripples against the rim.

"You don't suppose it would trade." I say this more to the cider than Nigel. In fact, I nearly hope he won't hear me.

"What?" His face contorts into a scowl. "I'm not sure what you're thinking, but—"

"Nothing, nothing," I say. "But I wonder. That thing was inside you. You wouldn't know its name, would you?"

Nigel slumps in his chair. "Oh, no. No, we're not going there. Look, even if I did know its name, it wouldn't let me tell you. It would be in the part of my memory it erased when it was inside me. Don't go fishing for this thing."

"I don't have a choice." I touch the spot on my left cheek. "It's coming back for me."

Nigel looks away. He must know that's true. He might even know why —that the reason behind its return is tied to my affection for Malcolm. I press a hand over my heart as if it's a tender thing I must protect. As I hold my hand there, something swells inside me. The notion is small, a tiny bit of hope struggling through all my doubt. But it takes root. I feel it grow.

It's a spring sapling of an idea. I barely think on it. I certainly won't speak it out loud. I must protect it from the icy wind. But when I'm at last in bed and shut my eyes, I know this.

It could work.

I'm filling the fourth thermos with coffee when Belinda wanders into the kitchen the next morning.

"And I thought yesterday's was good." She accepts the cup I hand her.

"Fresh beans from the Coffee Depot," I say. "They finished roasting them this morning."

She slumps against the refrigerator and sighs. "God, I could get used to this. Do you need me to scrub toilets or something? Because you could pay me in cups of coffee to do that."

I almost laugh. The only thing that stops me is the question swirling in my mind, the one I must ask Belinda but dread doing so.

"Actually," I say, "I could use your help."

"Sure."

She pulls up a chair, but before she can sit, I spring my question.

"How do you talk to ghosts?"

Belinda lands hard, chair legs stabbing the kitchen floor. Amazingly, she hasn't spilled a drop of coffee. She takes a long sip, staring down at the liquid in the cup.

"You really want to know?" she says at last.

"I need to know."

"They like small talk. Maybe because they're not fully there?" She shrugs. "When I was younger, I would prattle away, you know, like some little kids do." As she did back at the police station, she holds up her hand as if it's a talking puppet. "My dad was always working. My mother was always organizing this party or that committee or whatever. The ghosts were my friends."

"What happened?"

"What didn't? Middle school, maybe? Somewhere along the line, I graduated from small talk to gossip to rumors. Instead of playful sprites, I started attracting the nastier ghosts. Oh, God, Katy, they say some awful things. Things you know aren't true, but can't help worrying that they might be."

I nod. I remember Belinda in middle and high school. When a particularly mean ghost would attach itself, her hair lost its luster, her skin went ashen.

"When I discovered that drinking made them shut up, I thought I'd solve my problems for good." She shakes her head. "You know the rest."

Yes. I do.

"Small talk." Of all the things I might have to tackle today, this seems like the most formidable.

Small talk is not one of my strengths. My grandmother was good at it. And it was Malcolm who revived the business with sales pitches and marketing and simply talking to people while I chased ghosts around with cups of coffee and Tupperware.

I continue to fill thermoses and pack them in the field kit.

"Can I ask where you're going?"

I set the carafe of Belinda's security coffee on the table. "Nothing should bother you today, but just in case."

She stands and crosses her arms over her chest. "Again, where are you going?"

"On a pilgrimage," I say. "I need to talk to a few ghosts."

MY FIRST STOP is Springside Long-term Care. If my hunch is wrong, then I've wasted a great deal of money brewing a great many pots of coffee. If my hunch is wrong, Malcolm is lost forever. Everything depends on a hunch. The thought makes my stomach jump. My hands, however, are steady. I carry a single thermos with me of some of the best coffee I've ever brewed and head for Mr. Carlotta's room.

"Katy-Girl!" His face brightens when he sees me. "I was just talking to Jack. He's thinking about driving down from Minneapolis this weekend."

"How nice for you." I point to the brand new chess set on a side table. Its carved wooden pieces are glowing in the low lamplight. "Are you going to beat him again?"

"He's not coming down for this old man, Katy-Girl."

I shake my head, going for ignorance. This is not an entanglement I need today.

"You. He wants to see you again." Mr. Carlotta claps his hands together. "Give him a chance. Go out to dinner. He's not the boy you knew in high school."

"The one who set my hair on fire?" I strive for lightness, but it falls flat. I really am bad at small talk.

Mr. Carlotta snorts. "He's grown up. And when you grow up, you see things differently."

I choke back a frustrated sigh. I adore Mr. Carlotta, but he's a product of his times. He won't be happy until he has all his grandchildren married off, or at least his favorite one.

"He'd like to have dinner with you," he says.

"Then he should ask me that himself."

"He plans to. In fact—" The buzz of my cell phone cuts off Mr. Carlotta's words. He cringes and rubs his brow. "I told him not to text you."

I check my phone. Yes, Jack has sent me a text. Yes, he has asked me out to dinner.

"I can't." It's the answer I speak out loud and the one I text to Jack.

The room grows oddly silent. I glance up to find Mr. Carlotta staring at me, pain etched on his features.

"Oh, Katy-Girl, what's happened?"

"I…" I don't know what to say or how to explain what's happened in the past twenty-four hours.

"You look so much like your grandmother right now, that same stoic expression. Every time I asked her to coffee, every time she chased down my ghost. It didn't have to get romantic. I told her that … how many times?"

He asks this last to the air, or possibly his ghost. Certainly I don't know the answer.

"Don't cut yourself off like she did," Mr. Carlotta says. "No ghost is worth that."

But would a whole town be worth it? I know now what it is my grandmother gave up. The love of this worthy man. A chance for a new life. She kept the vigil, kept herself lonely. That photograph of my grandfather on her bedside table—an image of all she'd lost and all she could never have.

My eyes burn with a quick spate of tears. My stomach ties itself in knots. I struggle to pull in a full breath. Granted, this last might be nothing more than Mr. Carlotta's ghost.

And that ghost is the reason I'm here.

I try to work a smile onto my face. From the one Mr. Carlotta gives me, I know it's a weak effort.

"Mr. Carlotta, would you mind?" I gesture toward the door. "I'd like to speak to your ghost for a few minutes."

He nods. Without another word, he wheels his chair from the room. I shut the door behind him. For a moment, all I can do is press my palm against the wood. Then I reach for my thermos.

"No Tupperware today." I unscrew the cap and pour the coffee into the thermos's cup. "I just want to talk."

Aromatic steam rises into the air. Other than the entity, this ghost is the oldest I've ever encountered. It does not suffer fools gladly and is difficult to draw out, although I know it must be in the vicinity of Mr. Carlotta's Purple Heart. Technically, I suppose it haunts that rather than Mr. Carlotta. In this tiny room, it makes little difference.

By degrees, it oozes its way closer to the coffee. I add a touch more to increase the heat.

"I think it's some of my best," I say. "What do you think?"

In answer, the ghost drops onto the cup. The steam shimmers, creating a lopsided outline that looks as grumpy as this ghost often feels.

"I have a problem." I'm on my knees in front of the side table where the coffee is sitting. Oddly, I don't feel all that self-conscious speaking out loud to what is no more than glimmering air. Maybe it's because I've known ghosts all my life. And maybe it's time I got better acquainted.

"You're old enough that I think you know about this entity. I think you might know what it's called. Can you tell me that? I can't promise that I'll be the one to come back with more coffee, but someone will. You won't be ... alone."

I hold absolutely still, eyes closed, lips slightly parted. The ghost inches closer, the air around my face cooling as it draws ever nearer. Then, it's as if I inhale it. It places its icy caress against my eyelids, my cheeks—making certain to circumvent the spot on my left—and my lips.

A word enters my head, but this isn't Belinda's small talk. Slowly, as if this ghost must pull each syllable from a great depth, I have my answer.

"Thank you," I say, and my voice vibrates the shimmering air around me.

I ask Mr. Carlotta's ghost for one last favor, but I leave before it can respond. I'm working on trust now, and I have many more ghosts to speak to and many more favors to ask.

By two in the afternoon, I've located every ghost, spirit, apparition, and sprite in Springside Township. I raced around the abandoned barn near the edge of town, a thermos above my head as the wild ghosts that live there dipped and dived into the steam. I held a coffee klatch in a gazebo attended by a dozen sprites, leaving behind floorboards far damper and stickier than when I arrived. I even sneaked into Chief Ramsey's garden shed and offered a cup to the ghost that haunts the watering can. I've talked to them all.

Except one.

I'm tempted to return to the care facility and ask Mrs. Greeley if she's sensed my grandmother lately. But perhaps this is something my grandmother can't help me with. Maybe she's known that all along.

My next stop is the green and white Victorian. I expect some sort of barrier to entry. Crime scene tape. A large No Trespassing sign. A closed circuit camera like the one on Main and Fifth. What I don't expect is the bright yellow van with the black lettering and the riot of antennae in a gangly mess up on top. I don't expect Gregory B. Gone to be leaning against his van, arms crossed over his chest, his gaze trained on the house like a despondent lover.

I pull the remaining thermos of coffee from the field kit and grab two Styrofoam cups before I leave my truck.

"I hope you like it with cream," I say, balancing the cups on the hood of his van. "I have sugar, too, if you want it."

He purses his lips and I take that as a no. A butterfly bandage covers a wound on his forehead. The lens of his glasses is still splintered. A strip of silver duct tape keeps the whole thing from tumbling off his face.

"Thank you." He sips and then points the cup toward the house. "You know, that's the first time I've seen a ghost."

"I'm not sure that thing really is a ghost. It's something more." And perhaps, in a way, something less as well.

"Always wanted to," Gregory continues. "Everyone else senses the cold spots, hears the creaking stairs, freaks out and runs away. Me? I don't feel a thing."

I consider the man next to me, the van behind him proclaiming *Ghost B Gone*, and the naughty sprite whirling about his head.

"How do you eradicate ghosts if you can't sense them?" I ask. At this point, I think that's a fair question.

"Terese. She's very ... open to all things supernatural."

Yes. That turned out to be a problem, too.

"She broke up with me," he adds.

Broke up? "I didn't realize you two were a couple."

"Yeah, that might have been part of it. She said I cared more about the show than I did about her."

Well, he did leave her on the floor while he ranted like a madman about what had—and hadn't—been caught on video. But then I let that entity take Malcolm. I maybe shouldn't judge. Instead, I wave my fingers at the sprite, trying to get it to fly away.

"Go on, shoo," I say under my breath.

"Ouch." Gregory slaps his neck. "You'd think it would be too late in the season for mosquitos."

Mission accomplished, the sprite dances off.

"What are you going to do now?" I ask.

He shakes his head. "I wish I knew."

Despite the defeat in his words, his expression shifts. Maybe it's the scent of wood smoke that fills the air. A soft swoosh tickles my ears, the sound of a rake across dried oak leaves. The status quo, in Springside Township, can be an enticing thing.

"This isn't a bad little town," he says. "Maybe I'll stick around. Nice place to raise kids."

I refrain from pointing out that his girlfriend just broke up with him. I strive to keep my face bland, completely noncommittal. But something must bubble to the surface because he gives me a wry grin.

"Yeah ... another one of our problems. Or maybe it was just my problem. Maybe *I'm* the problem." He drains the last of the coffee and then crushes the Styrofoam cup. "Thanks, Katy. You make a damn good cup of coffee."

"Yes," I say. "I know."

~

I DON'T ENTER the green and white Victorian until the bright yellow of the Ghost B Gone van has disappeared down the road. Once inside, I'm drawn to the living area. Does it matter where I do this? Possibly. Possibly not. In any case, my feet lead me to where I last encountered the entity.

Enough coffee remains in the thermos for two final servings. No Styrofoam for this. I pull out two blood red Japanese cups. I think they're meant for tea, but I'm after elegance, not accuracy.

I fill each cup to the rim and set both on the mantelpiece. When I step back, my heel grinds a shard of glass into the wood floor. Then I stand in the empty space, paralyzed not so much by indecision—I've made up my mind—but by whether I'm being a coward in not saying goodbye to everyone. I'm not sure what will happen when I speak the name I hold in my mind, but I'm fairly certain nothing will be the same. I might not be the same.

I might not be here.

Eyes shut, I inhale deeply, then let it out with a whoosh. No sense in wasting time. The coffee's getting cold.

"Momalcurkan."

I stumble over the word. It feels awkward and unwieldy in my mouth, like it's not a real word at all. Just to be perverse, I add:

"I have some coffee for you."

The floorboards beneath my feet rumble. Plaster dust rains down. This time a spiderweb of cracks appears along the ceiling, marring its smooth surface. The bank will never be able to sell this place.

That inky mass oozes from the fireplace and creeps up the mantel until it reaches the coffee. The blob is nearly solid now, and the cups barely visible. The air grows stale. Around me, things flutter, wilder, more insistent than before. Bridal veils, every last one. White lace teases my peripheral vision until I look at it full on. Then, it vanishes.

The inky mass eases from the mantelpiece. One cup is overturned, but only a tiny stream of coffee flows onto the mantel. The other cup is completely empty. What sounds like an enormous sigh shakes the structure. The jangle of the pot and pan rack comes from the kitchen. The swinging door whooshes.

"Most delicious."

The words echo in my head and all around me. In front of me, the inky blob transforms, once again taking the shape of a handsome man. In this particular case, that handsome man is Malcolm, or a facsimile of him.

"Brava, my dear. Brava. You've managed a trick most necromancers spend years trying to accomplish and never do. Certainly your grandmother never managed it."

"I'm not half the ghost hunter she was," I say.

"Perhaps not. Perhaps you are something more."

"No," I say. "I'm not."

The entity regards me, its scrutiny silent and penetrating.

"It isn't time yet," it says.

My heart thuds, a furious beat in my chest. That proclamation gives me hope, just enough so I can speak my next words.

"I know. I want to make a trade."

"What sort of trade would that be? I see no one here who might entice me. The humans in this place are puny and uninteresting."

"Really?" I say. "No one? Not even me?" I turn in a slow circle like I'm a runway model, despite my hiking boots and coffee-stained jeans.

"Well, that's another matter. What is it you have in mind, my dear?"

"Me for Malcolm, but I have conditions."

"Of course you do."

"He must be alive."

A rumble shakes more plaster from the ceiling, but the sound isn't threatening. Instead, it feels as if the entire house is chuckling and I'm a small child making ridiculous demands.

"Human and in one piece," I add. "And everything he was before you took him as a willing sacrifice."

"Including a liar?"

Three words, perfectly aimed. I press a hand against my stomach as if this thing has struck me there. I pull up everything I know about Malcolm, everything he is to me.

"He's my business partner, and my friend, and I think I've maybe fallen in love with him."

"No maybe about it, my dear. That he still exists means you have."

He still exists. I keep my breathing shallow. I don't want this thing to sense my relief.

"If he still exists, then we can trade. Right? If you return Malcolm, I'll be your willing sacrifice."

"You saw how he did it, what words he spoke?"

I nod.

The entity falls silent again, and everything around us with it. No birds sing outside the window. There's no traffic on the street. The entity in this space has obliterated every last whiff of wood smoke and the sound of crisp leaves. It's stale and cold and I wonder if this is my fate. Bed sheets. Bridal veils. The taste of metal against my tongue.

"Very well," the entity says. "I accept."

As it did with Terese, the entity peels away from the form that is Malcolm. He crumples to the floor, inert. I can only hope he is alive and breathing and everything else he should be. I don't have the luxury to check. Instead, I must hold up my end of the bargain.

I step forward and spread my arms. I tip my head back. "I am your willing sacrifice."

I hold still, mouth wide open, heart kicking up again. The entity oozes toward me, and my limbs lock in place as if I've been cast in bronze. A tendril inches toward my face, reaching for the cheek it marked.

"I've waited a long time for this, my dear."

In that moment, a ghostly stream fills the living area. My mouth is still open, and the first ghost to plunge in is Mr. Carlotta's. Oh, it's fierce, leading the charge like a true warrior. The shock of its memories rattles me. Before I can make sense of any of them, another ghost follows, and then another. The dozen sprites from the gazebo dive in all at once. I can't move, whether from the entity or all the ghosts inside me, I don't know.

Still, they come. The wild ones from the abandoned barn. The grumpy ones who haunt the dark alleyways of town. Sadie's two sprites.

An unearthly cry rends the air. The hold on my limbs loosens and I stumble backward. The ghosts catch me before I tumble to the floor.

"I can still take you, Katy," the entity says.

But Springside Township has a great many ghosts. The thing reaches for me again, but the ghosts don't stop. The entity's hold weakens, but it's still a match. Its power sputters, surges, sputters, surges.

With one last surge, it flows around me. I feel my existence falter, this world receding, and some other one rushing toward me. The light there is bright enough to blind, and yet it contains hidden recesses dark enough to wilt your soul. The house around me fades. I'm still standing in the living room, but I no longer feel the floor beneath my boots. And Malcolm? He's no more than a hazy outline. It's like looking at an old photograph in sepia. It's a world that no longer exists.

But the ghosts won't let me go. They keep me rooted in place until one last ghost dives into my mouth.

This is a ghost I know.

The entity's screech pierces my ears. I'm frozen in place now, my body in a full-on ghost infestation. My sight grows dim, my eyelashes heavy with frost. I feel as if I'm sinking into a dark, icy pool of water. Before I sink all the way, before I lose the last bit of light, I hear my grandmother's voice.

Goodbye, Katy-Girl. I love you.

~

"KATY? KATY, ARE YOU OKAY?"

The familiar voice pokes through the fog clouding my head, the sound of it low and familiar, although it lacks humor. And this is a voice I very much want to hear laugh. My eyelids flutter, my lashes no longer weighed down by ice.

When I open my eyes, the first thing I see is Malcolm. He's here. He's alive. I glance around and find the space warm, a hint of wood smoke in the air. Outside, a bird chirps. I push to sit up, and immediately he's at my side, helping me. I inhale nutmeg and Ivory soap, and I think I might collapse again.

"It's really you," I say.

"It's really me." He gives his head a little shake as if he can't believe he's looking at me. "I don't know what you did. I don't know why, especially since—"

I press a finger against his lips. "That doesn't matter."

He takes my hand, squeezes it. "Actually, it does. Which is why I can't
… I mean, I barely understand what happened. How—I mean, all the
ghosts? Did you capture them?"

"No."

"But how did they all—?"

"I just asked for their help."

Malcolm gives me a blank stare as if I've uttered nonsense.

"You kept telling me how much they like me, right?" I say. "I decided
to test that theory. I figured none of them wanted this entity around
either and they'd be glad to help me get rid of it, one way or another.
Also, I bribed them with coffee."

For a moment, that blank stare remains. Then Malcolm throws his
head back and laughs.

"You just … asked them." He shakes his head like I've done something
impossible. "I think you've made a breakthrough in necromancy."

"I keep telling you. I'm not a necromancer."

"So you say. This?" He raises his hand, indicating the house and
himself. "This proves otherwise." His attention turns to my face—or
rather, my left cheek. "Hold on," he says, words softer now.

Brow furrowed, concentration absolute, he raises his hand to my
face. He touches the spot on my cheek. I flinch inwardly, certain it will
burn him again.

He doesn't wince, doesn't shirk. Instead, he uses a finger to scrape
away at my skin. Something dislodges and falls to the floor. Between us,
a blue disc shatters into a million tiny crystals. A second later, those
million tiny crystals evaporate.

"Am I free?" I ask, my voice barely a whisper. I don't want to hope,
but find I'm doing just that.

"I think so."

I sigh, and we're so close that I sigh into his mouth. I inch closer so
my lips might brush his, so I might sample that nutmeg. Malcolm pulls
me in to him, one arm around my waist, a hand cradling the back of my
head. When he kisses me, I taste the nutmeg and the apology and the
thrill that we're both here, both alive, both human.

All kisses end, it's true. But this one? This one goes on for a very long
time before it finally does.

~

I POUR coffee into three bone china cups. The porcelain is so fine that the cups are nearly translucent. Wedding china. My grandmother's. At least, I think it is. I never asked. Now, regret tugs at me that I didn't.

I swallow back the sigh. I'm too full of caffeine to stay sad for long. I'm in Mr. Carlotta's room, the last stop on my pilgrimage to thank all the ghosts of Springside Township. They all helped, but it's this fierce warrior of a ghost who rallied them and led the charge. That deserves something special.

"Ah, Katy-Girl," Mr. Carlotta says. "I think your coffee may even outshine your grandmother's."

"I don't see how it could. She taught me everything I know about brewing coffee."

He sips again. "It tastes different today."

Perhaps it does. Or perhaps it's because today, his room feels lighter. Granted, his ghost is not a presence you can ignore, but the air doesn't feel quite so melancholy, my lungs don't struggle to draw a breath.

Still, I make the offer. "Do you want me to take your ghost when I go?"

Mr. Carlotta strokes his jaw, his eyes on the very spot where his ghost rests. "No, let him stay. He's not thickening the air quite so much, and I get the sense he needs the rest."

"All right," I say, "but there are some things you should know. Your ghost is a warrior."

"I knew it! He has the feel of an old soldier."

"Maybe," I say. "But your ghost is actually a she."

Mr. Carlotta's eyes sparkle with discovery. "A she? Are you certain?"

"Positive."

"An Amazonian, then?"

I shrug. "I don't know. All I know is this ghost is very old."

"Or perhaps Queen Boudica herself!" He nods. "Yes, I think she must be."

The ghost swells at this suggestion. Whether true or not, she certainly seems to like it—and Mr. Carlotta.

"She could use a little R and R," I say. "She fought a big battle the other day."

"I thought you were up to something."

Once we finish, I clear the cups and saucers, tucking each in bubble wrap before placing them into the field kit. I'm at the door, ready to leave, when Mr. Carlotta calls out.

"So, I was talking to Jack last night—"

I shake my head, but I'm smiling. He'll never give up. "I'm seeing someone right now."

He scrutinizes me. "So you are, Katy-Girl. So you are."

I'm halfway down the hall when he wheels his chair into the corridor.

"But you tell him for me that I've got my eye on him!"

When I reach *K&M Ghost Eradication Specialists*, Malcolm is outside, leaning against the door. The sun glints off the storefront glass and the lettering glows like pure gold. It's one of those rare November days that make you think winter will never invade. The air is warm, but it holds undertones of the cold to come.

"Have fun?" he asks.

I nod, but it's a distracted sort of gesture.

"You didn't find her," he says, "did you?"

I shake my head. "I think she's gone for good this time."

"Remember when you told me that the thing she wanted most was to take care of you?" Malcolm says. "Well, maybe she's done that. Maybe that means she can move on. Maybe ... oh!"

Oh? What does he mean by *oh*? "Tell me."

"It just hit me. Maybe she went to find your grandfather."

"Then you don't think that entity destroyed him?"

"Not with the way your grandmother loved him." He pauses and considers the sky. "I suspect his spirit is out there somewhere. It was her love that sustained him." He looks at me now, those brown eyes soft. "That made all the difference. I'm certain of it."

We each wear scars from our own battle with the entity. Silver strands thread their way through Malcolm's ebony hair, a bit a gray settling in around his temples. His eyes have more creases when he smiles. While the spot on my cheek is gone, the skin where it sat has a faint blue cast to it, a stain that no amount of scrubbing can remove.

He shifts and I notice the sign on the door behind him.

Closed for QBR.

"What's QBR?" I ask.

"Quarterly business review. It's been a busy three months."

Yes, it has.

"A lot has happened," he adds.

That, too.

"So, in a QBR you review the business, wins and losses, make plans. Basically, it's an honest look at where the business is at."

"Emphasis on honest?"

He clamps his mouth shut. That only lasts for a second. He bursts out laughing, hands propped on his knees.

"Yes," he says, catching his breath. "Emphasis on honest." He tips his head toward the sky again. "And since it's so nice, I thought we could have a picnic." He gestures toward his convertible.

There, tucked behind the passenger seat, is a wicker basket. Tucked next to it is a red and white checked blanket.

"So this would be what?" I ask. "A date?"

"Only if you want it to be."

I consider this, and Malcolm. I could weigh pros and cons, I suppose. I could walk a careful line between business partner and friend. Or I could trust that we'll figure everything out as we go along.

"Yes," I say. "Let's go on a picnic."

He keeps the top down and cranks the heat. We drive along Main Street until we leave Springside Township behind us. The sky is so blue, Malcolm's fingers laced in mine so warm, and the wind steals our laughter.

We drive so fast that—for once—the ghosts won't be able to follow us.

THE GHOST THAT GOT AWAY

COFFEE AND GHOSTS SEASON 2

PART I
GHOSTS OF CHRISTMAS PAST

COFFEE AND GHOSTS SEASON TWO, EPISODE 1

CHAPTER 1

IT'S TWO WEEKS before Christmas, and I'm crouched in our storefront display. Morning sunlight shines through the gold lettering on the glass and casts the words *K&M Ghost Eradication Specialists* along my arms. The velvet beneath my shoes makes it tough to gain purchase. My thighs ache. My palms sweat. The scalding cup of coffee I'm holding threatens to spill.

Passersby stop and stare, mouths open. I catch sight of Police Chief Ramsey, but all he gives me is a smirk. He doesn't believe in ghosts, not even when they're right in front of him. If I had any sort of presence of mind, I would've thought to print out a sign, something along the lines of: *Demonstration in progress.*

But that would be a lie. This is no demonstration. The sprite careening around the display window really is agitated. I really need to catch it. I'm really not certain this single cup of coffee will do it. Not this time of year.

There's something about December that brings out the worst in ghosts.

I'm about to admit defeat. The coffee's cooling too rapidly to tempt this one much longer. The sprite shoots back and forth, whipping around the samovar and percolator we keep on display, nestled in the velvet. It slips inside the samovar. The whole thing shakes, then teeters off its perch.

I pitch forward to catch it. My fingertips skim the metal. The coffee in my other hand sloshes, soaks my sleeve, and splatters the window. I'm flat on my stomach in the middle of the display. The sprite does a victory lap around my head and I glance up into the perplexed gaze of my business partner.

He's standing on the other side of the glass. His lips twitch. Malcolm Armand (the M in *K&M Ghost Eradication Specialists*) was once my rival and is now my partner—and sometimes there are benefits with that arrangement. He doesn't move from his spot outside our window. In fact, he looks like he's about to settle in for a show.

"Help?" I mouth.

I can't hear his laugh, but I can see it, head thrown back, the way it lights his eyes. He vanishes from sight and a moment later, the chime over our door rings out.

"Katy, what on earth?"

"We have a sprite," I say.

He sticks his head into the display area. "We have a sprite?" He glances about like he's tasting the air. "Oh ... we have a sprite. Any idea how that happened?"

"None."

The sprite shoots past Malcolm and heads for the conference room.

"Damn," he says. "Is Nigel in yet?"

"Not unless he came in the back way."

Without another word, Malcolm sprints toward the conference room. I crawl from the display as quickly as soggy velvet will allow. Nigel, Malcolm's brother, was once addicted to swallowing ghosts. Granted, there isn't much to a sprite, but it's better if he isn't tempted.

I'm at the threshold to the conference room when Malcolm emerges.

"All clear." He holds up a sealed Tupperware container. "Look what I got you for Christmas."

"Seriously? You caught it that fast?"

He shrugs. "I'm just that good."

He is, actually, but I'm in no mood to admit it. I cross my arms over my chest and stare hard, waiting for the rest of the explanation.

"And I think you wore it out," he adds.

I study the sprite trapped inside the Tupperware. It floats lazily about, giving me a single thump against the side in agreement.

The chime above our door rings for a second time that morning. Nigel strolls in. His shock of white hair always takes me by surprise. Although he's only a few years older than Malcolm, he wears the legacy of his addiction in his hair and in the lines around his eyes and mouth.

Today a grin brightens his face. He looks almost boyish. His steps are quick and light. I think he might break into a song or possibly execute some sort of dance step. Instead, he merely nods at the sprite as he passes by.

"Good work," he says, and heads into the conference room where we keep the computer.

Malcolm and I stare after him. A tune reaches my ears, the melody off key but buoyant.

"Is he whistling?" I ask Malcolm.

"I think so."

"Does he do that often?"

I've only known Nigel for about four months, Malcolm a touch longer. Both brothers still hold a great deal of mystery for me. I couldn't tell you if Malcolm whistles.

"I don't think I've ever heard him whistle before," he says.

Malcolm creeps toward the conference room door and peers inside. Then he whirls, eyes wide, lips pursed as if he's trying to hold in laughter. He crosses to the far side of the reception area, gesturing for me to follow. We bend our heads close together.

"Nigel went over to Sadie's for dinner last night."

I nod. This, I know. Sadie Lancaster is my neighbor. I swept her house for sprites about fifteen minutes before Nigel was due to arrive. It's become an evening ritual.

"Well," Malcolm says now. "He never made it back to the apartment."

"Never made it …" I trail off, the obvious hitting me with enough force I almost gasp. "You mean they … that he … he stayed the night?"

"That's exactly what I mean." Malcolm grins and leans in even closer. "I think it explains his mood, don't you?"

I clamp a hand over my mouth so I won't giggle or do anything else juvenile. Sadie deserves some happiness. So does Nigel, for that matter. Still, Malcolm and I are responding with all the maturity of a couple of twelve-year-olds.

Maybe that's because we haven't taken that step. We're not even close to that step. We are, by my calculation, at least five miles from that step. My gaze drifts from the conference room door to the display window. From here, I can make out the sodden velvet and the way the gold lettering makes it glow.

K&M Ghost Eradication Specialists

My eyes lock with Malcolm's. His are a deep brown, close to black, like an excellent dark roast. We both know why we haven't taken too many steps. What happens to *K&M Ghost Eradication Specialists* if K&M the couple doesn't work out?

"Katy," he begins. His voice is soft, devoid of that earlier glee. He sounds like he might say something quite serious.

Before he can, my phone buzzes in my back pocket. I tug it out, and Malcolm sighs. I can't tell if I hear regret or relief in it, so I focus on the text instead.

Sadie: Katy, can you come over

I hold the phone so Malcolm can read the message. "I just cleared them last night."

"Maybe it's time we took them farther out."

"Maybe."

Sadie's two sprites adore her. They are, I think, like the children she never had. But they're not children; they're sprites. Like the one thumping the Tupperware container Malcolm is holding, they cause trouble. Sprites love to play pranks, get a reaction, soak in attention.

"If Nigel ..." He nods toward the conference room. "I mean, if this is getting ... permanent, they can't hang around."

No, they can't. Nigel's addiction makes that impossible. But something about losing them for good makes my chest ache, just a little.

My phone buzzes again.

Sadie: Katy please

I tuck my phone back into my pocket and hold out my hands for the Tupperware.

"I might as well go. I have coffee at home, and I can lose this one and the other two while I'm at it." I give my soggy sleeve a shake. "And change. I should probably change."

My hands are on the container, so when he pulls it toward him, I come with it. We're close now, with just a sprite and some plastic between us.

"I probably smell like the Coffee Depot," I say, and my voice has gone all breathy.

"I'm not complaining."

Between us, the sprite thumps the sides of the Tupperware, and my heart picks up its beat. If I smell like the brew of the day, then Malcolm spices the air with a strange mix of Ivory Soap and nutmeg—it's warm and exotic all at once. Malcolm's gaze is locked on my face. I couldn't look away even if I wanted to.

And I don't want to.

My phone buzzes a third time.

Malcolm sighs again and then gives me a grin of resignation. We are *K&M Ghost Eradication Specialists* and this is how we pay the bills.

"I'd better." I wave a hand toward the door.

"Yeah. You'd better."

When I'm outside, with my truck rumbling to life beneath me, I can't tell if it's regret or relief that will follow me on this call.

SOMETHING GREEN IS HANGING from my door. The wreath looks festive, like Christmas, but it wasn't there this morning. The front walk bears the slightest imprint of someone's boots, a pair much larger than I wear. Instead of heading around back to the kitchen like I normally would, I follow those snowy footsteps up my walk.

A mistletoe wreath is hanging from a hook on my door. It's an old-fashioned arrangement, the perfect complement for the old Victorian house, and the sprig of holly berries glow blood red against the white of the door. In the center, stuck beneath a plaid bow, is a card.

I strip off my mittens and tug at the card. The entire wreath wobbles, then plunges to the ground. I balance it against one boot while I read the note.

For one speaker to the dead from another:
Did you know that the French once referred to a bough of mistletoe as a specter's wand? They believed that not only could the holder see ghosts, but could induce them to speak as well.
Of course, we don't need those sorts of tricks, do we? Still, what would the holiday be without such ornaments as this?

The card is unsigned. I turn it over, check the envelope, but there's no clue to who might have sent the wreath. Malcolm, possibly? Was that why he was a few minutes late this morning? I frown at the card. It doesn't really sound like him.

"It's bad luck, you know, to let mistletoe touch the ground."

A voice echoes around me, low and masculine. I shove the card into my coat pocket and whirl to face it.

No one is there. Not on the sidewalk or the street. No one has crept up behind me on the walkway, although my heart is thudding like someone has. I scan the area, my back to the door. Without taking my gaze from the street, I bend down and pick up the wreath. It takes three clumsy tries before it lands on its hook once again. Then I decide the best place to be is inside the house.

Without shrugging off my coat, I brew a quick pot of Kona blend. If Sadie's sprites are back so soon, I'll need extra enticement to get them to leave. They've been stubborn lately. Maybe it's the holiday. Maybe it's because they're lonely.

Maybe I don't blame them. I haven't climbed the stairs to the attic yet to bring down the decorations. I haven't bought a tree. Whenever my mind drifts to this first Christmas without my grandmother, I force myself to think of something else.

Like now. I'll go catch some sprites and breathe in all that is Sadie's house at Christmastime—sugar cookies and gingerbread houses, strings of popcorn and cranberries, spiced apple cider.

Although first I take a quick look around outside, but the street is late-morning quiet with children at school and people at work.

The door to Sadie's house is ajar. Warm, scented air greets me when I push it open all the way.

"Sadie?" I call out.

I stop at the threshold, pulling in a few deep breaths, tasting the air. Sprites have such a slight presence that sometimes it's hard to tell if they're in residence at all.

Something otherworldly is here. That much I can tell. Normally, when the sprites act up, Sadie will be somewhere they are not. I call out again.

Nothing.

I pull out my phone. On the screen is one final message.

Sadie: he

He? Is there someone—or *something*—else in the house? Or is it the start of a word—a word like *help*? I don't think, don't question what I should do next. I dash up the stairs to the second floor, taking the steps two at a time. I call out again, my voice ragged.

"Sadie, are you okay?"

I don't want to barge into her bedroom, but that's the most logical place to search. I push open the door, the sight that greets me freezing me in place.

Sadie, on the floor, clad in a silk robe of deep gold. Her face is far too pale. She is far too still. My thumb is on the phone, ready to dial 911. I step into the room, but before I can cross to Sadie, a force surges into me.

The cold envelops me first. This is no sprite. Its presence fills the bedroom with resentment and dread, the air so stale and sharp it pricks the inside of my nose. A hot trickle of blood runs down my lip and the quicksilver taste fills my mouth.

The thing shoves me against the shuttered doors of the closet. The flimsy wood buckles under my weight. I grip the frame and try to regain my balance, my breath, cursing myself for walking into an ambush.

This ghost is fierce and angry. It moans, the sound like an accusation. Then the room is silent.

In the quiet, I glance around. The thing is still here; that much I know. With my coat sleeve, I wipe away blood. My phone is where? I can't fight this ghost on my own. In fact, I haven't encountered one this aggressive for a while. I need Malcolm. Sadie needs an ambulance. But first, I need to cross the room to where my phone has landed, next to the vanity.

I'm halfway there when the air shifts behind me. It feels like a gathering storm. I launch myself those last few steps. All I need to do is send a text. The ghost slams into me, the force propelling me against the vanity and its mirror, with all its glass.

The room explodes in shards. My head slams against something hard. I crumple to the floor, lungs searching for air, fingers groping for the cell phone. The moment I reach it, an icy blast sends it skittering away.

My vision blurs both with tears and an approaching darkness. I need my phone. I need to tell Malcolm about this ghost.

But it's too dark and too cold and my phone is too far away. I close my eyes. I tell myself it's only for a second so I can catch my breath. But my eyelids are heavy, and the dark washes over me. I taste regret along with the blood in my mouth. What I want is to hear Malcolm's voice. That feels like the most important thing of all.

THE INSISTENT SOUND of the ringtone penetrates my skull. This is the fifth time someone has called my phone. However, it's only the first that I'm coherent enough to do anything about it.

My world is still very much a black tunnel. I crack open my eyes, wincing against the sun streaming through lace curtains. I don't dare move too much or too quickly. If this ghost is still here—and I suspect it is—I don't want to alert it that I'm now awake—or mostly so. Not that my head, in its current state, will let me move too much or too quickly.

I crawl, a slow, agonizing trek across the hardwood. Beneath me, I leave a trail, a smear of blood, I think.

My phone stops ringing.

I sag against the floorboards in defeat. But with my ear pressed against the floor, I hear the rumblings in the house. A scraping, a crash, a shattering of glass. It's the sound of a Christmas tree toppling over.

If the ghost is downstairs, then he can't keep tabs on me, not if I'm quiet about it. I renew my journey across the floor and toward my phone. When my fingers graze its edge, it rings.

My first impulse is to answer the call, cry out, but I still my hand. This ghost is too aware, too calculating. I feign unconsciousness, enduring each ring and praying that the caller has patience.

On the seventh ring, I answer.

"Katy? Where on earth are you?" Malcolm's voice fills the room and my head. My heart beats hard with hope and reassurance even as a spike of pain travels my skull. "Did you drive out of cell phone range? It's been hours."

Hours. I crane my neck but can only glimpse Sadie's feet. Malcolm's voice is so strong and sure—and loud. I feel the buzzing, that other-worldly static, fill the air before the ghost flows into the room.

"Sadie's," I cry out, but my voice is rough, the word slurred. The ghost plummets and sends the phone careening against the wooden footboard.

This time I know it won't ring again.

CHAPTER 2

SINCE MALCOLM'S CALL, I've drifted in and out of consciousness. I know I must move, crawl if I can't walk, stay awake if I can't do either.

But my eyelids are so heavy. The icy dread that fills the room makes it difficult to breathe. The ghost isn't letting down its guard this time around. Forming complete thoughts is a challenge, never mind forming a plan to escape this thing. My head aches every time I try.

I know my grandmother faced such ghosts during her life. I remember a showdown in an old barn on the outskirts of Springside when I was barely eight. I remember that particular ghost lifting my grandmother as if her bones were hollow and tossing her into an empty stall.

We hadn't even used coffee to defeat it, although we'd started there. We always started there. All ghosts want something. Sometimes that something is to simply feel human once again, which is why coffee works so well to catch them. The steam. The aroma. Maybe it's simply nostalgia. I never questioned my grandmother on why it works.

But sometimes ghosts want more.

That particular ghost wanted forgiveness, something my grand-mother figured out by lighting a bit of hay on fire and shutting the barn doors. The ghost whirled and swooped, pushing open the doors and urging nonexistent horses to escape. Then it charged my grandmother as if it could smother the flame with its ethereal form. I caught it with one of our extra-large Tupperware containers.

But what this ghost wants? I can't begin to say.

Panicked voices fill my head long before I can make sense of any words. Footsteps pound, the vibration traveling through the floor, along my jaw, around my skull.

"Sadie!"

I squint. Behind me, Nigel crouches, touches Sadie's forehead and brings his cheek to hers while his fingers travel her neck in search of a pulse.

"Thank God." He scoops her up into his arms and stands. "I'm going to take her next door to Katy's."

"I've called 911," someone else says, the voice familiar, but I'm certain it isn't Malcolm.

I push against the floor. I should help. I should at least walk out of here under my own power. My arms tremble and I collapse against the hardwood. Then a hand is on my shoulder and that voice is in my ear, a tenor with just a hint of a southern drawl.

"Katy? Katy Lindstrom?"

I push against the floor again. This time, two strong hands hold me steady. Slowly, I inch upward until I sit. I blink and the man who's holding me comes into view.

"You're not Malcolm," It's the only thing I can think to say.

The man gives a soft laugh and shakes his head. "No, I'm not. Sorry to disappoint. I'm a friend of his, though. Carter Dupree."

"Do I know you?" My head swims and Carter's face distorts. He has four blue eyes, then two. He is so very blond and bright it makes me wince.

"I'd remember meeting you." He grins at me, and even his teeth are bright, so much so that I want to shield myself from the glare. "Here. Can you stand?"

He offers his hand and I take it, my knees wobbly. For a moment, I sag against him, then stand on my own.

"Where's Malcolm?" I ask, my words mostly air.

"Downstairs, holding off the ghost until we get out of here."

"Is he okay? It's ..." I touch my head. My fingertips come away stained with red. "It's bad."

"I can see that. Let's get you out of here and to the hospital."

We pass Malcolm on the way out. On the threshold of the living room, a samovar sits, the aromatic steam filling the air, the scent exotic and distracting. The ghost rattles about, still angry, but the aroma diverts its attention.

Malcolm throws a worried glance over his shoulder. His gaze lands on me, his gaze stricken.

"Christ, Katy—"

"I've got her," Carter says. "Follow as fast as you can."

Behind us, something shatters. Carter urges me toward the entrance.

We step outside and into the crisp air of December. The midday sun makes me duck my head and hide my eyes. The wail of a siren grows closer. By the time I can crack my eyes open again, an ambulance has pulled to the curb in front of my house.

Carter holds me steady until the EMTs can load the stretcher with Sadie into the back of the ambulance. Then, they come for me.

"I—" My mind is too foggy to calculate the cost of an ambulance ride or remember if we even opted for this under our small business insurance.

"You need to go with them," Nigel says. He eases me from Carter's grip and toward the nearest EMT. "If not for yourself, then for Sadie. They won't let me ride with her because we're not related."

I let the EMTs lead me to the ambulance. Carter peers in after me.

"I hope the next time we meet it's under better circumstances, Katy Lindstrom." He touches his brow as if tipping a hat.

The doors shut. The ambulance pulls forward, rocking me back and forth. I reach for Sadie's hand and squeeze her fingers.

She doesn't squeeze back.

DESPITE MY PROTESTS, I'm admitted to Springside Hospital for an overnight stay.

"Observation," the doctor intones, looking very serious right before she winks. I've known her all my life, and this isn't my first trip to the emergency room. When she adds, "Your grandmother would never forgive me if something happened to you," I know she's sincere.

But I'm alone in my own room. No one will tell me how Sadie is. The room phone is out of my reach. I don't have my cell—and even if I did, it's probably broken—so I can't call Malcolm. The television makes my head ache even worse. Someone with a sense of humor selected my hospital gown. I stare down at the print.

Dozens of little ghosts and jack-o'-lanterns stare back.

I wait, worry eating away at my insides. My head is throbbing, so I shut my eyes and concentrate on the footfalls that echo outside in the corridor. Some whisper. Some clomp. Then I hear steps that have a familiar cadence, footsteps that have shadowed mine.

I open my eyes in time to see Malcolm enter the room. Part of his forehead is covered with a bandage. I open my mouth, but before I can say anything, he waves away my words.

"Just a graze," he says. "Damn thing threw a vase at me."

"And?" I'm certain this is not a full report.

"And maybe a few bruises." He pulls up a chair and sits at my bedside. He reaches toward me as if to brush hair from my face but pulls his hand back. "I'm fine. It's you I'm worried about."

"And Sadie? How is she?"

He sighs. "She's fine, physically, according to the doctors. But she's still unconscious. They'll run more tests in the morning, but she's not injured—well, not like you are. They're letting Nigel stay with her."

I start to nod, then my head decides that's a bad idea. I swallow back the pain. I want to talk, not be coddled, so I school my face.

"What do you think it is?" I ask. "I mean, is it more than a ghost?"

It wasn't so long ago that I freed Malcolm—and myself—from an entity. This ghost in Sadie's house doesn't feel as calculating or intelligent as that other being was. True, Sadie's new ghost flavored the air, but it didn't change it, didn't manipulate, didn't suck the life from everything. I remind myself that not only did I banish the entity, I'm the only one who knows how to invoke it. Even so, I feel as if I should glance over my shoulder once in a while, just to make sure it's truly gone.

"It feels like a ghost to me," Malcolm says. "Completely nasty, but just a ghost. We used to get the really horrible kinds once in a while when I was living in the frat house. I used to catch them—" He breaks off, eyes widening, a look of chagrin painting his features.

"In my samovar," he finishes. "I had all those ghosts in there when it exploded at Sadie's," he says. "What if this is my fault? Nigel will never forgive me."

"But that was months ago. Why now?"

"It hates Christmas? It's holiday central at Sadie's. Or at least, it was. The place is a mess."

"I don't think that's it, and I don't think it's your fault either."

His jaw tenses, his lips a thin line. No matter what I say, he'll blame himself. With my eyes closed, I cast my mind back to Sadie's bedroom. The ghost attacked so fast and so hard, I barely had time to get a read on it. But I spent plenty of time on the floor before help arrived.

"Suffocating," I say, testing the word for how it feels.

"Is that what it wants?" Malcolm asks.

"How it feels, what's left of its personality. Suffocating." I want to elaborate, but my thoughts are too fuzzy, my mind too dull to grasp the right words for it.

He nods as if I've made perfect sense. It's one of the things I love about working with him. He connects the dots between my random thoughts.

"And it's not leaving," he adds. "We'll have to eradicate."

"And clean up the mess." Not just the one it made, but the coffee-soaked one we're bound to create getting rid of the thing.

Malcolm manages a short laugh. "Yes, and clean. When you're up to it."

"Thank you," I say, something else occurring to me.

"What are partners for?"

"Well, that, but I meant the other, for the wreath. I just saw it this morning."

His brow crinkles. "What wreath?"

"The one on my door. You sent it, right?"

He gives his head a slow shake. "No, I didn't, but I'm thinking maybe I should have sent something."

"If you didn't send it …" My mind gropes for an answer or at least a clue. Then I remember. "My coat. I shoved the card into my pocket before I went to Sadie's."

Malcolm rummages in the built-in closet and pulls out an envelope.

"For one speaker to the dead from another," he reads before skewering me with a look. "Really, Katy? You thought I wrote that?"

"Who else would?"

"It's terrible." He makes a face. "Plus, it isn't signed. Trust me, when I send you something, you'll know it's from me. This?" He waves the card in the air. "This is just creepy."

I let out a breath, all relief and no regret. I knew it didn't sound a thing like Malcolm.

"But if you didn't send it, who did?"

Malcolm turns the card in his hands, studying it, holding it up to the light. His features shift from grim to amused. He throws his head back, but his laugh lacks its usual warmth.

"It seems they're courting you already," he says.

"Who's courting me … and why?"

"You met him today. So that's why he's in town." Malcolm shakes his head, self-recrimination painting his features. "I should've known."

"Who?"

"Carter Dupree."

"So he's a friend of yours?"

Malcolm snorts. "That might be pushing it."

"He said he was."

"Yeah, well, Carter says lots of things he shouldn't and not enough things that he should."

"Even without the head injury I'm not sure I'd know what that means."

He doesn't laugh, but the smile he gives me is indulgent and dazzling. After a quick glance at the door, he scoots his chair closer to the bedside.

"He's like us," Malcolm says. "A necromancer."

"I'm not a necromancer." We've had this conversation. Right now I'm in no shape to have it again.

"Whatever. Only with Carter it's different. He's part of a necromancer … guild, I guess you could call it."

"Such a thing exists? What do they do? Go through training?"

"Yes, but it's more like a consortium, or maybe a cabal, a syndicate."

"That sounds shady," I say.

He raises his hands, palms skyward. "It does, doesn't it?"

What is he saying, exactly, and why won't he spell it out? An awful thought strikes me, sends a second spike of pain through my head.

"Are *you* part of this thing? Is Nigel?"

He leans forward, so close I can smell the Ivory Soap laced with his sweat from this afternoon's battle. He is both warm and safe. I'm praying he won't say something to change that.

"Honestly? I don't think I ever made it onto their radar. That's maybe just as well." He pauses as if considering his next words. "Besides, the Armands have always been ... free agents. We'll consult with each other occasionally, but this is the longest Nigel and I have ever worked together." This time when he reaches out, his hand does travel my forehead and sweeps strands of hair from my face.

Shady cabals and families filled with lone wolves. Both options strike me as unbearably sad. There are many reasons I refuse the label of necromancer. I've now added two more to the list.

"Why is he here?" I ask.

"Ghost gossip."

"Ghost gossip?"

"You can't banish an evil entity without that fact getting around. One sprite told another, that one told a ghost who told another who has a ... pact with a necromancer."

"And then that necromancer tells all the others."

"Well, in this case, yes. I'm surprised it took them this long, now that I think of it."

"What do they want?"

"You."

"Me? What on earth for?"

"Less earth, more otherworldly. You called forth that entity once, right?"

Despite the ache in my head, I manage a small nod. Yes, I did, and we both wear the scars from that. There's still a faint blue cast to my left cheek from where the entity marked me. Malcolm's ebony hair has a touch of gray, especially around the temples.

"That means you can do it again," he says now.

"I don't want to do it again. That would be stupid."

"They don't think so. In fact, that's how they ... work things. They find the most powerful ghosts they can and then use their membership to leverage them."

"That sounds awful. It sounds ... cruel."

Again, Malcolm raises his hands. "I'm not disagreeing, just telling you how it is."

Dinner arrives then, in a clattering of the cart across the linoleum floor (*loud ... so loud*) and the scent of turkey with gravy. The meal includes pumpkin pie with a dollop of whipped cream on top. I plan to skip straight to dessert.

"That looks almost edible," Malcolm says.

The remark earns him a glare from the nurse entering the room.

"I think, young man, it's time to end your visit."

He turns one of his dazzling smiles on her and melts some of her ice. Her own smile in return is indulgent.

Oh so predictable.

"I just wanted to make sure Katy's okay for the night," he says.

"We'll be watching her." The nurse holds up her hand, five fingers extended. "Five minutes and no more."

Malcolm leans close as if to give me a goodbye kiss. Instead, he says, "We'll sort through this tomorrow."

I start to agree, then a panicked thought strikes me. "I left a sprite on the counter in my kitchen, and Belinda can't stay the night with that ghost next door."

Belinda Barnes is my roommate. She's also a magnet for the nastier ghosts that haunt this world. The one next door fits the profile perfectly.

"I called the Pancake House to warn her. She says she has a place to stay and will grab something to eat before she goes off shift."

She does? Before she moved in with me, that place was more often than not some back alley.

"Really?" I say, because Belinda having somewhere new to stay is a curious development.

He shrugs. "Don't think too hard on it."

With that, Malcolm leans even closer and places a gentle kiss on my forehead. I want to tell him he can do more than that—my lips are in perfect working order. But there's so much tenderness and concern in that one simple gesture that I decide to simply savor it instead.

"I'll be here in the morning to pick you up."

And then he's gone, out the door in five minutes as promised.

A HOSPITAL IS an eerie place in the middle of the night. I sample the air, but nothing supernatural flavors it. All that lingers on my tongue tastes antiseptic and medicinal. I want to ask for another piece of pumpkin pie, but except for the occasional shuffle of soft-soled shoes, the hallway is silent. I suspect the cafeteria is closed for the night.

I stare up at the ceiling, my eyes wide open, growing unease gripping my stomach. My limbs ache; I'm starting to feel the aftereffects of the attack. I reach for the call button, but I don't know what the night-shift nurse could do except hand me some Tylenol. Still, I clutch the cord. When a voice sounds near the end of my bed, I yank it closer.

"Good evening, Katy."

My heart pounds, feels as though it might shoot out of my chest. It's a good thing I'm not hooked up to any monitors—I would've sent the readings off the chart. I bolt upright. My entire skull protests the sudden movement. I sink back down against my pillow, fingers searching for the call button.

It's nowhere to be found. Or rather, the shadowed form at the end of my bed is holding the cord.

"I didn't mean to startle you," he says.

"Yes, you did." The accusation bursts from my mouth as my mind scrambles to assemble the pieces of the puzzle. I've met that slight southern drawl, recognize his voice. The light in my room is too dim for me to fully discern his features. Considering how bright Carter Dupree is, that's just as well.

"You're right," he says, his voice both quiet and filled with humor. "I did. And I apologize, but think of it as a demonstration."

"Of what? How to creep someone out?"

"No." This time, there's a slight edge to his voice. "The power of necromancy."

"I'm not a necromancer."

"That's not what we've been hearing."

"And you've heard what, exactly?"

I'm not up to this. After that jolt of adrenaline, my muscles are sluggish, and my head throbs. Despite being wide awake moments before, I feel waves of sleep crash over me.

"Ghosts talk. I'm sure you know that. We have a pretty good idea what happened."

"Great. Then you can let me sleep."

"Are you tired?"

"Very. Please leave."

"All right, Delilah," Carter says to the air. "That's enough."

All at once, a fog lifts. My eyes flutter open. My heartbeat climbs again, and I'm certain if I lunge, I can grab the call button from Carter. I also feel another presence in the room, unfamiliar, but definitely otherworldly.

"Delilah," I say. "I don't think we've met."

"She's not much for small towns. This may be her first trip down here," Carter says. "She's rather sophisticated."

"She's your ghost?"

"Not exclusively, but we work well together, so for all intents and purposes, yes."

Once upon a time, Malcolm had a ghost. Selena. She helped him play the stock market, propelled him into being named Broker of the Year. But that was before he came to Springside, before ... everything.

"Don't you see, Katy?" Carter says.

"You've lost me. I have no idea why you're here, in the middle of the night, and if I could call the nurse, I would."

"I'm here, in the middle of the night, without any detection or consequences—"

"None yet."

"Because of Delilah and the power of necromancy."

I glance toward the nightstand. It's still more than an arm's length away. I could try diving for it, but I'd only catch air. Next to the phone, something glimmers, but with Carter in my room, there's no time to investigate.

"Okay, great," I say. "You can sneak around."

"And throw my voice."

"Mistletoe and bad luck? That was you?"

"It was, and I can get you out of the way of a very angry ghost."

Delilah's presence is a tangible thing. She flits around the room. Strong—oh, she is very strong, and yet, at the same time, tethered, like she's on a leash.

"Thank you, Delilah," I say. "That was quite a shield you created."

"Hm." Carter folds his arms over his chest, the cord for the call button dangling from his grip. Any moment, he'll start tapping his foot with impatience.

"What?" I say. I'm in no mood to be grateful. "If you'd been there alone, that ghost would've thrown a vase at you, too."

The air vibrates, the feel of it like delight, like laughter building in the back of your throat. I think Delilah *is* laughing. I tilt my head because I'm not sure I've heard a ghost this strong laugh before. Sprites don't count. Their default setting is laughter.

All at once, the sparkle of the otherworldly drains from the room, as if it's being sucked up by some supernatural vacuum. Delilah's presence slips away, and the stale ordinary returns, the air filled with that medicinal, antiseptic odor.

Then I know. Carter has pulled her back inside himself, and the room is lonelier for it.

"There you go, Katy. The power of necromancy. Aren't you intrigued?"

"Not really."

"Don't you see what this means? What you can do?"

"I'm a ghost hunter. I separate people from ghosts." I pause, then add, "When they want to be separated." Lately, I've also brought people and ghosts together.

"So none of this tempts you?"

"Should it?"

"Oh, it should, and greatly. Perhaps I've done a poor job in showing you just how amazing necromancy is."

"No, I don't think it's you. It's me." I nod toward the call button. "You can give that back to me or I can start screaming. Either way, you're out of here."

Carter drops the call button on the end of my bed, then raises his hands in a gesture of surrender.

"You win, Katy, this round. But I came to Springside to convince you, and I'm not leaving until I do."

I pull the cord to me and hover my thumb over the button. "Three ... two ..."

Carter backs out the door. His footfalls are nearly nonexistent as he makes his way down the hall, but I catch a telltale hint of them. Delilah's doing, perhaps? It almost has the feeling of a gift. I wrap the cord around my wrist and sink back against the pillow.

Before I can close my eyes, that glimmer on my nightstand teases my peripheral vision. I sit up, lean across the bedrail, and inch the night-stand closer.

A single rose in a vase is sitting next to the phone. I pluck the card free with two fingers. There is just enough light that I can make out the scrawled message.

Katy,

Sleep well tonight. I'll see you in the morning.

Malcolm

I hold the card in my hand and do what he says. Despite my still-pounding heart and late-night visitors, I sleep amazingly well.

CHAPTER 3

IN THE MORNING, before leaving the hospital, I visit Sadie. Someone has dragged an actual armchair into her room. It's there that Nigel is curled, a thin hospital blanket tossed over him.

Sadie appears serene, or nearly so. Her mouth isn't slack, as it would be in sleep, but tight, like she's worried about something. My gaze drifts to Nigel. I wonder if that something is him.

I ease the bag I'm carrying onto the floor. During my short stay, I have collected an astonishing number of things: tiny lotions, fuzzy socks with sticky tread on the soles, discharge papers, and information on head injuries. In my other hand, I hold the vase and its rose. This I clutch close.

With my free hand, I touch the back of Sadie's. Her skin is smooth, not too cold, not too warm. Any other time, I'd agree with the doctors. There's nothing wrong with her.

Except for one extremely nasty ghost.

I step back and jostle the IV stand. I steady it, but it jangles, the noise loud enough that Nigel stirs. The blanket slips from his shoulders, and he sits up. He stares at me, bleary-eyed.

"Katy?"

"Sorry. I didn't want to wake you."

"No ... no. It's fine. I want to be awake." He nods toward Sadie. "I don't want to miss anything. I really don't want to miss it if she comes to."

"I don't think she has." I want to explain why, but before I can, his gaze moves from Sadie to my hand—or more precisely, the rose in my hand.

A smile lights Nigel's weary face. "I'm guessing that one is yours." He nods at the vase. "Not Sadie's."

Her room blooms with plants and flowers. I suspect the lovely fern is from Nigel himself, a replacement for the one her sprites constantly uproot. I glance at my rose. Heat washes across my cheeks, and I nod.

"From your brother," I say.

"Ah, I see he decided to go with 'low key and elegant'."

"There were other options?"

Nigel gives a soft laugh. "Lots of them. We grabbed some coffee in the cafeteria before they closed last night." He shudders. "Speaking of which, if you get a chance, will you bring me a thermos of yours?"

"Of course," I say, my mind half on coffee and half on Nigel and Malcolm discussing flowers.

A rap on the door has me turning. There Malcolm stands, pressed and presentable, as always. For a moment he grips the doorframe, not moving, a smile tugging the corners of his mouth.

"How are you this morning?" he asks, voice quiet.

"Better." I touch my head. "Still hurts. The doctor said that's normal." I hold up the vase, the rose swirling in the glass. "Thank you. It's beautiful."

I should say more. I should tell him about Carter Dupree's strange late-night visit, and get Malcolm to poke holes in my theory about Sadie's state of unconsciousness. But at the moment all I can do is gaze at him, and he seems content to do the same.

"I'm fine, too," Nigel calls out. "So thanks for asking and all."

Malcolm peers around me and skewers his brother with a look. But when he enters the room, his expression is nothing but concerned.

"Sadie?" Malcolm asks.

Nigel shakes his head. "The same. The doctors have no idea why she won't wake up."

"I do," I say.

I know I shouldn't blurt it like that. And as expected, my declaration gets attention. Nigel shifts in the chair. Malcolm frowns, touches my elbow.

"Katy, I don't think—"

"Hear me out," I say. "Please?"

I focus on Nigel and he gives me a tentative nod.

"I think it's the ghost in her house. She was unconscious when I found her, but she wasn't injured, right?" I glance toward Nigel. "The doctor said so."

He nods.

"But I was. I don't think the ghost wanted to hurt Sadie so much as to ... have her?" I'm not sure of this last, but it's odd that I was hurt and Sadie not at all. "I think if we can drain some of its power or even capture the thing, she'll regain consciousness."

Nigel's gaze goes from me to Malcolm and back again.

"It's a really strong ghost," Malcolm says at last. "It's possible that it has some sort of agenda and it's causing this." He gestures toward Sadie. "There are cases that back this up."

"Do you think you can capture it?" Nigel asks. "I was there yesterday. It's not going to be easy."

Now Malcolm turns toward me. "I don't even need to ask, do I?"

"We can try," I say. "Of course we're going to try."

WE'LL TRY, but not right away. This is Malcolm's only stipulation.

"I can't go in without you," he says, "and you can't go in until you're better."

This gives us time to plan a massive eradication. I order special beans from the Coffee Depot—the usual Kona blend and their new fair trade holiday blend. Malcolm makes a quick trip to Minneapolis to buy spices from A Taste of Persia, the restaurant and market where he gets all his supplies for tea. For this ghost, we'll need every trick in our arsenal.

He even sketches a floor plan of Sadie's house. We pore over it, looking for places a ghost might use to ambush us—and vice versa. We set a date for the Saturday before Christmas. With luck, we'll eradicate the ghost and be able to clean Sadie's house all before Christmas Eve.

And maybe she'll get to come home.

It's the eve before our planned eradication, and I've gone over our notes so many times, I can't stand the sight of them. I'm sitting on the sofa in the living room, playing with my new cell phone and listening for the scrape of a key in the kitchen door lock.

I gave Malcolm one a week ago, and now he enters, bringing a blast of icy air with him. He smells like snow and cold and outdoors. There's a sprinkle of snowflakes clinging to his dark hair.

He shrugs off his coat, revealing a button-down shirt newly decorated with splotches of coffee and tea.

"A rough go today?" I ask. He's been taking all our routine calls, insisting that I must rest. Now I wonder if that was wise. He's the one who looks like he needs a rest.

"There's an overabundance of ghosts at Springside Long-term Care," he says.

"Happens every year, especially after they show *It's a Wonderful Life* or *A Christmas Carol*."

"So, the ghosts think it's funny?"

"They do, and the residents are highly suggestive as well. It doesn't take much activity to get everyone in a frenzy. Plus, I sometimes think the residents are in cahoots with the ghosts." I've liberated my share of ghosts of Christmases past over the years, and I've chalked it up to holiday tradition. "And for some of the residents, ours is the only visit they get over the holidays. I mean, not counting the ghosts."

Malcolm's jaw tenses, and he gives me a terse nod. "Yeah, I guessed as much. Maybe we could go back the day after Christmas and—"

"Bring them some sprites?"

"Yes." He grins now. "We'll bring them some sprites." He taps the papers on the coffee table and takes a seat next to them. "What about you? Any new thoughts?"

"I just ..." I shake my head, wishing that would shake in the answers that elude me. "Why Sadie? I know she has her two sprites, so yes, there's that connection. But they adore her. If they weren't such pests, I could leave them be."

"I sent this thing's profile around to a few necromancer buddies to see if they recognized it, but came up empty." He takes up a perch on the coffee table. "It's not local because then you'd recognize it."

I would, or at least should. "I feel like I'm missing something." I consider Malcolm's statement, then ask, "When you say 'necromancer buddies,' you don't mean Carter, do you?"

He snorts. "No. I simply contacted a few other ... free agents. It's a courtesy as well. When we catch this thing, we'll have to set it free some-where. A heads-up is always appreciated."

There is so much I don't know—and I'm not sure I want to know—about necromancy.

"Malcolm, can I ask you something?"

Maybe it's the tone of my voice, or that I'm leaning forward, nearly off the sofa and onto the coffee table, but his eyes brighten. He gives me that smile, the one that can make you forget the next words you planned to say.

"You can ask me anything."

He may regret saying that when he hears my question.

"When you were with Selena, was she free to come and go?"

A shadow crosses his face, douses that grin. I don't know what it's like to have a long-term partnership with a ghost, only that it's an intimate thing, and this feels weird and awkward, like I'm asking about an old girlfriend.

"Part of our ... arrangement was that she'd be around during work hours. And of course, I held up my end by doing those things she want-ed." He gives a little shrug. "I think I told you art museums were her favorite. We went to a lot of gallery openings, too."

"But you didn't control her."

A frown crinkles his brow. He gives his head a quick shake.

"She wasn't a pet," I say to elaborate. "You didn't have her on some kind of leash."

"It's a mutually beneficial agreement. It's always been that way between ghosts and necromancers."

"Always? With all necromancers? Even that guild thing you told me about?"

He blows out a breath. "Katy, what are you getting at?"

"When I was in the hospital, Carter Dupree came to visit me and—"

"Wait!" Malcolm shoots up. "You're telling me this now?"

He paces the living room. His strides are long and each step holds frustration. "You're telling me this now," he mutters. "Seriously? Now?"

He continues the litany, although it's really more *about* me than *to* me.

"I forgot," I say when his steps and words slow. I tap my forehead. "Head injury, remember?"

Malcolm halts, hands on hips, eyes narrowed in my direction. I take that as my cue to tell him about Carter's visit, the parlor tricks, and the odd obedience of Delilah the ghost.

"It was horrid," I tell him. "Like she was a dog that he could tug along on a leash, or a servant ... or worse. I felt so sorry for her, and I liked her. She was strong, but she wasn't that sort of ghost." I gesture in the direction of Sadie's house. "And she did shield me from that thing over there."

Malcolm returns to the coffee table. He sits so close, our knees brush. He takes my hands in his, and his skin is so warm. He rubs my fingers, and the resulting heat threatens to obliterate all my coherent thoughts.

"It wasn't like that with me and Selena," he says. "It's never supposed to be like that. I don't know what, exactly, Carter and the rest of his bunch do, but it's a power I've never learned, or at least, it's not one my grandfather taught me."

"Do you miss her?"

He hesitates, his gaze drawn to the ceiling, before he speaks again. "I did, especially when I first came to Springside and didn't know anyone here."

"You came to Springside and ended up the most popular guy in town."

"That doesn't mean I had any friends."

How lonely was he during those first weeks in town? All I could focus on was how he was stealing my clients. I never considered that someone new in town, someone so good with people *and* ghosts, might lack friends.

"You do now," I say.

He eases one hand from mine and uses his fingers to tuck a strand of hair behind my ear. And even though we have things to do, things to discuss, for a moment, the two of us together, like this, is enough.

"So, tomorrow," he says at last, his voice quiet. "Do we risk brewing on the premises?"

"I think we'll have to." I cast a glance toward the kitchen. "Even with the thermoses and the short walk, the coffee will cool too much by the time we get it over to Sadie's. We'll need it fresh-from-the-percolator hot."

"As much as I hate the risk, I agree."

"I'm going to use the Kona blend," I add. "I don't want to tackle this thing with an untested coffee."

He nods. "Agreed."

"What about your samovar? That seemed to distract it."

"Let's hope I can replicate the recipe."

Malcolm stands, the movement so sudden, the coffee table scoots backward in his wake. "I should let you rest, and I promised Nigel I'd stop by the hospital for a bit."

"There's a thermos of coffee if he wants it," I say.

"I'm sure he does."

I walk Malcolm to the kitchen and then to its door. We stand there with it wide open, snow swirling. I wonder if he might kiss me. I even rise on my toes as if my feet have anticipated such a thing. But after a moment, I wonder why he won't.

"I have no plans to become a necromancer," I say to break the silence. "Especially that kind."

Why he might doubt this, I don't know. But it's like he wants something from me. My only guess is he wants to hear this. He tilts his head, but the smile on his face tells me that the message has been received.

"I know." He leans in and plants a gentle kiss on my forehead. "I've always known that." With that reassurance—and no other kiss—he leaves.

I hold in my sigh until the door has closed behind me.

Really, my lips are in perfect working order.

BETWEEN US, we maneuver a crate with all our supplies from my back-yard to Sadie's. We have a key from Nigel, and Malcolm unlocks the kitchen door and opens it in increments.

"At least it's not keeping us out," he whispers.

There's that. Battling this thing and a full-on ghost infestation might be more than the two of us can handle.

Slowly and with as much stealth as possible, we lug all the items we'll need into Sadie's kitchen. Percolators and the samovar. Freshly ground coffee. Sugar and half and half. I've added in a set of twelve china cups I picked up at Goodwill. I don't want this ghost destroying any more of Sadie's things.

And, of course, the Tupperware container with an extra tight lid.

I'm standing in the middle of the kitchen when the feeling of the place washes over me. The walls have absorbed the ghost's malevolence, the atmosphere like that of an abandoned building, of some place that is truly haunted.

"I don't like this," Malcolm says, his words barely audible.

I don't either. "Start the samovar. That will help."

Once upon a time, I would've sworn you couldn't catch a ghost with tea—I mean, who ever heard of such a thing? But Malcolm can and does, and some ghosts (the odd ones, admittedly) prefer his concoctions of tea leaves and exotic spices. In any case, the aromatic steam will do this place—and us—some good.

"It's a Christmas blend," he says.

"Sadie would like that."

Without another word, we get to work. Malcolm starts the samovar going near the kitchen entrance. If the ghost interrupts our preparations, it will need to breach the steam. That will slow it down and give us time to react.

Or so we hope.

I brew the coffee; we'll need lots, so I set three percolators going at once. Between the scent of freshly brewing coffee—the Coffee Depot's very best blend, their Kona blend—and Malcolm's tea, the kitchen glows with steam and warmth. It feels like Sadie's kitchen again.

"Better?" he says, scooting past me, a hand on my waist.

"Better."

"Where do you want to start?"

While we've talked through the options, you really need to breathe in a place this haunted before making a final decision. I do that now, shutting my eyes and inhaling.

"The dining room. There seems to be an abundance of ..." I trail off, the word elusive.

"Resentment," Malcolm finishes.

"Yes. That. That's it, exactly." I turn to him, and I'm certain I look as curious as he does. "I can't imagine Sadie making anyone or anything feel resentful." I inhale again and consider our other options. "Living room, and master bedroom. Those are the three main spots."

Coffee brewed, we set to work. Always twelve cups, always the same combinations: three black, three with sugar, three with half and half, and three extra sweet and extra light.

I pour while Malcolm follows, adding and stirring. His touch is deft. I don't think the man has sloshed coffee into a saucer even once. My grandmother would've been impressed.

He insists on the master bedroom, leaving me with the task of placing cups in the dining and living rooms. The air grows tense, as if it would love to absorb this warmth we're offering but something is holding it back.

"Do you feel that?" Malcolm calls from the bedroom.

"I do. Be care—"

A crash cuts off my warning. A howl shakes the house. Picture frames rattle against the walls. China in its cabinet clatters. Above my head, the chandelier sways and jangles, the trajectory threatening. Any moment, the thing will come crashing down on the table—and me.

Malcolm pounds down the stairs. The apparition looming behind him is so strong, so angry, it appears nearly solid. Except for the entity of a few months back, I've never encountered anything with so much substance.

Just a ghost. Just a ghost. I chant it silently, over and over. Just a ghost. Out loud, I say, "Living room."

I've already deployed the four cups of coffee in there. There's a couch to hide behind and several other pieces of furniture to use as shields.

Malcolm dashes past me. Before I can follow, the ghost diverts its course and flows into the dining room. It swirls around the chandelier. The crystals cry out almost like they're in pain. Why this thing hates the dining room so much, I can't say.

But it does. I glance around, trying to discern why. What is so offensive about this space? Sadie had—and has—an open invitation. After a long day of ghost hunting, my grandmother and I ended up here more often than not. And more often than not, it was the three of us, since Sadie's philandering husband was usually out ... philandering.

Malcolm's footsteps sound in the hallway. A moment later, he bursts into the room. He glances upward, eyes wide.

"Damn."

That one word sums up both our feelings. The ghost covers the entire ceiling, its form churning as if it's being boiled. The chandelier makes a pathetic sort of jingle.

"It doesn't seem to be going for the coffee," he says.

No, the coffee hasn't helped at all. If anything, it's as if we've fed its anger and resentment. Steam is still rising from the cups, but if the ghost isn't tempted, won't dip down for a taste, then we can't capture it. I'm about to suggest the samovar and tea when Malcolm's cell phone buzzes.

"What the—" He pulls out the phone, brow furrowed. "I don't get it ... I don't know what ... It's Nigel, but I don't understand what he's saying."

"What does he say? Is it Sadie?"

At my words, the ceiling quakes. Plaster rains down and coats my arms and the table, and covers the coffee in a light dusting.

"It's just one thing, over and over again." He looks up at me. "He says: It's Harold, it's Harold, it's Harold."

Harold? My gaze is drawn upward. Nothing in the whirling form looks familiar or even remotely human. But I sense it the moment the name pops into my head.

Harold Lancaster. Sadie's husband. The man who died in another woman's bed. The anger, the resentment—they simply don't add up. Sadie was the wronged party. Even Harold would've admitted as much. But this thing festering inside the house? Where does its resentment and anger come from?

"It's Harold Lancaster," I say, "but I can't figure out—"

"I can." Malcolm tucks the phone back into his pocket. "I recognize the feeling now. It's not resentment. It's jealousy."

"Jealousy?"

"Because Nigel slept with Sadie."

And Harold slept with half the town. "That's a bit hypocritical."

"Some people ... ghosts ... are like that."

Something pings in the back of my mind. I've forgotten something, I'm certain, something important. On the table, the dusty coffee is cooling. What's there now wouldn't tempt the most desperate sprite, never mind a ghost of this caliber.

"I haven't tapped into the third percolator yet," I say.

"I'll get it. I'm closer."

When he leaves, the room seems to contract as if I'm not enough to fight this thing on my own. I widen my stance, plant my hands on my hips, and stare upward. The ghost is everywhere, easy to see, and yet I feel as if I can't keep track of it.

I hear the clank of a percolator. Cups and spoons rattle. It's then that I remember. It's then that I know this is absolutely the wrong move. Malcolm enters the dining room and I meet him, hands outstretched to take the percolator from him. I will grab it and run. Before I can, it slips through my grasp and shoots toward the ceiling.

One moment, I'm staring, open-mouthed, as the percolator zooms on a collision course with the decorative plaster. The next, I'm on the floor, Malcolm sheltering me from the coffee that's raining down.

Scalding coffee.

He swallows back a cry, but I hear the pain in his voice. He sits up, his fingers fumbling with the buttons on his shirt. I have no time for such niceties. I grip the sides of his shirt and yank. Buttons scatter across the floor. He shrugs off the sleeves, grips his t-shirt, and pulls it up and over his head.

"Let me look." I don't dare touch him for fear of causing more pain.

His back is bright pink, all of it. Scalding is an occupational hazard, but a burn this large means a trip to urgent care.

"We've got to," I begin, but a rumbling from the ceiling drowns out my words.

I glance upward. This is bad. This is very bad. Of its own volition, my hand finds Malcolm's. More plaster falls. With his back both bare and damp, the dust sticks. No doubt it stings. The lines around his eyes and mouth are carved with pain, but he doesn't utter a word or a cry or even a protest. All he does is give my hand one quick squeeze.

"I'm sorry," I say.

"It's not your fault." His breath is ragged, but the words come out strong.

"Actually, it is. I forgot."

"Forgot what?"

"Harold Lancaster hated coffee."

His gaze meets mine. We don't discuss. We don't even need to confirm. We leap to our feet at the same moment and run.

Harold's ghost follows us as far as the front door. With a burst of supernatural wind, we're shoved from the house, down the porch steps, and into the snow-covered yard. Malcolm flops onto his back and releases a sigh.

He knows as well as I do the best method for treating scalds; rolling around in the snow isn't one of them. But I let him. We've been through too much in too short a time. And if I'd been thinking, this wouldn't have happened at all.

I gaze up at Sadie's house, then turn to track the flashy yellow van rumbling up the street. On its side the words *Ghost B. Gone, Gregory B. Gone, Proprietor* remain, although Gregory has traded his so-called ghost evictions for substitute teaching at Springside High School.

The van jerks to a halt and both Gregory and my roommate Belinda hop out.

"Katy?" Belinda rushes over, her boots stabbing the snow, her hair a blonde explosion between two neon green earmuffs. Her gaze falls on Malcolm. "What happened?"

"Scalding," I say. "I'm fine, but I need to get Malcolm to urgent care."

"Or just leave me here," Malcolm says. "Here is good."

"Frostbite isn't going to help." I reach down, offer him my hand, but he waves it away.

"One more minute." He shuts his eyes. "That's all I ask."

"I take it the eradication was a no-go," Belinda says.

"You'll need to stay ... somewhere else. I may need to stay somewhere else. That." I point at Sadie's house. "Is the ghost of Harold Lancaster."

"Seriously?

"Malcolm thinks it's because Nigel slept with Sadie."

Belinda's eyes go wide, her mouth an o. I consider that maybe I shouldn't have blurted that, but it's too late now.

Her expression shifts, a knowing smile lighting her face. She nods. "Yeah, he's right. Some guys are like that. I can totally see Harold Lancaster being one of those guys."

Gregory kneels next to Malcolm. He urges him to sit up and he gives Malcolm's back a quick inspection. His eyes narrow, and I have to fight my own urge to tramp across the lawn and check on him myself.

I'm about to ask Belinda where it is she's been staying when rotating lights and a single whoop of a police siren catch all our attention. A patrol car pulls up and out steps Police Chief Ramsey.

He doesn't so much look at us as judge us, and that judgment passes from Gregory to Malcolm to Belinda. At last, it lands on me. Of all of us, I suspect I'm the biggest disappointment.

"Call came in about some vandalism and a possible home invasion," Chief says.

Yes, because tiny Springside Township gets so many of those.

"Thought I'd check it out myself, seeing Sadie is in the hospital and all."

He strides past us, up the porch stairs, and rattles the handle to the front door. Nothing. It's locked. Or rather, my guess is it's supernaturally frozen. The brass glimmers, and I suspect a full-on ghost infestation. Usually you need a bevy of ghosts for that. But this thing? This particular ghost is strong enough to pull one off all on its own.

Chief Ramsey walks around to the back door, presumably to repeat the same exercise with the same results. Handcuffs jangle at his side. A frown creases his brow. He takes in the four of us again, and I think he regrets not being able to use them.

"And what are you doing in Mrs. Lancaster's yard?" He directs this at Malcolm, who is still shirtless and sitting in the snow.

"We're making snow angels," Belinda says, her voice light and sweet. "For Sadie, as a way to welcome her home. You know how she loves Christmas."

Chief exhales, shakes his head, then points a finger at each of us in turn. "You four are more trouble than the kids from the high school. And you." He points again at Gregory. "Are double-parked."

No one says a word as Chief Ramsey lumbers down the sidewalk and into the cruiser. In another burst of lights and siren, he leaves. The quiet in his wake feels ominous. Sadie's house appears benign, and it's just as well that Chief Ramsey couldn't peek inside. It's a coffee-soaked, plaster-covered mess.

Of course, that means we're not getting back inside either, at least not anytime soon. My normal procedure of warming up a ghost infestation? Plenty of Kona blend. I have no idea how we'll rid Sadie's house of Harold's ghost. But first ...

"Urgent care?" I direct this at Malcolm. He's shut his eyes again.

"I'm ... fine."

"No, you're not," Gregory says and turns to me. "I can drive him over, or we could call 911..."

Malcolm opens his eyes and we exchange a glance. No, we can't afford another ambulance ride, not so soon after the last one. He pushes to his feet.

"No ambulance," he says.

"Why don't you ride with Gregory," I say. "Belinda and I will follow in my truck."

It's only after they've left that I turn to Belinda, and it's only now that I notice the bag slung over her shoulder.

"So ... you've been staying where?" I ask, but I have a fairly good idea.

She holds up a hand. "Don't even start with me."

"I thought you said he was obnoxious."

"I did."

"But?"

"But he's the least mystical person I've ever met. It's like he repels ghosts. Sprites can't even stand him. You should probably send him in there." She points to Sadie's house and then shrugs. "It's a relief, really, not to have to worry about waking up to Casper the less-than-friendly ghost."

"And?" This can't be the whole story.

"And I figured it was just a rebound thing. He and Terese were together for a long time. I'm not looking for anything serious. So ... it works." She adjusts the bag's shoulder strap. "I was actually just going to switch out some clothes and stay over for another night—or two."

"You *should* stay somewhere other than here tonight." Here is bad for Belinda, especially with Harold's ghost so recently agitated, especially since I'm the one who caused all that agitation. Revenge isn't out of the question.

"What are you going to do?" she asks.

I study Sadie's house and shake my head. "I don't know."

"Know what I'd do?"

"What?"

"Get out of here for a night and offer to play nursemaid to Malcolm. He's going to need someone to wrap his back in gauze and check for blistering, right? That might as well be you."

Despite the cold and the light breeze, my cheeks burn.

"Tell me you didn't notice him in all his shirtless glory," she adds.

"I take it you did."

She raises her hands as if this goes without saying.

"We're business partners," I say. Now is not the time to think of Malcolm's naked back. It only makes my cheeks burn harder, and Belinda smirks.

"*Just* business partners?"

I don't answer. I'm not sure I know the answer. Instead, I head for my house. I can't imagine Malcolm wants any coffee, but Nigel might. I need to check on both of them, and Sadie too.

Belinda falls into step next to me. "Five minutes and I'll be ready."

"Take your time," I say. "I need to brew some coffee for Nigel."

I also need to think, and consider, and grope for answers. The kitchen is a good place for that. But as I stand in its center, listening to the percolator work its magic, I can't conjure up anything that might resemble a solution to all this. Even if I had an idea of our next steps, I doubt it would work.

There's something about December that brings out the worst in ghosts.

CHAPTER 4

Nigel hasn't even poured the first cup of coffee when he tells me this.

"When?"

"About one thirty, I think."

"We were at Sadie's then," I say. "Just our presence must have drained some of its power, at least at first."

"She called out his name." He stares down at the thermos as if he doesn't want me to see his face. "I thought at first she was calling *for* him."

Oh, poor Nigel. I hadn't thought of that. "But it wasn't that," I say. "Right? It was a warning."

Nigel pours and considers the coffee in his cup. I think he won't meet my eyes, but a moment later, he glances up, gives me a wan smile, and offers the thermos to me. I shake my head. I've had enough of coffee for one day.

"Didn't think so," he says. "I'm guessing Malcolm won't want any either."

"You're right."

A voice comes from the doorway. There Malcolm stands, hand braced against the frame, his grip tight as if he's holding himself up.

"How are you?" I ask.

"Not in the mood for coffee."

"But how are you?"

"Lucky." Now he grins, and if it isn't as bright as it normally is, it's still just as warm. "Only two small blisters, and the rest like a bad sunburn. You ripped my shirt off me in time."

"You know," Nigel says, and he takes a long draw of his coffee. "Under different circumstances, I might want to know more about that."

For the second time that day, I feel the rush of blood to my cheeks, like tiny pinpricks. I eye Nigel, who only laughs, and then work up the nerve to look at Malcolm.

His smile hasn't faded and he holds out a hand. "I feel like I'm about seventy, though."

I grab his hand and help him to a chair.

"Sadie woke for a bit," I tell him. "She tried to warn us about Harold."

He nods. "So that confirms the connection."

"I'm thinking that if we can drain its power, capture it, and take this thing far, far away, that will do it." My gaze drifts to Sadie's form, so still in the bed. "He'll let her go—or be forced to. Whatever this connection is, it won't hold."

We fall silent. I'm hounded by the notion that all ghosts want something, but I can't figure out what it is Harold wants. Is it this? Sadie in a forever sleep, like some fairy tale queen? Or is it something else, something I'm missing?

I was so young when Harold and Sadie moved in next door. She seemed old to me. She was, in a way—a married grownup, after all. Harold was even older. It's only recently that I've begun to think of Sadie as my friend rather than my grandmother's. It's only recently that I've seen how young she still is. The man keeping vigil at her bedside has a lot to do with that.

We sit. After a while, Malcolm's hand finds mine. I find Nigel's. The vigil doesn't help Sadie, but we're not doing it for her. I think we're doing it for us.

~

It's nearly ten at night when I return home. I'm clutching the takeout containers left over from dinner at Sadie's bedside. The spicy scent of Szechuan chicken warms the air and stings my nose.

I stand on the sidewalk outside Sadie's house. The windows are black. The place looks curled in on itself, as if it might crumble into dust. I remain there for so long, cold sneaks through the soles of my boots until my toes ache.

"He's gone, you know."

The voice makes me jump. My heart thuds, the beat of it quick and annoyed. This is a voice I recognize, and this is the third time it has startled me. I swallow my first question, which is: *He is?* I go with the one that I think will irritate Carter Dupree as much as he irritates me.

"Who's gone?" I ask.

"The ghost." And there he is, Carter Dupree, sliding soundlessly to stand at my side.

"What ghost?"

"Don't play dumb with me, Katy. We both know what's been going on." Although it's dark, I think I detect an eye roll. "Please. I carried you out of there."

He points to Sadie's house. Then, as if to prove a point, he strides up the walk. He halts on the porch, strips off his gloves, and touches the doorknob with bare fingers. He doesn't bend over in pain. His hand doesn't suffer from frostbite.

The door swings open. With the house so dark, I can barely see the decorative wreath Sadie keeps just inside the entryway. The infestation truly is gone. Now that I can taste the air from inside, I realize that so is Harold's ghost.

"See?" he says, and closes the door. "No ghost."

My fingertips itch. I want to pull out my phone. I want to text Malcolm or call him so he can eavesdrop. Instead, I tilt my head and keep my expression as bland as possible.

"Oh." It's all the reaction I plan to give him.

"You wouldn't know what happened to him, would you?" he says.

"Are you asking me or baiting me?"

"What do you think?"

"I think I'd rather talk to Delilah. Is she here?"

If she is, I can't sense her. The air is so devoid of anything supernatural, I'd almost welcome the appearance of Sadie's mischievous sprites.

"Delilah is always with me."

"Even when you sleep?"

The streetlamp casts a yellow glow. There is just enough light that I can see his left eye twitch. It isn't much of a tell, but it's enough to go on.

"Even then," he says at last, the words clipped.

"How can you be sure? I mean, you're asleep, right?"

A touch of the otherworldly invades the space between us. It doesn't warm the air, of course, but it gives the cold some extra bite.

"Delilah," I say, letting my voice ring loud. "Next time you want to hang out, just wait until Carter goes to sleep and come on over. We don't have much nightlife in Springside, but I can brew you some Kona blend."

The air around us shimmers, the feel of it light and joyful. I think it must be Delilah. Even with the lockdown Carter has on her, he can't suppress every last reaction. My guess? She's laughing.

"Hm." His voice is terse. "You may regret that invitation."

"I doubt it."

"Then I'll leave before you do."

Without another word—and with that strange threat in the air—he turns from me. I'm determined to track his progress up the street. I see no car. All the houses are dark, front porch lamps extinguished for the evening except for my own. I hold Carter Dupree in my sights for as long as I can, eyes wide open.

The air is so cold, his walk so long that tears brim in my eyes and travel down my cheeks, hot trails against chilled skin.

Then he vanishes. He isn't so far away that I merely lose sight of him. One moment he's beneath a streetlight, the next nothing is. I stare at the empty space until my gaze is drawn, once again, to Sadie's house.

My feet start moving before I've really decided. I walk to her porch, touch the knob for myself, and then step inside.

~

THE FIRST THING I do is lock the door behind me. The second? Pull out my brand-new cell phone and speed-dial Malcolm. I'm halfway to the kitchen door when he answers.

"Jesus, Katy, are you okay?"

"Relax. I'm fine." I lock the kitchen door as well and flip on the lights.

Coffee stains the countertops. On the floor, near the refrigerator, a pool of half and half has congealed. I tuck the takeout containers inside and continue my inspection. My boots crunch spilled sugar and shards of broken china. One Goodwill cup remains, the lone survivor of the mêlée.

"It's a mess in here," I say, more to myself than Malcolm.

"What's a mess? Where are you? Don't do this to me."

"Sorry, sorry. I'm at Sadie's. Harold's ghost is gone."

"How do you even—?"

"I ran into Carter Dupree. He told me." I crunch my way from the kitchen, intent on inspecting the rest of the house.

Malcolm swears, colorfully and for several seconds. "Funny how he shows up when I'm not around."

"Yeah, it feels less like courting and more like stalking."

The line goes silent. This worries me, as does the coffee stain on the living room's cream-colored rug. The spot is the size and shape of a Great Dane. It's going to take more than a can of carpet cleaner to get rid of that.

"Malcolm?"

"Still here. I'm just ... worried. Are you sure you should be at Sadie's?"

"The ghost isn't here. Carter isn't here. Besides, I locked the doors."

"And he has a powerful ghost at his disposal."

"Delilah? I like her."

"Well, don't get too attached. One, she's under his control. Two? The powerful ghosts are the most capricious."

"Was Selena?"

He falls silent again. I don't think he expected that question. Maybe it was unfair of me to ask it.

"She was," he says at last. "A little high maintenance too, as far as ghosts go."

"I think Harold's ghost has her beat."

To my relief, he laughs, the sound of it warm and sweet, a dark roast on a cold day sort of a laugh.

"Speaking of Harold," I say, although I hate to hear the humor drain from Malcolm's voice. "Carter was asking whether I knew where he ... it ... the ghost went. Why is he so interested?"

Malcolm swears again.

"What?" I prompt when he doesn't elaborate.

"I'm starting to think that this has been a setup."

"You mean Harold's ghost."

"That's exactly what I mean."

I move on to the master bedroom. Compared to the rest of the house, the damage is minimal in here, the most significant being my blood on the corner of the vanity and the floor. Jars and bottles are scattered everywhere, but everything is made of plastic or thick glass. Nothing is broken.

Except the mirror. I did that. Or rather, Harold did that, using me. Who gets that piece of bad luck?

"So, are you saying that someone like this necromancer cabal or whatever it is, tracked down Harold's ghost, captured it, and then set it free at the moment it would do the most damage?"

"That's exactly what I'm saying."

I step over shards of shattered mirror. "Do you know how paranoid that sounds?"

"Do you have a better theory?"

I don't, except that Sadie falling in love might have triggered something like this. Even in death, Harold has managed to control major pieces of her life. He owned the house she lives in, the car she drives. What happens when the grieving widow no longer grieves? What happens when her attention turns to someone else? Someone alive and worthy and oh so perfect for her?

"Is this something this guild thing is capable of?" I ask Malcolm.

"Possibly. Probably. Okay, yes. They've been in existence for a hundred years. They have ... accumulated wealth. But it's not like they advertise their abilities, not like we do. They don't want people knowing what it is they do or can do."

"Then why?" I ask. "Why do this to Sadie?"

Silence on the line greets my question.

"Malcolm?"

"It's not so much Sadie as it is you," he says, and reluctance is thick in his voice. I wonder if there are things he's not telling me. "It all comes back to you."

"I'm nothing."

"Don't say that. You're not only powerful, but ghosts like you."

"Not all ghosts."

"Forget Harold's ghost. Those kinds of ghosts don't like anyone. You know that. You have a sense for ghosts. You draw them out. Seriously, you keep us in business."

"You're good with ghosts. I couldn't do this without you."

"Thanks. My ego needed that. But how many times do sprites hit me on the head during any given week?"

Okay, the answer to that is: more than I can count. I see the gesture as a ghostly buddy-shove, but maybe Malcolm has a point.

"I can catch ghosts," he says. "I was a pretty good necromancer. Not so good that the cabal started courting me, but I held my own. They want you, Katy, because you have an innate affinity I don't think any of their number has. It's a whole lot easier when the ghosts come to you."

I'm in the dining room now. I've saved this space for last. The chandelier is hanging by wires. I don't dare turn on the lights, but the ones in the hallway shed enough light that I can see. Coffee has dried all over the dining table, ruining its finish. My silver percolator is resting on the floor near the sideboard, dented and concave. I will have to retire this one from service.

"Okay," I say to Malcolm. "Let's say this is a setup, and Carter brought Harold here. Where is Harold now? Not under his control, that's for sure."

"I don't know." Doubt echoes in his voice.

"Sadie," I begin. I'm about to dash from the house and rush over to the hospital.

"I'm with her, and Nigel will be back soon. He needed a shower and a change of clothes. I said I'd sit with Sadie until he got back. But I'll stay the night. I can't sleep on my stomach, so there's not much sense in going home."

"I feel like I'm missing something." I scan the dining room as if that something is here, spelled out in the coffee stains on the walls and across the floor. There's more to this than Malcolm's crazy conspiracy theory. I'm certain of it.

"Why don't you go home?" he says. "Get some sleep. There's not much you can do at eleven at night."

He's right, of course. But after we've hung up, I can't force myself to leave Sadie's house. If Malcolm can't sleep because of his injured back, then I can't sleep, period.

I spend the night cleaning what I can. The big chores—like the Great Dane on the carpet—will have to wait until the stores open in the morning. But at sunrise, when I leave, at least the place no longer reeks of stale coffee.

CHAPTER 5

BELINDA BRINGS THE steam cleaner. She and Gregory carry it up the front porch steps and into Sadie's house. They head straight for the living room.

All this in response to a single text I sent her an hour ago:

Ghost gone. You can come home.

"How did you know?" I ask, raising my voice to be heard over the rumble of the machine.

The thing throws steam into the air. Too bad Sadie's sprites aren't here. They'd love to dance in that.

"Did you look in the mirror anytime yesterday?" Belinda says.

Okay. She has a point. I may not be able to wear those jeans again—except on another eradication. My hair held so much plaster it needed three washings.

"I figured the house had to be worse," she adds.

With patience and undeniable practice, Gregory sets to work on the Great Dane. Already the stain has shrunk to standard poodle size. Chihuahua can't be far off.

I nudge her. "Man knows how to use a vacuum."

"Shut up."

I laugh, but I do shut up because she bites her lower lip and the start of an honest blush creeps up her cheekbones. I won't tease her about this, not too much. Still, he's only been in town for a few months. He can't be too obnoxious if he's willing to pitch in and clean a near stranger's home.

We're in the kitchen, scrubbing coffee stains from the floor tile's grout, when Malcolm stumbles in.

And he does stumble. Gregory holds out a hand to steady him, but Malcolm waves away the offer. He blinks against the scent of the cleanser as if it stings his raw and weary eyes. His normally smooth hair is rumpled; so is his normally pressed shirt.

I open my mouth. I'm about to ask. I'm sure the question is there on my face.

"Been driving around all night," he says before I can utter a word. "Went out to the old barn, even drove all the way over to the mausoleum." He shakes his head. "Nothing. I didn't see any signs of a ghost that powerful. I didn't even run into any sprites."

And we haven't received any calls, either. Some people ignore the sprites, chalk up their mischief to bad luck or Mercury in retrograde, but most can't ignore a ghost so powerful it can toss people against walls and mirrors.

"Well, if he showed up here and then left," Belinda muses, "maybe he went back to his old job?" She looks to me, both eyebrows raised. "Do ghosts do that?"

"Sometimes, but usually only one thing drives them, one passion from their old life."

"Have you tried the bars?" Gregory offers.

"The bars?" I say, skeptical. I'm pretty sure my grandmother never eradicated a ghost from a bar, and I certainly haven't.

"So, passion, right? He comes here." Gregory waves a hand, indicating Sadie's house. "Then Sadie leaves."

"Actually, the ambulance came to get her," I say.

"Narrow the lens." He brings his hands together. "The ghost doesn't know that. All he can see is betrayal and abandonment. It doesn't matter if he caused all the problems; he's still going to throw himself a pity party, and he's going to do that with alcohol."

The room falls silent. Belinda's expression shifts to something both thoughtful and tender.

Gregory strokes his beard, his own expression contemplative. "Trust me, I know a little something about that."

Malcolm clears his throat. "What do you say, partner? Want to hit the bars later tonight?"

I feel as if I'm missing something crucial in all of this. We all are. But I nod.

"Sure," I say. "Let's go out drinking."

MY TRUCK IS IDLING in front of the Last Ditch Bar and Grill. The neon illuminating the D barely flickers, so Malcolm and I peer up at the Last Itch Bar and Grill. My hands are on the steering wheel, his on the dash. So far, Finnegan's Pub, the American Legion, and the bowling alley have yielded zero ghosts but plenty of questioning looks.

I'm stiff from the cold and too little sleep. Malcolm's head bobs. I suspect the dash appears as tempting as a pillow at this point. But he heaves a sigh and pushes himself upright.

"Maybe I should go in alone," he says.

"Why?"

"This place looks a little … rough."

The bar is technically outside of Springside Township, but there's a Dairy Queen a quarter mile down the road, so I'm fairly certain the clientele can't be too questionable.

He doesn't move. Neither do I.

"What do you know about Harold?" he says instead.

"I told you most of it. I remember his lawn. He was forever doing something to the lawn, and when he ran out of his own, he moved on to ours. And I remember Sadie coming over for coffee. I remember the tears." As I speak, my voice lowers, and I catch the echo of the confused child I used to be. "I wasn't supposed to be eavesdropping, and there was so much I didn't understand."

I do now, of course.

"Sadie didn't grow up here, didn't have many friends," I add. "That can be hard."

"Yeah. Tell me about it."

Again, I swallow back a dose of guilt.

"She has a sister in Illinois," Malcolm says. "Nigel's been talking to her, keeping her up to date on Sadie's condition."

"This just seems so unfair, for both of them."

"You know," he says, his voice lower, filled with what sounds like admiration, "the nurses on the floor call him Sir Nigel since he's hardly left her side and he's so gallant."

Now it's my turn to heave a sigh. "We've got to fix this." I undo my seatbelt.

"You—"

"I'm coming with you." Before he can launch a protest, I switch off the ignition and hop from the truck.

The wind batters us. My jacket with its down filling feels thin and flimsy. The neon from Last Itch drowns out even the chance of stars, and I squint in its glare. It's late; we're both exhausted. And this feels like a fruitless effort.

"We really should be home in bed," I say.

My words hang in the air for so long that I think they might freeze and shatter on the ground. Then it hits me: what I've just said, what it sounds like.

"I—" My cheeks blaze, and even with the wind and the icy air I'm not sure they'll cool any time soon.

Malcolm laughs, grabs my mittened hand, and gives it a squeeze. "Come on. It's cold out here."

A haze of beer and hard liquor flavors the air. But the brass along the bar gleams, and the mirror reflects an array of colorful bottles. The few patrons look depressed rather than dangerous.

"Sense anything?" he asks.

I shake my head.

Malcolm nods toward the bartender. "Let's see what he has to say."

We navigate the maze of chairs and tables. At the bar, a large man is sitting, head down. He wobbles his beer bottle back and forth as if this is his sole entertainment for the evening.

The moment we reach the polished wood, the large man glances up, his gaze meeting mine in the mirror's reflection.

Police Chief Ramsey.

My grip on Malcolm's hand tightens until I'm certain I'm cutting off his circulation.

"Katy, what the ... *oh*."

Chief Ramsey spins around, wobbles, then rights himself. Although his gaze is a little bleary, it's just as relentless and judgmental as ever.

Malcolm tugs me closer. "Well, this is different."

Chief Ramsey points his beer bottle at me. "What are you doing in here? You're underage."

"No, I'm not."

"Well, you should be," he says. "And you." The beer bottle shifts and accuses Malcolm. "This is no place to bring a girl."

"Actually, we drove here in my truck," I tell him, "so technically, I brought Malcolm."

Malcolm snorts and gives my hand a quick squeeze.

Chief harrumphs, swivels in his seat to face the bar, and continues the back and forth dance with his beer bottle.

"Pity, party of one?" Malcolm whispers, but his tone is compassionate rather than cruel. "Chief's married, right?"

"As far as I know."

"*Still* married?"

The wedding band on his left ring finger would indicate yes, but people—and ghosts—have a hard time letting go.

"I don't know."

I wonder if I should start paying more attention to relationships in the here and now. I have no ambition to become the town gossip, but if the ghosts insist on making it personal, maybe I need to as well. It might make our job easier.

Malcolm tugs me closer still, his gaze scanning the booths, the pool table in the back, the ancient jukebox in one corner that has an *Out of Order* sign duct-taped to its front.

"Why don't you pretend to head for the restroom and do a quick circuit?" He nods toward the bar. "I'll talk to the bartender."

He lets me go and I do just that, my path through the place haphazard, as if I haven't noticed the sign for the restroom. Since it's an index finger with the words *Little Ladies This Way* painted on it, I'd have to be fairly dim not to.

No one here cares. Even the guys playing pool don't seem all that invested in their game, despite the bills stacked to one side. Near the back, I catch the sensation of the otherworldly, the presence slight and light.

I whirl, searching for the source. Nothing stands out. I take a few steps, and a pitcher of beer catches my eye. Normally, they don't wobble of their own volition, but this one does. I inch closer to confirm my suspicions, but don't get too close. I know what comes next.

The pitcher upends, coating the tabletop, the floor, and the two guys sitting in the booth.

One of them shouts. The other swears. At the front of the room, the bartender slaps the counter with his rag in frustration.

"Really, guys? Really? That's the third time tonight."

The sprites careen toward me, pleased and drunk and seeking attention.

"Not funny," I tell them.

They ruffle my hair and stream off, unconcerned. I don't have coffee. My Tupperware containers are in the truck. They know I'm not here for them. And I know, thanks to them, that Harold's ghost can't be here. Sadie's two sprites still haven't returned to her house. Sprites will not be where that particular ghost is.

I thread my way back to Malcolm, who's standing at the bar, head bent in conversation with the bartender and Chief Ramsey. Malcolm takes an occasional sip from a Heineken. I suspect he paid with a twenty and let the bartender keep the change.

Chief has moved on to something amber in a tumbler. The bartender is drinking Perrier. And as odd as this threesome is, the second I'm in earshot, their chatter dies. All three turn to gaze at me. I feel as if I've forgotten to pull on pants, or possibly zip them, but resist the urge to check.

The bartender smiles, then Chief does, and the whole thing goes from odd to creepy.

Malcolm raises an eyebrow. It's a small, almost-not-there sort of gesture, but it floods me with reassurance. He bids the men goodnight and heads for the door, catching me on the way with a hand at the small of my back.

"Outside," he says before I can ask.

The cold clears my head and my lungs. After the dank and murky bar, the air feels crisp and I think I could spend a good ten minutes in deep breathing exercises.

"That was interesting," Malcolm says.

"You had a nice chat, then?"

"No ghost, at least not the one we're looking for," he says. "I managed to find that out before Chief Ramsey butted in."

"Two sprites," I say. "You probably saw them."

"I offered our services, but Jeff—the bartender and owner—wasn't interested. They actually make him money. People keep buying new pitchers to replace the spilt ones. He promised to call if something other than that starts happening."

Sprites are one thing, but I think Harold's ghost might be bad for business.

"So ... what did you three guys talk about?"

He nods toward the truck. "I'm freezing. Get in and I'll tell you."

He's dragging this out, but I comply. Malcolm's expression is both mirthful and a bit mystified, and he knows how to leave me in suspense. He doesn't start speaking until I put the truck in gear and pull onto the highway that leads back to Springside.

"I was getting a little fatherly advice," he says at last.

"About?"

"You."

"Me. For real?"

"Apparently," he says. "According to them, I'm going about it all wrong."

"Going about what?"

"Everything, if you believe them."

The tires hum against the road. Wind carries snow across the double lane. The flakes swirl in the headlights. The effect is hypnotizing. I need to keep the conversation going, if only to stay awake.

"So, are you going to take their advice?" I ask.

Malcolm coughs out a laugh. "Not at all. One." He holds up a finger. "I want you to keep speaking to me."

"Do I even want to know?"

"Trust me, you don't. And two." He adds a second finger. "Chief is sleeping at the station tonight. You don't want to know about that, either. As for Jeff, he's on..." He trails off, touching his thumb to each finger, first on one hand, then the other.

When he reaches double digits, I ask, "Wives? Girlfriends?"

"Yes."

"Wives or girlfriends?"

"Wives *and* girlfriends."

"At the same time?"

"Often."

I can't help it. I laugh.

"When I take advice," Malcolm says, "I like to consider the source. And in this case—" He casts me a sidelong glance. "I'll wing it."

The heat returns to my cheeks with a vengeance, and it doesn't fade until I pull up in front of Malcolm's apartment complex.

"It looks like we've hit a dead end." He shields his eyes against the glare of the streetlamp and gazes through the windshield. "Can you think of any place we haven't tried?"

I can't.

"Maybe Belinda was right about his work," Malcolm says. "He was in sales, right?"

"I think so. He made a lot of money. That's all I really know."

"I'll call around in the morning to some of our business contacts, see if they're having any issues."

Our contacts? More like *his*. He's the one with the gift for networking and talking and generating leads. I shift in my seat so I can look at him full-on. We're in the black this month, even with my hospital stay. Some of that is the holiday bringing out the ghosts.

A lot of that is Malcolm.

"Thank you." I mean to say it forcefully, like a business partner. It comes out soft, more like a friend.

"Hey, it's what we do, right?" His grin starts off businesslike but transforms into something far sweeter.

That sweetness invades the cab of the truck. I feel as if I should hold my breath or make a wish or something. Every part of me insists I should lean closer to him. He seems caught by something and reaches out a hand to brush a strand of hair from my cheek.

I remain absolutely still. It's so quiet I'm certain I can hear my heartbeat. I think I might hear his.

"It's late," he says, breaking that stillness. "Even ghost hunters need sleep."

He unhooks his seatbelt and opens the passenger side door. "See you in the morning ... well, later this morning."

I swallow hard and nod.

He jumps down from the truck. I wait until he's inside the building and the light flickers on in his apartment's living area.

"It's what we do," I echo, putting the truck in gear.

I drive home, certain that when it comes to both this particular ghost and Malcolm, I'm missing something crucial.

THE CALL COMES at three in the morning. No name, just a local number that blurs before my eyes. I don't think I can handle a ghost eradication on only two hours of sleep. But it's December, and that brings out the worst in ghosts. I answer because—to quote Malcolm—it's what we do.

"Is this Katy Lindstrom?" a voice asks, husky and feminine and completely unfamiliar.

"Yes." I'm oddly reluctant to respond. Maybe it's the hour or the woman's tone. I blink and taste the air. I almost never end up with even a playful sprite, but something feels off kilter to me.

"And you're the ghost catcher, right?" the woman says.

"I am, along with my partner, Malcolm Armand."

"Oh, he's the cute one."

I haven't conducted an actual survey of how many cute guys live in Springside, but I'm pretty certain Malcolm isn't the only one. Besides, he's more ... suave than cute.

"Yes," I say, because the woman has fallen silent. "Can we help you? Do you have a ghost?"

"I think so ... I mean, I've never had one before, but I'm pretty sure this is one. I'm Misty Sandborne, by the way."

Something about her name pings in the back of my mind. I don't know her; she's obviously not a repeat customer. Yet, as the silence extends, it's clear she's expecting me to respond.

When I don't, she adds, "I ... knew Harold Lancaster."

Oh? *Oh.*

"Yeah, I know," she continues, although I haven't said a word. "It doesn't make me the most popular girl in town. I could tell you stories, though, about some of these so-called upstanding citizens—"

"The ghost?" I prompt.

"Right. Of course. Well, this guy said he could handle it."

"Guy?" I ask.

"A real cutie—not your cutie, but a different one."

See? Springside does have more than one cute guy.

"I don't have a cutie," I feel compelled to add, but I'm not certain Misty hears me.

"Anyway," she continues, "he said he could handle it and now he's out cold on my living room floor, and this ghost thing is ... pouting."

"Pouting?"

"Just hanging in the air. You can see its outline and everything and it's just ... sulking. *Gawd*, it reminds me of the way Harold used to get."

I bolt upright, then freeze. For a moment everything seizes: my muscles, my thoughts, any words I might say.

"You still there?" Misty asks.

"Yeah ... I am, and my partner and I will be right over."

"Oh! You're bringing the cute one?"

Yes. Yes, I am.

～

I TEXT Malcolm Misty's address and add:

It's Harold's ghost. Bring extra Tupperware. And anything else you can think of.

In the kitchen, I consider the percolator, the Kona blend, our field kit for toting coffee when we don't brew on the premises. But Harold Lancaster hated coffee, and his ghost has shown us—in no uncertain terms—how it feels about the stuff.

Coffee won't work. Maybe nothing will.

Misty lives in a duplex a few blocks from Malcolm's apartment. He's on the porch, stamping his feet against the cold and blowing air against his hands when I pull up in my truck. He has a bag slung over one shoulder filled with Tupperware and a small electric samovar.

I've arrived empty-handed.

"She's not answering?" I ask when I reach the porch.

"Decided to wait for you. What's up?"

"I'm pretty sure it's Harold's ghost," I say.

"And he's here ... why?"

"Misty Sandborne was one of the women Harold had an affair with."

So, yes, Malcolm is suave, the sort of guy who's hard to ruffle. But in this instance, I manage to do so. His mouth hangs open, and he blinks a few times before an incredulous look spreads across his face.

He recovers, because Malcolm always recovers, and says, "We're missing something, aren't we? Something obvious."

"There's ... yes, something. A connection? A pattern?" I shake my head. "But what it is, I don't even have a clue."

Malcolm rings the bell and we wait. A shuffle sounds behind the closed door, then it opens as far as the security chain will let it. I peer inside but can't see a thing.

"Hi, I'm Katy Lindstrom, and this is my partner, Malcolm Armand. We spoke on the phone? You have a ghost?"

"Oh, thank goodness!" the husky voice from the phone greets us.

The door shuts, the chain rattles, and then the way is clear.

"Watch out for the body," Misty says as we make our way down the hall.

Three feet inside, where the entryway meets the living room, a body is sprawled face down on the carpet. Malcolm steps over it first and then offers me his hand.

"Oh, a real gentleman," Misty coos.

We ignore her. We're too riveted by the sight of the inert form just lying there as if it's part of the decor. The question in Malcolm's eyes mirrors my own.

What the hell is Carter Dupree doing here?

I crane my neck to get a better look. With slightly more presence of mind, Malcolm takes a knee and checks for breathing and a pulse.

"Oh, he's fine," Misty assures us. "Just out cold."

I decide not to ask why or how. In that moment, the real reason we're here oozes its way into my consciousness. I recognize Harold's ghost. From the way it surges forward, I suspect it recognizes me as well. I brace, waiting for the inevitable—a vase careening toward my head, another encounter with sharp-edged furniture.

Instead, the thing simply hunkers down, morose and melancholy, filling the room with undeniable gloom.

"See?" Misty says. "I'm supposed to live with that? I was going to call you from the start, honest." She adjusts her emerald silk robe and gives Malcolm a little finger wave. "But he"—she points at Carter—"said he could fix everything."

"What happened?" Malcolm asks.

Misty shrugs. "He was muttering some things, crazy words—I'd never heard them before—then he opens his mouth real wide, like he was trying to swallow the thing whole. Then, boom!"

"Boom?" I say.

She extends a hand toward the body on the floor. I notice then that her long, lacquered fingernails match her robe exactly. "Out cold."

A knowing look crosses Malcolm's face. He gives his head a shake, like he can't believe the thought that's just crossed his mind. His sardonic smile tells me he does.

"Remember my theory, Katy, about why Carter's appearance coincided with Harold's ghost?"

I consider the events of the past few weeks, from the wreath on my door to Carter Dupree unconscious on Misty Sandborne's floor. My gaze travels from him to the dour mass that is Harold's ghost. I'm not entirely certain I believe Malcolm's conspiracy theory, but the proof of it is right there on the floor.

"But why? Why would he do that?"

Malcolm stands and nudges Carter's side with the toe of his boot. "You'll have to ask him that."

"Then what happened here?" I point at Carter and then to the ghost. This, I suspect, is a necromancer thing.

With movements practiced and cautious, Malcolm eases toward the ghostly shape. Its form covers the sofa and it seems to have settled there, its focus on the flat screen television rather than us. I have a strange urge to hand it the remote control.

"I think," he says, reaching a hand out, gauging the ghost's strength, "that it overpowered him. It's grown stronger in the past few days." He turns to me. "Do you feel it?"

I do, and the idea fills me with dismay. We've been doing all the wrong things with this eradication.

"Carter can't hold it and his other ghost at the same time, not anymore." Malcolm gestures toward the floor. "That's the end result. Only a really strong necromancer could do that. Nigel could, before the addiction took its toll."

At these last words, Misty places a hand on Malcolm's arm, her green nails shining like Christmas ornaments against his white shirt. "Oh, sweetie, that must have been so hard. Your brother, is it?"

Malcolm gives an awkward sort of nod, pats Misty's hand, and backs away with all the grace of Frankenstein's monster. I realize then what he probably has from the start.

Misty is wearing absolutely nothing beneath that emerald silk.

The ethereal form on the couch roils at this interaction. Misty whirls, silk swirling, hands on hips.

"Now, Harold Lancaster, you behave yourself. Yes, I know who you are and I'm not impressed."

The ghost shimmers, the result throwing a glow over the three of us. We stare, caught up in this spectral lightshow. It has our attention, and that's what most ghosts want, one way or another.

I cast my mind back to when I was younger. I didn't understand

Harold's philandering back then. Even when I did understand the concept, it was only much later that I truly understood—the pain, the sorrow, Sadie's tears, my grandmother's troubled looks.

But I also remember Harold Lancaster, the man who always ran his snow blower along our sidewalk and driveway every winter. He would—assuming he was home—come over to take something down from a high shelf, or lug the Christmas decorations from the attic. He'd oil the hinges on the garden gate without anyone asking him to.

"Malcolm," I say, working to keep my voice even. "Can you go grab some Tupperware?"

He backs toward his bag, more stuttering monster steps. "What do you have in mind?"

"If I can drain its power, do you think you can catch it?"

"Depends on how much you drain it, but yes, you do that, and I'll do the rest."

I turn to Misty. "Do you have an apron?"

"I have one left over from a French maid's costume I wore at Halloween."

Of course she does. "Can I borrow it?"

She heads toward the bedroom and I call after her.

"And a hair binder or two?"

When she returns, I knot the apron around my waist and use the rubber bands Misty hands me to secure my hair into a bun at the nape of my neck.

Malcolm raises an eyebrow at my impromptu costume. "I'm afraid to ask what it is you think this ghost wants."

"Trust me?"

He gives me one of those sweet, dark-roast grins. "Always."

I bustle into the kitchen area of Misty's apartment. The only thing dividing it from the living room is a long breakfast bar. I'm in full view of everyone. I turn, stand on tiptoes, and strain toward the top shelf above the sink.

"Oh, if only there was someone around who was tall enough," I say, making my voice quake the way my grandmother's used to, all low tones and a certain amount of bite.

"I'm sure he's tall enough." Misty jabs a finger toward Malcolm.

I shush her. "Now, Katy-Girl, don't you go crawling on the counters. That's dangerous. You might fall and hurt yourself."

A choking sound comes from Malcolm, like he's trying very hard not to laugh. Misty stares, wide-eyed. She throws Malcolm a questioning look, and her hand twitches, like she's *this close* to calling 911.

"I would love it if someone would help me." I punctuate this with little jumps toward the shelf.

Behind me, a groan sounds, eerie and possibly irritated. There's a rumble. A moment later, a soft exhale escapes Malcolm.

"Whoa," he says.

I peer over my shoulder to see the ghost slide from the couch, its form spreading out over the floor, like a bank of fog rolling in from the ocean. It flows from the living area to the kitchen until the mist is swirling around my feet.

Then the ghost pulls itself together into an almost humanlike mass.

"Oh, Harold! It's you!" I clap my hands together. "You're here to help!"

Harold's ghost rattles the dishes on the top shelf. One teeters and plunges to the floor, missing me by mere centimeters. It splinters into pieces.

"Hey!" Misty cries out. "That's my Martha Stewart collection!"

Another choking sound comes from Malcolm. I turn in time to see him jam the Tupperware under one arm and pull out his wallet. He hands Misty twenty dollars. She takes the bill and tucks it inside her cleavage.

How it remains there is a physics problem I don't care to contemplate. Besides, I have an entire kitchen yet to ruin.

One hand on my hip, I use the other to point, direct, cajole, and praise. Harold's ghost pushes the broom across the floor before shattering three glasses within the confines of the sink. The refrigerator door flies open. Cartons inch forward and then fall over the edge. Yogurt splatters across the tile.

With each effort, I praise. With each effort, Harold's ghost shrinks until at last it's opaque and puny. It still wants to help, circles me as if begging for another chore. This might be the saddest thing of all. It would do anything if only I praised it one more time.

My gaze meets Malcolm's, and I give the barest of nods.

He launches himself across the room, Tupperware clutched in both hands. His aim is perfect. He catches Harold's ghost in the exact center of the container and crashes to the floor.

With the ghost trapped, the otherworldly presence in the apartment dissipates. I draw a full breath. So does Misty.

"It's like smoke clearing." She fans herself, those long green nails blurring with the effort.

I glance down at Malcolm, still on the floor, still gripping the Tupperware for all he's worth.

"How'd you know?" he asks.

I shrug. "I didn't, not really. It was a guess, something I remembered from when I was little."

I think it was one of the reasons my grandmother always looked both sad and troubled around Harold. Yes, he hurt Sadie—and badly, too. But how awful is it to go through life craving constant praise and attention?

I kneel next to Malcolm to help him secure the container's lid. The Tupperware rocks, but the fight has mostly drained from this ghost. The only thing left to do is drive it somewhere far away. I unknot the apron and pull the rubber bands from my hair. Malcolm double-checks the container's lid. We're both eyeing the door.

"And I suppose you expect me to clean up this mess?" Misty is standing in front of us, hands on hips, emerald silk robe dangerously close to not being there at all.

Malcolm reaches for his wallet again, but she laughs.

"Oh, honey, I was kidding. I'll clean up. I'm just so glad to get that thing"—she flings a hand toward the container—"out of here."

"What about him?" I nudge Carter's foot with my own.

Misty cocks her head. "Naw, you can leave him. He's a cutie."

"He's kind of a jerk," I say.

"So was Harold."

Malcolm clears his throat. "It was nice to meet you, Misty." He extends a hand, the one not clutching the Tupperware.

"Oh, a real gentleman," she coos in a reprise from earlier.

I want nothing more than to leave, drive Harold's ghost far, far, far away, and then sleep for eighteen hours. But I turn to Misty and say brightly, "Call if you get anymore ghosts!"

Malcolm shrugs on his coat and steps over Carter Dupree. I do the same, a mere three feet behind him. The door opens, blasting us with icy, predawn air. He steps outside. I'm about to do the same when the door slams shut.

THE DOOR'S OAK paneling frosts over immediately. I know a ghost infestation when I see one. Even so, I touch the doorknob. I yank my hand back, fingers stinging with freezer burn.

I'm about to pound with my bare hand, but think better of it. I pull on a mitten and start hammering on the door.

"Malcolm! Are you okay? Did the ghost escape?"

"Did it ... what?" The door—and whatever else is between us—muffles his voice. "I have it right here."

"Then what is this?"

The door is now hoary with frost, and crystalline patterns spread across the doorknob. Even through the mitten, the cold brass bites my skin. I try the knob several times, because none of this makes sense and I'm feeling more stubborn than smart.

"Katy, Katy, stop it. You're not helping."

He's right. I give the knob one last rattle for good measure before giving up.

"Do you sense anything?" I ask through the door.

"Not a thing. Look, I'll do a circuit around back. You look inside."

I turn to face Misty. Her face is nearly as pale as her frosted door. Her hands clutch her arms, the nails fading into the green of the robe. I find myself contemplating that rather than my current predicament. I don't know where to look or what I'm looking for, and my mind is so clouded from lack of sleep, I'm not sure what I'd do if I found something.

"I could use a cup of coffee," I say.

That's when an icy glimmer chases across my neck.

"Maybe I'm not the only one?" I ask the air.

"Who ... who are you talking to?" Misty demands.

"I'm sorry," I say—to her this time. "But I think you have another ghost."

I hover impatiently by the door until Malcolm completes his circuit. His thump against the wood makes me jump, heart thudding.

"Nothing," he calls out. "We could maybe try the neighbors—"

"I think it's a ghost."

"But—"

"What happened to Carter's ghost when he passed out?" I ask before he can say more.

Silence greets this question. After a moment, I hear some stomping and throat clearing.

"Are you telling me that it was there in the apartment the whole time and we didn't sense it?"

"*She* was there the whole time, and no, we didn't, because I think that's her specialty."

I turn in a slow circle, my gaze scanning Misty's apartment. Other than that glimmer across my neck—and the frozen door, of course—I have nothing else to go on. But I doubt it's Carter Dupree who has been the master of stealth all this time.

"Delilah? Is that you?"

The air shimmers and sparkles, Delilah's presence filling the small space. She's strong, and lovely, and awe-inspiring. Misty gazes at her, slack-jawed, and I feel very much the same.

"I hope I'm that hot when I'm dead," she murmurs.

I ignore this and call through the door to Malcolm. "It's her. It's Delilah."

"Well, get her to let you out," he says.

"How am I supposed to do that?"

"Oh, come on, Katy. What do most ghosts want? What do most ghosts want from *you*?"

Is he crazy? Can't he feel how strong she is? Why would a ghost with so much power want a measly cup of coffee? Then I cast my thoughts back to that night when I invited Delilah to my house and the air shimmered with her ghostly laughter.

"Delilah?" I say. "Would you like some Kona blend?"

The door springs open. Malcolm reaches for me. Before he can grab my wrist, I'm yanked backward, a set of deadly green nails puncturing my down jacket.

"That one, honey?" Misty whispers in my ear, voice urgent and fierce. "He's a keeper. Grab him while the grabbing's good. You'll regret it if you don't."

With the force of the supernatural at my back, I'm ripped from Misty's grip, propelled down the steps, and dumped into the snowbank at the edge of the walkway.

I emerge from the snow, eyelashes fringed with flakes, cold rivers running down my spine. Malcolm stares, his gaze filled with concern. But really? Beneath that concern, I think he's trying very hard not to laugh.

"Here," he says, a hand extended. He pulls me from the snow and I topple forward into his arms.

I peer up at him, still snow-covered. Now he does laugh, but it's soft and sweet. With the gloved fingers of his free hand, he brushes the melting snow from my face.

"You okay?" he asks, and there's something more in his question, something I'm missing.

I nod. Cold sneaks through my jacket. The back of my shirt is soaked. I probably look like I tumbled from bed and into that snowbank. Malcolm doesn't seem to mind.

"Katy, I—"

Before he can say more, that supernatural force batters us both, urging us toward my truck.

"I think someone wants her coffee." He adjusts his grip on the container and takes my hand.

When we reach my truck, the entire thing is frosted over. He grabs my wrist before my fingers graze the door handle. I turn to him.

"If she wants coffee, why is she freezing my truck?"

He gives his head a slow shake and searches the air. The space around my truck shimmers and sparkles. The truck itself glows like it's been doused in glitter.

"I don't understand," I say. "I thought she wanted coffee."

"You could ask her."

"Ask ... her." I take a step away from him and fold my arms over my chest. "You mean necromancer style?"

"That's exactly what I mean," he says.

"I'm not a necromancer."

"Come on, Katy. You've done it before."

"I was trying to save your life. There are exceptions to rules."

"Why is it a rule in the first place?"

"It's not what I do. It's not who I am."

"It truly won't hurt you," he says.

"Addiction?"

Doubt clouds his eyes. It was, perhaps, a low blow to remind him of Nigel like that.

"You're stronger than that," he says.

"You don't know that." I believe there's a reason my grandmother never told me about necromancy, that she did it to keep me safe. Until I understand why, I'm not about to dabble in it.

My jeans are stiff with cold. Malcolm winces against the light breeze that chases a few flakes into his hair. And my truck shines like the star on top of a Christmas tree.

Then he holds up a hand as if conceding—for now. "All right. Maybe she'll talk to me." He turns in a circle, projecting his voice. "Delilah, would you agree to a simple exchange of information?"

The air vibrates; Malcolm smiles and hands me the Tupperware. He stands straight, eyes closed, head tipped back slightly, arms at his sides, the palms turned skyward. The glimmer descends on him. He stiffens before relaxing again. Then he laughs, low and rich, his coffee laugh.

"Yes," he says. "She's very stubborn ... We manage, despite that."

What? Are they … talking about me? I want to interrupt. I want to defend myself, but I don't know what I could say.

"Oh, of course," Malcolm continues. "I should've thought of that. I think Katy will be more than amenable once she understands."

Understand what? This is driving me crazy. Part of me regrets not speaking to Delilah myself.

The glow fades from Malcolm. He doubles over, releasing one giant cough. Then he stumbles backward, against my truck. He braces a hand on its side and then sinks to the ground.

"It's been a while since I've done that." His breath is ragged, cheeks flushed. His eyes hold a glazed look. He blinks as if he can't quite focus. "Wow. She's strong."

"Um, maybe you two would like to be alone?"

Malcolm coughs out a chuckle. Around us, the air shimmers with glee.

"A little help?" He holds out a hand.

I tug him to his feet. At the last second, I decide not to pull him in to me. It's tempting, but I'm too curious about what Delilah said. He's still too shaky. Besides, I doubt I can compete with something that sparkles the way she does.

He brushes off his trousers. "Here's the thing. She's only ever dealt with necromancers. Since she's accepted your offer of coffee, she needs to provide you something in return."

"Really? Like what? How does that work?"

"Usually it's something comparable."

I shake my head. "I don't need anything." I turn, addressing the air around me. "I'm sorry, but I can't think of anything."

"Here's the other piece of it. She's still tethered to Carter, but if you complete the pact, accept something from her in return, she'll be free to go."

"Free and not have to go back to him?"

"Exactly."

"Oh, Delilah. Okay, hang on, let me think." I squeeze my eyes shut. I take several deep breaths, the scent of wet wool and stale ice surrounding me. What I need is that cup of coffee waiting for us at home. I'm pretty sure I haven't had a coherent thought since before Misty's phone call of hours before.

I open my eyes and find Malcolm's. "Comparable, right?"

"Yes."

"So it doesn't have to be a huge thing."

"Not at all. Just a fair trade."

"Like the coffee."

"Sure." He gives me a wary look. I must sound punch-drunk to him. "Like the coffee."

Oh. *Coffee.* Of course.

"Delilah, I know I promised you Kona blend, and you can still have some, but I bought a new holiday blend from the Coffee Depot the other day. I have no idea if ghosts will like it. Will you give it a taste test for me?"

The air around us sparkles with renewed vigor. A moment later, all the ice on my truck evaporates.

Two thermoses of the Coffee Depot's holiday blend rest between Malcolm and me on the truck's front seat. It's his turn to drive, so I clutch the Tupperware container that holds Harold's ghost. It swirls inside, still fairly weak. I thought about offering it a hot chocolate, but I don't dare crack the lid.

After much debate among the three of us—me, Malcolm, Delilah— we decide to head east into Wisconsin. The highways are clear in that direction. North is out of the question. It makes no sense to head toward the Twin Cities and the necromancers who would no doubt like to capture both Delilah and Harold's ghost.

East also isn't quite as desolate—or dangerous—as the Dakotas. Snow, wind, a sudden storm, and we could end up trapped for days.

When we cross the Mississippi, Delilah ricochets around the cab of the truck. She gives us each a ghostly kiss on the cheek before streaming through the crack at the top of the window.

"Goodbye!" I call after her. "It was nice to meet you."

Malcolm laughs.

"What?" I say, rolling up the window. "It's true."

"She ... you ... you've made a powerful ally."

"I don't want an ally."

"I'm afraid you have one."

"I just wanted her to be free," I say.

"Which is why you have an ally."

"My grandmother always said that we're doing everyone a favor by separating people and ghosts. I always took that to mean the people benefited." I stare out the window, twisting in my seat to see the Mississippi wandering south. "I wonder if she meant the ghosts as well."

"Well, there's a lot of good haunting between here and New Orleans. Delilah should have a grand time."

"It wasn't that hard to free her," I venture. Really, a taste test?

"Well, Carter was unconscious, so his additional hold on her—whatever that was—had weakened. Also, he might be more skilled, but I think you have more innate ability."

"So, what you're saying is that it wasn't a fair fight this time around."

"Maybe not, but, Katy, don't doubt your ability as a necromancer."

"I'm not a necromancer." I sigh. How many times must I say this?

"You don't have to act on it." He casts me a sidelong glance. "But you should probably acknowledge it, for your own ... safety."

"My safety? Am I in danger?"

This time, Malcolm doesn't glance my way. His hands grip the wheel in the classic ten and two position, his knuckles tightening beneath the leather gloves, his gaze straight ahead.

"I don't know," is all he says.

WE DRIVE WITHOUT DESTINATION, leaving behind the towns close to the river and heading into the prairie. At last I spot a sign for a nature preserve. I point.

"Romance Prairie State Nature Area," Malcolm says. "Are we allowed to drive in?"

"Will it matter?"

His sigh sounds as weary as I feel.

"I have cross-country skis," I say. "I can ski to a secluded release point."

"You're not going alone. You have rules about necromancy? Well, I have rules, too, and one of them involves not wandering into a deserted nature preserve alone."

He's right, of course. It's a foolish thing to do, especially in the winter with a dangerous ghost along for the ride.

"You're not dressed for this." I'm wearing boots, at least, and I have the ski gear in the back of my truck.

"Doesn't matter. I don't think we'll have to go far."

Malcolm has an unerring sense for these things. The truck jostles over snow-packed ruts and careens onto something I'm not certain is an actual road, but after a quarter of a mile it lands us in a parking area.

The space is forlorn, abandoned. Wind whips my hair, nearly steals the Tupperware from my grip. No one is coming out here until spring. I glance at Malcolm.

He nods, once. Yes. This is the place.

I wade into the snow-covered prairie, pushing through matted grass and drifts that reach my knees. I walk far enough that sweat blooms along my spine and the cold air makes my lungs ache. I find a dip in the terrain, a shielded area, and turn around. I hold up the container.

"Do we uncover it?" My voice rings hollow in the empty air.

That's always been our policy. Catch and release. But this isn't a normal ghost eradication. This is personal. Back in Springside, Sadie is still in a coma. I don't know which is the worse fate for a ghost—released into the wilds or trapped inside a plastic prison. I suspect the latter but really have no proof.

Sadie's my friend, but Nigel is Malcolm's brother. I'll give his wishes more weight.

If he'll tell me, that is.

He stands there contemplating the surroundings. I shiver, the wind biting into my skin through my jeans. My arms tremble slightly, although the container isn't heavy. His gaze scans the horizon to the east, passes over me, and surveys the west. Then his eyes lock with mine. He's far enough away that I can't read their expression.

"Crack the lid," he says.

"Are you sure?"

"No. Not in the least. But to do it any other way would be ... violating something."

So I do. I ease back one corner enough that—if the ghost wants—it can stream through to freedom. Instead, Harold's ghost churns, slow and sad. Waves of dejection roll off of it. A surge of pity hits me.

"There are other ways to get attention." I place the container in the snow, digging it in so the wind won't catch it and tumble it across the prairie. "You know that, right? You don't have to hurt anyone."

I clomp from the field, collecting weeds and clumps of snow along the way. When I reach the edge of the parking lot, Malcolm pulls me up and out of the snowbank. He holds me close against his chest. I nestle there, arms around his waist.

"Thank you," he says, his breath warm against my scalp.

I'm not sure what I've done, but I nod anyway.

It's hours later when I wake in the crook of Malcolm's arm. The remains of our breakfast litter the table in front of us. The half booth we're snuggled in shields us from most of the diner's other patrons, but the clatter of dishes reaches my ears. The pancakes I ate are heavy and warm inside me. My lips taste like maple syrup. I feel grubby, un-show-ered, and I'm not exactly sure what my hair is doing, but I'm certain it's frightening.

All I want to do is close my eyes again, because in this moment, I'm content.

"You awake?" Malcolm says, his voice low. From its tone I know that he'd let me sleep for as long as I like.

"Just woke up. How long have we been here? Are they going to kick us out?"

"Only an hour and a half." His fingers play with the sleeve of my shirt. It's a slow, comfortable caress and might be the reason I fell asleep to begin with.

"The rush is over, so they don't really care," he adds. "Besides, I sweet-talked our waitress."

Of course he did. Sweet-talking waitresses is one of Malcolm's many skills.

"She keeps trying to serve me coffee." He shudders. "It smells like someone dipped a brown crayon into hot water. You've ruined me, Katy. I will never drink restaurant coffee again."

I can't help but laugh, and he tugs me closer. A slight buzzing comes from the pocket of Malcolm's jacket. He shifts without letting me go.

"Hang on, let me get this."

He pulls out his phone. Because I'm resting against his chest, I feel his quick intake of breath. It's an excited, happy thing. Before I can ask, before I can crane my neck to peer at his phone, he turns the screen toward me.

Nigel: She's awake. Whatever you did, it worked. Thank you.

Malcolm pulls me closer still, folding me into his arms. He squeezes, just once. "Looks like it's going to be a Merry Christmas."

THE TWO SPRITES float lazily in the Coffee Depot's holiday blend. They've had their fill, and I will need to scoop them back into their container soon. For now, I let them bask in the steam and Sadie's attention.

"They missed you." I realize now that the sprite bent on destroying the K&M storefront display was one of Sadie's. "This one—or maybe this one." I point. "Tried to warn me."

"They tried to warn me, too," she says.

Sadie is sitting at the kitchen table, her chin in her hand. Her salt and pepper curls are tipped in red and green. Tiny replicas of Christmas ornaments dangle from her ears. She's been baking all day long and her entire house smells warm and alive again. Rich chocolate, something savory with sage and onion, and something else that's gingery with a lot of bite. No wonder the sprites love it here. I'm not certain the coffee is enough to tempt them away.

Her gaze is tender as she watches them dip and dive in the steam. "When Nigel left that morning—" Here, a blush colors her cheeks.

"They burst in and tore around the place. I couldn't get them to stop. I'm afraid I scolded them."

"Sprites are immune to scolding."

"I'm just glad…" She trails off and sighs. "And sorry. I'm so sorry Harold hurt you and Malcolm."

"It wasn't really Harold," I say, "but his ghost. There's a difference."

I've tried to explain this to her already. Harold's ghost was alone and confused—and possibly under Carter's influence. With time, he might make a fine ghost. But now that doesn't matter. What matters is Sadie's quiet Christmas with Nigel, so I scoop up my charges and pull on my coat.

"It's so cold out," Sadie says. "I hate the idea of the nature preserve."

I hold the Tupperware at eye level and frown at the two sprites. "I do have another idea, but they'll have to behave themselves."

It's sunset on Christmas Eve. My truck meets hardly any traffic as I drive to the Springside Long-term Care facility. There, it's quiet too. Many residents visit family over the holidays. I wave at the night manager on my way in.

"I don't think you've ever brought us any ghosts before," he says to me.

"These two could use a little mothering. If they get out of hand, I'll come back. I'm on call over the holiday if you need me."

Mrs. Greeley's room is dark, but I doubt she's asleep. She's blind, and my guess is that she's heard my clomping boots from the moment I entered the facility.

"Katy, dear? Is that you?"

"It is," I say. "And I've brought you something." I've barely eased back the lid before the two sprites spring out, darting about like puppies or five-year-olds.

"Oh, my. They *are* active."

"They could use—"

"A visit with a grandmother?" Humor fills her voice.

"Exactly!" I pull up a chair. "I've already told them that they need to behave."

"It will be like having my own here, although at least I don't need to worry about finding them snacks."

"I'll stop by with some coffee." I eye the glimmer near the television set. "Do you two hear that? Behave and you get the Kona blend."

Mrs. Greeley's own grandchildren are away this holiday, at Disney World. I decide that when I come back tomorrow I'll spend the day with everyone. Belinda is up north with her mother at some fancy lodge. Malcolm has gone to visit a fraternity brother. Sadie and Nigel are spending the first of what I hope are many Christmases together.

"How about you, my dear?" Mrs. Greeley asks.

"I'm okay."

"That doesn't sound like an honest answer."

It isn't.

"I miss her," I say.

I want to add a litany of things to this list beyond how I miss my grandmother. How I haven't decorated the house, or put up a tree, or even have a single sugar cookie to eat. How none of that matters since my grandmother isn't here to celebrate. I don't want decorations or a tree or any cookies, not without her.

I hoped her ghost might return for Christmas, but I know that was wishful thinking.

Mrs. Greeley doesn't tell me everything will be okay. Instead, she takes my hand, the way my grandmother used to, and gently strokes my fingers.

I stay until the last of my tears have dried against my cheeks, leaving the skin scratchy and raw and my heart empty.

CHAPTER 7

I SEE THE FIGURE on my porch when I'm half a block from my house. For a second, my heart leaps. Tall, broad-shouldered. I'm certain it's Malcolm. But when he glances around—in a way that looks more than a little guilty—I know it can't be.

Besides, Malcolm has a key.

I park the truck three houses from mine, slip out, and ease the door closed. The temperature has dropped, so I tug my hood up and over my head. My boots squeak against the snow. In the quiet, the sound is loud, but whoever is on my porch doesn't seem to notice.

By the time I reach the end of my walkway, he's doing something with the mistletoe wreath, the one that I haven't bothered to take down and toss on the compost heap. Beneath the glow of the porch lamp, his hair gleams. I take a deep breath. Then I yell out.

"Boo!"

Yes, it's childish. But when Carter Dupree jumps about three feet into the air, it's worth it. He recovers, bracing a hand on the stair rail, then pulls it back because his fingers are bare and the metal handrail is like ice.

He's still blowing on his fingers when I land on the porch.

"Nice trick," he says.

"There's no trick."

"Really?"

"Yes, really. I'm not a necromancer."

"That's where you're wrong."

"Why did you bring Harold here?" I ask, deciding to skip over the small talk. "Why would you even do anything like that?"

"To show you your potential, to show you how you're *wasting* your potential." He shakes his head as if he can't believe my naïveté. "Besides, don't you have a powerful friend to call upon?"

I don't know what he means, but I also don't want to admit that—not to Carter Dupree. "So the part with the hospital means what? Nothing?"

"And everyone's okay, right?"

"Coma, concussion? Sure, we're great," I say.

He stands there, arms crossed over his chest, one eyebrow cocked in a look that's both smug and condescending. "And, speaking of necromancy—"

From the mistletoe wreath he pulls an envelope, different from the first one I found there a few weeks ago. He hands it to me. The edges are embossed in gold. The paper feels heavy in my hands. The whole thing has the elegance of a wedding invitation and the gravitas of a summons.

"Go on." He nods toward the envelope. "Open it."

I do, enough to read the gold lettering on the top of the card inside.

The Midwest Necromancer Association

Really? The shady cabal exists? And they have such a ... boring name?

You are cordially invited to a gathering of prospective members...

I read no further. Instead, I shoot Carter a glare.

"You're a shoo-in, you know," he says, "being legacy and all."

"Legacy? How can I be legacy? My grandmother wasn't a necromancer."

"No, she wasn't."

"Then?" I point to the invitation.

"Think about it, Katy. Think about what 'legacy' means and how that can apply to you."

I nod, but I have no plans to think about any of that.

We stand there in the cold, the night so still around us I can hear the faint crack of an icicle as it falls from the eaves. I suspect he wants me to invite him inside—yes, after everything. So I stand there, chin tilted in a gesture that means he should start walking down my porch steps.

"I'll be seeing you around, Katy." He brings two fingers to his brow in a salute. "You can count on that."

I remain on my porch until he's ducked inside a black sedan and driven away. Only then do I pull out the card.

You are cordially invited to a gathering of prospective members. Come meet your fellow necromancers for an evening of networking and socializing.
Learn what the Midwest Necromancer Association can offer you—and what you can offer us.
Black tie recommended.

Oh. Well. I guess I'm not wearing the skater skirt, then. I roll my eyes, not that there's anyone around to see.

Below the embossed lettering is a handwritten scrawl:
You have something of mine. I'd like it back.

My gaze is drawn to where Carter's car was sitting moments before. Doesn't he know I set Delilah free? I think about what he said, something about a trick and a powerful friend, and realize that no, he thinks I'm using Delilah.

Because that's exactly the sort of thing he'd do.

I'm about to trek back down the sidewalk to my truck when my phone buzzes.

The text is from Sadie. The moment I see it, my heart seizes.

Sadie: Katy, can you come over? We need your help.

Oh, no. *No.* I told them to behave. I divert my path, heading for Sadie's instead of my truck. When I pass the recycling bin, I drop the invitation and its matching envelope inside.

It's not Sadie who greets me at the door. It's not Nigel. No, it's Malcolm. Malcolm, who's supposed to be in the Twin Cities. Malcolm, who's standing there in a pressed shirt and trousers, not a hair out of place and a shave so fresh, the lingering scent of shaving cream fills the air between us.

Humor lights his eyes. This is most likely because I'm standing there speechless. The cold against my teeth and tongue tells me my mouth is hanging open.

He grabs my hands and pulls me inside. With gentle fingers, he eases the hood from my head. I manage to unzip the thing on my own and hang it on the coat rack.

"What are you doing here?" I ask. "I thought—"

"Seriously, Katy? Did you think we'd leave you alone on Christmas? *This* Christmas?"

From the living room comes a laugh, full and throaty.

"Is that—?"

"Belinda," Malcolm confirms. "Gregory's here too. And of course Nigel. We even invited Chief Ramsey."

"No. You're kidding."

"He was alone in the station when I was locking up the other day. I felt kind of sorry for him." Malcolm shrugs. "He brought a Yule log and some rum for the eggnog."

I laugh and start for the living room, but he slips his hand in mine and tugs me back.

"Katy," he says, and now his eyes are darker than I've ever seen them.

We're in the shadows of the entryway, the space filled with the aroma of pine. I stare up at him, trying to fathom the expression that crosses his face. He looks like a man teetering at the edge of a cliff.

"What I'm trying to say—" he begins. "What I've been trying to say for a while now is—"

"You don't know what comes next?"

"That's just it. I do. This comes next. You, and me, and ghost hunting. People search a lifetime trying to find something meaningful to do, a calling. I used to think that was necromancy. I used to think that the next big market win would make me happy. But it never did, not like this."

"So ghost eradication is better than being Broker of the Year?"

He laughs, head thrown back, that rich, dark roast of a laugh. I want to drink in the sound of it, memorize it, remember it forever.

"Much better," he says, "believe it or not."

I do. That's why the rest of it—the part where it's Malcolm and me without the ghosts—is so hard.

"But then there's us," I say. "You and me. No ghosts."

His forehead rests against mine. "And then there's us."

"Do you want there to be an us?" I don't like how small my voice sounds, but there's no helping it. My question comes out small because part of me hopes he won't hear it.

He does, of course. "That's the question, isn't it?" When I don't respond, he adds, "What do *you* want, Katy?"

Is this what he's been waiting to hear all this time? I've been answering one question, but he's been asking another. My throat tightens. I'm not certain I can push words through it. My heart pounds in my chest so hard, I'm afraid it might bruise my ribs.

"I want there to be an us."

Can you feel someone smile? Does it change how they stand, how they breathe? In that moment, Malcolm shifts. He inches me closer. His hands thread through my hair.

"Look up," he whispers, his breath soft against my cheek.

I do. Above our heads, a tiny, perfect bough of mistletoe is hanging from a velvet ribbon, a silent witness to our entryway confessions.

He kisses me then, a kiss full of nutmeg and spice, his warm Ivory soap scent mixing with the pine. This is what Christmas smells like and feels like, and I'm relieved to discover that yes, my lips *are* in perfect working order.

For the record?

So are Malcolm's.

PART II
THE GHOST THAT GOT AWAY

COFFEE AND GHOSTS SEASON TWO, EPISODE 2

THE DISPLAY WINDOW of *K&M Ghost Eradication Specialists* is littered with hearts. Pink hearts. Glittery hearts. Blood-red hearts. The sign suspended above the Valentine's Day explosion reads:

Don't let the ghosts of past loves haunt you.
Two-for-one eradication special.
Now through the end of the month.

I doubt Springside Township is teeming with the ghosts of past loves, but my business partner, Malcolm Armand, assures me seasonal advertising is the way to go.

Inside our office, things are quiet, if no less glittery. A trail of the stuff runs from the display window back to our conference room and work area. We still can't afford a receptionist, so the front desk sits empty. The clatter of the keyboard tells me Nigel, Malcolm's brother and our tech support, is already hard at work.

"Katy?" he calls from the conference room. "Is that you?"

"It is."

"Malcolm with you?"

I hesitate a fraction of a second before responding. "No."

Nigel appears in the doorway and crooks a finger at me. "I want to show you something."

I shrug off my coat and follow him into the conference room. I'm guessing he's found an interesting ghost sighting online or has updated our website. But he doesn't head for the computer. He simply stands there, gaze landing everywhere but on me, fingers tapping against his thigh.

"Nigel?

"What?" His eyes are a little wide, as if he's startled or wary. The shock of pure white hair only makes him look that much more anxious.

"You wanted to show me something?" I prompt.

"Yeah ... yeah. I do." Those nervous fingers reach into his jeans pocket. "This. I want to get your opinion on this."

From the depths of his pocket he pulls out a velvet-covered box, one small enough to rest in the palm of his hand. With a deep breath, he eases open the lid.

"What do you think?" he says, his words rushed. "Is it good enough? Big enough? What do you think of the design?"

Inside the box, nestled in midnight-blue velvet, sits a diamond engagement ring. Marquee cut, I think, although I hardly ever wear jewelry and I barely know anything about gemstones. Despite this, something tells me the ring is perfect for its intended recipient.

For a second, I can't actually respond. My mouth is an o. Then I exhale, words and breath coming at once. "It's gorgeous. When are you going to ask her?"

He shrugs. "Maybe Valentine's Day, but then I thought that's too cliché."

I give my head a quick shake. "Sadie loves the holidays. Valentine's would be perfect."

"You think?"

Now I nod, just as vigorously, and run the risk of injuring my neck. "Of course."

"And you really think I should propose?" The doubt in his voice chills me more than the negative ten degrees outside did.

"Why wouldn't you?"

For a long moment, Nigel studies the ring and then snaps the lid shut. He tucks the box into his jeans pocket and leans against the conference room table.

"Honestly?" he says. "I'm not sure I'm good enough for her."

I can't imagine why he thinks this. He is kind, gentle, attentive. When Sadie was in the hospital, he only left her side to eat and take the occasional shower. He was so devoted that the nurses dubbed him Sir Nigel. He's the opposite of Sadie's first husband, Harold Lancaster, who wasn't the best human being and made an even worse ghost.

The expression on Nigel's face, the worry in his eyes, tells me this is more than cold feet. This doubt runs deep.

"Look at me, Katy." He holds out his hands. "What can I offer her? I'm a recovering addict and I work for my little brother."

I cringe, inwardly, because technically, yes, that's true. He wears his former addiction—to swallowing ghosts—in the white of his hair, the deep grooves around his mouth and eyes. These facts don't do justice to who Nigel Armand really is, on the inside.

"Sadie sees all of you, not just those things. Those things don't matter."

"They do matter. A lot." His fingers start their tapping against his thigh again. "I can't give her what she deserves."

"You know what? She was married to someone who could give her everything." Only now that I'm older do I realize just how rich Harold must have been. "We both know how that turned out. She needs you. I've never seen her this happy."

He purses his lips, mouth tight with disbelief. Before I can launch another round—for Sadie's sake if not his—the bell above the front door chimes.

Nigel's eyes take on a renewed panic. "Promise me that you won't tell Malcolm anything."

"But—"

"Promise me."

"Don't you want him to know?"

"Eventually, yes. If things ... work out, I want him to be my best man."

"Then—"

"It's a brother thing. Trust me?"

I nod. I'm an only child, raised by my grandmother. Siblings are a mystery to me. The Armand brothers in particular? Even more so.

"And promise?" he adds.

I nod again. "I'll even run interference."

I dash out of the conference room and run smack into Malcolm. The cold clings to his wool overcoat. When he grips my arms, the icy leather of his gloves penetrates the sleeves of my shirt. My skin erupts in goose bumps, but that isn't entirely from the cold.

"Whoa," he says. "Hang on." He adjusts his grip so I'm embraced in a proper hug. "Morning kiss."

Then my business partner kisses me full on the mouth. This routine, this morning kiss, is one of the ways we manage the transition from couple into business partners.

"How are you this morning?" he asks, his lips at the corner of my mouth.

"Good."

"You were that last night, too."

I laugh because in truth, we merely indulged in an evening kiss. Granted, those last longer than the morning ones. Still, we're navigating our dual roles with caution. As K&M ghost eradication specialists, we work so well together.

We don't want K&M the couple screwing that up.

But I'd be lying if I said morning and evening weren't my favorite times of day.

Malcolm pulls back and smiles at me. It's that warm smile, the one that reminds me of a sweet, dark roast. If you could pour it into a cup and drink it down, it would sustain you for days. The crinkles around his eyes deepen and his gaze scans my face.

"You look like you have a secret," he says.

Oh, I'm so transparent. I consider how to respond and decide on the truth.

"I do, but it isn't mine to tell."

He opens his mouth, prepared to cajole, I'm certain. Malcolm is a world-class cajoler. The bell above our door chimes once again. Instead of breaking our embrace, he grips me tighter. We don't often get walk-ins. When the silhouette of two men in dark overcoats comes into view, I'm certain my expression is as confused as his.

"Oh, excuse me." The voice has a certain lilt, one that's out of place in Springside. "Are we interrupting something?"

My insides go as frigid as the air now swirling around our reception desk. I know that southern drawl. As the man steps closer, I recognize the glossy hair and overly white teeth. Carter Dupree gleams; he shines.

Right now, I wish he'd do it somewhere else.

Malcolm eases away from me, but the move is protective, not guilty. He stands, his body half-blocking mine. It's kind of endearing. It's also unnecessary.

"They don't have any ghosts with them," I say, my words low, only meant for Malcolm.

"Are you certain of that, Ms. Lindstrom?"

Carter's companion steps forward. He's an older, smoother version of Carter. He doesn't gleam quite as much, his hair gray rather than blond. His words, his steps—both carry weight. Despite myself, I want to stand up straighter, smooth out the wrinkles in my jeans.

"I'm certain," I say. Or as certain as I can be, under the circumstances.

"In this instance, you're correct. And I've been remiss. Allow me to introduce myself. I'm Orson Yates."

Malcolm sucks in a breath and chokes on it, his cough muted but clear.

"What a place you have here." Orson Yates surveys the front area, his gaze moving from the empty reception desk to the threadbare couch to the glitter on the floor. "It's ... quaint."

"Can I help you with something?" I tilt my head in mock concern. "Are you having problems with a ghost?"

I collect the stares of all three men. Yes, I'm pretending I don't know who this guy is, that I haven't spent the last two months deleting his emails—or rather, the ones I'm sure some assistant sends for him. I'm pretending I don't know that Orson Yates is the chairman of the Midwest Necromancer Association.

Orson himself breaks the silence with a laugh that sounds as brittle as ice.

"Oh, she's funny. Really, Carter, why didn't you tell me she was funny?"

Probably because Carter Dupree hates me.

"But I'm distressed that you didn't attend our gathering in January. You didn't even RSVP." Orson's tone implies I have all the manners of a five-year-old. I'm bracing for the *kids these days* speech, but decide to take the offensive.

"It was black tie. I didn't have anything appropriate to wear," I say. That, and I tossed the invitation into the recycling. "I only own a skater skirt."

"You gentlemen missed out," Malcolm mutters, low and under his breath.

I shoot him a look, but his entire focus—his whole being—is on the two men. He won't let down his guard, not even to receive a glare from me.

"I see," Orson says. "Perhaps the fault is ours. It's been a while since we've had a woman in our ranks. Then again, we don't have that many men, either. We're exclusive that way." He pauses, his gaze darting to Malcolm before landing on me. "Still, I can't remember our last female necromancer. I would, however, like to rectify that now by possibly adding you to our list."

"I'm not a necromancer." Really, I've said this so many times and to so many people. Why no one listens, I can't say.

Catching ghosts is my business, one my grandmother taught me. Using ghosts? To play the market, intimidate people, and who knows what else? That's necromancy, and I'm not interested.

But I'm at the point where I might invest in a nametag, one that reads:

Hello, my name is Katy.
I am not a necromancer.

And I would wear it every day.

When no one responds, I add, "I told Carter that, too. More than once."

Orson chuckles, a patronizing sort of laugh. "My child, you have no idea what you're capable of. Why restrict yourself?"

"Why would I want to be a necromancer?"

Orson spreads his hands wide. "Security. Wealth. A way to make your mark on the world."

"Why do I need your little club to do that?"

A spasm hits Orson's left eye—a tic that distorts his features for a moment. Then he's smooth again, but the façade looks more brittle than before. Malcolm steps closer and takes my hand.

"Easy," he whispers in my ear. "He's a powerful necromancer, and they're here for a reason."

I have a horrible feeling that reason is me, and they won't go until I say yes to whatever it is they want.

Before I can utter another word, or think of a way to get them out the door, Nigel emerges from the conference room. His gait is steady and strong, hands tucked casually in his jeans pockets. His shoulders are square, his mouth grim. His stride never falters as he passes us and halts before the two necromancers, effectively cutting them off from me.

"Ah, Nigel," Orson says. "Carter mentioned you were slumming it these days. Addiction, was it?"

I cast a glance at Malcolm, but his gaze is on Nigel, eyes wide with shock.

"You're not wanted here," Nigel says, tone bland as if he's merely discussing the weather. "You know that. You've known that from the moment you walked through the door."

"Your ward. Yes, I felt it. Did you think it would keep us out? This is a place of business, after all."

"It's not meant to keep you out, it's meant to encourage you to leave. You have no true business here. You can catch your own ghosts." Nigel casts me a glance. "Although these days, Katy is probably better at it than you are."

Nigel is so calm, hands still tucked in his pockets, but his words hold an authority I've never heard before—his last volley provoking a second eye twitch from Orson. I've only ever known the recovering addict, the sweet man who is quietly courting my neighbor.

I don't know this Nigel Armand at all.

Orson snorts. "What happens if I refuse?"

"You can't," Nigel says simply. "You know you can't."

Orson holds up his hands in apparent surrender. "All right, you win. For now." He clears his throat. "I'm afraid, Ms. Lindstrom, that you've aligned yourself with the wrong sort of necromancer. Pity, that. You have such potential."

He turns to leave, Carter Dupree shooting me a nasty look before he heads for the door as well. The bell chimes, and I swear I've never heard anything so wonderful as that sound. I'm about to sigh with relief when the door rings yet again.

"Now I remember!" Orson Yates declares, features bright, cheeks flushed. "Our last female member was your mother, and quite the necromancer she was, too."

The door whooshes closed as all the breath leaves my lungs.

WE STAND THERE, the three of us staring at each other, all of us searching for words. I don't know where to start. Nigel as some sort of badass necromancer? My own mother?

All of it is too much. I turn to Malcolm, who is still clutching my hand.

"Do you have any tea?" I ask, and it's a plaintive sort of question.

He gives my fingers a quick squeeze. "Let me brew some. Then maybe we can figure out what's going on."

This last is directed more at Nigel, who raises his eyebrows as if he's nothing but innocent.

Within minutes, aromatic steam fills the conference room. Malcolm does the honors, from brewing to pouring to pressing a glass into my hands. Warmth sinks into my fingers, which feel cold and stiff. For a moment I simply hold the tea, inhale, and let the steam fill me.

"This is different." I sniff, trying to work out what spices he's added this time around.

"It's my comfort tea," he says. "Secret recipe, emergency use only."

I manage a laugh. Malcolm pours two more glasses. Before Nigel can grasp the drink, Malcolm pulls it back, just out of his brother's reach.

"Ward?" he says. "I've never felt it."

"That's because you're not trespassing. I have one on the apartment and Sadie's house as well." Nigel's tone is still bland, but there's an undercurrent of resolve I've never noticed before. "After Carter came to town, I figured I should establish my territory."

"The apartment, too?" Malcolm shakes his head. "I should've thought of that."

Nigel rolls his eyes. "You've never been very good at them."

Malcolm scowls at this, but it's mostly in jest because a moment later he nods and relinquishes the tea. "True."

"Territory?" I ask Nigel. "Does it keep people … necromancers out?"

"No, it establishes your right to certain spaces. Another necromancer is free to violate that, but if he or she does, there are consequences. It's like a No Trespassing sign. It's all good until Chief Ramsey catches you."

"Could you put one on my house?" I ask, leaning forward in my chair.

This, I think, would be good. This might keep Carter Dupree from leaving creepy offerings on my doorstep.

"No, I can't," Nigel says.

I deflate and he laughs.

"I can't because it's your territory as a—"

I raise a hand. "Don't even say it."

"It doesn't make it any less true. But I could teach you how, if you like. Don't ask Malcolm. He's lousy at it."

I glance toward Malcolm and he gives me a rueful smile.

"I kind of am," he admits.

I swallow down some tea, the liquid nearly scalding the back of my throat. "Why are they here?"

I have my suspicions, but all of this is still so new to me. Necromancy, an association, wards. My thoughts linger on my grandmother and why she never told me about any of this.

A look passes between Malcolm and Nigel. Some sort of silent brother debate is waged. There's a tightening of lips, a barely visible nod, then Nigel takes a deep breath.

"You, Katy," he says. "They're here for you."

"But I told them 'no' already. I don't want to be in their club."

"Keep calling it that and you'll give Orson Yates a nervous breakdown. He takes the association very seriously," Nigel says. "Then again, a hundred years and a billion dollars is a serious thing."

"A billion *what*?" I try to wrap my mind around that. I remember what Malcolm once told me: many successful stockbrokers are necromancers. In fact, before he came to Springside, he was a broker as well. Judging by the clothes he wears and the fancy red convertible he drives, he was good at it, too.

But that was before he lost Selena to Nigel's addiction.

"Maybe they haven't noticed," I say, "but we don't make a whole lot of money eradicating ghosts."

"That's not why they want you," Nigel says. "It's your ability with ghosts. It's the fact that you invoked an ancient and powerful entity—and could do so again. Do you know what sort of power that would give them? We're talking power on a global scale."

I shake my head. "That thing's name dies with me. I will never say it again."

Even thinking about the entity makes me nervous. I know I shouldn't, but sometimes the harder I try, the more I actually *do* think of it, like when someone tells you not to think about elephants—that's all you can do.

"We should've anticipated this," Nigel says, his voice quiet, the words meant for Malcolm. "Springside is just so..."

"Nice," Malcolm finishes.

"Exactly. I was hoping they'd chalk it up to nonsensical sprite gossip, even after Carter came to town." Nigel shakes his head. "I've been stupid."

"I thought they'd give up after Katy sent him packing," Malcolm adds.

"Why would I even want to align"—I draw quotes in the air—"with someone who would hurt one of my friends? They must think I'm insane, or unfeeling, or something."

The ghost Carter unleashed—that of Sadie's dead husband—was about as strong a ghost as I've ever confronted. That it was immune to coffee made it all the more difficult to catch.

The furrows around Nigel's mouth grow deeper. "I should've been there."

"Too soon." This comes from Malcolm, the words quiet, apologetic.

I suspect for Nigel it might always be too soon before he can confront another ghost. He acknowledges this with a nod, then rubs his hands across his face.

"Do you think they've brought other ghosts to town? Could they hurt someone like Belinda?" My roommate attracts the nastiest of ghosts. If something like this is in their plans, I'm not sure how we'll cope.

Both Nigel and Malcolm swear, same word, same time, and they're so like brothers in that moment, I can't help but laugh, just a little. Their eyes meet and they both give a grudging smile.

"They're here under the guise of courting you," Nigel says. "I don't think they'll try the ghost trick again."

"If by courting you mean creepy and vaguely threatening, then yes, that's what they're doing."

"It's a show of power," Malcolm says. "Like with Harold's ghost. That was meant to impress you."

All it did was piss me off.

"They have a narrow view of what motivates people," Nigel adds, speaking like someone who knows a great deal about them. "Wealth, power, sex. For someone with a different temperament, and probably gender, the whole Harold thing might have worked. They show you their power. You prove your worthiness."

"Sounds like hazing," I say.

"Yeah." Nigel nods as if the word fits what he's been thinking all along. "It kind of does."

"What did they use on you?" I ask.

Nigel starts. Next to me, Malcolm leans forward. It was no more than a guess, but wariness crosses Nigel's face, followed by a half-smile of acknowledgement.

"They did court you, didn't they," Malcolm says, admiration and envy warring across his features. "Why didn't you ever tell me?"

"Because it was a non-starter. It never went much past the New Year's gathering." Nigel shrugs. "What can I say? The Armands are free agents. These guys have rules and practices I don't agree with. Since then, I've had a few run-ins with Orson or one of his flunkies—hell, you know Carter."

"Yeah, well, Carter gets around. Before today, I'd only ever heard of Orson Yates. I'd never actually met him."

"There's a reason for that."

Malcolm is sitting so close that I can feel his posture stiffen. "You ... is that why I never got an invitation? Because of you?"

Nigel drains his tea glass, stands, and crosses to Malcolm.

"There's a lot you don't know about necromancy, baby brother." He pats Malcolm on the cheek and leaves the room.

CHAPTER 2

I TRY TO BROKER a peace between the brothers with sandwiches from the deli next door. Nigel eats his lunch, nose inches from the computer screen—not that I've given him anything to do.

Malcolm sits in the outer room, inspecting each layer of his sandwich and putting it back together before bringing it to his mouth. Then, without taking a bite, he sets the sandwich down and begins the routine all over again.

Despite our haunted love advertising, we have no calls to distract us. It's so cold out, I'm certain the ghosts must be behaving themselves rather than risk a trip out to the nature preserve where we do our usual release.

I wait until Malcolm stops playing with his food to say quietly:

"Would you really want to align yourself with that sort of necromancer?"

His lips twist, his expression contrite. "No. I wouldn't."

"But it would've been nice to have the acknowledgement?" I venture. "For them to come courting?"

"I knew Carter at the U of M. We were both in the business program, both in a frat—different ones." He studies the sandwich and takes a bite before continuing. "You could say there was some friendly competition."

Or not so friendly. "And he got an invitation and you didn't."

This isn't a question. The whole scenario plays out in Malcolm's expression, the tensing of his jaw, the shadows in his eyes.

"I always thought I was the better necromancer." He gives me a wan smile. "And you've met Carter. As you can imagine, he rubbed it in."

"So, it's sort of like being asked to prom even if you don't want to go. It would've been nice, right?"

"Sort of." A bit of humor lights his eyes. "Speaking of which, you've never told me why you turned down Jack Carlotta."

Oh, there were so many reasons for that, the main one being I knew he'd end up at prom with Belinda—no matter who his actual date was. No one wants to be second place, second choice, a second thought. But I don't want to explain all this now, so I go with the answer I hope will make him laugh.

"Oh, you know, the only thing I had to wear was a skater skirt."

Malcolm laughs, head thrown back, and I know I've hit the mark. A moment later, when Nigel joins in, I think I may have brokered a peace. I bite my lip and try not to move, try not to jinx it.

"I was feeling protective," Nigel says. "I'd just come off a nasty encounter with Orson. I didn't want you near him and vice versa."

Malcolm nods, gaze locked on his lunch.

"They would've tapped you, if it's any consolation."

Now Malcolm shrugs.

"Oh, come on," I say. "Would you really want to be like Carter Dupree?" I wave my hands in the air. "All shiny and fake?"

"You don't think he's handsome?" And the way Malcolm says this has me tilting my head and leaning forward to catch the meaning in his words.

I wrinkle my nose. "He's *handsome*, I guess."

Malcolm's face goes blank. Really, I don't think I've ever seen him without some sort of expression.

"But you're the truly handsome one." He is. Women go nuts for him. The female residents and staff at Springside Long-term Care practically have their own fan club for him. "And you're interesting. You can brew tea and do magic tricks and make people laugh."

I lean closer to touch the gray at his temples. It's so recent and premature; I think maybe he's self-conscious about it.

"Listen to Katy if you're not going to listen to me," Nigel adds.

Malcolm laces his fingers through mine. He kisses them quickly, a there-and-gone brush of the lips. Then he lets go as if K&M the couple never made an appearance.

"I've been thinking," Nigel continues, "and doing a little searching over lunch. We haven't talked about the bait they're using on Katy." He looks at me now, his expression tender, brotherly. "Do you have any evidence to support their claim?"

I know so little about my parents. Pestering my grandmother with questions only deepened the frown she so often wore. I hated to do that to her.

"They died soon after I was born, in a car accident."

Again, they do that brother thing, eyes meeting, Nigel mouthing a silent question, Malcolm nodding his answer.

"Malcolm told me about necromancers dying in car accidents," I say.

"Leading cause of death. Never get into a car with an angry, uncontained ghost."

This, I know. This is why we trap ghosts in Tupperware to begin with and they ride in the back of my truck when we head out to release them. There are rare exceptions—like when we caught Harold's ghost. In those cases, they need to be contained and always in sight. You don't want ghosts of that caliber bouncing from the flatbed and vanishing into some cornfield.

"Do you have things like birth certificates, and—" Nigel hesitates.

"Death certificates?" I finish for him.

He winces, then nods.

"I can get all that for you. Social Security numbers, that sort of thing?"

"Yes, I'll use all that when I search. Are they buried here in Springside?"

"Next to my grandmother," I say. "There's…"

The words, *there's an extra plot*, freeze on my lips. It was the one meant for my grandfather. A chill runs through me. I try to shake it off and shake off the notion that the person who ends up in that extra plot will be me.

At last I do chase away the chill and gaze up at the two men. I have their full attention, their full concern.

"You know what I think?" I say. "I think I've aligned myself with the right sort of necromancer."

THAT NIGHT'S evening kiss tastes sweeter and lasts a whole lot longer than any before it. We're in my truck outside Malcolm's apartment building, engine rumbling against the cold. We've done a good job of fogging up most of the windows.

He cups my cheek, fingers threading into my hair. "You okay?"

"Why wouldn't I be?"

"After today? Your parents? I thought you might be feeling ... sad."

"I never really knew them. My grandmother raised me, and I miss her. I'm curious, and skeptical, but really, if it means banishing Orson and Carter from Springside, I'd be fine with never knowing."

He pulls me close for another kiss. "You're something else, you know that?"

I smile against his lips, my entire face on fire with a blush I suspect not even the dark can hide.

"Hey," he adds, voice low. "I just thought of something. Let's go somewhere for Valentine's Day."

"Uh, where?"

Springside is a wonderful small town with much to offer. Romantic restaurants don't make the list.

"We could drive up to the Cities, maybe eat at A Taste of Persia. I need supplies for tea, and I want to pick up some basmati rice."

"You know," I say, not entirely certain how to broach the subject. "Last time we went to the Twin Cities, there was that necromancer surprise."

His laugh is soft and maybe a little apologetic. "What if I promise, no necromancer surprise? Will you go?"

Considering what we've been through since then, and the fact I don't think there are many surprises left—at least not necromancer ones—I can't think of a reason not to go.

"Yes," I say at last. "I will."

"We'll go early, right after my appointment at Springside Long-term Care. Drive up, have dinner, walk around, and drive back?"

"I'll wear the skater skirt."

"I was hoping you'd say that."

He leans in for another kiss. The moment our lips meet, the cab of my truck fills with flashing red lights. The rearview mirror reflects the image of a patrol car. Between the dark and rotating lights, I can barely discern the bulky form of Police Chief Ramsey.

"That's my cue." Malcolm steals a quick kiss. "Text me when you get home."

He hops from the truck and strolls over to the patrol car. The lights cut off. Malcolm crouches to speak to Chief. I take that as my opening, put the truck in gear, and drive home.

I STAND on the sidewalk in front of my house, an old Victorian that belonged to my grandmother. Icicles hang from its eaves. Snow shrouds the lilac bushes. The windows are dark.

And once again, Carter Dupree is standing on my porch.

"Good evening, Katy." He's as cool as an ice statue, gleaming in the light of my front porch lamp.

I feign disinterest by pulling out my phone as if someone far more interesting than Carter Dupree has sent me a text message. Instead, I start one to Malcolm. I get as far as *Carte* when he speaks again.

"You have something of mine."

His words make my fingers jerk. I press send by accident but don't have time to follow up with an explanation. Beneath the calm tone lies a threat. Without looking away from him, I tuck my phone back into my pocket.

"I don't have anything of yours," I say, and my reply sounds lonely in the night air.

I'm cursing myself for not asking Nigel to show me how to create a ward. Not that it would do me any good now. Carter is already inside my territory and blocking my way.

"Delilah," he says. "What have you done with her?"

"I haven't done anything with her. She's a ghost, not your property."

"Where is she?" He takes the stairs with deliberation, each step making my heart spike. His hands are tucked in the pockets of his overcoat. Somehow, this makes him all the more threatening.

"She isn't here," I say. "I don't have her. I let her go."

At my words, he halts. Three feet of icy air separates us, but the way Carter glares at me lowers the temperature by ten degrees.

"You let her go?" His voice is so brittle that it cracks.

"Why wouldn't I?"

"Do you understand how powerful she is, how valuable?" He tips his head back and sends his disbelief skyward, as if I'm the stupidest person he's ever met. "I can't believe you did that."

His Adam's apple bobs. I think he might be crying; I think he might be experiencing actual remorse, but when he looks at me again, the smile on his face is like nothing I've ever seen. It goes beyond icy.

He takes a step forward. I take one back. I dart a glance toward Sadie's house. The windows are glowing with warmth. She's home. I suspect Nigel's there, too. I'm in boots; Carter is wearing loafers. I can run across the ice and grit of the sidewalk much better than he can.

Before I do, headlights flood the street. A red convertible careens to a stop, one wheel bumping up and over the curb. Malcolm bursts from the car and races across the yard.

He slams into Carter, the force of it sending them both into a snow bank. A shower of ice fills the air. And then it's arms and legs and fists. I inch forward, but when they roll in my direction, I jump back. Someone's foot connects with my shin.

I stumble toward the sidewalk. When my boots find purchase, I run. I'm out of breath when I reach Sadie's. I pound on the door, but my mitten absorbs all the sound. I yank it off with my teeth, try again, and I still have a mouthful of wool when Nigel opens the door.

"Katy, what the—"

I point to the battle currently being waged in my yard. Nigel grabs his coat and follows me. But when we reach my sidewalk, he simply stops, sticks his hands into his pockets, and watches, an amused smile on his face.

"Aren't you going to…?" I gesture toward the fight. "Help?"

Carter lands a punch that makes me wince, but Malcolm rallies with a knee to Carter's stomach. They roll again, snow spreading across the shoveled walk, flakes dancing in the air.

Nigel tilts his head as if considering. "No, I don't think so. He seems to be holding his own."

I release a disgusted sigh. "Really?"

He shrugs.

Before I can cajole or break up the fight myself, Sadie tears from her house, a huge pot clutched in her hands. She marches down the sidewalk, her destination clear. She takes a wide stance before Malcolm and Carter and heaves.

Water splashes. Steam rises. Shouts and curses echo in the night.

Carter staggers to his feet first, whirling on Sadie. "Holy hell, woman! It's below freezing out."

Now Nigel moves, inserting himself between Carter and Sadie. He shoots an arm out, connecting a palm with Carter's shoulder.

"Leave." Nigel's command is sharp, cold, and nonnegotiable.

Carter is drenched. He steps back, wiping a hand across his brow. Malcolm surges forward, but Nigel catches him around the waist.

"You, too, baby brother. Get out of here before someone calls Chief Ramsey at home."

"But Katy—"

"Is a grown woman and can take care of herself," he finishes. "Besides, Sadie's right next door, and so am I."

Carter remains immobile, an ice statue once again. Malcolm pants, breath ragged, a bruise forming beneath one eye. The sound of a car engine fills the night, and momentary panic grips me. I'm convinced someone has already made that call. This is Chief Ramsey, and Malcolm is headed for a night in jail.

Instead, a yellow van with black lettering pulls up. My roommate Belinda jumps from the Ghost B Gone vehicle. Gregory rounds the front, his form cutting through the van's headlights. They cast each other a look as if retreating back into the van is the better option.

I don't blame them. It probably is.

Nigel turns to Carter. "Where are you staying?"

Carter simply scowls.

"You can answer that," Nigel says, "or we can wait for Chief Ramsey to show up."

Carter wipes his mouth with the back of his hand and leaves a smear of pink across his cheek. "Springside B&B."

Gregory surveys the scene, his gaze going from me to Carter and then to Malcolm with his budding black eye. A crooked grin spreads across Gregory's face as if everything he needs to know is here in its aftermath.

"Need an escort service?" Gregory asks Nigel, with a nod toward Carter.

"Would you?"

"Leaving now." He pecks Belinda on the cheek and then takes Carter by the elbow. "That your fancy car down the block?"

Carter gives a single, terse nod.

"Then let's go."

At the wheel of the Ghost B Gone van, Gregory tracks Carter's progress down the sidewalk and into the sleek black sedan. The wheels squeak against the packed snow, and in the quiet that follows, I can hear Malcolm's still-ragged breathing and the soft rumble of his convertible.

"Now it's your turn," Nigel says to him.

"But—"

"Go. You'll see Katy tomorrow."

"Don't worry," Belinda chimes in. She drapes an arm around my shoulder. "I've got her."

Malcolm shoots me a look, one filled with doubt.

"Text me?" he mouths.

I nod.

We wait until Malcolm drives off. Only now do I feel the cold. I shiver against it, the chill penetrating through my coat and all the way down to the bone. Nigel picks up the pot and takes Sadie's hand. He nods at us, and together they retreat back up the walk and vanish inside Sadie's house.

Then Belinda and I are alone in the night.

"What was that?" she asks me.

I shake my head. "I don't know."

"Don't you?" she says, and her voice turns sly. "Didn't you once say you weren't the sort of girl guys fight over?"

"I'm not."

"Doesn't look that way to me."

I sigh, but it comes out more like a growl.

Belinda laughs. "Come on." She tugs me toward the door. "Let's go inside."

Before I shut the door, I scan my yard and the legacy of the fight. I wonder if I should dash over to Sadie's and ask Nigel to teach me how to create a ward. But I don't think I could make one big enough to hold the entire town of Springside.

CHAPTER 3

THE NEXT MORNING I'm the first one through the door of K&M Ghost Eradication Specialists. I pace between the front window display and the conference room, tracking glitter in my wake.

I peer out at the street, searching for that head of ebony hair. Even in the winter, Malcolm walks to work in the morning. When he doesn't appear, I pull out my phone and reread his final text from last night.

Malcolm: I'll apologize again in person in the morning. Meet me early?

Meeting early promises an extra-long morning kiss. So I wait. I pace. My heart jumps at the sound of footfalls on the sidewalk outside. At last, the bell above the door chimes. I whirl around.

And find Nigel shaking off the cold.

"Eventful night last night," he says.

I roll my eyes.

"He means well," Nigel adds. "Malcolm, that is. I don't know what the hell Carter wants."

Oh, but I do. I swallow back the dread. I haven't seen the last of Carter Dupree.

299

"Malcolm already apologized for going crazy," I say. "And it's not that..."

Although I worry that Carter might press charges. I worry he's done so already and that's why Malcolm hasn't walked through the door.

"This is new for him, Katy." Nigel hangs his coat on the rack.

"It's new for me, too," I say.

"Thing is, he knows how to get a girl's attention, but he hasn't had much practice in keeping it." He drapes his scarf over the coat. "Partnering with Selena ... well, it kind of kept him from figuring out the whole relationship thing. A ghost girlfriend is a whole lot easier than a real one. And as far as Carter goes, it's only natural that Malcolm would see another necromancer as a threat."

"Can he really be jealous of Carter?" I ask. "I don't even like Carter as a human being, and he really doesn't like me."

"Doesn't matter." He crosses to me and cups my shoulders. "Give Malcolm some time. He'll come to realize that he doesn't need to surround you with a ward or beat his chest or any of that."

I nod. I'm not as upset about last night as maybe I should be. I don't know what Carter planned to do, or what would've happened if Malcolm hadn't shown up. I glance toward the door. We are officially open for the day and the prospect of an extra-long morning kiss is diminishing by the second.

I reach for the canvas bag I use for porting thermoses of coffee. Today I've included a folder of information that Nigel asked for.

"It's all I could find." I hand him the folder and he pages through the contents.

"Have you thought of asking around?" he says, peering over the top at me.

"Asking ... around?"

"Springside. The people who knew your grandmother. The older residents." He slaps the folder against his leg. "What about the long-term care facility? Mr. Carlotta or Mrs. Greeley? They might know."

Of course they might, but I wouldn't know how to even start asking. I nod and tell Nigel thanks. I'm still leaning against the reception desk, my thoughts far away, when Malcolm flings open the door and brings in a flood of cold and energy. He shrugs off his coat, tosses it onto the rack, and then crosses the room to grab my hands.

Then he's swinging me around, his expression joyful. A deep purple bruise lines one eye, but that can't hide the delight in them. He's saying something, but his words are so rushed, so frantic, I can't make them out.

At last our whirling slows, as do his words.

"She's back! She's back. She's back, Katy. We were up all night."

I shake my head. I don't know who he's talking about or why he's so excited.

"She's here right now. Don't you feel her?"

I pull my hands back, tilt my chin up, and sample the air. With the cold and Malcolm's excitement, I missed the otherworldly presence that fills the space. Although how I could have is hard to say. It's so strong I suspect that if I reached out, my fingers would meet resistance.

"Selena's back," Malcolm says. "She found me."

"Selena," I echo, and my voice is thin.

"I couldn't wait for the two of you to meet."

Oh, I could've waited. Judging by the way Selena flows and buzzes around me, my guess is she could have as well. Her form shoves me, a cold caress that radiates up my spine. This Selena is territorial. If she could, I suspect she'd create a ward around Malcolm.

"Nigel's here," I say. "I don't think a ghost should be, especially this one."

While neither brother has admitted it, I believe that when Nigel—in the throes of his addiction—swallowed Selena, it caused a falling out between them. It wasn't long after that that Malcolm left Minneapolis and came to Springside.

He cringes. "You're right. I wasn't thinking. I'm just too ... I mean, I'll"—he points to the doorway—"just take her ... somewhere."

"Why don't you take the day off?" I suggest. "You were up all night, right?"

"Yeah, but I'm not even tired."

Maybe, but his eyes gleam with a frantic look, like someone who has taken a hit of a mind-altering drug. A crash is inevitable.

"Go on. Take the day." I nod toward the door. "Get reacquainted."

Part of me insists this is the wrong thing to say. That part insists I bring out my thermos of Kona blend, find some Tupperware, and catch this Selena. Then I'd go somewhere—preferably somewhere far, far away—and drop her off. And if she's lucky, I might crack the lid.

"Are you sure?" he asks, and his eyes appear preternaturally bright.

A drug, I think, and a powerful one. "Of course."

"You're the best."

He kisses me, a quick peck on the cheek, and dashes out the door, one arm flailing to find the sleeve of his coat.

I sink against the reception desk because suddenly my legs won't hold me. I stare at the closed door, the hint of cold—and supernatural—hanging in the air. I'm still there when Nigel ventures from the conference room.

"Katy? Was that Malcolm?"

"It was."

"And he left?"

"He did."

He takes a few cautious steps forward. "Is everything okay?"

"Selena's back."

Nigel exhales and swears under his breath. "This won't change anything. It really won't."

But he doesn't meet my gaze, and I know:

It already has.

THE VERY BEST place to drown your sorrows is the Springside Pancake House. I get a booth to myself, in Belinda's section, and she doesn't even bother to take my order. She knows.

All-you-can-eat dollar-sized pancakes and a large orange juice.

She eases the plate in front of me, her smile fading. "You okay?"

I manage a nod.

"I'd say you look like you've seen a ghost, but that's kind of every day for you."

Now I manage a laugh.

Her gaze flits toward the entrance. "Malcolm?"

I shake my head.

"Last night? I mean, did you guys fight or something?"

"No, it's ... complicated."

Really, how do I explain? That I'm jealous of Selena? That I'm afraid she'll ruin everything? That I risk losing my business partner and a friend and ... something more than that, something I haven't really given a name to. I didn't want to jinx it.

I suspect this is the reason why.

"Tonight, we can talk if you want," Belinda offers. "You know me. When it comes to guys, I never run out of advice."

And when it comes to guys, Belinda never needs it.

I'm almost done with my first plate when a well-tailored figure slides into the seat across from mine. In the late morning sunshine that streams through the windows, Carter Dupree gleams fiercely. He grins, teeth so white that I hold up a hand to ward off the glare.

"Could you turn that off?" I say.

"Rough night last night?"

"I could ask you the same."

"Rough morning?" His voice is sly and smooth.

I peer at him, searching for signs of last night's scuffle. Malcolm got in several good punches, but not a single scratch mars Carter's face. His knuckles are free from bruises, his nails short but perfectly manicured.

"So," he says, inspecting the cuticle of one of those manicured nails. "Did Malcolm like my present?"

Once, not too long ago, a ghost—an entity, really—choked me, cut off all my breath, made it impossible to breathe. Like then, I can't pull any air into my lungs. I want to claw at my throat, but I know that won't do any good. That I can't actually speak is a blessing. Any words I might say would come out garbled and pathetic.

"You met her, of course," Carter says. "I mean, he can't help himself." He taps his head. "He's not very bright that way. He thinks you'd want to meet her, and vice versa." Carter rolls his eyes.

"I don't know what you're talking about."

I'm proud of these words, but they wash right over him and leave me hollow.

"Not that I blame him," Carter continues. "Selena is one strong, sexy ghost. She's literally the one who got away. There's a special bond between a necromancer and the right ghost." He props his chin on a fist and contemplates the air somewhere above my shoulder. "Having the perfect woman inside your head, one who understands all your thoughts, your feelings? Indescribable, really. Delilah and I had that."

"Of course." I manage an eye roll of my own. "That's why she couldn't wait to leave."

Nothing. Not a twist of the lips or an eye twitch. He's nearly as icy as he was last night.

"It seems like we've both lost something, then." He leans forward, hands clasped now. "I'd call that even."

Belinda comes bustling by, her gaze flitting over Carter. The only evidence that she's seen him is the slight crease in her brow. She whirls, and the pitcher she's carrying tips precariously.

Orange juice splashes from the rim and drenches Carter's white dress shirt. He bolts upright, rocking the table between us. My plate and glass skitter and slide, but I catch them, one in each hand.

"Oh, I'm so sorry, sir." Belinda pulls a rag from her apron. "Here, let me help—"

He holds up both hands. "That won't be necessary. I was just leaving."

She beams at him, gives him the dazzling Belinda smile, and his scowl softens. He almost looks human like this, a little rumpled, not so shiny and pulled together. He eases from the booth and studies her nametag.

"Belinda, is it?"

She tilts her head, her explosion of blonde hair bouncing in its ponytail, customer-service smile still in place.

"I'll be sure to remember that," he adds.

And I don't like the way he says it at all.

We're silent as he leaves the restaurant. And there it is: a telltale limp in his gait. Only when the door has closed behind him do I let myself lean back against the booth. I wish she hadn't done that, but I can't find the words to tell her so.

Belinda, on the other hand, whistles while she wipes down the table.

She gathers up my plate and glass and returns moments later with a fresh version of each.

I cut my pancakes into tiny pieces. I dip each bite in maple syrup and contemplate how vindictive Carter Dupree actually is.

My guess is *very*.

CHAPTER 4

Don't let the ghosts of past loves haunt you.
Two-for-one eradication special.
Now through the end of the month.

I STUDY THE VALENTINES scattered in our display window and wonder if I can hire myself to eradicate a ghost. Although, really, if I could, would I? As if in answer, my reflection shakes its head.

No, I don't want to be someone's second choice, a second thought, a better-than-nothing. I also can't face Nigel's pity, and that's what it will be, no matter how hard he tries to hide it. Down the street, I catch sight of Chief Ramsey pushing through the doors of the Springside Police Department.

If I can't face Nigel's pity, then the least I can do is take his advice.

Inside the police station, Penny Wilson darts about as if Chief has given her twenty different tasks and she's uncertain which one to complete first. I stand at the front desk, head tilted, and taste the air. The space is close and dank, filled with the scent of stale snow mixed with sand. The aroma of charred coffee comes from the sideboard.

The two spites that normally haunt here? Hunkered down and miserable. I don't blame them. Penny has such a high tolerance for the

307

otherworldly that she doesn't notice their existence. Chief doesn't believe in the supernatural. As a result, I'm never around, offering up the Kona blend.

Something feels off, so I taste the air again. Scared? Yes, they both are. I glance around, searching for a reason, but before I can uncover anything, Penny halts in front of me.

"Oh, Katy!" Penny juggles today's newspaper, which I gather is for Chief Ramsey, two coffee cups, and a container of non-dairy creamer.

I should come back with some real coffee and half and half. It would be a public service.

"Can I help you with something?" she asks.

"Is Chief in? I mean, is he busy? If not, I'd like to talk to him."

"I ... I can check." Doubt flavors her words, her expression. She gives me a once-over, perhaps checking for trauma.

Chief and I have often had words, and in that, I'm merely following in my grandmother's footsteps. She never stopped by for a chat. To needle him? Maybe. But not like this, and not like what I have in mind.

Penny vanishes inside Chief Ramsey's office. She's gone for so long, I suspect the answer will be no. She's gone for so long, I consider investigating what has these two sprites on edge. Not even my full attention is enough to draw them from their hiding spot.

Penny emerges from his office minus one coffee cup and the newspaper. She nods. "You can go on back. He doesn't have anything scheduled until noon."

Chief is bulky, his office tiny. He's sitting behind his desk, gaze on his coffee cup, his expression dour.

I don't blame him; it smells terrible. I'm afraid the aroma might damage the inside of my nose.

He shakes his head and sets the cup down. "She means well, but..."

"The Coffee Depot delivers," I say.

"It would break her heart."

"I could teach her?" I venture. Maybe. I've tried to teach Malcolm, but when it comes to coffee, I'm either the world's worst instructor or he's an unusually slow learner. Why he can concoct amazing tea but his coffee tastes like a vending-machine special, I'll never know.

"You didn't come here about the lousy coffee," Chief says.

"No." I'm grateful for the excuse to shove Malcolm from my thoughts.

"So maybe it's about the disturbance in your yard last night?"

Of course some tattletale called Chief Ramsey. "Disturbance?" I go for all innocence, making my eyes wide and voice light.

He grumbles a sigh, rubbing his temples with his left hand. The wedding band is there, where it should be. But whether this means he's still married or is simply bad at letting go, I can't say.

"I have a personal question. If you don't mind, that is." I don't wait to see if he does. "You knew my mom, didn't you?"

Something changes in that moment. Chief drops his hand. His spine straightens. He leans toward me, as much as his bulk and the desk will allow.

"Yes, I did. We went to high school together."

"Same class?"

He nods. "She was the first person who ever spoke to me at school, maybe in all of Springside." Chief pauses as if he's considering what to reveal, or perhaps how much. "It wasn't the easiest thing, moving from Minneapolis to Springside. At least, not for me."

"So, what did she say?"

"That they gave me the haunted locker and to let her know if I wanted her to take care of that."

"Oh, yes. Locker 35. It's always been haunted."

The spirit that occupies the space is so benign, most people can't feel its presence. Except on pep rally days. Then it expels the contents of the locker as if it can't contain its excitement.

Chief eyes me, but continues. "She waved me over to her table at lunch that first day." His lips compress into a grim line. "I'm embarrassed to admit I thought the school administration put her up to it, so I just ... walked on past. But that wasn't your mother. I figured that out later."

This woman I never knew is starting to captivate me. We walked the same halls, the same streets, eradicated ghosts from the same school lockers.

"And when she came back to Springside after college, already engaged, she broke a lot of hearts, too."

Chief's included? His eyes hold a tenderness I've never seen before.

"Did you know my dad?"

"I did. He was a fine man. Trust me, I would've had something to say about it if he hadn't been."

Oh, yes, I think. Chief included.

He smiles at me now, the look indulgent and fatherly. "Why all the questions, Katy? Surely your grandmother—"

I give my head a vigorous shake. "She couldn't talk about it. It … hurt her, so I stopped asking. But recently, I've been curious about my mom, my dad, and what they were like."

"I understand, perhaps more than you realize." He stares out the small window as if the icy patterns on the glass enthrall him. He keeps his eyes there when he speaks again. "Their car accident. I was the first officer on the scene. I was still green, too. So green, this was the first time I'd ever…"

Something clicks in my mind. I wonder if my grandmother blamed Chief for not being able to save my mom. I don't know. I doubt I'll ever know. But all their years of animosity take on a fresh meaning.

We're both silent. I nod so Chief knows he doesn't need to continue the story. I've heard enough, and I can see this is a wound that has never fully healed.

After a moment, he coughs, clears his throat. Then he straightens again. He is less fatherly and more Police Chief Ramsey.

"It's interesting that you're asking me this now," he says, and his tone is far more no-nonsense than a moment before.

"Is it?"

"Because yesterday, I see this fancy Mercedes roll down Main Street. I get curious when a stranger comes to town driving a car that costs more than most of the houses around here. So, I ran the plates."

My heart is thumping so hard it makes my ribs ache. My throat is tight, and I have that feeling where I can't breathe again.

"Orson Yates," Chief says. "Thought the name sounded familiar, so I had Penny do a search on our old case files. Know the last time he was in town?"

Something tells me I do know, but would rather not acknowledge it. I shake my head.

"The week of your parents' accident. I interviewed him as a witness.

He saw the car plunge into the ravine. You know the one, outside of town on the way to the nature preserve."

I know that ravine. I drive past it every time we do a catch and release. I wonder how my grandmother drove by it for all those years—there's no other route to the nature preserve, no other close-by place to release ghosts.

I wonder at her strength.

"What caused the accident?" I ask. "Can you tell me?"

"Faulty brakes. Your grandmother ... pushed for a more thorough investigation, but there was no denying bad brakes on an old car."

Could a ghost do that? Could a powerful one lie dormant until the perfect moment? Could you unleash something like that, the way Carter unleashed Harold's ghost on Sadie?

Not to mention unleashing Selena on Malcolm. I bite my thumbnail in thought. This is information I never expected. It's information I can't use. It simply is; a past I can't change.

"Katy, what's going on?" Chief is frowning now, his expression both fatherly and official.

"I really don't know."

"Give the word and I'll start the paperwork for a restraining order."

And how would that work against ghosts?

"I don't have..." What? I'm not sure of the word I'm looking for, but at last I go with, "I don't really have any evidence. Orson Yates hasn't done anything except stop by K&M Ghost Eradication Specialists. His ... friend, Carter Dupree, is creepy, but it was Malcolm who started the fight last night."

At this, Chief actually chuckles. "I know. Carter Dupree was in earlier, asking for one against Malcolm."

Of course he was. I lean forward, wondering if this is yet another problem. "And?"

"I told him if he didn't like the residents, he could leave town." He jabs a finger at me. "But you tell that young hothead of yours to watch it."

"He's not mine," I say.

"Sure he isn't." Chief settles back in his chair, far too smug. "Tell him anyway. And you tell me if something else happens. Anything, even if you think it's no big deal. Call the dispatcher and they'll call me at home."

I nod. "Thank you. I ... hope I won't need to."

I'm at the door, ready to leave, when Chief calls out one last time.

"Katy? Know what I think?"

I shake my head.

"Your mother would be proud of you."

I leave the police station with my eyes damp and my heart beating a strange, erratic rhythm in my chest.

THE SETTING SUN is painting the snow pink by the time I reach home this evening. The windows of Sadie's house are glowing brightly, the light warm and inviting. Two shadows move from one room to another. When they meet, they pause for what I guess must be a kiss.

I hate to interrupt that.

I trudge up her steps anyway. A moment after Sadie flings open the door, she pulls me inside and into a hug.

"Oh, my dear. Nigel said you had a rough day."

Over Sadie's shoulder, I spear Nigel with a glare. He shrugs and mouths an apology while she rocks me. At last, I push away with gentle hands on her shoulders.

"I'm fine," I say. "Really."

"Still, you shouldn't worry," she says, patting my arm in a consoling manner. "A ghost can't replace a human being."

This I'm not so sure about, but I nod.

"And stay for dinner. I baked pecan pie for dessert."

Because I haven't drowned my sorrows in enough carbs and sugar yet today. This might push me over the edge.

"Actually," I say, "I was hoping Nigel would show me how to do something. A necromancer thing."

He raises his eyebrows. "A ward, perhaps?"

"Yes, a ward. Would you?"

"You don't have to ask twice." Already he's reaching for his coat and within a minute, we're outside, trudging through snow in the winter dusk.

We walk the perimeter of my property, along the picket fence between my yard and Sadie's and the taller, cedar fence of the neighbor to the rear. Occasionally Nigel stops, crouches, touches something—the base of a pine tree, the lilac bushes, the garden shed I never use because I never garden.

"Interesting," he says at last. "Your grandmother must have been extremely powerful. I'm picking up remnants of a ward she put in place years ago."

"But she wasn't—"

"A necromancer?" He gives me a sly look. "Are you one?"

I concede his point, although I don't consider this true necromancy. This has nothing to do with ghosts and everything to do with other human beings.

"So, she had a ward in place?" I ask.

"Several, I think, over the years. The vibe I'm getting is 'back off, big city necromancers'."

Despite myself, I laugh. That sounds like my grandmother. "I don't sense anything."

"Well, you wouldn't. This has always been your home. I'm only sensing it now because I'm searching for signs of a ward. It's not intact and its hold has depleted, which is why I haven't noticed it before."

"And Malcolm, too, right? He would've noticed it if it was intact."

"And my stupid brother, yes."

"He's not stupid," I say, although why I'm defending Malcolm is beyond me.

"All right, he's acting stupid and if he doesn't stop, he'll regret it."

"So how does a ward really work if a necromancer can walk right through it?" I want to change the subject. I want to know how this is going to help if someone like Orson Yates can breeze into K&M Ghost Eradication Specialists without recourse.

"This is important," I add. "Belinda spilled orange juice on Carter Dupree this morning."

Nigel snorts. "On purpose?"

"Yes. That's why it's a problem. I don't know if he recognized her from last night, but he made note of her name."

He swears, and his breath chases snowflakes from the slender branch of a sapling. "And that will lead him back here."

"Exactly. She's been ghost-free and alcohol-free for months now, but it wouldn't take much. One nasty ghost and she'll lose everything all over again."

"I know how that goes," he says.

"So, how does it work? Is it like insurance?"

"Sort of. The reason most necromancers won't violate a ward is the threat of retribution. Other necromancers will band together and deliver ... justice. Even if we can't stand each other, we'll work together to set things right or make sure it doesn't happen again. It's the principle of the thing."

"Retribution," I echo. "That sounds unpleasant."

"Trust me, it can be."

"This retribution wouldn't be one of your run-ins with Orson Yates, would it?"

Nigel laughs. "Very astute. Even he thinks twice before violating a ward, but he's one of the worst offenders."

"Speaking of Orson," I say, "I don't think he's bluffing about my mom."

The story comes tumbling out, everything Chief Ramsey told me about my parents and Orson Yates. We stand in the cold, the sun fully set, the yellow glow of the back porch light from Sadie's house illuminating us.

Nigel grips my arms as if he needs me to hold him up as much as I need someone to steady me.

"Katy, I'm sorry. I spent the day searching, but I haven't come up with much. I also reached out to some of the older necromancers I know, but I haven't heard back yet. Some of them don't even use email or the internet."

"But how do they—"

"Sprites, ghosts, telephone." He shrugs and gives me a crooked grin. "This time around, I used the telephone. I left lots of voice messages."

I want to laugh at this but only manage a sigh. "I suppose in the days before telephones and telegraphs, that could make a necromancer pretty powerful."

"You suppose right."

"And today, too," I add, thinking of Malcolm again and his time as a stockbroker with Selena retrieving information for him.

Will he go back to that? Part of me insists he won't; he loves what we do, even if he doesn't ... I can't finish the rest of that thought. Part of me wonders how anyone could resist the temptation. He could work for another brokerage firm or even start his own business. Scratching out a living as a ghost catcher can't compare.

"Hey." Nigel's voice is as soft as the snow. "Let's get your ward in place."

I shake off my thoughts and the cold eating at me. "What do I need to do?"

"A couple of things. A ward is deceptively simple. You pick a few anchor items, place the ward on them, and call it done. But it's all in the choosing of the right items, truly identifying what belongs to you, and not picking something that will up and leave—or get uprooted—any time soon."

I scan my property. "So, everything inside the anchor points is under protection?"

"Yes. This is where Malcolm always messes up. He'll pick things in a hurry and not truly consider how permanent something is, or whether it's his to begin with. For instance, the picket fence. That belongs to Sadie, which makes it a poor choice for you."

I walk toward the fence, place my hand on it. I turn and glance over my shoulder at Nigel. "But a good choice for you?"

"Try it without the mitten."

I pull off my mittens and shove them into my coat pocket. With bare fingertips, I touch the fence. The paint feels brittle, and my skin aches with the cold. Beneath all that comes a sensation. Words and images fill my head. I laugh.

"What do you sense?" he asks.

"Something along the lines of: *Go away! She's my girl.*" I spear him with another look. "That's very ... middle school."

He shrugs, hands in pockets, expression mild.

"And kind of chauvinistic. Sadie can take care of herself."

"I know. Still." He tilts his head toward the fence. "Message received, right? Short, no room for questions. Complicated wards disintegrate too quickly and are too easily circumvented."

"I'm guessing the one on K&M Ghost Eradication Specialists isn't so … strident."

"No, because you might want to collaborate with necromancers and … others. But you're right. It's more complicated and will wear off more quickly. Together we should be able to keep a solid one in place. So?" He raises his eyebrows at me. "Ready to try?"

I point to the items I've identified as anchors. "Willow tree."

"Good," Nigel says.

"Lilac bushes."

"Another good choice."

"The handrails out front, by the sidewalk?" This one I'm not so sure of, but I would love nothing more than to never see Carter Dupree on my porch again.

"You'll need to reinforce it with a few more anchors," he says. "Let me show you how to place a ward, and then we'll move to the front."

We start with the willow tree. Nigel kneels at its base and digs through the snow until he exposes the trunk near the frozen earth.

"Most necromancers will respect a ward placed anywhere on an anchor, but others will simply duck under one placed up high and then claim they never felt it."

"That sounds like a technicality."

"It is."

"It sounds like something Orson Yates or Carter Dupree might do."

This time, Nigel grins. "Absolutely."

He takes my hand and places it against the cold bark. "Now concentrate. Pick a few words or a phrase that encompasses your message."

"Does it matter what it is?"

"Not as long as it's clear."

I close my eyes, letting thoughts and images fill my head: Belinda, Sadie, Nigel, Malcolm. Friends. Safety. Protection.

"Whoa," Nigel breathes. "Glad I'm your friend."

"You're getting the message?"

"Loud and clear. Let's connect the dots so everyone else will too."

We trudge through the snow. By the time we're done, I've placed six anchor points around my property. We stand on the sidewalk staring up at my home as if we can admire my handiwork.

"You can come over for dinner," he says. "I owe you that. You know how it is. Sadie asks about my day, and things just come out."

"You're like an old married couple already." I cast him a look from the corner of my eye. "I'm guessing you haven't—"

He sighs. "Not yet. Valentine's, for sure."

"Or tonight," I say. "You could always ask her tonight."

He laughs, a self-effacing sound. "Not tonight, but dinner still stands."

"I'll order some pizza when Belinda gets home."

"All right. Goodnight, Katy."

"Goodnight," I echo. "And thank you."

He raises a hand as if to wave away my gratitude. I watch as he enters Sadie's kitchen and she envelops him in a hug. I remain on my front walk, gaze touching each anchor point. It's a start, but a shield isn't enough, not one as insubstantial as this.

I want Orson Yates out of Springside, and that's going to take something more than a flimsy ward. I know of only one thing powerful enough. My fingertips come to rest on my left cheek, on the faded blue mark the entity left.

I refuse to let my thoughts drift any further.

CHAPTER 5

THE MORNING AIR is bitter, the sun brilliant. My face aches from the short jaunt from my truck to inside the office. I'm pressing my fingertips against my cheeks in an effort to warm them when Malcolm bursts through the front door.

The bell chimes; his face is glowing from excitement and the cold. He scoops me into a hug, tucking me inside his overcoat.

"You owe me a morning kiss and an evening kiss," he says.

Inside the wool, the world is warm and safe. It smells of nutmeg and Ivory Soap frosted in winter. I nuzzle closer, intent on remembering how this feels, his arms around me, the thrum of his heartbeat. I hold still, hold on to the moment—this exact moment, the one before everything changes.

"Hey." He clutches my chin and raises my face to his. "What's wrong?"

"Carter Dupree brought Selena to Springside," I say, because delaying will only make it worse. "On purpose. To..." I trail off. To what? Hurt me? Obviously. To distract Malcolm? Maybe. But what else? Is there something I'm missing?

I brace for denial, for an outburst—for Malcolm to call me a liar. Instead, he tips his head back and laughs.

319

"Is that all? I already know that. Besides, Carter only thinks he's done that. Selena used him to find me. She told me all about it. He thinks he's this slick necromancer." Malcolm laughs again and gives his head a shake. "Trust me, he's not half as good as he thinks he is. Remember how easy it was to free Delilah?"

I nod slowly. This, I'm not so sure about. But Malcolm is as bright and brilliant as the day. He positively glows. That's when it hits me.

I've never seen him look so happy.

"Is that what's bothering you?" he asks.

"I'm worried," I say. "I'm worried that they came to town and haven't left and I don't know how to make them leave. I'm afraid they'll hurt even more people."

He cups my face. "We won't let them. Me, you, Nigel. We won't. I promise you that."

He kisses me then. I don't know if I believe the promises in either his words or his kiss. But I do know this:

There is nothing in the world I want to believe more.

It's too cold out for over-the-knee stockings. I grew up in Minnesota, and any sensible Minnesotan knows that winter weather and bare skin don't mix. Still, part of me is tempted to show some of that skin, opt for the stockings rather than the far more practical—and thicker —tights.

Part of me knows it's too late for that. It's the same part of me that has Carter Dupree's voice on a constant loop in the back of my mind:

Selena is one strong, sexy ghost ... there's a special bond between a necromancer and the right ghost.

Not that Malcolm has canceled the date. But the only time he's mentioned it all week was to insist that, weather permitting, we would drive up in his car, not my truck.

"My pickup is better in the snow," I said.

"My convertible is better for everything else," he countered. "It's Valentine's Day. I want to zip you up to the Cities in style, not in your grandmother's old truck."

Even I had to admit that my grandmother's old truck isn't all that romantic.

Now I stand in the living room, shutters partly open so I can see the street. I won't miss the flash of red. Malcolm's convertible is very hard to miss. Even so, I pace, gaze darting to the curb outside my house, dread building in my stomach. Every so often, I glance down, inspect a leg, and reconsider whether the black tights with pink hearts are cute enough.

He's fifteen minutes late.

I force my mind to turn to other things, like the lack of customers this month. Perhaps on Valentine's Day, everyone wants to cling to past loves. Our two-for-one eradication special hasn't brought in any business. Even the sprites are behaving themselves. I haven't gone out on a single annoyance call all week.

Worse, a fancy Mercedes is still sitting outside Springside B&B, although Carter Dupree has not darkened my doorstep since I put the ward in place.

Nigel has still not asked Sadie to marry him. He has nine hours left in the holiday to do so.

Malcolm is twenty-five minutes late.

At the forty-five minute mark, my cell phone rings. My heart leaps, my fingers fumbling with the phone. I answer so fast, all I catch of the caller is one small fact:

Not Malcolm.

"Katy, I'm sorry to bother you at home." It's Vanessa, the manager of Springside Long-term Care. "And really, I hate to bother you at all. I know you don't charge for your visits."

Springside Long-term Care has always been a gratis account; my grandmother insisted.

"What's wrong?" I ask. Perhaps this is where all the past loves have taken their haunting. That makes a certain amount of sense.

"Malcolm was scheduled to visit this afternoon. We were going to have a little party. Many of the residents wanted to give him valentines."

By *residents*, I'm sure she means the female residents and members of his fan club.

"Oh, and you have a valentine, too, Katy. From Mr. Carlotta."

Yes. I have a fan club of one.

"They were so disappointed, but I'm certain something came up. I told them that the two of you must have gone out on an emergency eradication, but they insisted I call and—"

"Vanessa, hang on. Are you saying Malcolm didn't show up today?"

"He was scheduled for one o'clock, like always."

Malcolm never misses his weekly visit, although truthfully, he does so little eradication while he's there you could hardly call it part of our business. It's all coffee and tea taste tests, magic tricks, and of course, a massive amount of flirting.

"Katy?"

That earlier dread—born of jealousy—shifts, turns cold. I close my eyes and see that black Mercedes in front of Springside B&B.

"Is everything okay?" Vanessa prompts.

"I don't know," I tell her. "But can you let everyone know that he didn't forget? It wasn't on purpose."

"Of course."

I hang up and immediately send Malcolm a text:

Are you okay?

I wait a whole thirty seconds before calling him. His phone rolls straight to voice mail. For a moment, my mind blanks. I don't know what to do next. I peer out the window, like an idiot, as if Malcolm will suddenly pull up in the convertible, like the last hour hasn't happened.

Then my limbs spring to life. I pull on my coat, pull the keys for my truck from the hook by the kitchen door. I throw the deadbolt and push the door open ... and a force sends me backward, into the kitchen table and onto the tile floor.

The otherworldly presence that has invaded my space is so strong that it looks like a layer of fog is covering the ceiling. I stand and flick on the light, but the glow is anemic, at best.

The ghost whirls; the walls shake. Waves of frustration roll off the thing. I don't know what it wants. I reach upward in hopes of gauging its intentions. My fingertips meet icy resistance, and I jerk my hand back.

This ghost?

Does not like me.

Then a shiver crawls down my spine, the sensation familiar. Now I know why this ghost doesn't like me.

This ghost is Selena.

But if she's here…

"Selena? Is that you?"

The walls rumble again, and I take that as a yes.

"Where's Malcolm?"

The shaking moves into the foundation. I'm fairly certain she'll shake my house to pieces at this rate.

"Stop, stop. I don't understand you. Where's Malcolm?"

As if in answer, the fog on my ceiling descends. It forms a shape that's vaguely humanlike, or more accurately, womanlike. Curves. This ghost has curves, and she's stalking me in what looks like an otherworldly pair of high heels.

She surges against me, shoving me back toward the living room. She pushes, and I stumble, until at last I land on the couch.

I try again. "Where is he?"

She whirls around while flyers, junk mail, and napkins from the takeout pizza place swirl into a small cyclone. The temperature in my house has dropped at least ten degrees. We're about to go into a full-on ghost infestation at this point.

I don't think even my best Kona blend will stop her.

I hold up my hands in surrender. "Selena, listen. I get it. Something's wrong, but I can't understand you the way Malcolm does. Spell it out. Assume I'm stupid."

At this last, the air shakes with what feels like laughter. Oh, she already thinks I'm stupid.

Her presence contracts until she's a nearly solid form across from me, perched on my coffee table, one ghostly leg elegantly crossed over the other. Tendrils that look very much like fingers extend from her, their trajectory on a collision course with my face.

This could be a bad idea. Even so, I hold still. She reaches me, wisps of her flowing around my head, invading my ears, my nose, my mouth.

That's when the images flash, one after the other. The road to the nature preserve. A red convertible in the parking lot. A dark-haired body slumped over the wheel.

I spring up. For a moment, the two of us occupy the same spot. More images, a jumble of them. I get a flash of other places, other people. The Minneapolis skyline. Carter Dupree. An old warehouse on some lonely road. The Springside Cemetery.

Selena shoots toward the ceiling and takes the images with her. I gasp for breath, winded, although I've done nothing more than view these things. But I'm still in my winter coat. I still clutch the keys to my truck. I study the shoes on my feet. Mary Janes.

That won't do. I kick them off, shove my feet into boots, and race out the door.

AT THE TURNOFF for the nature preserve, the steering wheel freezes. I yank on it, feel the ache in my shoulders from the effort before noticing the cloud around my legs.

"I can't go that way!" I kick with my left foot, for all the good it will do me. "I'm not a ghost. I have to drive the long way around."

The cab shakes with Selena's frustration.

"Go on ahead," I tell her. "Check on him. I'm right behind you."

She sticks with me as if she doesn't quite trust that I'll follow through. The truck rocks down the road. I'm grateful for the light traffic—and the fact that I've made it this far without encountering a patrol car.

It's only when I tap the brakes for a yield sign and meet no resistance that another notion creeps into my mind. Instead of Carter Dupree haunting my thoughts, I hear the echo of Nigel's warning:

Never get into a car with an angry, uncontained ghost.

And I've done just that.

I swallow back my panic and try for nonchalance, although certainly Selena can tell this is an act. I grip the wheel and sense its range tightening. Soon I won't be able to turn it at all. My brakes are all but useless. I pump them to no avail. All I can do is ease off the accelerator. Even that becomes a chore. My foot feels like it weighs fifty pounds.

Thoughts batter me from all sides. Can ghosts lie? Sprites play pranks, but can ghosts fabricate the way Selena has, showing me images of things that don't exist? Is Malcolm actually hurt? Is he even at the nature preserve?

Or is this an elaborate trap that I've walked right into? One orchestrated by Orson Yates and Carter Dupree?

The ravine is coming up on my right, that same ravine where my parents died. Like this? I wonder. An old car, an angry ghost, and no hope. Except I do have hope. I have Malcolm.

"Let me steer," I say to Selena, my voice as stern as I can make it. "If you don't let me steer, I can't save Malcolm."

She buzzes about the cab, agitated, her worry a tangible thing. Yes, Malcolm is hurt.

"You can't save him," I add, "but you know I can. That's why you found me, right? But if you don't let me drive, I can't do that."

Up ahead a sign looms, the one alerting me to take the turn at twenty-five miles per hour.

I'm going fifty.

"Selena, let go of the steering wheel. If I drive into the ravine, you might get rid of me, but there won't be anyone around to save Malcolm. Carter Dupree won't. Orson Yates won't."

The tires inch from the asphalt and onto the gravel of the shoulder. The silver guardrail flashes into view. I'm wrenching the wheel so hard, I'm nearly flat against the driver's side door with the effort.

All four tires are rolling across gravel now. The front grill of the truck will meet the guardrail first. At this speed, I'll plow right on through. My seatbelt is buckled, but I doubt that will matter.

I'm gripping the wheel with all my strength. When it turns freely in my hands, I'm thrown sideways against the window. The wheel slips through my fingers. The truck's grill scrapes the guardrail. I jerk the wheel farther, and then I'm jostling back onto the asphalt. The truck crosses both lanes and bumps against the row of pines that line the opposite side of the road.

I pull into my lane, heart pounding, hands shaking. Either my windshield or my vision is fogged. I swipe a hand across the glass and consider that maybe it's both. Cold sweat blooms across my skin. The sharp taste of copper fills my mouth. I wipe at it with the back of my hand and leave a smear of red across my skin. I'm bleeding, but don't have time to figure out from where or how much.

The fogged windshield clears and Malcolm's red convertible comes into view. The truck jumps forward, although I can't tell if it's Selena or me doing the driving. We skid into the parking lot, fishtailing to a stop.

I leap out and circle Malcolm's car. I try each door. I pound on the driver's side window. He's slumped over the steering wheel, absolutely still, his bulky winter coat blocking my view of possible injuries.

Except for the blood. I assume it's blood. A dark stain is spreading across one leg of his trousers. I pound some more, but he doesn't stir. With the coat in the way, I can't tell if he's breathing.

I pull out my phone and call 911. I don't stay on the line after I give the dispatcher the basics. I go back to circling Malcolm's car, trying the door handles again, tugging on the trunk's latch.

Selena is a blur above us.

"He's bleeding," I say to her, although I'm certain she knows this. "Can you get in? Unlock the door? Something?"

Certainly she's strong enough, but she flutters around as if there's a barrier keeping her away from the vehicle. I pull off a mitten and press my hand against the icy glass of one window. A cold ache invades my fingers, and I detect something else, something that feels supernatural.

What it is, I can't say. But if Selena can't get in, that leaves me. I race back to my truck and scramble into the back. Could I smash a window? Slice through the convertible's top? I find the flat tire kit first. The tire iron is heavy and cold in my hands.

It's perfect.

On the passenger side, I take up a wide stance and swing at the window. The blow bounces off the glass and the force sends me backward. All I manage is a tiny crack. I don't see the sense in trying again, but Selena is pushing at my hands, forcing my arms upward. Although I can't truly hear her, the air vibrates with the message.

Try again.

I do.

Another blow, another crack. The chip in the glass is deeper, a spider web of fissures branching across the window.

Again Selena urges me, so I swing a third time. If the crack is any deeper, I can't tell. I'm no closer to breaking the window than I was before I started. My arms ache, the tire iron weighing them down. I strain my ears in hopes of a siren, but hear only wind chasing ice crystals across the snow and the sound of my own ragged breathing.

"I can't break it," I say into the air.

Instead of urging me on, Selena spirals into tighter and tighter circles until at last she appears as thin as a wire. I'm certain if I touched her, she'd have actual substance.

I see then what her target is. Perhaps I've broken more than I thought. Or maybe it's just enough. She burrows into that small crack; it's a hole, not only in the glass, but also in the supernatural field that surrounds the car. Her form spreads through the fractures.

Then, with the force she demonstrated in my car and my kitchen, Selena vibrates. I don't think to turn away or step back. When the glass shatters, I'm standing right there. Shards rain down on me. I duck behind my hands, but glass tangles in my hair, cuts my skin, sticks to my tights.

I ignore it all in my lunge for the door. I yank it open from the inside and crawl across more glass to reach Malcolm.

I ease him back from the steering column. He is so heavy in my hands. My fingertips snake along his collar and dip beneath it. I hold my breath while searching out a pulse. It's there, strong beneath my fingers. With my cheek next to his, I feel his warm exhale against my skin.

Flashing lights fill the car. A siren I can only now hear wails. I manage to unlock the driver's side door before someone tugs me from the car. Two EMTs take over, leaving me in the cold and underneath the glare of Police Chief Ramsey.

CHIEF RAMSEY TOWERS OVER ME, unsmiling, arms folded across his chest. This is not the man who laughed at ghost stories on Christmas Eve. Neither is he the man who shared his memories of my mother mere days ago.

This is a man who may pull out his handcuffs and slap them on my wrists. He has a fierce look about him, a mix of disappointment and something I can't name. He takes deliberate steps and stops when the toe of his boot bumps against my phone. He leans down and picks it up.

"I thought I told you to call me."

He hands the phone to me and I tuck it into my pocket. Beneath his glower, I can do little more than swallow hard and nod. The urge to turn from him nearly overwhelms me. I want to track the EMTs' progress with Malcolm, make sure he's okay. I don't dare, not even when something clanks and rattles. A stretcher, I think.

"What the hell happened here?" Chief is still glowering at me, still fierce and unrelenting.

"I ... we..." I glance around.

Selena's presence no longer fills the air. She is either gone or has made herself so slight, I can't detect her. A wave of sudden exhaustion fogs my mind. I'm not sure I can make up a story, not one that will satisfy Chief.

But I try. "Vanessa from Springside Long-term Care called me because Malcolm missed his weekly appointment. I got worried when he didn't answer his phone, so I went looking for him."

There's nothing in my statement that isn't true. I take a breath, relieved I've made it this far with Chief.

"What about this." With a foot, he taps the shattered glass that litters the parking area. In the sunlight, the shards sparkle, and the light crunch of stretcher wheels running over the debris reaches my ears.

"This is safety glass," he continues. "Do you know what that means?"

I shake my head.

"It means that there's no way you used that"—he points to the tire iron—"to shatter the window so ... completely. Mind telling me what really happened here?"

I can only stare back at him, mute. No, I can't tell him what really happened; he'd never believe me. My legs shake as if the adrenaline is already seeping from my feet and into the ground. I may follow, curl up into a Katy-puddle among all the shards of glass.

"Hey, Chief," one of the EMTs calls out. "We're about ready here, and I'd like to check Katy, make sure she isn't injured."

Chief Ramsey blinks, gives one terse nod, and turns his back on me. The EMT leads me to the ambulance with a gentle hand on my arm.

"Are you okay?" she asks.

"I think so. I'm covered with glass." I wave a hand up and down. As if on cue, a few splinters from the window fall to the ground.

"You should probably come in to the ER. The glass might have scratched your eyes."

"Is Malcolm—?"

She nods. It's a noncommittal sort of gesture and I take it that way. Malcolm still is. For now that's enough.

"Why don't you ride in the back with him?" she says.

"But my truck—"

"I'll take care of your truck," Chief says.

How he went from convertible to ambulance without my seeing him, I don't know. But I think it means that, yes, I *should* ride in back. I should go to the ER. Even so, I turn and call out a second protest.

"And Nigel—"

"I'll call Nigel," Chief replies. "He'll probably beat us to the hospital."

Feeling chastised and childish, I let the EMT direct me into a seat next to Malcolm's stretcher. I can reach his hand, and for this I'm grateful. His skin is warm against mine.

I hold his hand for the entire ride to Springside Hospital. Every few blocks I give his fingers a gentle squeeze.

He doesn't squeeze back.

CHAPTER 6

A NICE NURSE PRACTITIONER helps me pick the glass from my hair and clothes. She cleans all the cuts and scrapes. A doctor is confirming that my eyes are scratch-free as Sadie arrives with a change of clothes and an extra-large hot chocolate.

"Oh, Katy, dear." Her hug is a cautious, gentle thing but so warm and safe that for a moment, tears fill my eyes.

"Malcolm?" My voice rings plaintive and scared around us. I haven't sounded this way since my grandmother died.

"In a room, recovering. He has some broken ribs and a concussion. They want to keep him for a few days to make sure there isn't any internal bleeding. Nigel's up there now."

"Can I ... I mean, will they let me see him?"

Sadie smiles at me and cups one side of my face with her hand. "They'd better. He's been asking for you. He's more concerned about you than his own injuries."

I clasp Sadie's hand—the left, I realize. It is smooth and unadorned. There will be no proposal tonight, I'm certain. The thought adds a layer of sadness to the entire day.

Nigel meets us outside the door to Malcolm's room. He pulls me into a hug, one with far more intensity than Sadie's.

"Thank you," he whispers. "Thank you. We have our differences, but he's—"

"Your baby brother," I finish.

He grips my shoulders. "Yes. That. And you." His fingers hover over the scrapes on my face. "Are you okay?"

"Mostly."

"Would seeing Malcolm get you all the way there?"

"I think it would."

"They've got him doped up on painkillers. If he falls asleep, don't take it personally."

"I won't," I promise.

Nigel releases me and I slip through the small opening in the door to Malcolm's room. The lights are dim. Beneath the antiseptic hospital odors, I catch a hint of something, something that smells like nutmeg and Ivory Soap.

Dark lashes grace his cheekbones. Both eyes are bruised now. A bandage is wrapped around part of his skull, and I wonder if that was the source of the blood. But his mouth looks soft, relaxed.

This might be the result of the painkillers.

His eyes flutter open, and he gives me a smile just this side of goofy.

It's most definitely the painkillers.

"Hey," I say, keeping my voice low and quiet.

He twitches his fingers, a *come here* sort of gesture, and I inch forward.

"There you are." His voice sounds rough. "Lifesaver."

I shake my head. "It wasn't just me. Vanessa called, and Selena—"

He grips my fingers and gives them the squeeze I so longed for in the ambulance.

"You," he says, a simple statement to end my protests.

I pull up a chair as close to the edge of the bed as I can. Malcolm takes my hand again, laces our fingers.

"What happened?" I ask. "Do you remember?"

"I was ... showing Selena what we do, my new life here. How we catch and release, although I couldn't even find a sprite to demonstrate. Our next stop was the party at Springside Long-term Care. Something attacked us, or really, me. It had no interest in Selena."

"A ghost? Something else?"

"A ghost, I think. A really nasty one."

"So, not like that entity?"

Malcolm shuts his eyes. "I don't think so. I think if it were something that strong, I'd be dead right now. It probably had a little direction and a boost from a necromancer, though." He sighs. "How did you get me out?"

I cringe to even say it. "A tire iron."

His eyes fly open. "You what? Smashed a window? Have you been working out in secret?"

I shake my head. "I could only make a tiny crack, but it was enough for Selena to sneak in and do the rest."

"Necromancy," Malcolm says. "A containment field. It can be used to keep ghosts out—or in. I used one on my samovar. It's how I stored so many inside there."

"A samovar is pretty small," I point out, "compared to a car."

"An easy trick for a powerful necromancer."

Our gazes lock, although we both remain silent. We don't need to confirm out loud what we're both thinking, how we happen to have two too many necromancers in town.

"I remember promising you no one else would get hurt," he says.

I think I might cry. Tears from earlier—from this entire week, really—blur my vision. I sniff, once.

"Hey, don't. Don't do that." He touches my cheek and catches a teardrop. "It's okay. I'm okay."

Except it's not okay, and he's clearly not okay.

A soft knock on the door has me sitting up a bit straighter, although Malcolm clutches my hand, keeps me from going too far.

"You need your rest," a nurse says to him, her admonishment gentle but firm.

This is my cue to leave. I don't want to. The hardest thing I've ever done is let my fingers slip from his. I'm at the door when he calls out, voice scratchy but filled with humor.

"Can I get a rain check on that date?"

I nod, push tears from my cheeks with my palms, and then I'm alone in the hallway. I stand there, outside Malcolm's room. I don't know what to do next. I don't know where to turn.

I don't see Nigel and Sadie on my way out. In truth, I don't search for them. I'm halfway down the sidewalk in front of the hospital when I spot my truck in the visitors' parking lot.

The keys are on the front seat, weighing down Chief Ramsey's business card.

~

I sit cross-legged on the reception desk of K&M Ghost Eradication Specialists. It's far too early to be open for the day, but it's also far too early to visit Malcolm, which is the only item on my agenda. The only other business open at this hour is the Springside Pancake House. I have a takeout container of pancakes and a large orange juice, courtesy of Belinda.

And I have coffee, courtesy of my own kitchen. I will use the time to think, to plan, to strategize. That black Mercedes is still sitting outside the bed and breakfast. I'm starting to loathe the sight of it, its presence a dark, malevolent thing.

I'm five minutes into strategizing—with not much to show for it— when the bell over the door chimes.

Orson Yates walks in, black wool overcoat dusted with a few snowflakes, a fedora giving him a polished air. He pauses at the threshold, removes the hat, and then tilts his head.

"Oh, my. That's an impressive little ward you've got going there."

"Then you know you're not wanted here."

He's quite possibly the last person I want to see—well, second to last. I dislike Carter even more.

"Ah, but the rules differ for a place of business." He drops his hat onto a coat rack hook as if he plans to stay a while. "Trust me. We have business."

"Did you lose a ghost or just your shadow?"

Orson purses his lips as if he's trying to swallow a smile. "Yes, Carter. I left him behind this time. I believe he has a tiny crush on you." Orson pinches his index finger and thumb together. "His judgment is off."

My appetite is off. My stomach rolls over on itself, and I'm afraid I'll lose all of my breakfast pancakes. I shut the lid on the remaining two and push the container to the far side of the desk. The thought to call Chief flashes across my mind, but Orson hasn't broken any laws—that I know of. He hasn't threatened me.

And informing Chief that Orson Yates is the most powerful necromancer in town, and therefore the most likely suspect in the ghost attack on Malcolm, simply won't work.

I have no choice. I must listen to what he has to say. I lean back and pull a paper cup from the desk drawer. When the top of the thermos opens, the rich aroma of Kona blend fills the space. The moment the scent reaches Orson, his features soften; an eyebrow arches. Oh, he's interested.

It might not be alcohol, but sometimes coffee works just as well.

"Would you like some?" I ask, going for professional. Or as professional as someone can be while wearing jeans and sitting on her own reception desk.

"I would. Believe it or not, the coffee-making ability of the Lindstroms is legendary. Your grandmother had quite a reputation for excellent brew, and there was more than one man who would've married your mother for her coffee alone."

I don't like that this man knew my mother. I don't like that he knows things about her that I may never know. I really don't like that he's old enough to be my father.

I offer him a cup anyway. "How do you take it?"

"Black."

Lucky for him. I'm not about to hop off the desk and fetch sugar and half and half. I pour a cupful for him and top off my own before closing the cap of the thermos.

Orson takes the coffee, inhales, and his expression is so rapturous it's nearly obscene.

"Your grandmother taught you well." He raises the cup. "In this, at least. Why she neglected a large part of your education, I can't honestly say. It baffles me."

"I don't know what you're talking about."

"I think you do. I think you've been wondering the same thing yourself. Have you ever asked yourself, why coffee?"

"Because it works."

"If that were the case, why not use instant or those new K-cups?"

I make a face. "You'd just end up with a mess and a pissed-off ghost."

"But ask yourself: is it the coffee, or is it the container?"

Orson points to the storefront display where, along with the hearts and glitter, an old percolator of my grandmother's rests next to Malcolm's samovar with the blown-out back.

"And why Tupperware?" he continues. "There's nothing special about it."

"It contains the ghosts until we can release them." Really, this is ghost-catching 101.

"Yes, but why, Katy? Not everyone can scoop up a ghost and seal it away for transport or ... whatever."

I shrug. "Does it matter?"

"It might, considering you claim not to be a necromancer. What if I told you that every time you catch a ghost, you commit an act of necromancy?"

"But I'm not—"

"So you say. But what keeps the ghosts in check once you catch them? Why doesn't it work for most others? It's you. Call it your touch, your innate ability. If you trap a ghost in something, it will stay there until you release it."

"Are you saying I'm magical?"

"Not exactly. What I'd like you to consider is this. Your friend Belinda Barnes can sense ghosts just as well as you can. Why can't she catch them? It would make her life so much easier."

The pit of my stomach ices over. I clutch my cup and sip, desperate for something warm inside me. I don't like that he knows about Belinda. And while his words are perfectly reasonable, his tone holds something else, something that sounds like a threat.

"You, my child, are a necromancer. Why your grandmother didn't inform you of this, I don't know." He gestures toward the display window. "That's how we stored ghosts, originally. The coffee or tea kept them from grumbling too much until the time came to pull one out and put it to use."

"I don't use ghosts. I set them free. Catch and release."

"Really? Springside has an unusual number of ghosts. Oh, and don't they adore you. I've never seen a necromancer who inspired so much affection and loyalty. If I didn't know better, if I didn't know of your aversion to necromancy, I'd say you were amassing an army."

"A ghost army?" The idea is ludicrous. "What on earth would I do with a ghost army?"

"On earth? A great many things, actually. But the fact you're amassing an army on the border of my territory ... concerns me."

"It shouldn't, and it isn't an army."

"But they've come to your aid before, have they not?"

This is something else Orson shouldn't know. Only a few people know how the ghosts of Springside helped me free Malcolm from the entity.

"They may be loyal," he adds, "but ghosts aren't very discrete."

Tattletales.

"What do you want, Orson? You said we had business. I've already told you I don't want to be a part of your club."

With this last, I set off the twitch again. He uses his ring finger to smooth his left eyebrow. He casts me a look, his expression that of someone much older and much wiser dealing with a rebellious child.

"So, what do you want?" I ask when he doesn't respond.

"It's quite simple, my dear. I can't allow you to collect so many ghosts so close to my own area of operations, so I will simply appropriate them from you. It's not like this"—he waves a hand, indicating K&M Ghost Eradication Specialists—"was going to pay the bills for long, or at all."

Will appropriate ... or already has? My mind goes to how few customers we've had this month, especially since Orson and Carter rolled into town. I think of the cowering sprites in the Springside Police Department reception area. I think how I haven't chased Sadie's two from her house in a week.

"You can't take my ghosts," I say.

"*Your* ghosts?" He raises an eyebrow. "So, you *are* amassing an army. In that case, I'm afraid I can and I will. Do you know what happens to a loyal, affectionate ghost after a few months—or years—in isolation? Oh, they become nasty, indeed. I believe you may have met a few."

My mind goes to Harold Lancaster's ghost. Then an image flashes in my mind, one Selena shared with me of a warehouse, gray and dingy.

How many ghosts could you store there? I feel as though I've walked right into this—whatever this is—and don't know the way back out.

Orson Yates drains his coffee and crushes the cup in his hand. He lets the crumpled paper drop to the floor and returns his hat to his head.

"Good day, Ms. Lindstrom." He nods once. "It was a pleasure doing business with you."

～

I'M CROUCHED in a far corner of the Springside Police Department reception area. Penny Wilson's chair sits empty—for now—and the scent of yesterday's charred coffee is a lingering memory in the air.

I pop open the thermos and the rich smell of Kona blend banishes it completely.

"Come on, guys," I say. "I'm not going to catch you. I just want to talk."

Sprites have such a slight presence, they're often difficult to detect. But these two are still here, cowering behind a file cabinet. I doubt they've played a prank all week.

"No one's here," I add. "At least not Carter Dupree."

I suspect Chief is in his office, although the door is shut tight. I keep my voice low and encouraging.

"He's not coming back. Chief Ramsey doesn't like him. As long as you stay put, they can't take you."

I hope what I've said is true. Carter must know two sprites haunt here. He no doubt sensed them when he stopped in for the attempted restraining order against Malcolm. I wonder at that, wonder if that was simply a way to barge into one more place and take an inventory of ghosts.

After a moment, a ghostly shimmer appears in the crack between the metal cabinet and the wall. The sprites ease out, skittish, their forms barely visible. Oh, they are so puny and scared. This is nearly the same as isolation.

"Here." I place the thermos next to them.

In the rising steam, they gain substance. One whirls. The other starts a dance. I let them soak in their fill.

"Can you tell me if Carter Dupree came here more than once?" I ask them after they start floating, full and sated.

The question prompts another flurry. They twirl about, crashing into each other, rising with the steam and then sinking back down. As answers go, this is one I can't decipher.

"Bob up and down for yes," I say. "Let's try this again. Did Carter Dupree come back here?"

The bobbing is unending.

"More than once?"

Even more bobbing.

"Yesterday?"

The bobbing slows. That might be too precise a question, especially for a sprite. I've always suspected ghosts lose track of time, one day flowing into another for them.

"If he comes back, don't go near him. Same goes for Orson Yates." I doubt Orson is running around collecting sprites—that sounds like a job you'd give to a minion. "Hide back here, or in Chief's office, or even in the holding cell."

"Oh, my word! Katy! What on earth are you doing?"

I jerk up, my head connecting with the edge of a desk. Stars flash before my eyes, and I blink until my vision clears. I peer up at Penny Wilson, my fingers investigating the sore spot on my scalp.

"I..." I glance behind me. The sprites bob encouragingly. "I thought I spotted a mouse."

Penny clutches her hands together and backs up several steps. "A mouse! I'll go get Chief."

"No!" That's the last thing I need. "I think it's gone now."

But Penny is knocking on his door.

"I have to go," I tell the sprites.

This time when they bob, I swear they're laughing at me. I grab a Styrofoam cup from the sideboard and pour them some more coffee anyway. I wedge it into the crevice as best I can so it won't spill.

"Hide," I say, "and be good."

"What's this about a mouse?" Chief's booming voice fills the room. He folds his arms over his chest and locks a glare onto me. "Expanding your eradication services?"

I hop up. "No, I'm good. Thanks, Penny, for all your help."

I tread my way to the front door, hoping Penny won't ask how she helped, praying Chief won't demand an explanation. If he does, it comes after I'm out the door and on the sidewalk. The bump on my head throbs, but the cold clears my jumbled thoughts.

I don't have a plan, but at least I know what I'm going to do next.

AFTERNOON SUNLIGHT FILTERS through the window blinds, most of it spilling onto the floor. Even in the shrouded room, Malcolm winces, raising a hand now and then to shield his eyes.

"Bad?" I ask. "Can I get you something?"

"No. I just feel useless, and I hate feeling useless."

"Don't baby him," Nigel says. "He'll start to expect it."

Malcolm narrows his eyes at his brother. "Shut up."

Nigel merely laughs.

We've gone over everything we can, established that other than the sprites in the police station and Mr. Carlotta's ghost in the long-term care facility, all the ghosts of Springside are gone. I even snuck into Chief Ramsey's garden shed to confirm that the ghost who haunts the watering can was missing. The wild ghosts on the outskirts of town, in the old barn, are also absent. Perhaps they were the first to go.

Something about that makes this all unbearably sad.

"He's overstepped his bounds," Malcolm says. "Certainly we can call on someone."

Nigel shakes his head. "I tried, believe me. No one wants to go up against Orson."

Malcolm scowls and then rubs his temples as if the expression made his head hurt. "Cowards."

"Not entirely," Nigel says. "Part of it is Katy."

"Me?" My gaze darts to Malcolm, but he glances away. "What have I done?"

"They see Orson's point," Nigel continues. "You've amassed an army of ghosts here in Springside."

"But I haven't—"

"Technically, you have." Nigel holds up his hands, halting my protest. "The others in the necromancer community don't understand how you keep so many ghosts in one place and how they can be so loyal."

"Maybe because I don't actually keep any of them."

"You're an unknown quantity," he continues as if I haven't spoken. "Your grandmother was powerful, with a reputation to match, even if she didn't practice necromancy. Add in your parents' mysterious death, and they'll believe Orson before they believe you."

I turn toward Malcolm, hoping he'll see the pleading in my eyes.

He shrugs as much as the broken ribs allow. "I hate to say it, but Nigel's right—sort of. When I first came to Springside, I thought you were crazy for releasing all those ghosts. You had so many, and I couldn't believe that you'd let them slip through your fingers like that."

"My grandmother always said everyone was better off that way, ghost and human." I study my hands for a moment, noting that the most recent scald on the back of the right one is fading. Then I confront both brothers. "Do you suppose she never told me about necromancy because she wanted to change the way things were done?"

"If so, it backfired," Nigel says. "Everyone I talked to is quite baffled by you. They think you've developed some new technique and will hoard both that knowledge and all the ghosts."

"Necromancers are a suspicious lot," Malcolm adds.

Nigel nods. "One of the many reasons the Armands have always been free agents."

"But you." I point at Nigel. "And you." I target Malcolm. "They know you. Can't you tell them?"

Nigel casts his gaze downward. Malcolm's expression twists. He plucks at the bandage around his head, his hand blocking his eyes.

Then it occurs to me. Malcolm came to Springside out of desperation. Until recently, Nigel was in the throes of his addiction. Neither man was at the top of his game. And now, they catch ghosts rather than use them. I don't know much about the world of necromancy, but from what I've seen, status, power, money—it's all very important.

And it looks like we're on our own.

"I'm sorry," I say, voice contrite and soft. "If it's any consolation, I still believe I've aligned myself with the right sort of necromancer."

Nigel glances up and gives me a half grin. Malcolm's dark eyes are unreadable, the expression in them like nothing I've seen before. I can't tell if they hold regret or self-recrimination, or even disgust. Whatever it means, it's steely and unrelenting.

"Nightstand drawer," he says.

I open it and pull out a box, one that contains a Bluetooth earpiece. I don't ask how he ended up with it. No doubt a nurse or a volunteer or someone was more than happy to do him this favor. I hold it up in question.

"For your phone," he elaborates. "So you can take me with you, hands-free."

"Take you with me where?"

"When you go find our ghosts."

MALCOLM HAS BEEN in my head all morning. He whispers in my ear, tells me jokes. I try not to laugh so passersby can see. I keep my responses muted as much as possible. But the whipping wind and the traffic on Main Street make that difficult.

Still, I try. I'm already *the girl who catches ghosts*. I don't want to add *the girl who talks to herself* to the list.

We've traveled through and around town at least three times. Or rather, I have. Malcolm's taken a virtual ride thanks to my new Bluetooth earpiece.

We haven't found a single thing.

On this circuit, something's different. The black Mercedes is missing from in front of the Springside B&B.

"It's gone," I say to Malcolm.

"What is?"

I keep forgetting he can't see what I'm doing. "Orson's car. It's not parked at the bed and breakfast."

"Did they go for pancakes?"

I make an illegal U-turn and rumbled down the opposite side of Main Street. All the spots in front of the Pancake House are filled, but none by a black and menacing Mercedes.

"I want to go to Springside Long-term Care," I say. "I'm worried about Mr. Carlotta's ghost."

I've warned Mr. Carlotta, of course, along with both the day and night managers. It's not like they're in the habit of letting creepy visitors inside, no matter how well-dressed they are.

Still. Of all the ghosts Orson Yates could catch in town, the one that haunts Mr. Carlotta's Purple Heart is the most valuable. I make another U-turn and head away from Main Street.

The parking lot of Springside Long-term Care is also free of that black Mercedes. I hop from my truck, thermoses of coffee jostling in the canvas bag I use as a field kit. The wind whips my hair around my face, batters strands against my cheeks. With a finger, I make sure the earpiece is in place.

Inside, I'm assaulted. I'm barely past the double entry doors when residents begin to push envelopes into my hands, the paper a bright array of reds and pinks and others a more somber blue. These last, I suspect, are get-well-soon cards.

"Katy, dear, how is Malcolm?" one of the residents asks. Actually, they all ask this, in their expressions at least, each one waiting for my answer.

"Much better," I say. "The doctors say he's healing quickly, and he's sorry he missed the party."

This inspires a round of tut-tutting with suggestions for an even bigger party once Malcolm is out of the hospital. I can't possibly answer all the questions or respond to every last one of the well-wishes. They echo around me, fill the space with warmth.

"Are you getting all this?" I whisper, hoping only Malcolm will hear me.

"I am." His voice is filled with mirth. "Are you able to get to the resident rooms, or are they going have to call out the National Guard?"

I laugh and earn a frown or two. A few of the residents are proprietary when it comes to Malcolm. In their eyes, I'm an interloper, at best, and I certainly shouldn't be laughing. I push on through, collecting the belated valentines and get-well cards as I go, stashing them in the field kit.

At last I reach the hallway to Mr. Carlotta's room. The corridor is serene compared to the front lobby. I can hear myself think, hear myself talk, not to mention hear Malcolm.

"They love you," I say to him. "You know that, right? I've added five pounds to my bag with all these cards."

My boots scuff the carpet as I walk. The rattle of a wheelchair and the drone of a television fill my ears. What I don't hear is Malcolm. I touch the earpiece again.

"You still there? Did we get cut off?"

He clears his throat. "No ... no, I'm a little overwhelmed, is all. I didn't realize—" He breaks off and coughs.

"That they'd end up meaning so much to you?"

"Yeah. That. You always know what I'm thinking."

Not always. I hold in a sigh.

"Katy-Girl!" Mr. Carlotta greets me, as always, with the nickname my grandmother used. He's in his wheelchair by the window. I suspect he's tracked my progress all the way from the parking lot.

I bend so he can kiss my cheek. This also gives me a chance to take in the room, gauge it for an otherworldly presence. Ah, yes. Mr. Carlotta's ghost is still here. As soon as I sense her, something inside me unclenches.

Mr. Carlotta pulls two envelopes from the nightstand. He hands them both to me.

"One for you," he says. "And a get-well card for"—he coughs—"that young man of yours. I hope he's recovering."

"Are you kidding me?" Malcolm says in my ear. "I got a card from Mr. Carlotta? And he didn't call me a name?"

"He probably wrote something rude on the inside," I whisper.

Mr. Carlotta doesn't entirely approve of my relationship with Malcolm. Much of that, I suspect, is because he'd prefer I be in a relationship with his favorite grandson, Jack.

"What, dear?" Mr. Carlotta says.

"Nothing, nothing," I say, feigning innocence.

Then I hold a finger to my lips. I have Mr. Carlotta's full attention. We're being sneaky, which is one of his favorite things. From my pocket, I pull my cell phone and put it on mute. I remove the Bluetooth earpiece. I give both to Mr. Carlotta.

"I need to talk to your ghost," I tell him. "No one else can hear."

He eyes the phone cradled in his hands.

"Not even Malcolm. It's for his safety, everyone's safety."

He gives me a solemn nod and wheels himself from the room. I shut the door gently behind him. A bit of guilt tugs at me. I've debated this question before: to tell Malcolm or not to tell him.

No one knows how I learned the entity's name. Malcolm has never asked, although certainly he knows I did something to find it. I tell myself that he believes as I do: the fewer people who know that being's name, the better.

That goes for ghosts, too.

I pour a cup of coffee for Mr. Carlotta's ghost. She's an old thing, ancient, possibly. He calls her Queenie, after Queen Boudicca. Although this ghost was a warrior, I have no idea if she really was a warrior queen.

She is, however, particular and morose, her presence weighing the air. As of late, she is, if not happy, lighter. The air is easier to breathe in Mr. Carlotta's room. I no longer catch and release her to give him some space. They've found a certain companionship with each other, these two old soldiers.

She oozes from her hiding spot. Most days, she's content to stay put in the nightstand drawer, attached to Mr. Carlotta's Purple Heart.

"You know what's going on," I say to her.

She continues to ease forward. I take that as a yes.

"You can't let them catch you. I know you're strong, but they're willing to wait for years, decades, even."

Queenie reaches the coffee and begins to smother it. Kona blend is her favorite, and I've splurged with fresh-roasted beans straight from the Coffee Depot. The steam glimmers, her form lumpy.

"You wouldn't want to leave him all alone, would you?" I nod toward the door.

Her form expands. She is either enjoying the coffee or I've angered her—or both. With this ghost, both is always a possibility. I know the moment she's drunk her fill. With a ghostly finger, she knocks the cup over so coffee splatters on the side table, the floor, my jeans.

"I'm telling you something you already know, right?"

I get a bounce in response, one that's almost worthy of a sprite.

"I'm just worried," I tell her. "No one knows what we know, and I'd like to keep it that way." I'm about to stand when another question occurs to me. "You wouldn't know where they're keeping the other ghosts, would you?"

Queenie's form contracts. She looks smaller, if not diminished. She retreats away from me and back into the nightstand drawer, to the Purple Heart. If this is an answer, I don't know what it means.

I pick up the cup, open the door, and then go in search of paper towels. By the time I return, Mr. Carlotta has Malcolm on speaker and is cross-examining him.

"So, she takes you around with this thing in her ear? It looks like something from *Star Trek*."

"Yes, she takes me around with that thing in her ear." Malcolm's patience is starting to crack. "That way, I can talk to her."

"What you need to do is get out of the hospital so she isn't out here on her own." While Mr. Carlotta doesn't call him anything rude, it's all there in his tone. Despite two cracked ribs and a concussion, Malcolm is slacking.

"I can take care of myself," I interject. "Besides, this way, Malcolm can look things up on the internet."

"Or even dial 911," he adds.

"See?" I say. "It's kind of handy."

Mr. Carlotta harrumphs at us. I hold out my hand. With some reluctance, he returns my phone and the earpiece. Before I can leave, he grips my wrist.

"Be careful, Katy-Girl."

"I will. I always am."

"I don't like these characters.," Mr. Carlotta continues. "They came to town before, you know. Well, not that young one, obviously. But the other one. He's all sleek and self-satisfied, was like that back then too. I remember—" He glances away.

"What do you remember?" I ask, not certain I want the answer.

"I remember how losing your mother and her husband nearly killed your grandmother. If not for you, Katy-Girl..." He trails off.

I don't ask him to elaborate.

"This isn't a coincidence, is it?" he asks.

"No." I see no reason to lie. "It's not."

"Be careful," Mr. Carlotta demands again. "And, young man? You keep your ears open."

"I will," Malcolm says before I take him off speaker and secure the earpiece once again.

Outside, I sit in my truck, letting it warm up. Or at least, that's my excuse.

"Katy." Malcolm's voice is soft in my ear. "Are you okay?"

"Thinking, or trying to."

"Your chat with Mr. Carlotta's ghost go as planned?"

"I ... sort of. I did ask her where they were keeping the other ghosts, and she drew in on herself, went back to hiding."

My first idea was to search out that warehouse from the images Selena shared with me, but there's nothing like it in Springside. After I described it to Malcolm, his guess was somewhere outside the Twin Cities. It had the look of an abandoned industrial park. If the building is close by, it's nothing I've ever seen.

"Let's assume they haven't moved the ghosts from here," I say. "You're the necromancer. Where would you store a bunch of ghosts before you could take them somewhere?"

"I used to store them in the samovar."

"And we both know what happened when it got too full."

His laugh warms my ear. "So we're looking for something bigger than a samovar."

"The high school?" I suggest.

"Too busy."

"What about the Ghost B Gone house? It still hasn't sold."

"It would work, but it's also on Chief Ramsey's radar. I'm sure they're trying to stay out of his way, not call attention to themselves. It's going to be somewhere we wouldn't think to look."

None of this inspires confidence. "Where wouldn't we look for ghosts?"

"Oh, Katy ... you're brilliant."

If I am, this is news to me.

"Where wouldn't we look for ghosts," Malcolm says, his voice taking on a new energy. "Almost never, but the one place everyone else thinks is haunted?"

It hits me then. Yes, hide the ghosts in plain sight. "The Springside Cemetery?"

"Exactly."

"Wait!" I shut my eyes, try not to see what I want to see. But no, I remember. I'm certain of it. "Selena showed me that, along with the other images. I'm almost one hundred percent sure."

I put the truck in gear and back from the parking space. I make one final illegal U-turn and rumble down the road toward the Springside Cemetery.

"You're right," I say to Malcolm.

Actually, I whisper it, which is silly since I'm still in the truck, still several yards away from the cemetery parking lot, but close enough to spy the Mercedes. It's like a sleek black beetle, the paint gleaming in the late afternoon sun.

I stop the truck and put it in reverse. I inch backward and park on a lightly traveled side street.

I take my field kit even though I'm not certain what good coffee will do. The thermoses rattle. I unwind the scarf I'm wearing and weave it between the metal containers.

"I'm going to hop the fence so they don't see me coming," I tell Malcolm.

"You might as well," he says. "According to the web page, the cemetery locks the gates at four."

"Really?" I ask. "They have a web page?"

"Why not? We do."

I walk the perimeter until I find a section of the rock wall that isn't much taller than I am. I unsling the field kit and ease it up and over before attempting the climb myself. In boots and mittens it's a precarious thing. My feet skid against the icy rocks. I have zero purchase with my mittens. I tug them off, and with a mouthful of damp wool, I scale the wall and tumble to the other side.

A snow bank swallows me. I am breathless and cold. For a moment, I stare up at the sky. I almost feel like a child, ready to make a snow angel.

"Katy? You've gone silent on me. Say something."

"I landed in a snow bank, but I'm okay."

I dig my way out and find the field kit, all to the sound of Malcolm's chuckle. But then he grows silent himself.

"Malcolm?" I touch the earpiece again. I'm about to pull out my phone and check it when he finally speaks.

"Maybe you shouldn't do this."

"We need to find the ghosts."

"But you don't need to have another run-in with Orson and Carter," he says. "I don't like that you're there alone. You're outnumbered."

"What are they going to do to me?"

"That's just it, Katy. I don't know."

A bit of trapped snow slithers down my neck. A shiver follows.

"I can't ... we can't just let them do this." I take a few steps forward, brushing snow from my coat and kicking it from my boots. "What if I'm sneaky?"

"You'll have to be very sneaky. They'll probably have a spy or two out."

"You mean a ghost?"

"That's exactly what I mean, so stay on high alert for all things super-natural."

Ghosts as spies. This is new. "What other necromancer tricks haven't you told me about?"

His sigh fills my ear. "Several, I'm sure. I grew up with necromancy, the same way you did with catch and release. It's not that I'm hiding anything. It simply doesn't occur to me to tell you."

He has a point—and he still can't do a release without some ghost cuffing him on the back of the head.

I shuffle forward in the snow. The gravestones around me are worn and weathered, their inscriptions barely legible, each wearing a cap of snow. Except for some crisscrossed tracks of squirrels and birds—and my footsteps—the blanket of snow is pristine. This is the old part of the cemetery, and it doesn't see much traffic.

This might be why I sense the presence immediately. It might be why I know who this ghost is. I halt. Really, I have no choice in the matter. It's like an otherworldly wall has been built in front of me. I'm not moving forward; I'm not going around, either. We regard each other, human to ghost. Then I speak very softly, just loud enough for Malcolm to hear.

"It's Selena," I say. "She's here."

"Put me on speaker," he says. "Can you? Turn down the volume if you have to, but this will go better if she can hear my voice."

I scan the cemetery. No matter how low I turn down the volume, the sound of voices will carry. But I'm not moving forward without Malcolm's help.

"Okay." I pull out my phone and tap the speaker. "It's on."

"Selena, sweetheart, is that you?"

His voice kicks up a frenzy, a mini blizzard of snow. Ice crystals strike my cheeks and his words strike a dull ache in my chest.

"I think the answer is yes," I manage to choke out. "She's causing a snowstorm."

"I'm alive and in the hospital. Thanks to you and Katy. Everything's going to be okay." His voice is patient and calming. Even though he's not speaking the words to me, I relax, if only a little. "Can you help Katy? Tell her what's going on?"

The whirling subsides. Selena's form shimmers in the light slanting through the trees. If anyone else spotted her, they might believe she's an angel.

"She ... hovering," I say.

"Did Orson or Carter send you out as a spy?" Malcolm asks.

This is clearly the wrong thing to ask. The blizzard starts up again, this time with such force, I'm afraid she'll knock over a headstone. Instead several branches drop from the tree above my head.

"I have no idea what that means," I tell her.

Selena vanishes into the snow. A moment later, something tunnels through the smooth canvas in front of my feet. First one letter, than another.

N O

"She says no," I say to Malcolm. "Also, she thinks I'm stupid."

"I'm sure she doesn't," he insists.

The glimmering, gleeful presence says otherwise.

"Do they know you're here?" he asks.

She swirls around the letters.

"No, they don't," I say.

"Have they trapped the ghosts?"

With a single whoosh, she creates a line across her letters.

"I'm guessing that they have." I consider Selena—and consider whether she's lying. If she isn't trapped or a spy, why is she here in the cemetery?

"Do you know where Malcolm is?" I ask.

The storm she kicks up is the worst yet. I duck, clutch my hands over my head, and wait it out. Snow invades my mouth, creeps down the back of my shirt. I'm cold and achy and the wind chill in this section of the cemetery must be well below zero.

"Can ghosts navigate?" I'm still crouched, but the battering of snow diminishes.

"There's a reason we drive the truly nasty ones into the middle of nowhere, right?" Malcolm says. "We're hoping they won't find their way back."

Sometimes they do. Sometimes they seem to know where they're going, like with Delilah and the Mississippi River. But sometimes...?

"She can't find you," I say. Maybe she never could, from the first time they were separated. Carter must have enticed her with that when he caught her. I think back to when Nigel finally gave up all the ghosts and they went streaming into the air. We were nowhere near Springside. Besides, Selena didn't know Malcolm had moved away from the Twin Cities.

How long has she been searching for him? Months, certainly.

The snowstorm dies, and the cemetery is quiet again, Selena a shimmering form in front of me. From the moment Malcolm burst into K&M Ghost Eradication Specialists with her, I knew I was going to lose him. But I never imagined I'd lose him like this, here in the cemetery.

I stand, put the phone on mute, and then bring up the map. I switch to satellite view and zero in on downtown Springside.

"Here's what you do." I trace the route with a finger. "From Malcolm's apartment, go to the police station and then to our business." I glance up at her, uncertain ghosts can read maps. "See?"

Selena bobs, her excitement sparking. In this moment, she does look nearly divine, the spot we're standing in bathed in a golden glow.

"Keep to this road," I say. "You'll pass a park with a playground, and then at the end of the street, you'll see the hospital. Malcolm's on the fourth floor, room four forty."

She swirls, another frenzy that sprays snow in an arc. She follows its path. It glimmers in a rainbow of color before the whole thing collapses to the ground in an explosion of ice crystals.

"You're welcome," I say. "And kiss him for me?"

I'm pretty sure I've had my last.

Selena buzzes around the treetops as if comparing that view to my map. She swoops down one last time and swipes at my cheek. Something fizzles against my skin.

I realize she's caught a tear. If I don't get a grip, there will be several more. I press a hand against my eyes and wait for the cemetery to fall silent. When I'm alone, I push forward through the snow once again.

It takes another five minutes before I can switch the phone off mute.

You have no business here. **Turn back.**

The thoughts pop into my head unbidden. I can't account for them. They're strange, authoritative declarations. I glance around, although I'm positive no one has spoken. Slowly, I move forward.

You have been warned. Turn back. Mind your own business.

I freeze again. I peer over my shoulder. A sensation of being watched crawls across my skin. I feel like a naughty child breaking any number of rules.

"Someone's telling me to stop," I whisper to Malcolm.

"A ghost?"

I raise my chin and sample the air. "No. Nothing like that. It's a voice, only not."

"Oh," he says, and he sounds almost amused. "Remember when Nigel taught you how to create a ward?"

"Yes."

"Well, you've just walked into one."

"Whose? Orson's?"

"What does it sound like?" Malcolm asks.

"Authoritative, yet vague. It's a *go away and ask no questions* sort of vibe."

"Yeah, that's Orson."

"But how can he create one in the cemetery? No one owns the cemetery. It's not keeping me out, right?"

"What did it make you do?"

Slow down. Stop. Talk to Malcolm. "It's a distraction."

For a moment, I consider what to do next. Do I sprint forward, or is that, too, part of the plan? Will that lead straight into a trap? The other danger is moving too slow, arriving too late to save the ghosts.

I run.

The snow hampers my steps, clings to my boots. My lungs ache with the cold. I sense something otherworldly. It's not a spy, not a single ghost, but something much more than that.

I burst through a row of pines. The toe of my boot catches on what feels like a tree root. I pitch forward and let out a yelp. Snow crashes down on me, followed by the muffled sound of Carter Dupree's laughter. Malcolm's voice is frantic in my ear.

"Katy? Katy? Who is that? What's going on?"

My face stings. My jeans are soaked. I yank at my leg to free it and dislodge another cascade of snow. I crawl forward, try to shake off the excess and blink the fringe of flakes from my eyes. I only stop when I reach a pair of legs and an extended hand in a leather glove.

Carter Dupree is as bright and smooth as ever. I refuse the offer of help, partly out of pride, partly because my attention has been caught by what's behind him.

In the center of the clearing, where some of the larger tombs form a semi-circle, there's a wall of glimmering white. I squint, picking out forms—tiny sprites, larger ghosts. Near the top, I recognize the wild spirits from the old barn. They strike what looks like air without breaking through.

They are confined, all of them, in a ghostly sort of prison.

"What have you done?" I push to my knees, my gaze never leaving that solid mass of ghosts.

They swoop and swarm as best they can in the confined space. Some, I'm certain, are calling for help. The air holds a plaintive echo, sad and heart-rending.

"What have you done?" I ask again.

"Katy, what is it? What's going on?" Malcolm's voice is low in my ear. I shake my head in answer, which is stupid because he can't see me.

"Ah, Ms. Lindstrom. I see you have no regard for wards yourself. We have that in common, then."

Orson Yates steps forward.

"Oh," Malcolm says. "That's what's going on. Be careful."

I nod, which makes me look like I'm agreeing with Orson. But I don't care. All I want is to figure out what they've done to my ghosts. I struggle to stand, again ignoring Carter's proffered hand. I take a step and then another until I'm close enough to reach out and touch the ghosts.

Except I can't. My mittened fingers meet resistance. I can't push through, and although several of them try, the ghosts can't push out. I place my hands against the invisible barrier and gaze at all the ghosts and sprites and spirits inside. How many are in there? All the ghosts of Springside minus three?

Orson moves to my side. I don't bother to glance in his direction.

"I simply can't fathom it." He waves a hand toward the ghosts. "Such loyalty, such affection. You know, of course, that all ghosts want something."

Now I do look at Orson, just barely, from the corner of my eye.

"What these ghosts want is for you to capture them, over and over again. I suppose that's a viable business model, as long as the good citizens of Springside don't catch on."

A few of the fiercer ghosts ram the barrier opposite where Orson is standing. He merely chuckles.

"You know, my dear, the offer still stands, despite everything. Your powers, while undisciplined, are impressive. Most necromancers must work for years to establish the sort of rapport with ghosts that comes naturally to you."

"Have you considered that it comes naturally because I don't want to use them, not like you do?" I turn to Orson and stare at him straight on. "I don't want money or fame or whatever it is you're offering."

"Not even the affections of a certain disgraced necromancer?"

My throat tightens. I suppose my feelings for Malcolm are hardly a secret, not with the way ghosts gossip. What about his for Selena? How much have the ghosts already gossiped about that? How much does Orson know?

"You can't buy someone's affection," I say.

"Oh, that's where you're wrong. You most certainly can, after a fashion."

"I don't want to buy anyone's affection."

"I wonder," he says, as if my declaration holds all the weight of a child's.

It's then that I notice the voice in my ear has gone silent. Has Malcolm heard everything from the past few minutes? Are we still connected? A flush invades my cheeks, a fierce one that I hope looks like the result of the cold.

I'm pretty sure it doesn't.

I don't dare speak Malcolm's name, not with Orson a few feet away and Carter within earshot. I'm afraid of what I might betray if I do say his name. Instead, I turn to Orson, arms folded across my chest.

"I've said this before, and I'll say it one last time. I don't want to join your club."

There's no eye twitch this time. The look he gives me is colder than the air. The ghosts at my side whip themselves into a fruitless frenzy. They crash against the barrier, not that they can reach me—or Orson.

He gestures with a hand. "Carter, if you will."

Carter clenches his fist. His fingers glow. I'm not sure what comes next, but I feel the hum of the otherworldly, and a fierce, angry sensation sweeps across the snow

Before Carter can take a step toward me, flashing lights paint the snow pink. A siren fills the air for a second before cutting off, and the bulky form of Chief Ramsey emerges from a patrol car.

Another patrol car pulls up, this one with Officer Deborah Millard. Orson's eyes narrow. Carter drops his hand, the glow subsiding along with that unearthly threat. I feel the cold against my tongue and teeth, and I know my mouth must be hanging open.

"Evening, gentlemen," Chief says, unlocking the cemetery gates. "I hate to inform you, but the cemetery is closed for the day and you both are trespassing. I'm going to have to ask you to leave."

I can't imagine Orson Yates hopping the cemetery fence. I study the perimeter and consider that they've been waiting for me to spring this trap, possibly for most of the day.

"And Ms. Lindstrom as well?" Orson sweeps a hand toward me. "She is also here after hours."

"Katy is a resident of Springside, and her parents and grandmother are buried here. She has permission to visit at all hours." He nods to me before turning back to Orson. "You, on the other hand, do not. In fact, trespassing is a serious offense in Springside, but I can offer you one of two options." Chief ticks them off on his fingers. "One, leave now, and by leave, I mean Springside; or two, spend the night in jail."

"You can't do this," Orson says. "It's ridiculous."

"I *can* do this, and I will." Chief pulls out his phone and taps the screen. "Hello, Daisy? This is Chief Ramsey. You have two guests, Orson Yates and Carter Dupree. They need to leave unexpectedly. Could you have someone pack their things? They'll be by in about ten minutes to pick them up on the way out of town."

Chief hangs up and tucks the phone away. He regards Orson. Something passes between the two men, although both remain immobile. The cemetery grows colder, the sun slipping lower in the sky.

"Ah, small-town, petty tyranny," Orson says. He brushes nonexistent snow from the sleeves of his overcoat. "When it works, it works. Come along, Carter."

Carter hesitates, and he shoots me a glance. I can't read his expression. In this instant, I have no idea how he feels or what he's thinking. The moment before he turns from me, Carter Dupree rolls his eyes.

Orson pauses in front of Chief. "Ramsey, is it?"

"It is."

"Good to know."

"Officer Millard will escort you to the bed and breakfast and then to the edge of town." Chief touches the brim of his hat. "If I were you, I'd remain gone."

We wait in silence while they leave. The rotating lights on top of Officer Millard's patrol car promise it won't be an inconspicuous exit. When at last the lights have faded and quiet has returned to the cemetery, Chief speaks.

"You okay, Katy?"

"I am."

"Did they threaten you?"

"I ... I don't know. You arrived before anything could happen. And how—"

"That young partner of yours. Something about a Bluetooth earpiece and I don't know what, but he made it sound convincing enough for the dispatcher to call me."

Malcolm. Of course. I touch the earpiece, but the line is still oddly silent.

Chief stares into the center of the cemetery. I'd say he's studying the ghosts, except he doesn't believe in them. Then he speaks again.

"Can you handle that?" He nods toward the site where all the ghosts are corralled.

"You can see them?" I shout the words, my voice echoing in the cold air. This is a breakthrough.

He clamps his mouth shut, his lips a hard, straight line.

"What do you see?" I ask, making my voice as gentle as possible. This can't be easy for Chief, admitting he's been wrong about something.

He shakes his head. "I'm not sure. It looks like fog, or snow, and if things weren't always so ... strange around you, I might believe it's nothing more than that. It's odd. I went to the shed yesterday to pull out an extra shovel, and the space felt so empty, like I was missing something."

"You have a ghost that likes your watering can," I say.

He grimaces at this.

"It's not a bad ghost," I add. "It just likes your shed. I think it feels comfortable there. Some ghosts are funny that way."

"Is it in there?" He points. The ghosts swirl in response.

"I don't know. Probably."

Chief nods. "I'll leave you to it. You'll be okay?"

"Yes." I touch the earpiece again, although it remains stubbornly silent. "I have my backup."

I wait until Chief has left before placing my hands against the barrier. Ghosts swarm around my palms, but I can't break in and they can't get out. The last of the sun sinks below the horizon. I'm alone in a cemetery, in the dark, with nearly every ghost in Springside.

And I have no idea what to do.

THE SOUND of Malcolm's voice in my ear sends my heart pounding.

"Katy! Are you there? Is everything okay?"

"I'm here."

"Did Chief—"

"Ride in like the cavalry? Yeah, he did."

I tell him about the trespassing and the two patrol cars and even how, after everything, Orson still wanted me to join his club.

"You know," Malcolm says, his voice warm with relief and humor, "it's not really a club."

"Yeah, I know, and I also know it bothers Orson when I call it that."

Steam from one of the thermoses rises in the air. The scent of Kona blend is intoxicating in the cold, and it's all I can do not to drink down the entire thing. Instead, I hold it next to the barrier. With a hand, I push the steam toward the ghosts only to watch it dissipate against the invisible wall between us. They wail in frustration.

"Where'd you go?" I ask. I try to blow the steam toward them, but that doesn't work either.

"They make me get up and walk around. I put the phone on mute and stuck it in my pocket."

"Your hospital gown has a pocket?"

"I talked them into letting me wear some scrubs."

Of course he did, especially if "they" happened to be female. I roll my eyes at the ghosts across from me and shake my head.

"Have you made it home yet?" he asks.

"I'm still at the cemetery."

"But—"

"The ghosts are all here."

I place a hand on that invisible barrier, and despite this problem, something inside me relaxes. Malcolm didn't hear everything about the ghosts, which means he missed Orson's taunts as well. Relieved as I am, part of me is ... disappointed. In myself? Maybe it's better to be honest, tell him how I feel. Or maybe it's simply better to go on as K&M Ghost Eradication Specialists.

And right now, they have a huge job.

"They are?" he asks. "What are they doing?"

"They can't leave," I say. "They're ... trapped. It's like an invisible container or a barrier or—"

"Like the containment field that kept Selena out of my car?"

"Only in reverse, and much, much bigger. They're all trapped inside it."

"And they're going to stay that way. That's a necromancer trick I never mastered beyond the samovar. It must be Orson's doing. Carter isn't that good."

"But ... we can't leave them like this. I can't even get through to them."

"And I can't leave the hospital. That trek down the hall winded me. Even if I could, I'm in no shape to attempt something..." He trails off and the line goes silent again. Then he exhales and swears.

"What?" I prompt.

"I'm not strong enough for something like this, but I know someone who is."

I don't need to ask, but I do anyway. "Nigel?"

"Exactly."

"But." I point, which is utterly ridiculous. "Nearly every single ghost in Springside is in there. He can't possibly—"

"Too late. I'm calling him on the hospital line."

The second he switches to mute is obvious this time. I hear nothing. I'm destined never to know what passes between them, these two brothers. I stomp my feet and pace. I blow more coffee steam toward the ghosts, although it's cooling too fast to tempt them for much longer.

So I drink it down. I need its heat, its caffeine, its smooth warmth against my cold lips. I need to be ready. If Nigel can free the ghosts, I'll need to protect him from them.

And I'll need to protect the ghosts from him.

CHAPTER 8

"YOU KNOW THAT'S not going to work."

Nigel's voice, as always, is measured. I cap the thermos and turn to him.

"I know, but they seem to like it anyway."

Several ghosts bob and dance opposite me. I don't know if they can smell the coffee or if it's simply the idea of it that sets them off. Nigel's gaze locks on the swirling mass before his eyes clear.

He takes a few steps closer, his boots dragging in the snow. When he's at my side, he removes his gloves before reaching out and touching the barrier.

"Yes, this is Orson's work. I recognize it."

"He planted a ward, too, but I think it was more of a practical joke. I fell for it."

Literally.

"For all his pretenses, he's really nothing more than a schoolyard bully on most days."

"Chief was going to toss him in jail for trespassing," I add.

Nigel snorts, but his attention soon turns to the ghosts. He exhales, his breath fogging the air, and for a moment, it looks like the barrier has been breached.

"I can't do this, Katy."

"But—"

"I can't do it, but *you* can."

I shake my head. "I can't. I have no idea what to do. I wouldn't know where to start." I hold up the thermos as proof. "See? I think coffee will work."

His laugh is warm and indulgent. "You can do it. You just don't know how. Those are two different things. Malcolm said that Orson still tried to court you, after everything. If you'd agreed, this"—he waves a hand at the barrier—"would've been your first lesson."

I look at the ghosts; I can't leave them here like this. I glance at Nigel. I can't endanger him, either.

"I'll talk you through it," he says. "Think back to when you found Malcolm in his car. What did you do?"

"I beat on the window until there was a crack. Selena did the rest."

"See that?" He gestures toward the barrier.

"No, that's the point. I can't."

"Try again."

So I do. I squint, tip my head one way and then the other. I'm about to admit defeat when the slightest outline appears.

"Oh." The word comes out with a sigh. "I never saw it around Malcolm's car."

"You didn't know what to look for. With Malcolm's car, you forced a crack in the barrier, which is pretty impressive."

"I had a tire iron," I say. "But it's in the back of the truck."

"You don't need a tire iron. Sure, you cracked the window with it, but it was your will to break through the containment field that did everything else. In some ways this"—he gestures toward the barrier again—"is easier."

"Because it's bigger?" Doubt fills my voice. I cannot imagine breaking something so big.

"Actually, yes. Something this large is hard to keep intact. Fissures, hairline fractures, cracks. It needs constant tending by the necromancer who created it. With enough time, the ghosts themselves would find holes and slip out. All we need to do is find a vulnerable point."

We trudge along the perimeter, stopping every few feet to inspect its surface. Now that I'm aware of it, the containment field seems painfully obvious. Nigel is right. It's not a perfectly round and smooth globe that traps these ghosts, but a flawed and ragged construction, hastily built.

He kneels and pushes snow away from the ground, clearing a path from our feet to the barrier.

"Do you see that?" He runs his fingers down the side, and I swear, the surface sparkles in their wake.

I nod.

"You try," he says.

I kneel next to him, pull off my mitten, and let my fingertips travel the same path. A spark kindles beneath my skin, that same glimmering light defining the crack in the barrier.

"That's your target."

We retreat a few feet back. Nigel eases behind me, positioning me by the shoulders so I face the flaw in the barrier straight on. He leaves one hand on my shoulder, the grip firm.

"I'm right here. I'll talk you through it. But if I let go of your shoulder, I want you to promise me that you'll run—"

"I won't."

"Katy, please, you don't understand—"

"Your addiction? I was there, remember? You won't let go of my shoulder. I won't let you." I lock my hand on his.

"Malcolm's right," he murmurs. "You're really stubborn."

I don't deny it. My grandmother was stubborn. I figure it's a family trait. "Now what?"

"Concentrate on the crack. Don't close your eyes, but visualize it getting larger. Think about where it's weakest, how you can chip away at it."

"Can I imagine a tire iron?"

"By all means, go right ahead."

I think about that, about breaking through that small fissure in the barrier. I remember how I created that spider web of cracks to free Malcolm. I think about how much I would like to break this thing, this prison, because I don't want anything of Orson Yates in Springside.

Nigel's grip tightens on my shoulder. "Keep going," he whispers. "You're doing it."

The outline of the barrier vibrates. I force my concentration on that weak spot, willing it to grow larger. I think of all the ghosts inside. I think about coffee, about how the steam from Kona blend might slip through and entice the ghosts out.

There's a rush for that space, the ghosts crowding so close they look like a solid bank of snow. I think maybe I've started a ghostly riot. Then that fissure expands and sends out tendrils through the barrier, one after another, until the surface resembles glass on the brink of shattering.

And then, all at once, it does.

Instinct has me ducking. I clamp down harder on Nigel's hand. I won't let him run toward the ghosts, but there's not much I can do when they come flowing out and head straight for us.

Or rather, for me. Some I recognize; their personalities are that strong. Others whip by so fast I can't get a read on them. But it's all the same, all ruffled hair and otherworldly kisses against my cheeks. A few rattle around in the field kit, searching out Kona blend.

"Go," I tell them. "Get out of here before someone else catches you." I promise them coffee—and lots of it—if only they leave now. They do, in groups and alone, until at last, all that's left are two little sprites.

These two are more than familiar.

"Go on. That includes you. I'll bring you some coffee tomorrow."

With that, the last two ghosts—Sadie's sprites—leave the cemetery.

I'm still clutching Nigel's hand. His fingers curl around my shoulder, the grip tight. His breath is ragged.

"You did it," I say.

At least, I think he has. I don't think a ghost slipped past me and into him. He turns me slowly, hand never leaving my shoulder. It's as if he still needs that last bit of reassurance. Lamplight from the street filters into the cemetery. Despite the dark, I can see the gravestones, the path we made around the now-broken barrier, and Nigel's expression.

His smile steals my breath.

"I did it," he says, his voice almost hesitant.

"You did it," I echo.

"You know why?" He releases me and digs in his pocket. "It was thanks to you, and this." In his hand, he holds the box with the diamond engagement ring. "Don't you see? Now I know. For certain. I can ask

Sadie to marry me and I'll never worry that something might happen, that I'll relapse and abandon her."

I throw my arms around him. "Do it now. Ask her tonight."

Nigel nods. "Yes, tonight. I need to go find her."

A soft hum fills my ear, followed by a voice.

"She's here, at the hospital."

Even though I know it's Malcolm, I let out a yelp.

"What?" Nigel asks. "Is everything okay?"

I touch the earpiece and listen. Nigel leans closer, as if he can hear Malcolm as well.

"Sadie's visiting," Malcolm says. "She brought me something to eat. Come now. I'll make up an excuse to keep her here."

"The hospital," I say to Nigel. "She's visiting Malcolm. I'll meet you there."

He pockets the ring and races through the snow. I start the trek back to my truck.

"You okay?" Malcolm asks.

The cemetery is empty and dark. I follow the path I made through the snow on my way in. For a moment, the thought crosses my mind to visit the graves of my parents, of my grandmother, but I've had enough of ghosts for one night.

"Yeah, thanks to Nigel. And who knows, maybe business will pick up now."

He laughs.

"Orson said something," I begin, my voice thin in the cold air, "about the ghosts here in Springside wanting to be caught, that they want to be caught by me." I pause, my discomfort with the idea growing. "Are we cheating people?"

"I think the ghosts like your coffee, which is why they're willing to be caught. If you were using them in some way, they'd make it that much harder. Besides, we get our share of the mean ones."

I nod even though Malcolm can't see me.

"Unless a necromancer can find a compatible ghost," he continues, "catching them isn't all that easy. Even corralling them like Orson did wasn't simple. Why do you think he recruits necromancers in the first place? The more he has, the easier it is."

I'm not entirely convinced. And yet, I'm not unconvinced either. I want to ask how he found Selena, but I suspect she was the one to find him.

"See you soon?" he says after I've fallen quiet.

"I need to say thank you to someone first."

"Well, hurry. You don't want to miss anything."

No, I certainly don't.

THE SPRINGSIDE POLICE DEPARTMENT feels as empty as the cemetery did, although all the lights are blazing. Penny's workstation is tidy, her computer screen dark. I swipe a Styrofoam cup from the sideboard and pour some Kona blend into it. The coffee is still hot and the steam warms my cheeks.

I know the sprites are still here. Their presence flavors the air. I breathe in their relief. True, they're still hiding behind the file cabinet, but I think that's so they can watch me crawl on my hands and knees to bring them another cup of coffee.

Sprites aren't above such things.

But I don't mind, not today. When I swap out the cold cup for the new one, their joy makes the air glimmer. Tomorrow they'll go back to playing pranks and tormenting Penny. But tonight, they're grateful.

And so am I.

On my way to Chief's office, I pull out my last thermos. His door is shut, but light sneaks through the space beneath it. I hear a squeak and the rustle of papers.

He answers my knock with a gruff, "Come in."

When he sees me, I get an almost-smile. "I hope this means you took care of the ... problem at the cemetery."

"I did."

He nods, once. "Good."

"I wanted to say thank you, for today."

He waves away my gratitude. "Just doing my job. I was looking for a legitimate way to escort them from Springside. This was as good an excuse as any."

"Even so, I want to say thanks." I uncap the thermos and pour him a cup. "This is still hot. It still tastes the way it should because it hasn't been cooking all day long." I point toward the outer office and the coffeemaker that Penny tends and then set the thermos on Chief's desk. "And it's all yours."

I'm at the threshold when Chief calls after me. He's followed me from his office and he now shadows the doorway.

"Katy, you tell me if Orson Yates turns up again, or if they contact you. I don't care what it is. Okay?"

"I will," I promise.

CHAPTER 9

SOMEHOW, I BEAT NIGEL TO the hospital. Sadie is fussing over Malcolm. His bed has precise hospital corners. She's arranged all the items on his tray table. His nightstand is spotless, and in its drawer a dozen snacks are hiding for later. She is now rearranging all the flowers everyone has sent.

When she sees me, her eyes widen. "Oh, Katy! You're soaked through. Here, let's get you dry."

She takes me by the shoulders and directs me toward the room's radiator. I cast a glance back at Malcolm.

"Oh, thank God," he murmurs. "She has another patient."

I can't help but laugh.

Sadie forces me out of my boots and socks and into a pair of fuzzy hospital ones with treads on the soles. She hangs my coat, my mittens, and my socks over the heater to dry. During all this, I send a questioning look toward Malcolm.

"Nigel?" I mouth.

He shakes his head.

"Cold feet?" Again, I mouth the words.

Malcolm shrugs.

The tiniest bit of worry worms its way through me. What if nearly every ghost in Springside was too much of a temptation for Nigel? And if so, what can I do about that?

I cast another look at Malcolm. He knows his brother better than I do, and even if he wants to, he's not going anywhere. Neither am I at the moment. All we can do is wait.

"Don't worry," he says, low enough that only I can hear.

But I do worry. For Nigel to relapse—after everything—feels like failure. It isn't fair, not for him, or Sadie, or Malcolm, for that matter.

I'm contemplating this and possible next steps when a wolf whistle sounds in the corridor.

"Looking good, Nigel," one of the nurses calls. "Or should I say *Mr. Armand?*"

Nigel's laugh echoes in return. My heart rate picks up. A curious smile tugs the corner of Malcolm's mouth. Sadie, on the other hand, is busy adjusting my damp clothes and finding me a blanket.

When Nigel enters the room it's perfectly clear why I beat him here. He's resplendent in a three-piece gray suit, a red tie knotted at his neck. His shoes gleam. His hair—as brilliant white as his pressed shirt—is smooth, not a strand out of place.

I don't think I've ever seen him in anything but jeans and sweatshirts, and maybe a button-down at Christmas. This? This is impressive. This is Nigel Armand, world-class necromancer.

This is a man on a mission.

Sadie turns, and the blanket slips through her fingers and pools on the floor.

"Nigel?" she says, uncertainty lacing her voice.

He hushes her. "Let me say this?"

She nods.

Nigel drops to one knee, that velvet-covered box open in his palm. I inch closer to Malcolm. I reach out and my hand meets his.

"Sadie Lancaster," Nigel says, "would you do me the honor of becoming my wife?"

Sadie blinks, once, twice. Her face goes pale before a blush blazes up her cheeks. "What?" she says, although it sounds more like a cry for help.

"Will you marry me?"

Malcolm squeezes my fingers, and I clutch back. I'm not sure how this will end. Even the hallway has gone quiet. We're all waiting for Sadie's reply.

"You want to marry me?" she says.

"More than anything."

When he says those words, I know they're true. He wants this more than anything, more than all the ghosts in Springside.

Sadie falls to her knees and cups Nigel's face. "Oh, my beautiful boy, you can't mean that."

"I do. I'm asking you to wear my ring, put up with all my faults, and spend the rest of your life with me."

Something cracks in Sadie's resolve. Her gaze darts downward, lands on the ring. Gently, she plucks it from the velvet and holds it up to the light.

"It's beautiful."

"Not as much as you are."

Her gaze moves to Nigel, her eyes filled with doubt. His fingers join hers, so they both hold the ring.

"Wear my ring, Sadie?"

She gives a shaky nod and together they ease the diamond onto her finger.

"Marry me?" Nigel places a kiss on her hand. "Please?" He places another kiss there before lifting his face so it's even with hers. "Spend your life with me?"

His hands thread through her curls, frame her face. He kisses her, and it's so tender, I have to look away. A moment later, Sadie's whisper fills the room.

"Yes, I'll marry you."

It's as if the entire hospital staff has been waiting for these words. Nurses pour into the room, along with orderlies, volunteers, and even a few doctors. All the nurses who tended to Sadie while she was in her coma are here. Someone breaks out an industrial-sized jug of cranberry juice and we toast the couple with plastic cups.

Tears stream down Sadie's face. Nigel holds her close, tucked in his arms. There are so many people in the room that I start to wonder if anyone is taking care of the other patients.

Malcolm tugs my hand. "How long have you known?"

"A few weeks. He wanted my opinion on the ring, like I know anything about rings."

"How does it feel to you?" He nods toward Nigel and Sadie.

I consider the question, although I already know the answer. "It feels right, has from the start."

"I think so too."

At last the nurse for Malcolm's floor clears everyone out, her voice stern.

"This young man needs his rest." She eyes him. "He's been doing far too much today."

The hospital staff vanishes nearly as quickly as they appeared. Nigel helps Sadie into her coat and they leave together, hand in hand. I'm turning toward the radiator, intent on my still-damp things, when Malcolm's fingers catch mine.

"Doesn't apply to you," he says.

"What?"

"Stay." He tugs me closer.

"I thought that maybe you'd want ... I mean, you and Selena—"

"Selena's gone."

"She's gone?" True, I haven't felt her presence, but I guessed she was hanging back, waiting for everyone to leave. "But ... where did she go?"

"Somewhere safe, where Orson or Carter won't be able to capture her. She told me about the map, how you showed her how to find me." His laugh is soft, a bit rueful. "She didn't understand why you did that."

"I wanted you to be happy."

He releases my hand and inches himself to the far side of his bed. He winces with the effort. I want to tell him to stop, but I know he won't.

"Right here." He pats the space left empty.

"But—"

"It'll be therapeutic, really. Good for me and all that. Besides, we need to talk."

I take up a perch on the edge of the bed. This, however, isn't sufficient.

"All of you," Malcolm says, "feet included."

I scoot all the way onto the bed until at last I'm flush with Malcolm, feet tucked by his ankles, my right hand coming to rest gingerly against his chest, fingertips lighting on the spot above his heart.

His sigh rumbles beneath my fingers. "Much better."

He is, as always, so warm, and still smells of nutmeg. My heart pounds because I'm not sure what comes next. I'm not sure what he'll say, only that he thinks we need to talk.

"Do you know what I was doing that day when you found me at the nature preserve?"

I give my head a slight shake.

"I was showing Selena my new life here, what it means to me, trying to explain why I wasn't moving back to the Twin Cities. I wanted her to see what I did at Springside Long-term Care, and how we catch and release."

"I thought that when she came back, you'd want to ... I don't know, go back to investing."

"I still invest. I'm not killing it, but don't you have a pretty decent start on a retirement account now?"

It's true. I do, thanks to Malcolm.

"You looked so happy when she came back," I say. "I thought you'd—"

"You thought what? That I'd want to be with her?"

I nod.

Something rumbles in his chest, another sigh perhaps. "Maybe at one time, before I moved to Springside, I would have. And I admit it, when I was living in Minneapolis, I thought having a relationship with a ghost was the answer to everything. When someone is literally in your head half the time, you never have to explain yourself. But you know what it isn't?"

I shake my head.

"Real. I was relieved when Selena came back. I spent a lot of time worrying someone like Carter or Orson might exploit her. But seeing her again made me realize what truly makes me happy."

I wait to hear what that is, my heart still thrumming, fingertips against his chest. Part of me almost wishes he won't speak. I would freeze this moment so I can stay nestled here forever in the crook of his shoulder.

"You don't know what I'm talking about, do you?" he says.

I give my head another shake.

"It's you."

"Me?"

"Of course you. I know I'm not very good at this relationship thing, but I'm willing to try if you're willing to put up with me."

"Put up with you?"

"It's a lot to ask, I know."

"You don't have to ask."

My heart pounds so hard, I'm afraid it might burst from my chest. I'm afraid Malcolm must be able to feel it. But then again, his heart is thumping beneath my fingers, its rhythm matching mine.

The lights are turned down low. Visiting hours must be over. But when a nurse bustles in on her rounds and checks Malcolm's blood pressure and pulse, it's as if I'm not even there.

"As long as you're quiet," is all she says on her way out.

"Stay the night?" Malcolm asks when the room is ours again.

"I don't think that's allowed."

"It is tonight, at least for me."

"You get away with so much."

"Well, I did bribe them, and you're going to have to bring in some Kona blend tomorrow."

I laugh, the worry, fear, and dread I've been storing inside me loosening their grip. I'm warm, all the way through, from my toes to my heart. I don't need to freeze this moment in order to savor it; I get to live it for the next eight hours.

"Stay with me, Katy?"

"Yes," I say. "I'll stay. I'll stay for as long as you want."

Malcolm closes his eyes, dark lashes gracing his cheekbones. His mouth is soft and curved with the slightest hint of a smile.

"In that case," he says, "it looks like you're stuck with me for a very long time."

PART III
THE WEDDING GHOST

COFFEE AND GHOSTS SEASON TWO,
EPISODE 3

THERE'S A STRANGER standing on the sidewalk, staring up at my neighbor's house. In a town as small as Springside, any stranger is greeted with wariness. Ones who stare up at houses? Even more so.

Which is why I'm tracking this particular stranger from behind my screen door. I'm cradling a cup of coffee in my hands, but my phone is in my back pocket, the police chief's personal number on speed dial. Lately, whenever a stranger wanders into town, something bad always follows them. I want to make sure nothing has followed this one, because in less than a week, my neighbor, Sadie Lancaster, is getting married.

No one, not even this well-dressed stranger, will stop that. Not if I can help it.

With a shoulder, I push open the screen door and step onto my porch. The man is still planted on the sidewalk. He hasn't strayed onto the walkway itself. It's like there's an invisible barrier, one he doesn't plan on crossing. A tweed blazer is draped over one arm. His hair is dark, and smooth, and styled. All in all, he's so pulled together that I suspect I know *what* he is, even if I don't know his name.

"Can I help you?" I call out. Because, well-dressed or not, a stranger is a stranger.

His dark eyes light onto me. He smiles and then treads the distance between Sadie's house and mine, never straying from the sidewalk. He halts, turns, and clicks his heels together.

It's meant to make me laugh; I can tell. I purse my lips together in order not to. I'm still in stranger = creepy mode.

"You must be Katy Lindstrom," he says.

I swallow the urge to nod.

"I'm a friend of Nigel's," he adds, his voice low and melodious. He sounds as if he finds everything—me, Springside, this spring morning—slightly amusing. He nods toward the ground. "That's an impressive ward you've got going there. It rivals Nigel's." He waves a hand toward Sadie's house.

"And you are?" I ask.

"A necromancer who respects wards."

Well, I guessed the necromancer part. I still don't know his name or if he's truly a friend. Necromancers seem to collect a great many friends who turn out not to be all that friendly. I try again.

"And you are?"

He laughs. "Oh, of course. Forgive me. I'm Prescott Jones, and I do know Nigel. Honest." He digs around in the blazer's pocket and pulls out a wedding invitation. The gold embossed lettering glints in the morning sunshine.

My fingers unclench, slightly, from around the coffee cup. I take a sip and let the caffeine clear the last of the sleep from my head. I'm in pajama bottoms and a cami. I'm completely sloppy compared to this Prescott Jones, and I really should be getting ready for work. Instead, I remain on the porch.

"Is that the famous Lindstrom brew?"

He raises an eyebrow, a request if there ever was one. I tilt my chin in answer—a solid *no*. It's bad enough he's on my sidewalk. I will not invite a strange necromancer inside my house.

"We've met, you know," he says as if in response to my thoughts. "I was about ten years old and you were maybe ... ten months? Our parents were friends. Did you know that?"

I give my head a slow shake. "You knew my parents?"

"Not very well." He shrugs. "I was ten. I wasn't interested in what the grownups were doing, but I remember them." He pauses and looks not at me, but somewhere past me. "I remember when they died. We went to the funeral." Now he looks around as if he's just discovered where he is. "It was here, in Springside."

I'm not sure what to believe of this tale, if anything. But my heart thuds like it knows the truth of it. I grip the cup harder. My fingers feel cold and I try to catch the last of the coffee's warmth.

"And I remember." His voice has grown quiet. He speaks so softly that I can barely hear him. I want to rush down the porch steps and stand right across from him so I don't miss a word.

I stay put.

"I remember," he says again. "They—the grownups—had me play with you. We were in some side room or something, a nursery, maybe, during the actual service." He tilts his head as if seeing me for the first time. "I don't suppose that's something you'd remember."

I don't suppose it would be. My throat is tight. My heart is still thudding. And the soft words from this stranger have me transfixed.

Then something glimmers by his head. A smile replaces the pensive look, and he holds out a hand as if to catch an invisible bird.

"We also have a mutual friend. Go on, Frederick. Go say hi."

That glimmer fills the space between us, stretching thin, until it reaches me. Then I know for certain. A sprite—one with an amazing amount of strength. It—or rather, he—whizzes around my head in greeting before settling on my shoulder.

"Oh, I've caught you before," I say to him.

Frederick whirls around, the force picking up a few blades of grass and lilac blossoms. The tiny cyclone fills the air with the scent of spring—fresh-mown lawn, the light perfume of early blooms, and something that reminds me of hope.

He lands on my shoulder again and then swan dives into my cup of coffee. It's barely warm enough to tempt a sprite, never mind an actual ghost. But steam is rising in the air, and I'm drinking Kona blend, which is a ghostly favorite.

"You're quite rude, too," I say to Frederick as he floats on the coffee's steam.

Oh, this one is. This is the sort of sprite that has us using the Tupperware with the opaque sides when we go out on a call. Some sprites won't stop playing pranks—even after they've been caught—and will manifest obscene images. Some things are better left unseen.

Prescott Jones chuckles. "He is, isn't he? But he makes me laugh, so I let him tag along."

He snaps his fingers. Frederick rockets from the steam, whirls around my head once more, and then gives me a ghostly kiss on the cheek.

"I won't detain you any longer." Prescott nods. "I hope to see you before the wedding, but if not, perhaps we can speak more then."

With that, he retreats down the sidewalk until he reaches a flashy yellow car. I watch until the car and its driver are well out of sight. Even then, I remain on the porch, ears strained for any stray sound, my gaze taking in my yard and then Sadie's.

Once I've stepped inside, I bolt the door. I should shower, head in to work, ask Nigel about all of this. But Prescott's appearance has knocked me off-kilter. For the longest time all I can do is peer through the curtains at the quiet street.

No one hears me come in. I'm certain of this. I barely hear myself walk through the door, or the chime that rings above my head. Shouts echo from the conference room. The voices blend together, but I do know this. One belongs to Malcolm, my business partner, and the other to his brother, Nigel, our tech support.

"I can't believe you've been doing this. It's unconscionable. Really, I don't have words for it."

Since Nigel keeps on shouting, it appears that he does have more words. But they're no match for Malcolm's.

"Would you just listen? It's a simple investment. It's like getting venture capital without jumping through all the hoops of getting venture capital. In a couple of months, it will all even out and everything will be fine."

"Oh, really. And have you told Katy this? Because if you haven't told her any of this, then it isn't simple and it certainly isn't fine."

An icy silence fills the conference room. That same ice invades my veins. My fingers turn cold again. I don't know what the fight's about, but I do know this:

Malcolm hasn't told me anything.

I sigh and sag against the reception desk, the thermoses in the canvas field kit jangling. We're still not making enough money each month to hire an actual receptionist, not that we have anything for him or her to do. After all, I'm the one who makes the coffee around here. As a precaution, I've filled several thermoses this morning. Unexpected necromancers make me nervous.

To be honest, I've been dreading something like this. Malcolm is more than my business partner, and has been for a couple of months. It's been gnawing at the pit of my stomach. Needless worry, I've told myself, about mixing business and … well, pleasure.

Maybe not so needless after all.

I almost turn around. I almost sneak out the door. For several seconds, I consider leaving and heading over to the Pancake House, because even if all-you-can-eat dollar-size pancakes don't solve anything, they certainly can't hurt.

But I want to make sure Nigel truly does know someone named Prescott Jones. I want to ask about my parents, and what Nigel thinks of this new connection, one we haven't managed to uncover on our own. I really want to talk about the wedding, complain about the final dress fitting, and all the rest.

I don't want to talk about this thing—whatever it is—that Malcolm has done. But I have no choice. I push off the reception desk and head into the conference room.

I find both brothers glaring at each other. Nigel has his hands planted on the conference table (really, it's someone's old dining room table). Malcolm is on the opposite side of the room, leaning against the wall, arms crossed over his chest.

"Oh, look," Nigel says. "Here's Katy now. Would you like to tell her, or should I?"

No one speaks.

"Tell me what?" I ask.

I can't imagine what could be so bad that they won't talk to each other. Malcolm is Nigel's best man. If they don't start speaking, it will make for an awkward wedding ceremony.

"My brother thinks he's clever," Nigel begins. "He thought we wouldn't notice, that I wouldn't notice, that *you* wouldn't." He turns to me. "Who owns this business?"

"We both do. Malcolm and I. It's a limited liability company. Malcolm filed the paperwork and everything." I cast him a hopeful glance, but the smile I receive in return is full of guilt.

"Then do you know that he's been floating the business for the past several months?"

Floating ... the business? I'm not certain what that means, but it doesn't sound good. To be honest, I've let Malcolm manage the money aspect. He has a business degree. He understands profit and loss and knows when to file the taxes.

I know how to brew a damn fine cup of coffee. I'm not sure our contributions are equal.

"What does that mean?" I say at last.

"It means we're not making any money. Malcolm has been keeping the business afloat with his own money—"

"Like an investment," Malcolm says. "If you would just—"

"What?" Nigel slaps the table. "Pretend it isn't happening? Pretend you haven't been lying?"

"Have I lied?" Malcolm turns, first toward me, and then back to Nigel. "Have I? I'm the business manager. I'm managing the business."

"We're not making money?" I say, and my voice is incredibly small compared to theirs. "But I thought ... didn't you say ... I mean..."

I'm not sure what I mean, since I can't remember—exactly—what Malcolm has told me about the business. But business was good in December; he said so. I do remember that.

"All small businesses struggle at first," Malcolm says. "Ours is no different. I'm simply providing the capital to get us going. Once we have a steady income, the business can pay me back."

"That's fine for you," Nigel says. "But you know what? It doesn't work for me. It means my baby brother is essentially giving me a handout. I'm getting married in less than a week." He pauses, scrubs his face with his hands. "I've come to terms with the fact that I'll be living in the house that Harold Lancaster bought, but I'll be damned if I'm not earning an actual salary."

Oh. *Of course.* It's not about Malcolm at all. Well, it is. Malcolm excels at lies of omission, but I've known that for a while. But this?

This is all about Nigel and Sadie, the wedding, and the specter of Harold Lancaster—who was rich, and as it turns out, an actual specter as well. We've dealt with the latter problem, at least for now.

I'm not sure how to deal with this one. This isn't the sort of ghost you can catch with some excellent Kona blend and a Tupperware container. This is the sort of haunting that can ruin a marriage.

I glance back and forth between them. I need to fix this. I give Malcolm a half-smile, just to let him know I'm working on a solution, but he won't meet my eyes. Before I can say anything—and really, I'm not sure what I plan to say—the chime over the door rings. A booming voice follows.

"Katrina Lindstrom! I respect your ward. I ask for your permission to enter your place of business."

The anger drains from Nigel's face. The smile that replaces it makes him look like he should: a man who's about to marry the love of his life. He rounds the table and grabs my hand on the way to the front entrance.

"Katy, come on. There's someone I want you to meet."

On the threshold stands the largest man I have ever seen. He must be six-foot-five, at least. In both height and girth, he's even larger than Police Chief Ramsey. This man is big and burly, with graying hair and skin a lovely shade of brown. His shirt is pressed, as are his trousers. The polish on his shoes reflects the light.

He's pulled together, the way I've come to expect from a necromancer, except everything is at least twenty years out of date.

"Katy Lindstrom," Nigel says, gesturing toward the man. "This is my good friend and mentor Reginald Weaver. As you might have guessed, he's a necromancer."

Reginald studies me, eyes narrowed and filled with discernment. "Oh, so this is the little lady causing all the trouble."

I really should take offense at that, except I don't think he means to be offensive. His tone is measured, without a trace of sarcasm. Although

I would argue that I'm not the one causing trouble—that's squarely on the necromancers who keep showing up in town.

"It's nice to meet you?" I ask, and I do say it like that, as a question. Honestly, I'm not sure it's going to be nice at all.

"You have to invite him in." Nigel nudges me. "He's old school. He won't cross a ward unless invited."

"What?" I glance around as if I can see the ward I've placed on our storefront. I can't, of course. "Come in," I say, and then gesture toward my field kit. "Would you like some coffee?"

Reginald takes a giant step across the threshold. "I would, almost as much as I want to see my good friend married." He hugs Nigel then and despite Nigel's height, he's swallowed by Reginald's embrace.

Aromatic steam fills the air as I uncap the thermoses. I let everyone pour their own cup, noting that Reginald likes his coffee extra sweet.

"I didn't think you'd get word in time," Nigel says to Reginald. "We have more than our fair share of sprites in Springside, but a reliable ghost?" He shrugs. "It was secondhand, too, since I still can't—"

Reginald cuts off Nigel's words with a strong hand to his shoulder. "You don't need to explain. Malcolm's ghost came through, although apparently there was a promise of some Kona blend?"

"Did I promise a ghost some coffee?" Again, I glance around. I don't detect a presence, but I've recently learned that some necromancers can hide their ghosts.

"I'm sure Malcolm did it for you and then 'forgot' to tell you about it." Nigel draws little air quotes around *forgot*, and the anger from earlier invades his voice.

Reginald's chest heaves with a sigh. "Nothing really changes. After the ceremony I will retreat to the woods once again. In five years' time, I will emerge, perhaps to attend your wedding, Katrina Lindstrom, and these two"—he points at Nigel and then Malcolm, who is shadowing the conference room door—"will still be fighting. I miss nothing."

"Are you the one who only communicates by ghost?" I've been fascinated by that ever since Nigel told me about the necromancers he knows. Some don't use phones or computers or any sort of technology. If you want to contact them, you send a ghost.

"Yes. I seldom venture from my woods, and then only to procure supplies. This trip to Springside is quite an adventure for me."

He speaks so formally that it's clear he hasn't had an actual conversation in a while. I wonder what it is he does out there, alone in the woods, then decide not to ask. I'm about to suggest the Springside Pancake House—which isn't actually adventurous, but the all-you-can-eat will keep him fed—when the door chime rings out once again. I suppose it's too much to hope for that it's an actual customer.

It is. Springside is being overrun by necromancers. Prescott Jones stands in the doorway, the toes of his wingtips just touching the invisible line of my ward. He's doing that on purpose. The smile on his face tells me so.

"I won't dare cross a ward, not with Reginald Weaver around to bear witness. I value my life more than that."

Nigel snorts, but Reginald's expression is devoid of humor.

"You should never violate a ward. No true necromancer does."

I've heard of necromancer justice—retribution, as Nigel calls it. If Reginald is the one who dishes it out, no wonder most necromancers respect wards.

"Katy." Nigel waves a hand. "This is my friend, Prescott Jones."

"We've met," I say, but Prescott doesn't budge from the entrance, so I add, "Would you like to come in for some coffee?"

Prescott needs no more from me. He's across the room in a moment and has Nigel in a tight embrace.

"Oh, it's good to see you. So good. I thought we'd lost you there for a while."

"I thought I'd lost me," Nigel admits.

Prescott holds Nigel at arm's length. "And I see that love agrees with you. You look like you should."

I pour Prescott a cup and refill Reginald's and Nigel's. I can't help but agree: love has done wonders for Nigel. His hair is still pure white, a legacy of his addiction that will never go away. But he isn't as gaunt as he was last fall, and his eyes never appear glazed over, focused on nothing, like they used to. You can see his beauty now. Both brothers are terribly handsome—all olive skin and lush eyelashes.

The thought draws my gaze to Malcolm. He hasn't joined the group, and when I offer up a cup of coffee, he shakes his head.

Malcolm never turns down my coffee.

A moment later, he nods toward the front door and slips out without the three other men noticing. Something tightens in my chest. I've repaired rifts between these two before. I know they love each other. But this time? I'm not sure I can fix this, not before the wedding on Saturday.

"Orson's not going to like this."

The proclamation—from Prescott—pulls my attention away from Malcolm and the door closing softly behind him.

"Not like what?" I ask.

"So many powerful necromancers in one place," Prescott says. "He'll think you've recruited us for the ghost army you're amassing."

I wrinkle my nose—all the consideration Orson Yates truly deserves. "I'm not amassing an army, and I'm pretty sure you know that and he knows that."

Prescott laughs. "Of course I know that. So does he. But you've already seen how he operates. Orson finds the truth inconsequential."

A thought occurs to me, one that involves Orson Yates, his version of the truth, and Prescott. "You knew my mother, right?" I say to him.

"Yes, both your parents."

"And you knew she was a necromancer?"

"I was ten, but yes, I remember that. It was ... she was ... remarkable."

"Was your mother a necromancer?"

Prescott laughs at this, but it's a soft laugh, filled with the warmth of reminiscence. "My mother was old school. She kept the house, kept all of us from killing each other, and only took a job after we all graduated. There were five of us. She should've received hazard pay."

"You didn't answer my question."

Prescott glances away. "It's ... she never practiced the craft, so no, technically she wasn't. We ... those of us who do—" He waves a hand, indicating the group of us. "You take it for granted." He looks to Nigel now, and Reginald, his gaze searching. "The sensing and the communication, it's like any skill. If you don't use it, it fades."

Nigel nods, but Reginald purses his lips as if he doesn't quite agree.

"Why aren't there female necromancers?" I point to Nigel, who does an excellent job of avoiding eye contact. "Do you have any female necromancer friends? Did you invite them to the wedding? According to Orson Yates, the last woman necromancer in his association was my mother. That had to be—"

"Twenty-five years ago," Reginald says. "And I can't answer your question, Katrina Lindstrom, except to say that life is unfair."

"Is it deliberate?"

"Depends on whom you ask," Prescott says. "In the case of Orson Yates, I'm going with yes."

"What about your grandmother?" Nigel's voice is gentle, as if he knows this is a wound that hasn't healed. "Clearly she knew about necromancy. If she wasn't one in her youth, then she certainly had the skills to be one. Why didn't she ever tell you?"

It's a question that keeps me up at night. Before Malcolm and Nigel came to Springside, I'd never heard of this sort of necromancy, speaking to ghosts, partnering with them for fun and profit, using them to do your bidding. Although I'm capable of talking to ghosts, I seldom do so necromancer style, by inviting them inside my head. I prefer my way, which more often than not resembles a game of charades.

"I don't know," I say. It's this that hurts the most. Why didn't she tell me, if only to warn me?

The men fall silent. I open my mouth in hopes of steering the conversation back to lighter things, but Prescott claps his hands together.

"So, bachelor party. There's going to be one, right?" He nudges Reginald and then Nigel. "I have an excellent bottle of scotch that says there must be a party."

Nigel shakes his head and laughs.

Reginald rubs his eyes. "I'm still recovering from your last excellent bottle of scotch."

"Oh, come on," Prescott says. "Just you, me, Reggie here, and we'll even let Malcolm tag along."

At the sound of Malcolm's name, Nigel scowls. I take that as my cue to pour a fresh cup of coffee and head for the door. Before I can leave, Reginald touches my shoulder.

"You take one brother, and I'll handle the other. I've done this before." He winks. Or at least, I think he does. It's a there-and-gone sort of gesture, one that seems out of character.

Almost.

I step outside. The sun is already heating the sidewalk beneath my feet. Malcolm is sitting on the curb next to his convertible, head in his hands. Maple syrup from the Pancake House is floating on the air. Traffic is light, the only real noise the bell of a bicycle ringing out.

It's not a bad morning to sit curbside. So I do, easing next to Malcolm. He doesn't move.

"Hey." I hold out the cup of coffee.

I get a half-sigh, half-growl in response.

I wave my hand across the top of the coffee cup in an attempt to force the steam in Malcolm's direction. It doesn't really work. I look ridiculous, but that's the point. At last Malcolm glances up and gives me a smile.

I offer him the cup. After a moment of hesitation, he takes it. Something inside me loosens. This feels, if not like a victory, then progress.

"I'm sorry," Malcolm says. The words come out with a rush. "I should've told you what was going on. I started to, a hundred times, then I'd think, well, one more month, and then it won't matter."

"Why didn't you tell me? We're partners. I should know these things."

"I didn't want you to worry. I knew you'd suggest cutting costs or not taking a salary, or something." With this last, his gaze fixes on our storefront. The sun strikes the gold lettering of K&M Ghost Eradication Specialists and the words glow.

"It's quite a bit of overhead," I say. "Isn't it? That's the right word? Overhead?"

"Yes. That's the right word, and yes." He sighs. "It's overhead."

"Then maybe—"

He holds up a hand, stopping my words. "Every time I think we should, I remember how you looked that day when you first saw it."

I remember tracing the letters with a finger, marveling at how amazing they were, and how amazing Malcolm was for making the whole thing a surprise.

"I must have stood outside and stared for half an hour."

"You did, and I stared at you," he says

I turn to him now, my eyes dazzled by the gold lettering and the sun.

"I'd never made someone that happy before," he adds, "and I wanted to keep on doing it. Still do."

"We have that small business loan, don't we?"

His mouth turns grim.

"Oh ... that's what you've been paying with your own money, right?"

"The interest rate isn't terrible, but it adds up. And Malcolm-backed loans are currently at zero percent."

I'm pretty sure that's a joke and that I should laugh, but I'm feeling out of my element. "I wish I were better at this. You do so much for the business, and I don't really contribute—"

"Katy, you're the reason we even have a business. Do you remember what I said that first time you showed me how to release ghosts? I'm all sizzle." He bumps my shoulder with his. "And you're the steak."

I turn toward him. His lips brush my forehead and then come to rest on the tender spot next to my eye. My hand finds his, and I trace his fingers, travel the path of a fading scar left over from our last eradication.

"Still, you shouldn't have to do this all on your own. I could take a business class." My voice is low and a little breathy. It's definitely not a profit-and-loss sort of tone. "But that would probably cost money."

"It probably would."

"Would you show me, then? Walk me through the basics? What would happen if you got sick?" That isn't out of the realm of possibility. A few months back, Malcolm ended up in the hospital with broken ribs and a concussion. "I should know what to do."

"I'd love to, especially if we end each session with an evening kiss."

"Oh, I think we could." I draw out my words as if the idea needs great consideration. It doesn't, of course. "Besides, I didn't get my morning kiss yet today."

"You can blame my brother for that." He sighs again, his breath warm against my cheek. "Damn. My brother."

"It's the wedding," I say. That's true, mostly. "Nigel's nervous, and I don't blame him. There's the age difference that everyone's talking about, and of course, Harold was actually well-respected in town."

Malcolm snorts. "I get it, but I don't. Everything I've heard makes me believe he was nothing but an ass and never deserved Sadie."

Everyone has been talking. Whispers about how it's too soon after

Harold's death. Whispers about a younger man and an older woman—I think those might hurt the most. Doubt shadows Sadie's expression when she thinks we're not looking. And while both brothers have been accepted in town—and Malcolm is everyone's favorite—technically, they're still strangers.

"It's almost like Harold is still haunting them," I say.

"You're right. Nigel's lashing out, and I happen to be handy. Under the circumstances, I would too." He nudges my shoulder again. "I think I already have. Last winter, anyone?"

"You're lucky Chief Ramsey didn't make you spend a night in jail."

"At least I got a few good punches in."

I hold back a sigh—and the worry that goes with it. I doubt we've seen the last of Carter Dupree or Orson Yates, but as the weeks have slipped by I've thought of them less and less. It's been wedding talk and sprites and the occasional stubborn ghost. It's the Springside I remember so well from when I was growing up.

Despite everything, I feel warm and content in the morning light. I close my eyes and lean in to Malcolm. We could spend the day right here, on the curb, the sun baking our heads.

A single whoop from a police siren has my eyes shooting open. In the street in front of us, a patrol car is idling. The window rolls down. I squint and can just make out the bulky shape of Police Chief Ramsey.

"Got a call about some inappropriate PDA," he says, his manner gruff, no-nonsense.

"PD—?" I begin.

"Public displays of affection," Malcolm fills in for me.

"We're not even holding hands," I say.

"Not hold them somewhere else."

Chief isn't budging, so Malcolm pushes to his feet and tugs me to mine. I peer into the police car. I can't get a read on Chief or even see his expression. All I have is the stern tone of voice and the posture that tells me this is nonnegotiable.

"You're kidding," I say to him anyway.

"Nope, I'm not. And in my day"—he jabs a finger at Malcolm—"we'd at least take our girl out for breakfast."

With that, the window rolls back up and the cruiser rolls down the street. I stare after it and watch the brake lights flicker before turning to Malcolm.

"He was kidding, right?"

"I think..." He laughs. "I think Chief has an odd sense of humor. Or he's trying to set us up. Or both." He holds out a hand. "But it's not a bad idea. Breakfast?"

"Can we afford breakfast?"

"I can afford the Pancake House. My treat."

The second my fingers touch his, he pulls me close. The sun has warmed his skin and that enticing mix of Ivory soap and nutmeg fills the space between us.

"Morning kiss?" he whispers, mouth inches from mine.

"Isn't that a public display of affection? Chief might come back and arrest us."

"Let him try."

CHAPTER 2

IT'S ONLY AFTER we've devoured platefuls of pancakes and Malcolm has left to pick up his tux and Nigel's that I notice the worry in our waitress's eyes. Annie's topping off my orange juice, and as she does so, she leans over and whispers.

"I'm covering for Belinda."

Belinda is my roommate—well, some of the time. Lately, she's been Gregory's roommate. When she's working the Pancake House, Malcolm and I make it a point to sit in her section. But she isn't here this morning.

"She didn't show up, didn't call in, isn't answering texts." Annie takes her time straightening the napkin holder, the salt and pepper shakers.

"She wasn't—" I begin. "I mean, I think she stayed over at ... a friend's last night."

Annie rolls her eyes. "Right. *Friend.* Thing is, we don't want her to get in trouble, lose her job, that sort of thing."

I don't want that either. Belinda has been ghost- and alcohol-free for months now, coming up on a year. The job here means so much to her. I can't imagine her blowing it off. And things have been so quiet that I can't imagine it's a ghost causing this trouble. Then I think of Carter Dupree and the orange juice Belinda spilled all over him and consider: maybe it could be.

"Could you check on her? I would, but—" Annie shrugs. "I'm working her shift."

"I will."

I check my phone. I have twenty minutes before I need to be at the dressmaker. That should give me enough time to stop at Gregory's apartment. I reach for my bag, but before I can pull out my wallet, Annie holds up a hand.

"He paid. Of course he paid. And the tip was..." She shakes her head as if the tip was so large, words alone can't describe it. "If you don't want him hanging around." She nods at the window, at the K&M Ghost Eradication Specialists storefront across the street. "You let us know. The girls in this town would line up for him."

"I'll keep that in mind."

I leave the Pancake House weighed down by worry and maple syrup.

FROM A BLOCK AWAY, I can see the bright yellow van Gregory drives. Even after all these months, he still hasn't removed the black lettering on the side that reads:

Ghost B Gone
Gregory B. Gone, Proprietor

I'm still not sure how he managed all those ghost "evictions"; he has no sense for anything otherworldly, and I suspect it was the other members of his crew who found the haunted locations—or simply used a bit a stagecraft to manufacture them.

How he feels about substitute teaching at Springside High School? I don't know. But I think he's here, permanently, since I'm pretty certain I know how he feels about Belinda.

I walk the one flight up to his apartment. I rap on the door. I wait. I lean forward, as if that will help me hear the telltale signs that someone's home. I'm debating between knocking again and turning around to leave when the door opens.

What I notice first is the long, flowing silver hair. Next is the robe, only because it doesn't fit the wearer's form at all. She's draped in it, like it's a Halloween costume. If she spread her arms wide, she might be able to fly.

I know this woman standing across from me. The last time I saw her, she kissed my cheek and then—unwittingly, it's true—unleashed an entity on me, Malcolm, and the rest of Springside.

"Terese?" I say.

A frown clouds her brow, but a moment later, a smile blooms across her face. "Katy, right? Gregory's been telling me all about the wedding. You must be so excited. I'll see you there. I'll have to run home, of course, for something to wear, but I'm his plus one."

I stand there, open-mouthed. I'm sure this is why Terese feels obligated to fill the space with so many words. I can't think of anything to say. Well, I can, but remarking that Gregory has an invitation because he was originally Belinda's "plus one" is most likely a conversation killer.

"Gregory," Terese calls over her shoulder. "Come see who's here."

I'm still standing in the doorway, speechless, when Gregory emerges from the hallway. He's wearing a pair of jeans ... and nothing else. In his hands he holds a towel and he's using that to dry his hair.

When his gaze lights on me, he freezes. The towel slips from his grip and lands on the floor. His mouth hangs open. I'm fairly certain that in this moment, our expressions are nearly identical.

"We were just talking about the wedding." Terese turns to me. "Did you need something from Gregory?"

An explanation might be nice, but I doubt it's forthcoming. I mouth a few things that aren't really words, then inspiration strikes.

"Actually, I was going to talk to him about the haunted locker at the high school, but I'm running late. I have to be at the dressmaker. So ... you know ... some other time."

"Oh, too bad. We were about to sit down for some coffee, and you're more than welcome to have a cup." She laughs at that and then shakes her head. "What am I saying? My coffee can't compete."

I have a single thermos left in my messenger bag—Kona blend, made with fresh beans from the Coffee Depot. It takes me all of half a second to reject the idea of offering it up.

"I'm sure your coffee's fine," I say. "But I really need to..." I gesture down the hallway, hoping for a quick way out.

"I understand. I'll see you at the wedding if not before."

Terese gives me a friendly wave. Gregory, who stands a foot taller, mouths what looks like an apology over her head. I'm in no mood to accept it.

Because if Belinda isn't here and if she isn't at work, I have no idea where she might be.

THE WOMAN DOING my final fitting doesn't mind that I have my phone out and I'm texting with the agility of a fourteen-year-old girl. My messages to Belinda go nowhere. I try Malcolm because I need to talk to someone.

Katy: Terese is in town.

I wait and wait. I can tell he's responding, or at least thinking about responding.

"Did you get taller?" the woman says to me around a mouthful of pins.

"I don't think so."

"Lose weight?"

"I just ate a big plate of pancakes at the Pancake House."

"Huh. Something's not right. Turn."

As I do, a message from Malcolm pops onto my screen.

Malcolm: Terese as in Mistress Terese of Ghost B Gone?

Katy: That's the one. She's staying with Gregory. Or at least, she's at his place and wearing his bathrobe.

The woman has me turn again, my dress swirling. It's a color best described as ice pink, and I'm not sure whether it makes me look elegant or like a four-year-old.

"Hold still," the woman says. "I need to take in this seam and I don't want to stab you."

Malcolm: Oh. That's ... bad. Belinda?

Katy: Can't find her, she isn't answering and skipped work.

Malcolm: Want me to look?

Katy: Would you?

Malcolm: Of course. You don't even have to ask.

I remain as still as I possibly can. This is easier now that Malcolm is out searching for Belinda.

"There. Got it. Why don't you head out and show Sadie before you change?"

The skirt of my dress held high in one hand, phone in the other, I tiptoe out of the fitting room and over to the larger one, the one they use for wedding gowns. Sadie is standing on a pedestal, while the owner of So-Sew Springside, Marguerite, inspects the dress's train.

"Katy, dear." Sadie holds out a hand to me.

I tiptoe a few more steps and grasp her fingers.

"Aren't you something?" She beams at me. Her flushed cheeks, the pink highlights in her salt-and-pepper hair, and the blush color of her gown conspire to make her appear a decade younger. "Malcolm won't be able to take his eyes off of you," she says.

"Well, he'd better if he doesn't want to trip while he's walking down the aisle."

Marguerite snorts a laugh. "She's trying to get you up on this pedestal."

Well, yes, she is, and has been playing matchmaker ever since Malcolm came to town.

"I think Nigel's the one who's going to have trouble walking down the aisle," I say. "You look incredible."

Sadie presses a hand against the beadwork of the bodice. "It's not too much?"

I give my head an emphatic shake. "Not at all. He wants this. You know that."

Sadie had the big wedding—with Harold. From what I gather, they did everything his way. This time around? Everything is mutual, from the size of the guest list to the filling between the layers of the cake (raspberry cream—pink, of course), to the location (Springside Community Center, not the country club), to a single attendant for each of them. Malcolm is Nigel's best man, and I'm Sadie's lone bridesmaid and maid of honor.

Assuming, of course, that Nigel starts speaking to Malcolm before Saturday.

"And the boys are ... fighting again?" she asks, although it's not really a question.

I'm not sure how she knows this, but she does.

"I'm setting the table for five tonight, or so Nigel informs me," she adds. "Nigel, his friends Reginald and Prescott, you, and me."

Oh. So that's how she knows. "He's not very subtle, is he?"

"No, he's not. And I wish..." She trails off and shakes her head, curls bouncing.

"I'll talk to him," I say, although I haven't had much luck brokering a peace between them.

They don't have much practice being friends. From what Malcolm has told me, while they were growing up, they were always in competition with each other. Each left home at eighteen, meaning to strike out on his own and earn acclaim as a necromancer. These days, they work together, and while they both work hard, neither has mastered the *together* part. I sometimes think the only reason they try is because of me.

"Or maybe," I add, now that I've given it more thought, "take me off your list. Malcolm and I might have some work to do tonight."

We might, of course. We might get an actual customer with an actual ghost. Or I can start learning about profit-and-loss statements and taxes in between evening kisses. This last sounds like an excellent way to spend several hours.

"Try to make the dinner if you can," Sadie says, "because no matter what Nigel says, I'm setting the table for six."

I nod, tiptoe from the dressing room, and check my phone.

Malcolm: No luck so far.

I'M HALFWAY TO K&M Ghost Eradication Specialists when the obvious hits me. I can't find Belinda because she's in the one place I haven't really checked:

Home.

I swing my truck around, certain this is the answer. She snuck in sometime last night, and now she's upstairs, in her room. Belinda Barnes, former Springside High School homecoming queen, isn't the sort of woman who cries her eyes red over a guy.

She might, however, like something to punch. Or some coffee. I don't know if she wants my company, but at the very least I can brew her a pot of one hundred percent Kona and offer up the couch cushions.

I'm so intent on this plan that I nearly miss seeing the necromancer in front of my house. I stop the truck in the middle of the street, shift into reverse, and back up.

There, on the sidewalk, a smirk on his face, is Carter Dupree. I don't bother parking. I kill the engine and climb from the cab. At the last moment, I grab my messenger bag. True, a metal thermos isn't much of a weapon, but it's better than nothing.

"Looking for someone?" he says.

I'm not about to admit anything to him. "If I were, it wouldn't be you."

He makes a face. I reach for the phone in my back pocket.

"Don't even think about calling your boyfriend," he says. "Unless you want me to kick his ass again."

For the record, it was a draw.

"Maybe I was going to call Chief Ramsey."

"And maybe I'll call my very expensive lawyer."

That's not an idle threat. I wish it were. But the BMW parked a few feet from my truck tells me Carter can afford an expensive lawyer. I know Orson Yates and the Midwest Necromancer Association can. I don't want to get Chief in trouble, so I leave my phone where it is.

For now.

"Do you ever read the ghost forums, Katy?"

I peer at Carter. This change of subject is too innocuous to be anything but double-edged.

I go with, "Sometimes."

Actually, scanning the ghost forums is part of Nigel's job. Combing through the misinformation, gossip, lies, and delusions on the forums could be a full-time job by itself. Add in the rest of the Internet? There's something about the Internet and ghosts that brings out the fraudulent and the frenetic.

"You know," Carter continues, as if he's telling me a slightly interesting story, "there are a lot of people upset that Ghost B Gone stopped webcasting. Apparently it had a lot of fans." He shrugs as if this fact is amusing.

It is, in a way, since Ghost B Gone never truly managed an eviction. The ghosts—mainly sprites—just got bored and left.

"Anyway, there's these rumors going around about Gregory and some blonde piece of fluff. Seems Mistress Terese has a lot of fans as well, and they're kind of outraged by this. I thought she might be interested in those message threads, so I sent her the link. She did the rest."

He raises his hands, palms skyward, as if this is some grand achievement on his part. I suppose it is, if your aim is revenge.

"You must be so miserable," I say.

His smile fades before rebounding. Now it looks a little strained. He points to the BMW. "Right. I'm the miserable one. I'm not the one whose business is failing and who can't afford a decent car"—he looks me up and down—"or wardrobe."

"Only a miserable person could enjoy hurting people the way you do."

This time, the smile doesn't fade; it grows sharp, dangerous-looking. He holds up his hand and makes a fist. It's a deliberate motion, but not aggressive—not yet, anyway. I've seen this move before, although I don't know what comes next. I suspect nothing good.

He lets each finger unfurl and as it does, the air around us starts to shimmer.

Goose bumps prickle my arms. The space around us is thick with the otherworldly. I'm not sure what registers first—the wave of anger rolling off this thing Carter has unleashed, or a single word, a command.

Duck!

I do, hands over my head. Even so, when the blast hits, it topples me to the sidewalk. The force knocks Carter off his feet. He flies through the air and lands in the middle of my front yard.

The ghost he's just released whips about, collecting twigs and pebbles in its wake, ripping tender leaves from the trees. Every time Carter tries to sit up, a gale force shoves him back down.

Grit stings my eyes, coats my lips. The ghost strikes anything it can. It rattles the picket fence, shakes the recycling bins. It crashes into the garbage. One can tips, spilling coffee grounds across the driveway.

Stale, days-old Kona blend fills the air. This fuels the ghost's anger even more. I'm puzzling out why when the obvious hits me.

It wants some coffee.

I tug the thermos from the messenger bag and crouch over the cup, shielding it from the debris in the air. I sniff, test the coffee with a finger. Still hot, strong and stout, without any sugar or half and half. I hope this ghost likes its coffee black.

I stand and hold out the cup. "For you. You can have the whole thermos. I can even make you a full pot, but you have to let me inside and you'll have to let go of Carter."

Not that I'm all that concerned about Carter, but I don't want him permanently pinned to my front lawn.

The whirling subsides. I take a tentative step forward. I feel as if I'm coaxing a wild and wounded animal from a trap. Its distrust thickens the air so much it's hard to breathe, and a lingering sadness fills me. This isn't your ordinary nasty ghost. I've encountered plenty of those. This is something else, something intentional.

"What have you done to this ghost?" I direct these words at Carter.

He props himself up on his elbows, the move slow and cautious. "I don't know what you're talking about."

The ghost surges toward the coffee, then, just as quickly, retreats. I try again, urging it forward with one hand. It skitters backward. After we've done this dance a few times, I set the cup on the sidewalk and take a few steps back.

"There," I say, keeping my voice gentle and encouraging. "It's all yours."

The ghost still hesitates. It doesn't point at Carter, not exactly. While strong ghosts can sometimes manifest humanlike forms, this one is in no state for that. But I feel my gaze tugged in his direction.

"I'll take care of him," I say to the ghost. I march over to where Carter is sitting on my lawn. "I don't know what you did to this ghost, but I want you to leave now."

He peers around me, his brow puzzled. "I don't know what you're talking about. It's just one of our reserve ghosts. We use them for ... whatever."

Whatever? I don't know what that means, and I'm not sure I want to. "I think it backfired this time."

Carter wipes his sleeve across his nose. The linen comes away streaked with bright red. A deep purple bruise is forming beneath one eye.

"Go," I say, "unless you want to stick around and have it kick your ass."

I stand between Carter and the ghost as he stumbles down my lawn to his car. He leaves us in a blast of loud music and a patch of burnt rubber along the asphalt. When at last it's quiet, I turn to find the cup nearly empty and the ghost huddled and scared.

I approach first with slow steps, and when that doesn't seem enough, on hands and knees across the sidewalk. I hope none of my neighbors are at home to witness this. Tiny pebbles prick my palms. I scrub them clean on my jeans before pouring a second cup.

"Here you go," I say. "It's all yours."

I'm out of my element with this terrified and damaged ghost. I sit back on my heels and consider what to do.

It's then my phone buzzes with a text message.

Malcolm: Still nothing. Any ideas?

I shield my eyes with a hand and study my house. The curtains are drawn across the window of Belinda's room. That doesn't really mean anything. We do it to keep out the heat.

Katy: Not sure, except now Carter Dupree is in town.

When the call comes mere seconds later, I'm not sure why it startles me. I'm not sure why I put the phone up to my ear. Malcolm's voice blasts from the speaker, and I wait until he's calm—or reasonably so—before I try again.

"Katy, what on earth? Are you okay? Where are you?"

"I'm fine, really. I'm outside my house, and Carter is gone. He didn't violate my ward, which I guess is to his credit."

I really hate to give Carter Dupree credit for anything, but it's true. Other than being blasted up and over the ward, he played by the rules— or at least the ones for wards.

"I'm coming right over." Malcolm's voice is frantic. "No, wait. I'm stopping at Springside PD and talking to Chief about a restraining order, then I'm coming right over. Or you come here. Or—"

I'm about to say something—with luck, something that will calm him down—when another voice joins the conversation.

"Easy, wild man."

The words are muted, but definitely directed at Malcolm. What sounds like a tussle follows. There's a scrape and a chorus of words I can't make out except for: "Let me talk to her." After a pause, Nigel comes on the line.

"Katy, I'm guessing you're okay," he says.

"I am." I fill in all the blanks for him and before he can even ask, say, "Sadie's still at So-Sew Springside. You don't have to worry."

"Trust me, this time around I'm not the one who's worried." He clears his throat. "It's all we can do to restrain him."

"Well, actually, I am kind of worried, but it's about this ghost."

It's letting me crouch next to it to refill the thermos's cup, but I'm running out of coffee fast.

"What about it?" Nigel sounds unconcerned, as if necromancers routinely unleash ghosts on unsuspecting people. "It sounds like one of Orson's attack ghosts, probably meant for Belinda."

Okay, so they probably do. "It's more than that. It's wild, and angry, and I'm not sure how to describe it, but ... damaged."

"Damaged? How so?"

I search for a way to explain what I feel whenever this ghost draws near enough that I can sense it. "It's the difference between an animal that's fierce and nasty because it's a predator and one that's fierce and nasty because it's been abused."

Silence greets my words.

"Nigel?"

"Yeah. Still here."

"I don't know what to do. I can't capture it and set it free somewhere. I don't think that would solve anything."

"It won't."

"Then—"

"Katy, do you have any idea who Reginald Weaver is?"

I blink, wondering what that has to do with my ghost problem. "Your friend ... mentor ... a necromancer?"

"He's one of the foremost necromancers in the state, probably the nation."

Through the speaker, I hear more of those muffled words.

"Oh, yes, and Prescott too. He's no slouch."

"Can they help me?"

The booming voice of Reginald Weaver fills my ear.

"Katrina Lindstrom, keep the ghost where it is. We will be there soon."

CHAPTER 3

I POUR THE LAST drops of coffee from the thermos and hope it's enough to placate this ghost. It hasn't shown additional signs of aggression, but then I've kept it full of Kona blend. I'm not sure what will happen after it finishes this last cup.

I'm still crouched on the sidewalk next to the ghost when two cars pull up: that flashy yellow one and a far more practical, although equally expensive, Land Rover.

Nigel and Prescott hop out of the yellow car. Nigel surveys the area and then points to Sadie's house.

"I'll be over here if anyone needs tech support."

Prescott squeezes his shoulder. "Good man."

From the corner of my eye, I track Nigel's progress up Sadie's porch steps and inside her house. His spine is straight, shoulders square. If he has any regrets about the life he used to live, they don't show.

This, I think, is a good thing.

Malcolm jumps from the Land Rover and rushes to my side. I hold up a hand, urging him to slow down.

"It's skittish," I say.

And, yes, the ghost wavers but otherwise remains in place.

Malcolm kneels next to me, his hand cupping the back of my neck, his lips next to my ear.

"Are you okay?" His whisper is fierce and frantic. "Be honest. I swear to God, if he hurt you, I'll—"

"I'm fine. Really. You're overreacting."

"I don't think I am."

"Everyone else does."

Or rather, Reginald seems completely uninterested in our ongoing drama. He stands at the edge of the ward around my property and appears to be inspecting it and my house, paying particular attention to the damage caused by the ghost. Prescott catches my eye and there's nothing but amusement in his.

Even the ghost loses some of its fear. I know an otherworldly laugh when I hear one.

"See?" I point toward the ghost. "Even it thinks so."

Malcolm manages a laugh of his own, one filled with self-deprecation. "Okay, you're right. I'm overreacting." He glances around the yard. "And you can clearly take care of yourself."

The last of the coffee is gone. I've served up coffee to everything from sprites to an entity so powerful I'm not sure you could call it a ghost. Most don't suck down an entire thermos's worth of the stuff, not even when it's Kona blend.

But this thing? It wants more, or at least that's my guess when it worms its way into the thermos.

"Do you want that pot of coffee I promised you?" I ask.

The thermos rattles and rolls along the sidewalk and bumps to a halt at my knees.

"I think that's a yes," Malcolm says.

Prescott surveys the street. "We should take this inside, and someone should move Katy's truck."

I hand Malcolm the keys and scoop up the thermos. I'm on the porch steps—alone—when I glance behind me.

Both Prescott and Reginald are standing on the sidewalk. Okay, so Prescott's wingtips are flirting with the edge of the ward. I suspect this is something he's known for. Reginald, however, is a respectful distance back. I suspect that's something he's known for, as well.

"Really?" I ask.

"Really," Prescott confirms.

So, once again, I invite them inside. Malcolm dashes up the stairs behind us. Before we can follow them, he pulls me close. It's an awkward hug—him, me, the screen door, and the ghost in its thermos.

I think he might question me again. Worry is radiating from him. It's there in the way his muscles tense as he holds me. Instead his lips come to rest on top of my head and brush strands of hair. When he does speak, his voice is low and warm.

"You smell like sunshine," is all he says.

WE'RE HALFWAY to the kitchen when a thought strikes me. The jolt of fear has me skittering to a halt. I turn, point, but Malcolm has already read my mind.

"You start the coffee. I'll check to see if she's home." He dashes up the stairs, and his footfalls echo overhead.

If Belinda is home, we'll have to send her next door—at the very least. If this thing in the thermos is some sort of attack ghost meant for her, we'll have to think of something to keep her safe. I peer into the depths of the thermos.

The ghost is cowering inside. I don't talk to ghosts, not the way Malcolm and the other necromancers do, but I don't need to do that to sense their feelings, their overriding desires. And right now, all this ghost wants is safety.

That's not something I've encountered before.

In the kitchen, I hand Reginald the thermos and start the coffee. Malcolm returns as I'm measuring out the grounds. He clears the threshold and then staggers backward as if the aroma from the freshly-ground beans has struck him in the chest.

"One hundred percent Kona?" he asks, eyes full of hope.

"I think we need it."

"When you say 'we', does that include humans as well?"

"Maybe," I say, but the scoop I'm holding should give him the answer

—as long as he keeps count. I'm making enough for five humans and one ghost. I'll insist someone run a cup over to Nigel.

"Belinda?" I mouth.

He shakes his head.

I don't know whether to be relieved or worried. "You don't suppose Carter has another attack ghost, do you?"

"Doubtful." Prescott hovers over my shoulder, and if Malcolm isn't counting the scoops, he certainly is. "Good God, that smells like heaven."

The kitchen in my old Victorian is cramped. With three men crowding around, the space feels even smaller. Reginald's so tall he jostles the pots and pans hanging from an improvised rack. Most of the counter space is devoted to brewing coffee and has been for as long as I can remember.

"So, you don't think he has another ghost?" I peer into the percolator, compare the amount of water with the grounds I've measured out. I go with a touch more filtered water.

"It's hard to manage more than one unless you're unusually skilled," Prescott says. "Carter isn't unusually skilled."

"Last time he tried, at least in Springside," Malcolm says, "he ended up unconscious and lost both his ghosts to Katy." He's pulling half and half from the refrigerator, and when he turns and confronts our stares, he nearly drops the container. "What? It's true. You captured Harold—"

"Actually, *you* did."

"*We* captured Harold's ghost, and then you made a pact with Delilah and set her free."

"Oh, Delilah." Prescott folds his arms over his chest and leans back against the counter. He shuts his eyes for a moment, a smile playing on his lips. "She's one hell of a ghost. I was wondering where she went. Anyway, I think it's safe to say that Carter came to town with one ghost. He lacks the skill for anything more."

"But where you find Carter with an attack ghost, you'll also find the man holding his leash." Reginald is still clutching the thermos. He strokes the sides gently, as if he's calming the ghost inside or coaxing it to come out.

"I don't think so, not this time." Prescott shakes his head. "Not with me, and not with you here. Orson's not that foolhardy."

"Are you certain it's foolhardy? Nigel can't fight. Malcolm is a young-ster, and Katy untrained. That leaves you and me. In one place. How hard would it be to take one—or both—of us out?"

"Is he going to—?" I begin.

"No, he's not," Reginald says. "At least, I doubt he will. I suspect it's another show of power. However, we shouldn't discount a move on his part, especially when we're distracted by wounded ghosts and upcoming weddings."

Reginald's words reassure me—to a point. I glance at Malcolm. His expression is grim, but when he sees me staring, he offers up a smile.

"Don't worry," he mouths.

But I think maybe I should worry, and a lot. I'm completely out of my depth with all this necromancer talk. I know ghosts, and I know coffee. I decide to concentrate on that, brew this ghost the best cup it has ever had, and maybe send it on its way healed, or mostly so.

The mood in the kitchen shifts as the aromatic steam fills the air. Prescott's shoulders loosen. Malcolm no longer looks so grim. The thermos wobbles in Reginald's grip.

When at last I've poured a cup for everyone, I think that maybe one problem is solved. The ghost emerges from the thermos and slips into the steam rising from its cup. As it does so, some of its fear slips away. It's like an exhale, a sigh of relief.

"This is quite good," Reginald says, the rim of the cup poised at his lips.

Prescott rolls his eyes. "What he means is, it's the best damn cup he's ever had. Katy, this is incredible. Really. You must be channeling all your power as a necromancer into brewing coffee."

"I'm not a necromancer." I swallow my sigh with a sip of coffee.

"You should rethink that," Prescott says, his tone dry.

"Well, this little one would agree." Reginald trades his cup for the one the ghost is basking in, easing it from the table with gentle hands. "It knows Katy's wishes, which is why it would like to speak to Malcolm."

Prescott makes a face. "Malcolm?"

Malcolm shoulders Prescott out of the way—a slight that only paints an amused smile on Prescott's face—and steps forward.

"Ready?" Reginald says.

Malcolm nods and reaches out. His touch is tentative. He shuts his eyes, mouth open ever so slightly.

"Technique, Malcolm. Technique," Prescott chides. "Ghost catching has made you sloppy."

Only the barest tensing of his jaw tells me Malcolm has even heard Prescott's words. A moment later, he steps back, eyes wide open.

"Katy, it's one of our ghosts!"

"Oh, so, you *are* amassing a ghost army." Prescott. Again.

Malcolm throws him a scowl. "I mean, it's a Springside ghost. They captured one from town, on purpose. That was supposed to make it fiercer because it would blame Katy for not protecting it."

"I suspect that backfired," Reginald says.

Malcolm nods. "It attacked Carter purely out of revenge, but it recognized Katy. I don't know which ghost it is. I couldn't get a good enough read on it. It's still pretty damaged." He looks to me. "Are we missing one?"

We have our regulars, it's true, those ghosts who either live such a quiet existence that we seldom eradicate them or those who are town fixtures that no one seems to mind—too much.

"I don't know." I review my last several calls. Naughty sprites at the long-term care facility. A ghost that was hoping to inspire awe at the community theater. I think it was going for *Phantom of the Opera*, but the effect was more irritating than terrifying.

Malcolm takes the cup and holds it in front of me. "You don't have to go all necromancer," he says. "Just do that sensing thing you do."

I reach out a hand. This isn't necromancy. At least, I don't think it is. I've always done this, gauged the feelings of ghosts, their driving desire, their personality. I close my eyes and concentrate on the cold sensation engulfing my fingertips.

I know this ghost. And then I know what it is Orson Yates and Carter Dupree have done.

"This is Chief Ramsey's ghost," I say.

"Chief has a ghost?" Malcolm tilts his head as if he needs a new perspective on the ghost still basking in the steam.

It's a fair question. Chief hasn't exactly embraced the idea of the otherworldly. He is, though, a bit more open these days. But he could barely sense the ghost that's been haunting his gardening shed, so he might not notice if it went missing.

"It haunts the watering can in his gardening shed," I say. "It never did much more than rattle the handle, and you know Chief."

Malcolm gives me a crooked grin. "Yeah. I do."

"May I?" Reginald holds out his hands for the coffee cup.

The ghost has returned to swirling in the steam, although I think a fresh serving might be in order. I pour another cup and the ghost abandons the first for the second. I hand both the cup and the ghost over to Reginald as gently as I can.

"I'm afraid this little one isn't the first to be abused by Orson and his association." He pauses and then nods as if he can hear the ghost without the trick Malcolm does.

He raises his gaze to mine and says, "It thinks the world of you, Katy."

"I don't really do anything," I protest. "I brew coffee and catch them. I've never bothered with this one because it's never caused any trouble."

"Ah, that's just it," Reginald says. "You maintain the order of things between humans and ghosts here in Springside. Things would be far worse if either side got the upper hand."

Malcolm cups my shoulder and gives it a squeeze. "Told you so," he whispers in my ear. "You're the steak."

"You know what a nasty ghost can do," Reginald continues. His gaze lowers to the cup still cradled in his hands. "Now you've seen what it is Orson Yates does."

"What do we do with it now?" I ask. "It doesn't seem ... strong enough to release."

Despite all the coffee it's sucked down—and it has made a full thermos and half a pot evaporate. I can't imagine driving it out to the nature preserve and letting it go, or even taking it back to its watering can.

"It isn't strong enough," Reginald confirms. "With your permission, I'd like to take it back up north when I leave. Prescott, go out to my truck and grab one of the cedar boxes."

Prescott's lips twitch as if he's contemplating a refusal. But he leaves without a word and returns with the box, all without comment or complaint. When he places the box on the kitchen table and opens the lid, the scent of cedar joins that of the coffee.

"Little one," Reginald says, voice low, mouth even with the rim of the coffee cup where the ghost is now floating. "Would you consent to spending some time in this box? You will be safe in there. No other necromancer will be able to breach its seal. I will take you home, and when you're better, if you wish, I'll bring you back to Springside."

The air shimmers as the ghost rises from the coffee's steam and eases into the cedar box. The inside is unvarnished but smooth. The whole thing feels safe, and I wonder if that's part of the seal Reginald has placed on it. Right before he lowers the lid, I blow the ghost a kiss.

Prescott bursts out laughing. My cheeks flame even as Malcolm's grip tightens on my shoulder. He throws Prescott another scowl.

"I didn't—" I begin, but my throat is tight. When Prescott holds up a hand, I'm glad for the excuse to stop speaking.

"It was just so charming. No wonder Orson can't figure out what it is you do. It's the opposite of everything he is and believes." He points to the percolator. "It would never occur to him to brew a ghost a cup of coffee, never mind send it off with a kiss."

Reginald studies the box. "No, it wouldn't. That, of course, is his great weakness, and why he isn't as powerful as he thinks himself to be." He turns to me. "Katrina Lindstrom, thank you for your hospitality. Your coffee lives up to its reputation. With your permission." He raises the box. "I will take this little one somewhere safe."

"Is that what you do?" I ask as I see both Prescott and Reginald to the door.

"It's not all I do, but lately, I seem to be running a rehabilitation center for the ghosts Orson or one of his associates have damaged."

"Could I visit your woods sometime? Learn how to do that?" I glance at Malcolm, whose expression has gone startled. Maybe I shouldn't blurt out every last idea that pops into my head, but this seems like a good one. "Maybe we could help some of the meaner ghosts instead of simply driving them out of range."

Reginald chuckles. "And here I thought you weren't a necromancer."

He leaves us with that, and says nothing else on his way out the door and down the porch steps. After a quick kiss on my cheek, Prescott follows. It's only after the exhaust from their cars has settled, and it's quiet again, that I turn to Malcolm.

"Is that necromancy?"

He shrugs. "I honestly don't know. Nigel studied with Reginald, but I never have. My grandfather was my mentor, in the same way you learned catch and release from your grandmother."

"What about your parents?"

I'm so used to being on my own—with or without my grandmother—that the fact that Malcolm and Nigel's parents aren't here for the wedding hasn't seemed odd, until now.

Malcolm sighs. "Let's see. Our father? Somewhere in South America. Or possibly the Falklands, but really, who knows? It's likely he hasn't heard about the wedding yet." He glances over his shoulder at Sadie's house before turning back to me. "Nigel had me send that particular ghost pretty late. I think it was on purpose."

I nod, although I really don't understand.

"And our mother. In Paris. She sent along a blue silk handkerchief for Sadie's something borrowed and something blue. She does approve of the whole younger man, older woman thing, so there's that."

"Oh." My voice sounds so small. I don't know what to make of this information or even how Malcolm feels about it. I want to say something to … comfort him, I guess.

That must show on my face, because he laughs and tugs me close. "Don't worry. It's … the way things are."

I peer up at him. "The Armands as free agents?"

"Something like that. My father never approved of Nigel's choice of mentor, which caused a rift. My mother had an affair, and that caused another, as you can imagine. By the time I needed a mentor, everything had fallen apart, so my grandfather stepped in."

"I'm sorry," I say.

"You know what's crazy? I'm not. Not anymore. I feel like I'm building a new family here in Springside. I mean, there's you, of course."

Here, I think I detect a hint of a blush, and my own cheeks burn again.

"But it's also everyone else, Belinda and Gregory—well, when he's not acting like an ass—Sadie, the residents at the long-term care facility. Even Chief Ramsey is starting to grow on me."

I like the idea of building the family you want rather than the one you ended up with. You can always expand, add new members. They don't, strictly speaking, need to be human.

"I'm wondering if we should go check on some of our family," I say. I think of the ghosts that might be missing, and of course, Belinda. "The human and the otherworldly."

Malcolm's lips find the top of my head again, and it's a shivering thing, this almost kiss of his.

"I think maybe we should."

CHAPTER 4

MY PHONE RINGS at three in the morning. The sound jolts me upright in bed, heart pounding. I grope the nightstand, missing the phone on the first three tries. My limbs ache and my head is fogged with sleep despite the adrenaline racing through my veins.

When I answer, my mouth is so dry, I can barely say hello.

"Hey, it's me. I'm sorry to call so late."

The voice makes my eyes shoot open. "Belinda! Where ... what? I mean—"

"Before you can ask, yes, I'm okay."

"I'm assuming you're not here." I strain my ears, but I already know the answer. If Belinda were here, she'd just knock on my bedroom door.

"You'd be right."

"Or Gregory's?" I hate to go there, but I want to know where she is.

She snorts. "No, I'm not there either. I'm at my mom's, actually."

I don't have a response for that, even if my thoughts are catching up to the rest of me. Belinda and her mother get along—up to a point. But there are several reasons she lives with me, and her mother tops that list. I stretch to turn on the bedside lamp, then squint in its glare. But the light chases away the dark and makes the house feel not quite so empty.

417

"Yeah, I know," she adds when I don't respond. "But I couldn't exactly bring Carter Dupree back to your place."

"You ... what?" My voice has returned, but I don't have any words for *that*. Carter and Belinda? "What's going on?" I ask at last.

"Apparently there are some badass necromancers staying at the bed and breakfast and he didn't want to sleep there tonight, not after what happened with that ghost."

"You know about that?"

"Yeah, he came into the Pancake House an hour before close."

"Annie was worried," I say. "She asked me to look for you."

"I know, and thanks. I took her shift to make up for ditching."

I scoot up and plump the pillows behind me. I still ache from trekking around Springside with Malcolm, and I suspect this will be a very long conversation. A dozen questions swirl in my head; I really don't know which one to ask first. Gregory and Terese? Belinda and Carter?

"Can we start from the beginning?" is the one I choose.

"So, yeah, I guess maybe we should." Her sigh fills my ear. "So, I get off shift the other night and Gregory's not there to pick me up. I think, no big deal, I'll walk to his place."

I know what's coming and I cringe. "Ouch?"

"Yeah. That. Terese was there, which was why he didn't pick me up after work."

"He could've said something, called, sent a text?" I can't help wondering if Belinda was greeted with the same sight I was: Terese swimming in Gregory's robe with him half-dressed in the background.

"It's complicated. I think I told you they were together for a long time. He was totally on the rebound. I knew that going in. If this works for them, who am I to stand in their way?" Her voice has the breezy quality of someone trying to convince themselves of something.

"Malcolm thinks he's an ass."

Belinda laughs. "He's the best. Tell him I said that next time you see him. Unless, of course—" Here, her voice turns sly. "All you need to do is nudge him."

"Don't even start on that. This is about you and Carter Dupree, for some reason."

"I'm going to get him off your back." That breezy quality turns steely.

"Don't be crazy. He came to town to hurt you. He had an attack ghost. He could have another for all we know."

"No, I was just a bonus. There's something else going on, and if I have to cozy up to him to find out what it is, I will."

"He's not going to tell you anything."

"See, I think you're wrong. Something happened today, with that ghost, and it's changed things for him. Do you know he's never been attacked by one?"

"Never been...?" My voice trails off.

I simply can't believe it. I started working with my grandmother when I was five. By the time I was eight, she was taking me with her on all her calls—even the bad ones. Getting attacked by ghosts is part of the job description.

"How can that be?" I ask.

"The way he was raised, I guess. It's all that necromancer stuff Malcolm and Nigel always talk about. Anyway, I thought he was going to break down at the Pancake House. I kept bringing him plates of pancakes until he looked semi-normal again."

"I don't like this. It could be a trick."

"Let's say it is. I'm a lot stronger than I used to be. A lot of that is thanks to you. I'll be okay. Trust me?"

"I really don't think—"

"You don't have to do it all yourself, you know," she says, that steely quality in full force. "The rest of us can help."

I hear the echo of something in her words, something I told Malcolm, perhaps.

"I'm just worried," I say.

"Don't be. I don't have many talents, but I do know how to get information out of guys, especially guys like Carter Dupree. Let me handle him."

"Do I have a choice?"

"Nope." With that, Belinda hangs up.

I stare at my phone until the screen goes black. I want to call Malcolm, but it's much too early. Even a text message will wake him up, so I refrain.

But I'm wide awake. I throw back the comforter and consider the empty side of my bed. I wonder how long it should stay empty. Both *not long* and *too late* fill my thoughts, competing for my attention. I don't know which one is right. Instead of thinking about either one, I head downstairs and brew the first pot of coffee of the day.

SPRINGSIDE at six a.m. is an incredible thing. I walk downtown because I don't want to disturb the quiet with the barely muffled sound of my truck. I want to take in the air, gauge it, search for what should be there —and what shouldn't.

Last night, Malcolm and I concluded that we might be missing some ghosts. The wild ones that haunt the old barn were absent. But, they're unpredictable, and I don't visit the site often enough to know their habits.

Fortunately, Sadie's sprites are still in residence. These days, they spend most of their time at the long-term care facility. They amuse Mrs. Greeley, and Mr. Carlotta's ghost keeps them in line. Queenie, as he calls her, was there too, a bit put out about her babysitting duties, but otherwise the same as always.

Of all the ghosts in Springside, that's the one Orson Yates cannot be allowed to capture. We both know the entity's name, although I'm the only one who can speak it and actually invoke the thing. But that one single word, in the hands of an unscrupulous necromancer? Nothing good would come of that. She's a strong ghost, but what would it take for her to give up that knowledge?

I don't know. I don't like the overabundance of necromancers in Springside, even if I do trust Nigel's friends.

I'm a block from the Springside Police Department when Chief Ramsey appears on its steps. He catches sight of me and possibly raises an eyebrow, although he's too far away for me to really tell.

I pull a thermos from my messenger bag and hold it up. It's a peace offering. I've used it before. Somehow, it never loses its effectiveness.

Chief sweeps an arm toward the station's door before heading inside. I jog the rest of the way, thermoses jangling at my side.

Chief is already in his office by the time I enter the station. On the sideboard in the reception area, yesterday's coffee has formed a charred sludge in the bottom of the carafe, burner still on low. For a few moments, I stare at the mess, uncertain whether I should do something about it.

"Ignore it," Chief calls from his office. "That's what I do."

"It's just so wrong."

That earns me an actual laugh. Those from Chief Ramsey are pretty rare.

"I have some Kona blend," I say.

"I might actually break a few laws for Kona blend."

I uncap a thermos and pour the coffee into a cup. It's then that the two sprites that haunt the police station come out of hiding. They swirl in the steam and between my fingers and make such an annoyance of themselves that I pour them a cup of their own.

That, of course, is exactly what they want. In truth, I don't mind. I'm glad these two are still here and still causing all sorts of trouble.

"There's strangers in town," I tell them. "You know what that means."

One lazes back and forth in the steam. The other one dances about. Neither is listening.

"It means you need to be careful."

The cup wobbles.

"Don't spill that," I say, "because you're not getting any more."

The cup rights itself.

What sounds like a cough comes from Chief's office. He may be more open-minded about ghosts these days, but not enough to believe in these two. I top off his coffee, and since it's always best to lead with your strengths, I enter his office coffee cup first.

I hand the cup to him and wonder again about showing Penny how to brew a decent pot. Or Chief. There's no law that says the police chief can't make his own coffee.

The Styrofoam cup looks tiny in his grip. He shuts his eyes and inhales. For a moment, his face loses its careworn expression.

"It always takes me back," he says. "Did you know that your mother would brew pot after pot when we were studying for finals?"

I give my head a slight shake.

"Well, she did. This?" He raises the cup. "Must run in the family.

Every year, a bunch of us would end up crowding around your grandmother's dining room table, and we'd spend half the night cramming."

I know so little about my mother, and these tidbits Chief shares always take me by surprise and leave me without words. These are small kindnesses, these glimpses into my mother's life. I wish I had a way to repay him.

"She was the only reason any of us got decent grades." He sighs and takes a sip. "But I'm pretty sure you're not here to talk about my GPA."

"Carter Dupree is back in town."

Yes, I know Belinda can take care of herself. And maybe I should trust her instincts on this. But I've seen how vindictive Carter can be, and I know where there's one necromancer with a nasty ghost, there are probably others.

"Ah, yes, and sporting a black eye. Please tell me that wasn't Malcolm's handiwork."

"It wasn't, actually."

Chief cocks his head. "Yours?"

"Not ... exactly?" I'm not sure how to explain an attack ghost to him. He barely believes as it is. "It did happen on my front lawn."

"Did you strike him in any way? Fist, rake, tree branch?"

I shake my head. "I didn't touch him at all."

"Good. Any witnesses?"

"Sadie wasn't home." Here, I shrug. "I'm not sure about anyone else. Most of them work during the day."

What would that attack ghost look like to someone watching from behind their living room curtains? A mini-tornado in my front yard? How would someone rationalize Carter flying through the air? Really, I hope there weren't any witnesses. It would just make everything that much more difficult to explain.

"Actually, I'm more worried about Belinda."

Chief's mouth forms a hard line. His brow darkens. So he must know as well. Springside is a small town, after all. By now, even the ghosts must be gossiping about Gregory, Terese, and Belinda.

"She's not drinking, is she?" he asks.

"I don't know. She's staying at her mom's."

"You two aren't fighting, are you?"

I shake my head. "She's trying to help me with ... something, but I'm not sure she should."

His frown deepens. He was close to her father, and I know he promised to look after Belinda when her father died. She hasn't made that easy.

"I'm not here on any sort of official business," I say. "I'm asking as a ... friend. You know, if we're both looking out for her? Maybe everything will be okay."

"I'll take you up on that." He stares at me, a patented Chief Ramsey stare, the sort that makes you think you've broken some obscure law. Then the look softens into an almost-smile. "Friend."

As I'm on my way out the door, he calls after me.

"Katy, you be careful too."

I halt, hand on the doorframe. "I will. I always am."

"I don't like that Carter Dupree is back in town."

If Chief only knew. "I don't like it either."

That earns me a laugh, but it's short-lived. "I want you to report anything out of the ordinary, no matter how small."

"Of course."

"I'm serious."

I'm about to turn around, to look at him again, but his tone shifts, and something about it keeps me frozen in place.

"I'd like to think your mom wouldn't mind if I looked out for you too."

His voice is rough, and I'm gripping the doorframe so tightly, my fingers ache. I don't dare turn around now, so I squeeze my eyes shut and give my head a vigorous nod. I hope that's enough.

I leave before discovering whether or not it is.

It's Friday, and the moment Malcolm walks through the door of K&M Ghost Eradication Specialists he pulls me into a hug and whirls me around the space. My boots thump against the reception desk and my skirt flares outward.

I'm not dressed for work, but that doesn't really matter. We made it through the week without another ghost incident. We made it through the week without Nigel and Malcolm having another fight. I made it through the week without a glimpse of Carter Dupree.

Even better, in a little more than twenty-four hours Sadie will walk down the aisle and marry Nigel. Nothing else matters.

"What's the occasion?" Malcolm asks.

"Occasion?"

"You're wearing my favorite outfit."

"This is your favorite?" True, I don't have a wide range of outfits, but if I had to guess, I'd say Malcolm's favorite involved the skater skirt.

"Well, you know how I feel about the skirt."

Yes. Yes, I do.

"And the boots are totally kickass, but it's those socks that get me every time."

I own exactly one skirt but many, many over-the-knee stockings. It's a cost-effective way to create a new look—or so I tell myself.

"Well, I have to wear the bridesmaid dress tomorrow." I roll my eyes. I'd really rather not wear the bridesmaid dress at all. "So, I figured I'd go with this today."

Malcolm blinks. "Wait. Assuming you weren't Sadie's maid of honor, would you wear your skater skirt to the wedding?"

"Why not? It's really all I own." I extend a leg and touch the stocking's pattern of smiling daisies. "I'd go with something else, though, something fancier, maybe with sparkles."

His lips twitch. He has an extensive—and expensive—wardrobe of his own. He's never uttered a word about mine. Until maybe now. I brace myself, but for what, I'm not certain.

Instead, he cups my face and gives me one of those sweet dark-roast smiles of his. "Just one of the many reasons why I love you."

All of a sudden, I can't breathe. I can't move. I don't know how to respond. No, that's not true. I do know. I know exactly what to do. My problem is, I'm frozen in place. I can't get my arms to throw themselves around his neck. I can't get my lips to kiss his.

I can't get the words I need to say to leave my mouth.

His thumb travels down my cheekbone. His expression is nothing but tender. I shake my head, but I'm not telling him no; rather, I hope he'll understand I've lost the ability to speak.

"Shh. You don't have to say it back. You don't have to say anything. Okay?"

"But what if I want to say something?"

"Oh, well, that's fine, too."

He pulls me close, and I bury my face against his neck. It's warm here, and that mix of nutmeg and Ivory Soap is both exotic and so familiar.

"I love you, too," I say against the sensitive skin of his neck. "I have for a long time."

"That's why you didn't need to say it. It's obvious."

"It is?"

"Seriously, Katy. People don't go around sacrificing themselves for others, or putting the other person's happiness first if they don't love them. You were going to step aside and let me partner with Selena again, if I wanted to. Am I right?"

I nod, and it's a miserable sort of thing. In that moment, I feel pathetic. I'm not so noble that I don't mind the mention of Selena. Malcolm notices. Of course he does.

"Hey, I know, I know." His lips brush my forehead. "I've had my moments with Carter."

True, but Carter was never a part of my life the way Selena was with Malcolm.

"Chief warned me that if it happened again," he adds, "he'd toss me in jail for the night."

"He didn't!"

"He did. I think it was supposed to motivate me."

"To do what?"

"Not sure, really. But right now, the only thing I want to do is this."

He kisses me then, and it's a dark and dizzying thing, much more an evening kiss than the normal morning one. In this moment, I'm thankful for so many things—that Nigel is off work, that I picked today of all days to pull on the skater skirt, that my heart is so full and that I could be so happy.

"I wish I didn't have to go to the bachelor party," he says several minutes later.

We've settled on the reception desk. The couch is more comfortable, but from our perch on the desk, we can see the storefront window and the gold lettering of K&M Eradication Specialists. My head rests on his shoulder, and we take turns tracing the scars on the backs of each other's hands.

"What do necromancers do at bachelor parties?"

"Show off, mostly, and drink, and then show off some more."

"The one with the most ghosts wins?"

"Something like that. I guess tonight we'll just drink Prescott's scotch and listen to him brag."

"It could be worse?" I say it like a question, too, because maybe it couldn't.

Malcolm laughs. "Yes, it could, but around them, I will always be Nigel's 'baby' brother. There's no escaping that."

I lace my fingers with his. "If it gets too bad, we could always text."

"There's an idea." His lips brush strands of my hair and his breath is warm against my scalp. "Better make sure your battery is charged."

CHAPTER 5

T HE TEXT COMES at midnight. I'm not surprised, really. I guessed Malcolm might have a better time than he thought he would. When I read the message, I know that's true.

Malcolm: We're having a ghost issue. We're all drunk. None of us can catch it.

Katy: Nigel? Is he okay?

Malcolm: Fine. But it would be better if we got it out of here. Would you mind?

Katy: It will take me a few minutes to brew some coffee, but I'll be over as soon as I can.

Malcolm: You're the best.

It's only as I ready the percolator that I wonder which of Springside's ghosts is causing the trouble. A naughty sprite? That seems likely. Still, if it's something more robust, it could be harder to catch, especially if I'm working solo. I pull out the Kona blend, start up the coffee, and then text Malcolm again.

Katy: Is it a sprite? Something more? One of our usual suspects?

My message sits there. No response. No notice that it has even been delivered. There could be a dozen reasons for that, starting with our spotty cell phone service in Springside.

The steam from the Kona blend is enough to clear my head, although I pour myself a to-go cup anyway. I pull the field kit together, adding in a container of sugar and a thermos of half and half just in case.

I'm halfway through my to-go cup and wide awake by the time I reach Malcolm's apartment building. Low lighting illuminates the stairs, but otherwise all the windows are dark—except one.

I stand on the sidewalk out front and stare up at the window of Malcolm's apartment and wonder if anyone is sober enough to buzz me in. The night air is cool, and I raise my chin in an attempt to get a taste of it. I don't sense anything otherworldly, but there's enough distance between the ground and Malcolm's apartment that I might not. It might only be a sprite, and their presence is so slight as to not be there at all sometimes.

When I turn to head inside, a figure blocks the path. I let out a yelp and leap backward. My heart races. The thermoses jangle in the field kit. I'm reaching for one when the figure across from me grasps my wrist.

Instinctively, I jerk back, but his grip is firm.

"Easy, there. The hangover's going to hurt bad enough." The voice is low, amused. "I don't need you adding to it."

My eyes adjust. I match a face to the voice, although in the dark, it's hard to pick out his features.

"Prescott? What are you—?"

"Malcolm sent me down to let you in."

"Is he ... is everyone okay?" I glance around, uncertain.

"Fine, fine, but we could really use the services of K&M Ghost Eradication Specialists."

Malcolm would come down himself to let me in. That's the way he is.

I doubt a couple of glasses of scotch would change that. He *might* send Nigel, if only to get him away from the ghost.

Prescott? No. Prescott isn't the sort of person who allows himself be sent on errands, especially by a baby necromancer or whatever he thinks Malcolm is.

For a moment, we remain like statues. In the slight breeze, I catch a hint of Kona blend, although that's only because the steam has scented my hair. What I notice most is the thing I don't smell.

Scotch. I've never been much of a drinker. Alcohol and ghosts don't mix. But I know the odor. I've caught the hint of it on Belinda far too many times not to.

Prescott is still holding my wrist. His grip is strong enough that I know, if I try to jerk away, he'll tighten it. But my left hand is free. I can use that to grab the canvas field kit, swing it around, and use the element of surprise to break free.

As soon as I think that, I wonder: when did things change? When did Prescott become someone I need to get away from? My arms and legs break out in goose bumps. I pulled on the skater skirt, thinking Malcolm would like that. Now I wish I'd chosen a pair of jeans, something more practical.

I think of Chief Ramsey and wonder if I should have alerted him. But a ghost crashing a bachelor party isn't out of the ordinary.

Except I don't think there's any ghost to catch.

With as much stealth as possible, I weave the fingers of my left hand around the strap of my bag. It's awkward, but it's the only shot I have.

I swing the bag, hoping the trajectory will connect with Prescott's head or neck—anything that will throw him off balance.

"Oh, no, you don't." Prescott ducks, and the jumble of thermoses glances off his head. He swears.

For one blissful moment, my wrist is free from his grip. I take a step, prepare to run, and crash into two people behind me.

"Grab her," he calls out.

Each seizes an arm. I open my mouth to scream only to find it stuffed with a handkerchief.

"None of that." Prescott rubs his head, fingers investigating the bump my collection of thermoses gave him. "Really, Katy, all you need to do is cooperate and everything will be fine. I give you my word as a necromancer."

It's not like I can agree—or disagree; not with my mouth full of high-end linen. My eyes water, and I can feel my pulse throbbing in my neck and in my temples. I want to gasp for air, but that only triggers my gag reflex. A muffled whimper finds its way around the handkerchief.

"Here." Prescott steps close. "If I remove this, do you promise not to scream?"

I remain absolutely still.

"The deal is this. You're coming with us—one way or another. You can ride in the backseat or the trunk. If you scream, you end up in the trunk. Understand?"

I nod.

"Are you going to scream?"

I weigh the options. I'm better off in the backseat, although, in truth, I'm better off not going at all. My gaze is drawn to Malcolm's window and the light illuminating the drawn shades.

Prescott follows my gaze. "Out cold, I'm afraid. Scotch will do that to Reginald. And Malcolm's in no condition to ride to your rescue, although I know he'd love to. You've put a spell on that boy." He turns to me. "So, what will it be?"

I glare at him. Really, how does he expect me to say anything with his handkerchief in my mouth?

"Yes, of course, forgive me. Let's try this again. Will you remain quiet?"

I inhale as deep a breath as I can manage and hold it for a moment. If I must go with them, then the backseat is better than the trunk.

I nod.

Prescott removes the handkerchief. I sputter and cough. I suck in a deep lungful of air but don't break my promise.

"Let's go," he says to the men at my side.

They haul me toward a car, not Prescott's flashy two-seater but a black sedan with dark windows. One man opens the door while the other grips me tighter. He places a hand on the back of my skull so I won't bump my head. The slight pressure tells me I'm supposed to duck.

Instead, I let my knees buckle. I'm in full-on damsel-in-distress mode. I don't cry out, but I give a little yelp. Despite the man holding me, I collapse to the ground under the strength of my own weight.

For one precious moment, my hands are free. I snake one into the messenger bag and tug out a thermos. I push it beneath the car where a tire won't hit it when we leave, but where no one will notice it either.

It's not much of a clue, but Malcolm will recognize the thermos, and anyone who opens the cap will recognize the Kona blend. I'm hoping that someone will be Chief Ramsey. I'm hoping he'll know what to do.

"Careful, gentlemen," Prescott says. "We don't want to break her, not yet, anyway."

I don't know what that means, only that it sounds ominous.

I'm yanked clear off my feet and half-shoved, half-helped into the car. The two men sandwich me into the middle seat while Prescott sits in the front next to a third man, the driver.

I glance behind me and wonder if the trunk might have been the better option.

We're on the outskirts of Springside when the man to my right pulls out a blindfold.

"That won't be necessary," Prescott says.

"Orders."

Prescott surveys the man before turning his gaze toward me. "I apologize, Katy." He nods at the man. "Go ahead."

With my sight cut off, I hear everything—the slight jangle of thermoses near my feet, the whir of tires against asphalt. I catch the overly spiced scent of someone's cologne. After a few turns and a few miles, I lose all sense of direction.

After a few more turns and a few more miles, I feel truly lost.

I AM LOST. With the blindfold, I can't tell how long we've been driving, but my legs ache. I'm folded in on myself in the middle seat. Every time I accidently brush against the man on either side of me, I curl my arms in closer to my body. I clutch my hands together to keep them from trembling.

I squeeze my eyes shut to keep from crying.

The ride is silent. No chatter. No radio. Perhaps it's the quiet that makes the otherworldly buzzing against my ear more pronounced. The presence has been along for the ride this entire time, but I've only just now felt it. Perhaps because it wants me to.

Perhaps because it's Prescott's naughty sprite Frederick.

It caresses one cheek and then the other, a ghostly version of a kiss. Each time it lands, it sucks up a tear. It feels like an apology.

"Frederick," Prescott snaps.

Frederick whizzes around my head before shooting off. I'm left with a single word echoing in my mind.

Sorry.

The car swerves into a turn and then rocks up and over what feels like a very large speed bump. From there, the ride turns rough. I'm thrown against each man in the back seat more often than I'd like.

Then everything stops.

The lack of motion leaves me feeling off-balance. I miss the hum of the tires. I miss the stasis the ride offered, the place between before and after. The car doors open and spring air rushes in, the cool morning bathing my raw cheeks. Through the blindfold, I detect the hint of a sunrise.

One man grabs my arm and yanks me from the car, the force of it resonating in my shoulder. I stumble forward and reach for the blindfold only to have someone slap my hand away.

"You're kidding me," Prescott says. "It's hardly necessary at this point. Hold still, Katy."

Fingers tangle with the blindfold's knot and strands of my hair. The material slides from my eyes and I squint into the morning light. Prescott balls up the blindfold and tosses it on the ground.

"Your part in this is done," one man says to Prescott.

"Oh, yes. Of course it is." The corner of his mouth turns up, but it isn't the sort of smile you should trust. "Thank you for reminding me."

A bemused expression passes over the man's face before he grabs my arm again. "Let's get her inside."

"You first, gentlemen." Prescott sweeps an arm toward the door of a building.

No. A warehouse. I lurch forward under the insistence of my escorts.

My feet trip each other up as I stare at the structure. I've seen this place before. It's the warehouse Selena showed me, as dingy and gray as her memory of it. The man yanks me forward, and I have just enough time to glance behind me at Prescott.

He winks.

That doesn't make me feel any better. He isn't along to save me. This isn't some sort of ruse. He is a world-class necromancer with an agenda.

The men lead me to the center of a large open area inside the warehouse and secure me to a support pole near its center, wrists bound behind me. I suspect I'm some sort of sacrificial lamb for whatever Prescott's agenda may be.

When Orson Yates emerges from a hallway directly across from me, I'm absolutely certain.

As HE WALKS TOWARD ME, Orson's dress shoes tap against the concrete floor. The sound echoes against the walls and the ceiling far above our heads. Around the perimeter of the room, men are stationed a few feet apart. I've lost sight of Prescott. And although I'm not alone with Orson Yates, it very much feels that way.

He halts a few paces from me. Out of spitting range, I note. Not that I'm that petty.

Actually, I am.

"I'm so sorry that it's come to this," he says.

He doesn't sound the least bit sorry.

"You could've cooperated. You could've been a part of this, like your mother was."

Yes, my mother, who died under mysterious circumstances. I strain against the zip tie that binds my wrists. My shoulders ache and the plastic is so tight, my fingers feel numb. The pole is cold and rough against my spine. I don't know if the metal edge is jagged enough to cut through the tie, but I ease my wrists back and forth in the hope that it can.

"I will ask you this once," Orson says, his words measured. "Invoke the entity. Do it now."

He doesn't say *or else*. It's there in his tone. I suppose he could hurt me, starve me, but he can't do too much of either—I'm the only one here who knows the entity's name. I'm the only one who can invoke it. Maybe that has put me in danger.

But it's also the only thing keeping me safe.

I remain silent.

"Invoke the entity, Katy."

"And here I thought you were only going to ask her once." Prescott's voice slices through the quiet, that amused tone present as always. "You have to understand what motivates an individual. Clearly, you have no clue about Katy."

Prescott walks closer as he speaks, and Orson turns from me, enough that I can see the tic in his left eye spasm.

"If she wasn't impressed by your show of force, why on earth would she respond now as the victim of that force?" Prescott stops a few feet away from Orson and shakes his head in mock dismay. "You've bungled this from the start."

"I don't recall asking for your opinion."

"But I recall being asked for my help." Prescott strokes his chin. "You want to know how I would've handled it? I would've approached Malcolm. As a necromancer, he's far more susceptible to this sort of thing. Convince him that he'd not only win untold riches, but also the affections of a certain ghost catcher?" Prescott raises his hands, palms skyward. "Really, it's no more difficult than that."

At the mention of Malcolm, my stomach seizes. I want to glance around. I want to make certain he isn't here, but I don't dare.

"You must be confused," Orson says. "Only Katy knows the entity's name."

I try to make myself as small and inconsequential as possible. It hasn't occurred to either of them to ask me *how* I know the entity's name. Do they think it's something my grandmother told me? Did my mother somehow know its name—and died because of it?

My insides turn to ice. My legs tremble. I'm a terrible liar. If they think to ask me, I'm not sure I can concoct a convincing story. So I pray they won't think to ask.

"Courting Malcolm would've been a waste of time," Orson continues. "He's not ... clever enough to woo the name from her."

Prescott closes his eyes and rubs his temples. "Because courting Katy has obviously been a good use of time. Rudimentary psychology, Orson. That's all this is."

"You want to see psychology in action?" Orson snaps his fingers. "Bring him out."

A door creaks open. Two of Orson's flunkies emerge dragging a third man between them. His head droops and his feet scrape along the floor. I can't see his face, but his hair is that deep ebony I know so well. This time when my stomach seizes, I think I may lose all the coffee I drank earlier.

I bite my lip to keep from crying out. When the men are halfway across the floor, Orson holds up a hand. They halt.

"Right there is fine, gentlemen."

They release Malcolm and he crumples to the floor, his head making a sickening thud when it strikes the concrete. It's then that I can't help it. It's then that I can't hold anything back. I forget my vow to be small and inconsequential. I scream.

"Malcolm!"

He pushes to his elbows before collapsing. His face is turned toward me now. The moment he registers my presence, his expression shifts from mere pain to something more, something darker. The defeat in his eyes is like nothing I've ever seen.

A line of bruises mars his cheekbones, and one eye is already swollen shut. His nose appears broken, and his bottom lip is split open and oozing blood. His right leg is twisted at an unnatural angle. I yank against the zip tie, but only succeed in making the plastic tighten around my wrists.

"There you go," Orson says. "Psychology 101."

"Orson—" Prescott begins.

"You doubt my methods? Let's see how well they work." Orson walks toward Malcolm. "It's too bad, really, that Nigel interfered all those years ago. Malcolm's not terribly clever, true." He kicks Malcolm in the stomach, and I flinch as if I've been struck. "But he would've made a good soldier."

"Leave the boy alone." Prescott's voice sounds steady, but it's very much a lone voice in this warehouse.

"Oh, I'm going to. There's someone else here who's eager to do the honors." Orson pulls a switchblade from his coat pocket and hands it to one of the men who dragged Malcolm into the room.

It's then that I take notice of this particular man. I was so focused on Malcolm that I missed the gleaming blond hair, the fading bruise beneath one eye. Carter Dupree accepts the switchblade and raises his gaze to stare straight at me.

He mouths something. My vision is so blurred by my tears that I don't know what he's said. A curse? A taunt?

"Slowly at first," Orson says. "We don't need to rush through this. It may take her a while to have a change of heart." He turns and addresses the men assembled around the room's perimeter. "Tell me, does anyone here know how long it takes to bleed out from a single slashed wrist?" Orson glances about, a schoolmaster expecting an answer. "No one? All right. Let's experiment." He turns his attention back to Malcolm. "Carter?"

For a moment, I swear Carter hesitates. For a moment, I think his lips move—in a whisper, in a prayer, in something nasty directed at Malcolm? Again, I can't tell. Salt from tears stings my cheeks. I throw myself against the pole, but it's a useless gesture.

When the tip of the knife touches Malcolm's wrist, I cry out.

"Stop! I'll invoke the entity. Just stop. Don't ... do this to him."

"Katy, no!" Malcolm's voice is ragged. He coughs, and his entire body shakes with the effort. "Once they have the entity, they'll only kill you ... and me. It will look like ... murder-suicide."

I jerk my head around, searching for Prescott. A glimpse of his expression should tell me whether or not this is true. But he's vanished, faded into the dark recesses of the warehouse, or perhaps he's left altogether.

"Carter..." Orson prompts.

Am I the only one who senses Carter's reluctance? The knife tip again grazes Malcolm's wrist. He recoils. Orson steps forward and crushes Malcolm's fingers beneath the sole of his shoe.

"There you go, my boy," he says to Carter. "Have at it."

I won't let there be a third time.

"Stop! I agree. I'll invoke the entity."

Orson eases his foot from Malcolm's hand. "Ah, now, see? I knew you could be reasonable."

"Katy, it's not worth it." Malcolm pushes against the floor again, but he's too injured to even crawl.

I wait until he looks straight at me. "You're worth it," I say. "It'll be okay."

I don't know that, of course. In fact, I doubt very much that things will be okay. But once I've invoked the entity, we'll all have bigger problems to deal with. It won't be pleased; this I sense without even speaking its name. And by invoking it now, I may be killing us all.

But if, in the chaos, Malcolm might escape? Well, that would be worth the price.

"We're waiting," Orson says.

I jut my chin toward him. "Are you sure?"

"Am I *what*?" He laughs and then turns and encourages everyone present to do the same.

Everyone does, lockstep, the laughter rising to the pipes and vents over our heads. Everyone laughs—except Carter.

"Yes, my dear." Orson is still chuckling, his words thick with condescension. "I'm quite sure."

"It's not going to be like you think."

"I doubt you know what I think."

That, at least, is true. I won't even pretend to understand Orson Yates or what he wants.

"And I'm still waiting," he adds.

I take a deep breath. It doesn't do much to clear my head. My hands throb. I tug against the zip tie again, but there's no escaping it. I do my best to calm my heartbeat, to focus on that one word Mr. Carlotta's ghost shared with me so many months ago.

My mouth is dry, and I lick my lips. Then, I say the entity's name. "Momalcurkan."

I speak as softly as I can. No one needs to remember it, assuming any of us live to do so.

An unearthly stillness descends on the warehouse. At first, I think

I've misspoken. I expected fire and brimstone, for the roof to be torn clear off. But something about this quiet feels more ominous than that.

"This isn't the time for pranks," Orson says. The sole of his shiny loafer inches toward Malcolm's hand. "Speak the name."

"She did."

The words are no more than a whisper, but they penetrate everything. I feel them vibrate beneath my feet, along the pole I'm tethered to, in the air around us.

"Then show yourself!" Orson demands.

I can't help it. I cringe against the pole. I know this entity, and it doesn't like to be bossed around.

Laughter ripples through the air, the sound of it menacing and cold. "You're right, my dear. I don't."

Like always, it can read my thoughts.

"I also dislike being invoked when I have no wish to be."

A spot on the cement floor liquefies. Dirt and concrete swirl to create what looks like a whirlpool. Its span grows, inch by inch. At first, I suspect I'm the only one who notices, but I can't stop staring to check. The rotation is hypnotic, and it reminds me of the mark this entity once made on my cheek. Although the blue cast of that has faded, I now feel it pulse beneath my skin.

Someone shouts. Orson spins around. I can't see his face, but I suspect he's gaping. He stumbles backward, away from the pool. Switchblade in hand, Carter darts off. The whirlpool expands until it touches the soles of Malcolm's feet.

I cry out, not that I can stop this thing. But perhaps I do, because the whirlpool's diameter remains static. Instead, a behemoth emerges from its center. The thing's surface is craggy and dark, like it has been formed from something elemental, from pieces of the Earth's mantle, or something much older than the Earth.

It turns its eyes toward me. They glow like lava, and its gaze burns. "I know you prefer a different incarnation, my dear," it says, "but I have work to do."

"Now!" Orson shouts.

From the perimeter, one of the men comes running. He must be one of Orson's necromancers. From his gait and the way he spreads his arms and opens his mouth, I know this:

He must be trying to capture the entity.

As soon as I think it, another thought strikes me:

He must be the most foolish person on earth.

But his aim is perfect. The craggy mass vanishes the moment the two collide. A grin spreads across the man's face, a look of undeniable pride at what he's accomplished.

"Well done!" Orson calls out. "Stand by, everyone. Stand by. We may need to do a handoff in short order."

The man takes one step and then another before he starts to stagger. What happens next is difficult to track. His hair fades from brunette to gray to pure white. He ages a good sixty years in a matter of seconds, taut jawline sagging into jowls, folds of skin obscuring his eyes.

He reels, his gaze accusing Orson before it lands on me.

I mouth, "I'm sorry."

He nods once before a bright flame consumes him. The entity peels away from the man a moment before his form disintegrates into a pile of gray ash.

"How many more children do you plan to throw at me, Orson?" The entity oozes forward. "You have very few whose desire is pure enough to hold me for more than a few moments. Indeed, there are very few in this room who could hold me at all."

Orson casts about. It's a jittery motion, and his gaze is just as frantic. From where I'm tethered, it's hard to see the perimeter, but I get the sense of people slipping away, the soft echo of footfalls down some distant corridor.

Certainly Orson is one of those whose desire is pure enough. But he simply stands there, mouth open, hand extended toward the entity as if he could hold it in place while he conjures up Plan B.

"Is my desire pure enough?" a voice asks.

The entity swings its head toward the far corner of the room. From the shadows, Prescott emerges. He strides forward, looking as pulled together and confident as he did on my sidewalk six days ago.

"Ah, Prescott Jones." The entity draws out the s, like the hiss of a snake, and I think yes, that more than fits Prescott at the moment. "You are opportunistic and conniving—admirable traits for a necromancer."

"But is my desire pure enough?"

"I think you know it is." The entity glides forward.

The contrast between its movements and its form is disconcerting. I blink, trying to fight my sudden dizzy spell, but I slump against the pole instead.

"But here's my conundrum," the entity continues. "There are others in this room whose desire is just as pure, perhaps even more so. Why should I limit myself to you?"

"Because you know it's going to be good." Prescott hasn't lost his poise, and the grin he gives this thing is downright seductive.

"Yes, it would be. I'll grant you that."

I'm so caught up in this exchange that the sensation of fingertips moving along my arms takes me by surprise. I yelp and jerk against the pole. I don't know who's behind me, but I want nothing to do with them.

"Shh, Katy. It's me." The words are low and tense, but spoken with a slight southern drawl that I recognize.

Carter Dupree?

"I thought—" I begin, not certain exactly what I thought, only that I'd never see Carter again.

"That I ran off like a coward?"

Well, yes, and that.

"Next on the agenda," he says. "First, I'm going to cut the tie. Hold still. It's so tight I'm afraid I'll end up cutting your skin."

I glance about, nervous someone will notice us, and that someone will alert Orson. But everyone is focused on the entity and Prescott and their little passion play. Orson stands like a man transfixed, one hand still extended, the other in his suit coat pocket. I can't see his face, so I don't know if he's concocting another plan or simply mourning his lost chance at the entity.

"Why are you doing this?" I whisper.

Carter doesn't respond. All I hear is the scrape of blade against plastic.

"You're on the list, aren't you?" I say. "How many people does the entity have to burn through to get to you?"

"Not enough. But, yeah, I'm on the list. But that's not why I'm doing this."

"Then—?"

"I don't want to go through life as a pathetic little shit."

In that confession, I hear the echo of Belinda. It's exactly the sort of thing she'd say, and Carter is exactly the sort of person she'd say it to.

Prescott has taken a step closer to the entity. His arms are hanging loose at his sides, but the tips of his fingers are twitching. He looks like an athlete about to perform a major stunt.

The knife slips through the zip tie and the blade skitters down the pole. A clang echoes. I hold my breath and Carter ducks, but no one glances our way.

"Don't move." He grabs my wrists so I can't pull my hands to me. "You still need to look tied up."

I know he's right, but rush of blood into my fingers is excruciating, like tiny needles of fire. Carter rubs my hands between his, his touch oddly tender.

"There," he says. "Better? Can you move your fingers?"

I try, bending the fingers and frowning with the effort.

"You should be okay in a couple of minutes," he says, "and then you can do what you need to do."

"What I need to do?" I repeat the words, but I don't know what they mean.

Before us, in the center of the warehouse, the entity and Prescott appear locked in negotiation. Their words are too quiet for the rest of us to hear. Orson has crept even closer, although his gaze darts around the perimeter now and then. I suspect he's looking for someone in particular, someone who's standing right behind me.

"You need to capture that thing," Carter says.

"I ... what?"

"Think of the power it has. Think of the kind of power Orson wants to wield. He wants it all: money, political sway. The world's bad enough —we don't need him adding to its problems."

"Prescott—?"

"Do *you* trust him?"

I barely know him, and since he's the reason I'm here, I can't say my trust extends all that far.

"I don't know what he'd do with that sort of power," I admit. But, judging by the way Prescott's grinning, I can't suppose it's anything good.

"Me neither," Carter says. "That's a problem. Then there's you. I don't know what you would do, but I know what you wouldn't. That's enough."

"But I can't—"

"There's no one else, Katy. No one but you."

He's right, of course. Malcolm's too injured. Besides, he was once this thing's willing sacrifice. I'm not sure he's capable of capturing it.

"Assuming I can capture it and it doesn't burn through me, then what?"

"Get it away from Orson."

"I don't know how," I say. "I'm not a necromancer. I don't know how to capture it."

"Just focus on what you want most. Don't second-guess. Go with that one thought—that's the pure desire—and then do what Perry did."

"Was that—?" I nod toward the pile of ash.

"Yeah."

"Were you friends?"

"Kind of." He rubs my hands one last time and then gives my fingers a squeeze. "Good luck."

He's gone before I can crane my neck to watch him leave.

Both Orson and Prescott are focused on the entity. I glance around, but no one is guarding the perimeter of the warehouse anymore. Slowly, I ease my hands in front of me and then, at last, rub my wrists and fingers myself. The skin is raw and swollen. I flinch at my own touch. My fingers still feel thick and numb.

Orson has eased even closer. He's given up looking for Carter, and his full attention is on the entity. Prescott's gaze has never strayed. They've both forgotten about me, but there's one person here who hasn't.

Malcolm.

My eyes meet his. He tries to push to his elbows again, but his arms tremble and he collapses. It takes all my willpower not to rush to him, gather him close, and find a way to get us out of here. For a moment, I contemplate doing just that. The two of us walking out the door and not looking back. We would leave this mess behind us.

The thought of it brings a spate of tears to my eyes.

With gritty palms I push away the tears and take a step forward, not toward Malcolm but the entity.

He shuts his eyes and shakes his head. "Katy, don't."

I don't know if he says these words or if I merely hear them in my head.

"I have to."

"Please." He tries to push up again, but he's far too injured.

I know that if he could, he'd follow me. This might be the only time when I'm glad he can't. Someone will find him and take him to a hospital. He'll be safe.

"Goodbye," I whisper. "I love you."

Then I turn toward the entity and break into a run.

I'M A FEW SECONDS into my sprint when I know it's no good. My thoughts splinter into half a dozen, and then a dozen. And then I lose count of all the things I want. Because I want it all: I want Malcolm healed; I want Springside safe; I want all my ghosts back. I want Nigel and Sadie happily married.

My hiking boots clomp against the cement floor. This is hardly a stealth attack. First Orson and then Prescott turn at my approach. Orson looks livid. Despite the dim light of the warehouse, his face appears bright red. He must know it was Carter who betrayed him, cut me free. Prescott holds up a hand as if he means to stop my advance.

"Katy, no! You don't know what you're doing." Prescott takes a step, a move meant to block my access to the entity.

In that moment, Orson barrels into him, slamming Prescott to the ground and clearing my path to the entity. Like that, I'm there. I rise up on the tips of my boots, spread my arms wide, open my mouth, and dive forward.

My world shifts as if I've plunged into deep water. I panic, claw at the air. The warehouse around me is bright, as if someone has switched on all the lights or opened the roof to let the sunshine stream in. I see minute cracks in the cement and imperfections in the ceiling's paint job.

I whirl and stumble. I want to cry out, but can't find my voice.

Shh. Relax, my dear.

The voice echoes around me, through me. I spin, inspecting the far corners of the warehouse that I know, logically, I shouldn't be able to see, but I can't find the source of the words that echo in my head.

"I don't know what to do." I half-cry, half-speak these words. No one's listening. Orson and Prescott are circling each other. Orson has what looks like a walkie-talkie in one hand and what is definitely a pistol in the other.

Right now, you need to run.

"But—"

You're in no shape to take on Orson's reinforcements, my dear, or his bullets. So run, and believe you can run faster than you ever have before.

The panic subsides just enough that I can see at least a dozen men file into the warehouse. Orson shouts and gestures with the pistol. My gaze zooms in on Malcolm, still on the floor.

"Malcolm—" I begin.

I guarantee his safety, but I can only do so if you run.

I have no choice. I do what the voice inside my head commands.

I run.

I FEEL the sun on my face, my hair streaming behind me. Grass and trees and fences blur. Tears flow from my eyes, carve tracks to my ears.

I don't think it's possible to run this fast. Somehow, I am.

I run until the warehouse is no longer even a dot on the horizon behind me. I run cross-country where no car can follow. I find myself in a wooded area, pine needles raking my cheeks and bare arms, soft earth cushioning my footsteps.

Slow down ... it's time to slow down.

I can't. All I can think of is the mess I've left behind, the fact that I left Malcolm, and yet I can't get my legs to stop moving.

My power might be supernatural, but you are very human, my dear. You will hurt yourself if you keep up this pace.

I stumble, my arms flailing, and the jerky movements slow my momentum. The words echoing in my head slow me down even further until, at last, I clutch a slender birch tree for support.

I cling to it, the papery bark rustling beneath my grip. I take heaving breaths, and I feel the miles I've run in the ache of my legs, the blisters on my feet.

I wait.

My heartbeat slows. The sweat that pours off my skin cools me until I shiver. It's good to stand still, to clutch this slender birch. It's almost peaceful. But the anticipation of what comes next haunts me. Will it hurt? I think of Perry and how his eyes accused us.

Oh, yes. It will hurt.

My dear, what are you doing?

"Waiting."

Whatever for?

"For you to burn through me."

Laughter reverberates in my mind. It's one thing to have someone laugh *at* you. But inside you? I shake my head as if that would dislodge this thing.

Let's review this morning's events, shall we?

"I don't think I have a choice."

Oh, my dear, I knew you'd be a delight. Now, tell me. Why do you think I'd burn through you?

"My desire wasn't pure enough."

Orson's certainly wasn't. He wants too many things—and he knows it. Why do you think he lined up so many children in an attempt to hold me? There's no way he can. He wants that which he can never have.

"Immortality?"

That would be in the realm of possibility. No, he wants youth, specifically his own youth. That's something I'm unable to give.

"Then how...?" I'm not sure what I'm asking. How was Orson going to use the entity if he couldn't control it himself?

He thinks he can leverage me the way he would an ordinary ghost. Up to a point, he may have been correct. But not just any necromancer can hold me.

"Is that where Prescott comes in?"

Ah, Prescott Jones. Now there's a necromancer with an unwavering desire.

Something clicks. I see what it was that Orson wanted all along. To use me, both to call the entity and have it reside within me—to do his bidding, whatever that would've entailed.

"So when I wouldn't cooperate and join his club, he looked for another way?"

Precisely.

"And Prescott convinced him he was that way?"

Opportunistic and conniving. Admirable traits for a necromancer.

I don't even need to ask. Of course Prescott never had any intention of honoring the deal he made. Orson was simply a means to an end.

And so was I.

I'm not sure where this leaves me, other than stranded in some unfamiliar woods, waiting for a powerful entity to burn through me. I wonder if anyone will be able to find my pile of ash.

So, tell me, my dear, what was it that you wanted?

"I wanted everyone to be safe, Malcolm, Springside, the ghosts. I want Nigel and Sadie married." I glance around, gauge the slant of the sun through the trees. It's only hours until the ceremony, assuming there will still be one. "I kept thinking what might happen to the world if Orson or Prescott captured you and ... see? Too many things."

That laugh reverberates in my head again. *My dear, that's all part of the same desire. Of those assembled in that rather nasty warehouse, yours was the purest desire of all.*

I'm not sure I believe that. In fact, I'm expecting a trick.

Ever the skeptic.

I sigh. It's bad enough that this thing could always guess what I was thinking—now it has a front row seat.

It's part of the pact.

"I'm not a necromancer."

In this particular case, you are, and we have a pact. I admit, it's a unique experience. Everything inside here is so ... benign.

"That sounds insulting."

Not necessarily. Besides, benign isn't banal. If I've been used for evil in the past, it's because I've been captured by evil men—and women. Women can be powerful necromancers, present company included. But they don't do a great deal of capturing. I've always wondered why that is.

"They're too busy doing other things?" I suggest.

The entity laughs again. I press a hand against my head to stop the throbbing.

"Not so loud."

Forgive me, my dear.

"And why so polite?"

In part because we've made a pact. I ... adjust my persona depending upon the necromancer.

"Do I want to know what your Prescott persona would be?"

In a word? No.

This time, I laugh. And I can't believe I'm laughing, that this thing has made me laugh, that it's made me curious. I can't say I like it. It once took Malcolm. It nearly killed Nigel. And just this morning, I watched it destroy someone.

But I'm intrigued.

And scared.

But not fearful. I know, in this moment at least, that it won't hurt me —or anyone I love. That's something.

"Now what?"

I believe you're due at a wedding.

"And Malcolm?"

We can return to the warehouse. Anyone with bullets or an agenda is now gone.

I turn to face the way I came, a hand still gripping the birch as if it's the only thing holding me up.

"I don't know where to go."

Oh, but I do.

"Do I need to run again?"

That would be fastest.

I retie my hiking boots, adjust my socks, and then pull in a deep breath.

"All right," I say. "I'm ready."

You've been ready for a while, my dear. It's about time you accepted your ability as a necromancer.

I run so fast that the air buzzes in my ears. I run so fast I can pretend I haven't heard the entity's words.

~

THE WAREHOUSE HAS the feel of a building long abandoned. I walk through the area where I was held, but the space is empty. There's the cut plastic tie and strip of duct tape hanging loosely from the support pole, as if someone has torn something away. On the floor a few feet away there's blood.

"Malcolm?"

My voice bounces back at me, too loud, too desperate.

"Is he here?"

I direct this question at the entity, but the presence inside my head is oddly silent. No, it's more than that. The entity is no longer there. I don't know when, exactly, it peeled away from me, but I can tell now that it has.

I turn in a slow circle, as if I could somehow spot it in the warehouse.

It's gone, but instead of relief, nothing but dread fills me.

My footfalls follow me as I walk the perimeter of the space. Every few steps I spin around, certain someone is following me.

No one is there.

The wail doesn't register at first, although I'm not sure why. There's nothing else to hear but my own breathing and the sound of my hiking boots striking the concrete. The cry is quiet and plaintive, but also familiar. I halt in my trek, tilt my head, and listen.

The sound grows louder, as if a chorus of voices has joined it. I know this cry. I've heard this cry all my life.

Ghosts.

They're here—I look around—somewhere. I jog toward the door Orson's men dragged Malcolm through. I push and it opens slowly, hinges creaking. I grope the wall for a light switch. The overhead lamp flickers on and its hiss and crackle fill the air in between the cries of the ghosts.

The corridor is lined with doors, each shut. I try the first, and while the handle turns, I can't open the door. That's when I'm struck with a double sensation—a ward, warning me to back off, and the shimmery outline of a containment field.

I ignore the first and concentrate on the second. Within moments, its hold wavers and then shatters. The door flies open. An otherworldly blast knocks me against the opposite wall as a group of ghosts streams out.

Several ghosts head straight for the open air at the end of the hallway. A few swirl around me, peppering me with icy kisses. I reach out a hand as if I could pet them. These are Springside ghosts, every last one. I jump to my feet and start in on the other doors.

I've just removed the containment field from the last door when the ghost inside comes barreling out. This one is so strong that we tumble across the floor. Even with the noise of my boots thumping, I hear familiar ghostly laughter.

"Delilah?"

She surrounds me so completely I'm encased in mist.

I know I won't understand her answer, but I ask anyway. "How did they catch you again?"

Her form vibrates, and it's dark and angry. But then she swoops around me, plants a kiss on my cheek, and shoves me—hard.

"What the—"

She keeps shoving, and this is no sprite I'm dealing with. The only option I have is to trip over my hiking boots and try to figure out where she wants me to go. She encourages me down a second hallway, more dank and dark than the first. I slap the wall for the light and it barely illuminates a path in front of me.

The doors here are open, all but one. Something about that feels wrong. I stop and peer inside a room. It's several degrees colder than the air in the hallway, and there's what I can only describe as psychic residue within its space.

I think of Chief Ramsey's ghost, how scared and scarred it was, and wonder if it spent time in one of these rooms.

Delilah won't let me contemplate that for long. She shoves again, and again, I trip down the hallway.

The door at the very end is locked, not with a containment field, but truly locked. I rattle the handle to no avail. I don't have anything with me to open it with, but Delilah continues to push me against the door.

"Okay, okay. I get it," I say to her. "Just let me..."

What? I test the door again. It swings inward, or would if it were unlocked. The wood sounds hollow when I knock on it. The handle is flimsy and the lock jangles. I consider my boots, the door, and how much space there is for a running start. Enough, I decide. I back up, push off the opposite wall, and aim my heel at a spot below the lock.

The thud echoes, but nothing budges. The jolt makes my leg ache from heel to knee and all the way to my hip. Delilah swirls around me. I hold up a hand before she can crash into me again.

"A moment." I suck in a breath. "I'll try again in a moment."

I back up for another run. I wince as my boot connects with the door, but this time something gives. The wood splinters. I kneel at the door and rattle the handle again.

Something clicks. I'm so relieved I won't need to take another run at the door that I let my forehead rest against the wood. The door creaks open and I fall forward with it.

There, on the floor in front of me, is Malcolm.

I crawl to him. My fingers find a pulse at his throat, and his soft exhale warms my cheek. I roll him gently onto his back and check his injuries.

At first, I can't see any. I squint, then stagger to my feet and switch on the overhead bulb. It doesn't add much to the light already streaming in from the hall, but there's enough that I can check for all the wounds I saw earlier.

They don't exist.

Well, not entirely. Beneath where his lip was split open, there's the tiniest of scars. The bruises along his cheekbones have faded to a dull yellow, and I can only see them because I know to look for them. A tiny bump mars his near-perfect nose. His leg, so mangled earlier, appears straight, resting as it should on the ground.

His dress shirt is tattered and torn and covered with rust-colored stains. I peel it back carefully to reveal his ribs.

Here, too, are only the remnants of wounds.

I sit back on my heels, a hand still anchored to Malcolm's chest. Instead of relief, terror zips through me. I can't account for this, and I search for the source of this magic, for the trick, the trap.

There's nothing but Delilah's soft swishing about.

"Thank you," I say to her.

Healed or not, I can't imagine what would've happened to Malcolm if I'd left him behind. I brush strands of hair from his forehead and then stand.

I have someone else to thank.

I step into the hallway. Except for Delilah and a few other ghosts milling about, I'm alone. I know that. I say the words out loud anyway.

"Thank you." I direct the words toward the sky, although why the entity should be up—and not down—I don't know. "I wanted Malcolm healed, and you did so." I squeeze my eyes shut to stop the tears flirting at their corners. I don't know why it means so much that he's whole and well and will be able to stand up for Nigel today, but it does.

"Thank you," I say one last time before ducking back into the room.

I FIND A KITCHEN AREA, some bottled water, and grab a fistful of paper towels. I sit at Malcolm's side and bathe his face and hands in the cool water until his eyelids start to flutter. All at once, his eyes fly open and he shields his face with a hand to block the glare.

"I'm sorry," I say. "I had to turn on the light to make sure you were okay."

"Katy?" His voice is rough and full of disbelief.

"It's me. I'm here."

"Katy?" He pushes up slowly, first to his elbows, and then to sitting.

"Yes, it's me. I'm here." I sound like an idiot, repeating myself. But giddiness bubbles up inside me because Malcolm is awake and whole.

He touches his temple and winces as though he expects it to hurt. He probes his cheekbones, his nose, and runs his hands along his ribcage. Gingerly, he bends his knee and inspects his shin.

"I ... remember being a whole lot more injured than this."

I nod. "You were."

"And I remember thinking"—he squeezes his eyes shut—"that I'd never see you again."

"Do you still hurt?"

I'm contemplating a dash for the kitchen area to search for some ice. In fact, I'm crouching to do just that when Malcolm's fingers wrap around my wrist, anchoring me in place. His skin feels right against mine, not cold and clammy, not heated with fever.

"If I think about it," he says, "I can remember it, remember them beating me, but it feels more like it happened in a dream than real life. I didn't know who they were or why they were doing it until they dragged me into that room and I heard you."

He cringes again, and I think I must as well. That's not something I care to remember. But his pained expression fades and he brushes a strand of hair from my cheek. His touch is so gentle it's like he's afraid I might shatter.

"Did they hurt you?" he asks, and something about his voice tells me he's bracing for the worst possible answer.

I hold out my wrists. "Only where they…"

I turn my hands first one way and then the other. I feel the ache from the zip tie, but the burns are gone. Malcolm holds my wrist close and runs a finger along the line where the plastic bit into my skin.

"Right here," he says. "This is from where they tied you up. You can barely see it."

His finger traces a path that sends a shiver through me. He tugs me close so I'm in his lap, his arms around mine. It's safe here in this pocket of warmth he's created, even in this dank room, even if the aroma of stale sweat and scotch reminds me of how we both got here.

"What happened today?" he asks. "What happened after they forced you to invoke the entity?"

I exhale and sag against his chest. "I'm still not sure. It's almost like I need a scorecard to keep track. First, Prescott betrayed Orson, then Orson had a gun—"

"Are you serious?" A gun? He was going to shoot Prescott?"

"I think so, at some point. But Prescott and the entity seemed to be negotiating, and Orson just stood there. It was weird."

"Oh," Malcolm says. "Of course."

"Of course what?"

"A ghost or entity is most vulnerable right after making a pact with a necromancer. The deal must be set. If something happens to the necromancer before that, things … get out of balance. It's possible Orson could've contained it without too much effort. He was waiting for Prescott to make a move."

"And the entity was waiting for me."

His arms tighten around mine. "What happened, exactly?"

The story comes out much like that of a dream, nonsensical except to the dreamer. As I speak, I feel Malcolm react as if what I'm saying makes sense. He nods, murmurs something to himself. When I've finished, he shifts and takes my face in his hands.

"Where's the entity now?" he asks.

"I don't know. I got back here and—" I wave a hand toward the door and start to turn that way, but Malcolm tugs me back.

"Look at me, Katy. Look at me right in the eyes."

I relent and allow myself to simply stare into those dark eyes of his. In the dim light they appear nearly black. I want to erase the worry I see there, but for the moment hold still.

He searches my face, runs his finger along my left cheek. From the way he traces the mark so perfectly, I know the faded blue reminder of that encounter remains.

"Do you sense it?" he asks.

"No. I got back here and it was like it had vanished. Delilah helped me find you—"

"Damn, they caught her again?"

"They did." I search the air around us for something otherworldly, but don't detect anything strong enough to be Delilah. "She might be gone by now, and even though it had vanished, I thanked the entity for healing you—"

"Wait." Malcolm scoots back as if he needs to survey my whole being. "You *thanked* the entity?"

"It healed you. Malcolm, you were—"

"Close to dead. I know." His lips compress into a hard line, but almost immediately soften. "Maybe that's it," he says. "By thanking the entity, you honored the pact. It needed to get away from Orson just as much as you did. It healed me, and you." He brushes the tender underside of my wrist with his lips. "You thanked it and set it free."

"Do you think that's it?"

"Maybe? I don't know. Reginald might, and so might Nigel."

"Who's getting married in ... how many hours?"

Malcolm scoots me back and pushes to stand. When he offers a hand and I take it, he pulls me into a hug.

"Cell phone?" he asks.

"Nope."

"Same here."

"There's a kitchen area. There might be a landline."

Without another word, we leave the room. On our way out, I shut off the light and close the door. It seems like such a silly thing to do, and the hinges screech as if in agreement. But it feels good to shut all that behind us.

In the kitchen, Malcolm picks up the receiver of the phone that's hanging on the wall. The whole thing sheds a layer of dust. He blows on the keypad and creates another cloud.

But then he turns to me, one of his sweet, dark-roast grins on his face.

"Dial tone," is all he says.

"R EALLY?" MALCOLM GLANCES at me and raises an eyebrow. "Do we warrant a police escort?"

I don't know if we warrant it, but one is winding its way up the long road to the warehouse. The lights of the patrol car are flashing. It's leading the convoy, followed by Reginald's Land Rover. Dust billows behind them, painting the clear air a dull brown.

We've only just stepped into the sunlight after spending the last hour huddled over the phone in the kitchen area. We took turns relating the tale, from Malcolm's kidnapping—in the guise of a faked pizza delivery—to mine, to the entity's appearance and then everyone's disappearance.

Nigel's and Belinda's still-panicked voices filled the line, punctuated by Reginald's more measured tone. We learned how Nigel had found my thermos and called Chief Ramsey when he couldn't find Malcolm, how Belinda had called Nigel when she discovered the guest room Carter was staying in was vacant and I wasn't at home. How Reginald had sent ghosts to track down Prescott, Malcolm, and me—without any luck.

During all of that, Malcolm held me close, his cheek next to mine, his lips brushing the sensitive skin at the corner of my mouth. His sigh was half worry and half relief, but toward the end of the call, held nothing but elation.

Now, as we stand here in the sun, I feel it too, even if a patrol car is making its way toward me.

Both vehicles pull to a stop in front of us. Nigel and Belinda spill out of the Land Rover. Nigel staggers a little before lurching toward Malcolm and gripping him in a strong hug.

Belinda captures me in a hug of her own before pulling out her cell phone and aiming it first at the two of us and then at Malcolm and Nigel.

"See?" she says into the camera. "They're both safe."

A strangled cry, a flash of pink, and I know that it's Sadie on the other end.

"I don't know what you said to Carter, but if it wasn't for you," I say to Belinda, "I'm not sure what would've happened."

"Right. *Please*." Belinda rolls her eyes. "I'm not the one facing down power-obsessed necromancers and scary lava entities."

I open my mouth to protest—because really, without her help, without Carter's change of heart, we wouldn't all be standing here—but she shushes me with a single glance, her *don't cross the homecoming queen* look.

So I don't.

Nigel is holding Malcolm at arm's length now, surveying him for any telltale injuries. "I don't care if you pay me in cups of Katy's coffee from now on. Just don't ... don't go getting yourself killed."

Their second hug is less frantic, but more healing. Malcolm is murmuring something that sounds like "I'm sorry."

I feel the urge to apologize too, although I don't know to whom or why. Then Chief Ramsey steps into view and I know the answer.

He doesn't speak, simply walks toward me and extends my thermos in one hand.

"Yours, I believe," he says.

I nod and take it from him.

"I think I remember saying to call if something out of the ordinary happened?" His tone isn't so much accusatory as it is disappointed and sad.

"I know," I say, and my words are miserable. "It was a trick. I thought it was Malcolm who was texting me."

I don't elaborate. Chief wouldn't believe most of the story anyway.

He pulls something from his pocket and hands it to me. My cell phone. My mouth drops open and I stare up at him in question.

"You need to change your code," he says. "*Coffee* is too obvious."

I turn the phone over in my hands. The last time I held it, I tucked it into the field kit, which ended up on the floor of a dark sedan. "But how...?"

"Someone turned it in," Chief says as if reading my thoughts.

"Someone?"

He shrugs. "Placed it on Penny's desk when she wasn't looking."

"You don't have any surveillance footage of that?"

"Maybe I do, maybe I don't, and maybe, at this point, it doesn't matter."

And maybe he's right.

"Unless we're going to talk about pressing charges."

"Charges?"

"Kidnapping, for one."

I shake my head, not in denial, but because I'm at a loss. "I wouldn't know where to start. I don't think anyone involved will be easy to find."

"That's not your job." He jabs a finger at me. "You got that? Not. Your. Job."

"Can it wait until after the wedding?"

My words find their mark. A rare and genuine smile brightens Chief's face. "It can," he says. "Besides, I need to walk the bride down the aisle."

Nigel's at my side then, and his expression steals all my thoughts. I forget to thank Chief. I can't do anything but deal with the man in front of me, the man I very much want Sadie to marry this afternoon.

"Katy ... I'm so sorry. I know how Prescott is, but I never imagined he had any sort of agenda, otherwise, I would've never—"

"It's not your fault."

"If you don't, I mean, if you'd rather not—"

"Not what? Not be part of the wedding?" Once again, my mouth hangs open. I glance about, hoping for some help.

Malcolm's eyes are uncertain, and his skin holds a pallor. Belinda frowns. Reginald steps forward, abandoning his spot in the shade of the Land Rover. He places a hand on Nigel's shoulder, securing him in place.

"My friend, you're handling this badly." Reginald turns to me. "What Nigel means is, he'd understand if all you want to do is return home and not attend the wedding tonight."

"But your wedding saved me." I point at Malcolm. "It saved us. It's all I could think about. Carter said I had to hold one thought in my head to catch the entity, but I couldn't. It was Malcolm and you and Sadie, and everyone. My last thought was about the wedding. But it worked, and now that's all I want to do."

Reginald places a gentle hand on my shoulder. "In other words, she is very much looking forward to the wedding."

I can't help but crack a smile, and Nigel gives me one in return.

"Will you?" Nigel says to Reginald.

"Of course, with her permission." He turns to me. "Katrina Lindstrom, I ask your permission to search for the entity. Do you grant it?"

I nod. "Yes, please. I think it's gone, but I don't know for certain."

"See? She's willing," he says to Nigel. "A good sign."

Reginald positions himself across from me. His form blocks the sun. He's as big as Chief Ramsey, and I sense Chief himself stir, move forward, as if he doesn't quite trust Reginald.

As Malcolm did, he takes my face in his hands and stares into my eyes. His scrutiny unnerves me. I want to pull away but, at the same time, resist that urge. This is important. And if the entity isn't truly gone, I want to know.

"Malcolm did this," I say. "He checked."

"I have more years of practice than your young beau."

A blush erupts in my cheeks, one I'm certain Reginald can feel beneath his fingers. At last his gaze shifts from my eyes and centers on my left cheek. He turns my face toward the sun and draws a thumb along the perimeter of the faded blue spot.

At last he steps back. "I detect nothing."

Nigel exhales. Malcolm's eyes brighten, his natural color returning.

"That's no guarantee," Reginald adds. "This is an entity, and an ancient one at that, not a ghost. The rules differ."

"You only deal with ghosts?" I ask.

"I try to. They can be capricious, but their wants are few and often predictable." He nods to the thermos I'm still clutching. "As you already know. Dealing with an entity like this is more like dealing with a very powerful, very exacting human being. You mentioned that you thanked it?"

"I did."

"Perhaps that was all it needed."

"Then we're good to go?" Belinda strides forward. She surveys each of us, hands on hips. "Because there's a wedding in a few hours and a maid of honor in desperate need of a makeover."

Nigel laughs and pulls both Malcolm and me into a hug. Reginald looks serene, if somber, and even Chief manages a smile.

Before we leave, I uncap the thermos. Steam rises into the air and against my face. The Kona blend is perfect drinking temperature. The thermos itself is one of a set of precision-made German ones designed to do just this—keep the coffee hot for as long as possible.

When no one is looking, I set the thermos on the ground, cap at its side. I'll buy a new set, I decide, to replace the one I've lost. And I will leave this one behind because I don't need a reminder of this place.

As we drive off in Reginald's Land Rover, I turn to peer out the back. A glimmer streams from the dark recesses of the warehouse. And around the thermos, I swear I see at least one ghost dance.

C H A P T E R   8

T HE BRIDAL CHORUS might be the most wonderful thing I've heard all day. I've just reached the makeshift altar when the first strains fill the Springside Community Center ballroom.

Nigel is a statue as he waits for Sadie to walk down the aisle. Only the slight tapping of fingertips against his thigh betrays his true state. His pure white hair matches his tuxedo shirt, and the tux itself looks tailor-made for him.

And then there's his brother. I sneak a glance at Malcolm and feel my cheeks burn brighter than my dress. He's always pulled together, but this takes it up a level. His hair gleams like ebony, and between the jacket, shirt, and bowtie, he looks as if he's stepped out of a fashion magazine. I predict there will be a long line of women at the reception wanting to dance with him.

He catches my gaze and gives me a wink. Then he tilts his head as if he's considering me, the ice-pink bridesmaid dress, and the single pink rose I'm carrying. He raises an eyebrow, nods, and mouths the word, "Nice."

And I'm blushing all over again.

I know when Sadie begins to walk down the aisle on the arm of Chief

463

Ramsey, because a gasp goes up behind me. I'm not supposed to turn to look, so I don't. Nigel appears petrified in place.

And then she's there, the blush-colored wedding gown like pink foam, the two dozen pink roses in her bouquet, and the pink highlights in her salt-and-pepper hair bathing her in their glow. When Nigel turns and sees her, his entire demeanor changes. The smile vanquishes the worry from his face, and the love in his eyes is so intense, I feel it like a stab in my stomach.

This. They almost lost this. *We* almost lost this. This moment. I suck in a breath and I swear I don't release it until after Sadie and Nigel have recited their vows, after the judge has pronounced them husband and wife, after Nigel has kissed Sadie and they're heading back down the aisle in a shower of rose petals.

I nearly sag against Malcolm when he takes my arm and we follow them.

"You okay?" he whispers.

I manage a nod.

"Fair warning," he continues. "I have it on good authority that the bridal bouquet will be headed your way like a heat-seeking missile."

That makes me laugh.

"You're beautiful," he says.

"So are you."

"But you know what?" He leans down, his lips next to my ear in an almost-kiss. "My favorite is still the skater skirt with the hiking boots."

SADIE'S SPRITES have behaved themselves for the entire ceremony and reception—until now. I allowed them to attend as long as they didn't cause trouble. But they have all the willpower and attention span of a pair of toddlers. I track them overhead as they flit among the ballroom's light fixtures. When they land on the floor they are the "breeze" that kicks up the rose petals. When a centerpiece on one of the tables starts to wobble, I know I will need to act soon.

I scan the dance floor. Sadie is dancing with Nigel, her head on his shoulder, his lips in her hair. Belinda is swaying in the arms of Jack

Carlotta, who drove down from Minneapolis for the ceremony. Her eyes are closed, her expression content, even if her smile is wistful.

Maybe because at a table not too far away, Gregory and Terese are sitting side by side, fingers laced. Her gaze tracks the sprites as they careen around the room, and her face is lit with amusement. Gregory? He's oblivious, as usual.

I'm not sure I like these new-old arrangements, but I'm not sure I dislike them either.

Malcolm is executing a stately foxtrot with one of the women from the long-term care facility. There really is a line, and where he's finding the energy—after everything—to dance with each of them amazes me.

But it means I can sneak into the kitchen area and dig out the carafe of Kona blend that I promised Sadie's two sprites.

The kitchen is still in chaos, with dishes everywhere, slices of cake wrapped up for later, empty bottles of champagne and sparkling grape juice. Splotches of gravy speckle the countertops. Somewhere in this mess is a bowl of sugar, and in the fridge a container of half and half. Sadie's sprites like their coffee sweet and light—to match their personalities—and will refuse anything else. If I'm not precise, I'll end up with a coffee-colored bridesmaid dress.

I line up sugar, spoons, two cups, and the carafe itself. I'm turning for the refrigerator when an otherworldly blast propels me against it. My body thumps against the side, hip striking the door handle. I'm pinned in place, cheek against the cool surface, my hands immobile.

I can't move, can't speak. I take tiny breaths since at the moment, I can barely breathe. Icy fingers clutch my throat and tighten their hold inch by inch. It's a slow thing, this choking off of my air—and deliberate. I know this thing that has me in its grip, and it wants that acknowledgement.

It's the ghost of Harold Lancaster.

I open my mouth to scream, to call for help, to alert Malcolm, but nothing emerges. With eyes closed, I work to contain my panic and conserve what little air I have. It's not letting me speak, so I can't negotiate. Even if I could, Harold is one of the rare ghosts that hate coffee. After a moment, his hold wavers—slightly. He can't hold me off the floor and choke me all at once. When his grip lessens, I work my hands beneath me, hoping to push from the refrigerator and break the ghost's grasp. I freeze when footfalls sound behind me.

"It seems someone was left off the guest list."

The voice is smooth and controlled and belongs to Orson Yates. I'm not sure whether to be shocked or impressed that he has the gall to show up here. Chief Ramsey is in the next room, and while he might be in his dress uniform, he's certainly capable of slapping on a pair of handcuffs.

"You may have noticed that he's quite upset about that—and with you." Orson tsks, and the sound plays counterpoint to his shoes striking the linoleum floor. "I can't believe you, of all people, left a poor, defenseless ghost out in the middle of nowhere, in all that cold and snow. And you accuse me of cruelty."

He's at my side now, his face even with mine. "I only give them what they want, after all. That's more than you ever do."

With Orson's proximity, the hold on my throat grows ever tighter. My vision tunnels, and I know I'm not getting enough air to either fight or think. Waves of hatred wash over me, but at the moment, I know this: if Harold's ghost is here with me, he can't ruin Sadie's wedding.

"We'll deal with the rest of the wedding party later," Orson says, as if he's reading my thoughts. No doubt that small relief played across my face. "It'd be a terrible thing for Nigel to relapse before the honeymoon even started, but I think I can arrange that. As for your blonde friend, the one who got under Carter's skin? Oh, I have a particular ghost in mind for her."

I manage a muffled cry but nothing else.

"And, of course, Malcolm. This time around, he won't make such a miraculous recovery. But first you will die knowing you caused all that."

I try to shove against the refrigerator door. I try to draw a breath. My throat is closed. My lungs burn for air. Tears sting my cheeks, the skin raw.

"Let her go."

The words are inexplicably calm and soothing. While I recognize the voice, my panicked, oxygen-deprived mind can't put a name to it. Who is here in this room with us? Is he here to help?

"Think about it, my friend," the voice continues. "You are not truly angry with her, are you? She is not the one who engineered your pain, is she?"

The grip on my throat eases slightly. I gulp in a breath, and it rasps against my windpipe. My fingertips claw against the refrigerator's smooth surface. I can't find purchase, but that doesn't stop me from trying.

Something glimmering and cool touches my cheeks. Sprites—two of them—swoop around my face, dry my tears. Their presence registers and so does this new voice. I know who's responsible for my rescue. Sadie's sprites must have alerted Reginald, who now speaks to Harold's ghost in low, even tones.

"You're too late," Orson says.

"And you're not welcome here," Reginald counters. "As you already know."

"What? Did you place a ward around a *community* center?"

"I don't need to. You have no true power. Not over this ghost, not over anyone here."

Then, as if Reginald has commanded it, Harold's ghost releases its grip completely. I sink to the floor as it ricochets off the refrigerator and arrows straight into Orson.

He stumbles backward, and there's a crashing that I hear more than see. A dish shatters and pots clatter, but I don't check the damage. I'm concentrating on the floor, on pushing myself to my feet. The sprites swirl about me. In my current state, I can hear them clearly. Their chatter fills my ears, full of concern—and suggestions on how to fix my dress once I do stand.

Harold's ghost has gone beyond murderous. The gale it creates around Orson tears tiny pieces of his suit from his body, yanks strands of hair from his head.

Reginald claps twice, and the otherworldly cyclone stops all at once. The ghost retreats, returning to him, much like a dog might return to its owner.

"It's over now," Reginald says to the glimmer caught between his outstretched hands. "You can come with me and find the will to heal."

From the other side of the room, laughter rings out. "Is that what you do with your time? What *is* it you do, exactly, Reginald? Run a ghost rehab center?"

"What I spend most of my time on is fixing your mistakes and repairing the damage you do. You waste your talent."

"Odd. I was thinking the same about you."

"You have a single chance to leave," Reginald says. "Not only does this ghost want to destroy you, but the police might wish to arrest you."

"Whatever for?"

"Kidnapping, I believe. Assault, perhaps. I'm not sure of all the charges, but I'm certain they're serious."

"Yes, and when the story comes out about ghosts and entities and the like, I'm sure it will hold up in the courts. That's why we get to do what we do. The world is filled with nonbelievers." Orson adjusts his suit coat jacket and tugs at his cuffs so they shoot past the sleeves. "Trust me, I am not a man you want to fight in a court of law."

I listen with dismay. I know Orson is right. Chief has a hard enough time grappling with evidence of the supernatural, even with the two sprites that haunt the police station. Then there's everyone else in the system. I wouldn't ask him to put his reputation on the line, not for this, not when we can deal with Orson ourselves.

At least, I think we can.

I cast a quick look at Reginald. He's still holding the ghost between the palms of his hands. Malcolm and I once went up against someone who claimed to be a ghost whisperer. She was a fraud, of course. But Reginald? That's exactly what he does. Emotion drains from Harold's ghost. It quivers, and it's not anger that I feel roll off of it, but a deep exhaustion.

"Leave," Reginald says. "This fight is over, and if you persist, I promise you, the retribution will be swift."

"Really? You think you can gather enough necromancers to counter me?"

"I know I can."

"Perhaps you can, but I doubt they can counter this." Orson shuts his eyes. A second later, a word emerges from his mouth, a word only I should know.

"Momalcurkan."

"No." I whisper the word and look in panic to Reginald again.

His face appears waxy. I don't need to explain what that means. He recognizes the name for what it is, for what it can do.

But how? Orson was standing too far away to hear me speak the entity's name. I said it softly on purpose, to keep something like this from happening. An image of myself tethered to the pole fills my mind, and then, the zip tie curled at the bottom and a strip of duct tape flapping by a spot above my head.

"He recorded me," I say quietly.

Orson laughs. "Indeed I did, and thanks to you, I will forever have this entity at my disposal."

"It's not going to be happy," I mutter.

Orson scoffs. "Its happiness is not my concern."

Already, a spot on the floor is swirling as if it's made of liquid. Sadie's sprites zip past my face, each planting a quick kiss on my cheek, and zoom from the kitchen. I don't blame them. If I could zoom out of here like a sprite, I would.

The form that emerges from the spot is not the craggy, lava-eyed beast of the warehouse, but something more human, its shape bathed in a cloud of inky smoke. The smoke solidifies until at last what could be a handsome man in a well-tailored suit is standing in the center of the kitchen.

"You'll pardon my tardiness," the entity says. "I had to dress for the occasion." It turns to me. "And, my dear, I am always positively giddy to see you, although you do have more sense than to invoke me twice in one day, unlike some people."

Orson launches himself across the room. I scramble, but I'm too weak from my encounter with Harold's ghost, my ballet flats too slick against the linoleum, my dress too cumbersome. He reaches the entity first, spreads his arms and opens his mouth wide.

Reginald moves to my side as if together we might be able to fight Orson once he's united with the entity.

But instead of capturing it, instead of the entity vanishing before us, Orson simply passes through. His momentum carries him forward and he smacks the kitchen floor with his hands and knees.

The entity's form solidifies further, or at least the foot he aims at

Orson does. The toe of the entity's shoe connects with Orson's backside. The force propels him against a row of cabinets. Dishes and pans rattle inside.

We're making so much noise, I'm certain someone else must be able to hear. I glance over my shoulder at the swinging doors, peer through the small window. The wedding reception beyond is going on as if the four of us are trapped in an invisible, soundproof room.

"That was part of your desire, was it not, my dear?" the entity says. "A perfect wedding for your friend?"

"We still have a pact?" I ask, and I see the same question reflected in Orson's eyes, an incredulous expression clawing its way through the pain.

But I don't truly need to ask. My connection to this thing runs through me. I feel it now. I touch the faded blue spot on my cheek and wonder why I couldn't feel it before.

Reginald hangs his head. In shame? In despair? I can't tell, but this certainly isn't his fault. An entity this strong could hide itself from all of us. Reginald said so himself.

Across the room, Orson swears. When it gets personal, the entity flicks a hand in his direction and sends Orson slamming against the cabinets once again.

"Cease. You will not speak of my necromancer like that."

Orson staggers to his feet. "But the pact ... after—"

"After we escaped your murderous children? You expected Katy to sever the pact. Did you not orchestrate the entire encounter, even to the point of letting Prescott Jones believe he could double-cross you? It would be far easier to secure me from her than it would be from him."

Orson blinks and sways. He reaches for the counter, and when his palm makes contact, sags into the support.

"But you had to make certain, didn't you?" the entity continues. "No sense invoking me if I'm still claimed. That gets ... messy." It raises its hands, indicating the kitchen around us. "But you hoped Katy would be happy to be rid of me, isn't that right?"

"Actually, I was." I see no point in lying. This thing has always read my thoughts.

The entity laughs, and it's a strange, hollow sound. "That's why I left you alone. I'm an acquired taste, even for the most experienced necromancer."

"The pact was severed," Orson says. "It must be. The exchange was made; each side benefited. You should be mine."

"And yet, I'm not."

The entity walks about the kitchen. Anyone peeking through the window would think the four of us are simply standing in here, chatting about the wedding or refilling our champagne glasses. They would think the entity was an exceedingly handsome man, although they wouldn't be able to recall his features once they glanced away.

When it stares at me straight on, all I can see is a swirling black void. I want to blink or glance away myself, but I can't. It holds me in its non-gaze for a moment and then stalks toward Orson.

"I'll grant you that humans have only graced this planet for a short duration. Still, in all that time, not a single necromancer has bothered to display any gratitude. Until now. The pact remains. No, the pact is strengthened." The entity raises a finger. "Take note for next time."

"So, if I have a pact with you," I say, choosing my words carefully, "then no one else can. Is that right?"

"That's correct." It's Reginald who says this. He turns toward the entity. "Don't put this burden on her. Let her go. You can retreat to another plane and end your interaction with humans."

"Why would I do that? I haven't had this much enjoyment in eons. Besides"—he sweeps a hand in my direction—"it's entirely up to Katy."

I can't sever the pact, not with Orson standing there, not with Orson anywhere. I can't risk it; I can't risk someone finding the recording of the entity's name. I'm stuck with this thing, possibly forever.

"Oh, really, my dear. Stuck? I'm crushed."

I glower at it, and the thing has the audacity to laugh.

"Katrina Lindstrom, this is far more serious than you realize," Reginald says.

I shake my head. "No, I realize."

"It will want things from you."

I imagine it will.

"Your life won't be your own."

That, too.

I turn to Reginald then. "Do you know of some other way? If I sever the pact, then Orson will invoke the entity and use it to do who knows what."

"Or your friend here might be tempted to do the same," the entity says. "Oh, Reginald, think of the *good* you could do with me at your disposal."

Reginald goes waxy again and refuses to meet my eyes. Orson snorts. I see the temptation, feel the tug of it myself. Even now, the urge to flick my wrist in Orson's direction and have the entity dispatch him is nearly overwhelming. It would be so easy, so simple.

So wrong. The world doesn't work that way, and what you get you must pay for eventually.

I won't pay like that.

"Oh, this is going to be interesting," the entity says.

Before I can contradict it, Malcolm bursts through the kitchen doors. His eyes are wide with panic, and when he spots Orson, his expression turns downright lethal. He launches himself across the room.

Malcolm might be younger and stronger, but the last time I saw Orson, he had a gun.

"No!"

My voice rings out, and the world stops. Or, at least, part of the world does. Malcolm is frozen in midair. Orson has one hand in his suit coat pocket. He's always so calm and smooth that, at first, I don't realize he's frozen as well.

That's when I notice the bulge in his pocket.

The entity glides across the floor. Its hand appears to dissolve as it infiltrates the fabric of Orson's suit coat. A moment later, it pulls out a pistol.

"We can't leave this here, can we?" the entity says. "A round in the chamber is far too dangerous, what with children and sprites about."

The entity holds the pistol in its outstretched palm. A thousand tiny cracks form on the surface, then those splinter into a thousand more. The pistol shatters into nothing but a handful of dark grains.

The entity brushes the last bits of black sand from its hands and then inclines its head toward me.

"You see, my dear? A pact isn't such a terrible thing."

My heart races. I feel gutted, and I really don't know what's worse—that I've nearly lost Malcolm twice in one day or that I'm forever beholden to this entity for saving him.

The entity stalks toward me. It knows me, must feel my ambivalence toward it. Of course, it doesn't have an expression; there's nothing but that swirling black void where a face should be. So what it thinks, what it feels, will remain a mystery.

"It has been a rough day, has it not?" it says.

I give a single, numb nod.

"And you haven't danced once with your young man." It casts a glance toward Malcolm, still suspended, still trying to come to my rescue. "He is awfully pretty. I can see why you're so taken with him." It gives me a once-over. "But not like this."

Then, like a fairy godmother, it waves one of its hands. The wrinkles vanish from my dress. A tear along the hem repairs itself. I feel the sticky residue of salt leave my face, lips smoothed with a fresh coat of gloss, hair contained in a chignon.

"There we are. You're a picture, my dear." The entity touches my cheek, the left one, and I feel nothing but the void. "As for the rest, I believe the three of you can handle things."

In a puff of black, inky smoke, the entity vanishes.

Orson lets out a long gasp and clutches at his empty pocket. Malcolm's feet hit the floor with a thud. I rush for him, wrapping my arms around his before he can launch himself at Orson again.

Then the four of us—Malcolm, Reginald, Orson, and me—stare at each other. At last, Reginald clears his throat.

"You had the chance to leave, Orson Yates. Now you have another. This time, I suggest you take it."

Orson pats his suit coat, his trousers.

Reginald shakes his head. "It's gone. You'll have to buy yourself a new one if you wish to shoot someone."

Orson flicks a murderous glance in my direction.

"And don't blame her. She didn't invoke the entity." Reginald regards me for a moment, then turns back to Orson. "Think of where your greed has led you. Perhaps it's not where you wish to be."

I'm still clutching Malcolm tight, but now he turns in my arms and scrutinizes my face. "The entity?"

"He knows its name," I say. "Others do too." I nod toward Reginald. "Orson recorded me, so really, anyone could know."

Malcolm's gaze flickers about the kitchen as if he's aware of missing something crucial. "Then it isn't gone."

I shake my head. I want to cry, but can't find the tears.

Malcolm breaks from my grasp and strides across the room. He collars Orson, twisting the fabric of his suit coat in a tight grip.

"This is where I make a joke about taking out the trash," he says. "But I'm not really in the mood for jokes." He yanks on the coat and drags Orson from the kitchen.

In the quiet that follows, Reginald speaks. "This isn't over for you," he says.

"I know."

"The entity finds you intriguing."

"That isn't good, is it?"

"I'm afraid not." He releases a long breath. "You must tell Malcolm what happened."

"I will."

I peer through the window into the ballroom, where the reception is still in full swing. Nearly everyone is dancing. Nigel twirls Sadie, and I feel the bass thumping beneath the soles of my ballet flats.

I will tell Malcolm. We'll figure out what to do, together. But now? I want him to come back so we can rejoin the party. I want to dance at Sadie and Nigel's wedding. I want to drink champagne that matches the rose petals. I want everything in the room beyond, and certainly the entity knew that from the start.

Malcolm returns to the kitchen, winded, his gaze anxious until it lands on me.

"Katy?"

I hold out my hand. "Let's go dance."

"But—"

"Nothing's really changed, and Orson's gone, right?"

"Oh, yeah. He's gone."

Malcolm's expression is more than a little self-satisfied. I decide not to ask about the circumstances of Orson's exit. Instead, I nod toward the reception. "Then I want to be out there."

Before we can leave the kitchen, Reginald touches my arm.

"You must tell him," he says, his voice so low it only reaches my ears.

"I will."

But not tonight.

CHAPTER 9

THE SONGS HAVE SLOWED, and the crowd on the dance floor has thinned. An hour ago, Sadie tossed her bouquet at me. It went off course, and Chief Ramsey was nearly the lucky recipient until Sadie's two sprites intervened.

At the last second, and in a spray of petals, it split in two. I caught one half, Belinda the other. It makes me wonder what the sprites know that we don't.

Malcolm has shed his tuxedo jacket. I've left my ballet flats beneath a chair. He's held me close for the last five songs, and no one has tried to interrupt us. My head is resting against his chest and I've been playing a game where I tug at the end of his bowtie to loosen it.

"You've got to stop that," he says, repressed laughter rumbling beneath my cheek.

"Why?" I go for wide-eyed innocence. I'm not certain it works.

"Because I actually don't want you to stop."

Oh? *Oh.* I smile to myself before peering up at him. "What if I don't want to stop either?"

He slows our steps. "Katy, after everything that's happened today, I don't think—"

"Well, I do think, *especially* after everything that's happened today." I wrap my arms tighter around his neck. "I don't want to let you go, not after everything that's happened. So, will you stay with me? Stay the night? In the morning, I'll brew you some Kona blend."

He laughs and pulls me closer. I don't push the idea. I think, maybe, he needs to live with the notion for a few minutes. As a precaution, I cast my thoughts upward. Something about the entity has been bothering me. I suspect our connection goes back much further, before the warehouse, before it marked my cheek, before its appearance at the mausoleum.

Ah, very astute, my dear.

I can't imagine what the connection is, or how far back it goes. I won't ask. I doubt it would tell me, anyway.

You're correct. I won't.

But I want it to tell me one thing.

Do I have tonight? I send the thought skyward, through the pink balloons that are bobbing along the ballroom's ceiling, and into the warm spring night.

The echo of that metallic laugh fills the room. To everyone else, it must sound like the community center's ventilation system groaning to life.

Yes. You have tonight.

Relief washes through me. I clutch Malcolm ever closer.

Enjoy.

I sigh. I could really do without the commentary.

"Katy?"

Malcolm murmurs my name against my hair. His voice is tender and warm. The fragrance of rose petals mixes with his nutmeg and Ivory Soap scent, and the combination is a heady thing that makes me sway.

"Are you sure?" he asks, the question tentative.

"I've never been more sure."

I can't imagine pushing him away, even if—in the long run—that might hurt him less. At the thought, my heart feels sore, like it's bruised itself against my ribcage. But I want Malcolm to know how much he means to me.

No matter what, we'll always have this. Tonight is ours. That's more than enough.

And it will be worth everything that comes after.

NOTHING BUT THE GHOSTS

COFFEE AND GHOSTS SEASON 3

PART I
GHOSTS AND CONSEQUENCES

COFFEE AND GHOSTS SEASON THREE,
EPISODE 1

CHAPTER 1

My business partner is kissing the back of my neck. Since we spent the night together, this isn't much of a surprise. I'm curled next to Malcolm, his arm draped over my waist, his rich, nutmeg scent warming the air. I want to laugh at the audacity and joy of it all, but don't dare make a sound, don't dare move. His kiss is a soft, shivery thing. I don't want him to stop. So I remain absolutely still as morning light filters through the drapes and bounces off dust motes in the air.

I'd be lying if I said I didn't love this.

I'd be lying if I said I wasn't worried.

But I am. This is new. Our business is still new, not quite a year old. Beneath the joy is a thin wire of dread that insists this happiness can't last. We've made a huge mistake mixing business with pleasure, and once I confess what happened at Nigel and Sadie's wedding reception last night, it will change everything; it will change *us*.

I will confess. I know I must. But not before coffee. No one should talk about business or pacts with (possibly) demonic entities before coffee.

Malcolm's lips continue to explore the nape of my neck. I'm pretty sure he's awake. True, he's an expert kisser. Even so, no one has so much skill that they can execute what he's currently doing while asleep.

I've vowed not to move, but my toes begin flirting with his. They find the sensitive arch of his foot, and I'm rewarded with his exhale against my neck.

"You awake?" he says, voice low and still warm with sleep.

"I'm guessing you are," I say.

"How are you?"

The simple question betrays so much with its tone: *Are you okay? Was last night okay? Did we make a mistake?*

I'm sure there must be other doubts I'm missing, other things he's feeling. I go with a single word reply.

"Good."

"Hm. You were that last night, too, if I recall."

Now I turn to face him. I'm rewarded with that sweet, dark-roast smile, his eyes, shining at the sight of me. I can't help wondering: how did I get so lucky?

"I think I promised you some Kona blend," I say.

"You did, and I plan to collect. But first, I think I need my morning kiss."

Morning kiss. Evening kiss. It's how we juggled being business partners and a couple, although that was before we moved the arrangement into my bedroom.

"Well, we turned the lights off after midnight." I peer up at him, trying to school my face into absolute seriousness. "Technically, that's morning, so we've already had our morning kiss."

"Doesn't count unless the sun's up." Malcolm tugs me closer, folds me into his arms.

It is, by far, the longest morning kiss on record.

I'M NOT sure how many pots of coffee I've brewed. Thousands, certainly. On most days, I do it without thinking. Unless we're up against a truly powerful ghost, I don't need to pay attention to the particular blend (although Kona works best to eradicate ghosts) or how precisely I measure the water.

This morning? My hands tremble—just a bit. I'm in Malcolm's

tuxedo shirt. The tails skim my knees. Even with the cuffs rolled, the sleeves knock against things with a sweep of my arms. When I sprinkle coffee grounds all over the counter, I set down the scoop, close my eyes, and try not to cry.

"Hey." Malcolm's voice is gentle in my ear. He moves behind me, wraps his arms around mine, and then cradles me against his chest. "Don't worry. I think it's impossible for you to make a bad cup of coffee."

"I could if I tried," I insist.

"That's just it. You gotta *try*. Just toss in some Kona blend. You could make brewed mud this morning. Trust me. I wouldn't notice."

"You sound like you're in a good mood, Mr. Armand."

"I'm in a very good mood." He turns me in his arms and places a kiss on my nose. "I've never been in a better mood."

Something inside me loosens. Tension drains from my shoulders. I eye the coffee scoop and vow to make Malcolm the best damned cup of coffee he's ever had.

Only now I realize that it's okay if it isn't.

By the time the scent of Kona blend fills the kitchen, and Malcolm has two cups and the half and half ready to go, I feel like myself again. We'll drink our coffee, clear our heads, and then we can tackle the big problems left over from last night. We can do this, I'm certain.

Just as I think this, footfalls sound above our heads. Malcolm and I glance upward and then, at the same moment, our eyes meet.

"Belinda?" he says.

I give my head a little shake. "I didn't hear her come in last night. Did you?"

He opens his mouth as if to answer, then shuts it tight. I take that as a no. Because treading above our heads is more than one pair of feet. We could make a dash for the stairs, but we'd only meet whoever is on their way down. We could hide in the living room, but that seems cowardly.

Malcolm studies me, then he glances down at the T-shirt and boxer shorts he's wearing. His lips twitch. Before I can say anything—or toss him one of my grandmother's old aprons—Belinda charges into the kitchen.

"Okay, okay." Her words come out rushed, like she's trying to convince me of something she knows is wrong. "Before you say anything, I just want to say that I'm not..."

She stutters to a halt. Her gaze flits to Malcolm and back to me. For a brief moment, her mouth hangs open. But this is Belinda Barnes, so the shock is quickly replaced by an impish grin.

"Well, it's about time. High five?" She holds up a hand. "I think this deserves a high five."

Malcolm snorts. I scowl.

"There will be no high fives," I say, willing my cheeks not to flame. They do, of course. My entire face is on fire. Even my knees feel hot.

This only makes Belinda laugh. "Fist bump?"

I tilt my head and glare. It's then I noticed her attire, remarkably similar to my own. The man's dress shirt is a pale blue, and since she's six feet tall, hits her mid-thigh.

Then the shirt's owner clears the kitchen doorway, and the whole situation goes from slightly awkward to fairly mortifying.

Jack Carlotta stumbles over the threshold, not that there's anything on the floor to trip him up. To his credit, he swallows his shock almost immediately. Maybe that's a lawyer thing. Before he does, I see a flash of ... something in his eyes. I can't tell if it's regret or guilt or simply shame.

Once upon a time, Jack, Belinda, and I attended high school together, and once upon a time, Jack and Belinda were *the* couple. You know the kind—star athlete and homecoming queen. That was also before the ghosts started tormenting Belinda, before the drinking, before Jack left for college.

And before he started asking me out on a regular basis. By text message. I still have one on my phone from only a few weeks ago. I've never said yes. He's never stopped asking.

After last night? I'm guessing that might change.

Along with the warm scent of coffee, the air is thick with embarrassment. It's my kitchen, which I suppose makes me the one responsible for starting a conversation, offering my guests breakfast. I glance at Malcolm, but his brow is clouded with a low-grade glare aimed in Jack's direction.

They've never really liked each other.

"I have Kona blend!"

I blurt the words, and they ricochet in the tiny space. Then Belinda tips her head back and laughs. The sound of it slices through the embarrassment to the point where even Malcolm cracks a smile.

"Pour us some coffee," Belinda says, pulling on one of my grandmother's aprons. She winks at me. "And then get out of here. Jack and I will make brunch."

MALCOLM and I do end up hiding in the living room. A racket comes from the kitchen—the clatter of pots and pans, the sizzle of veggie bacon, and the aroma of biscuits baking. I cradle a cup of coffee, and if the steam doesn't do much to cool my cheeks, at least it clears my head.

Malcolm paces. He's set his cup on the mantelpiece and pauses after each lap around the living room for a sip.

"You know," he says, after he's logged at least a quarter mile. "This isn't the way I pictured the next morning. I was hoping to cook you breakfast in bed."

"I still had to get up to make the coffee," I point out.

He makes terrible coffee. For the life of me, I can't figure out why since he's so good at everything else.

"I make okay coffee," he says.

"No, you don't."

"I do. Ask Nigel."

"But—"

"I've been faking."

"Why would you...?" I trail off, my mind whirling at this new bit of information. "But we've spent hours in the kitchen."

A sheepish expression lights his eyes while that dark-roast grin spreads across his face. "Yeah, that was kind of the point. At first, you know, before ... everything." He waves a hand toward the ceiling and the general direction of my bedroom. "I just wanted an excuse to spend time with you."

I tilt my head and go for stern. "And then it got too complicated to explain."

He raises his hands in surrender. "I know, I know. Bad habit."

I grumble a sigh, and he laughs.

"Forgive me?"

"I'll think about it."

I'm expecting him to log another quarter mile around the living room while I do. Instead, he shakes his head as if he's shaking away a thought—and the laughter that goes with it.

"What?" I ask, bracing for another confession.

"I was just thinking that we should text Gregory and Terese and invite them over for the most awkward morning-after brunch ever."

Now, I do laugh and pat the spot on the sofa next to me. "Sit?"

He does, and not too much later, I'm snuggled in his lap. His chin rests on my head, and I'm flush against his chest. His heartbeat is a strong, steady thing against my back.

"Am I forgiven?" he whispers.

"Still thinking about it."

His laughter rumbles beneath me. I'm a terrible liar, and he knows it.

I contemplate the front lawn, the spring morning. I let my gaze drift. At first, the shadow doesn't register. At first, that's all I see, a shadow stretching across my lawn. It takes a few moments before it attaches itself to the man who is so clearly casting it.

He stands on the sidewalk midpoint between my house and Sadie's. In the past months, I've seen so many necromancers stand in that very spot that I'm pretty sure he's one as well.

True, he isn't pulled together as most others I've met. His canvas trousers are the color of damp sand, worn and patched. His hair is shaggy, dipping beneath his collar, and far more gray than black. He carries a backpack slung over his shoulders. But there's something in the way he tilts his chin, tucks his hands so casually in his trouser pockets that pings sudden recognition.

I don't know him. Certainly I've never seen him before, but he's familiar in a way I can't pinpoint.

"Malcolm?"

"Hm?" It's barely an answer. His lips are too busy brushing against strands of my hair, and his fingers are intent on caressing my arms through the long sleeves of his shirt.

"I think there's a necromancer on my sidewalk."

The caressing comes to an abrupt halt. His fingers curl around my arms, and he holds me steady.

"Where?"

I part the shutters to give him a full view of my front lawn, the sidewalk, and the necromancer whose gaze is doing a slow and steady survey of my house.

Malcolm doesn't speak. He doesn't move. He is so still that dread curls in my stomach. Up until now, a necromancer on the front walk has been a harbinger of bad things. Still, this particular necromancer doesn't look all that dangerous.

"Am I right?" I prompt.

"Yeah." He exhales. "You're right. That's a necromancer." With his grip still on my arms, he eases me from his lap. "That also happens to be my father."

I'm uncertain how long we stand in the living room; Malcolm's gaze is focused on the outside, while mine flits back and forth between him and the man on the sidewalk. Now that he's said the word, called this man *father*, I see the resemblance. In fact, I can't believe I didn't before. It's there in the tilt of the chin, the solid jawline, and the stance. More than once I've seen Nigel tuck his hands into his pockets and affect that very pose.

It's a deliberate move, one designed to make him look harmless.

The man doesn't budge, but then, neither does Malcolm. There are the wards, of course, the one around Sadie's house that Nigel put into place, and then my own that surrounds my property.

Malcolm's father hasn't dared to cross either. In my case, that makes sense. He's a stranger, and my ward is particularly strident when it comes to stranger danger, especially of the necromancer variety. But he's also Nigel's father. From what little Malcolm has told me, I know they had a falling out.

One so big he won't cross the ward and knock on the door?

"Should I invite him inside?" I ask, pitching my voice low so he can pretend not to hear the question.

Malcolm's mouth is nothing but a grim line, but he gives the slightest of nods.

I head for the door. I'm about to pull it open when I realize my state of dress—or undress as the case may be. I consider rushing upstairs to pull on some clothes. But really? That doesn't change the situation. Besides, Malcolm is still in his boxers and T-shirt and shows no signs of panic or embarrassment.

The porch is cool beneath my toes. A breeze catches the shirttails and chases them around my knees. I grip the rail for support and call out.

"Excuse me, Mr. Armand? Would you like to come in for some coffee?"

He abandons his contemplation of Sadie's house and turns toward me. He walks a careful line along the sidewalk until he reaches the walkway to my house.

"Are you granting me entry?" he asks. His voice is deep, a rich bass with a hint of an accent.

"I am."

He nods and continues up the walkway. At the porch, he pauses. He has the same eyes as Malcolm, dark and piercing, but where Malcolm's are so often filled with warmth and humor, his father's are flinty. Up close, I can see the years spent outdoors written on his face—entrenched grooves around his mouth, crows feet that deepen when his gaze takes me in.

"You're a Lindstrom, aren't you?" he says.

"I am."

His lips compress into a line. In that moment, he definitely resembles his son. "I was afraid of that."

I'm not certain what to say to this. I'm not certain I should even invite him inside. But he's here, on my porch, and whatever happens next, it's probably better if it happens inside.

"Malcolm's in the living room," I say. "I'll go get you a cup of coffee and be right there." I gesture toward the living room with the vain hope Malcolm will appear and do something about his father. He doesn't, so I'm reduced to asking, "How do you take it?"

"I don't suppose you have any tea."

I open my mouth, but before I can respond, he speaks again.

"No, I don't suppose you would. Extra sugar, no cream."

I give a numb sort of nod. My pulse is thrumming in my throat. My feet feel awkward and clumsy, and I'm afraid my next steps will send me tripping into the kitchen. I have no idea why this man is judging me—well, other than the fact I'm wearing his son's rented tuxedo shirt and not much else—but his gaze is not kind.

So I jut my chin forward and say, "I'm Katy Lindstrom, by the way." I hold out my hand.

He stares at it for a long moment. "Darien Armand." With what feels like reluctance, he takes my hand. "Short for Katrina?"

"It is."

He drops my hand as if he's just discovered it's covered in slime. "Like the hurricane. Seems appropriate."

Without another word, he turns toward the living room and vanishes inside.

I tiptoe a few steps closer, but nothing but silence comes from the room. I wasn't expecting a tender father-son reunion, but the absence of any reaction makes my stomach tighten once again, the dread heavier than before. There's something worse about no emotion at all.

THE KITCHEN IS A WARM, safe refuge. I'm tempted to pour that cup of coffee for myself (no sugar, just half and half), sit at the kitchen table, and send Belinda eye messages while she prepares brunch with Jack.

She's standing at the stove, clutching the spatula almost like a sword, as if she's ready to do battle. But it's Jack who speaks.

"Who the hell is that?" He's at the kitchen sink. Plump raspberries sit in a colander, their juice staining the white porcelain. He looks as if he's ready to charge into the living room, but his state of dress isn't much better than Malcolm's.

"That's Malcolm's father."

Belinda exhales and swears. "You're kidding."

"I wish I were."

A sardonic smile twists Jack's lips. "Well, that's awkward."

I spear him with a glare. "It's been an awkward morning."

A blush streaks up his cheekbones. He turns back to the raspberries.

"He's one of those badass necromancers, isn't he?" Belinda says.

I nod, slowly. "I guess so, but I don't know for sure."

"I do," she says. "He's got that vibe."

"What vibe?" There's a vibe? If so, it's news to me.

"You all have it." She turns back to the French toast on the griddle and starts flipping the slices of bread. A sizzle fills the kitchen, its steam scented with vanilla and a hint of cinnamon.

"We do?" I touch my fingers to my chest. "I do?"

"Sure. I mean, I never realized it until recently. I just thought it was something special about you and your grandmother."

"My grandmother wasn't a necromancer."

She raises an eyebrow but doesn't contradict me. "Then when Malcolm and Nigel came to town, it made sense that they'd have it too. But now I can tell it's different for each necromancer."

"I don't get that vibe." I frown, wondering if I simply haven't noticed it or if it's something I *can't* notice.

Belinda's sense of ghosts is as good as mine, even if she can't catch them. When she was little, ghosts—mostly harmless sprites—were even her friends. She chatted and played with them. Her parents chalked it up to imaginary playmates. But the fact she's so receptive makes her a target for the nastier spirits, the sort that will corner you, taunt you, truly haunt and torment you until they've drained all they can from you.

I know my grandmother tried to teach Belinda how to capture ghosts. While we've been roommates, so have I. I don't understand why she can't.

And I really don't understand what a necromancer vibe is.

I pull two cups from the cupboard and start in on the coffee. I suspect Malcolm will need a fresh cup. I'm dumping a couple of heaping tablespoons of sugar into the second cup when Jack makes a gagging sound.

"Whoa. Really?" His face puckers. "That's a lot of sugar."

"He said extra sweet." I pick up both cups and head for the door.

I can't help but wonder if this is the only sweet thing about Darien Armand.

~

AGAIN, I pause outside the living room entrance and soak in the quiet. Any other time, I'd say the space was empty. Except this silence feels spiteful. I glance at the cups in my hands. Kona blend can solve a multitude of problems.

I'm not sure it's up to this one.

Malcolm is at the fireplace, elbow propped on the mantelpiece, fingers rubbing his temples. Darien Armand is standing in the center of the room, his backpack at his feet.

I don't know what to make of this. I never knew my parents; they died before I was old enough to have even a fleeting memory of them. I don't understand the intricacies of a father-son relationship. I *really* don't know how to bridge the gap between these two men.

I know ghosts and coffee, so I will start there and hope something happens along the way.

I offer the extra sweet to Malcolm's father. "It's Kona blend," I say.

He takes the cup and inclines his head in what might be an acknowledgment.

"It's a favorite of ghosts." I cross the room to Malcolm and hand him the second cup. When I do, the pained expression leaves his eyes for a moment, but it returns far too quickly.

I turn so I can keep both men in my sights. "We use it on all our eradications—well, most of them. Some ghosts like tea, but you probably know that. Malcolm makes wonderful tea." The words pour from me like sugar might pour from an upturned canister, and I can't seem to stop them. They sound loud—and a little bit desperate—in this space. "We own a business together. Did you know that? K&M Ghost Eradication Specialists."

"Really?" Darien takes a sip of the coffee.

No face scrunch, despite the amount of sugar I dumped into his cup. Instead, he presses his lips together. His expression is deliberately bland as if he doesn't want to betray even a hint of admiration.

"So that would make you business partners," he says.

It's not his words so much as his tone that rankles. Malcolm lifts his head and stares at his father.

"Yes, we're partners," Malcolm says, and there's a force to his words I've never heard before. "Katy's my partner."

"I see." Darien takes another sip, and in that simple gesture is a world of condemnation.

Then it hits me. I remember Malcolm telling me about the Armands, how they've always been free-agent necromancers, how not so long ago, even Malcolm and Nigel were in competition with each other. Could that be it? Could their father disapprove of our partnership—and of me?

"You'll forgive my confusion," Darien continues. "I could've sworn it was your brother who was on his honeymoon."

A flush invades my cheeks, hot and unrelenting. Something flashes in Malcolm's eyes, something fiery and unforgiving—and flinty. In this moment, the two men are so alike that I'm scared of what might happen next.

"That's enough."

The measured tones come from the living room's entrance. I turn to find Nigel standing there, framed by the threshold, hands tucked in his pockets. I gape, wondering at his prescience, when I see Belinda over his shoulder.

She's holding up her cell phone and gives me a little shrug.

Nigel and his father stare at each other.

"You could offer me your congratulations," Nigel says.

"Yes." Darien lets the word hang in the air. He takes another sip of coffee before adding, "I could."

Are all father-son relationships this fraught? The air is thick with unspoken accusations. Beneath that, something else simmers, not so much anger, but a deep and relentless hurt. There are wounds here that haven't had the chance to scab over.

The racket from the kitchen makes me jump. I hear the timbre of Sadie's voice, and I know she's followed Nigel and has just commandeered my kitchen from Jack.

"Katy has graciously offered you her hospitality," Nigel says. Again, it's his tone that catches me.

It catches Darien as well. His skin is too weathered to truly show a blush, but his posture shifts, he nods in my direction and almost looks contrite.

"And my wife," Nigel continues, and when he says *wife*, his eyes light up, and he can't hide his smile. "My wife is a wonderful cook. Let's talk over breakfast."

I want to point out that, technically, it's brunch, but I suspect that those are only more nonsense words that won't help this situation. Before I can make things worse, Belinda darts into the living room and grabs my hand.

"Come on," she says.

We slip past Nigel, who raises an eyebrow and then winks.

"Trust me," Belinda says as we head up the stairs. "It's always better to meet the parents when you're fully dressed."

"And you know this how?"

She merely laughs and when we reach the landing, shoves me into my room.

~

Even without inviting Gregory and Terese, Belinda and I have managed to host the most awkward morning-after brunch ever. Malcolm has pulled on his tuxedo trousers, and the outfit looks stylish and deliberate. But he squirms next to me in his chair like a small boy who's nervous about the next words that might come from his father's mouth.

Belinda is breezy in a sundress. I opted for jeans and one of the few blouses I own. I usually pair it with a blazer when we visit the one and only law firm in town. (Lawyers end up haunted more often than you might guess.)

If not for Sadie, I suspect the entire meal would have disintegrated into sullen silence. She sits next to Darien and has somehow kept the conversation going despite everyone else's monosyllabic responses.

In fact, she's in her element. I imagine that back when she was married to Harold that she must have hosted dozens of awkward dinner parties. What's one brunch with a wayward father-in-law?

"Nigel tells me you've traveled all over the world," she says to Darien now. "That must be fascinating."

"It is."

"Do you have a favorite place?"

"Each region has its merits."

Malcolm nudges me in the ribs. When I glance at him, he rolls his eyes.

Sadie is undeterred. That, I think, is her strength. She continues as if he's just regaled us with a tale of scaling the Andes.

"Nigel and I will be leaving soon on our honeymoon." She pauses to beam at her new husband. When she does, Nigel loses the sour expression and smiles in return. He gives her a nod of encouragement before bringing his fingertips to his lips and blowing her a kiss.

"It's not much of a trip," she continues, "but we plan to stay in a bed and breakfast up north, perhaps do some antiquing. I like to restore old things." Sadie gives a little shrug. "It's a hobby."

Darien slices a thin strip of French toast, his silverware making the barest clink against the china. "I prefer not to be weighed down by material possessions," he says before taking a precise bite.

Malcolm pokes me again. Before he can treat me to another eye roll, Nigel tosses his napkin on his plate. He stands and plants his palms on the table.

"Stop being rude. You're a guest in this house. The least you could do is behave."

Darien tilts his head in Nigel's direction. "You sound like your mother."

Sadie places a hand on Nigel's arm. "He meant no harm. Everyone's allowed their opinion on subjects. I like to restore antiques. Your father does not."

"That's just it. He did mean harm. He meant to be rude." Nigel glares, but Darien doesn't return the gesture. Instead, his gaze is fixed on Sadie.

"Oh," Darien says, as if making a sudden discovery. "You're a sensitive, aren't you?"

Her brow crinkles. "A what?"

"He means you're sensitive to ghosts," Nigel says. He relents under the steady pressure of Sadie's hand and sinks into his chair. He turns to her, his expression gentle. "That you can sense them when others can't. Like with your sprites. You know when they've snuck in before I do."

"Yes, it's true. I do sense ghosts quite easily," she says to Darien. "Just ask Katy." She shoots me a quick look before returning her attention to him. "So I guess that makes me a ... sensitive."

"Nigel's and Malcolm's mother is one. It often works out that way, a necromancer pairing with a sensitive. It's a mutually beneficial arrangement." Darien gives Nigel a sidelong glance. "Given your ... predicament, I suppose this makes a certain amount of sense."

Nigel's eyes narrow. "You mean my addiction."

Through all this, Malcolm's hand has found mine. He laces our fingers together and tugs me just a bit closer.

"Your hand is cold," he whispers.

Both my hands are cold and have been ever since we sat down to eat.

"You okay?" he adds.

I nod, but I'm not certain that's a true answer.

"I guess that would make me a sensitive, too." Belinda gives us one of her homecoming queen smiles, looking anything but sensitive. "Just ask Katy," she adds, echoing Sadie. "So do necromancers always pair off with a sensitive, or do they ever marry or partner with each other?"

As if on cue, I feel everyone's gaze land on Malcolm and me. His fingers tighten around mine. I think the blush that started in the living room will become permanent.

"Usually not," Darien says.

"But it's not unheard of," Nigel adds, his words quick.

"I suppose it isn't, but necromancers are far too competitive. There's too much risk of betrayal. The Armands have learned that the hard way." Darien gives his head a shake as if he's shrugging off old regret. "Such arrangements never last."

Tension radiates from Malcolm's hand into mine. He leans forward, on the verge of jumping up. I'm poised to do the same arm-calming maneuver that Sadie performed on Nigel a few moments before.

Instead, Sadie stands and breaks the spell that has settled on all of us. "I think it's time for some coffee. Katy, that's your specialty. Will you help me in the kitchen?"

Malcolm gives me a quick nod. With his hands at my waist, he propels me to my feet. Belinda hops up, grabs the empty French toast platter, and rushes after us.

"I'll help too!" she sings out.

On my way to the kitchen, I peer over my shoulder at Malcolm. Despite everything, he gives me one of his sweet, dark-roast grins. It's meant to reassure me. I return the smile—or try to—but Darien's words ricochet through my mind, clouding my thoughts with words like *betrayal.*

And I wonder if he's right.

CHAPTER 3

In the kitchen, Sadie leans against the sink, hand pressed to her chest, eyes fluttering closed for a moment.

"Oh, my," she says. "He's a cool customer, isn't he?"

"He's an ass," Belinda says.

Sadie directs a pointed look at Belinda, but there's humor beneath the reprimand—and a sigh.

"At least this explains much about the boys," she adds. "Nigel's told me some, of course, but it's a sensitive subject." Sadie pauses, her mouth twisting on the words *sensitive*. "At this point, he sees Reginald as more of a father figure than his actual father. I'm beginning to see why."

"He doesn't like me."

I blurt the words without thinking, but I know the truth of them. Darien Armand does not like me.

Sadie crosses to me. "Katy, no. It isn't personal. I doubt there are many people Darien Armand does like." She pauses and considers the ceiling. "I think it's clear that he has a great deal of hurt he hasn't … processed yet. It has nothing to do with you."

Except, I'm pretty sure it does, but I can't pull the threads together to explain why. According to him, I'm a hurricane and a Lindstrom. The latter might be the worst of the two offenses. I can't say why he doesn't like me, only that he doesn't.

"More coffee?" Belinda says. "Seriously, the man simply hasn't had enough of your coffee."

I get to work brewing a fresh pot by pulling out the one hundred percent Kona. Even the rattle of the beans sounds expensive. It's the coffee equivalent to Dom Pérignon.

Forget Darien Armand. We have a newlywed couple to toast.

WE EMERGE FROM THE KITCHEN, a tray of cups and saucers jangling, the aroma of rich, sweet coffee paving the way for us. At least, that's what I hope it's doing.

Everyone is milling about in the living room. I peer into the dining room and see the dishes neatly stacked on the table and all the chairs pushed in.

Malcolm, I think, is responsible for these feats. Now, in the living room, he paces—or does when his father doesn't toss him a glare and halt him in his tracks. He looks desperate for something to do, and his face lights up when he sees us enter. He rushes forward and takes the tray from my hands.

"How's it going?" I whisper.

Malcolm's gaze darts toward Nigel and Darien. "Tense. It's tense, but civil. Probably because there are witnesses." He nods toward Jack, standing at the mantelpiece, who's managing to look both grim and grateful.

Belinda sets cream and sugar on the table and then crosses the room to him. Jack tucks her in the protective curve of his arm, and she snuggles next to him. Momentary worry pings at me, but this isn't high school. Belinda might be a sensitive, but she's nobody's pushover.

Malcolm sets the tray on the coffee table, and I pour two cups—one extra sweet and one with half and half. I hold out the cups as I approach. The slightest tremor in my hands ripples the coffee's surface, but I don't spill a drop.

I haven't spilled a drop since I was eight.

Darien inclines his head again, which makes me think that's all the acknowledgment I'll get from him. Nigel cradles his cup, his smile warm.

"Thank you, Katy," he says, the words directed more at his father than at me. "Katy makes the best coffee," he adds.

"The Lindstrom women always do." Darien takes a sip. He likes the coffee; I can tell. Also? It's killing him to admit it. "It makes one ponder nature versus nurture."

"Wait," I say. "Did you know my grandmother? My mother?"

"I grew up in the necromancer community," Darien continues. "Even though the Armands like to hold ourselves apart." His gaze scans his two sons before he returns his attention to me. "A community is still a community."

"But—" I'm about to protest that my grandmother wasn't a necromancer when a revelation pops into my head. "You knew my mother."

It's not really a question, but the silent answer plays across his features before he speaks.

"Everyone"—he clears his throat—"knew your mother."

Again, it's not so much what Darien Armand says, but how he says it. The words make my cheeks sting. I don't even know what he means by those words or his tone, but when Nigel's eyes go flinty, I do know this:

It was on purpose.

Nigel gives my arm a quick squeeze before he turns on his father. "Why are you here?"

"You sent a ghost, son. You invited me to your wedding."

"Which was yesterday."

Darien shrugs, the barest lift of one shoulder. "Blame the messenger."

With his words, all three of us look at Malcolm. He's the one who sent the ghosts since Nigel, with his addiction, can't interact with them.

"This isn't Malcolm's fault," Nigel says, "and you didn't travel halfway around the world simply to insult someone you've never met."

"Have I insulted anyone? I certainly didn't mean to. I can't be held accountable if they took offense."

Malcolm's hand comes to rest on the small of my back. His other hand wraps around my upper arm. I feel a tug, a precautionary sort of gesture, like he's moving me out of the way of an oncoming train. I brace for what comes next. Certainly, something comes next, what with the way Nigel is glaring and Darien is studiously ignoring both his sons, his full concentration on the rotation of his teaspoon in his coffee cup.

Nigel opens his mouth. Malcolm's grip tightens. The doorbell rings.

At the sound, Sadie lets out a little gasp. I feel a wave of relief. I don't know who it might be, and at this point, don't care.

"Excuse me," I say.

In fact, I flee the room with so much relief that it's probably obscene. It feels like escaping on the last day of school, or breaking out of jail, or something. Malcolm follows right behind me, although I'm perfectly capable of answering my own door.

The bell rings again.

"Why don't you let me get it," he says.

"It's my door, Malcolm. No one is on the other side, trying to hurt me."

"I know, I know." He scrubs his face with his hands. "I'm just edgy, okay?"

I wait. After a moment, he peeks through his fingers at me and cracks a smile. Then I take his hand, and together we answer the door.

On my porch stands a girl of maybe eleven. Her hair is a riot of braids, each secured with a plastic clip in the shape of a cat. I love them immediately and wonder if I'm too old for cat clips, then realize that yes, I probably am.

"You're Tara," I say. "Aren't you?"

She nods and her braids bounce.

"You sell me cookies every year."

She nods again.

I still have several boxes in the freezer. Malcolm is patting his trouser pockets. He glances around, almost in a panic.

"I left my wallet upstairs."

My eyes meet his. I know the moment we both remember *why* his wallet is upstairs, in my bedroom. A blush burns my face—yet again— and a flash of pink streaks up Malcolm's cheekbones.

But yes, he wants to retrieve his wallet because he's the reason my freezer is so full of cookies. He can't help himself. He will buy as many cookies as he can afford and I can stuff into my freezer. He's been in town for barely a year, and already the neighborhood kids know he's a soft touch.

"I'm not here selling cookies," Tara says.

It's only now I notice how somber she is, her dark eyes sad and serious. She clutches a little purse, one of blue and yellow and in the shape of a cat.

"I want to hire you," she adds.

I send Malcolm a questioning glance. He gives his head a little shake and mouths, "Why not?"

"Okay." I exhale and check the house behind me. It's filled with tension and stranger danger. "It's too nice to be inside. Can we talk out here?"

Tara nods and the three of us settle on the steps. The wood is warm beneath me, the breeze on the cusp of losing the morning chill. The scent of lilac fills the air. My nose twitches in response.

"I know it's Sunday," Tara says, "and you were closed for the wedding—"

"Wait," Malcolm says. "Did you walk downtown?"

She bites her lip. A *yes* if I ever saw one.

"We're not closed," I say, "because most ghosts don't take Sunday off. They really can't tell time."

That almost earns me a smile, but something is wrong. I can feel the weight, the burden this little girl is carrying around with her.

"They won't stop fighting," she says, all at once, blurting much like I do at times.

"Who won't?" I lean forward, not certain where this is going.

"My parents, but they don't make any sense, and it's cold in there."

"Where?" Malcolm asks, his voice gentle.

"The living room. It's like a movie, like they're actors saying lines. They don't sound like themselves. I mean, their voices do, but not the words."

My gaze meets Malcolm's over the top of Tara's head.

"Possession?" he mouths.

I don't nod. I don't shake my head. Despite the sun warming the porch step, my limbs are like ice. I'm cold, from my toes to the pit of my stomach. I've never dealt with a possession before. That's a caliber of ghost way out of my league.

I swallow hard. My grandmother fought a possession once, all on her own. She never told me what happened or what she did to separate the ghost from the person it had inhabited. The entire family moved from Springside not long after. I remember how my grandmother came home haggard and worn, how she crawled into bed and slept for nearly twenty-four hours.

How she refused to speak of what happened when she woke.

"I can pay." Tara opens the cat purse. Inside coins glint in the sunlight. A few dollar bills rustle. She holds the purse up to Malcolm. "See? I have enough ... I think."

"More than enough." He takes the purse and snaps it closed before handing it back to her. "But consultations are free. We won't know what to charge you until we see what's going on. Sound fair?"

She beams at him. So do I. For a moment, I think we both forget our troubles—possessions and entities and estranged fathers—and just admire how the sun makes Malcolm's ebony hair gleam, how sweet that dark-roast smile is, and the way his lashes reach his cheekbones when he closes his eyes.

Yes, we both have a crush.

"Is there any coffee left?" Malcolm asks, effectively breaking the spell.

"Yes, but..." Mentally, I ransack my cupboards. What I need is my field kit—my lost field kit. "I'll need to dig out some old thermoses."

"You do that, and I'll let everyone else know they'll have to get along without us." He grins at Tara. "We have a paying customer, after all."

THE THERMOSES JANGLE and jostle inside a reusable grocery sack. A small bag of sugar thumps against my thigh. I miss my canvas field kit. I miss my collection of precision-made German thermoses and their matching cups.

Tara lives only a few blocks away. We've opted to walk, although now I'm rethinking that decision. Malcolm stops every few feet, adjusts his shoes, tugs at the tuxedo trousers. He's pulled on the shirt, but it hangs loose and unbuttoned. Despite everything, he's managed to make the outfit look intentional.

"Sorry, sorry," he says after the fourth or fifth time. "These weren't meant for hiking." His stare turns grim as he considers the shiny black dress shoes and then the expanse of sidewalk ahead of us.

"They're not," I agree, "but you *are* rocking a James Bond thing."

His expression lights up, and I swear, a bit of a blush stains his cheeks. "I'll take that as a compliment."

"But you can run home and change," I add. "I'll go on ahead and meet you there."

"No, no. If this really is a possession, you shouldn't go in alone." His gaze flits to Tara. "No one should."

He's right. I know he is. Besides, I like having him at my side, even if he's still squirming like a preschooler.

A block later, he apologizes again.

"Sorry," he says. "I mean about this morning."

I'm about to tell him it's fine, that nothing about this morning is his fault, but his eyes are dark and sad. In this moment, he looks almost lost.

"It's funny." He scrubs his face again and then runs his hands through his hair. "I promised myself that the next time I saw my father, I wouldn't completely shut down. What happens?" He casts me a sidelong glance. "I completely shut down."

"You were ambushed."

"We sent the ghost, so I'm not sure why we were both so surprised he'd show up—except we didn't think he would. We even joked about it." Malcolm shrugs. "He didn't come for my graduation from the U of M. He didn't even respond when I asked for help with Nigel's addiction. It's like we send ghosts and expect nothing in return."

What they found to joke about escapes me, but then maybe it's easier to joke than to be constantly disappointed.

"How does sending a ghost work?" I ask, in part to change the subject —he looks so miserable—and in part because I'm curious. "I mean, we count on the fact that ghosts aren't very good at navigating."

"It's ... a necromancer thing." His mouth curves into a half smile.

Ah, yes. *A necromancer thing.* "I knew you were going to say that."

"Remember when you showed Selena how to find me?"

Yes. Unfortunately.

"It's like that, only inside." He taps his head. "A ghost can glean all the information you have on someone. So I knew my father was somewhere in South America or maybe the Falklands. I grew up with him, which provides even more information. The ghost takes all that along with some navigation points and heads off."

"So sending a ghost to someone in a known location would be much easier."

"Even then you need a reliable ghost. This isn't a job for a sprite. I wouldn't trust a sprite to get a message across the room."

Tara walks ahead of us, her steps slow enough I can tell she's eavesdropping. It's a trick I used when I was her age. I was so often in the company of my grandmother and other adults, working instead of playing, that it became something I did without even thinking.

"Are you interested in ghosts?" I ask her.

She stumbles to a halt before picking up her pace.

"It's okay to be interested in ghosts."

Her pace slows. She turns around and takes a few steps backward. "It is?"

"Of course. I'm interested in ghosts."

"Yes, but you're..." Tara pauses, brow furrowing as if she can't find the right word.

I want to say: *I'm the girl who catches ghosts*, because that's what I've always been. But Tara's next words take me by surprise.

"You're a grown up."

"I am?"

Malcolm snorts a laugh. It isn't the rich, full-throated laugh that tells me he's happy. Still, a laugh is a laugh, and the sound reassures me. He nods in my direction and then rolls his eyes at Tara.

"She's been a grown up for so long she doesn't even realize it."

"I don't feel like a grown up," I protest.

Tara nods like she understands. "Because your grandmother died."

At that moment, an eleven-year-old girl speaks the truth and strips everything away. That hollow space opens up inside me, a tender ache like a fresh bruise. I want to resist the urge to touch it, but of course, I can't.

"Yes," I say, "because my grandmother died."

"I miss her," Tara says.

"I miss her too."

"She would listen to me about ghosts."

"She would?"

"When she was out working in her garden or sweeping the sidewalk," she says. "I would talk to her sometimes on my way home from school."

"My grandmother had a thing about sweeping the sidewalk," I tell Malcolm. "It was weird."

"Maybe she was using it as cover for placing a ward," he says.

I open my mouth, but nothing comes out except exasperated air. I feel as if the wind has been knocked out of me, twice in a matter of minutes. I grip his arm.

"She was placing wards." I speak the words and feel the certainty of them. "Right in front of me."

How many other things—necromancer things—did she do right in front of me? Why didn't she ever tell me, show me, explain? I have no answers, and Tara is staring at us, wide-eyed. I give myself a mental shake. We have a job to do. Maybe I can't change the past—in fact, I know I can't—but I can help this little girl with her present, and possibly her future.

"You can always talk to us about ghosts." I point to Malcolm and then myself. "We'll listen."

"I thought that might cost money." Tara's grip on the cat purse tightens.

"Or," Malcolm says, drawing out the word. "Maybe it pays money."

Her face brightens. "It does?"

"Well, it has to be good information."

We fall into step with her and continue down the sidewalk.

"Can you sense ghosts?" I ask.

Tara nods hard enough the cat clips in her braids clack together.

"Can you see them?" Malcolm pitches his voice a bit lower, like this is a serious job interview.

Tara pulls herself up tall. "Sometimes. There's a shimmery outline." She waves her hands in the air.

"Have you ever tried to catch one?" I ask.

"With Tupperware," she says. "My mom got mad because I lost the lid. And I never ended up with a ghost, anyway. I always wanted one, for a friend. But now, now that I see ... I'm sorry I ever even wished..."

One tear, and then another. She stops walking, hangs her head, and I know she doesn't want us to see her cry—she especially doesn't want Malcolm to see that. I shoo him away and kneel in front of her.

"You didn't do this to your parents. Ghosts don't work that way. They're not ... smart enough. They only have room inside them for so many thoughts, and those thoughts are about themselves, usually something from before they were ghosts."

She nods, but her eyes still brim with tears.

"That's why it's so hard to catch them. You have to be able to sense them and be a good detective."

"And coffee," she says, the words thick with those tears.

"And you need coffee," I say.

"They really don't like instant," she adds.

"Not even sprites like instant," I confirm. "Have you tried that?"

"That's why my mom got so mad at me and told me to stop talking about ghosts." She peers up at me, the tracks of her tears staining her cheeks. "I stained the carpet."

"I've stained lots of carpets," I say. "Still do. I've been catching ghosts since I was five, which means you're old enough to help. In fact, Malcolm and I will need your help since we don't know your parents very well. So, will you?"

Tara nods again. The salt remains on her cheeks, but her eyes are filled with determination rather than tears. We start toward her house, a gray two-story with a bright blue door.

After a few steps, her small hand takes mine and we walk the rest of the way together.

CHAPTER 4

We don't barge in. Not only is that bad manners, but ghosts are unpredictable, even on their best days. I stand with Tara on the porch while Malcolm does a circuit of the house. Gingerly, I test the door with a brush of fingertips.

The wood is warm, the brass handle gleams from sunlight, not frost. At least we don't need to battle a full-on ghost infestation along with a possible possession.

"Things look normal from the outside," Malcolm says as he rounds the corner of the house.

And no raised voices come from inside. That could be good, or it could be very bad. I reach out and ring the doorbell.

Other than a soft chime, nothing happens.

Tara regards me with the contempt only a preteen can muster. "It's my house." She rolls her eyes for good measure, opens the door, and walks inside.

Now I can hear the voices, angry and cold, although the words are indistinct. I glance at Malcolm.

"Should we?"

"It's better than letting the whole neighborhood in on this." He takes my hand. "If it's truly a possession, we'll need to be careful."

"There's only been one in Springside that I know of," I say.

"What happened?"

"That's just it. I don't know. My grandmother handled it on her own. The family moved away." I shrug. "There hasn't been one since."

"Until now."

Yes. Until now. Until Orson Yates came to town. "Do you think—?"

"I don't know what to think." He shakes his head. "Not yet."

Together, we step over the threshold. We are only halfway through the foyer when Malcolm halts.

"Feel that?" He licks his lips like he's tasting the air.

The otherworldly presence is thick, cold and penetrating. I doubt my puny offering of coffee will even make a dent. Malcolm's brow crinkles, and he glances around.

"Something about this feels ... familiar."

"Does it?" I ask.

"You don't feel it?"

"No. All I feel is cold and sorrow and..." I raise my chin to sample the air. "Deliberate, like when you know someone well and know what exactly will hurt them."

We take a few more steps toward the raised voices and the source of the cold. The farther we move into the house, the colder the air gets. The skin on my arms prickles with goose bumps. Malcolm laces his fingers with mine, and it's the only warm, safe thing in this space.

In the living room, Tara's parents rage in front of a fireplace. Closer to the entrance, there's a playpen. Inside that playpen is a little boy who can't be much more than two. He has wild, loose curls and deep, black eyes, the sort that lend his baby face the seriousness of an old soul. His arms are outstretched, but Tara's shaking her head, telling him he's too heavy.

He lobs a stuffed bunny at her.

I kneel next to the playpen. "He's more trouble than a sprite," I say.

Despite the cacophony from the other side of the room, she smiles. "He can be."

"Will he let me pick him up?"

"You can try."

So I do. He is sticky and squirmy but comes to me without complaint. I sometimes think that toddlers are very much like sprites, or sprites like toddlers—I'm not sure which.

"Hey, little man." Malcolm holds out his pinky for the baby to grasp. "What's your name?"

"Thomas Junior," Tara replies.

Thomas Junior gurgles at the attention. He releases Malcolm's finger and takes a firm hold of my hair.

I settle Thomas on my hip and study his parents. Their father is stony, arms crossed over his chest, his eyes dark like his son's, but lacking any depth. They are flinty and cold. I understand now what it means to cut someone with your eyes.

Tara's mother is on the receiving end of that. Her hair is loose and wild, with curls to match her son's, only hers seem to coil, almost snake-like. She is saying something, something passionate, but it's like her words are bubbling up from underwater.

"Man, this is brutal," Malcolm whispers in my ear.

"You can understand them?"

He pulls back and gives me a wary look. "Can't you?"

I give my head one slow, firm shake. "No."

"Really?"

"It's all garbled. Like the words are filled with static, or they're speaking underwater."

"That's weird."

It is. It really is. Unease unfurls in my stomach. Only a ghost with tremendous strength could manipulate reality so that I hear one thing and Malcolm another.

"Usually a possession like this needs direction from a powerful necromancer," he says.

"We've had several of those in town recently." And still do.

"That's what's worrying me."

"Are all possessions caused by necromancers?"

"They start that way," he says, "but some ghosts take to them and keep on possessing people … well, forever, I guess, or until another necromancer stops them."

"What do you think this is?"

"Personal."

The word comes from Malcolm with so much force and feeling, I'm taken aback. I'm usually the one who blurts things with Malcolm following in my wake, connecting the dots of my thoughts and intuition, turning them into something logical.

I focus on Tara's parents again, thinking about what I can't hear and what Tara said. I touch her shoulder.

"How do they sound to you?"

Her lower lip juts out. "They don't fight like this."

"Do you understand their words?"

She casts me a look, one filled with relief. "Not ... really. It's a jumble. I mean, the words are real, but they're all out of order."

Well, that's more than what I'm getting from the conversation. Next to me, Malcolm has tensed. He stares at Tara's parents, not blankly, but with resignation, like he's shut down. Thomas is warm and solid on my hip. I adjust him so I can place a hand on Malcolm's upper arm.

Nothing.

"How is this familiar, Malcolm?" I keep my voice gentle.

"They always do this," he says. "They fight. He'll make her cry. He always does. He blames her for everything."

In his words, I don't hear Malcolm, my self-assured business partner, but a little boy who wishes desperately that his parents would stop fighting. Yes, this is personal. I glance from him to Tara's parents. But ... how?

I take a knee and let Thomas bounce on my thigh. I nod at Tara to come closer. When she does, I whisper.

"When did this start?"

"Late last night ... early this morning."

Up close, I can see the circles beneath her eyes and a hint of red that's more than from just tears.

"And this is new, right? They don't normally fight like this."

She nods.

Personal, I think. Familiar. Family. Could Darien Armand have brought this ghost to town with him? I can't fathom a reason why he would, and why he would unleash something like this on an unsuspecting and unrelated couple.

Thomas kicks his legs and jostles the thermoses in the grocery sack that's still slung over my shoulder. I ease him to the floor and consider where to set up. I'm not sure coffee will help. At the very least, it might clear Malcolm's head—and mine.

Thomas tugs at my shoelaces. We generally don't eradicate with toddlers underfoot. I wonder what my grandmother did all those years ago before I was old enough to help. Sprites as babysitters, perhaps? No. That could only end badly.

"Can you watch him," I say to Tara. "I need to get the coffee out. It's hot."

She clutches her brother around the waist. He flails against the confinement. A moment later, when she retrieves the stuffed bunny, he settles in her lap, content for now.

I scan the living room, searching out childproof ghost eradication sites. The mantelpiece is the most obvious place; it's also the most hazardous. Tara's parents haven't budged from the hearth. Her mother is gesturing, arms and hands wild. Her passion is no match for his stony silence.

Bookshelf, I think. I'll deploy a few cups there and work my way around the couple. Perhaps the steam will be enough to distract this ghost, so it releases its grip, if only momentarily.

Everything's a jumble in my sack, but I retrieve cups and thermoses and start pouring. The scent helps me, at least. The steam travels on the air, more around the couple than toward them. This, too, is odd.

I step forward, hand outstretched, testing the air for a possible barrier. Could a necromancer do that in addition to unleashing a ghost? Or is this simply proof of how strong this ghost is?

I don't have enough experience with necromancers or possessions to tell. My gaze darts to Malcolm, who certainly does have enough experience, but he hasn't glanced my way in minutes, hasn't reacted to the coffee. I decide I need him and cross the room with a cup laden with half and half.

He won't take it. I stand there, steam wafting beneath his nose. I touch his shoulder, gingerly. I don't want to startle him. I don't want him flinging his hands and sending the coffee flying.

Nothing. Panic grips my throat so for a moment, I can't speak, can't breathe. Dread is heavy in the pit of my stomach. I can't fight this thing without Malcolm. I'm not even sure that I can snap him out of this trance, or whatever it is.

I turn back to Tara. "You still with me?"

Her eyes are huge and worried. "Is he okay?"

"I don't know." I see no point in lying to her. My grandmother never lied to me. Well, no, that isn't true. She never lied while catching ghosts, at least, not to my knowledge. For now, that's good enough.

"It's like a trap," Tara says.

"It is, isn't it?"

"Don't fall in!"

Her plea almost makes me laugh.

Tara's mother breaks free of the hearth. She shakes out her hands as if Tara's father has been gripping her wrists this whole time.

"This is about the Lindstrom woman, isn't it?" she says.

These words shatter the air around us. These words I understand. These words make me flinch with guilt, although I can't explain why. I only know Tara as the little girl who sells me cookies every year. I've glimpsed her mother standing on the sidewalk behind her; I've never met her father.

"You're obsessed with her," she says, "with *it*. You can't go back. It's time to stop."

"I'm not the one who broke my vows." Tara's father is like granite in his response.

I don't know why I can understand the words now. I glance toward Malcolm and meet his questioning gaze.

"Katy?" He reaches a hand toward me; I set down the cup and take it. His fingers are frigid, and that, too, is strange. "What's going on? Why are they talking about you?"

Are they? Aside from a wave of irrational guilt, I don't feel like I'm being talked about. I shake my head, unable to answer. But now that he's here, with me again, maybe we can solve this together.

The coffee is cooling. Already the scent has left the air. Fresh cups, all around, I think. I'm about to suggest this to Malcolm when the tread of heavy boots sounds behind us.

Reluctantly, I turn. Over the past several months, I've come to recognize that stride. And yes, behind me, flanked by Officer Deborah Millard, is Police Chief Ramsey.

Malcolm and I stand on the sidewalk. We stand there even as a car pulls up and a woman with the same wild curls as Tara's mother rushes inside. We're still there when she emerges minutes later with both children and an overstuffed diaper bag slung over one shoulder.

Tara breaks from her and dashes toward me. She clutches me tight around the waist and slips something into my hand, a crumpled bit of paper. She presses a finger to her lips so that I won't betray a thing; this is our secret.

She races to the car, and before she ducks inside, turns to wave. Thomas squeals a goodbye from his car seat. The woman—an aunt, I'm guessing—gives us a cold stare. She leaves us in a cloud of exhaust.

I smooth the paper, frown at the row of numbers on it, and then tuck it into my pocket.

We remain in place as if there's a ward around the house. I cast a furtive glance at the neighborhood, looking for rustling curtains in living room windows or eyes peering from a kitchen door. Someone called Chief Ramsey at home. I'm certain of it. But we remain there, on the sidewalk, because he told us to.

At last he lumbers down the front porch steps. Behind him, Tara's mom carries an overnight bag, and Officer Millard is speaking to her in quiet, soothing tones. Chief escorts them to one of the patrol cars and sees them off. Only then does he turn his sights on us.

Malcolm's hand grips mine, but he does no more than that. He hasn't spoken since Chief Ramsey showed up. My mind has been such a jumble of thoughts that I haven't said much either. But now that strikes me as odd. We always talk things through, even when all we do is talk in circles.

Chief comes to a halt directly in front of us. "This is a domestic disturbance. You have no business here."

"But Tara—" I begin.

"I let you do your job within the bounds of the law." He points at the house behind him. "But this is not part of your job. It's part of mine."

"Does this happen often?" I doubt Chief will tell me, but I'm hoping something will give him away.

His gaze flickers, briefly, toward the house before he schools his face. No, I think, he wasn't expecting to spend his Sunday like this.

"That's none of your business," he says.

"You're right," I say. "It's not. I'm sorry. I wanted to help Tara." And catch a ghost; I still plan on catching that ghost, but Chief doesn't need to know that.

The crinkles deepen around his eyes. Chief doesn't smile, but then, he hardly ever does.

"She reminds me of you," he says. "Always trying to fix things on her own." His gaze darts toward Malcolm and the soft look vanishes. "Why are you still in your tux?"

Malcolm and I exchange glances. He opens his mouth, but Chief holds up a hand.

"Never mind. I'm better off not knowing." He shakes his head. "Go. Get out of here. Don't worry so much. Go ... be young."

With that, he heads for the remaining patrol car and leaves us there, on the sidewalk.

In the silence that comes after, Malcolm finally speaks.

"I did it again, didn't I? I completely shut down." He swears. "I can't believe I did that." His mouth goes grim, and he stares up at the sky.

"It was more than that, at least for a little while. It was like you were in a trance."

"A trance?"

"I was trying to give you a cup of coffee. You wouldn't take it."

"You were?"

"You don't remember that?"

He swears again and rubs his eyes as if they're sore or tired. "No. I don't."

"Do you remember telling me that you thought this possession was personal?"

I study him carefully, searching for any shift in his expression, any glimmer of recognition. He blinks. The clouds clear from his eyes.

"Almost? Does that even make any sense?"

Under the circumstances? As much as anything does. I hate to bring up my suspicions, but better they're out in the open now rather than festering inside me all day long. Besides, I'm not certain I can face Malcolm's father and be civil if I don't know for certain.

"Your father," I say, picking my way through each word with care. "He wouldn't—"

"Blow into town and unleash one of the most powerful ghosts we've ever encountered?"

"Yeah. That."

"He could. I mean, he's fully capable of doing that."

"But in this case?" I venture.

Malcolm scans the house, from the brick chimney to the rose bushes along the front and sides. The petals cast a rosy glow on the gray paint. From this far away, I can't feel the presence of the ghost.

"It doesn't feel like him. All necromancers have a signature." Malcolm raises his chin as if to taste the air. "Actually, this doesn't feel like anyone at all."

"Except familiar. You said it felt familiar."

"I think what I meant was the dynamic, the fighting, but not the ghost or its necromancer."

The living room curtains shift. I sense more than see Tara's father— or rather, the ghost possessing him—scrutinize us.

"We should probably leave," I say.

Malcolm nods and heaves a sigh. "Yeah. I ... it's like I'm not totally free of whatever it is."

The sun is bright on the sidewalk, and I dread going home. "I don't want to go back to my place."

It's wrong, I know, to shirk my hostess duties, but the last thing I want to do is field questions from Belinda, play referee between Darien Armand and his sons. And while I should really apologize to Sadie for ruining the first day of her honeymoon, I don't have the words for that, either.

Malcolm lifts one foot and then another. "My feet are killing me."

"We could go back to your place," I suggest. "It would be quiet, and you could change, and then we could talk this thing through."

He doesn't respond. At last, the silence forces me to turn from my contemplation of the sidewalk. He's standing there, one eyebrow raised, the smallest of smiles curving his lips.

"Are you trying to get me alone?" he says.

I laugh, and he holds out his arms.

"Come here."

So I do.

He holds me close, and I can feel his heartbeat beneath my cheek. It's warm and safe in his arms. I hang on tightly, like I'm clinging to a life raft.

"That's better," he murmurs into my hair. "Together. We'll figure out who did this together."

Perhaps it's the warmth of Malcolm's embrace, or the fact I'm secure here as nowhere else, but my mind whirls, pulling in pieces from the last forty-eight hours. I think of the necromancers who have been in town. I consider Malcolm's words, how this haunting feels familiar. I think of my name—or at least, my last name—tossed about.

"Prescott Jones?" I venture, the suggestion quiet and easily batted away.

"Maybe he doesn't care about me, but he loves Nigel," Malcolm says. "He would do a great many things, some of them ... questionable. But hurt Nigel? No."

"So that"—I nod toward the house—"hurts Nigel?"

Malcolm pulls back, holding me at arm's length. "Oh, you're brilliant."

Well, not really, but I nod again so he'll keep talking.

"This was meant to hurt Nigel," he says. "I'm certain of it."

"And whatever this thing is, it also hurts you because you're related."

"See," he says and tugs me close again. "Brilliant."

"Not Carter Dupree." This is another improbable suggestion. The last time I saw Carter, he was about to run for his life. He's out of the state by now, possibly the country.

"Not a chance. If I'm not strong enough for something like this, there's no way he is."

Not that there's a rivalry there or anything. I refrain from rolling my eyes.

"What about...?" I'm about to suggest Orson Yates when a memory flashes across my mind.

The warehouse—and all those empty rooms with their sticky, psychic residue. An abandoned torture chamber would contain less horror. I think of how Orson cornered me in the kitchen at the wedding reception, and in particular, his taunts. I grip Malcolm even tighter.

"Hey," he says. "What is it?"

"It's Orson. At the reception, when Harold's ghost was choking me, Orson was telling me how he planned for Nigel to relapse, and oh, God, he has a ghost for Belinda too, and you. He has something planned for you."

"Shh." Malcolm's whisper is gentle against my hair. "Don't move, don't make a sound. As far as anyone knows, we're just engaging in a little PDA."

"Do you think he has spies out?"

"There's a chance." He shifts and pulls his cell phone from his pocket. "I'm warning Nigel. My father might not like anyone, but he won't let an attack ghost hurt Belinda. And Reginald's still in town. They'll be okay."

"So this? This was meant for Nigel?" I ask the question simply to ponder out loud. Malcolm still has me in his embrace, his fingers texting furiously against my back.

"It might take a possession at this point," Malcolm says. "It would be a guaranteed way to force him into a relapse."

"How well does Orson know your family?"

Malcolm gives his head a little shake. "I never met the man until he came to Springside, but I grew up in the necromancer community—it's odd that I hadn't met him. True, my father isn't all that social."

Really? I hadn't noticed.

"He doesn't think much of the necromancer community in general," Malcolm adds. "He steered me away from it. Free agents and all that." He rolls his eyes. "And my grandfather respected that while training me. So here I am, left in the dark."

"Same with me," I say.

Where the words come from, I'm not sure. At that moment, I know: everything my grandmother did was deliberate. Malcolm eases back, tucks the phone into his pocket, and trains his gaze on my face. He touches my cheek, the left one, the one that still has the entity's blue cast to it.

"I think your grandmother went to great lengths to make sure that you wouldn't have any contact with the necromancer community."

"But why?"

His fingers rest on my face. He taps the blue spot gently as if he's afraid my cheek might shatter. "This is why. Mind catching me up on what happened last night?"

WE WALK to Malcolm's apartment in silence—or as silent as someone can be while his dress shoes are tapping against the sidewalk. Malcolm has his fingers laced with mine. With each step, his skin warms. I can feel the trance loosen its grip on him until—at last—he is fully Malcolm again.

We will need to consider how to eradicate that ghost. The thermoses jangle at my side, a reminder of how impenetrable this possession is. I can't fix this on my own; I can't afford to lose my partner, either.

At the door to his apartment, he fishes around in his pocket, and then with the key in the lock, turns to me.

"Would you like to come in for some tea?" His words are overly polite and formal, but his eyes glint with humor. His expression is open and warm like it was in my bedroom this morning.

At the thought, yet another blush attacks my cheeks. I nod, suddenly shy.

"Good."

He kisses me, swings open the door, and the force of the other-worldly smashes into us. An invisible hand yanks Malcolm from me and shoves him across the room. He crashes against the living room windows and the glass shakes.

I brace, certain it will crack or splinter, explode into tiny pieces. It merely wobbles, and so does he. Relief washes through me. I unsling the sack with the thermoses and try to track the ghost. Coffee hasn't done us much good so far today, but I can't imagine it will hurt.

Assuming I can pour even a single cup, that is. The ghost rolls toward me. It's like a tumbleweed, picking up bits and pieces of the apartment—junk mail and flyers for pizza delivery, receipts and bills. The thermoses spill from my bag and shoot in all directions across the floor.

The unearthly presence slams me into the front door.

"Katy!"

I sink to the floor, clawing the air for my breath, blinking hard to regain my vision. Malcolm reaches me in a flash, kneels at my side. He gathers my hands in his.

"Katy, are you okay? Say something."

I nod, unable to tell him I simply had the wind knocked out of me. Before I can stand, the ghost swoops in. I manage to point, all the early warning that Malcolm gets.

He ducks, yanks us both to the ground and covers my body with his.

"Coffee ... tea." Two words. That's all I can force out.

We work so well together that he knows what I mean. I'll distract with the coffee; he'll brew some tea. Will it be enough? If this is one of Orson's attack ghosts, I'm not certain it will.

Malcolm eases off me. He points. One thermos is under the futon, another by the flat screen television. The TV looks expensive and like it would make an excellent projectile for a ghost this strong. I opt for the thermos beneath the futon. Ghosts get enough ideas on their own.

Malcolm rummages in the kitchen. The metal clank of the samovar reverberates through the small space. I'm on my stomach, arms stretched beneath the futon, fingertips grasping for the thermos. I secure it just as an otherworldly wave washes over me. I'm flat on the floor, so other than a layer of cushions landing on top of me, I'm fine.

"Water's heating," Malcolm calls out.

Time. He still needs time. I grasp the thermos, pull up to sitting using the coffee table, then realize I have a single cup—the thermos's built in cover. That's not going to work. A strong ghost is also a thirsty ghost.

"Cup?" I send the plea toward the kitchen, which is on the other side of the breakfast bar.

Malcolm ransacks the dishwasher, pulls out something that's clearly breakable, and mouths, "Catch?"

Do I have a choice? I hold up my hands, certain this will sting, or I will drop the cup, and it will shatter.

He pitches it toward me. The cup flies through the air only to hit an invisible wall. It bounces, picks up speed, its trajectory on a collision course with Malcolm's head. He swears, ducks, and the cup explodes against the kitchen backsplash. Tiny fragments rain down into the sink.

"I'll just use the one cup," I say, my words small and contrite.

"Good idea."

I crack the thermos and release the scent of Kona blend. I yearn to close my eyes and inhale. The coffee's still hot, still fresh despite the rough morning. I don't dare lose sight of the thermos, its little cup, or the swirling fog above my head.

I pour the coffee, and steam rises from the cup. I decide not to cap the thermos. Instead, I let its steam join that from the cup. The extra amount might be enough to entice this ghost.

Oh, I have its attention. The ghost swirls above my head, its form still thick and foggy, but all its focus is on the coffee. From the kitchen, I hear a gurgle and a click. I catch a whiff of exotic spices. Until I met Malcolm, I never knew some ghosts like tea. We can only hope this is one of them.

The combined aroma absorbs the chill from the air. This ghost is still strong, still forming weather patterns on the ceiling, but we've drained some of its power. It wants something hot; it's tempted.

All at once, it swoops down. I yelp, cover my head with my hands.

The ghost drains the contents of the cup in mere seconds and then does a lap around the coffee table before diving into the thermos.

The thermos clanks and rattles. It wobbles along the surface of the coffee table. Each time I try to catch it, it slips through my fingers.

Before I can yell for help, Malcolm charges across the room. He's gripping a Tupperware container and launches himself at the thermos. The Tupperware hits the coffee table, captures the wayward thermos, and skids across its surface. Malcolm lands with a thud on the floor, thermos and ghost trapped. The air clears, the ghostly fog dissipating as if sucked up by a vacuum. The Tupperware rocks in his grip, so I join him on the floor.

The container surges upward. Lukewarm coffee splatters everywhere. The thermos spins across the floor. We crash down. The ghost bucks again, and again we crash. I can only imagine what his downstairs neighbors are thinking.

But the coffee and Tupperware do their trick. The fight drains from the ghost. The air in the apartment grows warmer. What sounds like a plaintive cry comes from within the Tupperware itself. Something about it sounds familiar and tugs at my heart.

"I thought this might be an attack ghost," I say when I catch my breath.

"Yeah, but it's too ... nice."

Nice being one of those relative terms.

"It was almost too easy." Malcolm scans the coffee-splattered living area and heaves a sigh. "Almost. I'm buying the tux, aren't I?"

I peer over his shoulder and inspect the damage. He now wears a white dress shirt that's been polka-dotted with dozens of coffee-colored splotches. The tuxedo trousers are damp. I bite my lip, uncertain how to break it to him.

"That's what I thought," he says, and his sigh chases strands of my hair from my cheeks. "I'm buying the tux."

"Sorry?"

"It's not like you unleashed this ghost."

"Are you sure?"

I think back to the warehouse, to all the rooms sealed with containment fields, all those rooms filled with Springside's ghosts. I set them all free. Most were grateful, but clearly not all of them were.

"Are you a Springside ghost?" I aim my question at the container.

The Tupperware rocks.

"Did I set you free from that warehouse?"

The container rocks some more, but this ghost is losing its strength—and its anger. I'm not certain it was angry at all, maybe just scared or alone.

"Are you lost?" I ask.

From inside the container comes a pinging as if the ghost is ricocheting off the sides. The sound isn't violent. If anything, it's filled with relief.

"So which one is it?" I ask Malcolm. "Can you get a sense of it?"

"I don't want to lift the Tupperware," he says. "It still feels too wild."

Wild? I consider the swirling mass beneath the plastic. Wild is the perfect description.

"You're brilliant," I say.

"I am?"

"This is one of the wild ghosts that haunt the old barn." I bring my mouth closer to the container. "Am I right?"

The ghost thumps its response.

Malcolm sags. He doesn't release the container, but his hold relaxes, the white draining from his knuckles. I hop up to find the lid. We can't release this ghost—not yet. It's still in a mood. But now that it's made its point—it wants to go home—I can snap on the lid.

I kneel and ready the lid. We'll have to finesse this. But Malcolm is still slumped over the container. He's shaking, and panic grips me. Maybe we've underestimated this ghost.

"Malcolm?" I place a hand on his shoulder. "Are you okay?"

I get a nod—and nothing else. He continues to shake.

"Malcolm?" The panic has moved into my voice, and his name comes out as a squeak.

He holds up a hand. "Sorry ... sorry." He gulps a breath, and the sound is full of laughter. "If you unleashed this ghost, then it unleashed the twelve-year-old boy in me."

He pushes off the container to reveal the ghost inside.

It's mooning us.

"Oh, very funny," I say to the ghost. "Aren't you clever." This is why we use Tupperware with opaque sides. Ghosts can manifest all sorts of images, especially when contained. At least this one is keeping it PG-13.

Malcolm is still chuckling as we snap on the lid. Once we do, he holds the container at eye level.

"You behave," he says. "Or I will personally drive you up north and paddle you into the boundary waters."

The ghost shimmers and then settles at the bottom of the container.

"So." He offers me his hand and pulls me to standing. "We're adding a trip out to the old barn to our agenda?"

"You could change first," I say. "And I think you promised me some tea."

"I did." He tugs me closer and folds me into an embrace. I snuggle against his chest, his T-shirt damp beneath my cheek. He smells of nutmeg and Kona blend.

"You know," he says, and I can feel the rumble of another laugh. "This really, *really* isn't the way I pictured the next morning."

"But it's ours, right?" I'm so relieved to have a next morning—going on afternoon—that I'm almost grateful to the troublemaking ghost that's gently rocking its container.

Malcolm's laugh is warm against my hair. "It is, isn't it? I guess it means we're still—"

"K&M Ghost Eradication Specialists?"

"Exactly." He gives me a quick kiss, no more than a mere brush of lips. "Let me change, let's have some tea, and then we can take it from there."

I pour the tea while he changes. When he emerges from the bedroom, I do a double take. He's wearing a pair of basketball shorts and a University of Minnesota T-shirt, one with fraying at the neck, its gold faded to a pale yellow. It looks soft and like it must be his favorite.

Not that I've seen it before. Malcolm is always so pulled together. Even when he helped me rake up all the leaves last autumn, he paired some high-end skinny jeans with a fancy fleece jacket.

He's confessed to me that when he can't sleep at night, he goes running. I know he jogs a couple of miles before work each morning. Still? I'm having trouble reconciling this.

"What?" he says, turning around as if he can see his backside. "Did I forget something?"

"I just haven't seen you so ... underdressed."

His smile starts slowly, barely a tug at the corners of his mouth. Then he treats me to that sweet, dark-roast grin. "Well, except for last night."

The blush attacks once again. He laughs and then takes my hands, pulls me to the futon. We settle in, a glass of tea for each of us.

"We should talk," I say when we've both reached the bottom of the second glass.

"I don't want to, not now. I want to do this." He takes the tea glasses and places them on the coffee table.

With the pillow plumped behind us, he tugs me down, spooning me.

"This is how I pictured the next day," he says, his words a mere whisper against the nape of my neck. "Some tea and an afternoon nap."

My eyelids are heavy despite the two glasses of tea. I don't want to talk either. I want to simply be with Malcolm, no thinking, no planning, no doing.

"We'll talk later," he adds. "We always do, right?"

"We always do."

I let the warmth and safety of Malcolm's arms lull me. I don't forget about the entity, or Orson Yates, or Malcolm's estranged father. I doubt he does either. But at this moment, those things don't matter.

All that matters is how content I feel right now. I fall asleep to the rhythm of his heartbeat against my back and the soft thump, thump, thump of a ghost inside a Tupperware container.

CHAPTER 6

A persistent buzzing wakes me. I'm not sure where I am, exactly. A large, flat-screen TV looms over me. It might be threatening if I couldn't see my reflection and Malcolm's in the darkened screen. But I can. I like the picture so much that I consider buying my own television.

The buzzing continues, pauses, then starts up again. My phone. On silent. I always turn the ringer off when we go out on an eradication. The last thing you want is the ringtone blaring right as you're about to make a catch.

"What *is* that?" Malcolm murmurs against my neck.

"My phone. It's ... somewhere." Not my back pocket, where I usually tuck it.

"Did it fall out when the ghost threw you against the door?"

Oh, of course. I push to get up only to have Malcolm capture my arms.

"Stay put," he says. "I'll get it."

He tumbles up and over me. When he lands on the floor, his eyes go wide. He paws the coffee table, which is empty—no tea glasses, no ghost.

I scan the floor and point. Two glasses have rolled to a stop next to the television stand. The ghost has vanished, Tupperware and all. I'm about to panic when Malcolm lets out a laugh.

"Take a look." He nods toward the end of the futon.

There, settled by my feet, is the ghost in its container. It appears to be snoozing contently, like an ethereal golden retriever.

"We need to get that thing out to the barn," I say. "It's nothing but a troublemaker, worse than a sprite."

"Let me find your phone." He scoops up the glasses and heads toward the kitchen area. "Ah ha! Found it." He holds the phone above his head so I can see it. "It's Nigel," he adds.

A pang of guilt hits me. "How long have we been gone?"

"Too long, I'm sure, and I'm sure I'm about to hear all about it." He balances the tea glasses on top of a stack of dishes in the sink and answers the phone.

"Hey," Malcolm says and then pulls the phone away from his ear. "Hold on. I'm putting you on speaker so you can yell at both of us."

"Where the hell have you been?" Nigel's normally measured tone is taut, filled with worry and laced with anger. "It's been hours. You can't leave to investigate a possible possession and not check in. You both know that, right?"

Well, we do now.

"Sorry, sorry," Malcolm says between outbursts. "We came back to my place so I could change and ran into another ghost."

For a blissful moment, the line goes silent. Then Nigel clears his throat. "Another one?"

"A stray from the warehouse. It couldn't find its way back to its usual haunt."

"You're certain," Nigel says. "Because I wouldn't put it past Orson to deploy a spy or a decoy or—"

"Positive," I chime in. "It's one of the wild ghosts from the old barn. We're going to drop it off there on the way home."

"Be careful, because that could be where the spy or decoy or actual attack ghost is waiting."

My gaze meets Malcolm's, and a chill washes over me. I hadn't even thought of that. I feel as though I've swallowed some of Nigel's worry. What else haven't we thought of?

"We'll be careful," Malcolm says. "We're heading out now and will be back at Katy's in half an hour."

"You guys okay? Have you been fighting it this whole time?"

The quiet that follows Nigel's question stretches long and guilty. I stand and check the little clock on the kitchen stove. It's late afternoon, and we've been gone much longer than it takes to change clothes and catch a ghost.

Malcolm coughs. "We ... also took a nap."

Now the silence is incredulous.

"A nap," Nigel says, his voice full of disbelief. "Really. A nap. Never mind that Dad's in town, Orson Yates just released an untold number of attack ghosts, and I'm supposed to be on my honeymoon, you two decided to ... *oh*, you took a nap."

Wait. I don't like how Nigel's voice has gone all sly. A wash of pink stains Malcolm's cheekbones. I feel as if I'm missing something, something crucial.

"Look," Nigel says, his voice softer now and highly amused. "I get that it's ... new for you guys, and it's great that you're together, but under the circumstances—"

"We took a nap," Malcolm snaps. "Really, it was just a nap."

"Sure it was. Stop arguing and get back to Katy's. It's your turn to babysit Dad."

With that, Nigel hangs up. Neither of us moves. We simply stare at the phone resting in Malcolm's palm.

"What does he think we did, then?" I ask.

Malcolm purses his lips, and his gaze darts toward the bedroom.

So it takes me another moment, but—at last—I connect all the dots. My face grows hot, and I wonder if I'll ever stop blushing.

"He thinks we—?"

"Yep, he does." He hands me my phone and then tugs me close. "Kind of makes me wish we had."

I cast a glance over my shoulder. The ghost is rocking in its container, the motion propelling it across the futon.

"Not in front of a ghost," I say.

"You're right." He threads his fingers through my hair, easing his mouth toward mine. "They gossip way too much."

∽

We approach the old barn cautiously, leaving Malcolm's convertible on the gravel shoulder of the county road. Although the sun won't set for several hours, a hush has fallen over the area, as if everything around us is holding its breath.

"Sense anything?" Malcolm whispers.

I shake my head. The air tastes serene. Sunlight dapples the tree-lined path in front of us, glinting off rainwater that remains in some of the deeper ruts. Even the hum of insects has faded to something soft, a lullaby of a sound.

"I don't like this." He holds the Tupperware container at eye level and peers into it.

The ghost floats, neither agitated nor happy to be home. I nod toward the barn.

"Let's just release it and run back to the car."

We both glance behind us. It's like we're worried the path back to the road will vanish, swallowed by the trees and underbrush.

"I don't like this," he says again. "It's too quiet."

Other than the copse of trees that leads up to the barn, the area is wide open. Behind the structure, fields stretch for miles. Corn this year, as far as I can tell. There's something reassuring about the pattern of bright green and dark, rich earth.

"It's kind of hard to haunt corn," I say.

"You haven't seen many horror movies, have you?"

I point to the fields. "This sort of corn. Does that look haunted to you?"

"It doesn't." He glances up, and his gaze fixes on the barn. "This, on the other hand?"

The old structure stands sturdily. My grandmother always said that it had good bones. I've taken that to mean that it's architecturally sound. The breeze turns to a moan through the open doors, and the mottled paint—of an indeterminate color—makes me think she meant something more.

"Things ... happened here," Malcolm says.

"We almost set the barn on fire once, my grandmother and I, that is."

"What?"

"It was an eradication. A new ghost was wilder than usual, causing problems over at the farm. I think it started a barn fire or maybe couldn't save the horses in one—during its life, I mean. I don't know." We're at the doors now, and I trace a smudge of gray that remains after all these years. "All ghosts want something, right? This one wanted to put out the fire."

"And save the nonexistent horses?"

I nod. "I caught it in some extra-large Tupperware."

Inside the barn, the air is cool against my cheeks and tastes dry on my tongue. Spring hasn't reached this far inside, not yet. By July, the place will feel like an oven, but right now a chill races down my spine and makes me wish I had a jacket.

"Here," I say when we reach the center. "Let's release right here." I peer into the rafters, searching out this ghost's compatriots. There are three, at least, that regularly haunt this spot.

"I still don't like this," Malcolm says, but he readies the Tupperware.

"Maybe you better let me."

He grimaces at the container. "Yeah, you probably should, but I got your back."

I smile at him. "You always do."

Before he can pass me the container, before I can crack the lid, the Tupperware shoots from Malcolm's grip. The container flies into the air with so much force that it crashes against the ceiling.

Malcolm's arms wrap around me, and he tugs me to the ground. We crouch there, hands over our heads and peer upward. The container bounces from rafter to rafter with no set pattern. A wail comes from inside the plastic, but there's nothing we can do except watch it volley back and forth.

"Do you sense anything?" Malcolm asks. "See anything?"

I raise my chin—well, as much as he will let me. Is there an other-worldly presence besides the one we brought in? Possibly. Then why haven't we detected it before now?

A hollow laugh reverberates through the space. The container makes a final pass among the rafters before bulleting toward the ground on a collision course with us.

Malcolm grips my arms even tighter and rolls me just as the Tupper-ware hits. It kicks up dust and hay and comes skidding to a stop at our feet. A thick coat of grit covers my lips, and an equally thick mist hangs in the air around us. I sneeze, once, twice, three times. From inside the container comes hammering and keening.

"Very funny," I say to the two ghosts that now surround us. "I suppose you left him behind at the warehouse too."

The outline of two shimmering figures appears. The ghosts bounce once and then sink to the floor as if they're dejected by my scolding. It doesn't last. With ghosts it never does.

Malcolm stands, brushes himself off, and then offers me his hand. I pick up the Tupperware, but before I crack the lid, I skewer the two ghosts with a look.

"Be nice," I say.

They dance about in anticipation. Tonight there will be all sorts of howling and goings on now that their brother has returned. I ease open the lid, and all at once, the ghost streams out.

It does a victory lap around the space before doubling back and cuffing Malcolm on the side of the head.

"Hey!" His fingers investigate the spot, and he winces. "What have I ever done to the ghosts of Springside?"

"You're a stranger," I say.

"After nearly a year?"

"I don't know. Maybe it's because you exist?"

He snorts. "You might be onto something." He takes the Tupperware and then my hand. "And I caught their ghost catcher after all." He aims his next comment toward the rafters. "Sorry, guys."

We walk from the barn, hand in hand, the ghosts dancing behind us.

It's close to dinner by the time we reach my house, and Sadie is in my kitchen. Honestly, I'm not certain she ever left. The air is moist, filled with the gentle slosh of the dishwasher. The countertops gleam. She has commandeered several of my Tupperware containers. They sit on the kitchen table, filled with chocolate chunk cookies, gooey brownies, and homemade pita chips.

I shoot a look of dismay toward Malcolm and try to muster a smile for Sadie. I'm certain it's nothing but guilty.

"There you two are!" She wraps me in a quick hug and Malcolm bends down so she can kiss his cheek. "I told Nigel not to worry. He's in the living room with your father."

This last she directs toward Malcolm, whose entire face puckers. He's teetering on the edge of shutting down again. I can feel him pulling away from all of us, not just his father.

"And"—I wave a hand at my kitchen—"This?" I can't fathom why she's been in my kitchen, baking all day long.

"Nigel doesn't want to grant our father access to Sadie's house," Malcolm says.

Sadie opens her mouth as if to deny this, but no words come out. She purses her lips and gives the barest of nods.

"So even though they're related," I say, "your father won't cross Nigel's ward?"

"Not this particular ward, and not unless he's specifically asked."

"That sounds…" I pause, trying to conjure up the right words, or at least, polite ones. I fail. "Passive aggressive."

Malcolm shrugs. "It pretty much is."

"Does your father plan to stay here?" I have a spare room, but I'm not certain I want Malcolm's father in it. I'm not certain I have a choice.

"No, if he can't find a place to camp, the most he'll do is ask to pitch his tent in your backyard."

"You're kidding," I say.

An evil sort of delight lights Malcolm's eyes. "Not at all."

"There's the campground out by the nature preserve," I offer up.

"That would be perfect. Maybe we could ask a sprite to act as an early warning system, let us know when he's on his way here. That way, we can be out on a call." Malcolm draws little air quotes around *out on a call*.

"Really," Sadie scolds. She slaps his shoulder with an oven mitt. "You're as bad as Nigel. Your father has … issues, but he's traveled all this way to see both of you, and that says something."

"It might say something," he mutters, "but I don't think either of us is interested in listening."

Sadie rolls her eyes at me. I don't think I've ever seen her do that. Right then, I know: it's been a long day for her, too. I'm about to offer to cook dinner, but I'm grimy from the old barn. Besides, the kitchen timer rings, and her face brightens at the sound.

"The rice is done. Go." She shoos Malcolm out the kitchen door. "Katy can stay to help, but I think it's time you joined the others."

He casts a single glance over his shoulder, mouths a curse word, but heads off to the living room.

Sadie sinks against the counter but rallies quickly. "It will be the four of us for dinner."

"Belinda?"

"With Jack and Reginald. He's keeping an eye on things, and once Darien leaves for the evening, she'll come back here."

"He *is* planning on leaving."

She opens her mouth and then closes it. "I believe so." She shakes herself and laughs. "Of course he plans to leave. Dinner is almost ready. Why don't you set the table and then brew up some coffee for dessert."

I do, pulling my grandmother's wedding china from the cabinet in the dining room. I set the table, a sudden pang of loss hitting me. Maybe it was Tara's words this morning, but the ache of missing my grandmother has grown over the past few months.

I wish she could've met Malcolm. I wish she were here to tell me about necromancy—or at least explain why she never told me about it in the first place. If she were here, I suspect Darien Armand would already be out at the campground, cooking his dinner over a fire.

But she's not here. Even with Sadie in my kitchen, Belinda staying in a spare bedroom, and Malcolm in the living room, I feel inexplicably alone.

DINNER IS A TENSE THING, full of clipped words and overly polite requests for the butter and salt. By tacit agreement, we limit our conversation to Sadie's cooking, which is fantastic. She even conjured up several of Darien's favorites, although his gratitude consists of inclining his head in her direction—and little more.

Nigel grips his fork, and I worry he might snap it in two.

Coffee in the living room afterward isn't much better. Steam from the

Kona blend fills the air, but it's like the aroma has lost its ability to entice or soothe. Darien clears his throat once, twice. He sets his cup on a side table, leans forward. For a moment, I think he's planning to leave, and my heart leaps with an inappropriate amount of joy.

"I suppose we should address the elephant in the room," he says instead.

I glance about, almost expecting to spot a real elephant charging across the floor.

"Elephant?" Nigel says, and he takes a sip of coffee. "Really? There's just the one?"

Darien inclines his head toward his son, an acknowledgment of sorts. "I'm speaking of the most recent transgression."

I dart a look toward Malcolm. He's standing at the mantelpiece, perhaps because it's the most neutral territory in the room. I'm perched on the edge of my grandmother's old rocker. Sadie and Nigel have the sofa. Darien has claimed a hardback chair.

In the silence that follows, it's clear no one else knows what transgression he's referring to. He sighs, clearly put out that he must explain himself.

"Once upon a time," Darien begins, "your grandfather"—he nods at Nigel and then Malcolm—"partnered with another powerful necromancer."

"Wait a minute," Nigel says. "The Armands have always been free agents."

"Not always, and not consistently." Darien directs this toward Malcolm, who appears absorbed by the bric-à-brac on the mantelpiece. "The truly powerful ghosts and the entities of this plane require more strength to control than one necromancer can muster on his own, even one as strong as your grandfather was."

Darien shifts in his seat. "And he was quite powerful." He says this to Sadie, whose eyes are wide with trepidation.

She nods, curls bouncing. The motion catches Nigel's attention. He releases her hand to capture one of her curls and lets it wrap around his finger. The tender move plants an ache in my heart.

"In this particular case, your grandfather had hoped that together they could use their combined strength to trap an entity of considerable power."

My head jerks up at this. An entity? Of considerable power? Dread fills my stomach. For a moment, I'm afraid I'll have to dash from the room because I can't hold onto all this dread and my dinner. I don't because I know who that other necromancer was, even if she never claimed to be one.

"That was my grandmother," I say, "wasn't it?"

Darien raises an eyebrow as if the dimmest student in school has surprised him with a correct answer.

Both Nigel and Malcolm protest at once, and their replies merge into one: *Katy's grandmother wasn't ... that's impossible ... what are you saying?*

Darien casts them both a disappointed look. "You've been believing the stories Ms. Lindstrom has been feeding you."

I open my mouth in shock. "My grandmother wasn't a necromancer, at least, not in my lifetime. I didn't even know about necromancy until Malcolm explained it to me."

Across the room, Malcolm cringes. Yes, that wasn't one of our finer moments as partners.

"Do you mean to say that Lena Lindstrom gave up the practice of necromancy, and yet here you are, strong enough to capture and control that very same entity?"

Darien shocks the words from me, obliterates all my thoughts. My mind whirls as I try to process these new pieces of information. My grandmother as a necromancer? My grandmother partnering with Malcolm's grandfather? Once again, my gaze darts toward him, but he isn't looking at me. His entire focus is on his father.

"Katy doesn't lie," he says.

At least not very well.

Malcolm's eyes go flinty, and his lips twist with what looks like disgust. "That's what I do."

I'm starting to understand why.

"She grew up without knowing anything about necromancy," he adds.

"Then why does the aura of the entity surround her?" Darien sits back as if he's just delivered the final piece of evidence that will convict me. Of what, I'm not certain. "She's been deceiving you, all of you. It's only a matter of time before she betrays you."

Now Malcolm's gaze meets mine. "You were going to tell me, weren't you?"

I nod.

"But not last night?"

"I wanted last night to be about us." I don't care who hears it. I would gladly climb to the roof and shout it across the whole of Springside.

Despite everything, his expression warms. His eyes glow, and he gives me that sweet, dark-roast smile. "That's what I thought." He turns toward his father and his expression cools. Flint returns to his eyes; it's icy and sharp.

"Because Katy has a pact with the entity, she was able to save my life," he says, his words clear, distinct. "More than once. She hasn't deceived me, and I don't think she's capable of betrayal."

"That's because you're young and not—"

"Not very smart? I'm nothing more than a second-rate necromancer? At least I'm not bitter."

The hostess inside me flutters with panic. This is not polite, after-dinner conversation. Sadie is biting her lower lip as if she, too, wishes she could reel the discussion back to safer topics. Nigel, on the other hand, glances from Malcolm to his father, a hand on Sadie's as if to stop her from doing just that. The corner of his mouth tugs into a smile he aims at Malcolm, one filled with approval and admiration.

"If I'm bitter, then I have cause to be," Darien says.

Malcolm rolls his eyes.

"In the past two days alone, Katy's saved my life, at least twice." He shoots a questioning look my way. "Orson had a gun at the reception, right?"

Sadie's eyes widen in outrage. Nigel leans toward her, whispers in her ear. Her brow furrows, and while I don't know what he said, I do know this: there will be words later.

"And then before," Malcolm says, "at the warehouse."

I manage a single nod, even as I try to push images of Malcolm, wounded and near-death from my mind.

"You see?" Malcolm turns to his father again. "Twice."

"Three times, actually, but it's gauche to keep score," says a voice that isn't mine and certainly doesn't belong to anyone currently in the room.

A chill invades the space, and the words themselves tremble the floorboards, the walls, the wood of my grandmother's rocker. I stand and hold up a hand as if that will somehow stop this thing from appearing. Because I know that voice, recognize the chill.

I'm not the only one. The cool arrogance drains from Darien's expression. Nigel appears wan. Malcolm grips the mantelpiece, but his gaze searches the room.

"Thank you," he says to the air.

"Acknowledged, although it's Katy who deserves the gratitude. You're a lucky man, especially since she's so willing to overlook your rather obvious flaws."

I don't know how Malcolm will react to that, but his laugh surprises me. He scans the ceiling as if he can zero in on the entity.

"Yes, I know. I'm lucky."

"There, you see, Darien? Your youngest isn't as dimwitted as you believe him to be."

I step forward, hands on hips. Since the entity hasn't appeared, I direct my outrage toward the sky. "But I didn't invoke you."

"No, my dear, you didn't. Call it boredom, or perhaps I'm a bit miffed you didn't invite me to your dinner party."

A spot in the center of the floor begins to swirl, a whirlpool of motion that—if you stared at it too long—might hypnotize you. The form that emerges is not the craggy beast from the warehouse. It's humanlike again, almost benign. If someone were to peek through my window, they'd only see an extra guest, one dressed in pressed slacks and shirt. Maybe you wouldn't remember the face, and maybe the white in the shirt blazes a little too brightly.

The faded spot on my left cheek pulses in recognition—this is my entity. It commandeers the center of my living room, standing there, adjusting the cuffs of that snow-white shirt as if it doesn't realize it has captured our attention.

Then it glances up, and I'm caught in the swirling void of where its face should be.

"You don't need to invoke me in order for me to make an appearance."

That's going to put a crimp in my social life.

The thing has the audacity to laugh. Really, it isn't fair that it can read my thoughts—and always could.

"I'll limit my appearances when you're"—it pauses and shifts its attention toward Malcolm—"occupied with certain matters."

"You said three times?" As much as I don't want to, I cast my thoughts back to the warehouse. "Did I miss one?"

"In a sense. You were busy. Do you remember when I promised to guarantee Malcolm's safety if only you ran?"

I nod.

"Then here's what you missed." The entity holds out its hand, and inky smoke rises from its palm.

It has done this before, shown me scenes of Springside. This time, a portal opens up, one that looks out onto the warehouse barely two days before. I feel the tug of the past. I want to resist, hold up a hand to stop whatever happens next. Even as I wish this, I know we don't have a choice.

All at once, the portal swallows us up. The entire room plunges through mist and into the dark recesses of the warehouse. Stale air invades my mouth. My wrists sting from where the zip ties bit into my skin. My leg muscles protest the sudden speed. I run from the warehouse because it's the only way to save Malcolm.

Then it's as if a force yanks my spirit from my body. I see it retreat, dust kicking up in the wake of my strides. I'm so amazingly fast that all I want to do is watch myself run, but the scene in the warehouse grabs my attention.

Sometime during my escape, Malcolm managed to sit up. He collapses, this time onto his back. His head strikes the concrete floor, and I cry out. But a smile fights through the pain on his face, and his eyes are alight with what looks like triumph.

He shouldn't be so happy that I left him behind.

Prescott Jones and Orson Yates circle each other. The others in the warehouse keep their distance. Prescott holds up his hand, and his fingers glow with an otherworldly presence. I've seen this before, and I think he's about to unleash an attack ghost.

Before he can, Orson's face contorts, his expression both cruel and crafty. He swings around and aims the pistol at Malcolm.

The rapport leaves my ears ringing. The shot must go wide, since Malcolm still breathes, and there's no evidence of a wound. Orson fires again.

This time, I see it. Something deflects the bullet, one that would've struck Malcolm in the throat. Everyone ducks as the bullet pings off the shield. It embeds itself somewhere in the ceiling.

In the noise, Prescott slips away. The sedan outside the warehouse rumbles. By the time Orson stumbles to the door, the car is halfway down the dirt road that leads to the highway.

Orson wastes another bullet firing after it, but he is agitated, or has lousy aim. The shot plows into the ground and sends debris into the air.

And then all is quiet.

Orson turns from the retreating car. "Time to decamp," he says, tucking the pistol into his suit coat pocket. "This space has served its purpose, but it's been compromised. Leave all the ghosts in the main hallway. They aren't worth much anyway. Contain the ones in the back rooms. I'll be around to collect them shortly."

He steps into the warehouse. The space is thick with the stench of gunpowder and blood. He walks to the support pole where I'd been tied up and yanks what looks like a digital recorder from a spot about six feet up.

Again, he smiles that crafty, cruel smile. His fingers curl around the recorder, and he pockets it.

"Put him in one of the back rooms," Orson barks. He aims the toe of his shoe in Malcolm's direction.

"But—" One of Orson's flunkies cringes as the word leaves his mouth.

"As long as you don't ... damage him, no harm will come to you." He levels his gaze at the young man. "Or don't you trust me?"

The man swallows hard. He doesn't nod; he doesn't shake his head. His gaze darts to Malcolm as if he's weighing his options—an absent entity or a very real gun.

"Besides," Orson continues, "he'll only last as long as the pact does, but let's not make him easy to find."

Four men surround Malcolm. I want to cry out. I want to race across the floor to stop them. I'm strangely immobile. Despite the speed that carried me from the warehouse, I can't move my feet. No words emerge from my mouth.

Two men cradle Malcolm's legs, the others his head and shoulders. They are so very gentle, as if they know their lives depend on carrying him like one might an injured child.

They ease him to the floor of the room where I found him later. The last man to leave flicks off the light.

Everything fades to black.

For a moment, that black is all I see. Slowly, my living room comes into focus. The sofa with Nigel and Sadie—he has her pulled close, tucked in his arm. Darien in the hardback chair, his expression like granite. Malcolm at the mantelpiece. And the entity, holding us all in its thrall.

"So you see," it says, its tone self-satisfied, "three times."

I draw in a deep breath. My legs ache as if I've just completed the run from the warehouse. I can almost taste the salt of my sweat, the grime from my time spent tethered to that pole, and the fear that burned the back of my throat.

"You can ... do that? Take us into the past?" My words are breathless, but even I can hear the curiosity in them. This is a notion that's both amazing and terrifying.

The entity brushes some imaginary lint from its shirtsleeve. "When I choose to."

"Three times then," Malcolm says. "I owe you, Katy."

I shake my head. "You don't owe me anything. I left you behind."

"And don't go thanking me again." The entity sighs, and its breath turns the air icy, devoid of scent. "It was the only way to get her to leave."

"She's stubborn like that," Malcolm says.

The entity swings its head toward Malcolm. For a moment, he can only stare. His eyes don't glaze over, but he appears caught in the void where the entity's face should be. Something passes between them. Malcolm's expression shifts, determination settling on his features.

"Yes." He speaks directly to the entity. The cold, stale air absorbs his reply. A moment later, he adds, "I will."

His words are so soft, I'm not certain he's said anything at all or even what it means.

"We'll see about that," the entity murmurs.

"Parlor tricks."

The verdict comes from Darien, and an icy pit forms in my stomach. I once accused the entity of that myself.

It was an incredibly stupid thing to do.

"Ah, Darien, you doubt what I am, my power?"

"No," Darien says. "I doubt Ms. Lindstrom is truly strong enough to hold you, which makes this"—he gestures toward the center of the living room—"a sham."

The entity places a smoky hand on where its chin might be, assuming it had a face. Darien won't meet my gaze, so I look toward Nigel, who does such a convincing act of avoiding my eyes that I almost believe him. I try Malcolm. He merely shrugs.

I'm glad I'm not the only one who doesn't know what's going on.

Then Nigel clears his throat, prompted, I think, by an elbow nudge from Sadie.

"What my father is trying to say is he doesn't believe you've truly captured the entity since you haven't..." Nigel trails off.

"Haven't what?" I ask.

"Sent him away, say back to the Falklands—it was the Falklands, right?" Darien gives a single nod.

"Or shown any concern about the three attack ghosts he has at the ready." Again, Nigel turns toward his father. "Did I miss any?"

"Your instincts, as always, are impeccable."

Only now do I see Darien's fingers glow with that unearthly light. A bit of static fills the air. In it, I taste the otherworldly. These ghosts are strong, but I can't count them, not like Nigel has. He's right. Until he mentioned it, I had no idea. The ability to hide ghosts like that is the mark of a powerful necromancer.

"But if I don't have a pact with the entity," I say, picking my way through this minefield of a conversation, "then why is it even here?"

"That's what I'd like to know," Darien responds. The light in his fingers fades, probably because Nigel called him out.

"You know, I am right here," the entity says.

"Would you tell us?" I ask.

"Well, no, but you don't need to talk around me."

I snort.

"And you're a terrible hostess. Have you even offered me a cup of coffee?"

What compels me, I can't say, but I cross to the coffee table, pour a fresh cup, and then hold it in my hands.

"Cream?" I've served this thing coffee once before, although I've never asked its preference.

"Add a little sugar as well, my dear," it says. "I'm feeling rather sweet tonight."

I do. Then I march the cup across the room and hand it to the entity. So far I'm the only one who has dared approach it. The cup slips from my grip and into the entity's, all without it brushing my skin. Even so, the vastness of this thing leaves me breathless. It holds the cup despite its ethereal form. I can see the outline of the window through the facsimile of the shirt it wears—or pretends to wear.

The moment the exchange is complete, something shifts. I feel lighter, somehow, like when I check my bank balance and see enough money to cover all the bills.

"Did I just ... pay for something?" I venture.

"Ah, you are astute." The entity doesn't so much sip the coffee as make it evaporate. "Nothing wrong with putting a little something away for a rainy day, is there now?"

I turn from the entity and face Darien Armand. He regards me, skepticism warring with shock in his expression.

"You treat it so casually. That's ... unwise."

The entity chuckles. The sound is hollow in the air and rumbles beneath our feet. "Katy and I have always had a casual relationship. Isn't that right, my dear."

The damned thing sounds so gleeful. I refrain from rolling my eyes. My focus is still on Darien.

"I could ask it to send you back to wherever right now, couldn't I?"

Darien tilts his head as if he's been expecting this threat.

"You could, my dear," the entity chimes in, "and I would gladly comply."

"I could get rid of the ghost haunting Tara's father and find the other ones that Orson has unleashed in town. Right?" My gaze remains locked on Darien.

"In mere seconds or we could draw it out, have a little fun. That part is entirely up to you."

"But that all costs something." I turn to include Nigel and Malcolm. "It's like having a credit card with a huge limit. It would be so easy to fix everything." I think of Tara and Thomas Junior. I think of Belinda and what we'll have to do to protect her. "But then you have to pay the bill."

I wonder if this is something necromancers don't understand. Even now, all three men stare at me like I'm talking nonsense. Only Sadie nods as if what I say makes any sense at all.

"And who knows what that bill is going to look like?" I add.

I already know what it's like to have impossible bills to pay. It wasn't so long ago I spread them all out on my dining room table and considered which was the better option: paying the electric company or the property taxes.

Oh, but it would be fun. That's my promise to you, assuming you decide on that path.

I shake my head and try to shake the entity's insidious words from it. "I might lose everything I was trying to save." In fact, I'm certain of it.

We would still have fun.

I turn back to the entity, arms crossed over my chest. "Really?"

It raises its hands in a gesture of surrender, although I doubt this thing has ever surrendered to anyone. "You can't blame me for trying. You, my dear, would be a delight to corrupt."

"I remain unconvinced." Darien. Again. "She's had no training. She can't even deploy a ghost. By any measure, she isn't even a necromancer."

Malcolm spins from the mantelpiece, eyes stormy and dark, and aimed at his father. I'm immobile, shock rocketing through me. Why is Darien provoking the entity? I can't imagine what proof he needs beyond this manifestation in my living room.

"She isn't even second-rate," he adds.

The entity stands in the center of the room as if it hasn't heard these words. It tilts its head toward the cup as if admiring both the container and the contents. Its form expands to surround the coffee. I know the second the last drop has evaporated, and I'm compelled to pour yet another serving.

"Thank you, my dear."

I stare into the void that should be its face. There's no expression. No telltale hint of feeling or emotion. Slowly, it nods at Darien then returns its contemplation to me. Its amusement fills the air. I suspect that—if it could—it would wink at me.

Malcolm looks ready to charge. Nigel leans forward as if he wants to leap from the couch. It's only Sadie's calming hand on his arm that holds him in place.

Then I know: Darien is not provoking the entity at all. He's provoking me—or trying to—the way he might his sons. But I'm not an Armand; I've never been anyone's son. His words don't strike me the way they so obviously do his own flesh and blood.

"I don't know what she's done, but the two of you"—Darien points, first at Malcolm and then Nigel—"have fallen for it. The gossip is ... distressing, at best."

"You're worried about gossip?" Nigel tries to shake off Sadie's hand to no avail. "Malcolm nearly died three times yesterday, and you're concerned about what a handful of necromancers are saying? Why do we even care? We're free agents."

"What one Armand does effects all of us. My business has been ... down as of late."

I want to ask what it is Darien does for a living, but Nigel glares at his father. I look first to him, then Darien, and at last toward Malcolm. I feel as if I'm missing something in all this. I suspect that missing piece might be something Darien is hiding, and that it has to do with my grandmother and Malcolm's grandfather.

I'm going to open my mouth and ask—what, I'm not certain. But I'm tired of talking around the subject. Before I can, the entity speaks.

"Yesterday almost ended very differently—for everyone involved. Would you like to see that, Darien?" The entity's words are soft, coaxing, like he's offering a wild thing a treat before springing a trap. "Would you like to see? Would you?"

Darien stares straight into the void where the entity's face should be. His eyes glaze over, and his mouth goes slack. He gives the entity a single nod.

And in that moment, I feel as if he's condemned us all.

This time, there's no portal or preamble. I'm plunged into the stale air and grime of the warehouse. Behind me, I hear the retreating footfalls, the sound of Carter Dupree running away. At my feet, the zip tie, a few feet farther, Malcolm.

My eyes meet his. He tries to push to his elbows, but his arms tremble, and he collapses. It takes all my willpower not to rush to him, gather him close, and find a way to get us out of here. For a moment, I contemplate doing just that. What happens if we walk out the door and not look back? Even as the idea crosses my mind, I know it isn't possible. Whatever this is, we must see it through.

I take a step forward, compelled not toward Malcolm but the entity.

He shuts his eyes and shakes his head. "Katy, don't."

I don't know if he says these words or if I merely hear them in my head. And while part of me knows I could choose a different path, I'm drawn forward.

"I have to," I say, and the truth in those words strikes me hard. I have to. I must.

"Please." He tries to push up again, but he's far too injured.

"Goodbye," I whisper. "I love you."

Then I turn toward the entity and break into a run.

My hiking boots clomp against the cement floor. First Orson and then Prescott turn at my approach. Despite the dim light of the warehouse, Orson's face appears bright red. Prescott holds up a hand as if he means to stop my advance.

"Katy, no! You don't know what you're doing." Prescott takes a step, a move meant to block my access to the entity.

This is where Orson launches himself at Prescott. This is where I bypass both of them and capture the entity. This is where I run away to safety.

Instead, Prescott catches my arm. My momentum whirls us around. I stumble, missing the entity by several feet. Prescott grips my elbow. I don't know if he means to pull me away from the entity or Orson.

Except there is no entity. The warehouse holds no trace of the craggy, lava-eyed beast, the air devoid of its presence. In front of us, Orson stands, the pistol pointed in our direction. The barrel flits first toward me and then to Prescott.

"He's not going to shoot us." Prescott's whisper is hot and urgent in my ear. For once, he doesn't sound convinced of what he's saying. "He wouldn't dare. Too many questions from the necromancer community, too messy."

Despite the reassurance, I can't swallow back the thick panic in my throat. My limbs are icy with dread because Orson Yates has already killed. I'm not sure how I know this, but the moment the thought passes through my mind, I know it's true.

Orson's expression shifts, that crafty, cruel look lighting his eyes. That's when I catch movement in my peripheral vision. That's when I see Malcolm sit up, attempt to stand. I want to yell at him to run, but I know he won't. Like always, he's trying to come to my rescue.

Orson swings around. I know where he's aiming the gun. I know what he plans to do. Without thinking, I launch myself forward. With luck, I'll have enough time. With luck, I'll be able to block the bullet or cause the shot to go wide. I slip from Prescott's grasp with no effort at all. A few more steps and I'm in between Orson and Malcolm.

For one second, I think someone has punched me in the back. But the sensation is too hot, too precise for that. Orson's bullet pierces us both, me through the spine and Malcolm through the shoulder. The rapport echoes, the sound bouncing off the warehouse walls and inside my head.

Malcolm stumbles backward, knees buckling, and he falls onto the floor. A cry lodges in my throat; my breathing stops. For a moment, my body hangs suspended in the air. Then I come crashing down, tumbling on top of Malcolm.

I can't feel him, but I sense his warmth; I'm grateful for it because I'm cold, so very cold. He holds me, one hand anchored at the small of my back, the other cradling my head.

In all of this, his murmur plays in my ear.

"Katy, Katy, Katy."

It sounds like a prayer.

Something inside me releases its grasp. I float upward, leaving my body behind. Malcolm still embraces me; he still chants my name, but I can see us now, there on the gray and dusty warehouse floor. A pool of blood spreads beneath him, growing ever wider.

Orson Yates stands a few yards away, pistol lowered but clutched so hard his knuckles are white. I wonder if this means I'm a ghost now. If so, I will haunt him until the day he dies.

A hush falls over the space. In the distance comes the rumble of a sedan, of tires churning up gravel. I don't need to look to know Prescott is gone. Everyone else is silent.

Except for Malcolm. Each time he says my name, his voice grows weaker, the syllables come slower. His fingers slip from my hair in a final caress. He mouths my name one last time. Then the light leaves his eyes.

No one moves. Outside the warehouse, a songbird warbles. Inside, wails echo in the hallway where all the ghosts are locked behind containment fields.

Orson shakes himself as if waking from a dream. The pistol slides from his grip and strikes the floor. The clatter shocks everyone else into action. They scurry about, frantic, gazes darting everywhere except where Malcolm and I remain crumpled on the warehouse floor. Orson walks to the pole and yanks the digital recorder free. He lets it rest in the palm of his hand before his fingers curl around it.

He looks up, stares through the very space where I'm floating. With deliberation, he tucks the recorder into his suit coat pocket.

Then, he smiles.

~

AIR RUSHES INTO MY LUNGS. The cry lodged in my throat emerges, and I sound like a wounded animal. I choke and gasp before doubling over. Instead of concrete, I see the living room's worn carpet and the floorboards that need to be refinished. The scent of Kona blend warms the air, and a hint of lilac sneaks in through an open window. I hold still because if this is an illusion, I don't want to break it.

Across the room, Malcolm coughs so hard he must grip the mantelpiece to remain standing. Sadie weeps against Nigel's shoulder. His eyes are damp, mouth a grim line. Darien holds himself rigid in his hardback chair like a man waiting for execution.

"A very different ending," the entity says. Its voice remains soft as if it has just finished telling us a bedtime story. "Imagine the gossip were this to have happened, Darien." The entity shrugs. "Ah, well, at least you would've arrived in time for the funeral."

Darien remains stoic. I can't tell if he's even heard the entity.

"You can ... show us things that didn't happen?" The words feel rough against the back of my throat, and the taste of the warehouse is stale on my tongue.

"If I am more prescient than mere mortals, it's only because I collect and synthesize a great deal more than they can. But in this instance, the outcome came down to a moment's hesitation on the part of Prescott Jones. So unlike him." The entity shakes its head. "If you ever see him again, my dear, you must ask him why."

"Can you show us things that will happen?" I ask.

"I can show you possibilities, but that is all." The entity spreads its arms. "The future depends on so many tiny actions made in the moment, as you've witnessed."

That makes sense, not that I plan to ask the entity for such a favor. That, I suspect, comes with too high a cost. Besides, no one here needs to be clairvoyant to guess what Orson Yates might do with any entity, never mind this one.

"Katy."

My heart leaps at the sound of Malcolm's voice. It has the same tenor, that same prayer-like quality as it did in the warehouse. In the warehouse that never was, I tell myself. Except I can't convince myself of that. Even though I'm standing here in my own living room, alive and whole, part of me knows that somehow, somewhere I died, that Malcolm died.

I meet his gaze. His eyes are dark, unfathomable. He grips the mantelpiece, but I think now it's keeping him in place rather than holding him up.

"Katy," he says again, like he can't believe this is our reality. He pushes from the mantelpiece and charges across the space.

Like before, I don't think. I run to him. I will always run to Malcolm Armand. There is something about him that feels like home; he is home. Even so, fear grips me, because before we touch, I doubt he's truly here, that he's still alive.

He is. He takes my head in his hands. His gaze is so intense that it steals all my words, my thoughts.

"Katy, don't, just ... if it ever comes to that, don't do anything like that again."

I shake my head as much as his grip will let me. Tears dampen my eyes. I can't promise him that because if there's ever a chance I could save him, I would.

He pulls me close and kisses me then. The feel of it is dark and dizzying, like we've plunged into the blackness again. Everything falls away until it's just the two of us, alone. And I wish with all my heart that it would stay like that.

Someone clearing their throat has no effect, although I register the sound in the back of my mind. I should probably ask everyone to leave, but can't muster the will. All I can do is hang onto Malcolm, ever fearful that if I let go, I'll lose him forever.

"Hey, you two." Nigel's gentle voice intrudes. He's there, next to us, although I don't remember him standing, walking. I don't remember Sadie, either, but she's there with him, her eyes swollen and worried.

Malcolm eases his mouth away from mine, but he doesn't let go. Nigel grips us both by the shoulder.

"We'll talk more in the morning, but for now, take care of each other." He squeezes and pulls us closer. "You." He gives Malcolm a tap on the head. "Stop being such a hero." He turns to me. "That goes double for you."

Nigel steps back to let Sadie hug us close. Sobs shake her body, and she plants a damp kiss on each of our cheeks.

Then it's just Malcolm, Darien, and me.

Malcolm's father doesn't speak. He doesn't embrace either of us. He does, however, give Malcolm a nod of what might be approval. I'm not sure it extends to me, but I doubt that matters.

At the front door, he hefts his backpack onto his shoulders.

We don't ask where he's going; he doesn't tell us.

The door closes behind him with a soft click. A moment later, Malcolm throws the deadbolt.

"I don't want to leave you," he says, but his hand still rests on the lock. I worry that he thinks too much has happened, that it's better if he does leave.

"Just because everyone else left doesn't mean you have to."

He turns then and sinks against the door. He curls his fingers in a come-here gesture.

I do.

"I don't have anything here," he whispers.

"I gave you a toothbrush."

"I mean clothes, pajamas."

"You have clothes." I pluck the hem of his shirt. "And do you really need pajamas?"

"I don't know." A warm, sweet smile tugs at his lips. "Will I?"

"I doubt it."

"If you say so." He buries his face against my neck. "Jesus, Katy, I can't shake the idea of it. I'm afraid this is an illusion, and if I move too fast or do too much, I'll shatter it."

I'm afraid that if I speak, I'll shatter this as well. So instead, I take his hands and urge him toward the staircase.

We climb the stairs at a glacial pace. Malcolm stops to sweep strands of hair from my face. I pause to tuck the tag of his shirt beneath its collar. I touch his cheek, find the pulse in his neck, press my palm against his chest and feel the rise and fall of his breath.

When we reach the landing, I realize the entity vanished without my noticing. It's just Malcolm and me, the two of us alone—the thing I wished for with all my heart. Something shifts in the air, a balancing of sorts.

My heart's desire, all for a cup of coffee.

Something tells me that, next time, the exchange won't be quite as easy.

I'm NESTLED in Malcolm's arms. Everything is warm and safe here, just as I wished for. A breeze flutters the curtains. The night outside the bedroom window is quiet except for an occasional cricket or dog bark.

I should sleep, but my mind whirls. I struggle to piece together everything I know and test it against everything I believe, but the gaps between the two are vast.

"What are you thinking about?" Malcolm's voice is a low rumble beneath me. The sound is rich and warm, and his breath chases those wayward strands of hair across my forehead.

"You're awake?" It's an inane sort of question, but he only laughs.

"Your thoughts are so loud that I'm surprised the entire neighborhood isn't awake."

I sigh. "Sorry. I'm just trying to pull everything together."

"I figured as much." His fingers stroke the line of my brow. "Don't think so hard."

"Can't help it. I'm just so ... I was wondering about everything, like back at the mausoleum. Remember when you said you were getting a vendetta vibe from the entity? Were you—?"

"Lying?"

I cringe. "Yeah. That."

"Given my track record, it's a fair question." Malcolm shifts and I roll to see his face.

In the dark, it's hard to discern his expression, but I detect no guile.

"I was telling the truth, at least about the vibe. I mean, I thought it was about you, which makes sense considering its actions back then. But I wonder. Maybe it just *involves* you somehow."

"How?"

He tugs me close for a quick kiss. "If we knew that, we'd probably know everything."

I suppose we would.

"I thought maybe tonight was part of a vendetta," I add, "putting us through that alternate reality."

"I suspect it was more of an object lesson for my father."

Or for me. I ponder this and the entity in general. I'm here, right now, alone with Malcolm, because of the entity, because I captured it, and because now I'm its necromancer—or so it says. I'm not cold and dead on a warehouse floor, and neither is Malcolm. Yes, I think, this evening was a not-so-subtle reminder of all that.

"I don't understand the entity, what it wants. It haunts me, it marks me, and now it does me favors—for a price—and it talks to me like—"

"Like it's trying to seduce you. Yeah, noticed that, don't like it." His chest heaves with an exhale. "This entity doesn't have a morality like humans do, but it does honor its agreements, and it's made one with you. But it's still going to get as much from that deal as possible."

"Sounds like a stockbroker," I say.

"Hey!"

"Or a necromancer. No wonder every last one of you is chasing it down. That's what you were doing, right? When you came to Springside."

"Yes, and no. I did come to speak to your grandmother, and rumors had surfaced about this entity. That must have been about the time she died, and it was free of the pact your grandmother made with it."

We're quiet for a moment, my mind filled with missing my grandmother. Malcolm strokes my hair as if that alone can take the sadness away.

"At first it was all about me," he says, his voice quiet. "Yeah, surprise, right?"

I can't help it. I laugh.

"Then I thought if I could catch it, I could make a bunch of money and impress you and then, you know, other stuff."

"Basically what we're doing now."

"Pretty much," he says and pulls me in for another kiss. "But the entity was right. My attention shattered. You shattered it. I could've caught it before Nigel did, but I think even then, I knew I wouldn't be able to hold it. Real life with you was better than my imaginary one."

Real life with Malcolm still astonishes me. I couldn't have imagined it, and some days can't believe it's true. I have no idea what my life would've been like if he hadn't zoomed into town in his cherry-red convertible.

"I think it goes back even farther," I say after a moment. Malcolm's fingers play up and down my spine. As distracting as that is, my mind is buzzing too hard to concentrate on anything other than the entity.

Well, almost.

"Something happened with my grandmother and your grandfather."

"I wouldn't trust anything my father says."

"Something happened, and..." I fight to put the thoughts I have into actual words. "And maybe instead of you chasing the entity, it lured you to Springside."

Malcolm bolts upright and sends me tumbling toward the edge of the bed. He swears. I flop back to wait until he works through most of his vocabulary.

"Christ, you're brilliant, you know that?" He reaches for me and settles us among the pillows again.

"Not really. If I were brilliant, I would've figured that out months ago."

"This changes things. This feels like we're onto something."

"Maybe. There's more, maybe something to do with my mother as well," I say. "Remember at Tara's house, and her mother talking about the Lindstrom woman? Let's assume she didn't mean me since I don't even know Tara's father."

"So, that leaves two Lindstrom women, right?"

Enough lamplight filters through the curtains that I see a curious smile curve Malcolm's lips. "Do all Lindstrom women keep their maiden name?" he asks.

"It's tradition. My grandmother made me promise that if or when I ever got married I wouldn't take my husband's name."

"You know that's a necromancer thing, right?"

"What?" This time, I bolt upright and nearly clock Malcolm in the jaw. "I can't believe you're telling me this now."

"I never really thought about it until now. Female necromancers ... I wouldn't say they're rare, but those who practice the craft keep their maiden names. Like your grandmother. And your mother."

"That's the second thing your father said to me. He asked if I was a Lindstrom."

"What did he say when you told him yes?"

"He said, 'I was afraid of that.'"

Malcolm's body shakes, but his laughter is a dark thing I don't much like.

"My father, always the diplomat. Jesus."

"Forget your father for a moment—actually, don't. I have the feeling you'll need to think about him if we're going to eradicate the ghost possessing Tara's father. Remember what Tara's mother said?"

Malcolm exhales. "Something along the lines of you're obsessed with her, with *it*."

"The entity?"

He falls silent.

"What does your father do? I mean, as a necromancer."

"He's an expert at tracking and capturing very powerful, very elusive ghosts—usually for a very high price." He meets my gaze then, but his eyes are shrouded both by his lashes and the dark. "These aren't Springside ghosts. These are ghosts who live in the jungle or the Sahara or wherever because they want zero interaction with humans."

"Could he catch the entity?"

"I don't know. Possibly? Probably?"

"Do you think he maybe wanted to at one time? Do you think maybe my mother did?"

"Huh. That's an interesting way to look at it."

"Maybe she hired him?" I suggest.

"Or maybe they were working together." His fingers continue to explore, caress, as if he could pull answers from my skin. "I mean, clearly, the Armands aren't the free agents we like to claim we are." He pauses, stares at the ceiling. "But why would they work together?"

I never knew my father; I didn't grow up with a grandfather. But I feel the loss of my grandmother acutely. Some days, the pain stabs as sharply as it did on that morning I found her. What if you felt that every day, but there was something you could do about it?

"My grandmother never had a funeral for my grandfather. There's a plot—an empty one—in the Springside cemetery that was supposed to be his. I don't know what she told everyone. I could ask someone, Mr. Carlotta or Chief Ramsey maybe. What if she—or my mother—wanted to get my grandfather back?"

Malcolm falls silent again. His mouth isn't grim, but it's lost its smile.

"I don't suppose that's something your father would tell us?" I prompt.

"You suppose right."

Just what Springside needs: yet another necromancer with an agenda. Malcolm's fingers thread through my hair. I know it must be late, but the night seems to stretch before us endlessly. He kisses my forehead and then my nose. I have so many thoughts about everything that I'm certain they'll all burst out at once.

I blurt the first one that feels the most crucial. "Orson Yates."

Malcolm snorts. "If you're trying to turn me on, that's not the way to do it."

I laugh and burrow closer to him. "I'm curious about what he might know about your family, or really, your parents' marriage."

"Everyone in the necromancer community knows enough, so that includes Orson. Their breakup was epic. We're talking drama on the level of a soap opera. My mother is ... dramatic. Imagine the polar opposite of my father."

Yet another person I can't wait to meet.

"And Orson doesn't much like Nigel," I say. "I mean, even before all of this, at least not from the sound of it."

"You didn't know Nigel before the addiction. Katy, he was amazing. His strength rivaled my father's. He was going to do great things."

"I can't imagine Orson liked that."

"No, not at all."

After only six months, Orson knows me well enough that, to hurt me, he stole all of Springside's ghosts, and then kidnapped and nearly killed Malcolm. How well might he know the Armands? What could he do with that knowledge?

"Why did this ghost attack Tara's family?" I ask.

"Orson ... left in a hurry." He shakes his head and laughs softly.

Yes, and Malcolm was a big part of that.

"He probably unleashed the ghosts he had with him and went somewhere to lick his wounds," he adds. "You know how bad some ghosts are at directions. Some can't find their way across town."

Or back to the old barn.

"And this ghost picked Tara's family because?"

Part of me wants to jab Malcolm in the chest, prod him to think harder on this. I scowl as if I can help him do that thinking.

He sighs. "Because there's something about her family that looks an awful lot like mine."

"And that would be?"

He takes my head in his hands and cups my face. "Katy, I just don't know."

"Or maybe you don't want to think about it."

"That. Exactly."

"You need to. You need to think about your father."

"No, no, I don't. The world is a better place when you don't think about my father. Trust me, I've had years of practice not thinking about my father."

He tugs me closer still. I open my mouth to protest, but he swallows my words with a kiss. He hooks a leg around mine, and we roll. I can't help but laugh again. There's something so wonderful about being with him like this.

He nuzzles my neck, kisses the hollow of my collarbone. So gentle. So soft.

"What are you doing?" I whisper, afraid to break the spell.

"Not thinking about my father." He peers at me, and we're close enough that I can see the warmth and humor in his eyes. "Doesn't this night feel like a gift?"

It does; it really does. On the breeze, I catch a whisper of something that sounds almost like an admonishment. My heart's desire, and I'm squandering it. I push away the fear of what might come next. Instead, I thread my fingers through Malcolm's hair and pull him to me.

"You're right," I say. "Let's not waste it."

CHAPTER 9

Everyone should wake up to the scent of cinnamon and a hint of lilac in the air. I haven't opened my eyes, but the mattress shifts with Malcolm's weight. The clean aroma of Ivory Soap joins the one from the cinnamon rolls.

At least, I hope it's cinnamon rolls.

The urge to open my eyes nearly overwhelms me. If I don't, then it's still, technically, last night. If I don't, then I can keep the problems of today in the recesses of my mind, if only for a few more moments.

But when the smell of coffee—real, percolator-brewed coffee—reaches me, I nearly fall out of bed.

The only reason I don't tumble to the floor is Malcolm, sitting on the edge of the bed, all pressed and gelled. He's immaculate, of course, white dress shirt and creased khakis. In comparison, I'm ... rumpled.

"Morning, beautiful." He holds up a tray. "Look. Breakfast in bed."

"You made me cinnamon rolls?"

"Well, sort of. I popped them from a can, but—"

"That counts."

"And I also made you some..." He lets the sentence trail and reaches for an insulated carafe. He pours and then hands me a cup. "Coffee."

The cup warms my fingers, and the scent fills the pocket of space between us.

Malcolm sits back, hands planted on his thighs. "Okay. I'm ready for your honest opinion."

I roll my eyes, but I do sip, tentatively at first. The dark roast is bold, with a hint of cocoa. And it's good. Really good.

"My grandmother would be proud."

"You're just saying that."

To prove my point, I down the entire cup and then hold it out. "More? Please?"

"So it passes muster?"

I merely nod because, by this time, I've snagged a cinnamon roll and my mouth is too full of cream cheese icing and flakey layers for actual words. The second cup clears away the gooey sweetness and the fog from my head.

"These are the best cinnamon rolls I've ever had."

"They're not really homemade."

"They're still the best," I say, and I hope he takes my meaning.

The smile he gives me is almost shy. "You win. They're the best."

"And this?" I say, waving a hand at the whole package that is Malcolm Armand, ready for business. "Does this mean what I think it does?"

"Probably. If you hurry, we might be able to eradicate this ghost in time for Thomas Sr. to make it to work."

We eradicate at all hours of the day—and night—it's true. An early morning one like this? It feels right. The ghost won't expect us back so soon and neither will Chief Ramsey. I plant a sticky kiss on Malcolm's cheek on my way to the shower.

Just before the door closes behind me, I hear his murmur.

"It's about time I started thinking about my father."

THE BLUE DOOR of Tara's house glows in the sunrise. The sight is hopeful —almost. Since yesterday, the color has faded a shade or two, but at least the paint isn't peeling. Not yet, anyway.

"Does it look like a full-on infestation to you?" Malcolm whispers.

I can't tell, not from this distance. The grass sports patches of brown that weren't there yesterday. Several of the roses droop, heads bowed as if in mourning, petals scattered along the ground.

"I don't know," I say. "It may not bother until we're committed."

That would trap us inside.

We continue to stare at the house, putting off that moment of commitment, probably because our plan is sketchy, at best. I carry a percolator and everything to brew coffee, but I don't think we'll need it. In this case, I think it will be the samovar and the tea that will make the difference.

"My grandfather showed me how," he says now, an echo of our previous conversation.

"Do you think you can?"

His mouth is grim. "If I can draw out the ghost, it will be up to you to catch it."

I shift the bag on my shoulder. The Tupperware containers rattle. Malcolm's never even witnessed a possession, but his grandfather did instruct him on what to do. That's more than what I know.

The sound of a car door shutting punctuates the air. I don't think much of it. Springside has its share of early risers. It's only when someone clears his throat behind us that I make the connection.

"Do you even have a plan for getting inside the house?"

The words are calm and measured, but they send my heart racing. I whirl at the same moment Malcolm does. Behind us, Nigel and Sadie stand, arms linked. An amused smile plays on Nigel's lips. Sadie has the look of a soldier going to war.

"What are you doing here?" Malcolm says. "Are you crazy?"

"No more than you." Nigel studies the house as if he can calculate the risks from the sidewalk. "I might be an addict, but I'm still a necromancer."

"World-class," Malcolm says, his voice soft, full of admiration.

"Neither of you have faced something like that." Nigel points to the patches of brown, bricks in the chimney that have turned gray. "The entity notwithstanding. Not only is this thing stronger than Harold's ghost, but this is also a possession. You have no idea what that means."

He's right, of course. Still. "And it was sent here to possess you," I say.

"Which makes me the perfect bait."

Malcolm gives his head a violent shake. "Oh, no. Not that."

"You think tea is going to work, baby brother? Amateur move. This thing already has substance and heat, in the form of a human body. Tea isn't tempting it. Even Katy's coffee won't tempt it. But its original target? It was sent here for me. It's the least I can do."

"It might be the least, but it's also the stupidest," Malcolm shoots back. "I already lost you once. I don't want that to happen again. I saw what happened when you couldn't stop swallowing ghosts."

"And I watched you die yesterday. I think that makes us even."

Their voices are rising with the sun. I cast a hasty look up and down the street, watch for curtains fluttering in windows and people peering out of doors. The last thing we need is a concerned neighbor calling the Springside Police Department yet again. I send Sadie a pleading look.

"Nigel." Sadie pats his arm. "Malcolm is only concerned. And Malcolm? Why do you think I'm here? I'm not losing him. Neither of us is."

They both scowl. Nigel makes a face. Malcolm rolls his eyes.

"Honestly," I say in disgust, "I sometimes think you two just like to fight."

"Yes, Katrina Lindstrom. They do."

My heart leaps again. Sadie lets out a little gasp. Nigel's eyes widen, more in recognition than surprise.

How Reginald Weaver came to be standing next to us I may never know. But he's here, sturdy and calm, his form casting a long shadow across the lawn.

"What are you—?" Nigel begins.

"You're quite predictable, my friend." Reginald nods toward Sadie. "Plus, your lovely bride was concerned."

Nigel glowers, but the look washes over Sadie. Instead, she beams at Reginald. His appearance eases the worry inside me. I step back and consider our little group. There's Malcolm, who's always at my side. Nigel, who was once addicted to swallowing ghosts, and Sadie, who has a lifelong fear of them. Add an enigmatic and reclusive necromancer? We're an unlikely team. Even so?

We might be able to do this.

"Who's coming inside with me?" I ask.

Nigel blinks. "You have a way in?"

From my pocket, I pull the crumpled piece of paper Tara shoved into my hand yesterday. "I do."

"Do you also have a plan?" he counters.

I give him a pointed look. "Isn't that why you're here?"

Nigel rubs his temples. "You're worse than Malcolm."

"Actually," I say, "I don't think we should all go in at once, or through the front door. I think it should just be me."

"Katy," Malcolm begins, "I don't think—"

"It put you in a trance yesterday," I say and then point toward Nigel. "He's this thing's target. It knows me, but it can't hurt me the way it can the two of you."

Reginald nods. "Yes, that is our best option. There's an alleyway around back. You can let us in through the kitchen door."

I tilt my head, curious about how he knows this.

"I, perhaps, did some reconnaissance last night." He nods in my direction. "You be careful, Katrina Lindstrom. Get to the back door as quickly as possible. Remember, the ghost will try to stop you."

Malcolm cringes as if the last thing he wants is to send me in alone. But he takes our makeshift field kit and slings the bag of Tupperware over his shoulder before tugging me in for a quick kiss.

"Let's do this," he says.

And then I'm alone, feet planted on the walkway, staring at the gray two-story house with the fading blue door.

A CHILL SHROUDS the front porch. It's not a full-on ghost infestation, but the house is rapidly aging, becoming haunted. It has the feel of a place long abandoned and unloved.

I study the series of numbers scrawled on the tiny piece of paper in my palm. The keypad barely registered yesterday. Despite my bravado on the sidewalk, I'm not one hundred percent certain I can get in.

I test the door with a brush of a fingertip, just in case I'm wrong about the infestation. The surface is cool, but not so cold I'll risk frostbite. Each key beeps as I press it. A light flashes. The deadbolt churns in the mechanism.

So far, so good.

Then, on its own accord, the door creaks open.

Or not so good.

The foyer is dim. The air is cold and stale and makes the back of my throat ache. This is what anger might taste like. And while I know Reginald told me to hurry, I can't force my feet to move any faster, not even when the door groans closed behind me.

I test out each step as if I could move through the air without disturbing it. I don't know where this ghost might be, except it must still possess Tara's father. That means it must be somewhere physical. Upstairs in bed. On the living room couch. But not in the ventilation system or floating along the ceiling.

A clatter echoes through the house, of someone ransacking cupboards or pulling items from a bookshelf. I freeze and try to gauge where the sound is coming from, but the noise clouds my head. It's everywhere and nowhere all at once.

Kitchen. I need to get there, let everyone in. A sliver of icy air curls around me. I inch forward, and it grasps at me again, twists around my ankles and knees. I don't trip, but each step I take is slower. My lungs must work harder to pull in a full breath. An icy tendril worms its way higher until I feel it caress my throat.

I grab onto the wall and drag myself forward. This thing knows my fear, that awful sensation of not being able to breathe. I close my eyes—briefly—and focus. But my heart still pounds; my breathing is ragged.

Frantic thoughts ping in the back of my mind. I'm not going to make it to the kitchen.

A menacing force builds behind me. I glance over my shoulder to no avail. I can't see this thing, but I sense it, and it's poised to pounce. Kitchen, I think. Get to the kitchen.

Up ahead is the living room, and beyond that, the entrance to the kitchen. I keep it in my sights, even as the hallway plunges into darkness. I go on instinct, clawing my way forward. I yank and jerk and pull free of the tacky air and burst into the wintry light of the kitchen—and nearly crash into Thomas.

I stumble backward, hands held up as if that will ward him off. He looms in front of me. Overnight, his hair has turned pure white. His skin looks as if it's been coated in wax. There's a human somewhere beneath all the layers, but he doesn't have enough warmth or strength to fight his way out. His lips are cracked and pale, fingers thick and clumsy.

But his eyes. Oh, his eyes aren't his own. Those belong to the ghost, and they regard me with perverse delight and cunning.

"Well, if it isn't the Lindstrom woman."

His voice slides through the space, adding a layer of frost to everything. Above our heads, icicles grow from the kitchen rack. They glimmer, their points deadly. Beyond Thomas, I spot the back door, its window obscured by thick fog. I can't see out. I doubt anyone can see in.

I contemplate Thomas again. Who am I supposed to be? My mother? My grandmother?

"I have a first name," I say.

The air in this space sucks all the moisture and strength from my words. I'm not even sure they reach Thomas, except for the smile that distorts his lips.

He laughs, the sound rippling through the air. The kitchen rack shudders, shaking loose several icicles. They shatter against the granite countertop, shards flying everywhere.

I duck behind my arms. The cuts come, quick and tiny, a series of searing pain along my forearms and the back of my hands. Compared to this kitchen of grays and whites, the blood that bubbles from my skin is so red.

So the ghost refuses to take that bait. Blood streams along my skin and I shake out my arms, speckling the floor with splotches of red. I don't know who I am in this strange reality, or what my mother or grandmother may have done—except for one thing.

"I didn't betray you."

These words come out with more substance. They're warmer, stronger. They meet the cold air in the center of the kitchen, and clouds form. Light flashes, and moments later, the room quakes with what can only be thunder.

The storm clears the fog from the back door. Through the windowpane, Reginald appears. Then he vanishes. I think I see the top of Malcolm's head.

Something flies at the window. I duck, instinct taking over once again. Glass splinters. The window explodes, and the kitchen door crashes against the wall.

"Get Katy," Reginald says. "Hide in a bathroom and tend to her wounds. Meet us in the living room."

"But—" I begin.

The four of them charge into the kitchen and overwhelm my protest. Reginald and Sadie shield Nigel from the ghost while Malcolm dashes for me, grabs my hand, and yanks me from the room.

"But—" I try again.

He doesn't even glance my way. We race through the downstairs hallways until Malcolm pulls me into a powder room. He locks the door behind us and starts pawing through the cabinets.

"I hope they have something in here, otherwise we're going to be ruining some fancy towels."

"They have two kids," I say. "There must be something. But I don't really need—"

"Jesus, Katy, look at your arms." Malcolm flings open the medicine cabinet and lets out a sigh of relief.

I do as he says, holding my arms out in front of me. Sheets of red rush toward my fingertips. I'm dripping blood onto the floor, so I move toward the sink. As I do, a wave of dizziness sweeps over me. I knock into Malcolm.

"Easy there," he says. "Let's clean you up. You okay?"

I nod and hold my arms still.

Water stings. Soap stings. The antibiotic spray Malcolm spritzes all over my skin stings.

"I'm not sure there are enough Band-Aids for this." He rattles a box and then dumps the contents on the edge of the sink.

"Gauze?" I suggest. Now that my arms are clean, I can see all the cuts —so small, so precise, so deadly.

"It will have to do." With gentle fingers, Malcolm wraps my arms, using an entire roll of gauze from the first aid kit. His mouth is grim, and his eyes focused on their task. I want more than anything to make him laugh.

"I look like a mummy," I say.

He swears. Not the response I was hoping for. Then he cups my face with a hand.

"Katy, just…" He trails off, and I can't tell if he's heartsick or angry. Before I can try something else, the smallest hint of a smile warms his face.

"Just be careful," he says.

And then he kisses me.

A grayish light filters through the hallway. It's not the blackness of before, but it's not natural, either. We've only been inside for half an hour, at most, and I acutely miss the sunlight. I'm starving for something natural and warm. I grip Malcolm's hand tighter since he must be the warmest thing in this house.

"Our presence is draining some of its power," he whispers. "If the ghost doesn't keep its guard up, Reginald will be able to capture it."

"Even while it's still possessing Tara's father?"

"It's ... messy, but possible."

We pause near the kitchen. The space is a disaster of pink-tinged puddles and splatters of red everywhere that make me think of crime scenes and serial killers. A light fog remains, clogging the skylights, barring the sun from entrance.

Malcolm shakes his head. "Nothing in here." He eyes me. "Except for your blood."

We move on, inching our way along the textured wallpaper. I glance behind me, but it's too dark to tell if I'm leaving bloody prints in my wake. We pause outside the living room. Malcolm presses a finger to his lips, and I nod. We hold still. We listen.

We hear absolutely nothing.

We wait in silence for ten seconds, thirty, a whole minute. The muscles in my legs begin to twitch. An urge—to rush in and confront this thing—nearly overwhelms me.

"It wants me in the living room," I say, my voice barely a whisper.

"I feel it too, only—" He breaks off and shakes his head.

"What?"

"Different. That's all."

Slowly, I inch my head so I can study him. He hasn't shut down, not yet anyway. But where I want to rush in, hands on hips, and scold—much like my grandmother might—Malcolm's reaction is wholly different. He glances at me, and I see the heartache in his expression.

He has the look of a little boy who knows he's going to lose his family. The hurt in his eyes is deep, and I want nothing more than to make it go away.

"What would you do when your parents fought?" I ask.

"Freeze, shutdown, hide."

"What would Nigel do?"

"Sometimes come get me, take me outside. We'd go somewhere or ride our bikes."

"In the winter?"

The moment I say the words, I realize that's where we are—or maybe it's *when* we are. Winter. Ice. The gray quality of the sunlight. Everything suggests the longest night of the year, of being trapped inside.

"Basement, or our rooms. When he was older, Nigel started trapping ghosts and letting them loose. My mother would sense them immediately, and their presence would distract my father. Funny thing is, when they realized he was doing it? He got nothing but praise. He was what? Eight, and already deploying attack ghosts—more or less."

That isn't the whole story. I hear it in his tone. Malcolm isn't telling me something, and I'm not sure what that something might be. But it will have to wait. The urge to storm the living room is strong. I can't imagine what Reginald is doing, but he probably could use some help.

I brace against the wall, ready to push off and barrel into the living room when an otherworldly presence anchors my shoulder in place.

"Not yet, Katrina Lindstrom." The voice—an ethereal version of Reginald's—echoes around us.

Malcolm manages a low chuckle. "He has a ghost watching you."

"He can do that? How does he do that?" Despite everything I've seen this morning, this may be the most surprising.

"He's a powerful necromancer. If he says not yet, then he means not yet."

"And he can deploy a ghost to say it to me?"

"Exactly."

So we wait. In the quiet that follows, another question occurs to me.

"Is eight young for a necromancer?"

"For directing them, the way Nigel was? Yes. He was considered a prodigy. But by eight, a necromancer should at least be able to capture ghosts."

"I started working with my grandmother when I was five."

"See?"

"And you?"

"What?"

"When did you start deploying ghosts?"

He falls silent. "I never did," he says at last. "Never have."

"But you and Selena—"

"Selena and I had an arrangement. I never deployed her or sent her on errands. Ghosts were my companions. I sensed them early, possibly earlier than Nigel did. There was a time when everyone thought I was simply a sensitive."

"And not a necromancer?"

"Exactly. Everyone thought I had inherited my gift from my mother, but none of the skills of my father."

I consider this—and all the things I know about the necromancer community—and the power and prestige that comes with being a necromancer. I suspect sensitives aren't granted the same status.

"Nigel was the smart one," he adds. "I was the pretty one."

"But, Malcolm, you're smart."

He gives his head a little shake.

At the moment, I don't have words to convince him otherwise. A reverberation comes from the living room. That otherworldly presence whips around my head.

"Soon, Katrina Lindstrom. You will need to catch the ghost once I've drawn it out and before it can enter Nigel."

I nod, although whether Reginald's ghost can relay this to him, I have no idea. Malcolm unslings the bag with the Tupperware and hands me the largest container. He hangs onto the lid.

"How did you find out you were a necromancer?" I ask.

"Nigel caught one of my ghosts, one of my friends, and it got mad. So when he unleashed it on my parents, it went crazy. It wasn't more than a sprite, really, but no one could catch it."

"Except you?"

The barest hint of a smile plays on his lips. "Except me."

"And that changed things?"

"Sort of."

In those two words, I hear it all: he was still the pretty one, the baby of the family. I think of Nigel, being so good at such a young age. Would the pressure of that build to a point where you couldn't take it? I glance at Malcolm and wish he could see himself the way I see him.

A buzzing fills the air, a crackling static that makes me want to drop the Tupperware and clamp my hands over my ears. Before I can ask what it is or what we should do, a single word rings out.

"Now!"

Malcolm grabs my hand, and we rush into the living room.

Nigel stands near the hearth. In front of him, Sadie is stationed. Her lips are pale, eyes wide and scared, but her curls are wild, fierce things. She stands in front of her husband like a sentry.

In the center of the room, Thomas Sr. shakes. Reginald is at his side, a palm on Thomas's forehead, a hand bracing his shoulder. Sweat runs down Reginald's face. His arms tremble. His stance is wide, but every few seconds he readjusts it, as if this ghost is on the cusp of overwhelming him.

I worry that maybe it is.

Malcolm points to the sofa and then to the bookcase opposite of it. I nod, let his fingers slip from mine as we take up a position in between Thomas and Nigel. We can't block the ghost's view of him. It's the only thing tempting it from its current home. But we can't be so far away we miss making the catch.

Reginald lets out a terrific roar. A wail comes from Thomas, unearthly and loud, but the sound diminishes as the ghost peels away from his body. Thomas slumps into Reginald, and the ghost that so recently occupied his body now occupies this space.

It fills the living room with its rage and power. The walls shake. Glass rattles in the windowpanes. Pictures swing on nails and crash to the floor. The ghost swirls, its form like winter itself, so cold and barren. Despite its ethereal form, the force feels like a blizzard, like icy snow striking skin.

The ghost rotates, tighter and tighter. It shoots across the room, a frigid arrow. It bounces off one wall, the next, building up speed. It ricochets off a family portrait, and this time, I know its target.

It's heading straight for Nigel.

Malcolm leaps, but the Tupperware lid slips through this ghost without slowing it down. It flies too far above my head for me to even attempt a catch. The ghost skitters along the ceiling, but its aim is clear.

Nigel doesn't crouch or flinch. He merely stands there, his hands locked on Sadie's waist. Her expression loses all its fear. The moment before this thing plunges into Nigel, the moment before it destroys the man she loves, Sadie raises her hands, like a center fielder, and deflects the ghost.

It careens straight for me, knocked off course and off kilter. I lunge, Tupperware clutched in front of me. I land on the floor with a thud. The container beneath me rocks. My fingers slip along the sides, and I'm desperate to keep a seal with the living room floor.

I think of what Orson Yates—of all people—once told me: that every time I catch a ghost, I commit an act of necromancy. The seal is more than physical. I concentrate on that, on not letting go, not with my hands and not with my mind.

The ghost bucks like it might throw me off. Before it can, before my arms give out, Malcolm joins me, his grip covering mine, reinforcing it.

The ghost quiets—or rather, it can't fight the two of us. We won't risk snapping the lid on anytime soon, but for now, everyone is safe.

At least I think so. I glance up. Thomas is stretched out on the sofa.

Already the glossy black is returning to his hair, and the layers of wax are melting away. His eyes are closed. My guess is he's unconscious.

Reginald is slumped on the floor next to him, rumpled and worn. He must see the question in my eyes because he nods, touches his fingers to his brow as if in salute.

By the fireplace, Nigel cradles Sadie. He cups her head in his hands. From my spot on the floor, his murmur reaches me.

"My brave and beautiful wife."

When Orson orchestrated this attack, I don't think he counted on Sadie's quiet fierceness, or love overcoming fear. Orson understands weaknesses; he miscalculates when it comes to strengths.

Late morning sunlight streams through the windows, chasing away the fog and warming the air. The scent of roses alone gives me hope that we've truly banished this thing, even if Malcolm and I can't move from our spot on the floor.

"Katrina Lindstrom, young Malcolm, can you continue to contain the ghost?" Reginald's voice quavers.

I dart a look at Malcolm and then peer at Reginald. He's still slumped against the sofa, legs stretched out in front of him, and his skin has a waxy cast to it that worries me.

"Are you—?" I begin.

"Yes, I will be fine, with time."

How much time? Worry eats away at my relief. The kitchen is a disaster, the living room not much better. Malcolm and I are planted on the floor. If anyone happens inside—Tara's aunt, her mother, Chief Ramsey —the consequences will be both real and otherworldly.

We need a necromancer, a ghost catcher, someone to secure the lid. Nigel can't, and at the moment, Reginald isn't strong enough.

"You're bleeding again," Malcolm says, his voice low.

Spots of red now dot the gauze along my arms. With the blood comes the pain, that stinging sharpness, and an itch that's nearly impossible to ignore. I want nothing more than to let go and scratch at my arms.

"It's okay." I close my eyes and take a deep breath. "It'll stop."

Maybe.

We hold on tight as sounds invade the space. Birdsong, the rumble of an occasional car, a bicycle bell ringing out in greeting. As long as we hold still, hold onto this ghost, everything will return to normal.

I don't relax my grip, but I let my head rest on Malcolm's shoulder. His lips brush strands of my hair. A bit of hope sparks inside me. We caught the thing, after all. The rest? The rest is easy.

The second that thought crosses my mind, I hear the front door rattle. Malcolm swears softly. He clutches the container tighter. Footfalls echo along the hallway. My back is to the living room's entrance. I don't see who shadows the doorway, but when Malcolm swears again, I'm certain it can't be good.

Except his tone is all wrong. He sounds almost amused and exhales a half laugh.

"I don't believe it," he says, the words low and quiet against my ear.

"What—?" I begin and crane my neck.

Standing at the threshold is Darien Armand.

He scans the mess, judgment sparking his expression. Oh, he does not approve—that is clear.

"As business models go," he says. "This seems to be a losing proposition."

Darien crosses the space, removes the lid from the floor, and takes a knee next to Malcolm and me.

"Do you accept my assistance?" he asks.

This must be one of those necromancer things. My gaze meets Malcolm's, and he gives me a slight nod.

"I do." Honestly? At this point, my arms ache too much to refuse. At this point, it would be foolish to refuse.

With the utmost care, Darien slides the lid beneath the container. The Tupperware snaps into place. The ghost rockets about, but a seal created by three necromancers is too much, even for it.

"I will also dispose of this ghost." Darien stands, bringing the container to eye level. "I have an interested client."

Just like that, he leaves, without a goodbye, or really, a hello. And without my permission to take the ghost—not that I want it. Still. Before Malcolm can stop me, I spring up and run after Darien.

I catch him on the sidewalk. He turns at my approach, but remains silent, a hand on each side of the Tupperware container.

"Can I assume your client isn't Orson Yates?" I ask.

"You can assume anything you like, Ms. Lindstrom."

I sigh. "What about your sons?"

"What about them?"

"Don't you want to know how they are?"

"They're both relatively unscathed. That's obvious. What's also obvious is the very large mess they must now clean up." He nods toward the house. "You might want to assist them with that."

My throat tightens with outrage. Words. Oh, I have words. Dozens of them, but I can't seem to push any of them out of my mouth.

"This is one of the reasons I left the necromancer community. I was forever cleaning up after everyone." Darien tips the container in my direction. "Of course, in this particular case, you can put an end to things before they become even worse."

"I don't see—"

"Don't you?" He raises an eyebrow. "A necromancer with the sort of powerful ally that you possess?"

"It doesn't work like that."

"Of course it does. You simply need to be willing to pay the price. Consider, Ms. Lindstrom, whether my sons are worth that price."

He leaves me with that. I don't follow him down the sidewalk; I don't argue. There's no point. So I stare after him, the sun beating down on my head. Without thinking, I unwrap the gauze from around my arms. The notion that the sunshine might heal the cuts is strong, if irrational.

"Katy ... Katy." Malcolm jogs up the walk. "What's going on?"

I shake my head.

He halts next to me, his gaze scanning my arms. With gentle fingers, he pries the wadded up gauze from my grip and swears softly. "What did he say to you?"

"Nothing I don't already know."

"Come on." He wraps an arm around my shoulders and urges me back up the walk. "Sadie has half the place cleaned up. There's not much we can do about the back door window. Nigel thought about making it look like some kids and vandalism."

Malcolm continues talking. I nod, burrowing deeper against his side. In this moment, I want nothing more than his warmth. The chill from the house, from this ghost, still haunts me. It's like I'm shrouded in that wintery ice.

But if I'm honest with myself, I know that it's more than just the house or the ghost. It's the words of Darien Armand.

I steal a look at Malcolm, and I know this:

He is worth that price.

CHAPTER 11

Tuesday morning, I sit on my front porch steps, a cup of coffee warming my fingers, the sun doing its best to warm my arms. The cuts are healing, but the only time I don't feel chilled is in direct sunlight.

Reginald assures me this will pass once every last cut has healed.

I sip my coffee and wonder if that's true.

The clacking alerts me long before I see Tara. She skips down the sidewalk. While I'm clearly her destination, she clutches a thin whip of a willow branch that needs to touch everything in her path.

She stops at the end of my sidewalk, braids swaying.

"Hi." It's a tentative greeting. The willow branch twitches nervously.

"You can come sit," I say, "unless you need to get to school."

"Summer vacation."

"Really? Since when?" I check the position of the sun as if I can glean that information from it.

"Yesterday." She takes careful steps up my walk, placing one foot directly in front of the other while, at the same time, avoiding all the cracks in the concrete. It's quite a feat.

She settles at my side, and the cat clips in her braids clack again.

"Thank you," she says, quietly, like this is a secret between just us. "I know it was you and Malcolm who got rid of the ghost."

"We had some help."

"But it was mostly you and him."

I decide not to contradict her since she's glancing around, searching for him, hope in her eyes.

"He's not here right now," I say.

She slumps. "He should be."

I bite back a laugh because that's how I feel most of the time. "Malcolm doesn't live here."

"He should. He really should. Then you wouldn't be alone."

"I'm not alone. I have a roommate."

"I mean here." She touches the left side of her chest, the spot that can only mean the heart.

Again, she shocks me with how cleanly and clearly she cuts through everything.

I sigh, and so does Tara. Then we eye each other and laugh. I tilt my head and consider her. As I do, she drops the willow branch and pulls that blue and yellow cat purse from her pocket.

"I need to pay you," she says.

I hold up a hand. "Hang on for a minute."

She shakes her head, jostling the cat clips. "My parents won't. They won't even believe me about the ghost."

"A lot of people won't, even when they've seen one." Or have been possessed by one.

"Why did that ghost pick us, my family?"

I've been pondering this, turning over what little I know about Malcolm's and Nigel's childhood, how my family and his intersected at some point.

"That ghost was sent to hurt Nigel," I say at last.

"Why would anyone want to hurt Nigel?"

I go with the truth, or as much of it as I can for an eleven-year-old. "That's a long story, but some people use ghosts in ways they shouldn't. In this case, I think there was something about your family that made the ghost think of Nigel."

As much as ghosts truly think. Was it the volatile relationship between Tara's mother and father? Or maybe Tara and Thomas Jr. somehow confused this ghost. I cast her a look—yes, the clever, precocious one and the beautiful baby. I consider what Malcolm said, about sending ghosts as messengers. Could you deploy an attack ghost in the same manner? Load them up with information about your target and send them on their way?

"I still need to pay you." She digs around in her purse.

I shake my head, wishing I had a set of cat clips that would clack and help me make my point. "How about this. Are you doing anything this summer?"

"No. We're having 'cash flow' problems." She draws little quotation marks in the air, and at that moment, she reminds me of both Nigel and Malcolm. "We're stuck here in Springside."

"That was me, every summer. It's not so bad, especially if you have a job."

"A job?"

"It's been almost a year," I begin, and the words catch in my throat. Even after all this time, I miss my grandmother with a fierceness that takes me by surprise. "And I never figured out the gardening and the weeding, and someone should really sweep the front walk."

"I could do that!" She shoots her hand in the air as if I've made this offer to her entire class at school and might miss her in the crowd of volunteers.

"Not only that," I say, "but it might be good if someone else in town knew how to catch ghosts. What if I get hurt?"

Tara frowns at the cuts on my arms.

"Okay, what if I get the flu? Who's going to catch Sadie's sprites?"

"I could do that?"

"I think you could."

Her entire face scrunches. "But I don't like coffee."

"Want to know a secret?" I wait until she leans close. "For the longest time, neither did I."

She laughs. The sound is like sunshine and ice cream and summer in Springside. I think it might be time to train the next generation of ghost catchers.

I think we might need them sooner rather than later.

Before I can down the last drops of my coffee, a shadow falls across the walkway. Tara sucks in her breath. There, on the sidewalk, stands her mother, Thomas Jr. on her hip. At the sight of his sister, he kicks his pudgy legs, lets out a squeal, and tugs one of his mother's gleaming, black curls.

"Tara! What are you doing?"

Tara bites her lip in response. "Just visiting Katy is all."

Her mother charges up the walk. "I'm so sorry. She's been talking about all this ghost nonsense, and..." She trails off. I see the moment the realization hits—that she's speaking to someone who makes her living from ghost nonsense. A hint of pink invades her cheeks. She averts her gaze.

"Actually," I say, "I was talking to Tara about a summer job."

"A job?"

I wave a hand, indicating the ragged hedges around my house, the shaggy lilacs, and the fact I'm cultivating more weeds than flowers.

"It could use some serious help," I add, "and Tara's perfect for the job."

"I don't know." Tara's mother shakes her head.

"Please, Mom! Please! I'll do my chores at home, too. Please!" Tara clutches her hands together, almost prayer-like.

"If you need references." I nod toward the Victorian house next to mine. "You can talk to Sadie."

Doubt still clouds her expression. So maybe my neighbor, friend, and best customer isn't a stellar reference. I ransack my thoughts, certain the only other references will confirm that I'm the crazy girl who catches ghosts.

Then the obvious hits me.

"Or Police Chief Ramsey. Talk to him. He's known me all my life." And scolded me for at least half that time.

Her look softens. She switches Thomas to her other hip and holds out her hand. "I'm Celia Davenport."

"Katy Lindstrom. Would you like to come in for coffee? I was just about to brew a fresh pot."

Celia hesitates. "I've been working from home all morning." She laughs softly, eyes darting first to Thomas and then Tara. "Or trying to."

"Then you could probably use a cup," I say.

"If it's no trouble."

"Of course it isn't," Tara chimes in on my behalf. "It's what she does."

I shrug. "It's true."

Celia pushes a curl from her forehead. "All right then."

I hold open the door and let Celia and Thomas in first. Tara skips behind them, and when she passes me, I whisper, "I'll show you how to brew Malcolm's favorite coffee."

Her eyes light up. Now this is an offer she can't refuse.

"It never fails to bring him around," I add.

"Really?"

"Really," I say.

But once inside, I send him a text—just in case.

PART II
A FEW GOOD GHOSTS

COFFEE AND GHOSTS SEASON THREE,
EPISODE TWO

CHAPTER 1

My business partner, Malcolm Armand, leans across the table and kisses the maple syrup from my lips. We're sequestered in a cozy booth inside the Springside Pancake House. They make the best breakfast for dinner, even today, when it's served with a side order of worry.

Malcolm would kiss away the worry, too, if he could. It's there in the way his thumb rubs the faded blue spot on my left cheek, the way his mouth curves against mine. His hands come to rest on my arms, and his skin is so warm against mine. With the utmost care, he traces the scars that remain on the backs of my hands and along my forearms. The wounds aren't tender, and when he strokes them, it doesn't hurt. Instead, it's almost like these scars are greedy for his touch, for his heat and his vitality.

"You okay?" he says.

I nod.

"Not too tired?"

I narrow my eyes at him.

"Sorry, sorry." Malcolm raises his hands in surrender. "I sound like a mother hen."

He does. But truthfully? I don't mind too much. Also? I *have* been tired ever since we exorcised the ghost sent to possess Nigel. The scars left in the wake of that are so tiny, and yet, unless I'm in direct sunlight, I can feel them draining me. It's a slow drip that fogs my thoughts and weighs down my limbs.

Malcolm nods toward the window. Across the street, his cherry-red convertible is sitting in front of our office. The gold lettering that reads *K&M Ghost Eradication Specialists* glows with the setting sun.

"I'll do the rounds," he says. "See if any of our usual suspects are up to anything."

"Be careful." I want to remind him that an attack ghost with his name on it could be lurking anywhere in Springside. Before I can, he scoots from the booth, holds up a finger, stopping my words, and then casts a look toward the ceiling.

Yes, he knows what I'm going to say.

"*You* be careful. I'll be back in an hour to pick both of you up." His gaze darts toward the rear of the restaurant. "Don't let her walk home again."

"I'll try."

It's a promise I might not be able to keep. Belinda Barnes is a force unto herself—all six feet of her.

I track his progress from the Pancake House door and across the street. The sunset paints Main Street in bands of pink and gold, and Malcolm's convertible gleams so brightly it could be on fire. He doesn't bother with the door. He simply launches himself up and over and into the front seat.

A low whistle sounds behind me. "Sometimes I think he just strolled off a movie set."

Sometimes I think that myself. "He has his faults."

Belinda snorts and starts clearing dishes from the table. She lifts Malcolm's plate and sends a twenty-dollar bill fluttering. Her sigh is tinged with exasperation.

"He already paid." She holds up the twenty, inspecting it with a critical eye. "He can't keep tipping me—us—like this." She nods toward Annie, the other waitress on shift. "He'll go broke."

"See?" I say. "He does have faults."

Belinda shakes her head as if she could shake away my words. "You know I'm closing, right?"

Of course I do. It's why I'm here, in this booth, nursing an orange juice. "I know."

"It's been a week. I don't think—"

"Well, I do."

"What if this ghost doesn't exist? What if Orson Yates was lying? What if it's lost and haunting someone else?"

We've considered all of that—Malcolm, Nigel, and me. Malcolm, who is out looking for otherworldly evidence; Nigel, who has postponed his honeymoon and is scouring the internet for any and all ghost sightings; and me. Tonight, my job is to make sure Belinda doesn't walk home —or to make sure she doesn't do it alone.

I've fought a couple of Orson Yates' attack ghosts, and I know this: we won't see it coming. If it's as strong as the last ghost, we might not be able to defeat it. All our precautions might add up to nothing.

This is why my orange juice is spiked with worry.

Belinda clears the table, scooping up the glass once I've downed the last drop. Annie waves a goodnight as she leaves. The front doors whoosh closed. Then it's the clatter of a few dishes, the swish of the mop, and row upon row of empty booths.

It's just a bit creepy. Also? I feel utterly useless simply sitting here.

"Can't I help?" I've asked this before. In fact, I've asked this every night for a week.

"And get me fired? No."

I sigh and turn my attention toward Main Street. I long to see a flash of cherry-red. Instead, my phone buzzes with an incoming text. If I can't have Malcolm here with me, at least I can have him on my phone.

Malcolm: All quiet at the old barn.

Katy: Too quiet?

Malcolm: I got showered with hay when I stepped under the loft, and there's a shredded cornstalk in the front seat of my car. Tomorrow you should check on them. They miss you.

I laugh. Cornstalks and mischief—it sounds like a routine summer haunting. If not for the threat hanging over us, if not for the possession of last week, I'd say things were normal in Springside, that none of us need to worry, least of all Belinda.

A clatter comes from the kitchen, followed by Belinda swearing. Her vocabulary is nearly as creative and extensive as Malcolm's is.

"Something wrong?" I call out.

"The door to the cold storage is stuck."

"Need help?"

I don't wait for an answer. I slip from the booth and make my way toward the back, past the counter with its swivel chairs, the short order cook area, and then the prep area.

I'm partway through the kitchen when a sensation washes over me, faint and shivery, like I've walked through a spider web. I halt, hold absolutely still, and breathe in the air. I tilt my chin in an attempt to taste what might be the otherworldly.

The presence is so slight, I'm nearly certain it isn't there at all, except for the goose bumps on my arms and the prickle of hair at the nape of my neck.

"Belinda?" I go for casual, working to keep the tension from my voice. With my gaze straight ahead, I pull out my phone and send Malcolm a quick text.

Katy: Can you come back?

A moment later the phone buzzes in response, but I don't look at the screen. Instead, I inch forward. Belinda hasn't answered me. It's possible she didn't hear me. It's also possible that she can't, that there's something in between us, something otherworldly.

I try again. "Belinda?"

The space feels so empty, like I'm the only living thing inside the restaurant.

My phone buzzes a second time. Logically, I know all incoming text messages sound alike, but Malcolm's seem to contain an extra hint of panic. My silence is making him nervous.

Malcolm: What's up? Something wrong?

Malcolm: Katy, don't go silent on me. What's wrong?

Katy: I don't know. Maybe nothing.

Malcolm: On my way.

I pocket my phone and touch the stainless steel worktable. A second later, I jerk my hand back, my fingers stinging from the bite of cold metal. I exhale; my breath fogs in front of my face.

And yet, the otherworldly presence is thin, the sort that suggests nothing more than a naughty sprite is in residence. Everything else points to a full-on ghost infestation.

I call for Belinda one last time. The space swallows my words. Nothing lingers from the day's dinner rush—no scent of warm maple syrup, no bacon thickening the air, no hint of coffee. (Which is just as well—the Springside Pancake House serves the worst coffee in town.)

The air is cold and stale against my tongue. I take small, quiet steps forward, willing my sneakers not to squeak against the freshly mopped floor. The lights above my head flicker and then dim. I pull out my phone and take a surreptitious peek at the battery life. That, too, is draining.

The cold storage is near the back of the restaurant; this I know from an elementary school field trip to the Pancake House. In my mind, I hear the echo of us all those years ago, the chatter and the noise, and Belinda's voice rising above it all, declaring that someday, she would work here.

Now the only sounds are the stainless steel racks creaking from the drop in temperature. I feel as if I've stepped outside in mid-January. The otherworldly presence is elusive. Tendrils of it slip through my grasp. I can't find its source, don't know where it is. I don't know *what* it is.

When I reach the cold storage unit, I realize I don't know where Belinda is, either.

CHAPTER 2

I indulge in a full sixty seconds of panic. I abandon any form of stealth and race around the kitchen, through the restaurant. I try every door that has a handle—the cold storage unit, the back and front doors, the restrooms. These last open for me, yielding up a blast of icy disinfectant and nothing else.

Fog creeps up the front windows, eats away at the view of Main Street, obliterates the rosy hues from the sunset. A full-on ghost infestation. It has to be. Everything points to it—except for the fact that I'm missing the ghost.

I pull out my phone. The battery life is currently at twenty-five percent. It was fifty only a few minutes ago. I should go look for Belinda, but this might be the only chance I have to let Malcolm know what's going on.

Katy: I'm trapped inside the Pancake House. Feels like an infestation.

I wait, but if he's driving, he won't see my text. With reluctance, I tuck my phone away. If I'm lucky, it'll still have power when he has the chance to reply. I steel myself against the cold emptiness of the restaurant and go in search of Belinda.

I do a quick circuit through the front. I peer into all the booths, kick open the stalls in the restrooms. I'm fairly certain I won't find her here. That leaves the kitchen area, where I do ridiculous things like opening up all the long metal cabinets to reveal the industrial-sized pots and pans. On tiptoe, I check top shelves.

The cold mounts. My phone is stubbornly silent. My options dwindle. Unless Belinda somehow slipped out the back before the doors froze shut, she should be here somewhere.

Then it hits me: the one place I haven't looked is *inside* the cold storage. I approach the unit, dread churning up the pancake special in my stomach. The taste of sour orange juice burns the back of my throat. I brush my fingers across the handle, fast enough that the icy burn doesn't quite register.

This is where the ghost is, inside the unit. My guess is, Belinda is in there too. I consider my options and start with the obvious. It's always good to start there—keeps you from overlooking it, as my grandmother always said.

I find a roll of paper towels and snag enough sheets to insulate my hand against the door handle. It moves, but the door doesn't budge. That, I suppose, would've been too easy. But it isn't locked, which means the only barrier is an otherworldly one.

I pull out my phone. Twenty percent. No text from Malcolm.

Katy: I think the ghost has trapped Belinda inside the cold storage unit. Ideas for getting inside?

I turn and survey the space. Normally, I'd be brewing coffee right now. Kona blend or, for a ghost this strong, possibly one hundred percent Kona. My gaze lands on a series of coffeemakers and the stove. The idea strikes just as Malcolm's text arrives.

Malcolm: You're in a kitchen, Katy. Start brewing.

He's right, of course.

Katy: You read my mind. Also, the ghost is draining my phone battery.

On my way to the coffeemakers, I pull a few of those industrial-sized pots from a cabinet and clank my way toward the sink. Water from the faucet sputters at first, but soon I've filled two huge pots. My arms protest as I waddle them to the stove. I waste precious moments puzzling out how to use it, but I need steam and lots of it, so I keep puzzling even as my phone buzzes at me.

At last I switch two burners to high and set the pots on top. I confront the coffeemakers then, more confident, even if they are automatic drip. Not my preferred method of brewing. I pull out the coffee only to find it comes pre-ground and in large packets, the topmost ones flirting dangerously close to the "Brew By" date. I tear one open and recoil from the sad aroma that greets me.

It's anemic, at best.

A sign above the Springside Pancake House marquee boasts fresh coffee all day long, brewed in small batches. Technically, I suppose that's true. In practice?

I'm not certain the coffee's going to help. I swallow back my despair and check my phone.

Malcolm: Alerting Nigel and Reginald.

He doesn't mention his father, which is just as well. Darian Armand hasn't left town. What he's done—or plans to do—with the ghosts at his disposal, I don't know. Unless …

I cast a glance toward the cold storage unit. No; Darian Armand may dislike me, but he has no reason to hurt Belinda. This is Orson Yates' attack ghost, and it has found its victim.

The screen of my phone dims. I blow out a breath—fifteen percent— and text Malcolm again.

Katy: I think it's Orson's attack ghost. My kingdom for some Kona blend.

I consider the row of coffeemakers, all lined up like soldiers ready for battle. Well, if the coffee won't help, it can't hurt. I pull out filters, rip open packets, and consider all the tricks my grandmother used for turning bad coffee into something drinkable.

A pinch of salt or a dash of cocoa in the grounds, and eggshells—something about crushed eggshells. The first two I have in bulk. The last? This is the Pancake House, after all. I'm certain they buy eggs by the truckload. I turn slowly, my gaze lighting on the cold storage unit. The eggs—and the half and half for the coffee—would most likely be in there.

Then I spy the refrigerators. And, for the first time since Malcolm left, I manage a smile.

I have no finesse when it comes to cracking eggs. The whites leave traces of slime on my fingertips. Bits of shell litter the countertop and float among the yolks, but I have what I need. I set all the pots brewing, one with cocoa, one with salt, one plain, and one with the eggshells.

The water on the stove is lukewarm, so I do another circuit of the kitchen area, spending extra time in front of the cold storage unit. I inspect the seams of the door and try the handle again. I wonder how airtight the room is and whether Belinda has enough oxygen.

She's fine, I tell myself. That would have to be some sort of safety violation. Right? I nod, reassuring myself. I'm about to return to the coffee and my pots of water when my phone buzzes again.

Malcolm: Katy? Are you sure you're inside the Pancake House?

CHAPTER 3

For a moment, I can only stare at the screen. What does he mean, am I sure? I glance around, taking in the flickering lights, the gurgle of the coffee starting to brew, the huge pots of water standing sentry behind me. Of course I'm sure.

Then my phone rings. I jump, heart soaring. When I answer and hear Malcolm's voice on the other end, I all but collapse against the counter.

"Katy, you okay?"

"Sort of."

"Are you hurt?"

"No, no, I'm fine. Worried, is all. I'm brewing coffee and heating water, but I don't know if it will help."

As I talk, I make my way from the kitchen to the front of the restaurant. Fog has completely obscured the windows. Shadows play on the other side, but I can't tell if that's Malcolm or merely an otherworldly illusion.

"Well, I'm standing right outside," he says, "and everything looks normal."

"You can see inside? You can't see the fog?"

"What fog?"

"The fog that's keeping me from seeing you."

He swears. "This is bad."

He doesn't need to say how bad. Any ghost that can conjure this sort of illusion during a full-on infestation is powerful indeed, maybe even more so than the ghost that possessed Thomas Davenport.

I slip into the booth that sits in the exact center of the restaurant and scoot all the way to the window.

"I'm underneath the N in *Pancake*," I say. "Can you see me now?"

Gingerly, I brush the window with my fingertips. The glass is cool, but not so cold it will give me frostbite. I press my palm flat and bring my nose close, willing the fog to clear.

Shadows continue to play on the other side. One grows darker and closer, the shape menacing.

I nearly jerk back. My fingers twitch as if they long to push away from the glass. I remain at the window because I know the only thing on the other side is Malcolm. I blow out a long breath, certain that won't help.

But, for a moment, it seems like it might. The glass clears. The menacing shadow solidifies into Malcolm. He's standing opposite me, his hand pressed against mine with the thick glass separating us. His gaze locks with mine. A smile lights his face even as his eyes fill with concern.

Then another thick cloud rolls in, icing the window. Fractured crystals form beneath my palm. The sting is like nettles, the frost sharp and thick. Malcolm fades into shadows once again.

"This is serious," he says, voice low.

I steal a glance at my cell phone. Ten percent. I know I should end the call and conserve the battery, but Malcolm's voice is the only warm thing in this frozen world. I don't want to let that go.

"It's draining my cell phone battery," I tell him.

"Hang up. We'll do this by text for as long as possible."

Before I do, I ask one last question. "What happens in the morning, when they try to open for business?"

"We'll have this fixed by then. I promise you. We'll have it fixed."

With that, he ends the call.

~

IN THE KITCHEN, the scent of coffee greets me. The water on the stove hasn't started to boil yet. When—if—it does, I'm not certain it will help. The only reason I can smell the coffee is that I've brewed four pots at once.

I pour half and half into one of the adorable cow pitchers the pancake house uses and then set about giving each pot a taste test.

I immediately wish I hadn't. I contemplate licking the sleeve of my T-shirt to remove the flavor from my tongue. I'd reach for an orange juice chaser, but I've already used supplies that aren't mine. I'd hate to add to that.

Only the last pot, the one with the eggshells, holds any hope. This coffee is weak but lacks the aggressive bitterness of the others. I pour it into an insulated carafe and switch the others off—nothing good can come from cooking the coffee any longer.

Then I confront the cold storage room's door. I stare at my reflection warped in the shiny metallic surface. I appear ghostly, or at least ghoulish, my head pinched in the center like an hourglass. My nose is huge; my feet are tiny. My hair is frightening, but that might be from the ride in Malcolm's convertible. The rest is getting a supernatural boost.

"I don't have Kona blend," I say, "but I do have coffee, and I can make some more. Lots more."

My voice echoes around me, the false notes in my promise grating against my ears. I uncap the carafe and hold it next to the seam in the door. I doubt the aroma can sneak in, and if it does, I doubt it would tempt even a sprite.

Steam mists the stainless steel surface. On impulse, I draw a smiley face on the foggy canvas. Then I add the word *please*. When the fog evaporates, I hold the carafe close and try again. I write *coffee* and *hot* and *steam*. This last sparks another idea.

I run back to the stove and find the pots of water on the verge of boiling. I lug one down and drag it across the kitchen, the tile floor screeching a protest.

Ghosts like coffee because the steam gives them substance. The flavor gives them so many other things—a link to their previous life, memories of that time, a sense of who they once were. But steam alone can attract them. I've witnessed more than one sprite dance on steam from a teakettle or float near a laundry room vent.

No matter how powerful this ghost is, I doubt it's enjoying the cold storage unit.

I do a quick calculation of the door's trajectory and place the pot out of its arc. The last thing I need is a scalding. Steam coats the metal surface with even more fog. I dart forward and back, writing notes to this ghost.

When the handle rattles, I'm torn between dashing back to brew more coffee and staying put to rush the door when it opens. Indecision causes me to take a step back. As I do, the door flies open.

An otherworldly presence bursts forth. Clouds of it stream from the room. Its form rumbles above my head, swooping around the restaurant. It locates the coffee pots and collides with each in turn.

The carafes go flying, each one crashing and cracking against the floor. When the ghost finds the second pot of water simmering on the stove, I consider whether the cold storage unit might be the safer place to be.

I use the pot of water to prop open the door and venture inside. It feels like winter. Frost covers the racks. Icicles hang from the ceiling. The air is stale, but breathable—for now, anyway. I scan the floor, peer into corners. With each step, my heart thuds a warning. Venture too far from the door, and I might find myself permanently inside.

"Belinda? Are you in here?"

My words echo even though I've only spoken in a whisper. I creep forward. The back of my throat is raw with cold. Every step away from the door makes my heart pound even harder. This could be a trap.

Finally, near the back, I spy the toe of a sneaker.

Belinda has wedged herself into a far corner between two tall racks filled with crates of oranges. They look like snowballs now, thanks to the cold and the frost.

"Belinda?"

She doesn't budge. Her knees are pulled up to her chest, her head buried against them. She's clutching herself, hands pale from the effort and the cold. I know this pose. When I was younger, I watched my grandmother coax Belinda from it so many times. In high school, I did the same.

"Can you hear me?"

It's possible she can't. It's possible this ghost has already taken up residence inside her head, and the only words she can hear are the ones it speaks. Horrid, cruel words. I kneel next to her and touch the back of her hand. My own fingers aren't much warmer than hers are.

"Hey, let's get out of here, okay?"

I ease my fingers beneath her grip. Immediately she clenches my hand so tightly I let out a yelp. In an instant, I'm transported back to high school—a girls' bathroom, the locker room, the orchestra room with all its music stands serving as silent witnesses.

"Kind of ... like old times." Her voice is soft, barely there, but it's her own voice, not that of the ghost.

"Yeah, just like old times." I brace so I can help her stand.

First things first: I need to get us out of the cold storage unit before the ghost figures out how to move the pot of water and lock us both in here. I consider the coffee. I'll need to brew some more. At the very least, it will warm up Belinda. The warmer she is, the better she can fight off the ghost.

"It knows things, Katy," she says.

We're inching our way out of the unit. Belinda takes shuffling steps. The urge to push or pull her along nearly overwhelms me, but that isn't the answer. That might tempt this ghost to shut her down completely.

"It's been in your head," I say. "It's going to know a lot."

"No, not like that. Different things, things I can't know, about you, and Malcolm, and even your grandmother."

"It's warmer in the front of the restaurant," I say, trying to keep my voice steady while my thoughts whirl. I'm not certain what Belinda means, but I do know that the nastier ghosts are adept at tailoring their taunting. And when it's an attack ghost?

"I bet it's only stuff it knows from Orson Yates," I say. "Don't give in to it."

"It's more than that." She sags against me, her free hand clutching one of the metal racks for support.

We're nearly at the door, which is still propped open by the pot.

Steam is no longer rising from the water's surface, and this worries me. A giant pot of ice water makes an excellent weapon for an irate ghost. The moment I think this, the pot starts to wobble.

"Can you keep walking?" I cast a look toward Belinda and back at the pot.

She nods and shuffles forward, the sound of her footfalls swallowed by the thump of metal against tile. Water sloshes over the edge of the pot. The wobbling increases to spinning. The silver of the pot's sides blurs into white—though whether it's from speed or frost, I can't tell.

All at once, the pot shoots into the air. I have no choice. I let go of Belinda and leap forward, my shoes skidding on the wet floor. I slam into the door and push. A clanking echoes through the restaurant, the sound of the pot striking the tile floor. Then, a force shoves the door back toward me. Its surface strikes my palms, stings the flesh, and snaps my wrists backward.

My arms ache from fingertips to elbows, but I press them against the door and hold my ground. The thing on the other side would—if it could—slice me in half between the door and its frame.

It can't, but it can make this hurt. The frame digs into my spine, the door itself into my hipbone. I press all my weight against the door, but can't budge it even an inch.

And then Belinda is there, next to me. Her skin is alarmingly pale, but her eyes are fierce. She adds her weight. Together, we move the door half a foot.

"On three," she whispers.

I nod and keep my eyes on her as she mouths the count.

"One ... two ... three."

We shove, our combined strength taking the ghost by surprise and giving us those few precious inches we need to escape. I slip again, my arms flailing, just as the door slams shut behind us.

We both cling to it despite the ice-cold surface. I pant, my breath clouding the air in front of my face. My hands and wrists are tender, and I let the frosty door numb the ache.

"The front," I say to Belinda once the pain has subsided. I don't trust my grip, so I loop an arm around one of hers and tug her gently from the door.

We don't run; we *can't* run. Our feet slosh through puddles and crack thin layers of ice. We make it to the front of the restaurant without slipping or sliding or encountering the otherworldly presence.

This, I realize, isn't a reprieve. A persistent, otherworldly mist hangs in the air. We are in a full-on ghost infestation. We're here for the duration—something this ghost already knows. It's biding its time, content to let us have these few moments until the next round.

I raise my chin and taste the air. Now that it's no longer hunkered down in the cold storage unit, I can get a sense of its personality. Conflicting feelings bombard me, everything from anger to anguish. But beneath all that is something else, something that's both calculating and gleeful, something that feels deliberate and cruel.

I settle Belinda in a booth and pull out my phone to give Malcolm an update. It's odd that he hasn't sent me a single text since we last spoke.

Then I see why. The battery is completely dead.

CHAPTER 4

I decide the best course of action is to brew a fresh pot of coffee—or rather, several fresh pots. We need what little heat the coffeemakers can generate. I sweep up the mess the ghost made—all coffee grounds mixed with shattered glass—and pull out new carafes.

The water on the stove makes an effort to simmer, but the cold rolls through the restaurant in waves, sucking up all its warmth. It's better than nothing, and when the aroma of the coffee joins the steam, my thoughts don't feel quite as frozen, although when I blink, I can feel the cold against my eyes.

I grab a cow pitcher of half and half and an order pad. I find two cups and, with deliberate steps, make my way to Belinda's booth.

She has her legs pulled up onto the seat cushion, but her wan smile suggests she's still with me.

"You might want to add some cream." I nudge Belinda's cup across the table. "And some sugar. It's hardly my best brew."

I take a sip, and my face puckers. Malcolm once compared restaurant coffee to a brown crayon dipped in hot water.

This tastes worse.

"It's hot," I add. "That will help. It will make you feel better."

Mechanically, she reaches forward and goes through the motions of

613

adding cream and sugar and then sipping. I wait, gauging her reaction. She closes her eyes, and a small sigh escapes her.

"Better?"

She nods.

"Is it inside your head?"

"It's gone silent, but that's not necessarily better. I know it's there. I can feel it ... lurking."

So can I, although I don't hear ghosts the same way Belinda does, and never have. I hardly ever use the necromancer trick of talking to them the way Malcolm sometimes does. This ghost is so strong that its presence is a tangible thing. It flavors the air, shrouds the lighting, pollutes the space it occupies.

I squirm in my seat. The small hairs on the nape of my neck prickle. I swipe a hand across the collar of my T-shirt. I'm tempted to turn, to see what's behind me, but I know nothing's there.

It's a trick, a garden variety one at that. This ghost is capable of so much more. I study the mist and wonder what's holding it back.

I press a palm against the window beneath the letter N and wonder if Malcolm is on the other side, if he can sense me. Everything feels so empty, so isolated. I look toward the door. Oh, to simply walk out of here and be done with this. I could return with reinforcements, with real coffee. I could ...

A thought strikes me. There might be a way we could leave. Even trapped inside a full-on infestation, I'm not without resources.

I push to stand. "I think I should—"

"Oh, no, you don't," Belinda says. She eases back, sitting upright now. She hugs her knees, but her gaze targets me. "You're not invoking the entity."

"But how—?" How did she know when I barely knew myself?

"It's all over your face—literally. That stupid blue spot is brighter."

Without thinking, I touch my left cheek and the place the entity marked so long ago. It's numb and slightly waxy. The entity has always read my thoughts. Now I consider whether this mark is one of the ways it does so. I cast my thoughts upward, testing, probing. Can it hear me? Would it come to my aid even if I didn't invoke it?

I'm greeted with silence that's as cold and hard as the air around us.

No, if I want its help, I must ask. The cost of that? I probe again. Something shifts in the air, almost like a whisper of an answer. While I can't articulate what it wants from me, I do know this:

I'm not ready to pay. Not yet.

"Plus, they've been chattering." Belinda unclenches her grip long enough to hold up her hands like they're talking puppets. "You know how sprites are, and they love to talk about you."

I'm about to respond when her words sink in. "Sprites?" I glance around, sampling the air. "Is there more than one ghost?"

Her eyes go wide with the notion. "I hear them, and yet…"

I scoot from the booth as if standing will help me gauge what we're up against. I don't get too far before pouring myself a second cup—I need something hot to hang on to. The caffeine might help me think, even if the taste is like licking a chalkboard.

"One ghost or many?" I scan the kitchen area behind the short order cook stove. The space looks arctic, like it's been in a deep freeze for months.

"I try to count them," Belinda says, "and they melt into one, but I'm telling you, there are several I recognize."

I turn from my contemplation of the kitchen. "From where?"

"Everywhere," she says, and her voice holds a plaintive note I haven't heard in years. "It's like every ghost that has ever haunted me is here, inside the restaurant."

IT TAKES another full cup of coffee for me to sort through what Belinda has said. I know I shouldn't drink so much. If the ghost—or ghosts—decides to freeze us out of the restroom, we'll be in trouble. Then again, ghosts do love toilet humor.

Either way? I don't plan to visit the restrooms anytime soon.

I return to the booth and start jotting on the order pad.

"What are you doing?" she asks.

"Making a list, an inventory of supplies I used, so I can reimburse the Pancake House."

"Are you kidding me? You're eradicating. They should pay you."

"They didn't hire me."

"I bet Malcolm's already alerted Samia and Jim." She reaches across the table and pulls the order pad from my fingers. "They'll understand."

I'm not so sure. I'm equally unsure about how we'll escape, and whether the Pancake House can open for business in the morning. But most of all, I'm uncertain about this infestation.

One or many? Now that Belinda's mentioned it, I get a sense of the other personalities—it explains the anguish and the anger. Then they all vanish into a single behemoth, and its presence is so overwhelming, it steals my breath.

"All the ghosts?" I say to her.

"A lot of them, at least."

I point to the pad she stole from me. "Make a list. Write down every last ghost you remember and every last one you sense here."

"And then what?"

"And then I'll go find them. I got rid of them once, right?" I raise my cup and down the last drops. "I can do it again."

Belinda chews the end of the pencil—it probably tastes better than the coffee—and scribbles a few lines. I decide on a little reconnaissance. I check the front door of the restaurant again, simply because it's foolish to overlook the obvious.

In this case, it's more than obvious that we're in a full-on ghost infestation. The entire front entrance is frosted over. The indoor-outdoor carpet crackles beneath my sneakers. I can't even see shadows through the windows. I certainly can't tell if Malcolm is on the other side.

"My sprites are here," Belinda calls.

"Your sprites?" I emerge from the entryway. I've eradicated a lot of her ghosts, but I don't remember any sprites.

"From when I was little," she adds. "They would play with me, keep me company. They were my friends."

"Then, why would they haunt you now?" I investigate the cash register for no other reason than it's the sort of item a ghost—or ghosts —would love to launch across the room.

She tilts her head as if considering both my question and the other-worldly presence in the air. "I'm not sure they are, not exactly." She glances at me, brow wrinkled. "Does that make any sense?"

"About as much as everything else," I say. "I think we can assume this is not a typical haunting or infestation."

Cash register secure, I move along the counter. Beneath it, the storage areas are open, filled with cups and saucers, placemats, and packets of crayons for children. As soon as I've taken this all in, I pretend it doesn't exist. No reason to give these ghosts any ideas.

Something breezes through the front of the restaurant. Belinda grips the cow pitcher, but packets of artificial sweetener fly about, striking the windows, the tables, the countertops—and me. I duck behind my hands, but this attack isn't so much malicious as it is mischievous. In its wake comes the hint of a giggle.

Belinda's mouth quirks into a half-smile.

"Your sprites?" I ask.

"Yes, but ... not. It's more like my memory of them."

Sprites have such a slight presence that detecting them is tricky, sometimes impossible. I usually can, and more often than not, they want that attention. But they're gone now, assuming they were here at all.

I point to the order pad. "Any others?"

"The one from Ms. Callahan's geometry class?"

The suggestion itself seems to cause the lights above our heads to fizzle and pop. Another otherworldly breeze scoops up paper placemats and scatters them throughout the restaurant. By rote, I chase after them. They slip through my fingers. I can't catch or collect any of them. As soon as I realize what I'm doing, I halt, breath ragged.

"I still say that one was trying to help you."

Belinda shrugs. "Maybe, but geometry was my best class—I actually wanted to take that test."

In the quiet of the restaurant, I hear the echo of that day—the screeches and cries, the laughter and cheers as the tests went flying across the room and eventually out the window.

"Like a memory," I say to Belinda now.

"Exactly."

"Any more that you sense?"

"Do you remember that one—totally horrid—in my Family and Consumer Science class? And it threw you..."

Belinda trails off, eyes widening in horror. I scamper toward a booth, my feet slipping on the slick tile floor. Too late. An ethereal fist catches me in the stomach, propels me toward the kitchen, and tosses me against one of the refrigerators.

I slide to the floor, hip smacking against that icy tile, my jeans crunching broken glass and pieces of eggshell. I fight for breath, and my vision tunnels to a single point before expanding again.

"Katy!" Belinda springs up and skids to a halt next to me. "Are you okay?"

I nod, barely.

"Did you get the wind knocked out of you?"

I nod again.

"Are you hurt?"

I gasp a breath and hold up a hand, stopping her questions. "It's like we're ... following a script." Word for word. I remember this ghost, and it *was* horrid. I remember this conversation as well. "You mention a ghost, and we relive its eradication."

Belinda sinks down next to me and leans against the refrigerator. "You're right."

"Don't say anything about the one in the boys' locker room."

"Promise. I won't."

The tile is so cold that my hipbones ache. After a moment, I nod toward the front of the restaurant. Before I can stand, Belinda clambers to her feet and offers me her hand.

Back at the booth, I pour more coffee. We both need another cup. At this point, I'm so cold that the coffee tastes, if not good, then passable. By tacit agreement, Belinda continues her list, and I double my reconnaissance efforts.

"Oh, God, I'm sorry, Katy."

Belinda's words are pitched low, filled with something other than fear or anxiety. I want to say guilt, but none of this is her fault. She's staring at her list like it's an exam with a failing grade.

"You didn't cause this," I say.

"I'm talking about back in the day, high school and all that."

"You didn't cause those hauntings, either."

I inspect the rack above the short order cook stove. The Springside Pancake House prides itself on being low-tech. The wait staff uses pencil and paper, and they stick each ticket to the spinning order wheel. This, at least, is secure.

Mostly.

"That's not what I'm talking about."

I turn to look at her. The otherworldly fog has rolled through here as well, and the air is thick and full of mist. But there's something else, something more between us.

"What are you talking about?" I ask.

"I'm making this list, right?" She waves a hand at the ghosts who will not be named. "And it's making me think of all the other things from high school, the things I didn't invite you to, the parties—"

I laugh. "Like the ones at the old barn?"

That was a spectacularly bad idea. Then again, eighteen-year-olds with a keg nearly always have bad ideas at some point. For a while, though, the parties were epic, and the wild ghosts that haunt that space behaved themselves—right up until they didn't.

It took my grandmother to eradicate everyone from the barn—the kids, not the ghosts. If the parties were epic, her scolding topped them. No one left unscathed, including Belinda. I might have been embarrassed, but I was too busy clutching Tupperware and chasing down a contingent of sprites to worry about it—too much.

"It wasn't just those kinds of parties." She ticks the items off on her fingers. "It was the sleepovers, the birthday and swim parties. It was prom—"

"I didn't want to go to prom, and I really didn't want to go with Jack."

"Would you, though, if I hadn't gotten back together with him?"

"If I truly thought he couldn't get a date? Maybe. But that's not Jack." I plant my hands on the counter and lean forward. "Belinda, what's this about?"

She shakes her head, ponytail swaying from side to side. Then she musters her homecoming queen smile. "I'm a lousy friend."

"You're a great friend. We were just ... different then. You did your thing, and I did mine."

And mine was catching ghosts with my grandmother. By then, I did all the chasing and the capturing since her fingers were too stiff and her legs too slow.

"Except when I needed you," Belinda says, "and then you were always there."

"It's what I do. Really, could you picture my grandmother letting me go to all those parties, anyway?"

"It's not like any of us had permission." She snorts. "My parents didn't know. Half the time, I told them I was going to your place to study."

I drop my gaze as if the countertop has become utterly fascinating.

"Wait a minute ... are you saying they knew?"

"Actually, I didn't say anything."

"Ha, ha. Seriously. What gives?"

I don't want to talk about this. Nothing good can come from this discussion. There are certain ghosts here that shouldn't be disturbed. But Belinda has me locked in her gaze and won't let go.

"It was my mom, wasn't it?" she says. "It would be just like her to put you up to it. Did she bribe you? Threaten you? Say the word, and I'll—"

I hold up a hand, cutting her off. Belinda and her mother have a rocky relationship. As easy as it would be to pin this on her, I can't.

"Your dad," I say at last. "He asked both me and my grandmother, but mostly me, to keep an eye on you, to let him know where you were, what you were up to. He was ... worried."

And it's difficult to deny a dying man that sort of request.

"You spied on me?" A curious look lights her eyes, like she's both incredulous and hugely pissed off.

"Not really."

"The ghosts did?"

"I didn't talk to them back then." But it's entirely possible that my grandmother did. "Your dad was worried," I add, "about the hauntings and the drinking—"

She swears and drops her head to her knees.

Viewed from the outside, Belinda had one of those charmed high school existences that everyone envies—homecoming queen, star athlete boyfriend, amazing wardrobe, indulgent parents.

But they barely spoke to each other. The ghosts would crawl inside her head. They would whisper their lies and fill her mind with so much chatter she couldn't think. When her father died of pancreatic cancer two months after high school graduation, she let the ghosts in for good.

"So, you spied on me." This time, her words come out as an accusation rather than a question.

I've always been a terrible liar, so I respond with the truth.

"Yes. I did. Because he asked me to."

That was enough for both my grandmother and me. Springside High was—and is—small enough that even if you weren't invited to all the parties, you knew where they were, who went, and what happened.

It wasn't that hard to let Belinda's dad know where she was at any given time. It was all over social media; I'm not sure you could really call it spying. Except, of course, it was.

A chill washes across my neck, the sensation filled with the supernatural. Speaking of both ghosts and spying, they must be loving this, or at least the meaner ones are. This sort of emotional discord gives some ghosts a charge. Some people might speculate that the ghosts feed on negative energy.

My grandmother always said that a cruel person in life makes for a worse ghost in the afterlife.

A chill also rolls off Belinda. I can't repair the damage I've done, not in the middle of this infestation. I need to get us out of here, then maybe I can salvage our friendship.

I push strands of hair from my face and consider my next tactics. I could use some help. I could really use Malcolm and his ability to talk and charm and brew tea. I survey the restaurant. The entryway is in ghostly lockdown. No one is coming in or out. But there's a kitchen entrance, an emergency exit ... and a window. Not the big bay windows that look out onto Main Street, but one I've seen in the alley behind the Pancake House.

"I'm going to look around," I tell Belinda, not that I expect her to answer.

She doesn't.

CHAPTER 5

In the kitchen, I add water to the pot and start on another round of coffee. The aromatic steam seems to help. At least it doesn't hurt.

Unsurprisingly, the kitchen door is glazed over. I'm not even tempted to try the handle or test the deadbolt. The emergency exit appears benign. Only a light dusting of frost covers the silver handle. As I stand in front of it, the urge to reach forward, to push the door open, nearly overwhelms me.

Why? I wonder. I yank my hands back before my fingertips brush the handle. The answer is staring at me from a sign in the middle of the door:

Alarm will sound.

That's all we need: nonstop sirens, the police, the fire department.

These ghosts are devious and bent on making us as miserable as possible.

The last option—really, the only option—is the window. Which is where? I scan the walls, matching them to landmarks outside. Then I realize why I've never seen the window from the inside.

It's in the men's restroom.

I retrace my steps, switch out the old coffee for the new, and set the fresh carafe on the table in front of Belinda. I get nothing for my efforts. I swallow back the dread with a few sips of hot coffee.

"Don't let them in," I whisper. "You're stronger than that."

Then I head off to inspect the men's bathroom.

The otherworldly presence in the restroom is thinner, the air easier to breathe. Disinfectant mixes with the aroma of the coffee I'm holding. My stomach rolls in response, and the combined flavor coats my tongue. I gag before dumping the rest down the drain and taking some quick, shallow breaths to keep my breakfast-for-dinner on the inside.

Then I spy the window. It's at the end of the row of stalls. High up, so I'll need to perch on the radiator to peek outside. When I do, I can see the brick of the neighboring building, Springside Hardware and Tools.

No frost covers the glass—not yet. The metal latch feels cool, but turning it won't give me freezer burn.

When a hand appears on the opposite side, I yelp. My feet skid on the radiator, and I tumble backward. I smack against the tile floor, the ache spreading from wrists to elbows once again. The spike of pain in my tailbone leaves me breathless and gulping for air.

What I saw registers. A hand! A hand that belongs to a person, a person who is most likely Malcolm coming to my rescue like he always does. I claw to standing, and then I clamber back onto the radiator.

My fingers are numb, but I work the latch. I push on the frame, but it barely budges, creaking a protest. From the other side comes the sound of scraping and scrabbling. Someone swears. Malcolm—it must be. From all the noise, it sounds like we have reinforcements as well.

No one has opened this window in ages. The layers of dried paint are as strong as super glue. A knife from the kitchen would help, but I don't want to alert the ghosts to what I'm doing. I dig in with my fingers.

Slivers of the dried paint stab beneath my nails. I push. The person on the other side tugs. The hinges screech, and a thin crack appears between frame and window. Warm air rushes through the opening. It smells like damp wood with a hint of rotted vegetables, but I breathe it in because it's real. Beyond the stench, I sense the summer evening and all the promises it holds.

A pair of hands grips the window frame. The hinges squeal a final protest before the window swings up and open. I jump down from the radiator as first an arm and then a leg poke through.

He comes tumbling down, much like I did earlier. It's an awkward, uncoordinated sort of entrance that's unworthy of Malcolm.

It's that thought that stops me from rushing to him. It's that thought that has me teetering on tiptoes, on the verge of falling forward.

"You're not Malcolm." I can barely believe the words I'm saying.

"No. I'm not." The honeyed drawl hangs in the air, almost seems to thicken it. "Sorry to disappoint. Again."

When he looks up, the force of it strikes me.

I'm here, in the men's restroom, with Carter Dupree.

MY FIRST IMPULSE is not to berate Carter or even to thank him, but to rush past him. I do, scrambling back up to the window. For a moment, I can see the alleyway below. There, standing in its center, is Malcolm. He's peering up at me, his gaze worried.

"Malc—"

Before his name can fully leave my mouth, the window slams shut. It freezes over, crystals forming on the glass before a solid wall of ice shrouds my view. It's thick and opaque, and I can't even detect shadows or shapes on the other side.

I teeter again, but this time, hands at my waist keep me from crashing to the floor. I don't want to say thank you. I really don't. So, I go with the other question pinging around in my head.

"What are you doing here?"

Carter raises his hands as if I've accused him of something. "Trying to help?"

"Wouldn't you be better off in Mexico or Canada or somewhere Orson isn't?"

He gives a little shrug. "He's not in Springside."

"Not at the moment."

Carter inclines his head. "No, not at the moment, which is why I figured it would be the last place he'd look. Besides, he's busy with other things."

"Like what?"

"You."

"Me?" I suppose that isn't a stretch, although I also suspect it isn't me—

exactly—that Orson Yates is after. "He wants the entity."

"He wants you, or, more accurately, wants to take you down."

This makes me laugh. Maybe it's because I'm stuck in the middle of a full-on ghost infestation and talking to Carter Dupree in a restroom, but the whole thing strikes me as ludicrous.

"You make it sound like I'm a kingpin or a crime boss or something."

"Actually, that's the way he's making it sound. He's put out a general call to all necromancers in the Midwest region."

"And that means what?"

"Retribution."

I've heard about that before, from Nigel and Reginald. It's what keeps necromancers from going rogue, as far as I can tell. And as far as I can tell, it's Orson Yates who's gone rogue.

"And you know this how?" I ask.

He holds up his hand like a talking puppet—very much the way Belinda does. "Sprites like to gossip." He tilts his head as if he can hear them whispering now. "And I like to listen."

"Did they tell you anything useful about this infestation?"

"They didn't have to," he says. "I helped build it."

"You helped..." I lose the thread of my response. Honestly, what would anyone say to that? Thanks for all the ghosts?

"I know. It was a shitty thing to do. In my defense, at the time, I thought I was doing the right thing."

"The *right* thing?"

"Okay, the most vengeful thing." He studies me. In the dull yellow of the restroom, his blue eyes look gray. He's sporting at least three days' worth of growth on his jaw. He's a far more tarnished version of himself than he was a few weeks ago.

"You're not supposed to be as good as you are," he says. "You know that, right?"

"So everyone's been telling me. But if I were really that good, I'd know how to deal with that." I fling a hand toward the door and the hallway that leads to the main area of the restaurant. "Are you really here to help?"

"I am."

I nod toward the door. "Then, let's go."

NEVER IN MY life have I imagined that I would be grateful to Carter Dupree even once, never mind twice. But I am. The air in the main area is heavy with ghosts—those from the infestation and those that still linger after my conversation with Belinda.

The moment her gaze lands on him, her eyes widen. She sits up straight and sheds her despondency. She utters several curses that rival Malcolm's.

"Yeah, it's nice to see you, too," Carter says.

"What are you doing here?" She shakes her head, ponytail swishing back and forth as if she could sweep him from her sight.

"He's here to help. He knows about that." I point toward the kitchen. "He helped ... build it." I turn to Carter now. "Did you build it? I mean, what is it, exactly? One big ghost, or lots of ghosts jumbled together?"

"Yes." A smirk lingers just beneath his bland expression.

"Oh, that's it." Belinda shoves herself from the booth. "He's just messing with us. Let me at him."

Carter holds up a hand as if to stop her, then turns it toward himself as if he's inspecting his manicure. "Please. Like you could make me if I didn't want to help."

Belinda plants a hand on her hip. "I know I can."

Something passes between them, an odd sort of exchange full of challenge, animosity, and something more, something that looks like compassion. Theirs is not a relationship I want to contemplate.

"Guys, please. We need to get rid of the ghosts. Ideally, we need to do that and clean up the place before Samia arrives to open for the morning shift. Right?" I turn to Belinda. "When does she usually get here?"

"It's insane, like four in the morning."

I glance around the restaurant. The bacon and eggs wall clock is ticking toward ten. I consider the mess I've already made—and the one that's sure to follow. Ghost catching is a sloppy business. Six hours, give or take. I bite my lip hard enough that the warm, coppery flavor of blood and the quick stab of pain clear my head.

"Okay," I say to Carter. "How do we fight this thing?"

"I'm not sure," he admits.

Belinda throws her hands in the air. "See? He's only here to mess with us."

Carter glares at her.

"Can you tell me what it is, exactly?" I ask. "One minute, it feels like a really powerful ghost, and the next, I can sense sprites and personalities, and..." I tilt my head. In that instant, I sense a chorus of spirits, as if the ghosts have been eavesdropping and want to send this particular point home.

I catch Belinda's eye. "High school."

"Yeah." Her gaze searches the air. "Just like high school."

We both turn and lock our sights on Carter. He mouths something indistinct and then rubs the stubble along his jaw.

"It's a necromancer thing," he says.

Of course it is.

"It's kind of like a Frankenstein monster version of a ghost. What you do, or really, what a powerful necromancer does, is take a collection of ghosts—any kind of ghosts, from sprites to really strong ones—and stitch them together."

"Stitch them together." I say the words more to myself than either of them. I try to picture it—ghosts, a needle and thread. I'm at a loss for how someone might do that.

"Yeah, it's not easy. It's not something I can do."

"But Orson can?" I say.

Carter nods. "It was ... he was ... teaching me the technique. After I got a lapful of orange juice"—he throws a scowl at Belinda—"I decided it might be fun to get a little revenge."

"You're nothing but charm," she mutters.

I send her a quick shake of my head. At the moment, we need Carter, whether we like him or not.

He continues as if he hasn't heard her. "Since I was collecting Spring-side ghosts anyway, I separated out those that had haunted Belinda. It wasn't that hard. Sprites like gossip and praise, so they were more than happy to tattle on the less forthcoming ghosts."

This I can see. Sprites love attention. They love shiny things. Not too long ago, Carter was nothing but shiny.

"And then what?" I ask. "You have all these ghosts, so how do you … stitch them together?"

"That's the part I can't explain. The rest is Orson's doing." He holds out his hand toward the kitchen as if he's detecting an invisible force. "Do you sense him? He has a distinct signature. Most necromancers with his kind of power do."

I hold out my hand and will my fingertips to discern something different about this haunting. I detect that undercurrent of cruelty, but like earlier, I can't put a name to it.

"Nigel could," I say, dropping my hand. "But I can't."

Carter scrutinizes me, his face scrunched up not in disgust but what looks like genuine curiosity. "You make no sense as a necromancer."

"Well, I keep telling people I'm not one. Nobody listens."

He snorts and continues. "What this is, essentially, is a big knot of ghosts. A strong enough necromancer should be able to slice through the knot. And then, poof." He holds up his hands. "No more knot."

"But a bunch of ghosts on the loose," I say.

"Most will want to leave."

I tilt my head toward the kitchen. I don't need to strain to pick up the wailing, the cries. Carter's right. The large majority of ghosts want nothing to do with this haunting.

"How, exactly?" I ask.

Carter once again stares as if my ignorance astounds him. "You broke the containment field in the cemetery, right?"

I nod.

"And the ones in the warehouse?"

"I did."

"Same idea, except instead of visualizing breaking through something, you concentrate on cutting through something."

"And that's it?"

"It's a precision sort of move, takes a certain amount of finesse."

Which I clearly don't—or at least shouldn't—have.

"Is this something you can do?" I ask.

Carter glances away as if the cash register has absorbed all this attention. "I'm not strong enough," he says, "but you are."

"I am?"

"It's why we didn't bother to deploy it sooner. Orson knew you could slice through it pretty easily, and then we'd lose all those ghosts."

"But now it's something to keep me busy while he's off planning retribution or whatever it is?"

Carter shrugs. "Whatever works, right?"

"So, what should I do? Find the knot and cut it in half?"

"More or less." Doubt clouds his expression. "I guess."

"Where is it?"

He raises his chin. It's a familiar move, one I've done and watched Malcolm do so many times before. Carter rounds the cash register and heads into the kitchen area. Belinda and I follow, walking the same wandering path that he does.

We pass the coffeemakers. He glances over his shoulder, nose wrinkled.

"That smells awful."

"Thanks," I say.

"When this is over," Belinda whispers in my ear, "let me at him. I'm telling you, I need an hour, tops, to ruin his life."

"I'm not even going to ask how you plan on doing that."

We move deeper into the kitchen, past the racks and the prep areas, and mounting dread tells me where this journey will end. Belinda's fingertips brush my hand, and then she grips it tight.

Our sneakered feet meet the ice-slicked tiles. The pot remains on its side, embedded in the slush around it. Carter skids, and his arms flail, but he catches himself. Then, he halts our trek.

In front of us is the door to the cold storage unit.

For a long moment, none of us speak. I don't relish the idea of going back in. But Carter's right. The knot is here, behind the stainless steel door.

"How are we going to get in?" Belinda whispers.

Before I can answer, the handle rattles, and the door creaks open. A gust of cold air rolls from the space, chasing strands of hair from my cheeks and making Belinda's ponytail sway. The breeze ripples through the kitchen, and the stainless steel racks shudder in its wake.

"Oh, this is bad," Carter mutters.

Inside the room, clouds hang in the air from ceiling to floor. I catch glimmers here and there—something in the shape of a sprite I once caught, a more robust ghost lurking near the back. In the center, a huge cluster of ghosts is gathering.

At least, I think they are. One moment, I can count dozens. The next, all I see is one large mass, roiling with rage and sorrow.

"Do I imagine a sword?" I ask him. "A pair of scissors?"

"I don't think it matters, as long as it works."

"Did Orson ever—?"

He gives his head a quick shake before I can even ask my question.

"Orson didn't work like that. He parceled out instruction. It kept us ... dependent on him."

"I'm guessing you didn't make it this far in the lesson."

"Sorry." The single word is laced not with sarcasm, but with regret.

"Yeah, me too." I survey the mass in front of me. No one has attacked or thrown anything our way. That, in itself, is a small miracle. I pull in a deep breath. "Okay. I'll try."

I think back to when I broke the containment field in the cemetery, only instead of chipping a virtual hole with a tire iron, I now imagine a sword, like something out of *The Lord of the Rings*. I picture myself holding it above my head, bringing it down...

A cry rends the air. Belinda grabs my arm.

"What was that?" we both say.

Carter glances away as if he suddenly finds the prep area fascinating. He won't meet my eyes.

"They're crying," Belinda says. "My sprites. I can hear them. My sprites are in there."

I nudge Carter. He starts but turns to face me.

"What happens to the ghosts when you slice through them?" I ask.

He stares as if I've asked a ridiculous question. "They're just ghosts, Katy."

"But what happens to them? I need to slice through some of them, so what happens to those ghosts in particular? Where do they go?"

He shrugs. "I don't know. When the knot is cut, most of the ghosts go free."

"And the others?" The frustration in my words is as thick as the ghosts hanging in the air.

"They ... vanish."

"Do they die?"

"They're *ghosts*," he says as if I'm dimwitted. "They're already dead."

"It hurts them," Belinda declares.

She's right; it's an honest hurt, one I sense in the pit of my stomach.

"Is there another way to do this?" I ask.

"There is no other way." He gestures toward the mass of ghosts. "You slice through. How else are you going to untangle everything?"

Another cry goes up. The shelving inside the cold storage unit rattles with the force of it. Even the meaner ghosts, the ones harboring cruel intentions, quiver at the suggestion.

"How else?" I consider the entwined mass. "By unraveling them?"

"I don't think that's possible," Carter says.

"Have you tried?"

He shakes his head, in warning rather than in answer. "That's part of this, the purpose behind this trick. Not only can you tie up all of a necromancer's ghosts, but you force him—"

"Or her."

"Or her." He sighs. "To sacrifice some to free the rest."

"What a terrible thing to do," I say.

"I didn't say it was nice."

"But in theory, I could go in there." I point. "And untangle each ghost from the others, right?"

"It will drain you. It will leave you vulnerable."

"To what?"

"A necromancer with an attack ghost."

Like Orson Yates or Darien Armand? I flirt with the idea of conjuring up the sword again, but I lack the will to even imagine myself imagining it.

"I could go in with you," Belinda says, her voice low.

I give my head an emphatic shake. "Oh, no, you couldn't."

"I could, and besides, you need me. Can you tell where one ghost ends and the other begins?"

I squint into the churning crowd of them. Even now, I can only catch the suggestion of a form, and certainly not several, distinct forms.

"Can you?" I ask Belinda.

She nods. "I'm a sensitive, remember? And this is what I do." She swings toward Carter. "Right? You guys use them all the time, I bet."

An odd half-smile lights Carter's face. "Huh. Orson has a couple of friends"—he draws little air quotes around *friends*—"that he consults on a regular basis. We always thought it was, you know, for a different kind of favor."

Belinda snorts. "In his case, it's probably both." She nods toward the cold storage unit. She looks fierce, but beneath the homecoming queen smile, uncertainty lurks.

"Want to give it a try?" she says.

Do I? I can't imagine the sword any longer. I don't want to slice or cut or damage these ghosts, not even that truly vile one near the back. I don't want to be like Orson Yates, so I do the one thing I'm sure he wouldn't.

I plunge in.

THE FOG of ghosts swallows us immediately. Carter is a shadowy figure backlit by the kitchen. His form morphs, growing fatter, then tall and thin. His nose stretches, Pinocchio-style.

Belinda breathes a laugh. "They're making fun of him," she whispers.

Why, yes. Yes, they are.

"Where do we start?" I ask. "Can you find a thread or a ghost to begin with?"

She extends a hand in front of her. Ghosts swarm and then retreat. One slithers by me, ruffling my hair, but when I try to follow its path, it fades into the cloud once again.

"Here," she says. "Let's start here with this one. Do you recognize it?"

She sweeps her hands around and around until the outline of this particular ghost takes shape. It shimmers except for those spots where it's stitched to the other ghosts in this tangle. And I do recognize it.

"Ms. Callahan's geometry class."

"You were such a troublemaker," Belinda says to it.

The ghost squirms, mewing in a way more suitable for a sprite than a full-fledged spirit capable of short-circuiting the overhead lights. For this sort of work, a sword—imaginary or otherwise—won't do. Even a pair of sewing scissors feels too brutal. I don't want to cut; I want to pull.

Hands, then. Fingertips and nails.

"Will you let me?" I ask the ghost. "I think I can set you free, but you've got to hold still."

The ghost floats between Belinda's cupped hands while I get to work. It's like grasping soap bubbles. The ghost is just substantial enough for me to touch it, but oh so fragile. I pluck at the seam between it and its compatriot.

The more I tug at the seams, the more I can sense them. As with containment fields, once I start to work, I can distinguish what is the otherworldly and what is courtesy of a necromancer.

I don't want to rip. I soon realize that the stitches holding these ghosts together are very much like those that hold fabric—and Orson is a master tailor who has stitched these ghosts together with a strength that's daunting. I free a section only to have a tangle emerge within the tangle. The ghost squirms, shoots away from Belinda. Its outline fades. I step back and exhale a long breath.

"Be good," she tells it. "We're trying to help."

I glance around the cold storage area, trying to follow the line of ghosts into the center of the knot.

"It's endless," I say. So many ghosts, and all of them so tangled together.

"It's not. I've been counting them in my head. Don't worry about the others. Just concentrate on the next one."

It's good advice, for ghosts and life.

"Thanks," I tell her. "Thanks for coming along."

"What's a sensitive for?" She reaches into the cloud of ghosts. "This one. Do this one next."

I do. I work, and the outline of each shimmers and fades, but my fingertips start to recognize the feel of the thread—for lack of a better word—that holds them together.

My shoulders cramp; my fingers ache. This is going to take all night. But the ghostly chatter has died away. The vile ghost in the corner pouts —there's no mistaking that—but it hasn't taken a swipe at either of us.

Because if I don't untangle them? They're stuck with each other. For eternity? This, I don't know, but they want to be free, and they're letting me work.

For now, that's enough.

Images flash through my mind as we get closer to the center of the knot. Scenes from past eradications, from all the mischief these ghosts have caused, but there's more. I pause, scanning the air, not certain what I'm viewing is in my mind at all.

"Can you see that?" I ask.

Belinda nods, loose hair from her ponytail hiding her face.

It's like a ghostly version of television, or the portal the entity once used. The scene plays out on a misty screen. There, a pre-school version of Belinda is laughing with three frisky sprites. They swoop and dart around her princess-pink bedroom, ruffle her blonde curls, and float above her pillow at night, casting a muted, otherworldly glow to ward off the dark.

"Are those yours?" I know the answer, but I ask anyway.

"My sprites," she says, her voice as insubstantial as the mist around us. She raises a hand toward the image, then lets it drop. "I should've never sent them away."

"You did? When?" I don't remember my grandmother eradicating sprites when it came to Belinda; I certainly haven't.

"I was four, maybe five. My mother said I was too old for imaginary playmates." She shakes her head, but I think she's shaking her hair loose so I can't see her face. "She doesn't have a sensitive bone in her body."

In more ways than one. I squelch the thought and barely manage to swallow back the accusation. Belinda's father was the one who made the calls, paid for the eradications. When he died, I thought the ghosts would move in for good.

"What about your dad?" I venture.

"I think he must have been." She peers through the fringe of hair at me. "Don't you?"

Around us, scenes play out as if in response to her words. The foggy image of Belinda's father on a cell phone, his face worried. That vile ghost in the corner tormenting Belinda. My grandmother pointing and directing as I slip through a crawlspace after it.

Then a scene appears that doesn't feature Belinda at all, but her father. He's standing in our living room, even though my grandmother has urged him to sit more than once. He balances a cup of coffee in one hand, one I've just given him.

"I wish," he says, and then sighs, the sound of it so heavy, I'm not certain how he can stand under the weight of it. "I wish I could get through to her."

"It's the age," my grandmother says, "and nothing more. Give her time."

"Yes. Time." Belinda's father sips the coffee and closes his eyes.

My grandmother winces, and I see her mentally chastising herself for the careless words.

"I could help."

It's strange to hear my own voice come through the mist. I remember now. Mr. Barnes didn't ask me to spy.

I volunteered.

The scene fades. But the ghosts aren't through with us, because the next thing to appear is a hospital room, one equipped with monitors and IVs and drawn shades.

Belinda's father is so thin, barely a presence beneath the woven hospital blanket. Belinda sits at his bedside, and there's a stack of books on the nightstand. She's been reading to him and now closes the book and grips it in her lap.

"Mr. Bauer will be so proud I finally finished *To Kill a Mockingbird*." She gives her dad a practiced smile, although it looks as if it might shatter. She looks like she might shatter.

"You always did things in your own time, and that's okay. Remember that."

"Dad—"

"Shh. Just remember that, pumpkin, okay? And don't worry about the rest."

The room darkens. Hours must pass by, but the next thing I see is Belinda resting her head on his bed, hand gripping his, the heart rate monitor switched off. If grief has a sound, it's not wails and sobs but the low hum of ventilation, of overhead lights, of a world where you can't hear the soft breathing of the people you love.

This scene, too, fades. My heart is pounding hard in my chest. The corners of my eyes are damp and hot. Belinda is trying to hold the ghost we've been working on, but her fingers are trembling. I tug her hands from the ghost. It dips and dives and ruffles her hair in an attempt to give her a ghostly kiss.

She doesn't bat it away. She doesn't shove me away, either, for which I'm grateful.

"I wasn't there for him," she says, and her voice is so small, it's nearly swallowed by the mist.

"Were the ghosts lying, then?" I ask.

She raises her head, but locks of hair shroud her face. "What?"

"You were with him at the end."

"Only the end. I was a terrible daughter."

"He never thought so, and that's the part that counts. He gets to decide that, not you. He thought the world of you. That's why he came to us. If he didn't love you, didn't think you worthwhile, why would he bother?"

The ghosts hang cold and motionless in the air, and their hush surrounds us.

"I thought I might find him here." At last, she pushes the hair from her face. Her cheeks sparkle with tears. "I thought maybe he'd come back and haunt me." Her gaze tracks the line of ghosts, all jumbled from our efforts to untangle them. "I'm pretty sure I'd sense him if he did."

Her determination to follow me in here starts to make sense, as does her drinking. I wonder what's harder to live with, the voices or the silence.

"Not everyone ends up as a ghost." I consider the ones floating around us. "My best guess is, not everyone needs to. In your dad's case, I think he knew you'd be okay, just in your own time."

Belinda hiccups a single sob and throws her arms around my neck. I rock her and let her cry. At some point, three spirits join us. They're tethered to the long line of ghosts; they're not going anywhere without all the others. But they're free enough now to push their way to us.

"I don't think you truly sent your sprites away," I say to Belinda before turning my face toward them. They're hovering about her, all chatter and concern. "You three were there, in the hospital, weren't you?"

In answer, they bob up and down.

"And you've always kept an eye on her, right?"

More bobbing.

Belinda eases from me. She pushes tears from her face and reaches out to push a few from mine. Then she turns her attention toward the sprites.

If they weren't knotted together, they'd probably do backflips. As it is, they shimmer and bounce and begin to dance as best they can. They're clumsy, like puppies, and careen and collide into each other.

"You know," I venture. "You're not a necromancer. It's not like you could end up addicted. You're not like Nigel."

"What are you trying to say?"

"That maybe you don't need to send these three away."

"I don't?"

"Do they scare you?"

"No."

"Do you like them?"

"Yes."

"Can you put up with their antics?"

She tilts her head and considers the trio. "Maybe."

"Then, there's no reason they shouldn't stick around." I pull in a breath, an odd weariness settling on me. "Of course, we have to untangle them first."

I scan the storage unit. Before, these ghosts resembled a large ball of otherworldly yarn; now it looks as though we've strung the shelves with strands of supernatural tinsel. Ghosts are everywhere, a little less tangled but not free, not yet.

Belinda pushes to her knees and then stands. I don't remember when, exactly, we landed on the floor, but the tile is frigid beneath my legs. My muscles ache with the cold. Belinda offers me her hand.

"Come on, ghost catcher," she says. "It's time to get back to work."

CHAPTER 7

An hour later, I decide that unraveling ghosts must be the most tedious task ever. At least, I think it's an hour later. There's no clock in the cold storage unit, but when I ask Belinda about the time, a couple of ghosts form an impromptu clock.

It's an ethereal two in the morning, assuming these ghosts know how to tell time. This I doubt. I do know we've been in here for a while. Fog shrouds the doorway. Carter's shadow wavers, but whether he's been there the whole time, I can't say.

I tug and pull at the seams that hold these ghosts. Each stitch is like its own containment field. My fingertips are numb, my thoughts as hazy as the air around us. Despite the cold, sweat trickles down my spine.

I swipe a hand across my brow. "No wonder most necromancers cut through the seams." I'm about to add something else to this when a whirlwind kicks up in the center of the room.

All at once, I'm thrown to one corner and Belinda to the other. Two spirits of surprising strength tether my arms. My hands are locked so far apart that I can't pull at the seams, never mind free myself.

"I didn't mean it, guys," I say. "But if you don't let me go, I can't finish. Unless you want to be stuck with each other for eternity."

The air roils around us. So much otherworldly chatter fills the space that I want to clamp my hands over my ears.

But, of course, I can't.

Some sort of supernatural debate rages and then simmers. The shackles evaporate. I rub my wrists, although there's no mark or bruise—just a ribbon of cold that stings and throbs.

"Belinda, too," I say, "or I'm not pulling out another stitch."

The ghost in the corner—the vile one—lets go so suddenly that Belinda flies forward and crashes into the metal racks. Something tumbles to the ground—something that sounds an awful lot like a dozen eggs.

She props her hands on her thighs and gasps.

"You okay?"

"Just ... get ... back ... to ... work," she manages between breaths.

The more I tug, the more I'm led back to Belinda's three sprites. Over and over again, I follow a line of ghosts only to return to them. The obvious strikes me; I feel foolish for not realizing it sooner, for not seeing what Orson has done.

Belinda's three sprites are at the heart of the tangle. I kneel in front of them and consider what Orson gleaned from them—from all these ghosts—and how he used that knowledge against both of us. How, if I had decided to slice through this tangle, I most certainly would've destroyed them.

I marvel at that, at how well he picks his targets.

"What if I worked from the inside out instead of the outside in?" I say this not only to the sprites but to the room at large.

The air quivers with excitement. Yes, I'm on to something. I inspect the stitches holding the three sprites. They're tighter, closer together, sometimes looped through all three sprites at once. Even so? I'm certain that if I untangle this particular knot, all the rest will fall away.

Belinda sits across from me, her hands cupping the sprites. Despite their predicament, they're positively giddy with the attention.

"Hold still," I tell them. "This is tricky. I don't want to hurt you."

"He's a real bastard," Belinda says. "Why would a ghost even go near someone like Orson or Carter?"

"Maybe they don't have a choice. Most people aren't as sensitive as you or Sadie. The hauntings are just that—random and scary."

"And when you're lonely…" She lets the sentence trail. "I guess some attention is better than none."

Yes, I think. Lonely. Maybe that's why I feel such a kinship with these ghosts, no matter the trouble they cause me.

I return my attention to the three in front of me. They're subdued now, much like five-year-olds with splinters, bravely submitting to the grown-up with the tweezers.

These three have been so loyal to Belinda that I don't want to damage them in any way. I gnaw on my lower lip in the hope that the pain will keep me alert. Bit by bit, I obliterate Orson's stitches. Bit by bit, their range of motion increases.

Then, at last, I tug the final thread, and it evaporates. For a moment, the sprites simply hang in the air as if they can't believe they're free.

Then, the unraveling begins. There's a popping and a shredding, a chain reaction where first one ghost and then the next is free. They zip around the cold storage unit, their joy contagious.

Belinda laughs. I want to, but exhaustion is weighing me down. It's hard to breathe with all the fog and mist that lingers.

"Go on!" Belinda shouts. "Get out of here. You're free!"

I expect a mass exodus, a rush for the door. If Carter is anywhere in their path, they'll flatten him. We'll be catching ghosts for weeks.

Instead, they spin in tandem, creating another whirlwind. The metal racks around us start to fade. The floor beneath our feet turns rocky. Above our heads, the ceiling vanishes, revealing bright sunlight and blue skies. I blink, the glare of the day hitting me, and raise a hand to my eyes.

The Pancake House slips away, but we're not on Main Street, and it's not the middle of the night.

It takes a moment, but I recognize the warning sign with the curvy arrow. I've taken the turn in this road a thousand times. A few miles farther on is the nature preserve where Malcolm and I do our releases.

Below our feet is the ravine. Several yards away, someone is standing, someone who looks like Orson Yates.

BELINDA GRABS my arm and yanks me down. We crouch at the side of the road, our gazes locked on Orson.

He's partially hidden from the road by a cluster of saplings, his eyes trained on the approach from town. He stares straight ahead, straight past us ... straight through us?

The sun is beating down, warm and bright after the cold storage unit. I blink once, twice, and then rub fingers across my eyelids. There's something odd about Orson, something I can't quite place.

"Does he look different to you?" I whisper.

"Younger?" she says. I sense more than see Belinda take in his full measure. "Definitely younger, like our age. I hate to say it, but he's actually kind of hot."

"Ew."

"In a retro kind of way. Look at him. Hello, it's the 90s calling, and they want their stone-washed jeans back."

I can't help it. I snort. Loudly.

We both freeze, but his gaze remains on the road. It's as if he can't even hear us. I turn to Belinda again.

"1990s?" I venture.

"Totally. I mean, look at that..." Her words fade. She pats the earth with both hands, the move frantic. "It feels real." She picks up a handful of dirt.

The gravel appears solid enough in her palm, but when she lets it slide from its perch, the image wavers until the pebbles and dust settle once again.

"What is this?" she asks.

"Like before?" I suggest. "In the Pancake House? The ghosts are showing us something."

"Why?"

I open my mouth to respond, but no words come out.

"And why is it so real?"

This, I have a sense for. Underneath the illusion, I catch a hint of the otherworldly, the echo of memories stitched one to the other. "They're working together, and they're just strong enough to make this feel real."

I think of how strong the entity must be, then, to have transported the group of us to the warehouse.

"They're your ghosts," I add. "Maybe they—"

"No, they're *our* ghosts, Springside ghosts."

Yes. Springside ghosts, every last one, not a single interloper in the group.

"And this is something they think we should see?" I ask.

"Maybe. Maybe they're thanking you for not slicing them to bits like a scary necromancer." Her gaze moves from Orson to me. "What happened back then that they'd want you to see?"

"I don't know. I was just a..." My lips go numb. The word I was about to say lodges in my throat. I don't even want to think the word, and I give my head a vigorous shake as if that will dislodge it.

It doesn't. No matter how much I don't want the thought in my mind, it takes up residence there.

Baby.

I leap forward. Belinda makes a grab for me, but I'm too quick. I dash into the center of the road.

"Katy, get back here. He'll see you."

"He won't. He can't." I spin in a circle, arms wide. "This isn't real. It's a memory, or several memories."

Pieces of the scene around us flicker in and out. The trees across the ravine are a fuzzy green, their leaves imprecise. Even though the ghosts of Springside have pooled what they remember into one collective memory, they don't remember everything.

"Guys, don't do this." I speak to the sky, to the air, to anywhere the ghosts might be. "I don't need to see this. Really, I don't. Okay? Can we go back now?"

"Katy, he's looking right at you."

"He isn't looking at me or for me."

"Then..." Belinda pulls herself up and inches to the side of the road. "What is he looking for?"

"My parents."

I turn, face Orson, and wave my hands over my head. I jump up and down. He keeps the vigil, his gaze focused straight ahead. It's unnerving to be caught in his unrelenting glare, even if I know he can't see me. Orson from the past can't be aware of Katy from the future.

At least, I don't think he can.

From behind me comes the roar of a motor. Something flickers in Orson's gaze. I whirl and face in the direction of the oncoming car.

"Katy, what're you doing?"

"Waiting."

"Get back here."

I purse my lips and shake my head.

"Katy, don't do this."

"I'm not doing anything."

"You can't stop this, whatever this is."

"I know."

Up ahead, sunlight glints off the car's windshield.

"Katy, come on."

The road beneath my feet rumbles. The roar grows louder, the noise of it shaking the air. The car is taking the turn much too fast. I know; a mere four months ago, I nearly skidded through this turn and pitched into the ravine below.

A screech fills the world then, one so loud I feel it in my lungs, my heart. The car flies around the corner, heading straight for me, the left two wheels lifting from the asphalt.

Belinda screams. A cacophony resounds; past and present merge. Light explodes before my eyes. For a moment, I'm in the dark, surrounded by the fog and mist of the cold storage unit.

Then bright sunlight fills my vision.

The car, the one that's carrying my parents, is behind me now.

Belinda sobs with relief. She races from her spot at the side of the road and captures me in a fierce hug. Together we watch the car smash through the guardrail and plunge into the ravine.

The sound of it guts me. The crunch is like nothing I've ever heard before. I rush forward but collide with an invisible wall. Fog covers the deepest part of the ravine, obscuring my view, and I feel as if I've had the wind knocked from me.

"I don't understand." I step back and address the wispy clouds flowing in random patterns. "I thought you wanted me to see this."

Silence greets my plea, from both the ravine and the ghosts below. Then, I hear it. Light steps on asphalt that break into a jog.

Orson Yates runs past us until he's teetering at the edge of the ravine, one hand gripping the branch of a tree. He scampers down a few feet only to crawl back up again. He frowns in the direction of the car, and an odd play of emotions flickers across his face.

I'm expecting that cunning and cruel smile of his, but it never materializes. In some ways, Orson looks as gutted as I feel. He slides down the ravine only to change his mind and claw his way back up. He does this once, twice, enough times that I lose count. He's a man caught in a trap of hesitation and doubt.

In the distance, the thin wail of a siren rises up. The sound draws closer until it's all we can hear. Orson freezes, near the top of the ravine now, his grip so tight on that tree branch he's bound to snap it in two.

A Springside patrol car draws up. An officer steps out. The bulk may be a little less, but the shoulders are just as broad, and there's no mistaking the towering frame of Police Chief Ramsey.

Make that Officer Ramsey. Like Orson, he looks so young. Too young, really.

"Sir, did you see what happened?"

"A car, it ... I mean—" Orson points. "Broke through the guardrail and..."

Chief is already on his radio, calling for support, an ambulance, the fire department. Orson appears jittery. He unclutches the tree branch and skids several feet down the ravine.

"Sir, stop!" Chief scans the area. He lifts his chin almost like I do when I'm sensing ghosts. "I smell gas. Let—"

It isn't an explosion, not like in the movies, but there's a crackle of flames. Smoke snakes up from the center of the ravine. I can't see the crash site, have no idea what it looks like.

I think that's just as well.

More sirens fill the air. Orson takes one last look at the ravine, his gaze hollow, nearly vacant. Then he pulls himself up the incline to the road. Chief Ramsey offers him a hand and tugs him the rest of the way.

Then, inexplicably, Chief lets go. Shock, rather than anger, fills Orson's expression. Chief whirls and starts down the road. Somewhere beneath the wail of sirens and the snap and pop of the fire, a plaintive cry echoes.

It sounds like a sprite, tiny and lost.

At first, I don't see what's making the sound. Chief kneels at the side of the road where the gravel meets a soft patch of grass. He freezes there except for one massive shuddering of his shoulders.

"I don't believe..." His words trail off, swallowed up by the snap and sizzle of the fire and the approaching wails of the sirens. He crouches, and when he does, I see what has caught his attention.

A baby is sitting in that soft patch of grass, one that's not quite as old as Thomas Jr., but not an infant, either.

All my rational thoughts stop. I can only stare at the scene. Belinda comes up behind me, grabs me around the waist, and holds on tight. It's as if she knows I need the support to stand.

Chief remains frozen in place. The baby clutches and unclutches one of his fingers. She blinks at him, in wonder, perhaps. He must fill her entire view, shading her from the sun. Although she's tiny, she probably shouldn't see the carnage in the ravine.

It's something she won't remember.

Orson comes up behind them. Chief surveys him over his shoulder, very much a guard dog sizing up a threat. His gaze sweeps over Orson, and the man halts.

Orson's brow furrows. "What is it?"

That's when Chief rouses himself. With gentle hands, he scoops up the baby and tucks her into his arms. He keeps Orson in his sights, but grooves line his mouth and anguish fills his eyes. He looks more like the Chief Ramsey I know than a young patrol officer at the start of his career.

Orson is a man petrified. He stands there staring at both Chief Ramsey and the baby. "That isn't ... I mean, it can't be. It isn't—"

"Possible?" Chief supplies.

"Was she in the car?"

"I don't see how she could've been." Chief rocks the baby gently in his arms, swaying slightly as he does. He and his wife never had children. A sudden sadness strikes me in the midst of everything else—he would've made a wonderful father.

"Then, how...?" Orson's mouth opens and closes as if he's struggling to breathe.

"You tell me," Chief says. "You saw the accident?" This is more a statement than a question, less of a friendly inquiry and more a detective across the table from a suspect.

Orson nods, but the gesture is absent-minded. He searches the air, the ravine, scanning the space, back and forth, back and forth. Clearly, he's searching for something. A glimmer sparks in his eyes. He takes a step away from Chief, and then another, intent on something.

"Sir, as a witness, you need to remain here. I need to take your statement." Chief jangles the handcuffs at his side. How? I'm not sure, not with his arms full of baby.

The light in Orson's eyes dims. He mutters a curse that Chief pretends not to hear. Before either man can say another word, a second patrol car pulls up, followed by a fire truck and the state troopers.

Chief points a finger at Orson in the way you might tell a dog to stay and heads for the second patrol car. He walks straight through Belinda and me. She gasps, but I'm too numb to feel anything.

The edges of the scene fracture, and the sphere of what we can see grows smaller and smaller. The green in the grass and the blue in the sky fade to pale imitations of color.

Only the center of the vision remains, the smoke-filled ravine. This, too, is quickly changing to mist and fog. The cold from the storage unit invades my bones.

Before the scene vanishes completely, the smoke clears from the ravine. On the other side, a man is standing. For a moment, my heart leaps. I recognize that ebony hair, the set of the jaw.

But the man is too gaunt, not quite tall enough to be Malcolm. No, it isn't Malcolm at all.

The man on the other side of the ravine is Darien Armand.

Belinda and I collapse onto the hard tile floor. Ghosts fill the room. In fact, not a single one has escaped. They swirl above our heads, and although I'm not listening—at least, I'm trying not to—their chatter is nearly deafening.

"Shh." Belinda holds a finger to her lips. It's an admonishment most choose to ignore.

Her three sprites crowd around us. They're unusually bold, shoving the other ghosts away and letting us catch our breath.

"Huh," she says, and the corner of her mouth turns up into an almost-smile. "They're worried about you."

"I'm fine."

"Yes. Of course you are." She rolls her eyes, a move meant for her sprites, and then points at me. "Yeah, I know. She's stubborn."

From somewhere deep inside me, I manage a laugh. At the moment, it's better than tears. Those can come later, preferably when I'm not on the floor of the cold storage unit.

"We need to get out of here," I say. "Right?" I aim this at the ghosts. "You guys want to go home?"

As a mass, they stream for the door. The whoosh ruffles our hair, and the sound of it is like an approaching train.

"I hope Carter isn't on the other side," Belinda says. Then she gives me an evil grin. "Actually, I kind of hope he is. Come on. Let's go see."

We find Carter outside the door, flat on his back in a puddle. He's craning his neck and scowling at us—and the world in general. Without hesitation or reluctance, Belinda offers him her hand.

He shakes out his limbs, wrings water from his shirt, and mutters a few curses for good measure.

He nods toward the cold storage unit. "What happened in there?"

I'm not certain we should tell Carter anything about what we saw. Before I can throw Belinda a warning glance, she gives him her patented homecoming queen smile. Then she runs her fingers through her hair, secures it in a ponytail, and says, "What didn't?"

Carter seems to have forgotten he even asked a question. I tilt my head and study Belinda. I'm pretty sure this is a trick I can never attempt, never mind master.

"Want to get out of here?" She wraps an arm around my waist, and together we take a few steps into the main kitchen area. "Are we good?" she adds, her voice so low, it's barely a whisper.

"We're always good."

"And you? After all of ... that? Are you okay?"

"Are you?" I counter.

"I'm not sure." Her gaze flits upward, toward where the three sprites are dancing along the ceiling. "But I feel better now that I have my sprites back."

"So do I." I'll worry less about her with these three keeping vigil.

She gives me a sidelong glance, and I muster a grin.

But I sigh with dismay when we pass the mess we made during this eradication. The coffee has brewed so long that a burnt odor lingers in the air. It's almost enough to put me off coffee for good. No wonder some people think it tastes terrible. In this case, they're right.

Through the windows, the lights of Main Street glimmer. It's probably my imagination, but I'm certain I see the gold lettering on the storefront of K&M Ghost Eradication Specialists. My heart beats harder at the sight. Because, even though it's technically night, and we'll be cleaning for the rest of it, somewhere on the other side of the door, Malcolm is waiting.

Carter reaches the entryway first. He rattles the handle. He rattles it again before jerking it back and forth. Then he plants a shoulder against the door and shoves.

"Come on," Belinda says, annoyance tingeing her voice. "Not funny at this point."

"Not a joke." Carter's voice is so tight that I think he might growl. "Trust me, I want to be as far away as possible from here."

Behind us, the ghosts are gathering. I'm pretty sure we haven't lost a single one. They jostle and swirl, each jockeying for a spot close to the door. All at once, they whirl, creating an otherworldly battering ram.

I call out, but it's too late. They smash into the door—and Carter. He's knocked to the floor for the second time in minutes. He sits there, knees bent, head in his hands.

"Hey, guys," I say to the thick fog obscuring the ceiling. "I know you don't like him, but—"

"Mutual," Carter says.

"And you're not helping," I tell him.

Ghosts are capricious. They'll keep us trapped in here out of spite, or because they think it's fun to watch the humans snipe at each other.

I brush my fingertips across the door, although since Carter was just yanking on the handle, I doubt we're in a full-on ghost infestation.

The wood is smooth, cool but not cold, and definitely not frosty. It locks from the inside, and nothing's engaged.

"Why can't we get out?" I wave a hand at the ceiling. "Why can't they?"

Carter lifts his head from his hands. His eyes are wide with fear. It might be the dim light in the foyer, but I swear, he's turned a sickly gray. He shakes his head, hard.

"No, no, no," he mutters. Then he turns his gaze on me, the look full of desperation. "Remember the cemetery?"

I nod, dread thickening in my throat.

"We're inside a containment field."

"So, a necromancer can trap humans along with ghosts?"

"Sort of. A necromancer can break free easier than ghosts can, but with enough necromancers, you can detain someone. It's how retribution is ... meted out." Carter peers upward. "Or, with enough ghosts, it creates its own sort of lockdown."

"Like an infestation?"

"They can't leave." He shrugs. "We can't leave."

"So, which one is this? Is there a group of necromancers outside the restaurant?"

"Not that I can see." Belinda's voice comes from the seating area. She's in a booth, leaning up against the window, hands cupped around her face.

"In this case, it's just one," Carter says. He slumps against the door, and his head thumps the wood. The sound is defeat itself. "I recognize the signature."

I'm glad someone does. "Orson?" I ask, although his posture alone has already told me the answer.

He gives one miserable nod.

"I thought you said he wasn't in Springside."

He shuts his eyes and groans. "I'm an idiot."

I'm tempted to agree. "Do you think he's close by?" I say instead.

"He must have been, probably while you guys were in the cold storage unit. That's why the field is so strong. He's been reinforcing it."

"But I'm sure Malcolm, and Nigel, and Reginald... They would, I mean—"

I don't know what I mean. Would they sense him? Is that something necromancers can do? I certainly didn't, and neither did Carter until a few moments ago. I don't even know if Malcolm had the chance to alert either of them.

"I suppose Reginald could deploy a ghost or two to keep watch," he says, "but Malcolm doesn't do that sort of thing."

No, he doesn't, and Nigel can't.

"So, the sneaky bastard slimed his way through the alley and trapped us?" Belinda suggests.

A laugh nearly chases the fear from Carter's features. "Yeah, that's exactly what he did."

"Then maybe we don't want to leave right now." I'm not sure what possesses me, but I lean down and offer Carter my hand.

He stares at it as if it might have some of that slime from the alley. Then he takes my hand. He looks toward Belinda and then at me again.

"No, we need to get out of here. This sucks." He gestures toward the ceiling and the ghosts churning there. "For everyone."

I point to the door. "And if Orson is on the other side?"

"Then I take a bullet or an attack ghost or whatever he has planned for me."

"I won't let that happen."

"We won't," Belinda echoes.

He doesn't say anything, but something shifts in his expression. "So, in the cemetery—" He coughs and clears his throat. "Do you remember what you did?"

I nod.

"This is a stronger field. Can you feel it?"

I lift my chin. At first, all I get is a wave of ghosts clamoring for attention. Oh, they're loud. Beneath the racket and chatter, I sense the containment field. It surrounds the restaurant, almost as if the Pancake House is contained in an industrial-sized snow globe.

"I do," I tell Carter. I probe it with my thoughts, the way Nigel showed me on that snowy February night in the Springside Cemetery. I can't detect a single crack, a flaw, a fissure. "I'm not sure I can break it."

"I can't either, not by myself, but there might be a way."

I wait for the explanation. Carter stares at the floor, then up at the ceiling. Something near the cash register catches his attention. He scowls and jabs a finger at the ghost floating there. "Yeah? Well, you're an asshole."

"Language," I say. "Remember the sprites."

He rolls his eyes. "You don't hear them?" He rubs his temples. "It's nonstop chatter."

I do, but it's all white noise to me, the words indistinct. I have no idea what that ghost said to Carter. I look toward Belinda in question.

She nods and casts her gaze toward the ceiling and the thick layer of ghosts there. "Yeah, they can't shut up. Most of them want to leave, but some want to stay and talk, and every single one has an opinion."

I tilt my head. I catch bits and pieces, a word here, a comment there, but only if I concentrate. It's easier to tune them out.

"It's probably why you're such a good necromancer," he adds. "Despite everything. No distractions."

I'm not certain how to take that—as a compliment? If it is, it's a back-handed one. Belinda mutters something and sends a look toward the bevy of sprites floating above her head. They shake with ghostly laughter.

Carter still doesn't say anything about the containment field.

At last, frustration overtakes me. "This way to break out?" I prompt. "Are you going to elaborate?"

"We have to hold hands," he mumbles.

"What?"

Behind me, Belinda snorts.

"We have to hold hands," he repeats, louder this time.

"That's it?" I sigh, the long night catching up to me. My limbs feel heavy. Keeping the fog from my thoughts is becoming a full-time job. "This isn't elementary school, and I don't have girl cooties."

"Yeah, well, I don't want your boyfriend charging in here and knocking me into next week."

"He won't." At least, I'm pretty sure Malcolm won't.

"I got this." Belinda scoots past us, giving my shoulder a squeeze. "You guys do your necromancer thing. I'll run interference." She plants herself in front of the door, hands on hips. She throws a glance over her shoulder, one aimed at Carter. "Better now?"

He glowers. I can't help it; I laugh. Then I hold out my hands, palm skyward.

"Ready?" I ask.

He murmurs something that might be *yes*, and then Carter and I link hands.

"There's a point near the back entrance," he says. "That's where Orson began the field, and it will be weakest there."

I close my eyes. Perhaps it's the combined power, Carter's and mine, but the image of the containment field pops into my mind. Near the back door, I sense the weak spot. It isn't much, not even the width of a hairline fracture.

"The field at the cemetery was kind of sloppy," Carter says. "Orson's good, and he had time to build this one and reinforce it."

"Nigel said that eventually the ghosts would find a way out."

"They would, but in this case, it would probably take weeks."

Of their own volition, my fingers tighten around Carter's. We don't have weeks. We don't have hours. I concentrate on that spot near the back entrance. A shadow is hanging over it, one that's the same size and shape as Orson.

I yelp, but Carter grips my hands before I can jerk away.

"It's an aftereffect," he says. "Don't let it spook you."

"Is that how you sense another necromancer?" If so, it's really creepy.

"It's one way."

"Uh, guys?" Belinda says. "Any luck?"

Both Carter and I remain silent.

"Because we might have a problem."

I don't want to ask, but I do anyway. "What sort of problem?"

"Samia's here."

CHAPTER 9

Even the ghosts go quiet. The chatter around us dies. The only sounds are the sizzle and pop of one of the coffeemakers and the rumble of Samia's minivan.

Then that cuts off as well.

"Is Malcolm outside?" I ask.

I hope and pray that he is. Malcolm can sweet talk and work his charm. He can convince Samia that all is well; I'm certain of it.

"Actually," Belinda says, her voice hesitant, "no one's out front. Well, except for Samia."

"Where is he?" I say this mostly to myself. It isn't like Malcolm to wander off in the middle of an infestation this large. It isn't like him to wander off at all. In fact, I'm surprised he hasn't been pounding on the doors and windows, trying to get in.

"Maybe something better came along." Carter. Of course.

Before I can say anything, before Belinda can, an otherworldly whoosh sideswipes Carter and sends him into the newspaper rack. He crashes to the floor, and the rack teeters and falls on top of him. The ghosts erupt, whirling and nattering and making a ruckus once again.

Hands on thighs, Belinda peers down at him. "What? You diss Katy in a room full of Springside ghosts? You really are an idiot."

"Nice." He makes no move to stand or even push the rack from his ribcage. He almost looks content there on the floor. "You know, I really wish I never came to Springside."

"We're all wishing that right now," Belinda says.

The room shakes with ghostly glee. Even I manage a laugh, but it catches in my throat when I glance toward the restaurant's front door. My eyes meet the dark, concerned ones of Samia.

I gape, wishing I had words to fill my mouth, words to explain to her what's going on in her restaurant. Even if I did, I'm not sure she could hear me through the closed door.

Belinda notices my stare and jerks around, and her shoulders slump in defeat. Then she gestures widely, something I'm sure means, *We can explain all this.*

Not that we can.

Samia's face vanishes from the window. Belinda rushes forward and peers out.

"What's she doing?" I whisper the words, which is ridiculous. It's not like Samia can hear us.

"She's got her cell phone out."

That's not good.

"I can think of two people she might be calling," Belinda adds. "Jim or Chief Ramsey."

Either way, I suspect I've seen the last of the all-you-can-eat pancakes, and Belinda may be out of a job. If only Malcolm were here to…

The thought strikes me so hard it hurts. I stare down at Carter, and I must look fierce, because he recoils.

"You said Orson was in the alley, right?" If he were standing, I'd grab him by the collar and shake the answer from him—that's how desperate I feel. "That's where he created the containment field?"

In response, Carter gives a single nod, and his Adam's apple bobs. I force back a wave of nausea.

The alley is also the last place I saw Malcolm.

~

I BOLT, jumping over Carter and the downed newspaper rack. My name echoes after me, but I don't glance over my shoulder. If I'm wrong, there will be plenty of time to explain later. And if I'm right?

I don't want to think about that.

With both palms, I shove open the door to the men's restroom. I dash to the window and scramble to the ledge. I kick my feet, trying for purchase. An otherworldly force pushes from behind, so I end up half in and half out of the window.

The ledge bites into my stomach. I wince, fight for a full breath, and scan the alley. It's not quite sunrise. The only light comes from a street-lamp near the alleyway's entrance. I breathe in that damp wood scent, catch a hint of rotted vegetables. To my left is a dumpster, the most likely source of the stench.

I grip the windowsill and lean out even farther. In front of me, the air wavers. Orson's containment field runs down the center of the alley. I stretch an arm and brush fingertips against the barrier. I scan the darkness below, searching for Malcolm.

Something shoves from behind—a ghost, no doubt, trying to be helpful. I teeter on the window ledge. My arms flail, and I let out a yelp.

Then, from below, comes a voice.

"Katy?"

"Malcolm?" Relief and fear course through me all at once. He's here, he's alive, but he doesn't sound like himself. "Are you okay?"

"Katy? Is it really you?" He sounds dazed, like he's just woken from a dream. "I was afraid you were dead."

Or a nightmare.

"I'm right here. I'm fine. I was worried about—"

"When I saw Orson—"

"You saw him?"

If Malcolm responds, I don't hear his answer. At that moment, the overly helpful ghosts at my back give me one last shove. I lose my perch. My stomach and then my thighs scrape along the sill. I tumble from the window.

I'm pretty sure I scream. At least the sound of it echoes in my head and burns my throat. Then something warm and solid stops my fall. My breath leaves me just as a solid oomph leaves Malcolm, and we crumple to the ground. His embrace is fierce and protective, and it's the only reason I don't panic.

"Katy, Katy." My name sounds like a prayer, and now I let in some of the panic. This isn't Malcolm. This isn't right. "I thought you were dead," he says again. "I thought Orson ... did something, and you—"

"Same," I manage, trying to banish all the images of Malcolm lying dead in this alleyway. My head is tucked in the crook of his neck, and his pulse is pounding erratically against my ear. I don't know whose heart is thumping harder, his or mine.

He holds me, an arm wrapped around my waist, a hand cradling the back of my head. We have so much yet to do, but we can take this moment, I tell myself. It isn't wrong to take one small moment.

I nuzzle closer. Despite his hours in the alley, he smells warm, like nutmeg, but like something else as well, something with a coppery tang. His fingers are oddly damp against my skin.

I pull back enough to peer up at him. I know worry must be reflected in his eyes, but the alleyway is so dark, I can't see it. That's just as well. I think it might undo me. Instead, I take one of his hands and study it.

I tug it into a thin beam of yellow lamplight. His fingers are stained, warm and sticky, his knuckles swollen. I take his other hand and inspect that too.

There's no mistaking blood.

"What happened?" I ask. His face is unmarred as far as I can tell. It doesn't look like he was in a fight. "Did Orson do something?"

He shakes his head. "That's just it. He didn't, at least not to me. I don't think he realized I was here in the alley until he was done creating the containment field."

So, when he trapped us, he trapped Malcolm as well. I reach a hand out and test the barrier again. Still there. Still intact.

"He came up behind me," Malcolm says. "I was busy trying to find a way up to the window." He points to the dumpster. "That wasn't budging, and the crates wouldn't hold my weight."

Splintered boards litter the alleyway, and there's a foot-sized hole in the side of a nearby orange crate.

"I didn't even notice him until he was standing right there." He gestures to a spot across from us. "I thought he might shoot me or unleash an attack ghost." Malcolm reaches out and taps the containment field. "This actually saved me. He couldn't do either without destroying this in the process."

"What did he do?" My gaze darts to Malcolm's hands. The wounds, the swelling—it all speaks to some sort of desperation.

"He just stared at me. Then he smiled that creepy smile of his and said, 'You're too late to save her, but that's the Armands for you—always too little, too late.' And then he left. I was trapped, my phone didn't work, and you were inside with Carter and who knows what."

He stares at the space where Orson must have stood and then slumps against the wall beneath the window. He pulls me closer, and I wrap my arms around his waist as tight as I dare.

"I went a little crazy," he whispers into my hair. "I tried to climb up the wall."

I think of how scraped his fingers are. "Climb or crawl?"

"Both. I tried to break through the containment field. When I couldn't, I started hitting it."

That explains the bruised knuckles.

"I thought I failed you." He utters this final confession in a voice so low that I barely hear it.

"You could never fail me."

A sigh makes his entire body shudder. "I thought we'd been set up. Carter came breezing in, all apologetic and with all the answers, and I was stupid enough to trust him because I didn't know what else to do. Then Orson showed up, and I really thought—"

"For the record, Carter's been helping."

Well, mostly, when he's not being passive-aggressive.

"Good." Malcolm heaves another sigh. "I'm in no shape to kick his ass."

I allow myself to simply rest against his chest and listen to his heartbeat, steady and sure now. In a bit, I'll tell him about Samia and how we need to break the containment field. In a bit, we'll get back to work.

Instead, Malcolm shifts. He takes my face in his hands, and I can feel the tacky residue of blood against my skin.

"Katy, I want this to stop. This thing with Orson is only going to get worse."

"I want it to stop, too, but I don't know how."

He stares at me. Even in the low light, I sense the force of it, the significance. I scramble to my feet and take a step back. There's a request in that look that I can't fulfill. I ask anyway.

"Do you want me to invoke the entity and order it to stop Orson?"

Malcolm stands. For a moment, he braces a hand against the wall. Then he reaches for me, but I slip from his grasp.

"You have to tell me that this is something you want. I won't do it any other way."

My throat tightens around a thick swell of what must be tears. I can't breathe. It feels as if that one solid, sure thing is crumbling beneath my feet.

He sags against the wall, hands slapping the brick. I wince because that's got to sting.

"Yes … no … I don't know." He clenches his fists, once, twice, frustration radiating from him. "I only know that if it were me, I would've made the deal by now, given the entity whatever it wanted, and—"

"Lost everything."

My words stop him. He shakes his head as if he doesn't believe me.

"Why, then?" he says. "Why have something like that and not use it?"

"Think about what you might have to give up. Think about what that does to you, to me, to Springside."

The silence stretches between us. He rubs his eyes, scrubs his face with his hands. His jaw tenses, and then he blows out a breath as if he's just considered several ideas and dismissed each one.

"There isn't one scenario," he says, his voice quiet, its frantic edge smoothed with what sounds like shame, "where I don't lose you." He swallows hard and peers skyward. "Maybe that's its gift to me. There's no way around that. I lose you, without a doubt. But if this keeps going, I'm afraid I'll lose you anyway."

"Then?" My throat remains tight, thick with tears on the edge of spilling over. I wait.

Malcolm curls the fingers of one hand, a barely there *come here* gesture. I'm wary, but I inch forward. When I'm close enough, he takes my hand and kisses the palm.

"I want this to stop so we can start." His lips find my palm again, and the eruption of butterflies in my stomach is fierce. "But I won't ask you to invoke the entity, no matter how tempting it is. It might be easy, but it's not the answer."

He pushes a few strands of hair from my cheek with a feather-light touch. It must hurt his fingers, but he doesn't even wince.

I hold on to him with all my might. I don't know who had the worst night, him or me. A thought flits across my mind: what would I have done, trapped in the alley with no way out? What would I have done if I thought Malcolm might die or already be dead? How long could I have resisted temptation?

I don't want to think about it, so I push those thoughts from my mind. I concentrate instead on the here and now. And right now?

We have a restaurant to restore.

I ease from his embrace and hold out my hands to him. He takes them without hesitation. "Are you up to breaking a containment field?" I ask.

He surveys the alley, his gaze zeroing in on the back entrance. "Weak point by the door?"

"That's the one. We were trying to break it when Samia showed up."

His grip tightens on mine. Malcolm closes his eyes and swears. "I'm sorry I wasn't out front. I would've—"

"I know, I know," I say. "Let's just do this and go home."

There's nothing awkward or weird about working like this with Malcolm. His skin is warm, his grip is secure, and the weak point comes into focus. Already I can sense a few fissures that weren't there moments before.

"This is so much better than holding hands with Carter."

Malcolm's grasp tightens imperceptibly. When I open my eyes, I find him looking at me, one eyebrow raised.

I bite my lip because, suddenly, all my words have fled. I try anyway. "What I mean is—"

He laughs, and it's nothing but amused. "You can explain later."

We resume our task. Within seconds, the containment field around us starts to shake. It's a low reverberation at first, one that penetrates the soles of my shoes. Fissures turn into cracks, and those travel across the surface of the field, branching in multiple directions.

The tremors grow, the vibration flowing through the space, through us. A sound like ice cracking fills the air, and then, all at once, the field shatters.

The helpful ghosts from the restroom flow from the window and circle around us. One ruffles my hair. Another plants a kiss on my cheek. Yet another bops Malcolm on the head. Then they stream from the alleyway, their numbers so great, it looks like early-morning fog.

We make our way from the alley, stumbling over smashed orange crates and tripping on discarded trash.

The doors to the Pancake House are wide open. Belinda is standing outside, waving to someone—or possibly something otherworldly. Samia is gaping at her restaurant. Amazingly, Nigel is there. I wonder who—or maybe what—alerted him. He has a hand on her shoulder. He gestures toward the entrance, and I can almost hear his comforting words.

We're sorry about the mess. Of course we'll help clean up.

Reginald is in quiet conversation with Carter, who seems reluctant to step from the man's shadow. I wonder what they're talking about, but most of all, I'm grateful we're free, that all the ghosts are free.

I turn a grin on Malcolm. His lips twitch. He's about to smile himself when something darkens his expression.

"Katy?"

He halts, and since we're holding hands, I do too.

"Are you okay?" he asks.

"Why wouldn't I be okay?"

Sure, I'm tired, but I don't think that's odd. It's been a long night.

"You look ... wrong."

"Wrong?"

Maybe it *is* exhaustion, or the power of suggestion. Or maybe it's something more. A wave hits me, one filled with cold nausea. My leg muscles go rubbery. I hold still, certain if I take a step, I'll collapse under my own weight.

The world narrows, the edges of my vision growing dark. I suck in a deep breath. At the moment, it seems very important that I keep breathing. I turn toward Malcolm. At the moment, it seems very important that I don't lose sight of him, either.

His mouth moves, but I can't hear any words. My legs go out from under me. I brace for impact, for asphalt bruising, scraping. Instead, I land in Malcolm's arms. He scoops me up and plants a gentle kiss on my cheek.

And then my world goes black.

CHAPTER 10

The sun is bright against my eyelids. I don't have the strength yet to open them. I've tried, several times. I want to reassure Malcolm that I'm fine. But since I can't speak—

or even open my eyes—I'm probably not fine at all.

It doesn't stop me from trying.

I'm resting in his arms. This I know for certain. I'm too warm and secure to be anywhere else. His fingers thread through my hair. Occasionally, he murmurs my name. I hear shouts, the rumble of a car. Then Samia's voice breaks through the fog in my head.

"Honestly, all of you," she says in her soft, lilting accent. "Bring her inside."

Once again, Malcolm scoops me up. I want to help. At the very least, I could loop my arms around his neck, but it feels as though lead weights are anchoring my wrists. I can't raise my hands. I can't do much of anything.

I'm not certain there's anything more frustrating.

Malcolm settles us in a booth. At least, the squeak of vinyl suggests this. I rest against his chest, his arms around mine.

"She is dehydrated, perhaps," Samia says. "Some water?"

Malcolm eases a straw between my lips. I sip, but the ice water is so cold, I recoil.

"Hey, there you are," he says, his voice low and hopeful against my ear. "I knew you were in there somewhere."

I manage the barest of nods. His chest rises and falls with a sigh of relief. Then, at last, I open my eyes.

Around me, everyone is hovering—Belinda, Samia, Nigel, Reginald, even Carter. Five pairs of intent eyes have me shrinking against Malcolm again.

"Maybe some of you could back off," he says.

"Of course," Samia says, and she beams at me. "Once I thank Katy."

For what? Not totally destroying her restaurant? Even now, the scent of burnt coffee lingers in the air. I don't detect any ghosts, but the aftereffects of the infestation remain.

"I'm sorry," I begin. "Especially for the mess—"

"Is nothing, not compared to what a ghost can do to the breakfast rush."

I concede she has a point.

"We will clean." She nods toward Belinda and points to the parking spaces outside the restaurant. "And Jim is here to help."

Belinda herself leans in and gives me a quick peck on the cheek. "We will clean," she echoes before lowering her voice. "And thank you. Thank you for being my friend."

She turns toward Carter, and I know she's assessing his damp clothes, the stubble along his jaw. Most of the shine has left him. What remains is possibly far more interesting.

"And you," she says before giving him a light kiss on his cheek. "You might make a decent human being after all."

"Nice." The scowl is back, but for a second, a wash of pink paints his features.

With that, Belinda heads toward the kitchen area, scooping up coffee cups as she goes.

Reginald studies me with concern. He's been quiet this entire time, but now he clears his throat.

"Katrina Lindstrom, can you tell us what happened in there?"

I do, as best I can, from the initial infestation to Carter's appearance to deciding to unravel the ghosts.

"Wait." Nigel holds up a hand and halts my words. "You didn't slice through them?"

"I didn't want to hurt or destroy any of them. Orson tied up Belinda's sprites at the very center. I didn't want to ... I mean, not kill them, but—"

Nigel whirls on Carter. "And you *let* her?"

"Whoa, man. I tried to talk her out of it. I told her it would leave her vulnerable." Carter folds his arms over his chest, and the frown is back. "Besides, have you tried talking her out of something?"

I push to sit up even though that takes me away from Malcolm's warmth. "No one *let* me do anything. I decided for myself. I didn't want to hurt the ghosts, especially since they were all Springside ghosts."

"You don't understand." Exasperation fills Nigel's voice, and he shoots Carter a quick glare before continuing. "It's not something necromancers do. It could take you weeks to recover."

I glance at Malcolm, who gives me a little shrug, and then turn toward Reginald. "What have I done?"

"Something most necromancers never attempt," he says.

"But why? It's not like the ghosts are—"

"Expendable?" Nigel says. "That's the thing, Katy. They are."

"No, they're not," I insist.

This, I think, is why I don't like necromancy. It's so casual in its cruelty. I know the ghosts are no longer human. I know they aren't even like pets (except for maybe the sprites). Still, they exist. They laugh. They wail. They celebrate. They mourn.

Even Reginald, despite all his kindness toward them, would've sliced through the tangle of ghosts that Orson created. I see that in his eyes even as he averts his gaze so I won't.

"To put it bluntly," Reginald says, "the ghosts feasted on you."

That *is* blunt. And untrue. I'm fine, or at least, mostly fine. If I could push up from the table and march out of the restaurant, I'd prove it.

"Feasted?" Malcolm sounds as skeptical as I feel.

"Her warmth. Her humanity." Nigel points at me. "Look at her. Really look at her."

Malcolm's gaze shifts toward me. He's already said himself that I look wrong. To be truthful, there's a hollowness inside me that I can't seem to shake off.

"It's often referred to as necromancer flu," Reginald adds. "And, like the flu, bed rest, fluids—especially hot ones—will help. No ghost catching or even interacting with them for a while."

"But she'll be okay, right?" Malcolm asks.

No one speaks. It's this, rather than the earlier scolding, that feeds my dread. My limbs are cold, my fingertips like ice. A pinprick sensation rushes along my scalp, followed by a shudder, but I stop it before my body can start to tremble.

"She'll be okay," Malcolm says again. This time, it isn't a question.

"It would be better if she weren't still healing from the previous encounter." Reginald nods at me, indicating the scars that remain on my arms. They've begun to ache, a dull sort of pain radiating from each cut.

"But, yes," he adds in what sounds almost like an afterthought. "With time and rest, she should make a full recovery."

The problem, I think, with being sick—even with something as ridiculous as necromancer flu—is that people talk about you rather than *to* you.

My gaze is drawn toward the window and Main Street beyond. The sun is rising, and in its glow, Springside is coming to life.

From my vantage point, I can see the police department and what looks like the bulky shadow of Chief Ramsey. I can't see his face, but I imagine he's studying the commotion at the Pancake House, and I imagine that he doesn't approve. Not so long ago, he spoke of my parents' death. He told me that he was the first officer to arrive at the crash site, and it was clear the pain of that hadn't faded.

Now I know he didn't tell me the whole story.

"Nigel," I say. "Is there some way you can access the police report of my parents' accident?" My non sequitur stuns everyone into silence, which gives me time to add, "And the newspaper reports, as well. I mean —" I look up and confront their stares once again. "I'm guessing there was something in the Springside newspaper, at least."

Nigel purses his lips and nods.

"Katy?" Malcolm's voice is gentle, his hand steady on my shoulder.

I turn to him. "Will you take me home?"

He gives me one of his sweet, dark-roast smiles. "You know I will."

He eases me from the booth. I can walk under my own power, but just barely. His arm around my waist keeps me upright until I'm secured in his convertible.

When we reach my house, however, he won't let me try the stairs.

"You won't make it," he says, "and you don't want to add broken bones to the list."

He's right; I know he's right. Even the idea of the porch steps is enough to exhaust me, never mind the ones that lead to my bedroom. For the third time that morning, he scoops me up.

"Under different circumstances," he says, pausing at the threshold, "this could be romantic."

His words ease the dread in my chest. I laugh. "It *is* romantic. Just having you here is."

He kisses me then. When he speaks, his voice is as soft and tender as his kiss. "I think so too."

With that, he carries me into my house and shuts the door with his foot, cutting us off from the world.

CHAPTER 11

What wakes me, I'm not certain. The air is rich with spice. I'm buried beneath my grandmother's down comforter. The sheets feel luxurious, as if I've just slipped between them after a long day—or night—of ghost catching. But I sense that I've been here for hours. Through the windows, light is streaming into the room, and its glow is gold with the sunrise.

I open my eyes and find Malcolm sleeping in an easy chair next to the bed, his feet propped on a worn footstool. His mouth is soft, but a furrow mars his brow, as if even in his dreams, he's worried.

I push to sit up—or try to. I have all the strength of a baby bird, and my biggest accomplishment is rustling the covers.

This is enough to wake Malcolm. His eyes flutter open. When his gaze finds mine, some of the worry melts from his brow.

"There you are," he says. His grin is warm and sleepy, but full of that dark-roast sweetness. "How are you feeling?"

I simply nod, since I'm still figuring that out. "How long have I been asleep?"

Malcolm taps his cell phone on the nightstand and studies the screen. "About twenty-four hours."

I don't bolt upright. I try, but I can't. It's like the air itself is heavy. Even so, the news is enough to get me into a sitting position.

"Hey, easy." In an instant, he's at my side, one hand supporting my back, the other adjusting the pillows. He settles me in and then takes a seat on the edge of the bed. "Better?"

The sight of him here, in my bedroom, leaves me dumbfounded—or maybe that's the necromancer flu. He's warm and rumpled, his faded U of M T-shirt wrinkled from a night in the chair. A few of his fingers are sporting bandages, and his knuckles are wrapped in gauze. It makes him look like he's been in a prizefight.

I nod toward the chair. "What are you doing there?"

He brushes the back of his hand along my forehead. "Keeping an eye on you."

"No, I mean instead of there." I let my gaze stray to the empty half of my bed.

A hint of pink highlights his cheekbones. "Well, you know, I always make a point of having an explicit invitation."

I muster all my strength and pat the space next to me.

He chuckles. "There's also the fact that Reginald's been checking on you every few hours, and that's—"

"Awkward?"

"Yeah. That." He shifts, pulling an insulated carafe and a glass mug from the nightstand. "But now that you're awake, maybe a little tea?"

He unscrews the cap, and the source of the aroma I smelled earlier becomes clear. It's Malcolm's fire spice tea. It's like drinking liquid Red Hots—without the sugar coma and mouth-scraped-raw aftereffects. Of all his tea recipes, this one's my favorite.

He hasn't made any since winter; just inhaling the steam is enough to make you break out in a sweat. Even now, perspiration dots his forehead. But I'm so cold—even sequestered under a down comforter and an extra blanket—that I can't wait to hold the mug in my hands.

"Easy," he says again, wrapping my fingers around the glass.

I force my hands not to tremble and hope my arm muscles will kick in. The glass is heavy, or rather, I'm inordinately weak, but the first sip sends a surge of warmth through me. I sink into the pillows and sigh.

"Good?" he asks. "Is it helping?"

"I think this is the best batch you've ever made."

The tea heats my stomach, the fire spreading from there. It's beating back the cold that's both freezing my limbs and sapping all my strength.

"I had some help this time. I've been chatting." He picks up the phone. "With my mother. She's nursed more than one necromancer through the flu. I have some necromancer stew going in a crockpot downstairs for when you feel like eating something."

"Necromancer stew? It's not made from actual necromancers, is it?"

Malcolm snorts a laugh. "It's more like turbo-charged chicken noodle soup, although I made this batch with vegetable stock. Prem swears by it."

"Is that your mother's husband?"

He gives his head a little shake.

"Partner?"

"Not really."

"Then what is he ... she...?"

"He." Malcolm heaves a sigh. "My mother likes to refer to Prem as her lover."

He's so uncomfortable—squirming like a little boy—that I laugh. The hot cinnamon spice slices through the layer of fog in my head. It sparks my curiosity, and I want to know more about the woman helping me. "What do they do in Paris? I mean, aside from the obvious?"

He squirms some more and throws me a scowl, but it's in jest—mostly. "They run a tour company."

"Tour company?"

"Haunted Paris."

"Oh! Ghosts?"

He grins. "Exactly. They cater mostly to tourists, but they also help necromancers in tracking down ghosts as well. And when the ghosts don't cooperate, Prem deploys the ones he keeps in reserve."

"Haunted Paris," I echo. My feet twitch as if they want to jump up and rush to the closet so I can start packing.

"You'd love Paris, Katy."

"You've been?"

"I lived there for a few months while I was growing up."

"Do you speak French?"

"Enough to order a decent meal."

I'm dumbfounded again, but maybe I shouldn't be. This might explain why Malcolm is so suave and pulled together. I can picture him in a café or catching ghosts along the Seine.

"We'll go someday," he says, and nods at my glass, urging me to drink. "But not until you're better."

I comply even as I narrow my eyes at him. "I don't think—"

"What? That we'll have enough money? Didn't you count all those ghosts you released? We're already getting calls and texts."

"We are?"

"Belinda helped me with an inventory, and it's clear Orson and Carter have been collecting them for months. This goes beyond the ones they had in the warehouse. No wonder business has been so bad."

This surprises me more than it should. I swallow down another gulp of tea as if that alone will return my strength. We have so much to do— and I have something important to confess.

I open my mouth to do just that, but Malcolm places a finger on my lips. "We can talk about your parents' accident later."

"Then—?"

"Belinda told me—and just me. It's not that I don't trust Nigel or Reginald, but for now, I think it's better if only the three of us know."

I shake my head, not to contradict him, but because there's more to this story.

Belinda didn't see Darien Armand. Only I did.

"It wasn't just Orson. Your father was there."

I blurt the words—it's the only way. If I wait too long or think too hard about it, I won't say them at all. Dreams of Paris will keep me from that.

Malcolm pauses in his reach for the carafe. For a moment, I don't think he'll move or say anything at all.

"What?" he says at last.

"The ghosts showed him to me. He was standing on the other side of the ravine. Belinda didn't see him. I don't even think Chief Ramsey or Orson saw him. But"—I shake my head as if that might shake away the image of Darien Armand—"he was there."

"My father was there." Malcolm's voice is a cold, hard thing. His lips form a thin line. "Of course he was."

For an instant, I think he's being sarcastic. The words have that sort of bite to them. Then he laughs, the sound of it so harsh and bitter, it steals the warmth from the tea. I almost wish he'd defend his father or refuse to believe. This acceptance fills me with icy sorrow.

"We could ask Chief," I say. "I mean, about me. I don't really know if I was there. What if the ghosts are playing a prank?"

"I don't think they are." He eyes me. "Do you?"

I give my head a quick shake and then lift the mug for another sip. There's nothing but a swallow left in the bottom, but I finish it off.

Malcolm's gaze lingers on my face, and his mood shifts. The bitterness leaves his eyes, and his mouth turns up in a smile. "The pink's coming back to your cheeks. That's good. That's real good."

I touch my face. And, yes, even though my fingertips no longer feel like ice, the skin beneath them is also warm.

He steals my glass and refills it. "Drink up," he says. "Because we have a trip to plan."

"I think we have other things to do first."

He nods as if conceding the point. "True. But the trip? That's pretty important. I've wanted to go back for ages, and I've always thought Paris would be the perfect spot for a honeymoon."

I freeze with the mug halfway to my lips and peer over the rim. "What does that mean?"

His hands join mine, and together we hold the mug. "Whatever you want it to."

In turn, we each take a sip of tea. Then Malcolm places the glass on the nightstand.

He kisses me, and it's a kiss to set the world on fire. Hot cinnamon spice mixes with his warm nutmeg scent. The combination may sweep me away. The combination may have me saying yes.

Not that he's asked. Not that he needs to.

I close my eyes and try not to dream too hard about Paris. It's a fragile thing, one that too many wishes might break.

I close my eyes and try not to dream too hard about Malcolm.

PART III
NOTHING BUT THE GHOSTS

COFFEE AND GHOSTS SEASON THREE,
EPISODE 3

CHAPTER 1

A week ago, my business partner, Malcolm Armand, may—or may not—have proposed marriage. This is something I'm not quite sure about, because, in truth, he merely proposed a trip to Paris.

But he claimed it was the perfect spot for a honeymoon.

Now, Paris at dusk fills the screen of my laptop. Buildings glow. Lights twinkle and throw stars on the water. It's enough to steal your breath. I'm not sure how much money you need to earn to own a view of the Seine. Apparently Malcolm's mother and the man she refers to as her lover, Prem, make more than enough. Even through the webcam, I'm mesmerized.

Malcolm's mother, Arianna, returns to her balcony and settles in the chair. "Yes, here it is." She thumbs through a hardback journal, one worn with age and use. "My grandmother kept meticulous notes."

I sometimes wish *my* grandmother had.

"Open," she says.

I comply, opening my mouth and leaning forward so Arianna can peer inside.

"Now the eyes."

I pull back my eyelids so she can examine the skin beneath.

"Still too pale." She presses a finger against her lips in thought. This doesn't mar her perfectly applied lipstick in a red so fierce it probably stops traffic. Her precision-cut bob sways, her hair a glorious silver. With the silk scarf knotted at her neck, she *is* Paris.

"I still don't like how slowly you're recovering," she adds. "You're young and healthy." She tilts her head, and the bob cascades along her cheekbones. "Show me your arms again."

So I do, holding each arm in front of the webcam so she can examine the scars that still linger.

Arianna frowns. When she does, the family resemblance is so strong that it startles me. Both her sons wear that same scowl.

"I'm feeling better." I'm hedging my bets. I've been locked inside my house for a week now. I'm allowed onto the porch, but only in full sunlight. Otherwise, it's cup after cup of tea and bowl after bowl of stew. "I could probably go on a few calls with Malcolm."

"No, you can't. You don't have the strength."

"I feel like I do. I'm going stir crazy."

"You *think* you have the strength. The moment you encounter anything stronger than a sprite, you'll undo everything we've done in the past week. No ghost catching, no interaction at all."

"Not even with sprites?" I venture.

"Not even that."

A thump comes from the living room, followed by a muted cry of, "I got it!" Tara's voice is triumphant, and Belinda's laugh is indulgent.

"Do it again," she urges.

My gaze flits toward the living room. I hope Tara doesn't decide to show me her latest catch. Back on the screen, Prem strolls into view. He has a full head of black hair, and his skin is a lovely shade of olive. I've speculated on the age difference, but Malcolm refuses to play along. No matter. It's clear from Prem's expression that—even after five years—he is dazzled by Arianna. Even so, he gives me a smile in commiseration before heading off screen to prepare for his evening.

"I'll send Malcolm another recipe to try," Arianna says.

"More tea?" I love Malcolm's tea—it's as warm and exotic as he is. His samovar now keeps my percolator company in the kitchen. I like the way it looks there on the counter, the glint of gold warming the cooler silver of the coffeepot.

But I've consumed gallons of the stuff in the last week. I'm not certain I can drink another cup.

She eyes me as if I've asked a silly question. Of course it's more tea.

Before I can protest, another crash comes from the living room, the sort that shakes the floorboards.

"I got them! I got them! Let's go show Katy!"

Oh, no. I open my mouth, hold up a hand, but Tara's only eleven, and these sorts of social cues zip right past her.

Belinda's eyes go wide. She lunges to catch Tara, but it's too late.

"Look!" Tara lands next to me, the cat barrettes in her braids lightly clacking. She holds up a Tupperware container. Inside, three mischievous sprites are swirling. "I caught them all at once!"

"You sure did!" I say, although I suspect the sprites might have had something to do with that. They're a friendly trio and probably think this is a game. Even so, it's good training, if only to learn the mechanics of catch and release. "Want to head into the backyard and let them go?"

She nods with more clacking from her braids. She takes Belinda's hand, and they rush out the back, the screen door thumping in their wake.

When I turn back to my laptop, Arianna's scowl greets me.

"What did I say about no interaction?"

"But I'm not the one interacting. I'm only training Tara how to catch them." When her scowl deepens, I add, "From a distance. It's all"—I place a hand on my hip and use the other to point—"like that."

Something softens in Arianna's expression. She regards me for a long moment, and in the silence, I can hear Paris at night. "You look so much like your mother."

My heart thumps a strange beat. In the week I've been video chatting with her, Arianna's alluded that she knew my parents. But with Tara and sprites about, Belinda hovering over my every move, and Sadie visiting several times a day, I haven't had the chance to ask her about them.

Honestly? I haven't had the courage.

I bite my lip, which earns me a finger wag from Arianna.

"No, no, stop that. It will absolutely ruin the look of your lipstick."

Yes, like I wear lipstick.

"I'm sending you some," she adds as if reading my thoughts. "Every woman should own a never-fail tube of lipstick."

I stop biting my lip—if only so I can bite back my reply. I like Malcolm's mother, but the woman could steamroll right over you. I'm glad there's half a continent—not to mention an entire ocean —between us.

The kitchen door opens. I turn, expecting Tara and Belinda. Instead, Malcolm steps through. I start at the sight of him. True, he's dressed impeccably—pressed trousers, a dress shirt. But he's also wearing what must have been a long day of ghost catching.

The white dress shirt is splattered with coffee, his loafers look as if they've been soaking in tea, and a series of grass stains has ruined his khakis.

Even the smile he gives me—one of his sweet, dark-roast ones— appears worn and tired.

I really need to get better.

On the laptop screen, Arianna lights up. "Oh, there's my baby boy."

Malcolm struggles to keep the grimace from his face. "Hello, Mother."

Arianna rolls her eyes and offers a cheek. "Kiss."

Dutifully, Malcolm air kisses first one and then the other cheek. It's very continental and sophisticated, even if it is through a webcam.

"I'm glad you're here," Arianna says. "I need to speak to you later, probably about midnight your time." She waves a hand toward the balcony doors. "It's tourist season, and we have two groups booked tonight. We won't make it back until morning."

"I—" Malcolm begins, but the Arianna steamroller bumps right over his protest.

"I want to move some of my investments around and ask your opinion on a few things, and I don't want to bore Katy."

He tries again. "But I—"

"There's a good boy. Well, I must be off. I need to help Prem prepare for this evening."

For an instant, it seems like all of Paris fills our view, and then the screen goes blank.

Malcolm's lips twitch, and he swears softly. "My mother doesn't need my help investing," he says.

"It sounds like she wants it," I offer. "That's good, right?"

This last week has been hard on Malcolm. Arianna is chatty, and I like her, but I sense a certain amount of strain when it comes to Malcolm and Nigel. Her affair with Prem was part of the reason behind her divorce from Darien. The aftershocks of that linger. I can see them in the vulnerable crinkles around Malcolm's eyes.

"Yeah, it's good. Technically, she was my first customer." He reaches a hand toward me, and I hop from the kitchen stool and step into his embrace. "But it means I have to sleep at home tonight."

"You can't talk to her here?"

"All her paperwork is at the apartment." He casts a look upward, toward the ceiling and the second story, where my bedroom is. "I'm sure she's guessed and everything, but it's—"

"Awkward?"

"Yeah. That. It's stupid. I shouldn't mind, but—"

"It's fine," I tell him. "I can survive a night on my own. Besides, Belinda is down the hall, and Sadie and Nigel are next door. It's not like I've been alone lately, anyway. "Plus," I add, patting the splotches on his shirt, "you could do some laundry."

He laughs and pulls me in closer. "You're right. I probably could."

"I should start going on calls with you. You've been working overtime all week." I wave a hand, indicating the number of stains he's currently wearing. "Was it bad today?"

"They're frisky, is all," he says, but his words emerge with a sigh. "Truthfully, I think they miss you and resent me. My wardrobe will survive, and so will I."

I peer up at him. "I don't like that you're going out alone. You're next on Orson's list."

That's the real reason I need to get better. We've faced two of the three threats Orson made at Sadie and Nigel's wedding reception—a possession meant for Nigel, and all the ghosts ever to haunt Belinda. I don't know what he might have planned for Malcolm, except that it must be deadly.

"Orson had his chance," Malcolm says. "In the alley. He could've broken his containment field, but he didn't." He cups my face with a hand. "It's you, not me, we should be worried about."

Maybe. I can't convince myself of it. If Orson truly wants to hurt me, he'll go after Malcolm. This is something he already knows.

"Speaking of which," Malcolm says, "are you ready to try some new tea?"

Am I? I heave a sigh. "Bring it on."

IT'S ONLY LATER, when I'm snuggled on the sofa with Malcolm, that regret truly starts to eat at me. I don't want him to leave. It's a purely selfish thought. If nothing else, he really does need to do some laundry. His wardrobe may be vast, but I suspect it's reached its limit. And it's not like I've never been on my own. I've become so used to having him here so quickly that the idea of giving him up for a night rankles.

"It's like the good old days," he says as if reading my thoughts. "Remember evening kisses?"

"It wasn't that long ago."

"I guess not." He shifts and settles me closer. His hands come to rest on my arms. Somehow, he knows without looking where the scars are. With his fingertips, he strokes each one as if that might heal it. His warm nutmeg scent is laced with Kona blend and a hint of Earl Grey. He smells like a long day at work.

"How are the ghosts?" I ask. "I mean, really."

"Like I said, they're frisky. I—" He breaks off, and I hear the echo of his next words. *I could really use your help.* "Maybe they're just happy to be away from Orson," he says instead. "Who wouldn't be?"

Yes, who wouldn't be? I fall silent, considering that, and what it might be like for the ghosts to be free, really free.

"Hey." Malcolm's voice is hushed. "What's up?"

"I was just thinking."

Beneath me, his chest rumbles with amusement. "When aren't you thinking?"

"I'm serious."

"So am I, and it's one of the things I love about you."

All the words melt in my mouth. My thoughts spin, and my heart thumps hard against my ribs. I want to say those words back, but I have a hard time making them leave my mouth. Every once in a while, I'll squeak it out. Malcolm doesn't seem to mind. His affection doesn't have a scorecard.

"So, what are you thinking?" he prompts.

This I have words for, so I tell him. "What's a necromancer without any ghosts?"

"Is this a riddle? Because I've never been very good at those."

"My grandmother always said it was better to separate ghosts from people, and she even told me she'd show me how after she died. I always thought she meant the people were better off." I shift so I can gauge his expression. "What if she meant the ghosts?"

"What's a necromancer without any ghosts?" He considers for a moment. "Unemployed?"

"What's Orson without any ghosts?"

"A bully without any reinforcements?" He eyes me. "I have other words for Orson, but I'll spare you."

I laugh and snuggle closer. "What does it mean to be free?"

"Okay, riddles are one thing, but existential questions are way out of my league."

"For the ghosts, I mean. My grandmother never even hinted at necromancy. I still don't talk to ghosts the way you do. It makes me feel like I'm violating one of her rules."

Malcolm shifts again so he can look at me straight on. "The ghosts would love it if you did. They adore you."

"Not all of them," I say.

"Most. Even the malicious ones have a certain amount of respect."

"She didn't want me to be a necromancer," I add. "That's pretty clear. But why?"

Concern replaces the warmth of Malcolm's gaze. He studies me, then brings a finger to my cheek and traces the faded blue spot that still lingers there.

"This is why," he says, his words solemn.

"But it happened anyway."

"Maybe she hoped it wouldn't."

"And left me unprepared." I strive to keep the grumble from my voice. I've worked so hard not to blame my grandmother for this. I miss her so much. Her death left a hole inside me that I haven't been able to fill—although having Malcolm in my life helps.

"Or not," he says, almost as an afterthought.

"Or not what?"

"Unprepared. You've been beating Orson at his own game."

"I've had a lot of help," I counter. "Plus, I'm not playing his game."

Malcolm grins at me. "That's why you're winning."

With both hands at my waist, he propels me from the sofa. He's about to stand when he flops back. He raises a hand with what looks like gargantuan effort.

"A little help?"

Oh, he's so tired, but, Malcolm being Malcolm, he wears even that with style. I help him to his feet and walk him to the door.

"Be careful," I say after one last kiss.

"Aren't I always?"

"I'm serious."

"So am I, which means you lock the door behind me."

I do. I also stand vigil until he's pulled his convertible from the curb and is heading down the block. I wait until the taillights have winked from view and then head into the kitchen.

Only the light over the stove illuminates the space. The air is still warm and fragrant with exotic spices. The samovar is switched off, but the gold sides glimmer—with something otherworldly.

I step closer and peer at the samovar. There, in the residual heat, floats one of Belinda's sprites.

"Shouldn't you be upstairs?"

The sprite swirls, crashing into the samovar and making it rock. I steady it and can't help inhaling another burst of that spice. I lean closer and sniff again. Then I pull the thing apart and inspect the tea leaves.

Beside me, the sprite bobs, puppy-like and curious about what I'm doing. I'm not exactly sure what I'm doing, except I know this:

I'm wide awake.

"What did Malcolm put in here?" I ask the sprite.

It flips over backward, apparently overjoyed that we're conversing.

"Actually," I say, "what did Arianna tell him to put in here?"

The sprite shoots toward the spice cabinet, slips inside, and then rattles the contents. The force of its effort flings the cabinet door open. Jars of spice and containers of herbs rain down on the counter.

"Stop! Stop!" I brace a hand on the door and use the other to collect the rolling jars. "You'll wake Belinda."

This subdues the sprite enough that I can clean up the mess. I consider dumping the tea leaves in the garbage. I consider texting Malcolm for the ingredients. Both can wait until morning.

"Come on," I say to the sprite. "It's time you were in bed."

I walk upstairs, the sprite weaving through the banisters beside me. At Belinda's room, I shoo it beneath the door.

"Go on. Take care of her."

I catch the telltale hint of a cry when it joins the other two. After the initial greeting, the room grows silent, the sprites now content. They'll keep an eye on Belinda, and certainly one will alert me if Orson sends another attack ghost her way.

Something tugs at me—regret again. It's so quiet up here, so lonely. I almost knock on Belinda's door. I consider waggling my fingers near the crack to coax out one of the sprites.

I opt for a heavy sigh instead.

There's no need to be alone, my dear.

I freeze halfway to my room. Then I give my head a vigorous shake as if that will knock the voice out of it. Because I know that voice, and I have no intention of inviting it in. Not now. Not when I'm alone.

I hold still while the house around me settles. If I stay this way, don't make a move, don't even allow myself to think, then everything will be okay. I wait, and all I hear is the pounding of my pulse in my ears.

Bit by bit, I relax. The voice in my head has faded. I take one step and then another toward my bedroom.

At the entrance, with my hand on the doorknob, I freeze again.

The bed I left rumpled is pristine—comforter smooth, pillows plumped. The clothes hamper has righted itself, and all the wayward socks have found their way inside. The blinds are drawn, and the windows have been opened just enough to let in the night breeze.

In the chair, the one Malcolm has occupied this past week, sits the entity.

The entity is in the form it thinks I like, that of a well-dressed man. And while it's true that Malcolm is almost always well-dressed, that's not the reason I like him. I'd like—I'd love—him no matter what he wore, even torn flannel and frayed jeans.

Would you, my dear? Would you really?

I scowl in the entity's general direction, but then turn my mind's eye toward Malcolm in torn flannel and frayed jeans. I try to bite back a smile, but it's no use.

I would very much like Malcolm in torn flannel and frayed jeans.

So predictable. It's always the pretty ones who get all the attention.

I ignore that. "What are you doing here?"

The entity spreads its arms wide. *I can't visit my necromancer?*

"I didn't invoke you."

True, but I think I mentioned that you don't necessarily need to.

"Plus, I'm not a necromancer."

Not true, but we're arguing semantics now.

Yes, we probably are, not that I plan to admit it.

I cast a glance down the hall. A hush has fallen over the rest of the house. It's as if the entity has created a bubble around my room, where there's light and sound and endless night.

I shut the bedroom door, although I suspect I don't need to. Belinda won't hear me—no one will.

Except for me, my dear. You're always forgetting about me.

Hardly. I try again. "Why are you here?"

The entity raises its hands in supplication. *To chat. We never get to chat. You're always busy with other things—being kidnapped or shot at or untying ghosts. You should consider a sabbatical.*

I skirt the bed to put it between the entity and me. Not that it's much of a barrier. In fact, it's a silly and obvious thing to do. I expect the entity to laugh at me.

It doesn't.

So I ease onto the comforter and then grab one of those perfectly plumped pillows as a talisman. I need something to hold on to, something that feels real, especially if we're going to chat.

Nothing good can come from that.

Oh, come now. Honestly? True, we've had our ups and downs, but you're my necromancer now.

I touch the faded blue spot on my cheek. I don't need a mirror to know exactly where it is. The skin there is slightly waxy, always cooler than the rest of my face, even now, when my fingertips feel like ice.

The entity tilts its head, conceding the point. *Yes, well, like I said, ups and downs. All relationships have them. Speaking of which, you might want to rethink your choice of partners—in and out of bed. Bit of a mama's boy, that one.*

I shoot it a look and several nasty thoughts.

It merely laughs. *So fierce. I wonder, does he know how lucky he is?*

The entity pauses and turns its head toward the ceiling as if in contemplation. It doesn't have a face, or, at least, it's never given this incarnation one. There's only a swirling void where a face might be.

Ah, the jury's still out. I guess time will tell.

I don't know what it means by that. Something about Malcolm? About me? The one thing I do know is, the entity won't tell me.

Another thing I know?

When it comes to Malcolm, I'm the lucky one.

You sell yourself short, my dear.

"So, we're going to chat?" I say, because I don't relish an endless night with this thing in my bedroom. Giving it what it wants is the only course of action.

But even as the thought crosses my mind, I notice how the lamplight is muted to a perfect glow. The air tastes sweet, and the breeze touches my cheeks in a way that's impossibly soft. It's all manufactured and gauzy, like a Hallmark card commercial, and yet...

You doubt my abilities?

"I don't, actually. That's the point."

I've been around for a very long time. It flicks a hand. Sparks light the air, ones that look like fireflies. They glow before winking out, the last one twinkling in front of my nose. *I've picked up a few tricks along the way.*

I consider what I might ask the entity. It would know everything, wouldn't it? From who assassinated JFK to the real reason Darien Armand is in town. In front of me, the entity glimmers as if in anticipation.

Excellent. We are *going to chat.*

Then it morphs—or, rather, its outfit does, from impeccably tailored suit to a velvet smoking jacket in midnight blue. A pipe appears in one hand, although, since it doesn't have a mouth, I'm not sure what good that will do.

Still, I can't help it. I laugh.

I'm simply getting more comfortable.

I almost hate to ask. "For what?"

For our chat, of course. You ask. I answer.

"For a price." I know how this works.

Not all answers come with a price—at least, not an exorbitant one.

It's almost like a game of truth or dare, sparring with this thing. Only it knows all the truth, and dares always have consequences.

You are far too cautious.

Maybe I am. Nearly everyone has urged me to use the entity, to make a deal, extract promises, take the easy way out and keep everyone safe. I want nothing more than to keep everyone safe.

I'm not convinced using the entity is the way to do it.

Why not, my dear?

I sigh. "Can I at least have some thoughts to myself?"

Not when they play so wonderfully across your face. I wasn't even eaves-

dropping. So, why not use me, when I'm here and oh so convenient, not to mention willing?

"Are you? Are you, really?"

Convenient? Why, yes. The entity raises a hand, indicating its form in the chair. *I'm right here.*

"I mean willing."

Excuse me, my dear?

"Are you truly willing?"

You're my necromancer, so, yes, of course I am. That's how it works.

"So, if Orson Yates were your necromancer, you'd help him ... do whatever—to me, to Springside, the world?"

The entity flickers. It has no face, so trying to gauge how my words affect it is a fruitless task. Still, it pauses a bit too long before filling my head with more of its words.

There are rules to how this works, Katy, ones that are far older and much deeper than you can possibly understand.

"That's not an answer." I know this thing is powerful. I know poking at it with a virtual stick is a stupid thing to do.

In my defense, it did say it wanted to chat.

The entity rumbles something that sounds almost like a human snort. *I did, didn't I? Here's my question for you, then. Why don't you trust me?*

Oh, for so many reasons. I could list them out. I could write an essay about all those reasons.

The one that pops out of my mouth surprises us both. "You're not my friend."

You wound me.

"I'm serious."

Apparently.

I crawl off the bed and leave the pillow behind. I no longer need the talisman.

"There isn't any bargaining between friends."

Are you certain about that? Isn't there a bit of bargaining going on between you and that so-called partner of yours? He's quite the charmer, but he isn't always ... how shall we say? On the level.

I cringe, because, yes, Malcolm has some issues with the truth. "We don't keep score."

Perhaps, and perhaps not. With him, who knows?

"But this isn't about Malcolm. I know him, and I trust him. All I know about you is that your loyalty depends on which necromancer currently has a pact with you."

A fairly straightforward proposition. You have no reason to doubt my intentions.

"But..." I open and then close my mouth, frustrated that I can't articulate my thoughts. They aren't even thoughts, really. What I want to say is more of a whisper than actual words.

"It isn't fair to you." I blurt this, not caring that it might not make sense.

The entity's form roils with laughter, the sound of it rich and indulgent, a parent amused by a toddler.

Unfair? To me? Could there be anything further from the truth?

"No, it isn't fair to you," I say again, warming to my subject. "You don't get to choose your necromancer, do you?"

Choose? No. Influence? Ah, now, that's a distinct possibility, and frankly, far more fun.

"But what if someone you despise catches you?"

That rarely happens.

"But it could."

There are rules for how I can interact on this plane. I abide by them because every once in a great while, they bring me someone like you.

Should that flatter me? Maybe. I think it's meant to distract me instead. Despite all the power the entity has, it needs a human conduit to do everything it might want to do. On our first encounter, it claimed to want simple things: the ability to drink a cup of coffee, to touch a cheek.

These aren't the desires of the power-crazed. Orson Yates doesn't want those things, or, at least, he just doesn't crave them.

"You're lonely," I say.

I know something about loneliness. I'm a girl who catches ghosts, raised by her eccentric grandmother, after all. Even when someone like Belinda included me, I always felt outside the circle, like there was a barrier between everyone else and me.

The entity flicks some imaginary lint from the cuff of its jacket. *Really, my dear? I've been around for ages.*

"Okay. Make that very lonely."

I know about that, too. That time still stretches out in my mind, the dark space between when my grandmother died and Malcolm and I became partners. What would it be like to have that same darkness without end?

I never thought I'd feel sorry for the thing that has haunted and tormented me for nearly a year. I never thought I'd understand it.

Your pity is wasted on me, my dear. As for your understanding? You have no more a chance of comprehending me than a sprite has of mastering calculus.

"Are you sure?" I ask. "About the sprite, I mean."

This time, the laughter is more muted, a warm chuckle. *See? It's things like this that make our exchanges more than equitable.*

The entity stands and walks forward, its strides fluid. It halts mere inches away from me. Its proximity buzzes the air, and its power is tangible, sharp and electric. The tiny hairs on the back of my neck stand on end. The urge to step back nearly overwhelms me.

I hold my ground.

Have I convinced you yet?

I shake my head.

Why ever not?

"The first thing you said to me tonight. 'There's no need to be alone.'"

You were mooning about, missing that partner of yours.

"You seem fixated on Malcolm."

That's because he takes up so much space in here. The entity gestures toward my head. *You sound rather lovesick most days.*

I ignore that. Behind me, the curtains rustle with the breeze. The air is cooler, as if the night has released the last bit of the day's warmth. The void where the entity's face should be swirls, the pattern shifting and changing to something more shrouded.

The bubble around us shatters. I feel the late hour in my legs, and it presses against my eyelids. And I consider: maybe it wasn't the tea at all.

I was wondering when you'd figure that out.

Without another word, the entity vanishes.

MY PHONE RINGS just as I reach for the lamp on the nightstand. The sound startles me, and I switch the light off, on, and then off again. My heart thumps a hopeful beat. No matter how tired I am, I want to talk to Malcolm more than anything. It must be him, calling to grumble about his mother.

The number is one I recognize, because I've seen it pop up on the screen several times this week. But it's not Malcolm.

It's Arianna. Calling me. At one thirty in the morning. And she wants to video chat. I decide to leave the light off.

"Oh, good, you're awake," she says the moment the connection goes through.

I want to say, *You just called and woke me up, so of course I'm awake.* Except that isn't true. I cast my thoughts toward the entity. Did it keep me awake and alert on purpose? For this?

I strain for a telltale hint—a rumble or a sigh or something in the air. The breeze kicks up again, and the curtains flap.

I'm not sure that's an answer.

"I apologize for the late hour and the ruse, but I simply must speak to you alone." She waves a hand, the gesture dismissive, and her mouth quirks into a knowing smile. "Like I don't know the two of you are sleeping together."

I don't want to talk about that, not at one thirty in the morning. And I really don't want to talk to Arianna about it, especially since she's as fresh as the Paris morning I can see behind her.

"This is important, Katy." She pauses and takes a sip from a white porcelain cup that could double as a soup bowl. Her lipstick leaves behind a perfect impression. "Before I say anything, you must promise never to tell Malcolm or Nigel what I'm about to tell you."

A secret? Oh, I hate those. I'm a terrible liar. Malcolm will know I'm hiding something. So will Nigel, for that matter.

I give my head a vigorous shake. "I don't think—"

"You need to know this, for their sake, if for no other reason."

"Their sake?"

"Will you promise me?"

I open my mouth, hoping for the right words, or any words, to come out. "Arianna, I can't. I mean, without knowing what—"

"I know you love my son."

If I'd hoped to find words, that declaration blows away any chance of it. She laughs, the sound light and airy. True, it's morning in Paris, but it's still far too early for this sort of conversation.

"I've been chatting with you all week long," she says by way of explanation. "It's fairly obvious, and I..." She trails off and becomes devoted to her cappuccino again. After a long sip, she continues. "I approve. You're good for him, and vice versa."

I give a numb sort of nod.

"Which is why you must promise, for his sake, and the sake of your partnership—both in and out of bed."

The echo of the entity's words shoots through me. That isn't a coincidence; it can't be. Once again, I'm wide awake. I feel as if I've downed a giant cappuccino like the one Arianna is drinking.

I push the pillows—still perfectly plumped—behind me and settle in. This, I suspect, will be a long chat.

"All right. I promise. I won't tell Malcolm."

"Or Nigel."

"Or Nigel," I add.

I wait, certain Arianna will launch her first volley. Instead, she brushes a few strands of hair from her forehead. She has, of course, an impeccable French manicure. She sips the cappuccino again. At last, she pushes back from the table and stands. For a brief moment, she vanishes from the screen. I hear the scrape of the balcony door, and she reappears in front of me.

"Prem knows this," she says, settling into her chair, "but I want to spare him the rerun." Arianna smiles, not the dazzling expatriate smile she so often wears, but one that's much sadder, more worn around the edges. "I'm sure someone has informed you about my affair by now, the one that ended my marriage to Darien."

I nearly bite my lip before remembering that it will earn me a scolding. "Malcolm mentioned it," I say. "He was trying to explain ... things about the family." I give in and gnaw my lip anyway. "Around the time of the wedding."

"Oh, my poor baby boy," she says. Her gaze darts to my chewed lower lip, but she ignores it. "Yes, that's exactly the sort of thing he'd do, and, of course, you've met Darien."

I nod.

"Some people wear their hearts on their sleeves. Darien? He likes to display all his wounds for everyone to admire."

Oh. Yes. No animosity *there*.

"I don't blame him," she adds. "Not when it comes to this. Because it wasn't my first."

Arianna falls silent, and I consider her words, trying to piece together the puzzle that is Malcolm's family.

"We did everything couples do when small children are involved: marriage counseling, fighting, more counseling. It wasn't until I met Prem that I realized how miserable we all were. And since, by that time, the boys were nearly grown and Darien traveled constantly." She raises a hand and lets it fall. "It was a step that, had I more courage, I would've taken years ago."

Arianna comes across so fierce, so sure of herself, that I can't imagine her a coward.

"But that's merely background." She glances away from me, toward the Seine. "I hate to burden you with this, but current circumstances dictate that I do." She returns her attention to me, staring at me straight on. Her gaze is like an arrow, and it pins me in place.

"About the time of your parents' deaths, I embarked on an affair with Orson Yates."

CHAPTER 3

The phone slips through my fingers and lands on the bed, screen down. How long I leave it there, I'm not certain. It doesn't matter. I don't have a single coherent thought in my head, never mind words to form into sentences and questions.

Malcolm's mother and Orson Yates? I don't need to worry about keeping this a secret from Malcolm. If I told him, he wouldn't believe me, not when *I* don't believe it.

I wonder if the call is still connected. Then I wonder if it would look too obvious if I brushed my thumb over *Cancel* and disconnected it. My stomach is a bundle of knots, and my chest feels tight. I don't want to talk about affairs and broken marriages. I don't want to know how it all relates to my parents' deaths.

Because clearly it does.

At last, I retrieve my cell phone. Arianna is still there, cradling the oversized cup in her palms.

"I'm sorry," she says. "An in-person chat would've been so much better."

Not really. This way, at least, I can hide most of my shock and all of my disgust.

"Orson Yates?" I mean it as a question, but the name comes out as an accusation.

"Orson was a much different man back then." Arianna regards me through the screen. "I know, it doesn't seem possible to you. For me? It doesn't seem possible he's changed so much. Or, rather—" She sets the cappuccino down and taps her lips with an index finger. "He's nurtured some traits at the expense of others."

I cast my thoughts back to the road and the ravine on the way to the nature preserve, or, rather, the version of it Springside's ghosts showed me. Orson was obviously younger, but there was something else about him, a kind of vulnerability. He was someone who, on the surface, appeared capable of both compassion and curiosity.

I peer at Arianna, and her expression shifts, a glimmer of approval lighting her eyes.

"I see you understand. Not everybody does. For some people, the world is black and white."

I wonder if that includes Darien Armand.

"The necromancer community was hit hard by your parents' deaths. In fact, I'm willing to say that it fundamentally changed the community. Things were never the same after that. Many of us left—not right away, of course." She pauses and contemplates the Seine. "But when we left, we left for good."

"I don't remember my parents." My voice sounds small and insubstantial, and I think the night breeze might be able to sneak in and steal the words away.

"I'm sorry for that. They were ... they were quite wonderful. Your father was one of those strong, silent types. But when he spoke, nearly everyone listened. Your mother was ... she..." Her gaze flits toward me and then back to the Seine. "Shall I tell you the ugly truth? I was quite jealous of her."

I'm not sure how to take that. I wasn't even a year old when my parents died. Still, I can't picture Arianna Armand being jealous of anyone.

"Not only did her ability rival that of all her peers—that includes my ex-husband—she had a way with ghosts, and, since I'm being honest, men." Arianna gives me a wry smile. "It's funny what we think matters, especially when we're younger."

I shake my head, not because I disagree but because I can't form a picture of my mother. She's more of a ghost than anything.

"Darien was quite obsessed with her. At first, I didn't understand why, or, rather, I thought it was for the typical reasons a man becomes obsessed with a woman who isn't his wife."

"Arianna, please, I don't—" I don't want any of this. I don't want to know about Darien Armand and my mother. I don't want to hear about this part of her. I don't need to pull back the veil and examine my parents' lives.

"Shh." She hushes me. "It's more, and less, than what you think it is."

I wait. My throat is tight, and my eyes are watering. I brace as if I'm waiting for a physical blow.

"Your mother very much wanted to bring her father back to this plane. It was that desire that drove her, I think, to hone her skills, to join the association. You may have noticed that they're not exactly egalitarian."

"Yeah. Orson made a big deal out of it when he came to Springside."

"Yes, he would." She regards me. "In a way, you've accomplished what she set out to do. You brought Malcolm back, after all."

I open my mouth, but Arianna holds up a finger. "I know all about that. Everyone does. In fact, when things … calm down, Prem would very much like to talk to you about it."

I nod. I would like to talk to someone about it, too, someone in addition to Malcolm. He doesn't remember his time with the entity, and our conversations about it are strained.

"But this was a special case. Your grandfather had been gone for several years, and the agreement between him, your grandmother, and the entity was complicated."

"Do you know why—?"

She holds up that finger again, halting my question. "From what I understand, it was a stopgap measure, but your mother was determined to bring him back, even up to and including sacrificing herself."

I swallow back the questions. It occurs to me that I can ask the entity about this. Oh, I could, certainly—for a price.

I ponder the timing of its visit this evening.

Again, hardly a coincidence.

I hold in my sigh and let Arianna continue.

"I don't know the whole story. There are pieces that I suspect only Darien knows, but I do know this. Your mother asked for his help, and he felt ... compelled to do so. I—" She shakes her head and then runs her fingers through her hair. The bob swings forward, the ends flirting with the corners of her mouth. "I thought that in addition to everything else, they were having an affair."

Her balcony door creaks open. Prem appears, bearing a plate of rolls, wisps of steam rising in the morning air. Without a word, he sets the plate on the table, kisses Arianna on the cheek, and then slips back through the door.

She sinks into her chair, releases a sigh, and blows him a kiss. "It doesn't make any sense, of course. You were an infant, and anyone looking at your parents could see how happy they were."

Arianna falls silent. She plucks a croissant from the plate and tears off a bite.

I work to peel away the emotions tangled in this story. My mother wanted to get her father back. What did she do? Possibly the same thing I did when I wanted to get Malcolm back.

Ask for help.

"So, my mother asked Darien if he could help her, since he's so good at catching ghosts?"

Arianna looks up from her croissant, surprise and relief playing across her features. "Yes, exactly. Darien was intrigued. Not so much with your mother, although he admired her skill, but with the entity."

Still intrigued? I decide not to ask.

"Of course, by the time I realized that, it was too late. Your parents were dead, and I found myself consoling the wrong man because of it."

Consoling?

"Here's something you probably don't know about Orson Yates. Not many people do. Unlike Darien, he's not very good at catching ghosts."

"He's not?"

She considers the croissant in her hand and picks up a butter knife.

"No. In fact, he's relied on others to do the more ... menial parts of the job for all these years. It's why he almost always travels with a protégé."

"Like Carter Dupree?"

"Yes, exactly like Carter," she says. "But when it comes to deploying ghosts, to training and motivating them? There's no one better than he is. It's a highly prized skill. You know how capricious ghosts can be. No one trains them like Orson does, and the Midwest Necromancer Association rewarded him accordingly."

I'm not sure where she's going with this. I'd guessed at the one. Orson's attack ghosts are fierce, and he's both cruel and cunning with them. With a little thought, I might have puzzled out the other, but I've always figured Orson preferred to have a minion to do the grunt work.

"I don't understand—" I begin.

Arianna cuts me off with another gaze that pins me in place. "Orson deployed the ghost that killed your parents, but it was Darien who caught the ghost in the first place."

CHAPTER 4

I drop the phone again. It bounces on the bed and vanishes in a fold of the comforter. Part of me wants to grab it and demand answers. Part of me wants to hang up and pretend the last half-hour never happened.

From within the down comes Arianna's muffled voice. I search out the phone, fingers snaking through the covers. For a long moment, I simply hang on to it. Part of me insists I already knew this fact, that it was obvious from the start. I don't need to hear any more.

Arianna's voice is more plaintive than crisp. She's revealed a great many family secrets to tell me all this.

I rescue the phone and turn the screen toward me.

"Oh, thank goodness, you're still there. Katy, I know this must be a shock, but keep in mind that the Orson Yates of two decades ago was a much different man, as was Darien."

Yes. That. Another secret to keep from Malcolm—and Nigel. At this rate, I'm going to lose track.

"I can tell you this for a fact: neither man knew the ghost would end up killing your parents. I didn't understand Darien's reaction at the time. It was only much later that I discovered he had been involved." She shakes her head as if that will shake away the past. "The association has always used strong-arm tactics, but the bullying never went too far."

"Except for when it did."

She sighs. "Yes, it did. It changed Orson, for the worse, obviously. But, at the time, he was bereft. He cared for your mother. I think I mentioned she had a way with men? You look so much like her. I imagine he must have a difficult time reconciling past and present."

Is that why he gave me so many chances to join the Midwest Necromancer Association? Then I wonder something else.

"Why would the association want to scare my parents?"

"Why have they been hounding you?" she says. "The entity, of course."

"Then, my mother—"

Arianna holds up a hand. She's still gripping the butter knife, and the sight of it gives her pause. She sets it carefully on her plate before continuing. "I don't know the answer to your question."

"I haven't asked it."

She laughs, but there's no humor in it. "If your mother didn't possess the entity at the time of her death, then she knew how to invoke it. That's all I can say on the matter."

"And if she possessed it? Then, wouldn't...?" I trail off. Wouldn't the entity save her?

"The entity already had a willing sacrifice in the form of your grandfather. Negotiations would've been protracted. Both the entity and your mother were vulnerable."

Malcolm has explained that to me, how, until a pact is set, things are out of balance. "So, when my mother died—"

"The pact remained in place, with your grandfather as the willing sacrifice."

"And no one else knew the entity's name."

Arianna gives me a wry smile. "Not until you figured that out."

Of course, the problem is, thanks to Orson—and modern technology —every necromancer in the entire world knows the entity's name by now. I'm back where I started, only with a heart weighed down by sorrow.

"You might speak with Darien." The suggestion is soft. It sounds more like an invitation than a decree. "Without Malcolm and Nigel around," she adds. "He won't speak about it any other way."

"He doesn't much like me," I say.

She laughs. It's the light and airy laugh I've come to expect from her. She sounds almost like herself again. "Oh, that? That's simply Darien being Darien. He doesn't like anyone, but he did admire your mother. As I mentioned, she had a way with men. Perhaps you do as well?"

I don't dignify that with an answer.

"Oh, my dear, I've kept you up so late. I think it's time we said *bonne nuit*." She squints at me, or perhaps at the change in the light that I only now notice. "Or, rather, *bonjour*."

She blows me a kiss, and then my screen goes black.

I sit on the bed, not moving, and watch the sunrise touch the street beyond the window. Then I kick off the covers and clamber to my feet.

There's no sense in trying to sleep. My mind is buzzing with too many thoughts. For the first time in a week, my legs feel strong, despite the all-nighter I just pulled. I tug back the curtains and kneel next to the window.

With both hands, I push the sash all the way up so I can lean out over the porch and its green steel roof. A car is inching up the street, pausing every few houses to jettison the morning paper.

I turn my attention toward the sky. Again, I don't know why I look up —rather than down or sideways—when I speak to the entity. I only know that I do.

"You could've said something." My voice rings out, breaking the quiet of the morning.

And where's the fun in that?

"Are you going to keep feeding me caffeine or whatever it is?"

Is that what I'm doing? Are you certain?

I'm not, actually, but something is fueling my thoughts and my limbs. All I know is that I feel, if not better, then more capable—at last.

"I don't suppose you're going to give me any hints."

As I said, where's the fun in that?

I sigh and consider all I have to do today, and how I'm going to accomplish all of that alone. I hate the idea of ditching Malcolm.

I don't.

"I wasn't consulting you."

An otherworldly chuckle fills the air, the sound of it fading into birdsong and the rustle of leaves. I need to do so many things today, but first, I'm going to start with some Kona blend.

Pour me a cup, won't you, my dear?

"I'll think about it."

~

THE MORNING IS STILL cool and Main Street still sleepy when I pull my truck into a parking spot in front of the Springside Police Department. I suspect Chief Ramsey is already in his office. If not, he's over at the Springside Pancake House.

I think about checking, but my entire system recoils at the thought. It will be a long time before I order all-you-can-eat dollar-size pancakes again.

I slip out of the truck and ease the door closed, each movement quiet and hesitant. Instead of dashing up the steps, I lean against the driver's side door and consider whether this is the best idea.

A week ago, Nigel dug up both the police report and the newspaper articles about my parents' deaths. In all of that, there wasn't a single mention of a baby at the scene. Which means what, exactly?

Either the ghosts lied, or someone else did.

I push off the truck, but, before I tackle the stairs, I reach through the window and grab my impromptu field kit and the two thermoses of coffee I made this morning.

Inside, the reception area is quiet. Penny Wilson's computer screen is dark, files and paperwork lined up neatly to one side. The ever-present scent of charred coffee lingers, thick enough that, at first, I'm uncertain if anyone—human or supernatural—is here.

I tilt my chin and sample the air. The hint of the otherworldly is slight, but definitely there.

A moment later, a force barrels into me. The two sprites that haunt the police station dart about so quickly, I can't track their zigzags. They crash into each other—an orchestrated move—before fanning out and leaving a glimmer in their wake that looks like fireworks.

"I'm happy to see you, too," I say to them.

They whiz past, ruffling my hair and dotting my cheeks with ghostly kisses.

They were caught up in the net Orson cast over Springside's ghosts. I wonder how he managed to snag these two. They almost never leave the police station, and I was surprised to find them among the mass of ghosts I untangled in the Pancake House's cold storage unit.

"You'll have to tell Malcolm sometime," I say. "Or just be extra careful from now on. Stranger danger and all that."

They whip past again and do a lap around the station, their forms narrowing. They look like arrows, and I'm their target.

Before I can sidestep or duck, each one bullets straight for an armpit. Oh. So. Cold.

The sensation is like a blast of ice water from a showerhead. Without thinking, I let out a yelp. A moment later, the door to Chief Ramsey's office swings open.

He surveys me, backlit by the sun filtering through the small window behind him, arms crossed over his chest. He's unusually unimpressed with me this morning.

"Please tell me you haven't made a mess in the Pancake House again."

I shake my head. The sprites are burrowing deeper under my arms, and keeping a straight face is a challenge.

"Been leaving cups of coffee in strangers' homes lately?"

"Anyone complain?" I counter.

For a moment, a smile tugs at the corner of his mouth. "Your coffee? No, they probably wouldn't."

I use that as my opening and rummage in the tote at my side. The sprites don't make this easy. They're nestled in good. Now that they're calm, I detect more than elation from them.

I think they might be scared. But with Chief staring down at me, there's no time to investigate why.

"Speaking of coffee." I pull a thermos free and hold it up in triumph. "Would you like some?"

Chief remains silent, his gaze assessing me. Then he retreats to his office.

"You know I do," is all he says.

I grab two Styrofoam cups from the sideboard and follow him inside.

CHAPTER 5

I pour us both a cup. He cradles his like it's the Holy Grail, inhales the steam like he's just discovered oxygen, and sips like it's the elixir of life.

"You should really let me give Penny a few lessons," I tell him. "You'd be surprised how much better the coffee will taste."

"But then you wouldn't visit me."

I freeze with the cup halfway to my lips. I set it back down on his desk. I don't trust my hands not to tremble. I don't trust my voice either, but I want to know what he meant.

"I'd still visit you."

"Would you?" He eyes me over the rim of his cup. "Seems to me, you stop by only when you need information."

"Well, you're the police chief. You have lots of that." I go for breezy, but the comment nags before solidifying into a guilty lump in the pit of my stomach. Have I been using Chief?

The sprites beneath my arms wiggle free and zip from the office. A moment later, a jangle comes from the reception area. Chief stares past me, frowns, and then shakes his head.

"What do you need, Katy?" The gruffness is in full force—the Kona blend hasn't helped at all.

"I ... need something?"

"You're here, with coffee, at barely past sunrise, and Malcolm isn't along. You either need something or you're about to get into some very deep shit."

I open my mouth to defend myself, but shock has stolen all my words. I don't think I've ever heard Chief swear before. To be honest, I've probably given him reason to swear—most likely, several reasons.

We're renegotiating something here, but what that something is escapes me. This is brand-new territory, and I'm not sure how to navigate it. So, I decide on the truth.

"I want to know something about my parents' deaths, and I think you can tell me."

Chief's hands lock on the Styrofoam cup. I'm afraid he might crush the flimsy sides and send coffee everywhere.

After a moment, his fingers release the cup, but his grip is nowhere close to relaxed.

"I've read the police report," I begin.

"Have you, now?"

"And the newspaper articles. I want to know one thing."

"And what would that be?"

"Was I there?"

Chief blinks as if I've startled him, as if this is the one question he never expected. He recovers, quickly, his police chief persona solidifying into place.

"Why do you think you were there?"

I sag. He always manages to ask the questions I can't answer. He won't believe me about the ghosts. I'm not sure *I* believe the ghosts, which is why I'm here in the first place. Even if the entity could tell me, I want to hear the answer from a human. Specifically, I want to hear it from the man who plucked me from the ground and cradled me like a father might.

"It's just ... something I've been wondering." I grope for an explanation. "Why wasn't I in the car? Were they going somewhere without me? Was I with my grandmother?"

"Katy, this case is closed. Has been for more than two decades. The particulars don't matter at this point."

"Or maybe they just hurt."

Chief rocks back, almost as if I've slapped him. His complexion is dark enough that it's hard to detect a blush—angry or otherwise. But he stares at me as if I've just inflicted some of that hurt.

"Yes," he says, and that single word comes out like steel. "They do."

"Then, I was there?" I venture.

Chief downs the last of his coffee. Without asking, I pour him a second cup. He regards it and then tips it in my direction, as if in a toast.

"There's nothing in the police report because no one knew what to make of it, and it was easy enough to keep it out of the newspaper."

"Keep what out of the newspaper?"

He continues as if he hasn't heard me. "Your grandmother arrived long before Springside's roving reporter did. Everyone just assumed that she..." He trails off and stares past me.

"Assumed what?"

He rouses himself. "That's the thing, isn't it? A car in flames, and a baby at the side of the road, unharmed. No one thought to ask. Not the first responders. Not the reporter. To this day, I don't understand it." His gaze centers on my face and locks me in place. "You shouldn't be here, Katy."

My heart thuds so hard against my ribcage, I'm certain it will bruise. I swallow, and my throat feels tender and raw.

"Your grandmother wanted us to arrest Orson Yates, and she was quite livid when we wouldn't. If I'd known he'd show up all these years later, maybe I would have. But there wasn't any proof he was involved. He was a witness and no more."

Well, sort of.

"I was there," I say, more to myself than Chief.

What the ghosts showed me was real. I think back on that misty scene that—if I let it—might solidify into an actual memory.

"It's not something you'd remember."

It wasn't, anyway.

"You were too young," he adds. He scrubs his face with his hands. "Katy, why bring this up now?"

That's a fair question, and I've plagued Chief so much that he deserves an answer. "I think something happened between my parents and Orson Yates."

Chief goes on high alert. He leans forward, and the keen interest of an investigator chases away some of the remorse in his expression. "Do you have any idea what that something might be? Proof? Something I can actually use?"

Well, yes, but it isn't something he'll believe. I pull in a breath and go for mostly true. "He thinks I have ... something. Something they left me, maybe?" I give my head a shake and hope I'm not overdoing it. "But I don't know what that something could be, and—"

Chief holds up a hand, and I clam up, grateful I won't have to dig a deeper hole. He wakes up his computer, and in the silence that follows, I'm lulled by the rhythm of his clacking on the keyboard.

"Huh." It's half a word, half a grunt, and completely mysterious.

"Did you—?"

"I want you to stay away from him." He swivels in his chair and jabs a finger at me. "Promise me?"

I nod. This is a promise I plan to keep.

"If he comes around, call me. If he harasses you, online, in the mail, anything, call me. It might be a good idea if Malcolm—" He pauses, clears his throat. "If Malcolm continues ... sleeping at your place."

My mouth drops open. My thoughts collide, outrage warring with embarrassment. "How do you—?" I begin, and then the obvious hits me. For the last week, Malcolm's cherry-red convertible has been parked on the street outside my house, day and night.

"Promise me, Katy."

I nod again. "I don't want to see Orson again or have anything to do with him."

"Good. With a little luck, maybe we can keep it that way."

I lean forward, but I can't see what Chief has on his computer screen. "What are you going to do?"

The remorse returns to his gaze, and the lines around his eyes deepen. "Something I should have done twenty years ago."

❧

I HEAD for my truck once it's become clear that Chief won't share his plans with me. I leave behind the thermos half-full of coffee. On my way out, the sprites dance about my head and ruffle my hair.

I hold up my hand in a wave to Penny and let them weave between my fingers.

"What's wrong?" The question is no more than a whisper, but it catches Penny's attention.

She looks up from her work, her expression bright. "Nothing, nothing. I'm fine. I'm about to make Chief some coffee. Want to stay for some?"

I open my mouth and then close it, nipping at the tail end of a sprite. I spit, and Penny's expression falters.

"Sorry, sorry," I say, trying to blow the sprite away from my face. There is no subtle way to do this. "Bug in my mouth."

I cast a sidelong glance at the coffeemaker. One of these days, I should really teach Penny how to make drinkable coffee.

"I can't." I gesture toward the door. "I have … things."

It's a poor excuse, but fortunately, it's enough for Penny, and when she goes to prepare the coffee, I conduct one last conference with the sprites.

"What has you so worried?" I ask them. "Is it Orson?"

They bob up and down, crash into each other. It's not much of an answer, but I get the gist of it. I suppose I could go all necromancer and let one of them into my thoughts. But sprites do nothing but chatter. I'm not sure it would help.

"Are there other necromancers in town?"

That's a no-brainer sort of question. Of course there are, at least in the form of Darien and Reginald. The sprites continue bobbing, adding a flourish, as if that will somehow help.

"Ones you've never seen before?"

Now they spin and twirl. I should've asked that first.

"Stay here," I tell them, "and you'll be safe."

I hope that's true. I don't like the idea of strange necromancers. Something always happens when one comes to town.

I blow the sprites a kiss and head for my truck.

Next on my list?
I'm going to go speak to one of those necromancers.

The nature preserve is the most obvious spot to find Darien Armand.

Even in the summer, it isn't too difficult to book a reservation in the campground. The space is vast, with everything from prepared campsites to ones that are no more than a clearing of tall grass in the dense woods. Today, the spots closest to the parking lot are teeming with Girl and Boy Scouts, families, and members of the Springside Senior Adventure Club.

The aroma of wood smoke mixes with scents of breakfast. My stomach grumbles, and I regret skipping the Pancake House. Children screech and laugh. Pots and pans clatter. Someone is singing a song about campground safety.

Something tells me Darien is somewhere far away from all this —*very* far away. That means a hike. I sit at a picnic table, tighten the laces on my boots, and consider whether my legs are up to the task.

I stand and gauge their strength with little bounces on each foot. Two little girls in pajamas and sneakers rush past, spot me, and then join in. We bounce in time with a song about doing chores until the singing comes to an end.

"Is this how you catch ghosts?" one of them asks.

"Not really," I say.

"Are you sure?" She points to something behind me, and then the two of them scamper off.

I turn around. Something glimmers in the air just above my head. I reach out a hand and let my fingers touch the ethereal form. The other-worldly sensation is unfamiliar.

"Have I caught you before?"

This ghost possesses far more maturity than a sprite, but its presence is so slight that it's hardly there at all. I glance over my shoulder, searching out the little girl. She's long gone, and I regret not asking her name.

"Maybe once?" I say to the ghost.

Its only response is to ooze forward, toward a path that leads away from the established campsites with their electronic hookups, restrooms, and shelters.

The second the buzzing starts in my ear, I remember the insect repellent in my truck and consider heading back to get it. Mosquitoes swarm as if I'm the only warm-blooded thing for miles around. I slap at my neck, my arms. I keep that up until I walk straight into the ghost.

It hovers around me. It's very much like being in the cold storage unit, inside the tangle of ghosts.

"Were you there?" I ask it. "Inside the Pancake House?"

Perhaps it's trying to tell me that. Its form quivers around me, but it only moves when I do, and I remain shrouded in its mist. It takes several yards—and a trek through a gnat-infested jumble of branches—before I realize that I haven't been bitten by a single mosquito.

"Thank you," I say.

It quivers once again. This one, I think, is not very talkative. I could live with a ghost like this. It bobs once, and I think: maybe I already am.

Despite my ethereal escort, sweat trickles down my spine. Perspiration blooms on my upper lip, and, while I'm grateful for the protection, the hiking boots are baking my feet. We must be a good half-mile from the main camping area when it occurs to me that maybe I shouldn't be following this ghost, that it's a stealthy Orson attack ghost.

Except it doesn't feel that way to me.

When we reach a hill, I'm certain I won't make it to the top. My legs are aching. A wave of exhaustion hits me, reminding me that despite its otherworldly cause, necromancer flu is very real, and I'm not fully recovered.

The ghost inches forward. I follow, gripping branches and stripping them of their leaves when my feet catch on the rocks. The path is an obstacle course of ruts and jagged stones. I'm nearly positive no one in their right mind would willingly make this climb. Except that someone has, since a thin stream of smoke is rising from the crest of the hill.

I claw my way to the top and immediately sink to my knees. My ghostly companion wanders off. I catch my breath, intent on following. But when I stand, a force slams into me.

My arms flail, and I nearly tumble backward down the hill. I skid, but catch myself, and take a moment to glance around.

There's nothing in front of me. I reach out a hand but meet no resistance.

I step forward and crash into the barrier again. Only it isn't a barrier. It's noise ... sound ... words.

You have not been invited, and, therefore, I do not wish to see you.

It's a ward, or, more precisely, Darien Armand's ward. I'm certain of it. Through the thicket of trees is a clearing, and in it sits a tent. When I step away from the ward and the noise leaves my head, I can hear the crackle of the fire.

"I'd like to speak to you, Mr. Armand," I call out. I don't suppose I need to shout; the noise is all in my head. But I'm sweaty, fierce, and annoyed; shouting feels good.

I step forward again only to get knocked back by that wave of sound.

You'd think I'd take the hint.

"I have coffee," I add, equally loud.

At least, I hope I do, and that the thermos hasn't slipped from my tote on the climb up. I grope the canvas sack, and when my fingers encounter the thermos, I let out a sigh.

All at once, the crackle of the fire is louder. A log shifts, sending sparks and a hiss of smoke into the air. Tent flaps rustle in the breeze. I try the barrier again, shuffling my way through, wincing in anticipation of that blast of sound.

I step straight through and continue to the campsite. The setup is quaint—a little tent with room for no more than two, a cheerful fire with a camp stool to one side.

Darien steps from behind the tent. He's wearing cargo pants and a T-shirt and has a towel draped around his neck. There are dots of shaving cream on his face, and he's holding a straight razor in one hand.

I try to pretend that this last isn't a threat, but my gaze locks on to the blade's edge.

The barest of smiles tugs at his mouth. With great deliberation, he folds the razor shut and tucks it away inside a backpack.

"You mentioned something about coffee?" he says.

I rummage inside the tote and pull out the thermos. I hold it up so he can see it. In response, he pulls out two flat disks from his backpack. With the flourish of a magician, he pops both into cups.

If he were anyone other than Darien Armand, I might applaud.

"Extra sugar?" he asks.

"Of course." I hold in a shudder. I don't like my coffee sweet, but at least it's Kona, and I'll be able to drink it.

"It's a long walk up here," he continues. "I can't imagine it would still be warm."

I hold up the thermos again. "German-made. It will still be *hot*."

"I'll let you do the honors, then."

I pour us two cups. Despite the muggy air and the excess sugar, the Kona blend works its magic. The aroma mixes with that of the campfire smoke, and the combination is heady. Whoever coined the phrase *the great outdoors* was probably holding a cup of coffee at the time.

I take a sip to fortify myself, then dive in. "Did you help my mother catch the entity?"

Darien raises an eyebrow. "I see we're skipping the small talk and preliminaries."

He strikes me as someone who loathes preliminaries, and small talk in particular. "I didn't know you were a fan."

"I'm not. Like most social niceties, it wastes time and is generally dishonest." He regards me. "You're very much like your mother in that."

"Did you help her?" I ask again.

"If you're asking whether she came to me for help, then, yes, that part is true."

"What part isn't true?"

"In the end, she caught the entity on her own."

"How?"

"One might ask you that same question."

My mind whirls, and I think back to how I discovered the entity's name. It was no more difficult than asking Mr. Carlotta's ghost Queenie.

I don't know, for certain, how long Queenie has been haunting him —although he claims it's been since Guadalcanal. What I do know is that she's ancient, if not an actual ancient warrior.

How she knows the entity's name is unclear. She's a prickly and particular sort of ghost. It would be just like her not to share the name or how she knows it with anyone. But she did with me, and—I'm guessing —with my mother.

"Ah, so you see?" Darien doesn't smile, but his expression shifts, and I know he must've read my mind. "It may be no more than Lindstrom blood. It started, after all, with your grandmother."

"My grandmother," I say, uncertain of where he's going.

"And my father. You'll excuse me if I don't feel much sympathy for your current plight. I see it as a just payment for a crime committed long ago."

"A crime." I'm somehow reduced to echoing him.

"But that's how the entity works. It bends and twists desires, makes you betray those you claim to love. How much longer until you betray Malcolm? I'm only here to pick up the pieces and ensure the damage isn't so great that he can't recover."

My heart thumps fast and hard, and the sweet coffee turns sour in my stomach. "What are you talking about?"

"It's what Lindstrom women do. Your grandmother and my grandfather, your mother and me, and now you and Malcolm."

The clearing grows silent. No early morning birdsong. No breeze rustling the leaves. Even the fire burns silently. The only sound is blood rushing in my ears.

"I may do many things wrong," I tell him, "but betraying Malcolm isn't one of them."

We stand in the clearing, glares locked in place. I don't budge, not even to sip the coffee. I could stand here all day. In fact, I plan to. I will wait until Darien Armand tells me everything he knows.

At last, he holds out his coffee cup. It's empty. I uncap the thermos and pour him a second serving. He sips, clears his throat, and starts speaking.

"Back when the Armands were part of the necromancer community, my parents and your grandparents conspired to bring a powerful entity to this plane." He peers at me over the rim of the cup. "I don't suppose I need to tell you which entity that turned out to be."

No, I don't suppose he does.

"My father never went into much detail about how they managed that, understandably. It was meant as a cautionary tale, not one to inspire curiosity. But have you wondered why it was your grandfather who ended up as the willing sacrifice?"

I give my head a little shake.

"Your grandmother betrayed my father. You've already seen the power the entity can wield, what it can do, and what a necromancer can do with all that power. You no doubt feel the pull of temptation."

I gulp coffee in a vain attempt to melt the ice in the pit of my stomach. My limbs are growing cold, and I shiver—both from too much sugar and the idea of it. Yes. The temptation. It's like a tug against my soul. I know I could flick my wrist and make the world the way I want it to be. I also know that, as a solution, it's ultimately false.

"Your grandmother was no different," he says. Energy infuses his words. It almost sounds like he's gloating. "She succumbed to the temptation and betrayed my father, but in the end, it turned out that her desire wasn't pure enough to hold the entity. To keep it out of the hands of other necromancers, your grandfather offered himself up as a willing sacrifice, with your grandmother keeping the vigil for the rest of her life. That was the pact, and it held until the day she died, despite your mother's attempts to break it."

Darien swallows the last of his coffee and flattens the cup between his hands. "And here we are today, waiting. What's that saying? Third time's a charm?"

I fight to weave all these new ideas together with what I already know—or think I know. It sounds right; all the pieces fall into place. And yet …

"If that's true, why would you want me to use the entity? Why did you encourage me to use it to stop Orson?"

A smirk curls his lips. He must have a devastating answer to that. But before he can speak, a thrashing comes from the path. Darien's eyes widen. I whirl around, certain it must be Malcolm and hoping it isn't at the same time.

Instead, Prescott Jones stumbles into view. He heaves a breath, wipes sweat from his brow, and then adjusts the suit coat jacket he has slung over one shoulder.

"Yes, I agree with Katy." Prescott nods in my direction. "I'm calling bullshit on your story."

CHAPTER 7

Darien sputters, an angry red washing across his face. "How did you—?"

"Please. Like I care about your ward." Prescott picks leaves from his shirt and then inspects his shoes with a sigh. "Hand-tooled Italian leather and completely ruined. You know, Springside has a perfectly lovely bed and breakfast."

"You violated my ward!" Darien's fingers flex at his sides.

"Call for retribution," Prescott says. "Oh, wait. That's right. You don't *need* the necromancer community." He turns to me. "Is there any coffee left?"

Stunned, I pull the thermos from my tote and give it a shake. "Little more than a cup."

Now Prescott turns toward Darien. "You wouldn't happen to have a third cup somewhere in there?" He waves a hand toward the tent.

Darien's expression is filled with outrage and ice.

"Go on," Prescott urges. "You know you want to get me that cup."

To my surprise, Darien spins and stalks toward the tent.

For a moment, I can't process any of this. I simply can't pull the pieces together. The last time I saw Prescott, he was speeding away from the warehouse. As for Darien? I can't imagine him doing anyone's bidding, but the sound of rummaging from the tent tells me otherwise.

"Odd how that third cup happens to be in the same spot he keeps his attack ghosts," Prescott says, his tone bland, as if we're discussing the weather.

Attack ghosts?

"Shall we let him ready one? Or two, for that matter," he continues. "I think yes. He'll be more relaxed, and we're not scared, are we?" He winks at me.

I can taste the humidity and the wood smoke, and I know my mouth must be hanging open. My gaze darts between Prescott and the wavering tent flaps. Yes, Darien is taking a long time to find a cup.

"You're not alone in all this," Prescott says, his voice softer now.

I'm facing the man who, less than a month ago, kidnapped me. Of course, he then let me capture the entity and save Malcolm along with everyone else.

The entity's voice echoes in my head.

If you ever see him again, my dear, you must ask him why.

So I do. "Why?"

I ask without preamble or explanation, trusting that Prescott will understand. The lift of one eyebrow tells me he does.

"Ah, that. I should apologize for the ... rough handling, although, at the time, I thought ... well, I thought differently, is all."

I wait, certain Darien will emerge from the tent and put an end to Prescott's explanation.

"It's a long story, one that involves a prince and begins with *once upon a time.*"

"But there's no *happily ever after?*"

He shifts the suit coat to one arm and pulls out his phone. He beckons me to step forward—within grabbing distance—and I'm compelled by some force; curiosity, most likely. That, and I'm pretty sure no one could look as mournful as he does and still be deliberately cruel.

On the screen, a man is staring up at us. The background is bright, full of blues and greens and a hot tropical sun. He is beyond handsome, possibly more handsome than Malcolm, objectively speaking, anyway. I don't think anyone could truly be more handsome than Malcolm. But the man in this photo, with his wavy dark hair and soulful, almond-shaped eyes, is a close second.

"Once upon a time," Prescott says, "I had someone who looked at me the way Malcolm looks at you. You might say my desire wavered at the last moment. I could've caught the entity. God knows I convinced myself it was the thing to do. And yet..."

"You let me do it instead."

"You caught the entity on your own. I merely stepped out of your way."

I nod toward the photograph. "Where is he now?"

"Toronto."

"Then, why are you here?"

Prescott's gaze flickers toward the tent. "Unfinished business."

"Is he a necromancer?" I ask.

"No, although he can sense the otherworldly and thinks what I do is rather amusing. Or at least, he did."

The tent rustles. Prescott tucks the phone into his trouser pocket. A moment later, Darien emerges, another flat disk in hand. He flicks it in our direction. Prescott plucks it from the air before it can soar over his head.

"Really, Darien, do I warrant three attack ghosts? I'm only here to chat. Besides, you could have thirty, and they would still be no match for the one Katy has."

Darien glowers. "What is it you want?"

"Me? I'd like to set the record straight. Or, rather, I'd like you to do so."

"I have nothing more to say on the matter."

"You forget. My mother and Katy's were best friends."

I suck in a breath, and the smoky air burns the back of my throat. I turn toward Prescott. "They were?"

"They roomed together in college. My mother was pretty broken up when your parents died." He pops open the cup and extends it in my direction. "I suppose it's loaded with sugar."

"It is, but it's also Kona blend."

"Then it will still be worth drinking."

I pour the last of the coffee into the cup. He takes a sip and sighs.

"Not even you," he says to Darien, "can ruin Lindstrom coffee."

Darien grimaces, and I feel sorry for him—almost. I wonder if he isolates himself because he truly enjoys being alone, or if it's the only way he knows how to deal with his loneliness.

I wonder if I have something in common with Darien Armand.

Prescott swirls the coffee in its cup like it's brandy or wine, or whatever it is people swirl in fancy glasses.

"So, do you want to explain the real reason Katy's grandfather ended up as a willing sacrifice, or should I?"

"There are two sides to every story," Darien says.

"Yes, but usually only one set of facts."

I'm not certain either man will speak. They stare at each other. Although Prescott is younger, I sense that, in necromancer terms, the two men are equal. The tips of Darien's fingers glow, a phenomenon that I've recently learned means he really does have at least one attack ghost.

It's only then that I notice Prescott's hands. They, too, possess an otherworldly halo.

"I've said my piece," Darien announces at last. "So, now, if you'll—"

A crashing comes from the underbrush. Darien gapes, and I imagine his outrage at not one, not two, but three uninvited guests. A frown creases Prescott's brow. He sets the cup down on a nearby log and turns to face the intruder.

Only it's no intruder. Instead, Malcolm bursts into the clearing. He takes one look at Prescott and charges.

I leap between them, arms outstretched to catch Malcolm before he barrels in to Prescott.

"Stop! Stop it! Malcolm, listen to me."

He doesn't, of course. I'm not sure he can hear anything at this point.

"He's trying to help, and if you don't stop, he'll sic an attack ghost on you."

I clutch Malcolm tight around the waist. Something otherworldly swirls between us, although it doesn't feel menacing. In fact, all this ghost does is smack Malcolm on the side of the head.

"Ow!" Malcolm blinks and glances around and then down at me. "You're okay?"

"I'm okay. More than okay."

The ghost makes a second pass. Malcolm ducks, but he's not the intended target. The ghost zips past, planting a saucy kiss on my cheek as it does.

Prescott snaps his fingers. "That's enough, Frederick."

Like that, the ethereal fades from the air, and there's nothing left but wood smoke and leaves and Malcolm's warm scent laced with sweat.

He's dressed in a T-shirt and shorts, feet clad in running shoes. His breathing is ragged, as if he's just sprinted up the hill.

"One of these days," Prescott says, "you'll get to be Katy's knight in shining armor. But that's not today."

Malcolm glowers at him before focusing on me again. "You're fine?" He strokes my cheekbone with his thumb and runs his fingers across my forehead. "The flu?"

"I feel better. The tea, maybe." Or the entity. Or possibly I'm healing on my own. The scars on my arms have faded and don't chill me quite as much.

He keeps me in the crook of his arm, but his posture and attention shift. "Nice ward, Dad."

I can't see Malcolm's face, but I'm pretty sure he's rolling his eyes.

"I value my privacy," Darien says. "That's all."

"Great. I'll give you your privacy," Malcolm says. "But I'd like to know one thing. Why did you catch the ghost that killed Katy's parents?"

I stiffen, uncertain how he knows that. I crane my neck to peer up at him in question.

"It's obvious, right?" he says. "Why else would he have been there that day?"

Both Prescott and Darien focus on us.

"When Katy was trapped inside the Pancake House, the ghosts showed her the accident." Malcolm releases me just enough to draw quotes around *accident*. "Orson was there." He zeroes in on Darien. "And so were you. There can only be one reason why."

"I did not deploy the ghost." Darien's voice is as smooth and cold as ice.

In contrast, I think Malcolm may erupt like a volcano. "But you caught it. For money."

"Which went into your college fund."

All at once, Malcolm's steam dissipates. He swears under his breath and grips me tighter. I place a hand on his back, hoping to reassure him, and my palm meets the damp cotton of his shirt.

"It's interesting, isn't it?" Prescott says. "Three generations of Lindstrom women and Armand men, and one entity. What's the common denominator here?"

"If Lena Lindstrom hadn't—" Darien begins.

"Yes, yes," Prescott says, his voice bored and dry. "We've heard the betrayal story. No one believes it."

Malcolm's gaze darts between his father and Prescott. His brow furrows. "What really happened? Do you know?"

"What I know came from my mother, who heard it from Katy's." Prescott nods at me. "What she understands of the story is this: at one time, your grandfather and Katy's grandparents conspired to bring an entity to this plane."

"Do you know why?" I ask.

"Here's the thing, according to my mother. They wanted to do good. This was the tail end of the sixties, after all. Peace. Love." Prescott lifts a shoulder. "I don't know, but it wasn't the usual prize most necromancers seek."

I only knew my grandmother as an older woman, someone who had seen a great deal of life and sorrow already, and someone who'd had the idealism knocked out of her.

"And then?" I prompt.

"And then, someone got greedy."

The words hang in the air. Malcolm shifts and pulls me closer, as if he's afraid I might bolt. The sun beats down, promising a hot day. The woods around us are still, as if the creatures there are waiting for the rest of the story.

"I think we know who that was," Darien says.

"No." Prescott brushes away Darien's words. "I don't think you do." He pivots so he can stare at Malcolm straight on. "I'm sorry. I know he was your mentor and meant the world to you, but instead of working with Katy's grandmother to harness the entity's power, your grandfather captured it."

I cast an anxious glance at Malcolm. He's standing immobile, like a statue. He gives Prescott a single nod. "Go on."

"He couldn't hold it. It would've burned through him in a few weeks, maybe a couple of months. He also couldn't unleash it into the world. There was something about this particular capture that went ... wrong. In the end, the entity accepted the offer of a willing sacrifice."

No one speaks. Above our heads, leaves rustle, the breeze skimming the tops of the trees, giving them a light caress. But there's more to it—a whisper, perhaps, an ancient and otherworldly one.

"But that's how the entity works," I say, breaking the silence and echoing Darien's earlier words to me. "It bends and twists desires. It makes you betray those you claim to love." I look at him. "Why did you agree to help my mother?"

I can imagine so many scenarios, from mere curiosity to the desire for revenge, but which it is, I don't know.

Darien's countenance is like slate. "The reasons don't matter," he says. "In the end, it was a quest that led nowhere and hurt everyone involved."

We'll never know. I sense that in Darien's stance, in his clenched hands, glowing eerily at his sides. He hasn't let down his guard. He won't. Not even to speak with his son.

Next to me, Malcolm blows out a long breath. "We're done here." He looks down at me. "Right? Is there anything left to say?"

I give my head a shake.

Malcolm kneels and picks up the thermos that has rolled to a stop next to my feet. I don't remember when or how it landed there, but I let him tuck it into the tote at my side.

"Let's go home." He takes my hand and, with great deliberation, turns his back on his father.

The walk down the hill is one of the longest I can remember.

WE'RE HALFWAY to the nature preserve parking lot when a supernatural flurry surrounds us. The air sparkles with the chaos that can only come from overexcited sprites.

"What—?" I hold out my hand, trying to gauge how many there are.

"Belinda's sprites," Malcolm says. He takes in the commotion, and a smile lights his face. It's good to see, but it's all too fleeting. "They saw you leave this morning, followed you, and then panicked after you left the police station."

"Oh, really?" I say to the air.

"They found me while I was out on my run."

Tattletales.

He falls silent. The guilt from last night's phone call and this morning's campfire chat is thick in my stomach. "Malcolm, I—"

He holds up a hand. "No, really. It's okay. It's just … everything is starting to make sense. It's taken me a while to realize that my grandfather didn't tell me half of what I should've known about necromancy."

"You know a lot," I say. Well, he knows more than I do, at least.

Malcolm shakes his head. "I just act like a know-it-all. That's different." The grin makes a brief return. "But now I realize that he never told me half of what he knew. I wish he would've trusted me with that. He always spoke with such sadness, like a man who'd been badly disappointed."

"With life?"

"With himself. He's the one who encouraged me to go to business school and partner with a ghost. 'Be practical,' he always told me."

That, too, makes sense, in the same way my grandmother's silence about necromancy does.

He takes my hand again, and we continue our trek, the sprites dancing about like it's a celebration. They have no decorum.

In the parking lot, Malcolm's convertible is sitting next to my truck. He takes the tote from my shoulder and swings it up and over into the flatbed. Then he leans against the driver's side door. He curls his fingers in my direction and raises an eyebrow.

"Morning kiss?"

Yes. I think we could use one. I step into his arms, and the bustle around us fades. The sun is bright against my eyelids. The air is filled with chatter and smoke. And my business partner, Malcolm Armand, kisses me. It isn't the longest morning kiss on record, but it comes close.

At last, I rest against his chest, his hand stroking my hair.

"I missed you last night," he says, fingers gathering the strands and letting them go.

The rhythm of it lulls me. The sunlight, hot on my back, conspires to send me to sleep, right here, where I'm safe.

"I missed you."

"I called, you know."

I pull back, ever so slightly. "You did?"

"Right after I called my mother back because I forgot to mention something about her investments. It went straight to voice mail. Then, when I called you, the same."

I don't like where this is going. My mind urges me to step away and sidestep this conversation. My body, however, is cozy right where it is and doesn't budge.

"So," Malcolm continues, "I'm curious. I mean, this isn't proof you were talking to each other, but it's just the sort of trick she'd pull."

I can't tell him. I absolutely cannot. Never mind my promise to Arianna. Finding out his mother had an affair with Orson Yates—of all people—right after learning about his grandfather? No. I can't. I won't. I won't do that to him.

But I'm a terrible liar. Even when I want to lie, when it might be in my best interests, my attempts at it are weak.

"Okay, so she did call you," he says, breaking up my thoughts.

"I never said—"

"You didn't have to. Jesus, Katy, you're trembling. What did she say to you?"

I peer up at him, struggling to find words—any words—I can tell him, but the concerned look in his eyes steals my breath.

"Hey, stop that." Malcolm cups my face. Then, gently, with his thumbs, he catches the tears that slip down my cheeks.

"She asked me not to tell you."

"Which is completely unfair to you. It can't be that bad, can it?" He gives me a grin.

I open my mouth to answer, but nothing comes out. Another tear slips down my cheek, and he catches this one with his thumb as well.

"Okay, it *is* that bad." Malcolm mutters a curse and stares at the sky. When he returns his gaze to me, his expression has shifted. He looks a little bit older and a lot more determined. "You know what? I'm an adult. *I'll* ask her. It's not going to be this thing that comes between us, okay?"

I give him a tentative nod, and when he urges me closer, I burrow into the crook of his shoulder.

"Hm. That's better," he says. "So, what else did you do this morning?"

"I talked to Chief Ramsey."

"I bet that was exciting, seeing how fond he is of me."

"Actually, he wants us to keep sleeping together."

Malcolm's hands tighten on my upper arms. He eases me back to stare into my eyes. "What? He *said* that?"

"Not in so many words. He said you should keep staying at my place. He thinks Orson is up to something." I push my palm across my cheek, catching the last wayward tear. "And ... he confirmed it. I really was there, on the side of the road. He found me."

"What did you tell him about Orson?"

"That I think he wants something my parents had, and now thinks I have it."

"About as close to the truth as it comes, at least the version he'll believe." He eyes me again, his expression both abashed and amused. "He really said that, though, about us sleeping together?"

"He really did."

"It's not a bad idea. I hated being away from you last night. It's why I went out for an early run." He plucks at the T-shirt. "I probably stink."

He doesn't, not really. He merely smells more like himself, that warm, rich scent of nutmeg even stronger. I burrow closer. "I don't mind."

Malcolm holds me, chin resting on top of my head, arms secure around me. We stay like that for several minutes, not speaking, but I swear, I can feel his thoughts churning.

"Where does this leave us?" he says at last.

"I don't know."

"If we only knew what Orson was going to do next."

"You," I say. "I think he plans to hurt you."

"I don't. He had that chance. It's you he's after."

I consider that, and something Carter said to me in the Pancake House pops into my head.

"What's involved with necromancer retribution?" I ask.

"Nothing good. Depending on the offense and the verdict, the necromancer community can decide to strip someone of their ability to catch and deploy ghosts, essentially reducing them to a sensitive."

Yes, it's like I suspected. There's no glory in being a mere sensitive. "And if they can't catch or deploy, they can't make a living."

"Exactly, and they're no longer a threat, assuming they were one to begin with."

"So, you could set someone up, right? Or accuse someone of something they didn't do?"

"You could, but you'd have to convince the rest of the community. It takes a quorum. It's no small thing to strip someone of their power. They're not getting it back once it's gone."

"Huh." I consider all that, and I wonder if I've been wrong about something all this time. It's not my friends that Orson wants to hurt.

"What, huh?" Malcolm says. "Katy, talk to me."

"In the Pancake House, Carter said that Orson put out a call to all necromancers in the Midwest region, that he was asking for retribution." I pause and lick my lips. My mouth is dry, and my head is buzzing with too much caffeine. "Against me."

Malcolm's grip on my arms grows tighter. "And you're telling me this now?"

"I..." I trail off. I've been more asleep than awake this past week, and so worried about Malcolm going out on rounds on his own.

"How did you find my dad this morning?"

"There was a ghost. I didn't recognize it, but it showed me the way. I don't think it was an attack ghost. It was completely benign."

"Unless it was a spy."

Was it? I consider that and how it wandered off once I'd crashed into Darien's ward. "But—"

"This is the first time in a week you've left your house," Malcolm says.

"So?"

"You're outside your ward."

Sweat from our trek down the hill prickles my skin. Dread ices the pit of my stomach, and my fingers turn cold.

Malcolm lets go of me and wrestles his phone from a holder secured to his upper arm.

"Let me text Nigel." He taps away, waits for five seconds, and then swears. "Forget that. Let me call Nigel."

He switches on the speaker, and the phone rings and rings until it rolls into voice mail.

He scans the area, a hand shielding his eyes. "Do you detect anything?"

I lift my chin. It's only now that I realize that Belinda's sprites have vanished. "Nothing."

He tucks the phone into his pocket and then walks around my truck and his car, fingertips skimming the metal. He crouches and inspects the underside.

"You try," he says to me. "You're better at detecting ghosts."

I'm not, not really, but I go through the motions. "Do you think—?"

"I think I'm not letting you out of my sight, so it's a matter of picking the best car." His gaze darts back and forth between the two. "Mine. It's faster."

"It's really conspicuous," I say. "My truck is better."

A hint of a smile lights his eyes. "Katy, your truck is one of the most conspicuous things in Springside."

Okay, so maybe he has a point. "Do you think either one is haunted?"

He shakes his head. "No, but that doesn't mean it isn't a target."

The drive back to Springside is far less treacherous than the one to the nature preserve. That doesn't mean we should risk getting into either car.

"If I ... die before I can invoke the entity, does that mean the pact is broken?"

"I assume so. That's the way it works with ghosts, but it's risky. If you invoked the entity, even injured or near death, it could save you, and the pact remains in place."

"Then, why didn't it help my mother?"

"Are you sure it didn't?"

His words stun me. I want to probe the meaning of them, but my mind shuts down. I'm not certain I can go there, imagine that, wonder what transpired in the ravine.

"You're here, you're alive." He closes the distance between us and cups my face. "And I think that has something to do with your mother and the entity."

I nod numbly. "Should I ... should I invoke it now?"

"Do you want to?"

I shake my head.

"As long as you can speak, you're safe."

"*We're* safe."

He smiles at me, that warm, dark-roast smile I haven't seen in a while. "Yes. We're safe." He heaves a sigh. "All we need now is a plan."

"Should we leave town? Head home? Will the ward keep us safe?" The questions pop out of my mouth. The practicalities, the reality of this, are far easier to deal with than contemplating my mother and the entity.

"Maybe? I wish Nigel would answer."

"Try Belinda," I suggest. "She's off today."

He does, and again, the call rolls to voice mail.

"Sadie?" My voice cracks on her name.

The call goes through, and he counts each ring under his breath. I close my eyes and wish with all my might that Sadie will answer, that she'll reassure us, invite us over for breakfast. When her voice mail picks up, Malcolm slaps his hand against the truck's side in frustration.

"I really don't like this." He shields his eyes and scans the area again.

The summer day is growing hot. Children have traded pajamas for swimsuits. The campsite is alive with sounds: the occasional pop and hiss of soda cans, the rattle of ice-filled coolers, squeals and laughter. Malcolm and I are the only oddities here, baking on the asphalt rather than relaxing in the shade.

Then the chill of the otherworldly invades the air. It's a presence I recognize, but I can't place it, not right away. Then, it speaks.

Katrina Lindstrom, you have been summoned by the necromancers of the Midwest region. You are to submit to examination, and, if found guilty, face retribution.

Malcolm pulls me close, but his warmth can't chase away the ice that has invaded my bones.

"This is one of Reginald's ghosts," I say.

Malcolm nods. "It is."

"What does that mean?"

Before he can answer, his phone buzzes with an incoming text message.

Only, there is no message. On the screen, a single photo appears. I recognize Sadie's living room immediately, with its comfy couch, the gleaming antique furniture, and the corner that Nigel has claimed as his own, strewn with programming books.

On the couch, Nigel, Sadie, and Belinda are sitting, all side by side, all gagged, their wrists bound. A bruise has bloomed around Nigel's left eye.

I pull my gaze from the photo and look up at Malcolm.

"I guess it means"—I cough, my throat so tight I can barely force out the words—"I guess it means we're going home."

CHAPTER 9

We're three blocks from my house when Malcolm kills the convertible's engine. He grips the steering wheel, his knuckles white as marble.

"I can't let you do this," he says at last.

"We don't have a choice."

"Yeah, we do. I have half a tank of gas and my wallet. We don't need anything else."

"But Nigel and Sadie, and Belinda—"

"Will be fine. It's only a threat meant to scare us. No one will hurt them."

I pull against the seatbelt and swivel to face him. "Orson nearly killed you, and in that alternate reality the entity showed us, he killed us both."

"He's not going to do anything, not in the middle of Springside. It would be stupid, too easy for the police to…"

His eyes light with the idea the moment it strikes me.

"The police," we both say at once.

Malcolm starts the engine and whips the car around.

"Do you think Chief will believe us?"

"At this point, I don't think it matters. Even a patrol car drive-by will help."

745

"Wait," I say. "Give me your phone. I have Chief's personal number on mine. I'll text him the photo and then call 911."

"I'm still driving us to the police station." He tosses the phone into my lap and floors the accelerator.

A moment later, Malcolm slams on the brakes. I let out a yelp, and both phones fly from my hands. One cracks against the windshield. The other skitters through the interior and lands somewhere near my feet.

I grope for it and my breath. My lungs feel tight, and I struggle to inhale. There's pressure against my throat, and I fight the urge to pull away some invisible hand. I touch my neck with fingers that feel like ice and peer through the fog clouding my vision.

A black sedan is blocking the intersection. Malcolm curses, throws the car into reverse, and whips us around again. At the end of the opposite intersection, another black sedan is sitting, the faces of its occupants shielded by tinted glass.

"I know you don't want to invoke the entity," he says, "but I'm thinking now would be a good time to do so."

I nod. At this point, we can't fight so many necromancers, not even with Springside's finest, assuming we could reach the police station. I don't know what it will cost me, but if everyone I love is safe, it will be worth it.

I open my mouth. The pressure on my throat grows. The fog is thicker now. I reach a hand to swipe at the windshield, but the glass is dry. I blink, but that doesn't help.

"Katy..."

I swallow—or try to. The pressure on my throat grows. That's what it feels like, too: a hand—an otherworldly hand—squeezing ever tighter. I take shallow breaths. I can't force oxygen into my lungs any other way. My vision tunnels to a single pinpoint before expanding again. I grip the dash and concentrate on getting enough air to say a single word.

"Katy..." Panic tinges Malcolm's voice.

I turn toward him. My hand flutters at my throat, and I mouth words, hoping he understands what's happening.

His eyes widen, and then he's leaning over the steering wheel and scanning the neighborhood. When he looks back at me, anger replaces the shock and panic.

"Stop it! Stop it now! She can't breathe." He unbuckles his seatbelt as if preparing to launch himself from the car. "If you kill her, I'll capture the entity. And my desire will be pure enough that I'll take the rest of you down before the entity can burn through me."

The pressure on my throat eases, but only slightly.

"Try now," Malcolm whispers.

I mouth, "Momalcurkan." The entity has a strange, nearly unpronounceable name to go along with its capricious, sometimes unfathomable nature.

The air remains still, the road steady and sure beneath us. There's no rumble. And while the otherworldly is here with us in the car, it's certainly not the entity.

"Think it, then. Think as hard as you can. Maybe that will work."

I double my efforts, both to think and speak the name. Nothing. It's almost like we're inside some sort of insulated room. I know my thoughts don't reach farther than the rag roof of the car.

That's when it hits me. We're inside a containment field. I tap Malcolm on the shoulder and then the car's top.

"Try the door," he whispers.

The handle moves uselessly. I press the button to roll down the window and the mechanism grinds, but the glass remains in place. Malcolm throws the car into gear and heads not down the road but directly for someone's lawn.

There's an alleyway behind this row of houses. I'm not sure what he has planned, and the convertible isn't exactly an off-road vehicle. But he grips the steering wheel with a determination I've never seen before. The front wheels go up and over the curb, and we rock back and forth.

Before he can tear through the yard, smoke billows from beneath the hood. It's oily and black, and its stench chokes me further. I can't cough it out of my lungs, so it lingers there, festering.

Young Malcolm, do not attempt to escape. If your speed exceeds fifteen miles per hour, the ghost that currently resides in your transmission will destroy it.

Malcolm slams the car into reverse. He inches away from the curb, and we bump back onto the road.

Please proceed to Katrina Lindstrom's house. That is where the examination will take place.

"Why?" I mouth. I don't know if he can read that single question, or understand the meaning behind it.

But this is Malcolm, and when he releases a heavy sigh, I know he does. "I don't know why Reginald is doing this. There isn't a quorum without him. There isn't retribution without him, either. He's more powerful than Orson. I just don't—"

Please proceed to the examination.

He slams his hands against the steering wheel. Under normal circumstances, the horn would blare. Now, there isn't even a squeak.

I tap him again and hold up my hand like a talking puppet. I tap him again, on the chest and then the lips.

He shakes his head, the move slow and full of regret. "I don't know the entity's name. I didn't hear you say it in the warehouse. I didn't hear Orson say it at the reception, and I kept myself from being curious. I thought it would be safer that way."

He's right. Under normal circumstances, it would've been.

"Jesus, I'm sorry, Katy. I'm so sorry—"

I place a finger over his lips. My feet scramble to find purchase on the car's floor so I can push myself far enough over the console to reach him. Then, I kiss him.

It's long and desperate and full of all the things I wish I could tell him. Stars shoot across my vision, and I'm lightheaded from lack of oxygen. None of that matters. I know this is goodbye. He cradles my face, and his thumbs can't keep up with the tears trailing down my cheeks.

Please proceed to the examination.

"Shut! Up!" He shouts the words at the sky before turning back to me. Softer now, with a tenderness that makes his voice crack, he speaks. "I love you, Katy. Nothing changes that. I will always love you. If there's a way to get us—get *you*—out of this, then I'll find it. I promise you that."

I touch his cheek and his lips, and he places one last feathery kiss against my fingertips. Then he puts the car in gear and inches us down the road.

That's when I know:

There's no way out.

THE SIGHT of a necromancer on my sidewalk has never been a good thing. Now, a dozen or so are lining the walk. They stand in between the road and my walkway, and—perhaps more importantly—they block access to the ward that surrounds my house.

What little hope I had left shrivels.

Malcolm doesn't bother to brake. He lets the car coast to a stop. It does so directly in front of my house. There, Orson is standing, and everything about the well-tailored suit, the starched white shirt, and the polished dress shoes exudes smugness. This is a man who knows he's won.

"Huh," Malcolm says. "He looks like crap."

He does? I mouth, "Really?"

"Look at his hair. It's a bad dye job, or maybe Grecian Formula. He's lost weight, but not in a good way."

I look again, and beneath the shiny exterior, I see the telltale signs of strain.

"He won't be able to hold the entity."

No, but then he couldn't before. I scan the assembled men—yes, they're all men—who will pass judgment on me and wonder which one here might be strong enough for that.

You may now exit the vehicle.

Malcolm gives my hand a squeeze. "I'll come around and get you."

The doors pop open, but there's no rush of summer air. The containment field extends beyond the convertible, maybe even encompasses my entire house. I squint at the sky, trying to discern its boundaries.

What I see appears to be layer upon layer of overlapping barriers. My gaze returns to the assembled necromancers. Each one must be contributing to the field.

Malcolm makes it as far as the front of the convertible. There, an invisible force slams into him, throwing him several feet into the air. He lands on the grass between the sidewalk and the road, his body crumpling.

I cry out—or try to. I scramble from the car, but fear and exertion steal what little air I have. I pitch forward, palms striking the asphalt.

The surface tears at the tender flesh, and I tumble away from the car. I roll, come to rest on my back, and simply stare up at the sky.

"Hold him!" Orson shouts. "Both of them!"

Footsteps pound, but no one approaches me. I wheeze, breath barely whistling through my throat. When I do sit up, I see that three men are struggling to hold Malcolm, while two others are gripping Nigel by the arms and shoulders.

He surrenders first, letting his arms go limp. The men don't let go, but their stances relax.

"There's a good boy," Orson says. He nods toward Malcolm. "Now him."

"Malcolm," Nigel says, his voice rough. "This isn't helping Katy."

Malcolm yanks a hand free and swings at one of the men. There's a smack of bone on flesh, and then a flurry where Malcolm ends up on the ground, arm jerked behind him, his face twisted with pain.

I rasp another breath. I want to scream and kick and fight back, but the grip on my neck is steady and strong, and I barely have enough air to think.

"Let him go," Nigel says.

Orson purses his lips in mock consideration. "You're in no position to demand anything."

"Katy won't cooperate unless you let him go."

This is true. I've clawed my way up the side of the car, and while I can't do much, not cooperating is still an option. My gaze meets Nigel's, and he mouths a single word.

Please.

I nod and then slap the hood of the convertible to get Malcolm's attention. When I have it, I shake my head.

"But—" He squirms against the men, and I know when another spike of pain hits by how his expression contorts. I give my head another shake, and I see the moment he gives up. His body goes limp, but what's worse is the defeat in his eyes.

From the group of necromancers, Reginald steps forward. His brows are drawn together; his mouth is turned down. The men on either side inch back. Even Orson falters, although he catches himself at the last moment.

"Katrina Lindstrom," Reginald says. "It is time for the examination." He points to a spot where the sidewalk meets my walkway. I don't suppose it's likely I can make that last leap over the invisible line of my ward, land on my lawn, and insist that everyone leave.

No, I don't suppose I can. I stagger forward, and my feet drag. The neighborhood is eerily silent. No kids are playing. No one is bicycling or walking their dog. I wonder at that, at how these men have managed such a thing. Is it the containment field or something else, something otherworldly?

And while everyone tracks my progress, no one steps forward to help me. I take another faltering step, lose my balance, and land hard on my knees. I press my palms against the ground even though they sting. My lungs scream for oxygen, and the burn runs through me. It's like drowning without the final relief of giving in to the water.

The light tapping of dress shoes sounds behind me. I brace for the inevitable. A kick to the head? Some of Orson's minions dragging me across the asphalt?

Instead, those dress shoes halt next to me. Wingtips. Possibly hand-tooled, from Italy. An outstretched hand reaches for one of mine. I take it.

My legs are wobbly beneath me, but I stand. Only then does my rescuer speak.

"Do I need to remind everyone that you don't have quorum without me?"

Prescott Jones scans the crowd, his hand at my elbow. When no one responds, he gives me a sidelong glance.

"Apparently, I do."

CHAPTER 10

"We don't need you to proceed." Orson steps forward, but Reginald halts his progress with the mere lift of one finger.

"We need a quorum. There is only one other necromancer in the area who could provide that."

"Darien Armand is no longer part of the Midwest region," Orson counters.

"As you say. Also, his connection to these proceedings may be too personal for him to be unbiased." Reginald inclines his head toward Prescott. "We welcome you, Prescott Jones."

"I doubt that," Prescott mutters, but I'm the only one who hears. "Orson's grudges are never pretty. Explains the manhandling."

Yes—I cast a quick glance at Malcolm—quite literally.

"Here," Prescott continues, louder now. "Let me help you to your spot." Under his breath, he adds, "In a moment, they'll transfer the full containment field to you. If you're found guilty, they'll use their combined power to strip you of your necromancer abilities."

And if I'm no longer a necromancer, then I won't be able to hold on to the entity. Anyone might invoke it—Orson, Prescott, Reginald.

Prescott takes in my expression. "I see you understand the consequences of that."

I can't let that happen. My gaze darts from Orson and back to Prescott. I know Orson's agenda, but I wonder just how mercenary Prescott is. I consider what he said earlier, about unfinished business.

"Yes, I know. I'm not to be trusted." His smile is brief and sad. "How much air are you getting?"

I hold my thumb and index finger half an inch apart. He turns toward the assembled necromancers.

"Let Katy breathe."

Orson snorts. "What? So she can invoke a powerful and dangerous entity, one that poses a risk to the entire necromancer community? No, I don't think so."

"Call off the ghost and transfer the containment field to her. Use that to gag her." Prescott glances over his shoulder at me. "You don't have a cold, do you?"

I shake my head.

"There you go. Perfect solution."

"Yes," Reginald says. "It's time to transfer the field."

A wave washes over me, and for a moment, I can't breathe at all. Then, with a whoosh, the otherworldly presence that has gripped my throat vanishes. Air rushes into my lungs, and I nearly sob with relief. As it is, a tear travels down my cheek.

My head clears, and although I'm tethered by invisible bonds and I can't move my mouth, my thoughts are sharp again. I search out Malcolm and try to convey what I'm feeling with just my eyes.

A bruise has disfigured his cheekbone, and a cut above one eye is weeping blood. One of Orson's minions is hovering at his side, but Malcolm is stoic, like a statue on my lawn.

Reginald moves to the center of the gathering. "Katrina Lindstrom, you stand accused of endangering the necromancer community. We will hear the evidence and, as a group, decide your fate."

The invisible gag remains in place. Apparently, I don't have a say in this. Of course, if I did, at this point, I'd invoke the entity. I imagine everyone here knows that.

"Orson Yates," Reginald says, "you may speak now."

Orson strides to the center of the group. He takes time to shoot the cuffs of his dress shirt from the sleeves of his suit coat jacket. For good measure, he fiddles with the cufflinks and adjusts his tie.

Despite the fact that nothing good is bound to happen, I meet Malcolm's gaze and roll my eyes.

He squeezes his own eyes shut. I know he wants to laugh, and I know if he did, it would be that sweet, dark-roast laugh tinged with sorrow.

Orson clears his throat. "We know the checkered history of the Lindstrom women. Three generations now have tried to control an entity whose power is beyond their capabilities."

I'd like to contradict that, but of course, I can't talk.

"That is not my concern," he adds.

Really? Because, if so, it's news to me.

"What concerns me, and always has, is Katy's distinct lack of education in necromancy. Let the record show that I offered her a spot in the Midwest Necromancer Association more than once, which she refused."

"Your supporting evidence?" Prescott asks. "I also refused a spot in the association. No one's accused me of a crime."

"Not yet," Orson murmurs. "But, to your point, I do have supporting evidence."

Orson lifts his hands. A glow surrounds his fingers, the halo that means he has a ghost—or several—at the ready.

It's then that I realize that he does possess several ghosts. Their wails and cries fill the air—sad and scared. These aren't attack ghosts. They're Springside ghosts, and they emerge into what must be a containment field suspended between Orson's outstretched arms.

The field flickers, images fading in and out. It's like watching a silent movie, one where the film is scarred, the projection jittery. The first picture to solidify is of me at the Coffee Depot, speaking with the assistant manager.

I'm glad no one can hear me declare that I plan to brew him the best damn cup of coffee he's ever tasted. Not that it matters. A moment later, the industrial-sized coffee maker erupts, spraying the entire café with lukewarm coffee.

That's just the start.

It's like a coffee-soaked greatest hits reel. The next images show the damage to Sadie's house in the wake of Harold's ghost, including splatters across the walls and plaster dust that make the dining room look like an ancient crime scene. The pictures flicker again, and there I am, holding my hands against the containment field in the Springside Cemetery. I'm trying to console the ghosts caught inside. When whispers ripple through the gathering, I realize that it must look like I'm hoarding them.

The images continue to flash across the ghostly movie screen, faster now, so discerning what might be my fault from that of a particularly nasty ghost is impossible. The Pancake House. Springside Long-term Care. Even the mess left behind at Sadie and Nigel's wedding reception. All of it, my fault.

"As you can see," Orson says, his voice taking on the quality of a concerned school principal, "she is untrained and undisciplined. She has hoarded ghosts for years in Springside. To what end is anyone's guess. She is unfit to practice the craft and, as such, a threat to the necromancer community."

You could see it that way, like I leave behind coffee-stained destruction wherever I go. But then, I've never claimed to be a necromancer, either.

Maybe that was a mistake.

Reginald nods at Orson. "Thank you, Orson Yates." He turns toward the assembled group. "Would anyone here like to speak on behalf of Katrina Lindstrom?"

Well, I would, but I don't suppose that's happening. Nigel steps forward, but Reginald gives him a sad shake of his head.

"No, my friend. Your association with her disqualifies you from speaking."

I don't see how, but apparently Nigel does. He deflates, and when my gaze meets his, he mouths, "I'm sorry."

So am I.

Then a throat clears. Prescott takes the steps up my walk and halts just inside Orson's personal space.

"Really?" Prescott adjusts the cuffs of his dress shirt with just enough of a flourish that Orson can't miss the mockery. "A threat to the necromancer community? You'd have us believe that?"

Orson remains silent. Perhaps he's not allowed to speak. Perhaps he doesn't care what Prescott has to say.

"Instead of being untrained, as my colleague claims, I would like to suggest that Lena Lindstrom was deliberate in how she educated her granddaughter." Prescott raises his hands, indicating the space around us. "Springside is small. Its ghosts, for the most part, are benign. And those that aren't?" He slides a glance in my direction. "Are dispatched with a minimal amount of fuss."

Well, sometimes.

"Katy has also formed a business partnership with a member of a well-respected necromancer family—"

"Perhaps not the best argument," Orson murmurs.

"—That provides a service to the town of Springside. A town this size needs this sort of thriving business. Strip Katy of her necromancer abilities, and you deny Springside of this vital service."

"But she can still serve Springside as a sensitive," Orson counters. "Her partner is an ... adequate necromancer."

The two men stare at each other. Prescott has his hands tucked in his pockets. I don't know if that means he has a ghost at the ready or if he's bluffing. Orson's fingers are still glowing with the ones he's trapped. In the quiet, their cries reach me, the sound so plaintive that, despite everything, my heart aches for them. No one else seems to notice.

"And I should like to remind the community of Orson's—"

"I'm sorry, Prescott Jones," Reginald interrupts. "This is Katrina Lindstrom's examination. Confine your comments to her."

Prescott presses his lips together. His eyes narrow as he takes in Orson and then the assembled group. "Then I should like to remind the community of the Lindstrom legacy, and how three generations have kept everyone"—his gaze flits toward Orson—"safer than they may realize."

It's not much of a defense. Even so, I'm grateful to Prescott. I can't move, can't speak or smile, but I stare at him with what I hope looks like gratitude. When he nods in my direction, I sense that he understands.

"Are there any others who wish to speak?" Reginald asks.

The group falls completely silent. Again, I wonder at the lack of traffic. I don't live on a busy street, it's true, but my neighbors come and go.

Someone must be working from home today. I eye the assembled group and wonder at the power they wield—and what that means for me.

No one else steps forward. No one speaks. After a long pause, Reginald coughs to clear his throat.

"Then it is time," he says. "Those who wish to stand with Katrina Lindstrom may do so now."

Nigel breaks free of the necromancers holding him. He shakes the men off. The glare he gives one of them is deadly, and his fingers curl into a fist. I almost expect Nigel to return the favor of the black eye. Instead, he catches up to Malcolm and helps him limp across the lawn.

They take up a position on either side of me. Malcolm's grip is firm, one hand poised on my waist, the other at my elbow. Nigel's voice is low and rough in my ear.

"I'm sorry, Katy. I'm so sorry. So is Reginald. He had to give in to Orson's demands for an examination. It's the way necromancer justice works. He didn't have a choice."

Didn't he? I take in Reginald's passive countenance and wonder.

After a moment, Prescott clears his throat, brushes imaginary lint from his suit coat jacket as if he's brushing off Orson, and comes to stand with us.

"I apologize, Katy," he says. "I didn't think it would come to this. Otherwise, I would've prepared a better defense."

No one else moves. It's clear my three supporters don't beat the dozen or so that Orson has.

"Don't worry about the numbers," Nigel whispers as if reading my thoughts. "All it will take is for Reginald to weigh in on our side. He holds that much sway."

"Quality versus quantity," Prescott adds.

Reginald's gaze finds mine. There's something in his eyes—a message, I think, that he's trying to convey. I don't understand it. I can't even show him I don't understand. He gives me a single nod and then looks away as if the sight of me hurts him.

"I find that I must stand with the necromancer community." With that, Reginald takes a single step and aligns himself with Orson's group.

Nigel cries out as if he's been struck in the gut. Malcolm's hold on me tightens, and he draws me closer. I don't even have enough air to feel breathless at Reginald's betrayal. The only thing keeping me upright is Malcolm's hands and his warmth.

"What are you saying?" Nigel launches himself forward, his momentum cut short by Prescott's grip on his shoulders. Nigel flails, and Prescott staggers, but his grasp never wavers.

"Let it go, Nigel. Let it go."

He whirls to face Prescott. "But—"

"Let it go. It's over," Prescott says with a finality that chills me. "You can't change things."

Because that's the way necromancer justice works. No one says that, but the implication is clear. Already, the other necromancers are lining up directly across from me, well-dressed and respectable, Orson as their center. He shoots me a smug look full of triumph.

My heart thumps hard in my chest. My mouth is dry. I can't lick my lips, can't really swallow, for that matter. I can't even sink into Malcolm's presence at my side, but I soak in his warmth.

"It is time," Reginald announces. "Move away from Katrina Lindstrom."

Prescott drags Nigel toward the front porch. Nigel digs his heels in, plowing furrows into the lawn.

"I won't leave her alone, and it's not like I need my ability."

"You might," Prescott says. "Someday." He grips Nigel around the waist, and it's all he can do to hold on.

"Move away," Reginald says, his voice stronger, sharper.

Malcolm inches closer. His grip on me tightens. He's been quiet this entire time, but his voice emerges strong and sure. "Make me."

Across from us, Orson looks like he wants to do just that.

"Young Malcolm," Reginald says, and now his words carry a hint of tenderness. "You risk losing your ability as well. This won't hurt her physically."

"Really? I don't believe that. And I'm not leaving her."

If I could, I'd shove him away. One of us needs to have some ability to catch ghosts. Then again, depending on who captures the entity, that may be the least of our problems. Maybe it doesn't matter.

Maybe Malcolm has already realized that.

Reginald glances at the assembled group of necromancers and then at Malcolm. A frown puckers his brow. He turns toward Prescott with what looks like a silent command.

"Oh, no," Prescott says. He still has a hand on Nigel's shoulder. "You can do this without me."

"The community has spoken."

"This is not my community anymore. I refuse to participate."

"Very well." Reginald returns his attention to Malcolm. "The choice is yours, young Malcolm. I do not have enough necromancers present to pull you away and carry out retribution. Step away now. This is your last warning."

Malcolm is solid and warm beside me. He doesn't budge, doesn't flinch. He's stoic again, remaining absolutely still except for the thumb that swipes a tear from my cheek.

"It's okay," he says, and I know he's speaking to me and not the group. "I want to do this."

Reginald sighs, the sound heavy and full of regret. "Then we shall begin retribution."

CHAPTER 11

The air crackles around us, the scent dry and sharp. A pulse radiates from the group of necromancers. The force of it strikes me in the chest, and it feels like barbed wire has encircled my heart.

Something tugs at my insides, as if this force is trying to remove a vital part of me.

And it's working. The ability I've always taken for granted slips away. I want to cry out, but I can't. I want to shout at them, curse them. I want to...

Malcolm throws himself in front of me. All at once, the sensation stops. A strangled noise emerges from his throat. I feel a rush of returning power, a loosening around my heart. I gasp for breath, and the shock of it washes through me.

I can move my lips, my tongue, my mouth. I can speak. I bring my fingertips to my lips, testing the feel of them. At that moment, I know what Malcolm has done. To hesitate now is to waste his sacrifice.

"Momalcurkan."

A hush falls over the neighborhood, maybe the entire town. Everything is so still. Malcolm wavers for a moment before crumpling on the lawn. No one moves, but I don't let that stop me. My knees hit the ground, and my hands search out his pulse, his breathing.

"Malcolm?" I roll him onto his back and, with careful fingers, wipe away the grime and blood as best I can. He's warm, and my hand rises and falls with each breath he takes. His pulse is strong.

I sit back on my heels. I'm about to ask someone—well, someone nice, like Nigel or Prescott—for help when I notice what's caught everybody else's attention.

In a matter of seconds, clouds have rolled in, blotting out the perfect summer sky. These aren't puffy cotton balls, either, but a thick and menacing blanket tinged green. The color reminds me of a bruise or an infection. It's the sky right before a tornado strike.

And yet, the air is so still. I can hear Malcolm's breathing and my own.

Someone coughs. A couple of the necromancers eye each other. I don't know if they doubt the entity's presence or are looking for a quick way out.

Orson raises a hand as if sensing their unease. "Hold steady. There's no need for alarm. The entity is capricious. It may not appear."

I shake my head. I know better. True, it will show itself when it feels like it, and not a second sooner. But to suggest it isn't even here? That seems foolish.

And yet.

Something that sounds like a sigh whispers through the branches. The breeze picks up again, lifting sweaty strands of hair from the back of my neck. My arms and legs tingle as if an electric current is running through the ground and into me. The air tastes like static.

A necromancer on the edge of the group takes a single step backward. He takes another. Then, emboldened, he bolts for the street and one of the black sedans parked in front of my house.

He makes it as far as the sidewalk.

His entire body jerks as if he's been struck by lightning. He collapses to the concrete, and his head strikes the surface with a sickening thud.

The remaining necromancers crowd together as if there's safety in numbers, or at least, safety in not crossing the invisible fence around my house.

"Don't panic," Orson says. "This will pass."

I'm not sure it will, not without my intervention.

"Stop it." I don't need to shout or command. I'm pretty sure the entity can hear me. Will it obey? That's something I don't know.

It hasn't made an appearance inside my head—not yet. But the air has that stale quality to it. The entity is here, even if it's playing coy.

At least, I think it's here.

Who sees it first, I can't say. Nigel has taken a knee on the other side of Malcolm and is repeating all the checks I've made. His gaze meets mine, and I see the question there. I can only shake my head. I don't know if Malcolm will wake up. I keep my palm against his chest. I count his breaths and let his heartbeat reassure me.

An urgent whisper catches my attention. As a group, the necromancers have stepped back yet again. They huddle around the bushes in front of my house, leaving Orson to stand alone in the center of my yard. Prescott is staring down the road, his skin sallow.

A block away, a man in a dark suit is strolling down the center of the street. Or, at least, it looks like a man in a dark suit. His image shimmers like he might be a mirage, a trick of the heat. His facial features are nonexistent. A pang of recognition strikes me. I know who—or what—is approaching.

His stride is deliberate and slow. A car—a black Mercedes—is blocking the most direct route to my walkway. With a finger, the almost man upturns it. Metal creaks against the asphalt, the sound lonely and hollow. The sedan tips over, crunching its roof.

The crash makes no sound. But the footfalls, the tap of men's dress shoes against cement, ring clear.

The almost-man halts on my walkway. The swirling void where a face should be surveys the surroundings, seeming to take more interest in my house than the people outside of it.

"Your little helper is doing an excellent job with the flowerbeds, my dear," the entity says at last. "You should give her a raise."

I manage a nod.

"Of course, there is all this debris scattered across your lawn, but I don't suppose she's to blame for that."

"You don't belong at this proceeding." Orson's words emerge with surprising strength.

The entity raises a hand, palm skyward. "And yet I've been invoked."

"This is necromancer business. The pact—"

The entity holds up a finger, halting Orson's words. "And what would you know of my pact with humanity?"

"No interference in matters of justice and retribution."

A single drop of sweat travels down the side of his face, but Orson stands firm. I think there must be truth to what he said. He's too sure of himself, too sure of those words, for them to be a bluff.

"Am I interfering?" The entity gestures toward the group. "Please, continue."

No one dares, of course. Prescott looks almost amused—a half-smile lingers beneath the pallor. Reginald has closed his eyes as if he wishes to shut all of this out.

Nigel's hand comes to rest on mine. He nods at Malcolm. "I'll take care of him."

When I meet his gaze, the full implication of his words sinks in. There's only one way to stop this. I lean close to Malcolm, kiss his warm, sweet lips, and whisper words I hope he can hear.

"I love you. Don't forget that."

Then I stand. My legs feel as if I've hiked for miles, but I walk without faltering until I'm standing across from Orson, completing the triangle made up of him, the entity, and me.

I see so clearly what could be. Instead of coffee-stained destruction, I could leave behind a trail of blood. It would be easy. A flick of my wrist in Orson's direction, and all of this would disappear. The weight of it squeezes my heart. What an awesome thing, this sort of power, how seductive.

And yet, it wouldn't stop with that. Someone else would want the entity, and then someone else after that. I wonder if this is what my grandmother realized all those years ago.

I cast a glance over my shoulder and take one last look at Malcolm. I'll miss everything about Springside, but my heart will ache the most for him.

I take a step forward, breaking the symmetry of the triangle. Orson wavers as if this is something he hasn't expected.

No, I don't think he would.

I turn toward the entity, spread my arms wide, and say, "I am your willing sacrifice."

Cries go up around me, although the entity itself betrays nothing.

"You ... you ... can't be serious." Orson stares at me, naked confusion on his face.

"Of course I am," I say, and then address the entity." I can do this, right?"

"Hm. What? Yes, undeniably you can, although it's a shame to leave things so untidy." It waves a hand toward the huddled group of necro-mancers. "While I don't generally get caught up in human affairs, in this case?" The entity surveys the group. "I should like to see that trail of blood you have in mind."

Orson blanches. I spare him a look. It would be *so* easy.

"You're quite sure?" the entity prompts. It doesn't need to read my thoughts, although I'm sure it has. How I feel must be plain to everyone here.

"I am."

"You can't return to this plane. The one being here who might muster that sort of love has already been my willing sacrifice."

I steal another look at Malcolm and then force my gaze away.

"And while he's pretty, he's a bit dull."

"He is not!" The outburst comes automatically, even though I know better than to let the entity goad me.

It laughs, the sound tinged with a sadness I find odd.

"In any case, he no longer qualifies. You leave with me now, Katy, and you forfeit your life here. You'll never see Springside, your friends, or Malcolm again."

"And no one on this plane can invoke you or capture you again," I say. "Right?"

This needs to be ironclad. No loopholes. No tricks. I leave, and everyone I love will be safe.

"That's correct," the entity says. "I promise you. No tricks."

I resist the urge to look at Malcolm one last time. If I do, I might lose my courage, my will to do this thing. So, instead, I focus on Orson. Two bright spots of color are sitting high on his cheekbones, as if someone has slapped him. His shirt collar is soaked with sweat.

But his eyes are as sharp and canny as ever. His fingers twitch as if he wants to reach for an attack ghost or a gun. I suppose it's to his credit he hasn't cowered before the entity.

Then I think of how many people he's hurt in Springside alone. I think of Sadie and Nigel and how Orson tried to destroy them both, of Malcolm nearly beaten to death, of all the ghosts locked away and tormented.

I want to call him names, lash out, seek revenge. So easy. It would be so easy.

"Guess what?" I say instead.

Orson looks at me, a hint of doubt creeping into his eyes. When I'm certain I have his full attention, I say the one thing I think will hurt the most.

"I win."

A burst of laughter comes from the entity, the sound strong enough to shake the earth. The air around us quakes. Leaves rattle in the trees. Car alarms blare.

"Very well, then, my dear. Say the words one more time."

"I am your willing sacrifice."

CHAPTER 12

There's a flash, and it's bright enough to blind. Then, what looks like a thousand stars streak across the sky. Darkness flows around me, and, while I can't see a thing, I sense hidden recesses black enough to wilt my soul. The air flashes hot and cold. I brace for what must be an eternity of torment.

But the air softens into something cozy and warm. I float, suspended in nothingness. Then I sink and feel the space around me solidify into something real. The sensation is like settling next to a fire on a crisp autumn day, head cushioned by pillows, legs tucked into a knitted blanket.

When I open my eyes, I discover that's where I am: in someone's den —or so it would appear. A fire is blazing on the hearth. The walls are lined with books, volume after volume. A china coffee service is sitting on an end table.

I'm alone.

I sit up and then push to stand. I pat my arms and legs, blink, tap my head, touch my nose.

I feel solid.

Shutters cover what must be a large window over the sofa. The cushions there are soft, the perfect spot for a nap, and the shutters are smooth and cool. I pull them open, expecting to meet nothing but a solid wall, convinced that this isn't a room so much as a perfect replica of one.

The shutters creak open, and I gape, transfixed. The space beyond is vast. And it truly is space, or maybe the universe, or eternity. I forget to breathe, to move, to think. I can only observe.

All at once, the shutters clatter shut. I fall back, land hard on the table, and jangle the coffee service.

"So curious," the entity says. "Always so curious. You are not ready for that, my dear. You will short circuit every last synapse in that brain of yours, and how tedious for me if you do."

Instinctively, I nod. Yes, the entity's right. Even now, my thoughts are zooming as if my mind is desperately trying to repair itself.

"What is it?" I ask. "Space? Time? The multiverse?"

The entity raises its hands, shrugs. "Yes."

I stare at the void where its face should be—only now, it's less of a void. There are planes and angles, reflecting surfaces. I see a field of stars, swirls of nebulae, pockets of endless dark and bursts of shattering light. I could stare at it for eternity.

The entity snaps its fingers. "Yes, but that would become boring." When it speaks again, its voice is softer. "It is rather marvelous, though, isn't it?"

"It is." No longer transfixed by either its face or the space outside this little room, I take a second look around. "This isn't bad, either. Where am I?"

"Think of it as your accommodations. You can adjust your surroundings as you like, but this was how your grandfather preferred things. I thought we'd start there."

"My ... grandfather?" Now I study each corner, the pattern on the rug, the books that line the shelves, as if all that could tell me more about the man I never knew. "It's like my living room, only not."

"That was our compromise. This version has enough familiarity without breeding despair." It gestures toward the coffee service. "Give it a try."

I kneel next to the table and lift the coffee pot's lid. A clink of china rings clear in the quiet room. Then I inhale. The scent of Kona blend washes over me. It strikes me like something physical, and I brace a palm against the table. This doesn't smell like something I've made, but a pot my grandmother brewed.

"Oh!" I clutch the lid in one hand and anchor the other on the end table. All I want at that moment is to be back in my kitchen, sitting on a stool, watching her concoct the perfect pot of coffee.

"Enough of that." The entity slips the lid from my grasp and replaces it.

The scent dissipates, and my senses return.

"There's a balance," it says, "with humans. Enough nostalgia to keep you sated, but not so much that you wallow."

"So, I'm a pet?"

"Oh, not at all, my dear." It shifts again, trading the suit coat for that ridiculous smoking jacket. Then it settles into a wingback chair next to the hearth. "You are my welcomed guest."

"For how long?"

"Pardon?"

"How long am I here? Until Malcolm stops…" I can't finish the sentence, so I barrel on to the next one. "Like with my grandfather and grandmother. She kept the vigil for him, and I kept one for Malcolm."

"But in this case, you were already my necromancer."

"So, there's a difference."

"A significant one."

"And that would be?" Honestly, could this thing spell it out?

"You came to me of your own free will, not under duress."

"I was under duress," I say. "A lot of it."

It chuckles, and the sound of it billows outward like pipe smoke. "Granted, but in this case, we merely shifted the locale, if you will, of our relationship. You are still my necromancer. We still have a pact. We're simply honoring it here."

"But for how long?"

"For as long as you like. Since you're human, you may want to … let go at some point. But, my dear, we'll have millennia together if you so desire."

Millennia? With this thing?

It laughs, but it isn't that grating, metallic laugh from Earth. Like before, the sound is an endless stream that ripples through the space—rich, warm, sustaining.

"Always so charming," it says.

I ignore the comment. "But with my grandfather, with Malcolm—"

"The essential difference is that neither one was my necromancer. It's to their credit that they both knew they couldn't hold me as such. And that Malcolm had a turn?" The entity tilts its head, and the stars dance. "Fitting, all things considered."

"Are you going to tell me all those things?"

"Would you like to know?"

Really, it has to ask? I'm about to insist when a thought occurs to me. The entity must know everything, or nearly so.

"Can I ask you anything?" I say.

"You can ask. I may not answer, at least not directly."

"For instance, who really assassinated JFK?" I don't know why that's popped into my head, but it's the first thing out of my mouth. I'm not sure I really care. It's more to see what the entity says.

The entity gestures toward the bookshelves. "Over there, somewhere. Far left corner, I think. It shouldn't take you too much time to find the correct volume." It crosses one leg over the other and adjusts a trouser pleat. "Time being one of those relative things here."

"I have to look it up?"

"Indeed you do, my dear. I will not be pestered by endless questions. Plus, it will sharpen your mind, keep you engaged. Trust me on that."

I scan the bookshelves, and, as my gaze inches upward, they appear never-ending. I peer over my shoulder at the sofa. I could spend an eternity reading, and the idea of it is almost enough to make me smile despite everything.

"Your grandfather felt the same way."

"Will you tell me about him?"

The entity sweeps a hand toward the sofa. "Sit, my dear."

I do, but I take up a perch on the end table instead and pluck a china cup from the coffee service. The porcelain is cool in my hands, the pattern that of my grandmother's wedding china. Something about that hurts more than I think it should.

"Yes." It draws out the *s*, and something about the entity's voice soothes my heart as if the sound is a supernatural balm. "In a way, it is," it adds. "The shock of leaving your plane alone would incapacitate you, and I certainly don't want you moping about, lovesick for that young necromancer of yours."

I'm not sure I like not being able to feel the things I should. The ache is there, but it's distant, wrapped in gauze and tucked away carefully where I can't pick at it.

"Exactly," the entity says. "If you agree to leave it there, I will agree to tell you about your grandparents and how all of this started."

"And how I ended up on the side of the road?"

"That as well."

I trace the rose pattern on the china cup before setting it next to the coffee pot. Then I pull my knees to my chin and wrap my arms around my legs. I'm ready, and I give the entity a single nod.

CHAPTER 13

"Once upon a time," the entity begins, "both the Lindstroms and the Armands were very active in the necromancer community, but I imagine you've guessed that already."

I should've guessed it sooner. "Did you lead Malcolm to Springside?"

The entity raises a finger. "One narrative at a time, please." It pauses, and something brightens in the field where its face should be. "But, yes, I did. He *is* fairly easy to lead about. I'm sure you've noticed that about him."

I scowl.

The entity chuckles before continuing. "Not only were your families active, but they were also powerful, poised to rule. That ludicrous club—"

"The Midwest Necromancer Association."

"Yes, that. Either one could've assumed leadership there, but they wanted more. More is always dangerous, especially when the parties concerned don't agree on what it means."

"What did it mean?"

"To your grandparents? Peace, prosperity, a more level playing field. Their reasoning was, why should the supernatural benefit only a small portion of the world's population?"

"All or nothing," I murmur. That was so like my grandmother. "And Malcolm's grandfather?"

"Oh, he started with the best intentions, but then, so many people do. Orson Yates, for example."

I make a face.

"I believe the feeling is mutual," the entity says. It sweeps a hand, and the air in the center of the room shimmers. A hole opens up, dark and swirling at first. Then images appear.

I recognize my grandmother by the set of her jaw alone. She's so young, and every time she turns her attention to the man at her side, her face lights up and her eyes soften. Her love is so tangible that I'm certain I could reach out, capture it between my palms, and have it glow. No wonder she was able to keep the vigil for my grandfather all her life.

Malcolm's grandfather looks so much like his grandson that my heart catches. For an instant, the pain breaks through and radiates around my ribcage. I whimper, but a moment later, that soothing balm rushes in. I flatten a palm against my heart as if I could bring the pain back, because part of me still wants to feel all the hurt.

In front of me, my grandmother is conferring with Queenie, Mr. Carlotta's ghost. My grandfather is digging through the stacks at a university library, handing off volumes to Malcolm's grandfather.

They gather at night in the nature preserve, in the very spot where I've been releasing ghosts all my life. Stars fill the sky. They are wide-eyed and solemn. For a moment, it's almost as if I'm viewing myself with Malcolm and Nigel.

"Hm, yes," the entity intones. "I believe the bond was that deep, which is why the betrayal hurt so much."

They link hands and then speak the entity's name, all three of them at once. I lean forward on the coffee table and plant my feet on the floor to steady myself. Something about this is different. Something about it feels ... wrong.

The image of the entity appears. This is neither the craggy, lava-eyed version from the warehouse nor the well-heeled gentleman that currently presides over this space. It doesn't look like a being at all; it's more like they ripped out a piece of the sky and brought it down to earth.

And, oh, it is not happy.

My grandmother notices first. Her mouth is set in an O of fear, but her eyes tell the story. Nothing but sorrow and shame is lingering there. She shakes her head as if she could undo all that they've done.

But, of course, they can't.

"They hurt you," I say to the entity.

At once, the images shatter, leaving us in that facsimile of a den.

"Pardon me, my dear?"

"The three of them invoked you at once. They ripped you from … where you live?" That must be it, I think, and there's no way that doesn't hurt.

"That is … correct enough."

"Vendetta," I say.

We've never really discussed the entity's behavior when I first encountered it, but the pieces of that fall into place.

"That's why Malcolm was getting that vendetta vibe from you at the mausoleum." I pause, casting my mind back to that eradication. It seems so long ago, when Malcolm was merely my business partner. "He thought it was about me, though. But was it about him? Or us together? Or our grandparents?"

The entity doesn't speak, although it hasn't moved from its wingback chair. It conjures a pipe, and smoke rings billow from the bowl. The scent is insidious, sweet and calming, and not at all like tobacco.

I yawn. But I'm not on Earth, so do I really need to sleep?

"Stop that!" I say.

"Hm?"

"You're changing the subject."

Now it laughs. "I'm doing no such thing."

"You are."

The smoke curls and wanders about the space. My thoughts follow. Part of me wants to abandon the conversation, pull a volume from the shelf, and settle in on the couch.

Instead, I slip from the table and approach the hearth. There's no place for me to sit, so I kneel a few feet from the entity. This makes me look like a supplicant or a pet, but maybe that's okay, considering what I have to say.

"I'm sorry."

"Are you, now? Whatever for?"

"For what we did to you."

"You haven't done a thing, my dear."

"My grandparents did, and so did Malcolm's grandfather. So, I'm apologizing for them. If someone ripped me from Springside, I'd be pretty angry."

"It seems someone has, or am I wrong in thinking you're not currently on this plane of existence?"

"I was a willing sacrifice, remember?" When it doesn't respond, I add, "Where are you supposed to be? Here?"

"Here is adequate. When you're ready, we can explore other worlds, other universes."

"But you don't have a place where you belong."

The entity turns its head toward me. Stars shoot across the surface where its face should be. I'm relieved that I no longer see that abyss, but the vastness I do see feels just as lonely.

"That's why there was a void where your face should be. Did we take that away from you?"

"You did nothing."

"My grandmother, then, and Malcolm's grandfather."

"They merely finished something that was started long ago," it says. "But to answer your question, yes. I ... lost the place where I belong. I hope to make my way back there." It raises a hand as if it might caress my cheek. "Perhaps you'll still be with me."

The entity stands. The pipe vanishes in a puff of blue smoke. In that smoke, I see the rest of the story. Malcolm's grandfather leaps at the entity, arms wide. I can't hear my grandmother shout, but the smoke ripples in response.

Malcolm's grandfather staggers. He can't hold the entity. It rages within him, will burn him through. My grandmother steps forward and presses a hand on his heart.

Although I can't hear her speak, her mouth forms an apology. She's speaking not to Malcolm's grandfather, but to the entity inside him. She leans close, as if she might coax the entity to emerge. I know what her next words will be; I spoke them not that long ago myself.

I am your willing sacrifice.

Before she can utter the phrase, my grandfather pulls her away. He kisses her with so much tenderness that it makes my chest constrict. Then, he takes her place.

I can't hear his words either, but the lights that flash in their wake illuminate the nature preserve.

In another puff of smoke, he and the entity vanish. My grandmother collapses to the ground, hands pulling at the earth as if that will bring my grandfather back, sobs wracking her body.

Malcolm's grandfather stumbles from the clearing. He knows enough not to try to comfort her. He knows this is his fault. He surveys the sky the way I would when I was searching for the entity. He could invoke it again; he could take my grandfather's place.

He doesn't.

He walks away, very much a man who has lost something crucial.

The last wisps of smoke dissipate, and I find myself alone in front of the fire. The wingback chair is empty.

I swipe at the air as if that will let me rewind the scene.

"They didn't invoke you," I say.

Nothing but the crackle of the fire greets me.

"This was different," I continue. I don't need to speak these words. No doubt the entity can read my mind here as well as it can everywhere else. But speaking them feels important.

"It wasn't a pact. It was something else." A word pops into my head. "Leverage." I think back to when Malcolm first told me about necromancy and explained how Orson and the Midwest Necromancer Association worked, how they leveraged ghosts, harnessed them to do their bidding. At the time, I thought it sounded cruel.

Now I know it is.

I swipe the air again, and my fingers leave tendrils of blue smoke in their wake. In the wisps, I catch sight of my grandparents and Malcolm's grandfather at the moment before everything changed. Again, I'm struck with how familiar the sight is, how I can see Malcolm and myself at the nature preserve, or the three of us—Malcolm, Nigel, and me—in the office, huddled around Nigel's computer.

I return my attention to the images shimmering in the blue smoke.

That could've been us.

"It was so quick," I say.

The blue smoke vanishes in the wake of my breath.

Betrayal often is, my dear.

I DON'T KNOW how much time passes. I discover that I have a never-ending pot of coffee. Once a day—at least, it feels like once a day—a treat appears on the table, although I don't need to eat, or even drink, for that matter.

It's a habit, it's comforting, and my guess is, the entity knows that.

I pull random volumes from the shelves and tumble into the past—not just of Earth. I could spend several lifetimes lost in these books. It's like reading on steroids—I feel the sun's heat and the icy rain, taste spring or gunpowder in the air, feel freshly mown grass beneath my feet.

All without leaving the sofa.

The history I want to find most is that of my mother. She must be in these volumes somewhere, because it appears that everyone is. The task is daunting. There is no index, no coherence, no alphabetical order, or really any order that I can see.

"Of course there's an order, my dear."

The entity's voice startles me. The book I'm holding slips from my fingers and lands on the floor. I'm guessing it's a floor; it looks like a floor.

The entity bends down and scoops up the volume. "Don't assume there isn't one simply because you don't understand it."

It has a point. Plus? I really don't understand anything anymore. "Where were you?" I ask.

"Someone thought to invoke me. I had to deal with that."

I'd thought maybe I'd chased the entity away with all my probing and questioning. "People can still do that?"

"They can try, but you're not only my willing sacrifice, you're also my necromancer. No one else can capture me unless you relinquish your dual roles."

"Then, why would someone invoke you?"

"Why did Orson, at the wedding reception? Why did Malcolm's

grandfather betray your grandmother?"

"But I invoked you when you had Malcolm."

"And I appeared, did I not?" The entity glides across the room, pointing at books I've left scattered about. They go flying back to the shelves. "That was also the day you became a necromancer."

"I ... what?"

I think back to how the ghosts of Springside came to my rescue. "I didn't command the ghosts or deploy them," I counter. "I merely asked for a favor."

"And they agreed, and their power was enough to thwart my ... plans for you. It wasn't quite the negotiation I was expecting. Considering you're your mother's daughter, perhaps I should have."

I latch on to that. I know I can't force the entity to tell me anything about her, but I so want to know. "What happened?"

The entity approaches the wingback chair. It hesitates, as if it can't decide whether to sit or not. Instead, it clutches the top of the chair in a manner so humanlike it surprises me.

"Your mother. Her desire was as pure as yours, although it was far sharper. Yours encompassed the whole of Springside. She focused on one thing for much of her life."

"My grandfather."

"That was her sole aim, why she trained with the necromancer association and partnered with both Orson and Darien. When your grandmother very wisely refused to reveal my name to her, she went off and found it on her own."

"Kind of like I did?"

"Indeed." The entity shakes its head, and again I'm struck with how humanlike the gesture is. "And she caught me. Exceedingly clever, your mother."

"But ... you had a willing sacrifice."

"Who refused to leave."

"But ..." I work to pull this all together. Wouldn't my grandfather want to come home? Didn't he yearn for Springside the way I do?

"He refused to let his daughter take his place, and that desire equaled hers. As a result, the negotiations became protracted—an in-between state for the necromancer and myself. Remember, in the warehouse?"

I nod.

"I could've easily been captured at that point by someone else. There were several necromancers in Springside that day. Orson Yates might have had a chance, had he been resolute enough to take it. I'm not sure he realizes that."

I think of Orson's hesitation on the side of the road, how he seemed unable to decide between the entity and the accident victims. I wonder: does that day haunt him like I think it must?

The entity doesn't need to tell me what happened next. A chase, perhaps? My parents trying to escape the way Malcolm and I did, their car haunted the way Malcolm's transmission was?

I can still hear the roar of their car engine, feel the crash in my bones, see that plume of smoke rising from the ravine.

"And in that instant," the entity says, its voice unbearably soft, "when the wheels left the gravel and met the air, all of your mother's desire transferred to you. Her one wish, her last wish, was that you would live."

And that's how I ended up on the side of the road, pinned in place, unharmed and alone.

"I didn't have to save you," the entity says.

"But you did."

"I did."

"Is that your vendetta? Is that really why I'm here now?"

"I dislike ... caring so much for something so small and puny and fragile as a human."

My heart hammers in my chest. I press my palm against it and wonder at that. Do I need a heartbeat anymore? Is it just the memory of one? The ache spreads, and I welcome it even as I try to hide the pain. I don't want another dose of that soothing balm—not yet, anyway.

But the entity has turned away from me, so perhaps it doesn't notice. Except, it notices everything, so it must be letting me hurt and cry and feel the tears scratch my cheeks.

The sorrow hollows out my belly. I'm empty inside, longing for Springside, for Malcolm, for the mother I never knew. And still, the entity keeps its back to me.

At last, I push the tears from my face and consider the coffee service. I've been using the same cup over and over again, but there are several on the tray—almost like the entity and I are some 1950s married couple, and we're expecting guests at any moment.

I pour a fresh cup and add some half and half from a little pitcher. It's fresh and cool and can't possibly be real. I approach the entity, the cup cradled in my hands.

The aroma of Kona blend must reach it first. I detect the slightest shift in its stance.

"You saved my life." I grip the cup, and the barest ripple travels the surface of the coffee.

"And now you're here."

"Well, yes, I am. But before this, I started a business and fell in love. I had a protégé and a best friend. It was a good life. And so"—I set the coffee down on a side table—"thank you."

I return to the couch and pick up the one book the entity didn't send back to the shelves. I turn the pages, more focused on the tactile experience than anything inside the book itself. I'm not sure I care about the Teapot Dome scandal.

When I look up again, the entity is gone. I find the cup empty—not even a drop of coffee remains in the bottom. Next to the cup, a puff of that blue smoke is floating. It shifts and swirls until, at last, it spells out the words: *You're Welcome.*

I blow on the words and watch the smoke shift to stars. They sparkle and shoot across the room and then fade.

I am alone. But not lonely. For the first time in a very long time, I suspect the entity isn't either.

WE HAVE A ROUTINE NOW. I know when the entity vanishes because extra treats appear. The soothing balm rushes in when my thoughts wander to Springside and especially when they wander to Malcolm.

The books on the shelves rearrange themselves, and it's as if the entity is directing my education. It's a bit passive aggressive, but it's effective. Besides, it only laughs when I complain.

There's so much more beyond this haven he's created for me. The books tell me that; my own senses do. When I sit on the couch, my feet twitch. When I felt this way in the past, back in Springside, I would brew up a pot of coffee, pull together the field kit, and go searching for ghosts.

"You're not close to being ready," it says when I broach the subject. "It will take decades, not that you'll really notice. About the time people stop invoking me. My name will fade from view, and I won't have to deal with these constant interruptions."

"Is it on the internet? Because if it's on the internet, it's never going away."

The entity laughs. "Ah, but you have to know what to look for."

"Could we go ghost hunting?" I ask. "When I'm ready?"

"Whatever do you mean?"

It knows. Of course it knows.

"My grandmother and grandfather. My parents?"

"Ah. Perhaps."

"Perhaps while we're looking for your home?"

Its posture shifts, and it settles deeper into the wingback chair. I take that as a yes.

Ours is a well-ordered existence. Nothing disturbs my daily treat. The coffee never gives me jitters. The otherworldly balm coats the rough edges whenever I feel too much. So, days ... weeks ... some time later, when something rocks the stability of the floor, I'm unprepared.

The carpets buckle. The force of the disturbance throws me off the sofa. I stare, hands planted on the table while the entity stands, its head tilted in curiosity.

A form emerges from the floor, billowing and misty. It reminds me of the chain of ghosts sewn together inside the cold storage unit of the Pancake House. The clouds expand and grow, solidifying around a central figure.

One by one, features emerge. My gaze snags on the strangest things —the set of the jaw, the lush, dark lashes against paler cheekbones, the sharp crease in the khakis, and a pressed white dress shirt.

It takes a moment, perhaps because I believed I'd never see him again.

When the clouds of mist fall away, they reveal the man who's now standing in the center of the den.

It's Malcolm.

I gape. I forget to breathe. I know it's Malcolm. My heart is thumping too hard, my throat is too tight, and my mind is scrambling for explanations. The most dire?

He's dead. He's dead, and he's here now because ... well, I'm not sure, exactly, except he's wearing the pallor of death and hasn't moved or opened his eyes. I want to ask the entity, but I can't drag my attention away from Malcolm.

Then, all at once, he coughs. With a fist, he strikes himself in the solar plexus, and a plume of mist is expelled from his mouth. Fog rises and swirls. He continues to hack like he has bronchitis or pneumonia. As he does, his skin returns to that lovely shade of olive. His hair gleams. He coughs one last time, clears his throat, and then looks at me.

"Malcolm?"

He gives me one of those sweet, dark-roast smiles.

"But ... you can't be here. Are you dead?"

"I don't think I'm dead."

"Are you real?"

He curls his fingers in a come-here gesture. "Try me."

I leap up and throw myself across the room. This is Malcolm, and I will always run to him. I take three steps before launching myself the last few feet. I half-expect to fall through him and crash to the floor, certain this is no more than a hallucination.

He catches me. His arms are solid and sure, his nutmeg and Ivory soap scent the best thing I've inhaled in ages. He is warm and secure and definitely my Malcolm Armand.

Behind me, the entity claps. The sound of it ripples through the space, buffeting us like waves in the ocean.

"Oh, well done, necromancer. Well done, indeed. Bravo, even."

I peer over my shoulder at the entity. Malcolm keeps his grip on me, but his scowl is fierce.

"Isn't he clever, Katy? Go on, tell him just how clever he is. You know he wants to hear it from you too."

Now I frown, out of frustration. I don't get it, don't understand how Malcolm can be here, warm and alive.

"You can't be a willing sacrifice," I tell him. "Besides, I wouldn't let you."

His gaze flickers toward the entity. "I'm not the willing sacrifice."

"Then ... how?"

He points to the mist that still surrounds us. "They are."

The fog shifts once again, revealing ghost after ghost and sprite after sprite. They careen around the den, rattling the coffee service, sweeping across the bookshelves, and twirling around me like an otherworldly cyclone.

"Ghosts?" Their forms collide and merge, split apart. Tracking them is impossible.

"Not just any ghosts," Malcolm says. "Every last ghost in Springside."

"Every ghost?"

Even as I ask the question, I know the answer. All at once, half a dozen sprites pepper my face with kisses—I count both Sadie's and Belinda's sprites among them. The ghost that haunts Chief Ramsey's watering can slouches along the perimeter. The wild ghosts from the old barn push books to the floor—a Sisyphean task, as the books magically reshelve themselves.

In the corner, I detect a grumpy group that roils and simmers, but for all their discontent, even these ghosts seem placid.

"Attack ghosts?" I venture. "They came, too?"

"Would you want to be a dog on a leash?"

No, I wouldn't, especially an angry, mistreated dog, and especially if Orson were holding that leash. Still, I stare at the group in wonder. "They were able to escape?"

"They were, plus I had a little coaching from Nigel. I walked and biked every street in Springside, searched every corner, alley, and store." Malcolm grins, and he looks downright devious. "And along the way, I picked up my father's ghosts."

Oh, no wonder he looks so self-satisfied. "All the way out to the nature preserve?"

"He moved in closer after ... everything. He set up camp in Sadie's backyard."

Oh, poor Sadie and Nigel.

"And I collected Prescott's and Reginald's ghosts."

At that moment, a mischievous sprite zips by, planting a naughty kiss on my cheek. It can only be Frederick.

"And even Orson's attack ghosts," he adds.

"All of them?"

"Every last one."

"Does that work?" I ease from Malcolm's embrace, although he keeps his fingers laced with mine. I turn toward the entity. "Can ghosts be a willing sacrifice?"

The entity has fallen silent. It studies the proceedings with a hand cupping its chin as if it's deep in thought.

"There is no reason why they can't," it says at last. "Before now, they never had a means"—the entity nods toward Malcolm—"a conduit, if you will, to speak my name. And this one"—it gestures toward a single ghost making its slow way toward the hearth—"is a most welcomed guest."

Queenie. Mr. Carlotta's ghost.

"So, you what?" I turn back to Malcolm. "Swallowed all the ghosts and invoked the entity?"

"Pretty much. Queenie helped. The ghosts of Springside love you, and they listen to her. Me?" He rubs the back of his head. "Not so much."

"Now what?" I ask.

The entity still appears deep in thought. The surface where its face should be sparkles and glitters in a way I've never seen before.

"There are so many," it says, its voice both solemn and soft. "So many lost souls."

"Can you take care of them?" The magnitude of what they've done—of what Malcolm has done—strikes me, leaves me breathless. What if there's no place for these ghosts in this plane of existence?

"Perhaps not this exact plane, my dear," the entity says, "but I assure you, they will find a home somewhere. I will be their devoted caretaker, if you allow me that role. They are your ghosts, after all."

My ghosts. All of them. I extend a hand, and a group of sprites weaves between my fingers. "They would do this for me?"

"They would," Malcolm whispers.

I'm dumbstruck. Words escape me. I search the space, this facsimile of a room that I thought might be my home forever. For a fleeting moment, I hesitate. Then I find my words. In all of this, there is only one choice.

"Can I say goodbye?"

The entity gestures to its wingback chair. I sit. One by one, each ghost floats past. The sprites chatter and twirl, and the ones from the Springside Police Department collect the stray tears that wander down my cheeks. Frederick steals another kiss. I say goodbye to the rowdy ones, the quiet ones, and even incline my head as the attack ghosts pass.

The very last ghost is Mr. Carlotta's Queenie. When she oozes to a stop in front of me, all I have left to say is, "I'll take care of him. He won't be lonely." I place a hand on my heart. "I promise you."

With that, I'm done. I'm about to stand when the entity offers its hand.

"It's not often that I learn something from a mere mortal."

I wait for it to elaborate, but of course, it doesn't. Instead, I take its hand.

"You were a worthy opponent, my dear, if a somewhat dull necromancer."

"Hey!"

Its chuckle is downright demonic. "Oh, the fun we could've had together." It pauses, seems to consider something. "And it isn't often that a mere mortal either surprises or delights me. You managed to do both." The entity touches my cheek—the left one, on the very spot it marked so many months ago.

"Off with you, then. Go be with your young man. He has proven himself after all. Imagine that."

"Will you ... will you be okay?"

"You have given me quite a gift. Let me return the favor."

There's a flash, and what looks like a thousand stars streaking across the sky. The air turns cold and then hot before shifting into something crisp and cool. What feels like grass cushions me, and short, thick blades tickle my palms.

When I open my eyes, the view of my front porch at sunrise greets me. I catch a hint of blue in all the gold and pink, the darker shadows of the green steel roof. When I turn my head, I see Malcolm on the grass, his body next to mine.

"You did it," I whisper.

"We did it." His gaze is so tender. With tentative fingers, he touches my cheek, the left one. "Huh. It's gone."

"Completely?" I ask, but I already sense the answer.

"Completely."

The void rushes in, stronger than I expected. The entity is no longer connected to this particular plane of existence, or to me. It would take more than merely uttering its name to invoke it.

I stare up at the brilliant blue sky, catch a hint of smoke in the air, notice how the leaves are rimmed with red and gold.

"How long have I been gone?"

"Six weeks."

Six weeks! I'm about to bolt upright. The urge to run around and check on everything nearly overwhelms me. But I stay put, back flush with the earth. Malcolm's hand finds mine, and he inches me closer, his hold on me suddenly protective.

A shadow falls across the lawn, and it stretches long and menacing.

Orson Yates is standing on my sidewalk.

And he's holding a gun.

Desperate, I scan the neighborhood. It's early morning, with curtains still shrouding windows, porch lights still on.

Orson takes one step and then another, a deliberate move across my ward.

"Don't move, don't scream." He aims the gun at Malcolm. "Or he'll be dead before you can take another breath."

Next to me, Malcolm tenses. His grip tightens as if he's building energy for an attack.

"Don't think about it," Orson says. "I can kill her just as easily."

"If you kill us, the police will catch you." The words emerge from my throat stronger than I think they should be.

"You've taken many things from me, Ms. Lindstrom, but not quite everything. I have ... resources, and it seems you are without any. Do you know what that means?"

I'm afraid to ask. My heart thuds, pulse roaring in my ears, and my thoughts race so fast I can't catch up to them. Malcolm grips my hand as if he, too, knows that we're out of options. Orson will shoot us. He will walk away. But before he does, he wants me to ask. So I do, if only to buy a few more seconds with Malcolm.

"What does that mean?" I say.

"It means—" That cunning and cruel smile lights his face. "That I win."

Maybe it's how his fingers are twitching that alerts me. Maybe it's his stance. The barrel is centered on Malcolm's chest. Fling myself at Orson? Tackle him around the knees? If only I had a branch, or a rake. A sword, even.

I grope the ground for something—anything—but only end up with a fistful of grass. Then Orson's own words cross my mind.

What if I told you that every time you catch a ghost, you commit an act of necromancy?

Containment fields. My imaginary tire iron that freed the ghosts in the cemetery. The sword that nearly sliced through them in the Pancake House.

I pick the tire iron and, with all my strength, picture smashing it against Orson's hand and knocking the gun from his grip.

The shot is deafening, the blood a bright red. Drops of it strike my face, the feel of it hot and sticky. A howl cuts through the ringing in my ears. My vision and thoughts clear just as Malcolm barrels into Orson.

There's no grappling. Malcolm clutches his shoulder, Orson his hand. They crash onto the lawn. Malcolm. Still alive. A burst of relief flows through me until I realize that the gun is missing—or, at least, I don't know where it is. I crawl across the grass, scanning the bushes, combing the ground, all in search of it.

Another bang rings out. For one terrifying moment, I fear Orson has found the gun and has used it. But the sound isn't as sharp or as loud.

A moment later, Darien Armand lands on Orson, followed by Nigel, and all I can see is arms and legs and the brightness of that blood. Darien jerks Orson's hands behind his back; Nigel sits on his legs.

Malcolm rolls to the side, hand clutching his arm, and stares up at the sky. His chest heaves. Pain is etched on his face.

But he's alive, and the relief comes rushing back.

I push to stand, take a step, and my foot finds the gun. I ease off it, but the last thing I want to do is pick it up.

I think someone should. I'm bending to retrieve it when Nigel calls out.

"Don't!"

I glance up.

"You don't want your prints on it."

"But—" I point at Orson.

"He's not going anywhere." Nigel shifts his weight and pulls out a phone. "We need to call for an examination."

"Shouldn't we call the police instead?"

Even now, I'm surprised one of my neighbors hasn't, but other than the commotion in my yard, the street quietly slumbers on. I glance up, wondering if there is—once again—some necromancer magic going on.

"Not if we don't have to." Nigel glances at his father, who nods.

I keep my foot on the gun, uncertain if we're doing the right thing.

"It's me," Nigel says when the call goes through. "Yeah, he made it back, and with Katy." He pauses and gives Malcolm a look filled with admiration. "You're right. It *is* damned impressive. Call Reginald. We've got Orson. Tell him it's time."

Nigel tosses the phone to me. "Hang on to that, and don't lose sight of the gun."

"But ... Malcolm?" I point again, this time indicating the blood that's seeping through Malcolm's fingers.

Nigel raises an eyebrow at his brother. "You okay?"

Malcolm rolls to face us. "I can hang on."

"Good man."

"We ... like Reginald now?" I venture.

Malcolm gives me a wan smile, one meant to reassure me. I'm not certain it does. "I'll explain it later."

So I stand there, foot on the gun, and survey the neighborhood. As far as I can tell, the gunshot woke no one else. Curtains remain drawn, doors closed. No wail of a siren fills the air. Despite this, I half-expect to see Chief Ramsey round the corner and haul us all in to the Springside jail.

Instead, a flashy yellow car rumbles down the road, followed by a Land Rover and several black sedans of the German variety.

Prescott leaps out first. He dashes up the walk, throwing me a grin as he goes.

He helps Malcolm to his feet.

Prescott keeps a hand on Malcolm's shoulder. "Steady?"

Malcolm nods and staggers over to me. His entire left sleeve is drenched with blood, and the coppery scent of it heats the air between us.

"He shot you." This is stating the obvious. I realize that. At the moment, those are the only words I have.

"In the arm," Malcolm says. He lets go of the wound for a second and taps his chest. "Not here." He leans in and kisses me, and it's hot and salty, and for a second, I think I might cry.

The sight of necromancers filling my lawn has me blinking away the tears. Like before, they assemble in a solemn row. Only this time, it's Orson's turn for an examination. Once the entire group has circled him, Nigel and Prescott let go and step back.

Orson is still clutching his hand. Beneath his grip, the flesh is bruised, an angry purple radiating up his wrist.

"I would like to state for the record that Katrina Lindstrom used necromancy to attack me," he says. "My hand is broken. She is in direct violation—"

"You were going to shoot Malcolm!" I cry out. "You *did* shoot Malcolm! I—" I glance around, wondering if this is going to be about me yet again.

Reginald raises a finger, and I swallow back my protests.

"And we might wish to lodge charges against Malcolm Armand," Orson continues, "as he's the one who has stolen all the ghosts within a ten-mile radius." He narrows his eyes at the assembled group. "You might want to check to see which ones you're missing. My guess is, all of them."

Then again, maybe this is going to be about me, along with Malcolm. Anxiety pings inside me as I study each and every necromancer. As a group, they're not just solemn, but unsympathetic. Their stances are firm, their expressions passive.

"What's a necromancer without any ghosts?" I whisper to Malcolm.

"Usually pissed off."

"Even today?"

He blows out a breath, and I hear his uncertainty in it.

Darien Armand steps forward. He casts Orson a look so cold it should cover my lawn in frost.

"I am no longer part of the necromancer community," Darien intones, "and I will not participate in this examination except to say that if you cannot protect your ghosts from a … novice necromancer, perhaps you don't deserve the title yourself."

With that, Darien steps from my lawn and into Sadie's backyard.

"Are you sure you got all your father's ghosts?" I whisper to Malcolm.

He stares at the spot where Darien vanished. "I have no idea."

Reginald clears his throat. "Orson Yates, for too long you've been a blot on the necromancer community and its good name."

Orson snorts.

"You have already stood for examination in the past," Reginald continues. "More than once."

"And in the past, my name has always been cleared."

"That was our mistake," Reginald says. "You have been summarily examined. We, as a community, can no longer allow you to practice necromancy. You will submit to retribution."

Orson doesn't sputter or lash out. To his credit, he pulls himself up straight, although he cradles his injured hand against his chest. "Then I bow to the wishes of the community. Do your worst."

I expect a trick. Apparently Malcolm does too. A frown clouds his brow, but then a knowing look fills his eyes.

"Money," he whispers in my ear. "He doesn't need ghosts, or necromancy, or any of that. He has plenty of money. He's set for life."

The other necromancers line up across from Orson. Prescott takes his place among them, as does Nigel. Malcolm and I don't budge from our spot on the grass. My foot is still covering the gun.

"Katrina Lindstrom. Young Malcolm." Reginald gestures toward the group. "Take your place. We need all necromancers present for retribution."

Malcolm swallows back a sigh. I still don't move. My gaze meets Orson's. In it, I don't see the man who tried to kill us—more than once—but the one who hesitated on the side of the road, the one who couldn't choose which path to take, and so had a path chosen for him.

I take a step back, and then another. I'm on the sidewalk before anyone really notices.

"Katy?" Malcolm stares at me, his gaze full of concern. He's still clutching his arm.

"Someone shot you," I say simply. "I'm going to go get Chief Ramsey."

A murmur passes through the group. A few of the necromancers shift from foot to foot before Prescott clears his throat.

"Katy, this is retribution," he says. "It's how necromancer justice works."

I survey the group one last time. So many necromancers, and all of them on my lawn. Then I know my answer.

"I keep telling all of you. I'm not a necromancer."

I turn from them and head down the sidewalk toward the center of town. A moment later, Malcolm falls into step next to me.

Penny Wilson is holding the coffee carafe when we enter Springside Police Department. Her mouth hangs open, and the handle slips through her fingers. The pot shatters on the floor, sending coffee and shards of glass everywhere.

Then she screams.

Chief bursts from his office, scowling and perturbed. "Penny, what the hell—"

At the sight of me, he freezes. He moves a hand to his chest and, on reflex, clutches the spot over his heart. I think he might be having an actual heart attack. I can't make sense of it until I remember:

I've been gone for six weeks.

Then Chief does the one thing I didn't expect. He steps forward and pulls me into a hug.

It's awkward and weird, and I want to choke back the spate of tears that fill my eyes, but I can't. I'm reminded of the man who found me on the side of the road, who scooped me up and cradled me like I was his own daughter.

He recovers quickly and steps away, once again Police Chief Ramsey and all business.

Between Penny's scream and the impromptu hug, Officer Deborah

Millard has stepped into the reception area. She has a first aid kit. With the utmost calm, she cuts away the bloody sleeve and bandages Malcolm's arm.

"You should probably go to urgent care," she says, her voice level. "You might need stitches."

Malcolm nods, says thanks, and bestows one of his charming smiles on her. But then his gaze finds Chief, and his eyes turn steely.

"Can I assume this means I'm no longer a person of interest?"

"What?" Now I gape. "You blamed Malcolm?"

Chief glances away, but that's only to gather his strength. He spears me with a look. "You vanished without a trace."

"Well, I'm back now. I can't believe..." I trail off, all out of words, and simply wave a hand at Malcolm.

"Standard in cases like this. We look at the ... significant other. Mind telling me where you were for the past two months? Or is this one of those things I won't believe?"

It is, of course, so I blurt, "Someone shot Malcolm."

"I can see that."

"It was Orson Yates, and he's in my front yard."

THE RIDE in the patrol car is fast, but not fast enough. By the time we've returned to my house, all the fancy sedans are gone, minus one. Prescott's yellow sports car is sitting in front of Sadie's house. Prescott himself is on the front porch, fluttering the pages of a newspaper.

Chief lumbers up the walk, plants his hands on his hips, and demands, "Is Mrs. Lanca ... Armand home?"

"She's packing," Prescott says. He folds the paper and places it on the seat next to him. "As is Mr. Armand. For their honeymoon."

Chief's mouth forms a hard, thin line.

"I'm housesitting, you know, keeping an eye on things." The move is subtle, but none of us miss the nod in the direction of my place.

Some of the fierceness leaves Chief's expression. "Got a report of a gunshot. You hear anything?"

"I only woke up a few minutes ago." Prescott stretches as if his limbs are heavy with sleep. It's a fairly impressive show, but I don't think Chief is buying the act. "Must have slept through it."

When Chief turns to study my yard, Prescott winks at me.

I rush down the steps and onto my lawn. In the grass, the slightest impression of where Malcolm and I landed remains. There's a divot not too far away that—if you squint at it—could be the shape of a gun. Other than that, my yard looks well cared for and weed-free. I can't even find a single drop of Malcolm's blood, not in the grass and not on the sidewalk.

"It happened right here," I say to Chief.

Malcolm slides in next to me, his uninjured arm wrapping around my waist.

"No weapon, no suspect," Chief says. His gaze flits from me to Malcolm and back again. "No crime."

"But—"

"You know," Chief says, and now his voice turns contemplative. "I called up an old high school buddy a few weeks back, right before you did your disappearing act."

I blink and cast a sidelong glance at Malcolm, who gives his head a little shake.

"We graduated high school together," Chief continues. "He was also a friend of your mother's."

I hold very still, not daring to miss Chief's next words.

"These days, he works for the IRS. Someone has to, right?"

Numb, I nod.

Chief chuckles, and in it, I hear the echo of the entity's laughter. "Turns out Mr. Yates doesn't like paying his taxes, and the IRS would like to ... chat with him about that."

He turns from us, steps off my lawn, and heads down the sidewalk. He doesn't speak again until he reaches the patrol car.

"You two take care of each other. And for heaven's sake, go be young." He touches the brim of his hat and then slips inside the car.

Even after the rumble of the engine has faded, Malcolm and I continue to stand in my front yard. Prescott is no longer on Sadie's porch. The sun has just now crested the roofs and is painting the street in a golden glow.

"You know he arrested me after you vanished with the entity," Malcolm says at last.

"He *what?*"

"Handcuffs and everything."

"But—"

"Things were ... crazy. Orson wanted me to stand for retribution, for interfering with necromancer business." With his uninjured arm, he manages to draw little air quotes around *necromancer business*. "Chief did me a favor, really. He spent the night at the station, too. We talked until dawn." An odd smile lights Malcolm's face. "Chief's kind of deep, when you get right down to it."

That doesn't surprise me. I peer up at Malcolm. There's a bit more gray at his temples, perhaps a new crease or two at the corners of his eyes. I don't know if that's from swallowing ghosts or from the past six weeks—or both.

The magnitude of what he's done washes over me. I want to tell him everything I'm thinking, but the first thing to come out is:

"I should drive you to urgent care."

Another smile warms his face, this one richer and sweeter—a true dark-roast smile. "Yes, you should, you really should." But as he says it, he tugs me closer.

"We should probably figure out what to tell them, too." I nod toward his injured arm. "About that."

"Or we could tell them to call Chief." His gaze flits toward the street, but the patrol car has vanished. "He owes us."

Malcolm still hasn't budged, and I worry about infection and blood loss and—

His lips find mine. His kiss is so tender and sweet that it obliterates all the thoughts in my head.

"Urgent care?" I say, breathless.

"In a bit. Right now, I'm missing six weeks' worth of morning kisses, and I'd like to collect."

We spend the following week in the office, the gold lettering of K&M Ghost Eradication Specialists glowing in the window. Every time I see the words, my heart catches.

The phone is silent. So is our email inbox. No one has sent us a text. The implications of that gnaw away at my happiness at being back on Earth, in Springside and with Malcolm. He hasn't said anything, but then, he really doesn't need to. What are eradication specialists without any ghosts?

Out of business.

Instead, he catches me up on everything I've missed, explains how Reginald and Prescott hoped to turn the tables on Orson and use my retribution to launch one of their own against him.

"Reginald was hoping to act as a double agent, I guess." Malcolm shrugs. "That didn't really go as planned."

"He could've told us," I say.

"Not really. For it to work, he needed our reaction, Nigel's in particular. It's hard to fake that sort of response."

I think of how that felt, of how Nigel nearly doubled over as if he'd been struck in the gut.

"It was so quick," I whisper. I wait, wondering if I'll hear an echo of

Betrayal often is. I don't, but I tip my head toward the ceiling and search for it anyway.

On Wednesday, the bell above the door chimes. For an instant, hope surges through me. A customer? Someone with a ghost? Will we need the Kona blend? I'm halfway through my mental inventory of supplies when the sight of Darien Armand brings me to a crashing halt.

"Will you grant me entry?" His voice is level and deep; his words sound measured and more formal than usual.

It's only then that I notice he has the toes of his well-worn boots on the edge of my ward.

I nod.

Malcolm doesn't sigh or roll his eyes. He doesn't squirm. He merely stands and meets his father in the center of the reception area.

"I'm leaving town today," Darien says.

"Back to South America?"

Darien adjusts the backpack on his shoulders and glances out the window before speaking again. "By way of Paris."

Malcolm darts a look in my direction but remains absolutely still.

"Your mother and I have ... things to sort through. She's happy with Prem, and I don't wish to disrupt that, but it's time we talked."

A curious look lights Malcolm's expression, but he merely nods. "Have a safe trip."

Darien grips Malcolm's shoulder. They stand like that, father and son. Then Darien nods, and in it, I see all the things he can't say.

In it, I see approval.

He's at the door, the chime ringing out again, when he pauses. He considers the entryway, then turns and considers me.

"By the way, Ms. Lindstrom, your coffee is as good as your mother's ever was."

The door whooshes closed, the bell jangling one last time.

Malcolm is standing in the center of our office, arms slack at his sides. I go to him, and it's only then that he moves and captures me in a hug.

"You okay?" I ask.

He releases a long-repressed sigh. "You know what? I am. Strange as it sounds."

"It *sounds* like you had a rough six weeks. I'm sorry I wasn't—"

"Yes, because you decided to save the freaking world, I had to deal with my parents." He cups my face in his hands. "Are you kidding me? I can hardly believe you're here right now. If I had to go through six years of that to get you back, it would be worth it."

I think he might say more. In fact, I'm positive. But he doesn't. He merely plants a gentle kiss on my forehead and tucks me closer to him.

For a long time, we stand in the glow of K&M Ghost Eradication Specialists, and I know I could never want anything more than this.

ON FRIDAY AFTERNOON, after a week of doing nothing, we settle on the reception desk. We've never had enough money—or business—to hire an actual receptionist. The couch is more comfortable, but from here, we can admire how the letters in the window glow and follow the sun's patterns across the carpet.

"Hey," Malcolm says. "Why don't we do the rounds tomorrow?"

"The rounds?"

"Yeah, the whole town, all the usual haunts. I have an appointment at Springside Long-term Care. I'm hosting a..." He trails off and clears his throat. "A tea party."

"A tea party?"

"Well, there aren't any ghosts."

Not that he ever did actual eradications at Springside Long-term Care. It was all taste tests and flirting.

"But I hate missing an appointment, so a tea party and maybe some magic tricks."

And, of course, the magic shows. I laugh, but then I burrow closer to him. "This," I say. "This is why I love you."

Malcolm kisses the top of my head. For a moment, everything's as it should be, but that isn't this new reality. We need to confront that.

"It's over, isn't it?" I say.

"I ... yeah." A sigh rumbles in his chest. "I think it is. We don't have the cash flow to keep going, not with all this overhead and no new customers."

Or *any* customers. I consider that and all that's happened in the past year since my grandmother died.

"You know, my grandmother said she'd come back and show me how to get rid of all the ghosts in Springside. I'm not sure this is what she had in mind."

"Maybe it is. I guess she knew you'd have to face the entity one day, not to mention Orson."

"That *we'd* have to."

"She'd be proud of you."

Maybe. But that won't keep us in business. After everything, I so desperately want there to be an *us*.

Malcolm sighs again. "I didn't want to say anything today, but on Monday, I'm going to let the building manager know we won't be renewing the lease."

I swallow hard and nod.

"And talk to a lawyer about what we need to do to dissolve the business."

What then? How long will K&M the couple last if K&M Ghost Eradication Specialists is no more?

"So, tomorrow," Malcolm says. "One last hurrah. We'll go everywhere, see all the sights. Who knows, we might even find a ghost."

We might, but I doubt it. This sounds like a goodbye tour. But if it is goodbye, then I'll spend every moment of it with Malcolm.

"Let's," I say. "I'll wear my skater skirt."

"Oh, I was hoping you'd say that."

"I'll even brew some coffee, just in case."

WE START at the Pancake House with all-you-can-eat dollar-size pancakes and orange juice. Malcolm tries the coffee, just to be polite. When his face puckers in its aftermath, I shoot him a told-you-so look.

"Oh, that's terrible," he says under his breath. "That's really, really terrible."

I laugh.

In a far corner, Gregory B. Gone is sitting ensconced in a booth. He's spread all manner of papers and books on the table, and Belinda's been pouring him a never-ending cup of coffee. He's so engrossed that I don't think he notices the taste.

"Looks like he got the gig," Malcolm says.

"Gig?"

"Full-time at Springside High, Honors English and drama club advisor."

"So, he's staying ... and Terese is...?" I trail off. I've missed so much in the last six weeks.

"They went off on a long weekend for Labor Day. He came back. She didn't." Malcolm spears a bite of pancake. "I think she wanted to stay in the Cities."

I want to ask if that's what he wants, too, but I clamp my mouth shut when Carter Dupree enters the restaurant and takes a spot at the counter.

"And he's working at the brokerage firm," Malcolm says, pointing his fork at Carter.

I swivel around in the booth for a closer look. "Really?"

He picks up his coffee cup and raises it in Carter's direction. Carter responds with a rude gesture; Malcolm returns the favor.

"It's kind of crazy." Malcolm shakes his head and chuckles. I detect a grin lurking on Carter's face. "But Springside can really grow on you."

Or maybe it's Belinda. I raise my eyebrows at her as she passes. She makes a face. I turn back to Malcolm.

"This is very weird," I say.

"It is, and Jack Carlotta hasn't even shown up yet."

We decide to leave before he does.

At Springside Long-term Care, I'm sandwiched between Mr. Carlotta and Mrs. Greeley. From my vantage point, I can admire everything that is Malcolm. He's dressed impeccably, almost exactly like the first time I saw him, in a blazing white dress shirt and pressed khakis. He keeps touching his pocket as if he's making sure he hasn't lost something. It's an obvious tell, but his audience doesn't seem to mind—or notice, for that matter.

His samovar throws aromatic steam into the air. It's a heady sort of scent, and I don't recognize this particular brew.

"Oh, my, that *is* romantic," Mrs. Greeley says.

"What is?" I ask.

"The tea. Do you two have a picnic planned for later?"

"No."

I'm trying to wrap my head around the notion of tea being romantic when a gasp goes up. Malcolm has pulled silk flowers out of thin air at least a dozen times, but for the residents, the trick never gets old.

"And he's in fine form today," Mrs. Greeley adds.

She might be blind, but there's nothing wrong with her hearing. Malcolm really is in fine form, and his fan club is more than appreciative.

When the show is over and everyone's had their fill of tea, I wheel Mr. Carlotta back to his room.

He takes my hand and gives it a squeeze. "I miss her," he says.

I don't know if he means Queenie or my grandmother or both.

"Me too." I kiss his cheek and promise to visit next week.

On our way out of town, we stop at the Springside Police Department. I pull a thermos from my tote and jump from the convertible.

"This will only take a minute," I say.

"Just don't get yourself arrested."

I laugh and dash up the steps.

"I'm serious," Malcolm calls after me. "You know how he gets."

Inside, I find Penny Wilson in the reception area, contemplating the space where the coffeemaker used to sit. On the sideboard squats a sleek and shiny contraption of red and black. It looks so high-tech that you probably need a special degree to run the thing.

"What's this?" I ask.

"Chief brought it in this morning," she says, shaking her head at the sight. "Since the old pot broke, we've been getting deliveries from the Coffee Depot, but..." She raises a hand and lets it drop. "Now this."

I lean in close for inspection. The contraption will make espresso, cappuccino, steamed milk, and might just do your taxes if you ask nicely. But coffee is coffee.

"I'll stop by on Monday," I say, "and show you how to use it."

Penny gives me a numb sort of nod. I leave her to contemplate the beast and knock on Chief's door.

A grunt lets me know I can enter. I hold up my thermos to show him this is a social call.

"I guess you don't need this anymore," I say, but I set the thermos on his desk anyway. "That's a pretty fancy setup you have."

"I will never refuse Lindstrom coffee." He uncaps the thermos, inhales, and his shoulders relax. "Never."

"I'll show her how to use it," I offer, "and how to grind beans for it."

Chief waves away my offer. "You don't have to."

"No, I don't, but maybe I want to."

He assesses me over the rim of the thermos and gives me a nod. "All right. Deal."

I'm about to turn to leave when I notice his hands—or, rather, the left one and its ring finger. The wedding band is missing. Only a tender circle of flesh remains in its wake.

I close the door softly behind me and wonder what I can do for him. Nothing comes to mind until I catch sight of the black and red coffee-producing beast. I can start there.

As I leave, I pause at the door, raise my chin, and taste the air for any evidence of the otherworldly. I know I won't find it, but that doesn't stop me from trying. The air is bland, with only a hint of that burnt coffee odor, and I'm reminded that things end, even when you don't want them to.

WE SAVE the old barn for last. Perhaps it's out of hope that, of any place, a stray ghost might decide to settle here. Or maybe it's the brilliant September day—the blue sky, a scattering of fluffy clouds, the rich green of the fields, and the gold of the leaves starting to change.

It's hard to be sad here. Even so, I'm managing it.

The barn is empty, of course. Rodent tracks crisscross the cracked cement floor. Dust tickles my nose. A stall door creaks, but it's nothing more than the breeze.

Malcolm hazards a few rungs up the ladder and peers into the hayloft. He turns, catches me in his gaze, and shakes his head.

"Nothing. It's too—"

"Orderly," I finish. The air is crisp, but devoid of the supernatural.

Malcolm steps down the rungs, taking each gingerly. They groan beneath his weight but don't splinter. He approaches me, and his solemn expression sends my heart into overdrive. My palms start to sweat. I tell myself to take deep breaths, that I knew this was coming.

It's all I can do not to run out the barn doors with my hands over my ears so I won't hear his next words.

"Katy." He stops in front of me, examines the ground, then studies my face. "I've been trying—I mean, I don't know, exactly, but—"

"You're leaving. I understand. You need to find work. It makes sense." The words pour from me. Maybe if I say enough of them, his won't hurt so much.

He frowns. "What?"

"You're moving back to the Twin Cities, right? To get a job? Now that—"

"No, no, I'm not. I'm not leaving Springside. I'm not leaving you." He takes my hand. "Unless you want me to."

I shake my head so hard, strands of hair stick to my cheeks.

With gentle fingers, Malcolm sweeps them from my face. "Well, that's settled. Actually, what I'm trying to do is ask you something."

"Ask me something?" I must look dumb: mouth slightly open, eyes wide and confused. At least, that's what I think when he laughs.

"You have no idea what I'm talking about, do you?"

I shake my head again.

His eyes are dark and tender. "Just one of those things I love about you. Which brings me to my question—"

I never hear Malcolm's question. Before he can utter another word, a howl fills the space. The temperature drops by ten degrees. Goose bumps pucker the bare skin where my skater skirt ends and my over-the-knee socks begin.

We both tip our heads up and study the rafters. Swirling fog fills the space from hayloft to roof.

"It can't be," I say.

As if in response to that, a force blows through the barn, slamming stall doors open and closed, the sound so much like a shotgun that I want to cower on the floor. The otherworldly surrounds us, the flavor of it like static against my tongue.

I can't count the number of ghosts that crowd the barn, all of them unfamiliar. One zeroes in on Malcolm and cuffs him on the back of the head.

"Hey!" He whirls, but it doesn't matter. That ghost is long gone.

Another tugs at my hair and then shoves me against Malcolm. He catches me—barely. We cling to each other while chaos erupts around us. The ladder teeters and crashes to the floor, wood splintering. A group of sprites flings hay from the loft, and the presence of so many ghosts makes the dust sparkle.

"What's going on?" I grip Malcolm tight, afraid to lose my hold on him. "Where did they come from?"

"Nature abhors a vacuum." He shakes his head in wonder. "Maybe the supernatural does too."

From the entryway comes a shimmering laugh. I recognize the sound, although I haven't heard it since June, when I freed all the ghosts from the warehouse. Very few ghosts laugh quite like this one, and even fewer have the strength she does.

"Delilah?" I say. "Is that you?"

The storm she kicks up tells me it is. She circles us, embracing me in a ghostly hug, gracing Malcolm with a kiss.

"Did she...?" I begin, but can't find the words to finish.

"Bring us ghosts?" He surveys the barn. "I think she did."

"But ... why?"

"I think I told you once that you made a powerful ally by setting her free." He shrugs. "Maybe she's decided to repay the kindness."

"But—"

"Isn't this what you do?" He gestures toward the ghosts. "Isn't this what you want to do?"

"Yes, but things end."

"There's always going to be ghosts, and they're always going to need you to keep them safe—from themselves, from people exploiting them. For that matter, I need you." His grin starts a bit crooked, but it blooms into that sweet, dark-roast smile. "And with that in mind—"

Malcolm takes a step back. He clears his throat. His hand goes to his pocket again, and he pulls something from within its depths.

"I still have a question." His gaze darts to the object in his hands. "But I'm going to phrase it slightly differently."

He takes a knee in front of me.

I forget to breathe.

"Katrina Lindstrom, will you spend the rest of your life catching ghosts with me?" He offers up a velvet-covered box. Inside sits a ring with a stone that glimmers like the otherworldly.

His question steals all my words.

I should say something. Anything. Or nod. Or fling myself at him. But I stand there, frozen, the ghosts bobbing around us, quiet and waiting.

"It's a moonstone," he says. "And vintage, so it has history. I thought you might like that. I was chasing down a sprite and found it at an estate sale while you were gone."

The words jolt the thoughts back into my head. He found it, bought it, *while I was gone*. The magnitude of his love, of his faith in us, sweeps over me. I mouth a few words, but no sound emerges.

"Some people even call moonstone the ghost stone, and I thought that ... or if you'd rather have something different, or you need to think, or..."

He's babbling, probably because I haven't moved since he took a knee. Now I do fling myself at him, tumbling into his arms.

"Yes!"

"It's an art deco design, and it really is vintage, and—"

"Yes!"

"I know Nigel got Sadie that big diamond, and it—"

"Malcolm." I take his face in my hands. He peers at me, eyes wide and startled. "Yes."

He blinks. It takes a moment, but only just. He scoops me up and whirls me around. Then, with the utmost care, he sets me on my feet. He pulls the ring from its box and slides it onto my finger. The feel of it there is strange and wonderful.

The barn explodes in a flurry of supernatural activity. Ghosts zoom back and forth. Sprites shower more hay on us, and pieces of it float down like confetti.

Malcolm orders me to hold still and races to the convertible. He returns, tote slung over his shoulder, hands busy uncapping the first thermos.

The moment the aromatic steam hits the air, a ghostly cry shakes the entire structure. We let them drink their fill, placing all twelve thermoses throughout the barn. Then Malcolm swings me around again. There are so many ghosts that the air hums with their chatter, and we sway to the rhythm.

Tomorrow, I'll place an order for more Kona blend. I'll stock up on sugar and track down a new field kit. Tomorrow, we'll answer calls and scrub out the Tupperware.

But tonight, we'll dance with the ghosts. Tonight, we'll celebrate.

No matter what happens, tonight belongs to us.

All of us.

WHAT THE HECK IS COFFEE & GHOSTS?

Coffee & Ghosts is a cozy paranormal mystery/romance that is told over a series of episodes and in seasons, much like a television series. Think *Doctor Who* or *Sherlock*.

Ghost in the Coffee Machine, which I think of as the pilot episode, began life as a short story that first appeared in *Coffee: 14 Caffeinated Tales of the Fantastic*.

Once, a very long time ago, I wrote a murder mystery that involved a ghost. During the research phase, I came across a tidbit about catching ghosts using coffee and glass jars. The novel never went anywhere, but years later, when I saw the call for submissions for Coffee, something clicked. Katy, her grandmother, and their business of catching ghosts with coffee and Tupperware (a far more practical and, frankly, safer option) were born.

Not too long later I realized that I wasn't done with coffee and ghosts —or rather, they weren't done with me. They demanded their own type of storytelling as well.

Serial fiction is exciting and fun to write. It's different from a novel in that each episode has its own story arc but also supports a larger one for the season.

I've recently consolidated the episodes into three season bundles.

This makes both finding the episodes and binge-reading them much easier.

I can't tell you how much fun it was to write *Coffee & Ghosts*, and I want to thank you for reading and coming along on this journey with me.

ABOUT THE AUTHOR

CHARITY TAHMASEB has slung corn on the cob for Green Giant and jumped out of airplanes (but not at the same time). She spent twelve years as a Girl Scout and six in the Army; that she wore a green uniform for both may not be a coincidence. These days, she writes fiction (long and short) and works as a technical writer for a software company in St. Paul.

Her short speculative fiction has appeared in UFO Publishing's *Unidentified Funny Objects* and *Coffee* anthologies, *Flash Fiction Online*, *Cicada* and *Deep Magic*. She blogs (occasionally) at Writing Wrongs.

If you enjoyed the story, please consider leaving a review, no matter how short. All reviews are very much appreciated and helpful for prospective readers.